PLAYER'S HANDBOOK D&D DESIGN TEAM
Monte Cook, Jonathan Tweet, Skip Williams

PLAYER'S HANDBOOK DESIGN
Jonathan Tweet

ADDITIONAL DESIGN & DIRECTION
Peter Adkison

ADDITIONAL DESIGN
Richard Baker

EDITORS
Julia Martin, John Rateliff

EDITORIAL ASSISTANCE
David Noonan, Jeff Quick,
Penny Williams

MANAGING EDITOR
Kim Mohan

CORE D&D CREATIVE DIRECTOR
Ed Stark

DIRECTOR OF RPG R&D
Bill Slavicsek

BRAND MANAGER
Ryan Dancey

CATEGORY MANAGER
Keith Strohm

PROJECT MANAGERS
Larry Weiner, Josh Fischer

VISUAL CREATIVE DIRECTOR
Jon Schindehette

ART DIRECTOR
Dawn Murin

D&D CONCEPTUAL ARTISTS
Todd Lockwood, Sam Wood

D&D LOGO DESIGN
Matt Adelsperger, Sherry Floyd

COVER ART
Henry Higgenbotham

INTERIOR ARTISTS
Lars Grant-West, Scott Fischer,
John Foster, Todd Lockwood,
David Martin, Arnie Swekel, Sam Wood

GRAPHIC DESIGNERS
Sean Glenn, Sherry Floyd

TYPOGRAPHER
Nancy Walker

DIGI-TECH SPECIALIST
Joe Fernandez

PHOTOGRAPHER
Craig Cudnohufsky

PRODUCTION MANAGER
Chas DeLong

OTHER WIZARDS OF THE COAST RPG R&D CONTRIBUTORS

Eric Cagle, Jason Carl, Shawn F. Carnes, Michele Carter, Andy Collins, William W. Connors,
Bruce R. Cordell, Dale Donovan, David Eckelberry, Jeff Grubb, Rob Heinsoo, Miranda Horner,
Harold Johnson, Kij Johnson, Gwendolyn FM Kestrel, Duane Maxwell, Steve Miller,
Roger Moore, Jon Pickens, Chris Pramas, Rich Redman, Thomas M. Reid, Sean K Reynolds,
Steven Schend, Mike Selinker, Stan!, JD Wiker, Jennifer Clarke Wilkes, James Wyatt

Based on the original DUNGEONS & DRAGONS® rules created by E. Gary Gygax and Dave Arneson

U.S., CANADA,
ASIA, PACIFIC, & LATIN AMERICA
Wizards of the Coast, Inc.
P.O. Box 707
Renton WA 98057-0707

EUROPEAN HEADQUARTERS
Wizards of the Coast, Belgium
P.B. 2031
2600 Berchem
Belgium
+32-70-23-32-77

QUESTIONS? 1-800-324-6496   620-T11550

Visit our website at www.wizards.com/dnd

Contents

CHARACTER CREATION BASICS

Follow these steps to create a beginning, 1st-level character. You will need a photocopy of the character sheet, a pencil, some scratch paper, and four six-sided dice.

0. CHECK WITH YOUR DUNGEON MASTER

Your Dungeon Master (DM) may have house rules or campaign standards that vary from the standard rules. You might also want to know what character types the other players are playing so that you can create a character that fits in well with the group.

1. ABILITY SCORES

Roll your character's six ability scores. Determine each one by rolling four six-sided dice, ignoring the lowest die, and totaling the other three. Record your six results on scratch paper.

If you roll really poorly, you can roll again. Your scores are considered too low if your total modifiers (before changes according to race) are 0 or less, or if your highest score is 13 or lower.

2. CHOOSE CLASS AND RACE

You want to choose your character's class and race at the same time because some races are better suited to some classes. The description of each class in Chapter 3: Classes includes an entry labeled "Races." You can look there to see what class and race combinations are most common. Write the character's class and race on the character sheet.

Take some time to think about what sort of person your character is going to be. You don't have to develop his or her whole personality at this point, but now's a good time to start thinking about it.

The classes are barbarian, bard, cleric, druid, fighter, monk, paladin, ranger, rogue, sorcerer, and wizard. The races are human, dwarf, elf, gnome, half-elf, half-orc, and halfling.

3. ASSIGN AND ADJUST ABILITY SCORES

Now that you know your character's class and race, assign the scores you rolled in Step 1 to your character's six abilities: Strength, Dexterity, Constitution, Intelligence, Wisdom, and Charisma. Adjust these ability scores up and down according to his or her race, as indicated on Table 2–1: Racial Ability Adjustments.

Put high scores in abilities that work for your character's class. Each class description includes an entry called "Abilities" that points out important abilities for that class. You'll also want to assign abilities according to your concept of what sort of person the character is, and his or her strengths and weaknesses.

For each ability, record the character's modifier. See Table 1–1: Ability Modifiers and Bonus Spells. This number essentially tells you how far above (or below) average your character is in regard to that ability.

4. REVIEW THE STARTING PACKAGE

Look at the class's starting package at the end of each class description in Chapter 3: Classes. It offers a fast way to complete the next several steps of character design. If you like the feat, skills, and equipment listed there for a character of the class you've chosen, then you can record this information on your character sheet. You can also use it as a guideline for making your own decisions from scratch.

5. RECORD RACIAL AND CLASS FEATURES

Your character's race and class grant him or her certain features. Most features are automatic, but some of them involve making choices. Some decisions require thinking ahead about one of the upcoming character steps. For instance, to know whether you want to give a fighter Exotic Weapon Proficiency as a bonus feat, you need to know something about exotic weapons (described in

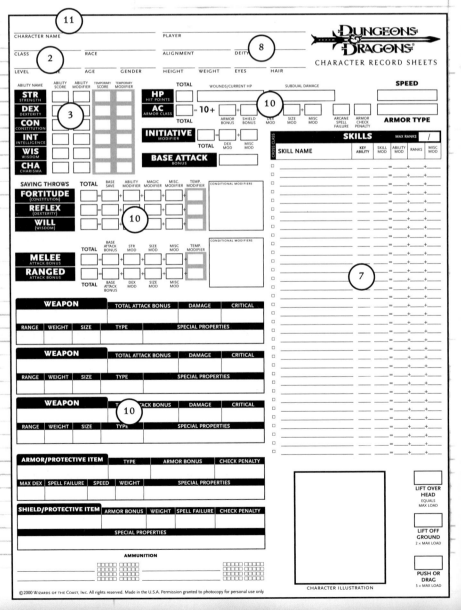

Chapter 7: Equipment). Look ahead when you need to, and don't be afraid to backtrack and do something over.

6. SELECT A FEAT

Each 1st-level character starts with a feat. See Table 5–1: Feats for a list of available feats. Some feats refer to equipment or skills, so you may need to look ahead at other chapters to decide whether you want one of those feats for your character.

7. SELECT SKILLS

Depending on your character's class and Intelligence modifier, you get a certain number of skill points to spend on skills as a 1st-level character. Skills are measured in ranks. Each rank adds +1 to checks (rolls) you make to successfully use that skill. At 1st level, your character can buy up to 4 ranks in a class skill (a skill from your class's list of class skills) or up to 2 ranks in a cross-class skill (a skill from some other class's list of class skills).

Your class skills are listed in the description of your class in Chapter 3: Classes, and all skills are listed on Table 5–2: Skills and described in Chapter 5: Skills.

Buying skills goes faster if you spend 4 skill points (your maximum) on every skill you buy, following the example of the skills in each class's starting package.

Each skill has a key ability associated with it. When you list the skills on your character sheet, fill in the space on the ability modifier column with the appropriate ability modifier (which you recorded back in Step 3).

8. REVIEW DESCRIPTION

Look over Chapter 6: Description. It helps you detail your character. You can decide these details now or wait until later, but they're at least worth reviewing at this stage.

9. SELECT EQUIPMENT

If you don't use the equipment in the starting package for your character's class, you randomly determine the value of his or her starting equipment (see Table 7–1: Random Starting Gold) and then select it piece by piece. You still might want to use the equipment listed for the starting package as a guide.

10. RECORD COMBAT AND SKILL NUMBERS

Based on your race, class, ability modifiers, feat, and equipment, figure out your saving throws, Armor Class, hit points, initiative modifier, melee attack bonus, ranged attack bonus, weapon statistics, and total skill bonuses. Fill in the character sheet with base attack and saving throw bonuses from your character's class table. Create a total bonus (or maybe a penalty) for each saving throw, for melee and ranged attacks, for attack and damage for each weapon, for each skill, and for initiative.

Determine the character's Armor Class (AC). This represents how difficult the character is to hurt in combat, based on his or her armor, shield, and Dexterity modifier.

Each character has hit points (hp), representing how difficult he or she is to kill. At 1st level, wizards and sorcerers get 4 hp. Rogues and bards get 6 hp. Clerics, druids, and monks get 8 hp. Fighters, paladins, and rangers get 10 hp. Barbarians get 12 hp. To this number, add your character's Constitution modifier.

11. DETAILS GALORE

Now invent or choose a name for your character, determine his or her sex, choose an alignment, decide how old he or she is and what he or she looks like, and so on. As Chapter 6: Description shows, there's no end to how thoroughly you can detail your character's looks, personality, and personal history.

There's no need to develop the character completely. With your DM's permission, you can always add, or even change, details as you play and as you get a better feel for your character.

CAMPAIGN

EXPERIENCE POINTS

GEAR

ITEM	ITEM

MONEY

SPELLS

SPELL SAVE

DC MOD

NUMBER OF SPELLS KNOWN (BARDS & SORCERERS ONLY)

0 ___ 1ST ___ 2ND ___ 3RD ___ 4TH ___ 5TH ___ 6TH ___ 7TH ___ 8TH ___ 9TH ___

SPELL SAVE DC	LEVEL	SPELLS PER DAY	BONUS SPELLS	SPELLS
	0		0	
	1ST			
	2ND			
	3RD			
	4TH			
	5TH			
	6TH			
	7TH			
	8TH			
	9TH			

LANGUAGES

SPECIAL ABILITIES/FEATS

NOTES

Introduction

Welcome to the game that has defined the fantastic imagination for over a quarter of a century.

When you play the DUNGEONS & DRAGONS® game, you create a unique fictional character that lives in your imagination and the imaginations of your friends. One person in the game, the Dungeon Master (DM), controls the monsters and people that live in the fantasy world. You and your friends face the dangers and explore the mysteries that your Dungeon Master sets before you.

Each character's imaginary life is different. Your character might

- explore ancient ruins guarded by devious traps.
- put loathsome monsters to the sword.
- loot the tomb of a long-forgotten wizard.
- cast mighty spells to burn and blast your foes.
- solve diabolical mysteries.
- find magic weapons, rings, and other items.
- make peace between warring tribes.
- get brought back from the dead.
- face undead creatures that can drain life away with a touch.
- sneak into a castle to spy on the enemy.
- travel to other planes of existence.
- wrestle a carnivorous ape.
- forge a magic wand.
- get turned to stone.
- get turned into a toad.
- turn someone else into a toad.
- become king or queen.
- discover unique and powerful artifacts of amazing magical power.

WHAT YOU NEED TO PLAY

To start playing the DUNGEONS & DRAGONS game, all you need are the following:

- The *Player's Handbook*, which tells you how to create and play your character.
- A copy of the character sheet.
- A pencil and scratch paper (graph paper is nice to have, too).
- One or two four-sided dice (d4), four or more six-sided dice (d6), an eight-sided die (d8), two ten-sided dice (d10), a twelve-sided die (d12), and a twenty-sided die (d20).
- A miniature figure, or at least something to represent your character in the game (even if it's just a mark on paper).

Additionally, the Dungeon Master needs the *DUNGEON MASTER'S Guide*, which is filled with advice, ideas, and guidelines, and the *Monster Manual*, which describes hundreds of monsters with which to challenge the players.

THE PLAYER'S HANDBOOK

This book gives you everything you need to create and play your character. It features the following chapters:

Abilities (Chapter 1): A single, streamlined system for determining how each ability affects combat, skills, and magic, plus rules for increasing abilities over time.

Races (Chapter 2): Seven distinct character races, each with unique features.

Classes (Chapter 3): Eleven character classes, each of which is available to each race. Each class has features to make it work well at both low levels and high levels. Also, a versatile system for multiclassing allows players to combine the skills and features of any classes.

Skills (Chapter 4): Dozens of skills that govern everything from the rogue's stealth to a wizard's arcane knowledge, including rules for gaining skills outside a character's class and for attempting to use skills in which a character isn't trained.

Feats (Chapter 5): Characters gain these special talents, such as Cleave and Lightning Reflexes, as they rise in level, allowing players to tailor their character's capabilities.

Description (Chapter 6): Details about your character's moral alignment, religion, personality, and physical description, including an array of gods from Heironeous, god of valor, to the demonic Erythnul, god of slaughter.

Equipment (Chapter 7): Weapons and armor from the common to the exotic—including the reliable longsword, double-bladed weapons, a repeating crossbow, and spiked armor—plus all the gear that adventurers need to stay alive.

Combat (Chapter 8): Critical hits, combat actions such as charge or full defense, multiple attacks for high-level characters of all classes, and rules for all the unpredictable maneuvers and challenges that adventurers face on the field of battle.

Adventuring (Chapter 9): Getting around the fantasy world, and gaining in power over time.

Magic (Chapter 10): Learning, preparing, and casting spells, plus rules for creating and discerning illusions, summoning monsters, and bringing back the dead.

Spells (Chapter 11): Spells from level 0 to level 9 for clerics, druids, sorcerers, and wizards, plus spells for bards, paladins, and rangers.

DICE

The rules abbreviate dice rolls with phrases such as "3d4+3" (which means "three four-sided dice plus 3," generating a number between 6 and 15). The first number tells you how many dice to roll (all of which are added together), the number after the "d" tells you what type of dice to use, and any number after that indicates a number added to or subtracted from the result.

Some examples include the following:

1d8: One eight-sided die (generating a number from 1–8). This is the amount of damage that a longsword deals.

1d8+2: One eight-sided die plus 2 (3–10). This is the amount of damage that a longsword deals when swung by a character with a +2 Strength bonus.

2d4+2: Two four-sided dice plus 2 (4–10). This is the amount of damage that a 3rd-level wizard deals with a *magic missile* spell.

d%: The "d%" ("percentile dice") is a special case. When you roll d%, you generate a number between 1 and 100 by rolling two different-colored ten-sided dice. One color (designated before you roll) is the tens digit and the other is the ones digit. A roll of 7 and 1, for example, gives you a result of 71. A 0 and 6 equals 6. A double-0 (two zeros), however, represents 100. Some pairs of percentile dice are both the same color. In this case, the tens digit is marked on the tens die in tens: 10, 20, etc., while the ones die has numbers from 1 to 0. With these dice, a roll of 70 and 1 would give you a result of 71, and a result of 10 and 0 would be 100.

THIS GAME IS FANTASY

The action of a DUNGEONS & DRAGONS game takes place in the imaginations of the players. Like actors in a movie, players sometimes speak as if they were their characters or as if their fellow players were their characters. These rules even adopt that casual approach, using "you" to refer to and to mean "your character." In reality, however, you are no more your character than you are the king when you play chess.

Likewise, the world implied by these rules is an imaginary one.

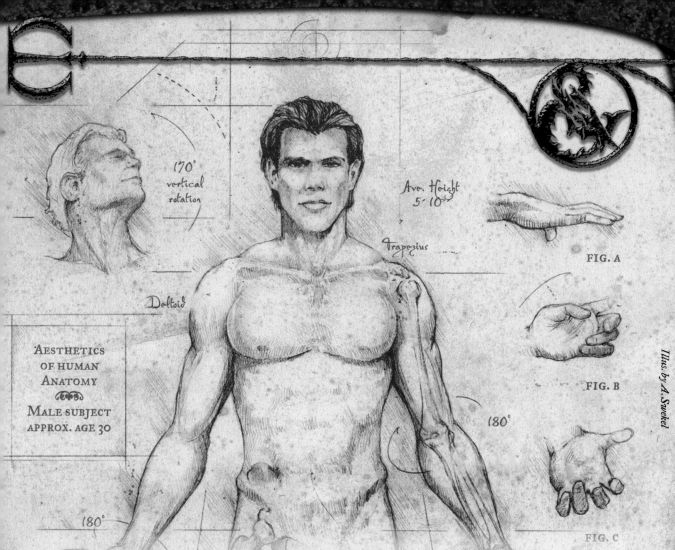

AESTHETICS
OF HUMAN
ANATOMY
⚜
MALE SUBJECT
APPROX. AGE 30

170°
vertical
rotation

Ave. Height
5'10"

Trapezius

Deltoid

FIG. A

FIG. B

180°

FIG. C

180°

Illus. by A. Swekel

Just about every dice roll you make is going to be modified based on your character's abilities. A tough character has a better chance of surviving a wyvern's poison sting. A perceptive character is more likely to notice bugbears sneaking up from behind. A stupid character is less likely to find a secret door that leads to a hidden treasure chamber. Your ability scores tell you what your modifiers are for rolls such as these.

Your character has six abilities: Strength (abbreviated Str), Dexterity (Dex), Constitution (Con), Intelligence (Int), Wisdom (Wis), and Charisma (Cha). Each of your character's above-average abilities gives you a benefit on certain die rolls, and each below-average ability gives you a disadvantage on other die rolls. You roll your scores randomly, assign them to the abilities you like, raise and lower them according to your character's race, and then raise them as your character advances in experience.

YOUR ABILITY SCORES

To create an ability score for your character, roll four six-sided dice (4d6). Disregard the lowest die, and total the three highest dice.

This roll gives you a number between 3 (horrible) and 18 (tremendous). The average ability score for the typical commoner is 10 or 11, but your character is not typical. The most common ability scores for player characters (PCs) are 12 and 13. (That's right, the average player character is above average.)

Make this roll six times, recording the result each time on a piece of paper. Once you have all six scores, assign each score to one of your six abilities. At this step, you need to know what kind of person your character is going to be, including his race and class, in order to know where best to place your character's ability scores. Remember that choosing a race other than human or

half-elf causes some of these ability scores to change (see Table 2–1: Racial Ability Adjustments, page 12).

ABILITY MODIFIERS

Each ability, after changes made because of race, will have a modifier ranging from –5 to +5. Table 1–1: Ability Modifiers and Bonus Spells (see the next page) shows the modifier for each ability, based on its score. It also shows bonus spells, which you'll need to know about if your character is a spellcaster.

The modifier is the number you add to or subtract from the die roll when your character tries to do something related to that ability. For instance, you add or subtract your Strength modifier to your roll when you try to hit someone with a sword. You also use the modifier with some numbers that aren't die rolls, such as when you apply your Dexterity modifier to your Armor Class (AC). A positive modifier is called a bonus, and a negative modifier is called a penalty.

ABILITIES AND SPELLCASTERS

The ability that spells relate to depends on what type of spellcaster you are: Intelligence for wizards; Wisdom for clerics, druids, paladins, and rangers; or Charisma for sorcerers and bards. In addition to having a high ability score, a spellcaster must be of sufficient level in order to gain a bonus spell of a given level. (See the class descriptions in Chapter 3 for details.) For instance, the wizard Mialee has a 15 Intelligence, so she's smart enough to get one bonus 1st-level spell and one bonus 2nd-level spell. (She will not

TABLE 1–1: ABILITY MODIFIERS AND BONUS SPELLS

Score	Modifier	0	1	2	3	4	5	6	7	8	9
1	−5	Can't cast spells tied to this ability									
2–3	−4	Can't cast spells tied to this ability									
4–5	−3	Can't cast spells tied to this ability									
6–7	−2	Can't cast spells tied to this ability									
8–9	−1	Can't cast spells tied to this ability									
10–11	0	—	—	—	—	—	—	—	—	—	—
12–13	+1	—	1	—	—	—	—	—	—	—	—
14–15	+2	—	1	1	—	—	—	—	—	—	—
16–17	+3	—	1	1	1	—	—	—	—	—	—
18–19	+4	—	1	1	1	1	—	—	—	—	—
20–21	+5	—	2	1	1	1	1	—	—	—	—
22–23	+6	—	2	2	1	1	1	1	—	—	—
24–25	+7	—	2	2	2	1	1	1	1	—	—
26–27	+8	—	2	2	2	2	1	1	1	1	—
28–29	+9	—	3	2	2	2	2	1	1	1	1
30–31	+10	—	3	3	2	2	2	2	1	1	1
32–33	+11	—	3	3	3	2	2	2	2	1	1
34–35	+12	—	3	3	3	3	2	2	2	2	1
36–37	+13	—	4	3	3	3	3	2	2	2	2
38–39	+14	—	4	4	3	3	3	3	2	2	2
40–41	+15	—	4	4	4	3	3	3	3	2	2
42–43	+16	—	4	4	4	4	3	3	3	3	2
44–45	+17	—	5	4	4	4	4	3	3	3	3

etc. . . .

actually get the 2nd-level bonus spell until she is 3rd level, the minimum level a wizard must be to cast 2nd-level spells.)

If your character's ability score is 9 or lower, you can't cast spells tied to that ability. For example, if Mialee's Intelligence dropped to 9 because of a poison that reduces intellect, she would not be able to cast even her simplest spells until cured.

REROLLING

If your scores are too low, you may scrap them and roll all six scores over. Your scores are considered too low if your total modifiers (before changes according to race) are 0 or less, or if your highest score is 13 or lower.

THE ABILITIES

Each ability partially describes your character and affects some of your character's actions.

The description of each ability includes a list of races and creatures along with their average scores in that ability. (Not every creature has a score in every ability, as you'll see when you look at the lists that follow.) These scores are for an average, young adult member of that race or species, such as a dwarven tax collector, a halfling merchant, or an unexceptional gnoll. An adventurer—say, a dwarven fighter or a gnoll ranger—probably has better scores, at least in the abilities that matter most to them, and player characters are above average overall.

STRENGTH (Str)

Strength measures your character's muscle and physical power. This ability is especially important for fighters, barbarians, paladins, rangers, and monks because it helps them prevail in combat. You apply your character's Strength modifier to:

- Melee attack rolls.
- Damage rolls when using a melee weapon or a thrown weapon. (Exceptions: Off-hand attacks receive only half the Strength modifier, while two-handed attacks receive one and a half times the Strength modifier. A Strength penalty, but not a bonus, applies to attacks made with a bow or a sling.)
- Climb, Jump, and Swim checks. These are the skills that have Strength as their key ability.
- Strength checks (for breaking down doors and the like).

TABLE 1–2: AVERAGE STRENGTH SCORES

Race or Creature	Average Strength	Average Modifier
Ghost	—	—
Toad	1	−5
Rat	2	−4
Weasel	3	−4
Small monstrous centipede	4–5	−3
Kobold	6–7	−2
Halfling or goblin	8–9	−1
Human	10–11	0
Half-orc	12–13	+1
Gnoll	14–15	+2
Small earth elemental	16–17	+3
Centaur	18–19	+4
Fire giant	30–31	+10
Nightshade nightcrawler	44–45	+17
Great gold wyrm	46–47	+18

DEXTERITY (Dex)

Dexterity measures hand-eye coordination, agility, reflexes, and balance. This ability is the most important ability for rogues, but it's also high on the list for characters who typically wear light or medium armor (barbarians and rangers) or none at all (monks, wizards, and sorcerers), and for anyone who wants to be a skilled archer.

You apply your character's Dexterity modifier to:

- Ranged attack rolls, including attacks made with bows, crossbows, throwing axes, and other ranged weapons.
- Armor Class (AC), provided the character can react to the attack.
- Reflex saving throws, for avoiding *fireballs* and other attacks that you can escape by moving quickly.
- Balance, Escape Artist, Hide, Move Silently, Open Lock, Pick Pocket, Ride, Tumble, and Use Rope checks. These are the skills that have Dexterity as their key ability.

Table 1–3: Average Dexterity Scores

Race or Creature	Average Dexterity	Average Modifier
Green slime	—	—
Gelatinous cube	1	–5
Colossal animated object	4–5	–3
Purple worm	6–7	–2
Ogre	8–9	–1
Human	10–11	0
Elf or halfling	12–13	+1
Displacer beast	14–15	+2
Blink dog	16–17	+3
Astral deva	18–19	+4
Elder air elemental	32–33	+11

CONSTITUTION (Con)

Constitution represents your character's health and stamina. Constitution increases a character's hit points, so it's important for everyone.

You apply your Constitution modifier to:

- Each Hit Die (though a penalty can never drop a Hit Die roll below 1—that is, a character always gains at least 1 hp each time he or she goes up a level).
- Fortitude saving throws, for resisting poison and similar threats.
- Concentration checks. This is a skill, important to spellcasters, that has Constitution as its key ability.

If a character's Constitution changes enough to alter his or her Constitution modifier, his or her hit points also increase or decrease accordingly.

Table 1–4: Average Constitution Scores

Race or Creature	Average Constitution	Average Modifier
Ghost	—	—
Grey elf	6–7	–2
Wild elf	8–9	–1
Human	10–11	0
Dwarf or gnome	12–13	+1
Carrion crawler	14–15	+2
Griffon	16–17	+3
Horse	18–19	+4
The tarrasque	35	+12

INTELLIGENCE (Int)

Intelligence determines how well your character learns and reasons. Intelligence is important for wizards because it affects how many spells they can cast, how hard their spells are to resist, and how powerful their spells can be. It's also important for any character who wants to have a strong assortment of skills.

You apply your character's Intelligence modifier to:

- The number of languages your character knows at the start of the game.
- The number of skill points gained each level. (But your character always gets at least 1 skill point per level.)
- Alchemy, Appraise, Craft, Decipher Script, Disable Device, Forgery, Knowledge, Read Lips, Scry, Search, and Spellcraft checks. These are the skills that have Intelligence as their key ability.

Wizards gain bonus spells based on their Intelligence scores. The minimum Intelligence needed to cast a wizard spell is 10 + the spell's level.

Animals have Intelligence scores of 1 or 2. Creatures of human-like intelligence have scores of at least 3.

Table 1–5: Average Intelligence Scores

Race or Creature	Average Intelligence	Average Modifier
Zombie	—	—
Carrion crawler	1	–5
Tiger	2	–4
Hydra	3	–4
Otyugh	4–5	–3
Troll	6–7	–2
Half-orc	8–9	–1
Human	10–11	0
Dragon turtle	12–13	+1
Invisible stalker	14–15	+2
Beholder	16–17	+3
Mind flayer	18–19	+4
Kraken	20–21	+5
Great gold wyrm	32–33	+11

WISDOM (Wis)

Wisdom describes a character's willpower, common sense, perception, and intuition. While Intelligence represents one's ability to analyze information, Wisdom is more related to being in tune with and aware of one's surroundings. An "absentminded professor" has low Wisdom and high Intelligence. A simpleton (low Intelligence) might still have great insight (high Wisdom). Wisdom is the most important ability for clerics and druids, and is also important for paladins and rangers. If you want your character to have keen senses, put a high score in Wisdom.

You apply your character's Wisdom modifier to:

- Will saving throws (for negating *charm person* and other spells).
- Heal, Innuendo, Intuit Direction, Listen, Profession, Sense Motive, Spot, and Wilderness Lore checks. These are the skills that have Wisdom as their key ability.

Clerics, druids, paladins, and rangers get bonus spells based on their Wisdom scores. The minimum Wisdom needed to cast a cleric, druid, paladin, or ranger spell is 10 + the spell's level.

Every creature has a Wisdom score.

Table 1–6: Average Wisdom Scores

Race or Creature	Average Wisdom	Average Modifier
Gelatinous cube	1	–5
Shrieker	2	–4
Orc	8–9	–1
Human	10–11	0
Owlbear	12–13	+1
Wraith	14–15	+2
Devourer	16–17	+3
Couatl	18–19	+4
Unicorn	20–21	+5
Great gold wyrm	32–33	+11

CHARISMA (Cha)

Charisma measures a character's force of personality, persuasiveness, personal magnetism, ability to lead, and physical attractiveness. It represents actual personal strength, not merely how one is perceived by others in a social setting. Charisma is most important for paladins, sorcerers, and bards. It is also important for clerics, since it affects their ability to turn undead.

You apply your Charisma modifier to:

- Animal Empathy, Bluff, Diplomacy, Disguise, Gather Information, Handle Animal, Intimidate, Perform, and Use Magic Device checks. These are the skills that have Charisma as their key ability.
- Checks that represent an attempt to influence others.

9

- Turning checks for clerics and paladins attempting to turn zombies, vampires, and other undead.

Sorcerers and bards get bonus spells based on their Charisma scores. The minimum Charisma needed to cast a sorcerer or bard spell is 10 + the spell's level.

Every creature has a Charisma score.

TABLE 1–7: AVERAGE CHARISMA SCORES

Race or Creature	Average Charisma	Average Modifier
Zombie	1	–5
Spider	2	–4
Dretch tanar'ri	4–5	–3
Triceratops	6–7	–2
Dwarf or half-orc	8–9	–1
Human or wolverine	10–11	0
Dragonne	12–13	+1
Storm giant	14–15	+2
Ogre mage	16–17	+3
Large barghest	18–19	+4
Great gold wyrm	32–33	+11

EXAMPLE OF GENERATING AND ASSIGNING ABILITY SCORES

Monte wants to create a new character. He rolls four six-sided dice (4d6) and gets 5, 4, 4, and 1. Ignoring the lowest die, he records the result on scratch paper: 13. He does this five more times and gets these six scores: 13, 10, 15, 12, 8, and 14. Monte decides to play a strong, tough dwarven fighter. Now he assigns his rolls to abilities.

Strength gets the highest score, 15. His character has a +2 Strength bonus that will serve him well in combat.

Constitution gets the next highest score, 14. The dwarf's +2 Constitution racial ability adjustment (see Table 2–1: Racial Ability Adjustments, page 12) improves his Constitution score to 16, for a +3 bonus, which gives him more hit points and better Fortitude saving throws.

Monte puts his lowest score, 8, into Charisma. The dwarf's –2 Charisma racial ability adjustment (see Table 2–1: Racial Ability Adjustments) reduces his Charisma score to 6, for a –2 penalty.

Monte has two bonus-range scores left (13 and 12), plus an average score (10). Dexterity gets the 13 (+1 bonus). That helps with attacking with ranged weapons and with Reflex saving throws. (Monte's also thinking ahead. A Dexterity score of 13 qualifies his character for the Dodge feat—see Table 5–1: Feats, page 79).

Wisdom gets the 12 (+1 bonus). That helps with perception skills, such as Spot and Listen (see Table 4–2: Skills, page 59), as well as with Will saving throws.

Intelligence gets the 10 (no bonus or penalty). An average Intelligence isn't bad for a fighter.

Monte records his character's race, class, ability scores, and ability modifiers on his character sheet.

CHANGING ABILITY SCORES

Over time, the ability scores your character starts with can change. Ability scores can increase with no limit.

- Add 1 point to any score at 4th level and every four levels your character attains thereafter (at 8th, 12th, 16th, and 20th level).
- Many spells and magical effects temporarily increase or decrease ability scores. The *ray of enfeeblement* spell reduces a creature's Strength, and the *strength* spell increases it. Sometimes a spell simply hampers a character, effectively reducing his or her ability score. A character trapped by an *entangle* spell, for example, acts as if his Dexterity were 4 points lower than it really is.
- Several magic items improve the user's ability scores as long as the character is using them. *Gloves of dexterity*, for example, improve the wearer's Dexterity score. (Magic items are described in the DUNGEON MASTER's Guide.) Note that a magic item of this type can't change an ability score by more than +6.
- Some rare magic items can boost an ability score permanently, as can a *wish* spell. Such a bonus is called an inherent bonus. An ability score can't have an inherent bonus of more than +5.
- Poisons, diseases, and other effects can temporarily harm an ability (temporary ability damage). Ability points lost to damage return on their own, typically at a rate of 1 point per day.
- Wraiths and certain other undead creatures drain abilities, resulting in a permanent loss (permanent ability drain). Points lost this way don't return on their own, but they can be brought back with spells, such as *restoration*.
- As a character ages, some ability scores go up and others go down. See Table 6–5: Aging Effects, page 93.

When an ability score changes, all attributes associated with that score change accordingly. For example, when Mialee becomes a 4th-level wizard, she decides to increase her Intelligence to 16. That gives her a 3rd-level bonus spell (which she'll pick up at 5th level, when she is able to cast 3rd-level spells), and it increases the number of skill points she gets per level from 4 to 5 (2 per level for her class, plus another 3 per level from her Intelligence bonus). As a new 4th-level character, she can get the skill points after raising her Intelligence, so she'll get 5 points for achieving 4th level in the wizard class. She does not retroactively get additional points for her previous levels (that is, skill points she would have gained if she had had an Intelligence score of 16 starting at 1st level).

INTELLIGENCE, WISDOM, AND CHARISMA

You can use your character's Intelligence, Wisdom, and Charisma scores to guide you in roleplaying your character. Here are some guidelines (just guidelines) about what these scores can mean.

A smart character is curious, knowledgeable, and prone to using big words. A character with a high Intelligence but low Wisdom may be smart but absent-minded, or knowledgeable but lacking in common sense. A character with a high Intelligence but a low Charisma may be a know-it-all or a reclusive scholar. The smart character lacking in both Wisdom and Charisma is usually putting her foot in her mouth.

A character with a low Intelligence mispronounces and misuses words, has trouble following directions, or fails to get the joke.

A character with a high Wisdom score may be sensible, serene, "in tune," alert, or centered. A character with a high Wisdom but a low Intelligence may be aware, but simple. A character with a high Wisdom but a low Charisma knows enough to speak carefully and may become an advisor or "power behind the throne" rather than a leader.

A character with a low Wisdom score may be rash, imprudent, irresponsible, or "out of it."

A character with a high Charisma may be attractive, striking, personable, and confident. A character with a high Charisma but a low Intelligence can usually pass herself off as knowledgeable, until she meets a true expert. A charismatic character with a low Wisdom may be popular, but she doesn't know who her real friends are.

A character with a low Charisma may be reserved, gruff, rude, fawning, or simply nondescript.

FIG. A

FIG. B

FIG. C

FIG. D

FIG. E

FIG. F

FIG. G

Illus. by A. Swekel

RACES CHAPTER TWO

The elven woods are home to the elves and their allies. You won't find many dwarves or half-orcs there. In turn, elves, humans, halflings, and half-orcs are hard to find in underground dwarven cities. And while nonhumans may travel through the human countryside, most country folk are humans. In the big cities, however, the promise of power and profit brings together people of all the common races: humans, dwarves, elves, gnomes, half-elves, half-orcs, and halflings.

CHOOSING A RACE

After you roll your ability scores and before you write them on your character sheet, choose your character's race. At the same time, you'll want to choose his or her class, since race affects how well he or she can do in each class. Once you know your character's race and class, assign your ability score rolls to particular abilities, alter the abilities according to race (see Table 2–1: Racial Ability Adjustments), and continue detailing your character.

You can play a character of any race or class, but certain races do better pursuing certain careers. Halflings, for example, can be fighters, but their small size and special features make them do better as rogues.

Your character's race gives you plenty of cues as to what sort of person he or she is, how he or she feels about characters of other races, and what might motivate him or her. Remember, however, that these descriptions of races only apply to the majority of people. In each race, some individuals diverge from the norm, and your character could be one of these. Don't let a description of a race keep you from detailing your character as you like.

RACIAL CHARACTERISTICS

Your character's race determines some of his or her qualities.

ABILITY ADJUSTMENTS

Find your character's race on Table 2–1: Racial Ability Adjustments (see the next page) and apply the adjustments you see there to your character's ability scores. If these changes raise your score above 18 or below 3, that's okay. *Exception:* Intelligence for characters does not go below 3. If your half-orc character would have an adjusted Intelligence of 1 or 2, make it 3 instead.

For example, Lidda, a halfling, gets a +2 racial bonus on her Dexterity score and a –2 racial penalty on her Strength. Knowing this, her player puts her best score rolled (15) in Dexterity and sees it increase to 17. She doesn't want a Strength penalty, so she puts an above-average score (12) in Strength. It drops to 10, which carries neither a bonus nor a penalty.

FAVORED CLASS

Each race's favored class is also listed on Table 2–1: Racial Ability Adjustments. A character's favored class doesn't count against the character when determining XP penalties for multiclassing (see Experience for Multiclass Characters, page 56).

For example, as a halfling rogue, Lidda can add a second class later on (becoming a multiclass character) without worrying about an XP penalty.

Illus. by T. Lockwood

Human   Half-Orc   Half-Elf   Dwarf   Elf   Gnome   Halfling

TABLE 2–1: RACIAL ABILITY ADJUSTMENTS

Race	Ability Adjustments	Favored Class
Human	None	Any
Dwarf	+2 Constitution, –2 Charisma	Fighter
Elf	+2 Dexterity, –2 Constitution	Wizard
Gnome	+2 Constitution, –2 Strength	Illusionist*
Half-elf	None	Any
Half-orc	+2 Strength, –2 Intelligence**, –2 Charisma	Barbarian
Halfling	+2 Dexterity, –2 Strength	Rogue

  *A wizard who specializes in illusion spells.

**A half-orc's starting Intelligence is at least 3. If this adjustment would lower the character's score to 1 or 2, his or her score is 3.

RACE AND LANGUAGES

In a big city, visitors can hear all manner of languages being spoken. Dwarves haggle over gems in Dwarven, elven sages engage in learned debates in Elven, and preachers call out prayers in Celestial. The language heard most, however, is Common, a tongue shared by all who take part in the culture at large. With all these languages in use, it is easy for people to learn others' languages, and adventurers often speak several tongues.

All characters know how to speak Common. Dwarves, elves, gnomes, half-elves, half-orcs, and halflings also speak a racial language, as appropriate. Smart characters (those with an Intelligence bonus) speak other languages as well, one extra language per point of bonus. Select your character's bonus languages (if any) from the list found in his or her race's description later in this chapter.

Literacy: Unless your character is a barbarian, he or she can read and write all the languages he or she speaks. (A barbarian can become literate by spending skill points.)

Class-Related Languages: Clerics, druids, and wizards can choose certain languages as bonus languages even if they're not on the lists found in the race descriptions. These class-related languages are as follows:

Cleric: Abyssal, Celestial, Infernal.

Druid: Druidic.

Wizard: Draconic.

HUMANS

Most humans are the ancestors of pioneers, conquerors, traders, travelers, refugees, and other people on the move. As a result, human lands are a mix of people—physically, culturally, religiously, and politically. Hardy or fine, light-skinned or dark, showy or austere, primitive or civilized, devout or impious, humans run the gamut.

Personality: Humans are the most adaptable, flexible, and ambitious people among the common races. They are diverse in their tastes, morals, customs, and habits. Others accuse them of having little respect for history, but it's only natural that humans, with their relatively short life spans and constantly changing cultures, would have a shorter collective memory than dwarves, elves, gnomes, and halflings.

Physical Description: Humans typically stand from 5 feet to a little over 6 feet tall and weigh from 125 to 250 pounds, with men noticeably taller and heavier than women. Thanks to their penchant for migration and conquest, and to their short generations, humans are more physically diverse than other common races, with skin shades that run from nearly black to very pale, hair from black to blond (curly, kinky, or straight), and facial hair (for men) from sparse to thick. Plenty of humans have a dash of nonhuman blood, and they may demonstrate hints of elven, orc, or other lineages. Humans are

Human · Half-Orc · Half-Elf · Elf · Gnome · Dwarf · Halfling

Illus. by T. Lockwood

often ostentatious or unorthodox in their grooming and dress, sporting unusual hairstyles, fanciful clothes, tattoos, body piercings, and the like. Humans have short life spans, achieving majority at about 15 and rarely living even a single century.

Relations: Just as readily as they mix with each other, humans mix with members of other races. Among the other races, humans are known as "everyone's second-best friends." They serve as ambassadors, diplomats, magistrates, merchants, and functionaries of all kinds.

Alignment: Humans tend toward no particular alignment, not even neutrality. The best and the worst are found among humans.

Human Lands: Human lands are usually in flux, with new ideas, social changes, innovations, and new leaders constantly coming to the fore. Members of longer-lived races find human culture exciting but eventually a little wearying or even bewildering.

Since humans lead such short lives, their leaders are all young compared to the political, religious, and military leaders among the other races. Even where individual humans are conservative traditionalists, human institutions change with the generations, adapting and evolving faster than parallel institutions among the elves, dwarves, gnomes, and halflings. Individually and as a group, humans are adaptable opportunists, and they stay on top of changing political dynamics.

Human lands generally include relatively large numbers of nonhumans (compared, for instance, to the number of non-dwarves who live in dwarven lands).

Religion: Unlike members of the other common races, humans do not have a chief racial deity. Pelor, the sun god, is the most commonly worshiped deity in human lands, but he has nothing like the central place that dwarves give Moradin or elves give Corellon Larethian. Some humans are the most ardent and zealous adherents of a given religion, while others are the most impious people around.

Language: Humans speak Common. They typically learn other languages, including obscure ones, and they are fond of sprinkling their speech with words borrowed from other tongues: Orc curses, Halfling culinary terms, Elven musical expressions, Dwarven military phrases, and so on.

Names: Human names vary greatly. Without a unifying deity to give them a touchstone for their culture, and with such a fast breeding cycle, humans mutate socially at a fast rate. Human culture, therefore, is more diverse than other cultures, and no human names are truly typical. Some human parents give their children dwarven or elven names (pronounced more or less correctly).

Adventurers: Human adventurers are the most audacious, daring, and ambitious members of an audacious, daring, and ambitious race. A human can earn glory in the eyes of his or her fellows by amassing power, wealth, and fame. Humans, more than other people, champion causes rather than territories or groups.

HUMAN RACIAL TRAITS

- Medium-size: As Medium-size creatures, humans have no special bonuses or penalties due to their size.
- Human base speed is 30 feet.
- 1 extra feat at 1st level, because humans are quick to master specialized tasks and varied in their talents. See Chapter 5: Feats.
- 4 extra skill points at 1st level and 1 extra skill point at each additional level, since humans are versatile and capable. (The 4 skill points at first level are added on as a bonus, not multiplied in; see Chapter 4: Skills.)
- Automatic Language: Common. Bonus Languages: Any (other than secret languages, such as Druidic). See other racial lists for common languages or Table 4–6: Languages for a more comprehensive list. Humans mingle with all kinds of other folk and thus can learn any language found in an area.

- **Favored Class:** Any. When determining whether a multiclass human suffers an XP penalty, his highest-level class does not count. (See Experience for Multiclass Characters, page 56.)

DWARVES

Dwarves are known for their skill in warfare, their ability to withstand physical and magical punishment, their knowledge of the earth's secrets, their hard work, and their capacity for drinking ale. Their mysterious kingdoms, carved out from the insides of mountains, are renowned for the marvelous treasures that they produce as gifts or for trade.

Personality: Dwarves are slow to laugh or jest and suspicious of strangers, but they are generous to those few who earn their trust. Dwarves value gold, gems, jewelry, and art objects made with these precious materials, and they have been known to succumb to greed. They fight neither recklessly nor timidly, but with a careful courage and tenacity. Their sense of justice is strong, but at its worst it can turn into a thirst for vengeance. Among gnomes, who get along famously with dwarves, a mild oath is "If I'm lying, may I cross a dwarf."

Physical Description: Dwarves stand only 4 to 4 1/2 feet tall, but they are so broad and compact that they are, on average, almost as heavy as humans. Dwarven men are slightly taller and noticeably heavier than dwarven women. Dwarves' skin is typically deep tan or light brown, and their eyes are dark. Their hair is usually black, gray, or brown, and worn long. Dwarven men value their beards highly and groom them very carefully. Dwarves favor simple styles for their hair, beards, and clothes. Dwarves are considered adults at about age 50, and they can live to be over 400 years old.

Relations: Dwarves get along fine with gnomes, and passably with humans, half-elves, and halflings. Dwarves say, "The difference between an acquaintance and a friend is about a hundred years." Humans, with their short life spans, have a hard time forging truly strong bonds with dwarves. The best dwarf–human friendships are between a human and a dwarf who liked the human's parents and grandparents. Dwarves fail to appreciate elves' subtlety and art, regarding elves as unpredictable, fickle, and flighty. Still, elves and dwarves have, through the ages, found common cause in battles against orcs, goblins, and gnolls; and elves have earned the dwarves' grudging respect. Dwarves mistrust half-orcs in general, and the feeling is mutual. Luckily, dwarves are fair-minded, and they grant individual half-orcs the opportunity to prove themselves.

Alignment: Dwarves are usually lawful, and they tend toward good. Adventuring dwarves are less likely to fit the common mold, however, since they're more likely to be those who did not fit perfectly into dwarven society.

Dwarven Lands: Dwarven kingdoms are usually deep beneath the stony faces of mountains, where the dwarves mine gems and precious metals and forge items of wonder. Trustworthy members of other races are welcome here, though some parts of these lands are off limits even to them. Whatever wealth the dwarves can't find in their mountains they gain through trade. Dwarves dislike water travel, so enterprising humans frequently handle trade in dwarven goods when travel is along a water route.

Dwarves in human lands are typically mercenaries, weaponsmiths, armorsmiths, jewelers, and artisans. Dwarf bodyguards are renowned for their courage and loyalty, and they are well rewarded for their virtues.

Religion: The chief deity of the dwarves is Moradin, the Soul Forger. He is the creator of the dwarves, and he expects his followers to work for the betterment of the dwarven race.

Language: Dwarves speak Dwarven, which has its own runic script. Dwarven literature is marked by comprehensive histories of kingdoms and wars through the millennia. The Dwarven alphabet is also used (with minor variations) for the Gnome, Giant, Goblin, Orc, and Terran languages. Dwarves often speak the languages of their friends (humans and gnomes) and enemies. Some also learn Terran, the strange language of earth-based creatures such as xorn.

Names: A dwarf's name is granted to him by his clan elder, in accordance with tradition. Every proper dwarven name has been used and reused down through the generations. A dwarf's name is not his own. It belongs to his clan. If he misuses it or brings shame to it, his clan will strip him of it. A dwarf stripped of his name is forbidden by dwarven law to use any dwarven name in its place.

Male Names: Barendd, Brottor, Eberk, Einkil, Oskar, Rurik, Taklinn, Traubon, Ulfgar, and Veit.

Female Names: Artin, Audhild, Dagnal, Diesa, Gunnloda, Hlin, Ilde, Liftrasa, Sannl, and Torgga.

Clan Names: Balderk, Dankil, Gorunn, Holderhek, Loderr, Lutgehr, Rumnaheim, Strakeln, Torunn, and Ungart.

Adventurers: A dwarven adventurer may be motivated by crusading zeal, a love of excitement, or simple greed. As long as his accomplishments bring honor to his clan, his deeds earn him respect and status. Defeating giants and claiming powerful magic weapons are sure ways for a dwarf to earn the respect of other dwarves.

Human Skull   *Dwarf Skull*

DWARVEN RACIAL TRAITS

- **+2 Constitution, −2 Charisma:** Dwarves are stout and tough but tend to be gruff and reserved.
- **Medium-size:** As Medium-size creatures, dwarves have no special bonuses or penalties due to their size.
- Dwarven base speed is 20 feet.
- **Darkvision:** Dwarves can see in the dark up to 60 feet. Darkvision is black and white only, but it is otherwise like normal sight, and dwarves can function just fine with no light at all.
- **Stonecunning:** Stonecunning grants dwarves a +2 racial bonus on checks to notice unusual stonework, such as sliding walls,

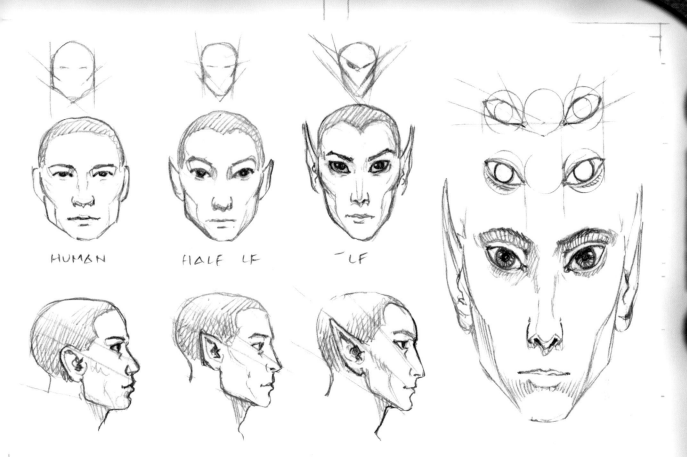

HUMAN   HALF ELF   ELF

Illus. by T. Lockwood

stonework traps, new construction (even when built to match the old), unsafe stone surfaces, shaky stone ceilings, and the like. Something that isn't stone but that is disguised as stone also counts as unusual stonework. A dwarf who merely comes within 10 feet of unusual stonework can make a check as if he were actively searching, and a dwarf can use the Search skill to find stonework traps as a rogue can. A dwarf can also intuit depth, sensing his approximate depth underground as naturally as a human can sense which way is up. Dwarves have a sixth sense about stonework, an innate ability that they get plenty of opportunity to practice and hone in their underground homes.

- +2 racial bonus on saving throws against poison: Dwarves are hardy and resistant to toxins.
- +2 racial bonus on saving throws against spells and spell-like effects.
- +1 racial bonus to attack rolls against orcs and goblinoids (goblins, hobgoblins, and bugbears): Dwarves are trained in the special combat techniques that allow them to fight their common enemies more effectively.
- +4 dodge bonus against giants: This bonus represents special training that dwarves undergo, during which they learn tricks that previous generations developed in their battles with giants. Note that any time a character loses his positive Dexterity bonus to Armor Class, such as when he's caught flat-footed, he loses his dodge bonus, too.
- +2 racial bonus on Appraise checks that are related to rare or exotic items: Dwarves are familiar with valuable items of all kinds (especially those made of stone or metal).
- +2 racial bonus on Craft checks that are related to stone or metal: Dwarves are especially capable with stonework and metalwork.
- Automatic Languages: Common and Dwarven. Bonus Languages: Giant, Gnome, Goblin, Orc, Terran, and Undercommon. Dwarves are familiar with the languages of their enemies and of their subterranean allies.

- Favored Class: Fighter. A multiclass dwarf's fighter class does not count when determining whether he suffers an XP penalty for multiclassing. (see Experience for Multiclass Characters, page 56). Dwarven culture extols the virtues of the warrior, and the vocation comes easily to dwarves.

ELVES

Elves mingle freely in human lands, always welcome yet never at home there. They are well known for their poetry, dance, song, lore, and magical arts. Elves favor things of natural and simple beauty. When danger threatens their woodland homes, however, elves reveal a more martial side, demonstrating skill with sword, bow, and battle strategy.

Personality: Elves are more often amused than excited, more likely to be curious than greedy. With such long lives, they tend to keep a broad perspective on events, remaining aloof and unfazed by petty happenstance. When pursuing a goal, however, whether an adventurous mission or learning a new skill or art, they can be focused and relentless. They are slow to make friends and enemies, and even slower to forget them. They reply to petty insults with disdain and to serious insults with vengeance.

Physical Description: Elves are short and slim, standing about 4 1/2 to 5 1/2 feet tall and typically weighing 85 to 135 pounds, with elven men the same height as and only marginally heavier than elven women. They are graceful but frail. They tend to be pale-skinned and dark-haired, with deep green eyes. Elves have no facial or body hair. They prefer simple, comfortable clothes, especially in pastel blues and greens, and they enjoy simple yet elegant jewelry. Elves possess unearthly grace and fine features. Many humans and members of other races find them hauntingly beautiful. An elf achieves majority at about 110 years in age and can live to be over 700 years old.

Elves do not sleep, as members of the other common races do. Instead, an elf meditates in a deep trance for 4 hours a day. An elf resting in this fashion gains the same benefit that a human does from 8 hours of sleep. While meditating, an elf dreams, though these dreams are actually mental exercises that have become reflexive through years of practice. The Common word for an elf's meditation is "trance," as in "four hours of trance."

Relations: Elves consider humans rather unrefined, halflings a bit staid, gnomes somewhat trivial, and dwarves not at all fun. They look on half-elves with some degree of pity, and they regard half-orcs with unrelenting suspicion. While haughty, elves are not particular the way halflings and dwarves can be, and they are generally pleasant and gracious even to those who fall short of elven standards (which, after all, consists of just about everybody who's not an elf).

Alignment: Elves love freedom, variety, and self-expression. They lean strongly toward the gentler aspects of chaos. Generally, they value and protect others' freedom as well as their own, and they are more often good than not.

Elven Lands: Elves mostly live in woodland clans of less than two hundred souls. Their well-hidden villages blend into the trees, doing little harm to the forest. They hunt game, gather food, and grow vegetables, their skill and magic allowing them to support themselves amply without the need for clearing and plowing land. Their contact with outsiders is usually limited, though some few elves make a good living trading finely worked elven clothes and crafts for the metals that elves have no interest in mining.

Elves encountered in human lands are commonly wandering minstrels, favored artists, or sages. Human nobles compete for the services of elven instructors, who teach swordplay to their children.

Religion: Above all others, elves worship Corellon Larethian, the Protector and Preserver of life. Elven myth holds that it was from his blood, shed in battles with Gruumsh, the god of the orcs, that the elves first arose. Corellon is a patron of magical study, arts, dance, and poetry, as well as a powerful warrior god.

Language: Elves speak a fluid language of subtle intonations and intricate grammar. While Elven literature is rich and varied, it is the language's songs and poems that are most famous. Many bards learn Elven so they can add Elven ballads to their repertoires. Others simply memorize Elven songs by sound. The Elven script, as flowing as the spoken word, also serves as the script for Sylvan, the language of dryads and pixies.

Names: When an elf declares herself an adult, usually some time after achieving her hundredth birthday, she also selects a name. Those who knew her as a youngster may or may not continue to call her by her "child name," and she may or may not care. An elf's adult name is a unique creation, though it may reflect the names of those she admires or the names of others in her family. In addition, she bears her family name. Family names are combinations of regular Elven words, and some elves traveling among humans translate their names into Common while others use the Elven version.

Male Names: Aramil, Aust, Enialis, Heian, Himo, Ivellios, Laucian, Quarion, Thamior, and Tharivol.

Female Names: Anastrianna, Antinua, Drusilia, Felosial, Ielenia, Lia, Qillathe, Silaqui, Valanthe, and Xanaphia.

Family Names: Amastacia ("Starflower"), Amakiir ("Gemflower"), Galanodel ("Moonwhisper"), Holimion ("Diamonddew"), Liadon ("Silverfrond"), Meliamne ("Oakenheel"), Naïlo ("Nightbreeze"), Siannodel ("Moonbrook"), Ilphukiir ("Gemblossom"), and Xiloscient ("Goldpetal").

Adventurers: Elves take up adventuring out of wanderlust. Life among humans moves at a pace that elves dislike: regimented from day to day but changing from decade to decade. Elves among humans, therefore, find careers that allow them to wander freely and set their own pace. Elves also enjoy demonstrating their prowess with the sword and bow or gaining greater magical powers, and adventuring allows them to do so. Good elves may also be rebels or crusaders.

ELVEN RACIAL TRAITS

- **+2 Dexterity, –2 Constitution:** Elves are graceful but frail. An elf's grace makes her naturally better at stealth and archery.
- **Medium-size:** As Medium-size creatures, elves have no special bonuses or penalties due to their size.
- Elven base speed is 30 feet.
- Immunity to magic *sleep* spells and effects, and a +2 racial saving throw bonus against Enchantment spells or effects.
- **Low-light Vision:** Elves can see twice as far as a human in starlight, moonlight, torchlight, and similar conditions of poor illumination. They retain the ability to distinguish color and detail under these conditions.
- Proficient with either longsword or rapier; proficient with shortbow, longbow, composite longbow, and composite shortbow. Elves esteem the arts of swordplay and archery, so all elves are familiar with these weapons.
- +2 racial bonus on Listen, Search, and Spot checks. An elf who merely passes within 5 feet of a secret or concealed door is entitled to a Search check to notice it as if she were actively looking for the door. An elf's senses are so keen that she practically has a sixth sense about hidden portals.
- **Automatic Languages:** Common and Elven. **Bonus Languages:** Draconic, Gnoll, Gnome, Goblin, Orc, and Sylvan. Elves commonly know the languages of their enemies and of their friends, as well as Draconic, the language commonly found in ancient tomes of secret knowledge.
- **Favored Class:** Wizard. A multiclass elf's wizard class does not count when determining whether she suffers an XP penalty for multiclassing (see Experience for Multiclass Characters, page 56). Wizardry comes naturally to elves (they sometimes claim to have invented it), and fighter/wizards are especially common among them.

GNOMES

Gnomes are welcome everywhere as technicians, alchemists, and inventors. Despite the demand for their skills, most gnomes prefer to remain among their own kind, living in comfortable burrows beneath rolling, wooded hills where animals abound but hunting is a very bad idea.

Personality: Gnomes adore animals, beautiful gems, and jokes of all kinds. Gnomes have a great sense of humor, and while they love puns, jokes, and games, they relish tricks—the more intricate the better. Fortunately, they apply the same dedication to more practical arts, such as engineering, as they do to their pranks.

Gnomes are inquisitive. They love to find things out by personal experience. At times they're even reckless. Their curiosity makes them skilled engineers, since they are always trying new ways to build things. Sometimes a gnome pulls a prank just to see how the people involved will react.

Physical Description: Gnomes stand about 3 to 3 1/2 feet tall and weigh 40 to 45 pounds. Their skin ranges from dark tan to woody brown, their hair is fair, and their eyes can be any shade of blue. Gnome males prefer short, carefully trimmed beards. Gnomes generally wear leather or earth tones, and they decorate their clothes with intricate stitching or fine jewelry. Gnomes reach adulthood at about age 40, and they live about 350 years, though some can live almost 500 years.

Relations: Gnomes get along well with dwarves, who share their love of precious objects, their curiosity about mechanical devices, and their hatred of goblins and giants. They enjoy the company of halflings, especially those who are easygoing enough to put up with pranks and jests. Most gnomes are a little suspicious of the taller races—humans, elves, half-elves, and half-orcs—but they are rarely hostile or malicious.

Alignment: Gnomes are most often good. Those who tend toward law are sages, engineers, researchers, scholars, investigators, or consultants. Those who tend toward chaos are tricksters, wanderers, or fanciful jewelers. Gnomes are good-hearted, and even the tricksters among them are more playful than vicious. Luckily, evil gnomes are as rare as they are frightening.

Gnome Lands: Gnomes make their homes in hilly, wooded lands. They live underground but get more fresh air than dwarves do, enjoying the natural, living world on the surface whenever they can. Their homes are well hidden, by both clever construction and illusions. Those who come to visit and are welcome are ushered into the bright, warm burrows. Those who are not welcome never find the burrows in the first place.

Gnomes who settle in human lands are commonly gemcutters, mechanics, sages, or tutors. Some human families retain gnome tutors. During his life, a gnome tutor can teach several generations of a single human family.

Religion: The chief gnome god is Garl Glittergold, the Watchful Protector. His clerics teach that gnomes are to cherish and support their communities. Pranks, for example, are seen as ways to lighten spirits and to keep gnomes humble, not ways for pranksters to triumph over those they trick.

Language: The Gnome language, which uses the Dwarven script, is renowned for its technical treatises and its catalogs of knowledge of the natural world. Human herbalists, naturalists, and engineers commonly learn Gnome in order to read the best books on their topics of study.

Names: Gnomes love names, and most have half a dozen or so. As a gnome grows up, his mother gives him a name, his father gives him a name, his clan elder gives him a name, his aunts and uncles give him names, and he gains nicknames from just about anyone. Gnome names are typically variants on the names of ancestors or distant relatives, though some are purely new inventions. When dealing with humans and others who are rather "stuffy" about names, gnomes learn to act as if they have no more than three names: a personal name, a clan name, and a nickname. When deciding which of his several names to use among humans, a gnome generally chooses the one that's the most fun to say. Gnome clan names are combinations of common Gnome words, and gnomes almost always translate them into Common when in human lands (or into Elven when in elven lands, and so on).

Male Names: Boddynock, Dimble, Fonkin, Glim, Gerbo, Jebeddo, Namfoodle, Roondar, Seebo, and Zook.

Female Names: Bimpnottin, Caramip, Duvamil, Ellywick, Ellyjobell, Loopmottin, Mardnab, Roywyn, Shamil, and Waywocket.

Clan Names: Beren, Daergel, Folkor, Garrick, Nackle, Murnig, Ningel, Raulnor, Scheppen, and Turen.

Nicknames: "Aleslosh," "Ashhearth," "Badger," "Cloak," "Doublelock," "Filchbatter," "Fnipper," "Oneshoe," "Sparklegem," and "Stumbleduck."

Adventurers: Gnomes are curious and impulsive. They may take up adventuring as a way to see the world or for the love of exploring. Lawful gnomes may adventure to set things right and to protect the innocent, demonstrating the same sense of duty toward society as a whole that gnomes generally exhibit toward their own enclaves. As lovers of gems and other fine items, some gnomes take to adventuring as a quick, if dangerous, path to wealth. Depending on his relations to his home clan, an adventuring gnome may be seen as a vagabond or even something of a traitor (for abandoning clan responsibilities).

GNOME RACIAL TRAITS

- **+2 Constitution, –2 Strength:** Like dwarves, gnomes are tough, but they are small and therefore not as strong as larger humanoids.
- **Small:** As Small creatures, gnomes gain a +1 size bonus to Armor Class, a +1 size bonus on attack rolls, and a +4 size bonus on Hide checks, but they must use smaller weapons than humans use, and their lifting and carrying limits are three-quarters of those of Medium-size characters.
- Gnome base speed is 20 feet.
- **Low-light Vision:** Gnomes can see twice as far as a human in starlight, moonlight, torchlight, and similar conditions of poor illumination. They retain the ability to distinguish color and detail under these conditions.
- +2 racial bonus on saving throws against illusions, because gnomes are innately familiar with illusions of all kinds.
- +1 racial bonus to attack rolls against kobolds and goblinoids (goblins, hobgoblins, and bugbears): Gnomes battle these creatures frequently and practice special techniques for fighting them.
- +4 dodge bonus against giants: This bonus represents special training that gnomes undergo, during which they learn tricks that previous generations developed in their battles with giants. Note that any time a character loses his positive Dexterity bonus to Armor Class, such as when he's caught flat-footed, he loses his dodge bonus, too.
- +2 racial bonus on Listen checks: Gnomes have keen ears.
- +2 racial bonus on Alchemy checks: A gnome's sensitive nose allows him to monitor alchemical processes by smell.
- **Automatic Languages:** Common and Gnome. **Bonus Languages:** Draconic, Dwarven, Elven, Giant, Goblin, and Orc. Gnomes deal more with elves and dwarves than elves and dwarves deal with one another, and they learn the languages of their enemies (kobolds, giants, goblins, and orcs) as well. In addition, once per day a gnome can use *speak with animals* as a spell-like ability to speak with a burrowing mammal (a badger, fox, rabbit, etc.). This ability is innate to gnomes. It has a duration of 1 minute (the gnome is considered a 1st-level caster when he uses this ability, regardless of his actual level). See the *speak with animals* spell description, page 254.
- Gnomes with Intelligence scores of 10 or higher may cast the 0-level spells (cantrips) *dancing lights*, *ghost sound*, and *prestidigitation*, each once per day. These are arcane spells, and as such the gnome suffers spell failure penalties for wearing armor. Treat the gnome as a 1st-level caster for all spell effects dependent on level (range for all three spells and duration for *ghost sound*). See the spell descriptions on pages 190, 209, and 238, respectively.
- **Favored Class:** Illusionist, which is a wizard who specializes in casting illusion spells (see page 158). A multiclass gnome's illusionist class does not count when determining whether he suffers an XP penalty (see Experience for Multiclass Characters, page 56).

HALF-ELVES

Humans and elves sometimes wed, the elf attracted to the human's energy and the human to the elf's grace. These marriages end quickly as elves count years because a human's life is so brief, but they leave an enduring legacy—half-elven children.

The life of a half-elf can be hard. If raised by elves, the half-elf grows with astounding speed, reaching maturity within two decades. The half-elf becomes an adult long before she has had time to learn the intricacies of elven art and culture, or even grammar. She leaves behind her childhood friends, becoming physically an adult but culturally still a child by elven standards. Typically, she leaves her elven home, which is no longer familiar, and finds her way among humans. If, on the other hand, she is raised by humans, the half-elf finds herself different from her peers: more aloof, more sensitive, less ambitious, and slower to mature. Some half-elves try to fit in among humans, while others find their identities in their difference. Most find places for themselves in human lands, but some feel like outsiders all their lives.

Illus. by T. Lockwood

Personality: Most half-elves have the curiosity, inventiveness, and ambition of the human parent, along with the refined senses, love of nature, and artistic tastes of the elven parent.

Physical Description: To humans, half-elves look like elves. To elves, they look like humans (indeed, elves call them "half-humans"). Half-elven height ranges from under 5 feet to almost 6 feet tall, and weight usually ranges from 90 to 180 pounds. Half-elven men are taller and heavier than half-elven women, but the difference is less pronounced than that found among humans. Half-elves are paler, fairer, and smoother-skinned than their human parents, but their actual skin tone, hair color, and other details vary just as human features do. Half-elves' eyes are green, just as are those of their elven parents. A half-elf reaches majority at age 20 and can live to be over 180 years old.

Most half-elves are the children of human–elf pairings. Some, however, are the children of parents who themselves are partly human and partly elven. Some of these "second generation" half-elves have humanlike eyes, but most still have green eyes.

Relations: Half-elves do well among both elves and humans, and they also get along well with dwarves, gnomes, and halflings. They have elven grace without elven aloofness, human energy without human boorishness. They make excellent ambassadors and go-betweens (except between elves and humans, where each side suspects the half-elf of favoring the other). In human lands where elves are distant or not on friendly terms, however, half-elves are viewed with suspicion.

Some half-elves show a marked disfavor toward half-orcs. Perhaps the similarities between themselves and half-orcs (both have human lineage) make these half-elves uncomfortable.

Alignment: Half-elves share the chaotic bent of their elven heritage, but, like humans, they tend toward neither good nor evil. Like elves, they value personal freedom and creative expression, demonstrating no love of leaders nor lust for followers. They chafe at rules, resent others' demands, and sometimes prove unreliable, or at least unpredictable.

Half-Elven Lands: Half-elves have no lands of their own, though they are welcome in human cities and elven forests. In large cities, half-elves sometimes form small communities of their own.

Religion: Half-elves raised among elves follow elven deities, principally Corellon Larethian, god of the elves. Those raised among humans often follow Ehlonna, goddess of the woodlands.

Language: Half-elves speak the languages they are born to, Common and Elven. Half-elves are slightly clumsy with the intricate Elven language, though only elves notice, and even so they do better than nonelves.

Names: Half-elves use either human or elven naming conventions. Ironically, half-elves among humans are often given elven names in honor of their heritage, just as half-elves raised among elves often take human names.

Adventurers: Half-elves find themselves drawn to strange careers and unusual company. Taking up the life of an adventurer comes easily to many of them. Like elves, they are driven by wanderlust.

HALF-ELVEN RACIAL TRAITS

- **Medium-size:** As Medium-size creatures, half-elves have no special bonuses or penalties due to their size.
- Half-elven base speed is 30 feet.
- Immunity to *sleep* spells and similar magical effects, and a +2 racial saving throw bonus against Enchantment spells or effects.
- **Low-light Vision:** Half-elves can see twice as far as a human in starlight, moonlight, torchlight, and similar conditions of poor illumination. They retain the ability to distinguish color and detail under these conditions.
- +1 racial bonus on Listen, Search, and Spot checks: Half-elves do not have the elf's ability to notice secret doors simply by passing near them. Half-elves have keen senses, but not as keen as those of an elf.
- Elven Blood: For all special abilities and effects, a half-elf is considered an elf. Half-elves, for example, can use elven weapons and magic items with racially specific elven powers as if they were elves.
- Automatic Languages: Common and Elven. Bonus Languages: Any (other than secret languages, such as Druidic). Half-elves have all the versatility and broad (if shallow) experience that humans have.
- Favored Class: Any. When determining whether a multiclass half-elf suffers an XP penalty, her highest-level class does not count (see Experience for Multiclass Characters, page 56).

HALF-ORCS

In the wild frontiers, tribes of human and orc barbarians live in uneasy balance, fighting in times of war and trading in times of peace. The half-orcs who are born in the frontier may live with either human or orc parents, but they are nevertheless exposed to both cultures. Some, for whatever reason, leave their homeland and travel to civilized lands, bringing with them the tenacity, courage, and combat prowess that they developed in the wilds.

Personality: Half-orcs are short-tempered and sullen. They would rather act than ponder and would rather fight than argue. Those who are successful, however, are those with enough self-control to live in a civilized land, not the crazy ones.

Half-orcs love simple pleasures such as feasting, drinking, boasting, singing, wrestling, drumming, and wild dancing. Refined enjoyments such as poetry, courtly dancing, and philosophy are lost on them. At the right sort of party, a half-orc is an asset. At the duchess's grand ball, he's a liability.

Physical Description: Half-orcs are as tall as humans and a little heavier, thanks to their muscle. A half-orc's grayish

CHAPTER 2: RACES

pigmentation, sloping forehead, jutting jaw, prominent teeth, and coarse body hair make his lineage plain for all to see.

Orcs like scars. They regard battle scars as tokens of pride and ornamental scars as things of beauty. Any half-orc who has lived among or near orcs has scars, whether they are marks of shame indicating servitude and identifying the half-orc's former owner, or marks of pride recounting conquests and high status. Such a half-orc living among humans either displays or hides his scars, depending on his attitude toward them.

Half-orcs mature a little faster than humans and age noticeably faster. Few half-orcs live longer than 75 years.

Relations: Because orcs are the sworn enemies of dwarves and elves, half-orcs can have a rough time with members of these races. For that matter, orcs aren't exactly on good terms with humans, halflings, or gnomes, either. Each half-orc finds a way to gain acceptance from those who hate or fear his orc cousins. Some are reserved, trying not to draw attention to themselves. Others demonstrate piety and good-heartedness as publicly as they can (whether or not such demonstrations are genuine). Others simply try to be so tough that others have no choice but to accept them.

Alignment: Half-orcs inherit a tendency toward chaos from their orc parents, but, like their human parents, they favor neither good nor evil. Half-orcs raised among orcs and willing to live out their lives with them, however, are usually the evil ones.

Half-Orc Lands: Half-orcs have no lands of their own. They most often live among orcs. Of the other races, humans are the ones most likely to accept half-orcs, and half-orcs almost always live in human lands when not living among orc tribes.

Religion: Like orcs, many half-orcs worship Gruumsh, the chief orc god and archenemy of Corellon Larethian, god of elves. While Gruumsh is evil, half-orc barbarians and fighters may worship him as a war god even if they are not evil themselves. Worshipers of Gruumsh who are tired of explaining themselves, or who don't want to give humans a reason to distrust them, simply don't make their religion public knowledge. Half-orcs who want to solidify their connection to their human heritage, on the other hand, follow human gods, and they may be outspoken in their shows of piety.

Language: Orc, which has no alphabet of its own, uses Dwarven script on the rare occasions that someone writes something in Orc. Orc writing turns up most frequently in graffiti.

Names: A half-orc typically chooses a name that helps him make the impression that he wants to make. If he wants to fit in among humans, he chooses a human name. If he wants to intimidate others, he chooses a guttural orc name. A half-orc who has been raised entirely by humans has a human given name, but he

may choose another name once he's away from his hometown. Some half-orcs, of course, aren't quite bright enough to choose a name this carefully.

Orc Male Names: Dench, Feng, Gell, Henk, Holg, Imsh, Keth, Ront, Shump, and Thokk.

Orc Female Names: Baggi, Emen, Engong, Myev, Neega, Ovak, Ownka, Shautha, Vola, and Volen.

Adventurers: Half-orcs living among humans are drawn almost invariably toward violent careers in which they can put their strength to good use. Frequently shunned from polite company, half-orcs often find acceptance and friendship among adventurers, many of who are fellow wanderers and outsiders.

HALF-ORC RACIAL TRAITS

- **+2 Strength, –2 Intelligence, –2 Charisma:** Half-orcs are strong, but their orc lineage makes them dull and crude.
- **Medium-size:** As Medium-size creatures, half-orcs have no special bonuses or penalties due to their size.
- Half-orc base speed is 30 feet.
- **Darkvision:** Half-orcs (and orcs) can see in the dark up to 60 feet. Darkvision is black and white only, but it is otherwise like normal sight, and half-orcs can function just fine with no light at all.
- **Orc Blood:** For all special abilities and effects, a half-orc is considered an orc. Half-orcs, for example, can use special orc weapons or magic items with racially specific orc powers as if they were orcs.
- **Automatic Languages:** Common and Orc. **Bonus Languages:** Draconic, Giant, Gnoll, Goblin, and Infernal. Smart half-orcs (who are rare) may know the languages of their allies or rivals.
- **Favored Class:** Barbarian. A multiclass half-orc's barbarian class does not count when determining whether he suffers an XP penalty (see Experience for Multiclass Characters, page 56). Ferocity runs in a half-orc's veins.

HALFLINGS

Halflings are clever, capable opportunists. Halfling individuals and clans find room for themselves wherever they can. Often they are strangers and wanderers, and others react to them with suspicion or curiosity. Depending on the clan, halflings might be reliable, hard-working (if clannish) citizens, or they might be thieves just waiting for the opportunity to make a big score and disappear in the dead of night. Regardless, halflings are cunning, resourceful survivors.

Personality: Halflings prefer trouble to boredom. They are notoriously curious. Relying on their ability to survive or escape danger, they demonstrate a daring that many larger people can't match.

Halflings have ample appetites, both for food and for other pleasures. They like well-cooked meals, fine drink, good tobacco, and comfortable clothes. While they can be lured by the promise of wealth, they tend to spend the gold they gain rather than hoarding it.

Illus. by T. Lockwood

Halflings are also famous collectors. While more orthodox halflings may collect teapots, books, or pressed flowers, some collect such objects as the hides of wild beasts—or even the beasts themselves. Wealthy halflings sometimes commission adventurers to retrieve exotic items to complete their collections.

Physical Description: Halflings stand about 3 feet tall and usually weigh between 30 and 35 pounds. Their skin is ruddy, their hair black and straight. They have brown or black eyes. Halfling men often have long sideburns, but beards are rare among them and mustaches almost unseen. They like to wear simple, comfortable, and practical clothes. Unlike members of most races, they prefer actual comfort to shows of wealth. A halfling would rather wear a comfortable shirt than jewelry. A halfling reaches adulthood in her early twenties and generally lives into the middle of her second century.

Relations: Halflings try to get along with everyone else. They are adept at fitting into a community of humans, dwarves, elves, or gnomes and making themselves valuable and welcome. Since human society changes faster than the societies of the longer-lived races, it is human society that most frequently offers halflings opportunities to exploit, and halflings are most often found in or around human lands.

Alignment: Halflings tend to be neutral and practical. While they are comfortable with change (a chaotic trait), they also tend to rely on intangible constants, such as clan ties and personal honor (a lawful trait).

Halfling Lands: Halflings have no lands of their own. Instead, they live in the lands of other races, where they can benefit from whatever resources those lands have to offer. Halflings often form tight-knit communities in human or dwarven cities. While they work readily with others, they often make friends only among each other. Halflings also settle into secluded places where they set up self-reliant villages. Halfling communities, however, are known to pick up and move en masse to some place that offers a new opportunity, such as where a new mine has opened up or to a land where a devastating war has made skilled workers hard to find. If these opportunities are temporary, the community may pick up and move again once the opportunity is gone, or once a better one presents itself. If the opportunity is lasting, the halflings settle and form a new village. Some communities, on the other hand, take to traveling as a way of life, driving wagons or guiding boats from place to place, with no permanent home.

Religion: The chief halfling deity is Yondalla, the Blessed One, protector of the halflings. Yondalla promises blessings and protection to those who heed her guidance, defend their clans, and cherish their families. Halflings also recognize countless small gods, which they say rule over individual villages, forests, rivers, lakes, and so on. They pay homage to these deities to ensure safe journeys as they travel from place to place.

Language: Halflings speak their own language, which uses the Common script. They write very little in their own language so, unlike dwarves, elves, and gnomes, they don't have a rich body of written work. The halfling oral tradition, however, is very strong.

While the Halfling language isn't secret, halflings are loath to share it with others. Almost all halflings speak Common, since they use it to deal with the people in whose land they are living or through which they are traveling.

Names: A halfling has a given name, a family name, and possibly a nickname. It would seem that family names are nothing more than nicknames that stuck so well they have been passed down through the generations.

Male Names: Alton, Beau, Cade, Eldon, Garret, Lyle, Milo, Osborn, Roscoe, and Wellby.

Female Names: Amaryllis, Charmaine, Cora, Euphemia, Jillian, Lavinia, Merla, Portia, Seraphina, and Verna.

Family Names: Brushgather, Goodbarrel, Greenbottle, Highhill, Hilltopple, Leagallow, Tealeaf, Thorngage, Tosscobble, Underbough.

Adventurers: Halflings often set out on their own to make their way in the world. Halfling adventurers are typically looking for a way to use their skills to gain wealth or status. The distinction between a halfling adventurer and a halfling out on her own looking for "a big score" can get blurry. For a halfling, adventuring is less of a career than an opportunity. While halfling opportunism can sometimes look like larceny or fraud to others, a halfling adventurer who learns to trust her fellows is worthy of trust in turn.

HALFLING RACIAL TRAITS

- **+2 Dexterity, –2 Strength:** Halflings are quick, agile, and good with ranged weapons, but they are small and therefore not as strong as other humanoids.
- **Small:** As Small creatures, halflings gain a +1 size bonus to Armor Class, a +1 size bonus on attack rolls, and a +4 size bonus on Hide checks, but they must use smaller weapons than humans use, and their lifting and carrying limits are three-quarters of those of Medium-size characters.
- Halfling base speed is 20 feet.
- **+2 racial bonus on Climb, Jump, and Move Silently checks:** Halflings are agile, surefooted, and athletic.
- **+1 racial bonus on all saving throws:** Halflings are surprisingly capable of avoiding mishaps.
- **+2 morale bonus on saving throws against fear.** (This bonus stacks with the halfling's +1 bonus on saving throws in general.)
- **+1 racial attack bonus with a thrown weapon:** Throwing stones is a universal sport among halflings, and they develop especially good aim.
- **+2 racial bonus on Listen checks:** Halflings have keen ears.
- **Automatic Languages:** Common and Halfling. **Bonus Languages:** Dwarven, Elven, Gnome, Goblin, and Orc. Smart halflings learn the languages of their friends and enemies.
- **Favored Class:** Rogue. A multiclass halfling's rogue class does not count when determining whether she suffers an XP penalty for multiclassing (see Experience for Multiclass Characters, page 56). Halflings have long had to rely on stealth, wit, and skill, and the vocation of rogue comes naturally to them.

SMALL CHARACTERS

Small characters get a +1 size bonus to Armor Class, a +1 size bonus on attack rolls, and a +4 size bonus on Hide checks. Small characters get an attack bonus because it's really relative size that matters in determining attack chances. It's no harder for a halfling to hit another halfling than it is for a human to hit another human because the attacking halfling's attack bonus counteracts the defending halfling's Armor Class bonus. Likewise, a halfling has an easy time hitting a human, just as a human has an easy time hitting an ogre, and an ogre has an easy time hitting a giant.

Small characters' lifting and carrying limits are three-quarters of those of Medium-size characters (see Bigger and Smaller Creatures, page 142).

Small characters generally move about two-thirds as fast as Medium-size characters.

Small characters must use smaller weapons than Medium-size characters. See Weapon Categories, page 96.

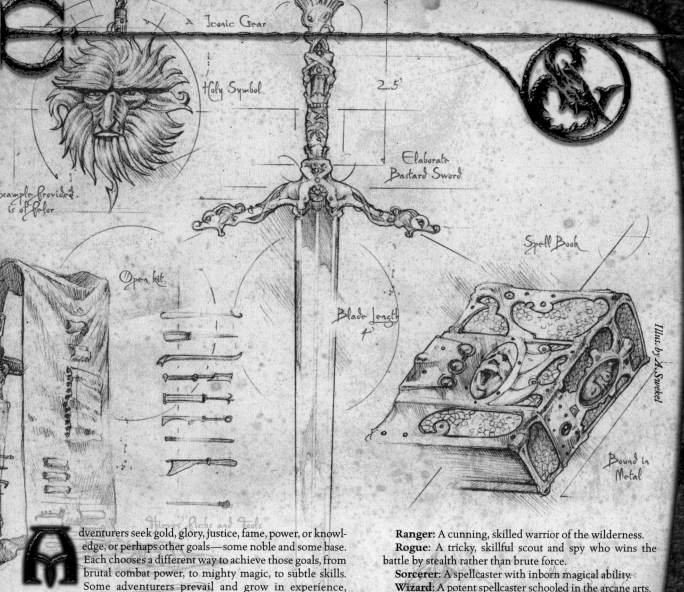

Illus. by A. Swekel

dventurers seek gold, glory, justice, fame, power, or knowledge, or perhaps other goals—some noble and some base. Each chooses a different way to achieve those goals, from brutal combat power, to mighty magic, to subtle skills. Some adventurers prevail and grow in experience, wealth, and power. Others die.

Your character's class is his or her profession or vocation. It determines what he or she is able to do: combat training, magical ability, skills, and more. Class is probably the first choice you make about your character (just ahead of race, or perhaps in conjunction with that decision). The class you choose determines where you should best place your character's ability scores and suggests which races are best to support that class choice.

THE CLASSES

The eleven classes, in the order they're presented in this chapter, are as follows:

Barbarian: A ferocious warrior who uses fury and instinct to bring down foes.

Bard: A performer whose music works magic—a wanderer, a tale-teller, and a jack-of-all trades.

Cleric: A master of divine magic and a capable warrior as well.

Druid: One who draws energy from the natural world to cast divine spells and gain strange magical powers.

Fighter: A warrior with exceptional combat capability and unequaled skill with weapons.

Monk: A martial artist whose unarmed strikes hit fast and hard—a master of exotic powers.

Paladin: A champion of justice and destroyer of evil, protected and strengthened by an array of divine powers.

Ranger: A cunning, skilled warrior of the wilderness.

Rogue: A tricky, skillful scout and spy who wins the battle by stealth rather than brute force.

Sorcerer: A spellcaster with inborn magical ability.

Wizard: A potent spellcaster schooled in the arcane arts.

Class Name Abbreviations: Class names are abbreviated as follows: Bbn, barbarian; Brd, bard; Clr, cleric; Drd, druid; Ftr, fighter; Mnk, monk; Pal, paladin; Rgr, ranger; Rog, rogue; Sor, sorcerer; Wiz, wizard.

THE MULTICLASS CHARACTER

As your character advances in level, he or she may add new classes. Adding a new class gives the character a broader range of abilities, but all advancement in the new class is at the expense of advancement in the character's other class or classes. A wizard, for example, might become a combination wizard/fighter. Adding the fighter class would give her proficiency in more weapons, better Fortitude saving throws, and so on, but it would also mean that she doesn't gain new wizard powers when she adds this second class and thus is not as powerful a wizard as she otherwise would have become if she had chosen to continue advancing as a wizard. Rules for creating and advancing multiclass characters can be found at the end of this chapter.

CLASS AND LEVEL BONUSES

An attack roll, saving throw, or skill check is a combination of three numbers, each representing a different factor: a random factor (the number you roll on

1d20), a number representing the character's innate abilities (the ability modifier), and a bonus representing the character's experience and training. This third factor depends on the character's class and level. Table 3–1: Base Save and Base Attack Bonuses summarizes the figures for this third factor.

Base Save Bonus: The two numbers given in this column on Table 3–1 apply to saving throws. Whether a character uses the first (lower) bonus or the second (higher) bonus depends on his or her class and the type of saving throw being attempted. For example, fighters get the lower bonus on Reflex and Will saves and the higher bonus on Fortitude saves, while rogues get the lower bonus on Fortitude and Will saves and the higher bonus on Reflex saves. Monks are equally good at all three types of saving throws. See each class's description to find which bonus applies to which category of saves. If a character has more than one class (see Multiclass Characters, page 55), the base save bonuses for each class are cumulative.

Base Attack Bonus: On an attack roll, apply the bonus from the appropriate column on Table 3–1 according to the class to which the character belongs. Numbers after a slash indicate additional attacks at reduced bonuses: "+12/+7/+2" means three attacks per round, with a base attack bonus of +12 for the first attack, +7 for the second, and +2 for the third. Ability modifiers apply to all these attacks normally, but bonuses from ability scores do not grant extra attacks. For example, when Lidda the halfling rogue is 3rd level, she has a base attack of +2. With a thrown weapon, she adds her Dexterity bonus (+3) and a racial bonus (+1) for a total of +6. Even though a +6 base attack bonus would grant an additional attack at +1, raising that number from +2 to +6 via ability, racial, or weapon bonuses doesn't grant Lidda an additional attack. If a character has more than one class (see Multiclass Characters, page 55), the base attack bonuses for each class are cumulative.

TABLE 3–1: BASE SAVE AND BASE ATTACK BONUSES

Class Level	Base Save Bonus	Fighter, Barbarian, Paladin, or Ranger Base Attack Bonus	Cleric, Druid, Rogue, Bard, or Monk Base Attack Bonus	Wizard or Sorcerer Base Attack Bonus
1	+0/+2	+1	+0	+0
2	+0/+3	+2	+1	+1
3	+1/+3	+3	+2	+1
4	+1/+4	+4	+3	+2
5	+1/+4	+5	+3	+2
6	+2/+5	+6/+1	+4	+3
7	+2/+5	+7/+2	+5	+3
8	+2/+6	+8/+3	+6/+1	+4
9	+3/+6	+9/+4	+6/+1	+4
10	+3/+7	+10/+5	+7/+2	+5
11	+3/+7	+11/+6/+1	+8/+3	+5
12	+4/+8	+12/+7/+2	+9/+4	+6/+1
13	+4/+8	+13/+8/+3	+9/+4	+6/+1
14	+4/+9	+14/+9/+4	+10/+5	+7/+2
15	+5/+9	+15/+10/+5	+11/+6/+1	+7/+2
16	+5/+10	+16/+11/+6/+1	+12/+7/+2	+8/+3
17	+5/+10	+17/+12/+7/+2	+12/+7/+2	+8/+3
18	+6/+11	+18/+13/+8/+3	+13/+8/+3	+9/+4
19	+6/+11	+19/+14/+9/+4	+14/+9/+4	+9/+4
20	+6/+12	+20/+15/+10/+5	+15/+10/+5	+10/+5

LEVEL-DEPENDENT BENEFITS

In addition to attack bonuses and saving throw bonuses, all characters gain other benefits from advancing in level. Table 3–2: Experience and Level-Dependent Benefits summarizes these additional benefits.

XP: This column on Table 3–2 shows the experience point total needed to achieve a given character level. For multiclass characters, XP determines overall character level, not individual class levels.

Class Skill Max Ranks: The maximum number of skill ranks a character can have in a class skill is equal to his or her character level + 3. A class skill is a skill frequently associated with a particular class—for example, Spellcraft is a class skill for wizards. Class skills are listed under each class description in this chapter (see also Table 4–2: Skills, page 59, for more information on skills).

Cross-Class Skill Max Ranks: For cross-class skills (skills neither associated with nor forbidden to the character's class), the maximum ranks are one-half the maximum for a class skill. For example, at 1st level a wizard could have 2 ranks in Move Silently (typically associated with rogues, and on that class's list of class skills), but no more. These 2 ranks in a cross-class skill would cost 4 skill points, whereas the same 4 points would buy 4 ranks in a class skill such as Spellcraft. The half ranks (1/2) indicated on Table 3–2 don't improve skill checks. They simply represent partial purchase of the next skill rank and indicate the character is training to improve that skill.

Feats: Every character gains one feat at 1st level and another at every level divisible by three (3rd, 6th, 9th, 12th, 15th, and 18th). Note that these feats are in addition to any bonus feats granted in the class descriptions later in this chapter and the bonus feat granted to all humans. See Chapter 5: Feats for more on feats.

Ability Increases: Upon gaining any level divisible by four (4th, 8th, 12th, 16th, and 20th), a character increases one of his or her ability scores by 1 point. The player chooses which ability score to improve. For example, a sorcerer with a starting Charisma of 16 might improve this to Cha 17 at 4th level. At 8th level, the same character might improve the Charisma score again (from 17 to Cha 18) or could choose to improve some other ability instead. The ability improvement is permanent.

For multiclass characters, feats and ability increases are gained according to overall character level, not class level. Thus, a 3rd-level wizard/1st-level fighter is a 4th-level character overall and eligible for her first ability score boost.

TABLE 3–2: EXPERIENCE AND LEVEL-DEPENDENT BENEFITS

Character Level	XP	Class Skill Max Ranks	Cross-Class Skill Max Ranks	Feats	Ability Increases
1	0	4	2	1st	—
2	1,000	5	2 1/2	—	—
3	3,000	6	3	2nd	—
4	6,000	7	3 1/2	—	1st
5	10,000	8	4	—	—
6	15,000	9	4 1/2	3rd	—
7	21,000	10	5	—	—
8	28,000	11	5 1/2	—	2nd
9	36,000	12	6	4th	—
10	45,000	13	6 1/2	—	—
11	55,000	14	7	—	—
12	66,000	15	7 1/2	5th	3rd
13	78,000	16	8	—	—
14	91,000	17	8 1/2	—	—
15	105,000	18	9	6th	—
16	120,000	19	9 1/2	—	4th
17	136,000	20	10	—	—
18	153,000	21	10 1/2	7th	—
19	171,000	22	11	—	—
20	190,000	23	11 1/2	—	5th

CLASS DESCRIPTIONS

The rest of this chapter, up to the section on multiclass characters, describes each class in alphabetical order. In each description, you'll first find a general discussion in "game world" terms, the sort of description that characters in the world could understand and the way such a character might describe himself or herself. These descriptions are general. Individual members of a class may differ in their attitudes, outlooks, and other aspects.

GAME RULE INFORMATION

Following the general class description comes game rule information. Not all of the following categories apply to every class.

Abilities: The Abilities entry tells you which abilities are most important for a character of that class. Players are welcome to "play against type," but a typical character of that class will have his or her highest ability scores where they'll do the most good (or, in game world terms, be attracted to the class that most suits his or her talents or for which he or she is best qualified).

Alignment: A few classes restrict a character's possible alignments. For example, a bard must have a nonlawful alignment. An entry of "Any" means that characters of this class are not restricted in alignment.

Hit Die: The type of Hit Die used by characters of the class determines the number of hit points gained per level.

HD Type	Class
d4	Sorcerer, wizard
d6	Bard, rogue
d8	Cleric, druid, monk
d10	Fighter, paladin, ranger
d12	Barbarian

A character rolls one Hit Die each time he or she gains a new level, then adds or subtracts any Constitution modifier to the roll, and adds the result to his or her hit point total. Thus, a character has the same number of Hit Dice as levels. For his or her first Hit Die, a 1st-level character gets the maximum hit points rather than rolling (although Constitution modifiers, plus or minus, still apply).

For example, Vadania gets a d8 Hit Die because she's a druid. At 1st level, she gets 8 hit points instead of rolling. Since she has a Constitution score of 13, she has a +1 bonus, raising her hit points to 9. When she reaches 2nd level (and every level thereafter), Vadania's player rolls a d8, adds 1 (for her Constitution bonus), and then adds the total to Vadania's hit points.

If your character has a Constitution penalty and gets a result of 0 or less after the penalty is applied to the roll of the Hit Die, ignore the roll and add 1 to your character's hit point total anyway. It is not possible to lose hit points (or not receive any) when gaining a level, even for a character with a rotten Constitution.

Lars Grant-West

Class Table: This table details how a character improves as he or she gains experience levels. Some of this material is repeated from Table 3–1: Base Save Bonuses and Base Attack Bonuses, but with more detail on how the numbers apply to that class. Class tables typically include the following:

Level: The character's level in that class.

Base Attack Bonus: The character's base attack bonus and number of attacks.

Fort Save: The base save bonus on Fortitude saving throws. The character's Constitution modifier also applies.

Ref Save: The base save bonus on Reflex saving throws. The character's Dexterity modifier also applies.

Will Save: The base save bonus on Will saving throws. The character's Wisdom modifier also applies.

Special: Level-dependent class abilities, each explained in the "Class Features" sections that follow.

Spells per Day: How many spells of each spell level the character can cast each day. If the entry is "—" for a given level of spells, the character may not cast any spells of that level. If the entry is "0," the character may only cast spells of that level if he or she has bonus spells (see Table 1–1: Ability Modifiers and Bonus Spells, page 8). If the entry is a number, the character may cast that many spells plus any bonus spells. Bonus spells for wizards are based on Intelligence. Bonus spells for clerics, druids, paladins, and rangers are based on Wisdom. Bonus spells for sorcerers and bards are based on Charisma.

A character can always choose to memorize a lower-level spell to fill a higher-level slot (see Spell Slots, page 148).

Class Skills: The number of skill points the character starts with at 1st level, the number of skill points gained each level thereafter, and the list of class skills. In each case, the character gets some number of skill points each level, such as 4 for a ranger or 8 for a rogue. To this number, add or subtract the character's Intelligence modifier for the total points gained each level (but always at least 1 skill point per level, even for a character with an Intelligence penalty). Remember that a 1st-level character starts with four times this number of skill points. Since the maximum rank in a class skill is the character's level + 3, at 1st level you can buy up to 4 ranks in any class skill, at a cost of 1 skill point per rank.

For example, Vadania is a druid, so she gets 4 skill points per level. She has a +1 Intelligence modifier, so that goes up to 5 skill points per level. At 1st level, she gets four times that amount, or 20 skill points. Her maximum rank for a class skill is 4, so she could, for example, divvy up her 20 points among five class skills with 4 ranks each. (It's more useful to have a higher score in a few skills than a lower score in many.)

You can also buy skills from other classes' skill lists, but each skill point only buys a half rank in these cross-class skills, and you can only buy up to half the maximum rank a class skill would have (thus, the maximum rank at 1st level for a cross-class skill is 2). Some class skills are exclusive, which means that characters of other classes cannot buy those skills. For example, Use Magic Device is exclusive to bards and rogues. Other characters can't buy the Use Magic Device skill. (See Table 4–2: Skills, page 59.)

Class Features: Special characteristics of the class. When applicable, this section also mentions restrictions and disadvantages of the class. Class features include some or all of the following.

Weapon and Armor Proficiency: Which weapons and armor types the character is proficient with. Regardless of training, cumbersome armor interferes with certain skills (such as Climb) and with the casting of most arcane spells. Note that characters can become proficient with other weapon or armor types by acquiring the various Armor Proficiency (light, medium, heavy),

Shield, and Weapon Proficiency (exotic, simple, martial) feats. (See Chapter 5: Feats.)

Spells: Wizards, sorcerers, clerics, druids, and bards use spells. Fighters, barbarians, rogues, and monks do not. Paladins and rangers gain the ability to use spells at 4th level.

Other Features: Each class has certain unique capabilities. Some, such as rogues, have few. Others, such as monks, have many.

Some abilities are supernatural or spell-like. Using a spell-like ability is essentially like casting a spell (without components). Using a spell-like ability provokes attacks of opportunity. Using a supernatural ability is not like casting a spell. (See Chapter 8: Combat, especially Attacks of Opportunity, page 122, and Use Special Ability, page 126.)

Ex-Members: If, for some reason, a character is forced to give up this class, these are the rules for what happens.

Starting Package: This section provides the default feats, skills, equipment, and other details for a 1st-level character of this class. You can ignore these altogether and create a character from scratch, or use the package as is for your first character (simply copying the details onto your character sheet), or take some portions of the package (such as equipment) and choose other details (such as skills) yourself. DMs can also use these packages for quickly creating 1st-level nonplayer characters.

The starting packages assume that you spend 4 skill points on every skill you start with (so as to excel in a few things rather than dabble in many), and thus they are expressed a little differently from the standard skill buying system. Even though the presentation looks different, you get a character with the right number of skill ranks.

Each starting package is associated with a race. Alternative starting packages show what changes to make to create a starting package for a character of another race. The packages do not take into account racial traits, so be sure to note your character's racial features (described in Chapter 2: Races), including ability modifiers and bonuses on skills. The package also does not list all class features, so note your character's class features as well.

"Gear" for the character means adventuring gear, not clothes. Assume your character owns at least one outfit of normal clothes. Pick any one of the following clothing outfits in Chapter 7: Equipment for free: artisan's outfit, entertainer's outfit, explorer's outfit, monk's outfit, peasant's outfit, scholar's outfit, or traveler's outfit. (See Clothing, page 111.)

BARBARIAN

From the frozen wastes to the north and the hellish jungles of the south come brave, even reckless, warriors. Civilized people call them barbarians or berserkers and suspect them of mayhem, impiety, and atrocities. These "barbarians," however, have proven their mettle and their value to those who would be their allies. To enemies who underestimated them, they have proved their cunning, resourcefulness, persistence, and mercilessness.

Adventures: Adventuring is the best chance barbarians have of finding a place in a civilized society. They're not well suited to the monotony of guard duty or other mundane tasks. Barbarians also have no trouble with the dangers, the uncertainties, and the wandering that adventuring involves. Barbarians may adventure to defeat hated enemies. They have a noted distaste for that which they consider unnatural, including undead, demons, and devils.

Characteristics: The barbarian is an excellent warrior. Where the fighter has training and discipline, however, the barbarian has a powerful rage. While in this berserk fury, he becomes stronger and tougher, better able to defeat his foes and withstand their attacks. These rages leave him winded, and he only has the energy for a few such spectacular displays per day, but those few rages are usually sufficient. He is at home in the wilds, and he runs at great speed.

Alignment: Barbarians are never lawful. They may be honorable, but at heart they are wild. This wildness is their strength, and it could not live in a lawful soul. At best, chaotic barbarians are free and expressive. At worst, they are thoughtlessly destructive.

Religion: Some barbarians distrust established religions and prefer an intuitive, natural relationship to the cosmos over formal worship. Others devote themselves to powerful deities, such as Kord, god of strength; Obad-Hai, god of nature; or Erythnul, god of slaughter. A barbarian is capable of fierce devotion to his god.

Background: Barbarians come from uncivilized lands or from barbaric tribes on the outskirts of civilization. A barbarian adventurer may have been lured to the settled lands by the promise of riches, may have escaped after having been captured in his homeland and sold into "civilized" slavery, may have been recruited as a soldier, or may have been driven out of his home by invaders. Barbarians share no bond with each other unless they come from the same tribe or land. In fact, they think of themselves not as barbarians but as warriors.

Races: Human barbarians come from the distant wild lands on the edge of civilization. Half-orc barbarians lived among orcs before abandoning them for human lands. Dwarf barbarians are rare, usually hailing from dwarven kingdoms that have fallen into barbarism as a result of recurrent war with goblinoids, orcs, and giants. Barbarians of other races are very rare.

Among the brutal humanoids, barbarians are more common than fighters. Orcs and ogres are especially likely to be barbarians.

Other Classes: As people of the wild, barbarians are most comfortable in the company of rangers, druids, and clerics of nature deities, such as Obad-Hai or Ehlonna. Many barbarians admire the talents and spontaneity of bards, and some are enthusiastic lovers of music. Barbarians don't trust that which they don't understand, and that includes wizardry, which they call "book magic." Barbarians find sorcerers more understandable than wizards, but maybe that's just because sorcerers tend to be more charismatic. Monks, with their studied, practiced, deliberate approach to combat, sometimes have a hard time seeing eye to eye with barbarians, but members of these classes aren't necessarily hostile to each other. Barbarians have no special attitudes toward fighters, paladins, clerics, or rogues.

GAME RULE INFORMATION

Barbarians have the following game statistics.

Abilities: Strength is important for barbarians because of its role in combat, and several barbarian skills are based on Strength. Dexterity is also useful to barbarians, especially those who wear light armor. Wisdom is important for several barbarian skills. A high Constitution score lets a barbarian rage longer (and live longer, because it gives him more hit points).

Alignment: Any nonlawful.

Hit Die: d12.

Class Skills

The barbarian's class skills (and the key ability for each skill) are Climb (Str), Craft (Int), Handle Animal (Cha), Intimidate (Cha), Intuit Direction (Wis), Jump (Str), Listen (Wis), Ride (Dex), Swim (Str), and Wilderness Lore (Wis). See Chapter 4: Skills for skill descriptions.

Skill Points at 1st Level: (4 + Int modifier) × 4.
Skill Points at Each Additional Level: 4 + Int modifier.

Class Features

All of the following are class features of the barbarian.

Weapon and Armor Proficiency: A barbarian is proficient with all simple and martial weapons, light armor, medium armor, and shields. Note that armor check penalties for armor heavier than leather apply to the skills Balance, Climb, Escape Artist, Hide, Jump,

Move Silently, Pick Pocket, and Tumble. Also, Swim checks suffer a –1 penalty for every 5 pounds of armor and equipment carried.

Barbarian Rage: When he needs to, a barbarian can fly into a screaming blood frenzy. In a rage, a barbarian gains phenomenal strength and durability but becomes reckless and less able to defend himself. He temporarily gains +4 to Strength, +4 to Constitution, and a +2 morale bonus on Will saves, but suffers a –2 penalty to AC.

The increase in Constitution increases the barbarian's hit points by 2 points per level, but these hit points go away at the end of the rage when the Constitution score drops back to normal. (These extra hit points are not lost first the way temporary hit points are; see Temporary Hit Points, page 129.) While raging, a barbarian cannot use skills or abilities that require patience and concentration, such as moving silently or casting spells. (The only class skills he can't use while raging are Craft, Handle Animal, and Intuit Direction.) He can use any feat he might have except for Expertise, item creation feats, metamagic feats, and Skill Focus (if it's tied to a skill that requires patience or concentration). A fit of rage lasts for a number of rounds equal to 3 + the character's (newly improved) Constitution modifier. The barbarian may prematurely end the rage voluntarily. At the end of the rage, the barbarian is fatigued (–2 to Strength, –2 to Dexterity, can't charge or run) for the duration of that encounter (unless the barbarian is 20th level, when this limitation no longer applies). The barbarian can only fly into a rage once per encounter, and only a certain number of times per day (determined by level). Entering a rage takes no time itself, but the barbarian can only do it during his action (see Initiative, page 120), not in response to somebody else's action. A barbarian can't, for example, fly into a rage when struck down by an arrow in order to get the extra hit points from the increased Constitution, although the extra hit points would be of benefit if he had gone into a rage earlier in the round, *before* the arrow struck.

Starting at 15th level, the barbarian's rage bonuses become +6 to Strength, +6 to Constitution, and a +3 morale bonus to Will saves. (The AC penalty remains at –2.)

Fast Movement: The barbarian has a speed faster than the norm for his race by +10 feet when wearing no armor, light armor, or medium armor (and not carrying a heavy load). For example, a human barbarian in studded leather armor has a standard speed of 40 feet. Normally, humans have a speed of 30 feet. His speed when taking the double move action is 80 feet (rather than 60), and his running speed is 160 feet (rather than 120).

Uncanny Dodge: Starting at 2nd level, the barbarian gains the extraordinary ability to react to danger before his senses would normally allow him to do so. At 2nd level and above, he retains his Dexterity bonus to AC (if any) regardless of being caught flat-footed or struck by an invisible attacker. (He still loses his Dexterity bonus to AC if immobilized.)

At 5th level, the barbarian can no longer be flanked; he can react to opponents on opposite sides of him as easily as he can react to a single attacker. This defense denies a rogue the ability to use a flank attack to sneak attack the barbarian. The exception to this defense is that a rogue at least four levels higher than the barbarian can flank him (and thus sneak attack him).

At 10th level, the barbarian gains an intuitive sense that alerts him to danger from traps, giving him a +1 bonus to Reflex saves made to avoid traps and a +1 dodge bonus to AC against attacks by traps. At 13th level, these bonuses rise to +2. At 16th, they rise to +3, and at 19th they rise to +4.

Damage Reduction: Starting at 11th level, the barbarian gains the extraordinary ability to shrug off some amount of injury from each blow or attack. Subtract 1 from the damage the barbarian takes each time he is dealt damage. At 14th level, this damage reduction rises to 2. At 17th, it rises to 3. At 20th, it rises to 4. Damage reduction can reduce damage to 0 but not below 0.

Illiteracy: Barbarians are the only characters that do not automatically know how to read and write. A barbarian must spend 2 skill points to gain the ability to read and write any language he is able to speak.

Krusk

Table 3–3: The Barbarian

Level	Base Attack Bonus	Fort Save	Ref Save	Will Save	Special
1	+1	+2	+0	+0	Rage 1/day; fast movement
2	+2	+3	+0	+0	Uncanny dodge (Dex bonus to AC)
3	+3	+3	+1	+1	
4	+4	+4	+1	+1	Rage 2/day
5	+5	+4	+1	+1	Uncanny dodge (can't be flanked)
6	+6/+1	+5	+2	+2	
7	+7/+2	+5	+2	+2	
8	+8/+3	+6	+2	+2	Rage 3/day
9	+9/+4	+6	+3	+3	
10	+10/+5	+7	+3	+3	Uncanny dodge (+1 against traps)
11	+11/+6/+1	+7	+3	+3	Damage reduction 1/—
12	+12/+7/+2	+8	+4	+4	Rage 4/day
13	+13/+8/+3	+8	+4	+4	Uncanny dodge (+2 against traps)
14	+14/+9/+4	+9	+4	+4	Damage reduction 2/—
15	+15/+10/+5	+9	+5	+5	Greater rage
16	+16/+11/+6/+1	+10	+5	+5	Rage 5/day, uncanny dodge (+3 against traps)
17	+17/+12/+7/+2	+10	+5	+5	Damage reduction 3/—
18	+18/+13/+8/+3	+11	+6	+6	
19	+19/+14/+9/+4	+11	+6	+6	Uncanny dodge (+4 against traps)
20	+20/+15/+10/+5	+12	+6	+6	Rage 6/day; no longer winded after rage; damage reduction 4/—

Ex-Barbarians

A barbarian who becomes lawful loses the ability to rage and cannot gain more levels as a barbarian. He retains all the other benefits of the class (fast movement, uncanny dodge, and damage reduction).

Half-Orc Barbarian Starting Package

Armor: Studded leather +3 AC, armor check penalty −1, speed 40 ft., 20 lb.

Weapons: Greataxe (1d12, crit ×3, 20 lb., Large, Slashing). Shortbow (1d6, crit ×3, 60 ft., 2 lb., Medium-size, Piercing). Dagger (1d4, crit 19–20/×2, 10 ft., 1 lb., Tiny, Piercing).

Skill Selection: Pick a number of skills equal to 4 + Int modifier.

Skill	Ranks	Ability	Armor
Climb	4	Str	−1
Wilderness Lore	4	Wis	
Listen	4	Wis	
Jump	4	Str	−1
Swim	4	Str	−11*
Ride	4	Dex	
Intimidate	4	Cha	
Intuit Direction	4	Wis	
Spot (cc)	2	Wis	

*−1 per 5 pounds of equipment.

Feat: Weapon Focus (greataxe).

Gear: Backpack with waterskin, one day's trail rations, bedroll, sack, and flint and steel. Quiver with 20 arrows.

Gold: 2d4 gp.

Alternative Barbarian Starting Package

Same as half-orc barbarian, except

Race: Human, dwarf, elf, half-elf.

Armor: Speed 30 ft. (dwarf only).

Skill Selection: Pick a number of skills equal to 5 + Int modifier (human only).

Bonus Feat: Alertness (human only).

Alternative Barbarian Starting Package

Same as half-orc barbarian, except

Race: Gnome or halfling.

Armor: Speed 30 ft.

Weapons: Battleaxe (1d8, crit ×3, 6 lb., Medium-size, Slashing) instead of greataxe.

Skill Selection: Pick a number of skills equal to 4 + Int modifier.

Skill	Ranks	Ability	Armor
Swim	4	Str	−5*

*−1 per 5 pounds of equipment.

Feat: Weapon Focus (battleaxe) instead of Weapon Focus (greataxe).

Gold: 6d4 gp.

BARD

It is said that music has a special magic, and the bard proves that saying true. Wandering across the land, gathering lore, telling stories, working magic with his music, and living on the gratitude of his audience: such is the life of a bard. When chance or opportunity draws them into a conflict, bards serve as diplomats, negotiators, messengers, scouts, and spies.

A bard's magic comes from the heart. If his heart is good, a bard brings hope and courage to the downtrodden and uses his tricks, music, and magic to thwart the schemes of evildoers. If the nobles of the land are corrupt, the good bard is an enemy of the state, cunningly evading capture and raising the spirits of the oppressed. But music can spring from an evil heart as well. Evil bards eschew blatant violence in favor of manipulation, holding sway over the hearts and minds of others and taking what enraptured audiences "willingly" give.

Adventures: Bards see adventures as opportunities to learn. They practice their many skills and abilities, and they especially relish the opportunity to enter a long-forgotten ancient tomb, to discover ancient works of magic, to decipher old tomes, to travel to strange places, to encounter exotic creatures, and to learn new songs and stories. Bards love to accompany heroes (and villains), joining their entourage to witness their deeds firsthand—a bard who can tell a marvelous story from personal experience earns renown among his fellows. Indeed, after telling so many stories about heroes doing mighty deeds, many bards take these themes to heart and assume the role of hero themselves.

Characteristics: A bard brings forth magic from his soul, not from a book. He cast only a small number of spells, but he can cast them without selecting or preparing them in advance. His magic emphasizes charms and illusions over the more dramatic evocation spells that wizards and sorcerers often use.

In addition to spells, a bard works magic with his music and poetry. He can encourage allies, hold his audiences rapt, and counter magical effects that rely on speech or sound.

Bards have some of the skills that rogues have, although they are not as focused on skill mastery as rogues are. Bards listen to stories as well as tell them, of course, so they have a vast knowledge of local events and noteworthy items.

Alignment: Bards are wanderers, guided by whim and intuition rather than by tradition or law. The spontaneous talent, magic, and lifestyle of the bard are incompatible with a lawful alignment.

Religion: Bards revere Fharlanghn, god of roads. They sometimes camp near his wayside shrines, hoping to earn some coin from the travelers who stop to leave offerings for the god. Many bards, even those who are not elven, worship Corellon Larethian, god of elves and patron of poetry and music. Good bards are also partial to Pelor, the sun god, believing that he watches over them in their travels. Bards given to chaos and occasional larceny favor Olidammara, god of thieves. Those who have turned to evil ways are known to worship Erythnul, the god of slaughter, though few will admit to it. In any event, bards spend so much time on the road that, while they may be devoted to a deity, they are rarely devoted to any particular temple.

Background: An apprentice bard learns his skills from a single experienced bard, whom he follows and serves until he is ready to strike out on his own. Many bards were once young runaways or orphans, befriended by wandering bards who became their mentors. Since bards occasionally congregate in informal "colleges," the apprentice bard may meet many of the more prominent bards in the area. Still, the bard has no strong allegiance to bards as a whole. In fact, some bards are highly competitive with other bards, jealous of their reputations and defensive of their territory.

Races: Bards are commonly human, elven, or half-elven. Humans take well to the wandering life and adapt easily to new lands and customs. Elves are talented in music and magic, so the career of the bard comes naturally to them. A bard's wandering ways suit many half-elves, who often feel like strangers even when at home. Half-orcs, even those raised among humans, find themselves ill suited to the demands of a bard's career. There are no bardic traditions among dwarves, gnomes, or halflings, though occasional individuals of these races find teachers to train them in the ways of the bard.

Bards are exceedingly rare among the savage humanoids, except among centaurs. Centaur bards sometimes train the children of humans or other humanoids.

Other Classes: A bard works well with companions of other classes. He often serves as the spokesman of the party, using his social skills for the party's benefit. In a party without a wizard or sorcerer, the bard relies on his magic. In a party without a rogue, he uses his skills. A bard is curious about the ways of more

TABLE 3–4: THE BARD

Level	Base Attack Bonus	Fort Save	Ref Save	Will Save	Special	Spells per Day 0	1	2	3	4	5	6
1	+0	+0	+2	+2	Bardic music, bardic knowledge	2	—	—	—	—	—	—
2	+1	+0	+3	+3		3	0	—	—	—	—	—
3	+2	+1	+3	+3		3	1	—	—	—	—	—
4	+3	+1	+4	+4		3	2	0	—	—	—	—
5	+3	+1	+4	+4		3	3	1	—	—	—	—
6	+4	+2	+5	+5		3	3	2	—	—	—	—
7	+5	+2	+5	+5		3	3	2	0	—	—	—
8	+6/+1	+2	+6	+6		3	3	3	1	—	—	—
9	+6/+1	+3	+6	+6		3	3	3	2	—	—	—
10	+7/+2	+3	+7	+7		3	3	3	2	0	—	—
11	+8/+3	+3	+7	+7		3	3	3	3	1	—	—
12	+9/+4	+4	+8	+8		3	3	3	3	2	—	—
13	+9/+4	+4	+8	+8		3	3	3	3	2	—	—
14	+10/+5	+4	+9	+9		4	3	3	3	3	1	—
15	+11/+6/+1	+5	+9	+9		4	4	3	3	3	2	—
16	+12/+7/+2	+5	+10	+10		4	4	4	3	3	2	0
17	+12/+7/+2	+5	+10	+10		4	4	4	4	3	3	1
18	+13/+8/+3	+6	+11	+11		4	4	4	4	4	3	2
19	+14/+9/+4	+6	+11	+11		4	4	4	4	4	4	3
20	+15/+10/+5	+6	+12	+12		4	4	4	4	4	4	4

focused or dedicated adventurers, often trying to pick up pointers from fighters, sorcerers, and rogues.

GAME RULE INFORMATION

Bards have the following game statistics.

Abilities: Charisma determines how powerful a spell a bard can cast, how many spells the bard can cast per day, and how hard those spells are to resist. To cast a spell, a bard must have a Charisma score of 10 + the spell's level. A bard gets bonus spells based on Charisma. The Difficulty Class of a saving throw against a bard's spell is 10 + the spell's level plus the bard's Charisma modifier. Charisma, Dexterity, and Intelligence are important for many of the bard's class skills (see below).

Alignment: Any nonlawful.

Hit Die: d6.

Class Skills

The bard's class skills (and the key ability for each skill) are Alchemy (Int), Appraise (Int), Balance (Dex), Bluff (Cha), Climb (Str), Concentration (Con), Craft (Int), Decipher Script (Int, exclusive skill), Diplomacy (Cha), Disguise (Cha), Escape Artist (Dex), Gather Information (Cha), Hide (Dex), Intuit Direction (Wis), Jump (Str), Knowledge (all skills, taken individually) (Int), Listen (Wis), Move Silently (Dex), Perform (Cha), Pick Pocket (Dex), Profession (Wis), Scry (Int, exclusive skill), Sense Motive (Wis), Speak Language (Int), Spellcraft (Int), Swim (Str), Tumble (Dex), and Use Magic Device (Cha, exclusive skill). See Chapter 4: Skills for skill descriptions.

Skill Points at 1st Level: (4 + Int modifier) × 4.
Skill Points at Each Additional Level: 4 + Int modifier.

Class Features

All of the following are class features of the bard.

Weapon and Armor Proficiency: A bard is proficient with all simple weapons. Additionally, the bard is proficient with one of the following weapons: longbow, composite longbow, longsword, rapier, sap, short composite bow, short sword, shortbow, or whip. Bards are proficient with light armor, medium armor, and shields. Note that armor check penalties for armor heavier than leather apply to the skills Balance, Climb, Escape Artist, Hide, Jump, Move Silently, Pick Pocket, and Tumble. Also, Swim checks

TABLE 3–5: BARD SPELLS KNOWN

Level	Spells Known 0	1	2	3	4	5	6
1	4	—	—	—	—	—	—
2	5	2*	—	—	—	—	—
3	6	3	—	—	—	—	—
4	6	3	2*	—	—	—	—
5	6	4	3	—	—	—	—
6	6	4	3	—	—	—	—
7	6	4	4	2*	—	—	—
8	6	4	4	3	—	—	—
9	6	4	4	3	—	—	—
10	6	4	4	4	2*	—	—
11	6	4	4	4	3	—	—
12	6	4	4	4	3	—	—
13	6	4	4	4	4	2*	—
14	6	4	4	4	4	3	—
15	6	4	4	4	4	3	—
16	6	5	4	4	4	4	2*
17	6	5	5	4	4	4	3
18	6	5	5	5	4	4	3
19	6	5	5	5	5	4	4
20	6	5	5	5	5	5	4

*Provided the bard has sufficient Charisma to have a bonus spell of this level.

suffer a –1 penalty for every 5 pounds of armor or equipment carried. Like any other arcane spellcaster, a bard can cast spells while wearing armor or using a shield but suffers a chance of arcane spell failure if the spell in question has a somatic component (most do).

Spells: A bard casts arcane spells from the bard spell list (page 159) according to Table 3–4: The Bard and Table 3–5: Bard Spells Known. He casts these spells without needing to memorize them beforehand or keep a spellbook. All bard spells have a verbal component (singing, reciting, or music). Bards receive bonus spells for high Charisma, and to cast a spell a bard must have a Charisma score at least equal to 10 + the level of the spell (Cha 10 for 0-level spells, Cha 11 for 1st-level spells, and so forth). The Difficulty Class for a saving throw against a bard's spell is 10 + the spell's level + the bard's Charisma modifier.

Illus. by J. Foster

Bardic Music: Once per day per level, a bard can use his song or poetics to produce magical effects on those around him. Depending on the ranks he has in the Perform skill, he can inspire courage in allies, sing a countersong to protect those around him from sound-based magic, *fascinate* a creature, make a magical *suggestion* to a *fascinated* creature, help others perform skills better, or inspire greatness. While these abilities fall under the category of bardic music, they can include reciting poetry, chanting, singing lyrical songs, singing melodies (fa-la-la, etc.), whistling, playing an instrument, or playing an instrument in combination with some spoken performance. As with casting a spell with a verbal component (see Components, page 151), a deaf bard suffers a 20% chance to fail with bardic music. If he fails, the attempt still counts against his daily limit.

Inspire Courage: A bard with 3 or more ranks in Perform can use song or poetics to inspire courage in his allies, bolstering them against fear and improving their combat abilities. To be affected, an ally must hear the bard sing for a full round. The effect lasts as long as the bard sings and for 5 rounds after the bard stops singing (or 5 rounds after the ally can no longer hear the bard). While singing, the bard can fight but cannot cast spells, activate magic items by spell completion (such as scrolls), or activate magic items by magic word (such as wands). Affected allies receive a +2 morale bonus to saving throws against charm and fear effects and a +1 morale bonus to attack and weapon damage rolls. Inspire courage is a supernatural, mind-affecting ability.

Countersong: A bard with 3 or more ranks in Perform can use his music or poetics to counter magical effects that depend on sound (but not spells that simply have verbal components). As with inspire courage, a bard may sing, play, or recite a countersong while taking other mundane actions, but not magical actions. Each round of the countersong, he makes a Perform check. Any creature within 30 feet of the bard (including the bard himself) who is affected by a sonic or language-dependent magical attack (such as *sound burst* or *command*) may use the bard's Perform check result in place of his saving throw if, after rolling the saving throw, the Perform check result proves to be better. The bard may keep up the countersong for 10 rounds. Countersong is a supernatural ability.

Fascinate: A bard with 3 or more ranks in Perform can use his music or poetics to cause a single creature to become *fascinated* with him. The creature to be *fascinated* must be able to see and hear the bard and must be within 90 feet. The bard must also see the creature. The creature must be able to pay attention to the bard. The distraction of a nearby combat or other dangers

prevents the ability from working. The bard makes a Perform check, and the target can negate the effect with a Will saving throw equal to or greater than the bard's check result. If the saving throw succeeds, the bard cannot attempt to *fascinate* that creature again for 24 hours. If the saving throw fails, the creature sits quietly and listens to the song for up to 1 round per level of the bard. While *fascinated*, the target's Spot and Listen checks suffer a –4 penalty. Any potential threat (such as an ally of the bard moving behind the *fascinated* creature) allows the *fascinated* creature a second saving throw against a new Perform check result. Any obvious threat, such as casting a spell, drawing a sword, or aiming, automatically breaks the effect.

While *fascinating* (or attempting to *fascinate*) a creature, the bard must concentrate, as if casting or maintaining a spell. *Fascinate* is a spell-like, mind-affecting charm ability.

Inspire Competence: A bard with 6 or more ranks in Perform can use his music or poetics to help an ally succeed at a task. The ally must be able to see and hear the bard and must be within 30 feet. The bard must also see the creature. Depending on the task that the ally has at hand, the bard may use his bardic music to lift the ally's spirits, to help the ally focus mentally, or in some other way. The ally gets a +2 competence bonus on his skill checks with a particular skill as long as he or she continues to hear the bard's music. The DM may rule that certain uses of this ability are infeasible—chanting to make a rogue move more quietly, for example, is self-defeating. The bard can maintain the effect for 2 minutes (long enough for the ally to take 20). Inspire competence is a supernatural, mind-affecting ability.

Suggestion: A bard with 9 or more ranks in Perform can make a *suggestion* (as the spell) to a creature that he has already *fascinated* (see above). The *suggestion* doesn't count against the bard's daily limit on bardic music performances (one per day per level), but the *fascination* does. A Will saving throw (DC 13 + the bard's Charisma modifier) negates the effect. *Suggestion* is a spell-like, mind-affecting charm ability.

Inspire Greatness: A bard with 12 or more ranks in Perform can use song or poetics to inspire greatness in another creature, granting extra fighting capability. For every three levels the bard attains beyond 9th, the bard can inspire greatness in one additional creature. To inspire greatness, the bard must sing and the creature must hear the bard sing for a full round, as with inspire courage. The creature must also be within 30 feet. A creature inspired with greatness gains temporary Hit Dice, attack bonuses, and saving throw bonuses as long as he or she hears the bard continue to sing and for

Devis

5 rounds thereafter. (All these bonuses are competence bonuses.) The target gains the following boosts:

- +2 Hit Dice (d10s that grant temporary hit points).
- +2 competence bonus on attacks.
- +1 competence bonus on Fortitude saves.

Apply the target's Constitution modifier, if any, to each bonus Hit Die. These extra Hit Dice count as regular Hit Dice for determining effects such as the *sleep* spell. Inspire greatness is a supernatural, mind-affecting enchantment ability.

Bardic Knowledge: A bard picks up a lot of stray knowledge while wandering the land and learning stories from other bards. A bard may make a special bardic knowledge check with a bonus equal to his level + his Intelligence modifier to see whether he knows some relevant information about local notable people, legendary items, or noteworthy places. This check will not reveal the powers of a magic item but may give a hint as to its general function. The bard may not take 10 or take 20 on this check; this sort of knowledge is essentially random. The DM will determine the Difficulty Class of the check by referring to the table below.

DC	Type of Knowledge	Examples
10	Common, known by at least a substantial minority of the local population.	A local mayor's reputation for drinking; common legends about a powerful place of mystery.
20	Uncommon but available, known by only a few people in the area.	A local priest's shady past; legends about a powerful magic item.
25	Obscure, known by few, hard to come by.	A knight's family history; legends about a minor place of mystery or magic item.
30	Extremely obscure, known by very few, possibly forgotten by most who once knew it, possibly known only by those who don't understand the significance of the knowledge.	A mighty wizard's childhood nickname; the history of a petty magic item.

Ex-Bards

A bard who becomes lawful in alignment cannot progress in levels as a bard, though he retains all his bard abilities.

Half-Elven Bard Starting Package

Armor: Studded leather +3 AC, speed 30 ft., 20 lb., armor check penalty –1, arcane spell failure 15%.

Weapons: Longsword (1d8, crit 19–20/×2, 4 lb., Medium-size, Slashing). This bard is proficient with the longsword.

Light crossbow (1d8, crit 19–20/×2, 80 ft., 6 lb., Small, Piercing).

Skill Selection: Pick a number of skills equal to 4 + Int modifier.

Skill	Ranks	Ability	Armor
Perform*	4	Cha	
Spellcraft	4	Int	
Use Magic Device	4	Cha	
Gather Information	4	Cha	
Listen	4	Wis	
Decipher Script	4	Int	
Diplomacy	4	Cha	
Knowledge (any)	4	Int	
Pick Pocket	4	Dex	–1

*Epics, lute, melody, storytelling.

Feat: If Dex 13 or higher, Dodge; if Dex 12 or less, Improved Initiative instead.

Spells Known: Cantrips: *detect magic, ghost sound, light,* and *read magic.*

Gear: Backpack with waterskin, one day's trail rations, bedroll, sack, and flint and steel. Three torches. Quiver with 20 arrows. Lute (common), spell component pouch.

Gold: 1d4 gp.

Alternative Bard Starting Package

Same as half-elven bard, except

Race: Human, dwarf, elf, or half-orc.

Armor: Speed 20 ft. (dwarf only).

Skill Selection: Pick a number of skills equal to 5 + Int modifier (human only).

Bonus Feat: If Dex 13 or higher, Improved Initiative; if Dex 12 or less, Skill Focus (Perform) instead (human only).

Alternative Bard Starting Package

Same as half-elven bard, except

Race: Gnome or halfling.

Armor: Speed 20 ft.

Weapons: Short sword (1d6, crit 19–20/×2, 3 lb., Small, Piercing) instead of longsword. This bard is proficient with the short sword.

Gold: 2d4 gp.

CLERIC

The handiwork of the gods is everywhere, in places of natural beauty and in mighty crusades, in soaring temples, and in the hearts of worshipers. Like people, gods run the gamut from benevolent to malicious, reserved to intrusive, simple to inscrutable. The gods, however, work mostly through intermediaries—their clerics. Good clerics heal, protect, and avenge. Evil clerics pillage, destroy, and sabotage. A cleric uses the power of his god to make his god's will manifest. And if a cleric uses his god's power to improve his own lot, that's to be expected, too.

Adventures: Ideally, a cleric's adventures support his god's causes, at least in a general way. A good cleric, for example, helps those in need. If, through noble acts, he can bring a good reputation to his god or temple, that's even better. An evil cleric seeks to increase the power of himself and his deity, so that others will respect and fear him.

Clerics sometimes receive orders, or at least suggestions, from their ecclesiastical superiors, directing them to undertake missions for the church. They and their companions are compensated fairly for these missions, and the church may be especially generous with casting of spells or divine magic items as payment.

Of course, clerics are people, too, and they may have all the more common motivations for adventuring.

Characteristics: Clerics are masters of divine magic. Divine magic is especially good at healing. Even an inexperienced cleric can bring people back from the brink of death, and an experienced cleric can even bring back people who have crossed over that brink.

As channelers of divine energy, clerics can turn away or even destroy undead creatures. An evil cleric, on the other hand, can bring undead under his control.

Clerics have some combat training. They can use simple weapons, and they are trained in the use of armor, since armor does not interfere with divine spells as it does with arcane spells.

Alignment: Like the gods they serve, clerics can be of any alignment. Because people more readily worship good deities than neutral or evil deities, good clerics are more numerous than evil ones. Clerics also tend toward law instead of chaos, since lawful religions tend to be more structured and better able to recruit and train clerics.

Typically, a cleric is the same alignment as his deity, though some clerics are "one step" away from their respective deities. For example, most clerics of Heironeous, god of valor (who is lawful good) are lawful good themselves, but some are lawful neutral or neutral good. Additionally, a cleric may not be neutral unless his deity is neutral. Exceptions are the clerics of St. Cuthbert (a lawful neutral deity), who may only be lawful good or lawful neutral.

Religion: Every common deity has clerics devoted to him or her, so clerics can be of any religion. The most common deity worshiped by human clerics in civilized lands is Pelor, god of the sun. Among nonhuman races, clerics most commonly worship the chief god of their respective racial pantheon.

Some clerics devote themselves not to a god but to a cause or a source of divine power. These clerics wield magic the way clerics devoted to individual gods do, but they are not associated with a religious institution or a particular practice of worship. A cleric devoted to Good and Law, for example, may be on friendly terms with the clerics of lawful and good deities and may extol the virtues of a good and lawful life, but he is not a functionary in a church hierarchy.

Background: Most clerics are officially ordained members of religious organizations, commonly called churches. Each has sworn to uphold the ideals of his or her church. Most clerics join their churches as young adults, though some feel themselves devoted to a god's service from a young age and a few feel "the call" later in life. While some clerics are tightly bound to their churches' activities on a daily basis, others have more free rein to conduct their lives, as long as they do so in accordance with their gods' wishes.

Clerics of a given religion are all supposed to get along, though schisms within a religion are often more bitter than conflicts between religions. Clerics who share some basic ideals, such as goodness or lawfulness, may find

Jozan

common cause with each other and see themselves as part of an order or body that supersedes any given religion. Clerics of opposed goals, however, are sworn enemies. In civilized lands, open warfare between religions occurs only during civil wars and similar social upheavals, but vicious politicking between opposed churches is common.

Races: Clerics include members of all the common races, since the need for religion and divine magic is universal. The clerics of most races, however, are too focused on their religious duties to undertake an adventurer's life. Crusading, adventuring clerics most often come from the human and dwarf races.

Among the savage humanoids, clerics are less common. The exception is troglodytes, who take well to divine magic and are often led by priests, who make a practice of sacrificing and devouring captives.

Other Classes: In an adventuring party, the cleric is everybody's friend and often the glue that holds the party together. As the one who can channel divine energy, a cleric is a capable healer, and adventurers of every class appreciate being put back together after they've taken some hard knocks. Clerics sometimes clash with druids, since druids represent an older, more primal relationship between the mortal and the divine. Mostly, though, the religion of a cleric determines how he gets along with others. A cleric of Olidammara, god of thieves, gets along fine with rogues and ne'er-do-wells, for example, while a cleric of Heironeous, god of valor, rankles at such company.

GAME RULE INFORMATION
Clerics have the following game statistics.

TABLE 3–6: THE CLERIC

Level	Base Attack Bonus	Fort Save	Ref Save	Will Save	Special	Spells per Day*									
						0	1	2	3	4	5	6	7	8	9
1	+0	+2	+0	+2	Turn or rebuke undead	3	1+1	—	—	—	—	—	—	—	—	—
2	+1	+3	+0	+3		4	2+1	—	—	—	—	—	—	—	—
3	+2	+3	+1	+3		4	2+1	1+1	—	—	—	—	—	—	—
4	+3	+4	+1	+4		5	3+1	2+1	—	—	—	—	—	—	—
5	+3	+4	+1	+4		5	3+1	2+1	1+1	—	—	—	—	—	—
6	+4	+5	+2	+5		5	3+1	3+1	2+1	—	—	—	—	—	—
7	+5	+5	+2	+5		6	4+1	3+1	2+1	1+1	—	—	—	—	—
8	+6/+1	+6	+2	+6		6	4+1	3+1	3+1	2+1	—	—	—	—	—
9	+6/+1	+6	+3	+6		6	4+1	4+1	3+1	2+1	1+1	—	—	—	—
10	+7/+2	+7	+3	+7		6	4+1	4+1	3+1	3+1	2+1	—	—	—	—
11	+8/+3	+7	+3	+7		6	5+1	4+1	4+1	3+1	2+1	1+1	—	—	—
12	+9/+4	+8	+4	+8		6	5+1	4+1	4+1	3+1	3+1	2+1	—	—	—
13	+9/+4	+8	+4	+8		6	5+1	5+1	4+1	4+1	3+1	2+1	1+1	—	—
14	+10/+5	+9	+4	+9		6	5+1	5+1	4+1	4+1	3+1	3+1	2+1	—	—
15	+11/+6/+1	+9	+5	+9		6	5+1	5+1	5+1	4+1	4+1	3+1	2+1	1+1	—
16	+12/+7/+2	+10	+5	+10		6	5+1	5+1	5+1	4+1	4+1	3+1	3+1	2+1	—
17	+12/+7/+2	+10	+5	+10		6	5+1	5+1	5+1	5+1	4+1	4+1	3+1	2+1	1+1
18	+13/+8/+3	+11	+6	+11		6	5+1	5+1	5+1	5+1	4+1	4+1	3+1	3+1	2+1
19	+14/+9/+4	+11	+6	+11		6	5+1	5+1	5+1	5+1	5+1	4+1	4+1	3+1	3+1
20	+15/+10/+5	+12	+6	+12		6	5+1	5+1	5+1	5+1	5+1	4+1	4+1	4+1	4+1

*In addition to the stated number of spells per day for 1st- through 9th-level spells, a cleric gets a domain spell for each spell level, starting at 1st. The "+1" on this list represents that. These spells are in addition to any bonus spells for having a high Wisdom.

Abilities: Wisdom determines how powerful a spell a cleric can cast, how many spells the cleric can cast per day, and how hard those spells are to resist. To cast a spell, a cleric must have a Wisdom score of 10 + the spell's level. A cleric gets bonus spells based on Wisdom. The Difficulty Class of a saving throw against a cleric's spell is 10 + the spell's level + the cleric's Wisdom modifier. A high Constitution improves a cleric's hit points, and a high Charisma improves his ability to turn undead.

Alignment: Varies by deity. A cleric's alignment must be within one step of his deity's, and it may not be neutral unless the deity's alignment is neutral.

Hit Die: d8.

Class Skills

The cleric's class skills (and the key ability for each skill) are Concentration (Con), Craft (Int), Diplomacy (Cha), Heal (Wis), Knowledge (arcana) (Int), Knowledge (religion) (Int), Profession (Wis), Scry (Int, exclusive skill), and Spellcraft (Int). See Chapter 4: Skills for skill descriptions.

Domains and Class Skills: A cleric who chooses Animal or Plant as one of his domains also has Knowledge (nature) (Int) as a class skill. A cleric who chooses Knowledge as one of his domains also has all Knowledge (Int) skills as class skills. A cleric who chooses Travel as one of his domains also has Wilderness Lore as a class skill. A cleric who chooses Trickery as one of his domains also has Bluff (Cha), Disguise (Cha), and Hide (Dex) as class skills. See Deity, Domains, and Domain Spells, below, for more information.

Skill Points at 1st Level: (2 + Int modifier) × 4.
Skill Points at Each Additional Level: 2 + Int modifier.

Class Features

All of the following are class features of the cleric.

Armor and Weapon Proficiency: Clerics are proficient with all simple weapons. Clerics are proficient with all types of armor (light, medium, and heavy) and with shields. Note that armor check penalties for armor heavier than leather apply to the skills Balance, Climb, Escape Artist, Hide, Jump, Move Silently, Pick Pocket, and Tumble. Also, Swim checks suffer a –1 penalty for every 5 pounds of armor and equipment carried.

Some deities have favored weapons (see Deities, page 90), and clerics consider it a point of pride to wield them. A cleric whose deity's favored weapon is a martial weapon and who chooses War as one of his domains receives the Martial Weapon Proficiency feat related to that weapon for free, as well as the Weapon Focus feat related to that weapon. See Chapter 5: Feats for details.

Spells: A cleric casts divine spells according to Table 3–6: The Cleric. A cleric may prepare and cast any spell on the cleric spell list (page 160), provided he can cast spells of that level. (Alignment restrictions mean that casting some spells may have unpleasant consequences.) The Difficulty Class for a saving throw against a cleric's spell is 10 + the spell's level + the cleric's Wisdom modifier.

Clerics do not acquire their spells from books or scrolls, nor prepare them through study. Instead, they meditate or pray for their spells, receiving them through their own strength of faith or as divine inspiration. Each cleric must choose a time at which he must spend an hour each day in quiet contemplation or supplication to regain his daily allotment of spells (typically, this hour is at dawn or noon for good clerics and at dusk or midnight for evil ones). Time spent resting has no effect on whether a cleric can prepare spells.

In addition to his standard spells, a cleric gets one domain spell of each spell level, starting at 1st. When a cleric prepares a domain spell, it must come from one of his two domains (see below for details).

Deity, Domains, and Domain Spells: Choose a deity for your cleric. Sample deities are provided on Table 3–7: Deities and in the descriptions on page 90. The cleric's deity influences his alignment, what magic he can perform, his values, and how others see him.

If a race is listed under "Typical Worshipers" on Table 3–7, the cleric must be of one of those races to choose that deity as his own (the god may have occasional worshipers of other races, but not clerics).

When you have chosen a deity and an alignment for your cleric, choose two from among the deity's domains for your cleric's domains. While the clerics of a particular religion are united in their reverence for their deity, each religion encompasses different aspects. You can only select an alignment domain (such as Good) for your cleric if his alignment matches that domain.

If your cleric is not devoted to a particular deity, you still select two domains to represent his spiritual inclinations and abilities (but the restriction on alignment domains still applies).

Each domain gives your cleric access to a domain spell at each spell level, from 1st on up, as well as a granted power. Your cleric gets the granted powers of all the domains selected. With access to two domain spells at a given spell level, a cleric prepares one or the

TABLE 3–7: DEITIES

Deity	Alignment	Domains	Typical Worshipers
Heironeous, God of Valor	Lawful good	Good, Law, War	Paladins, fighters, monks
Moradin, God of Dwarves	Lawful good	Earth, Good, Law, Protection	Dwarves
Yondalla, Goddess of Halflings	Lawful good	Good, Law, Protection	Halflings
Ehlonna, Goddess of the Woodlands	Neutral good	Animal, Good, Plant, Sun	Elves, gnomes, half-elves, halflings, rangers, druids
Garl Glittergold, God of Gnomes	Neutral good	Good, Protection, Trickery	Gnomes
Pelor, God of the Sun	Neutral good	Good, Healing, Strength, Sun	Rangers, bards
Corellon Larethian, God of the Elves	Chaotic good	Chaos, Good, Protection, War	Elves, half-elves, bards
Kord, God of Strength	Chaotic good	Chaos, Good, Luck, Strength	Fighters, barbarians, rogues, athletes
Wee Jas, Goddess of Death and Magic	Lawful neutral	Death, Law, Magic	Wizards, necromancers, sorcerers
St. Cuthbert, God of Retribution	Lawful neutral	Destruction, Law, Protection, Strength	Fighters, monks, soldiers
Boccob, God of Magic	Neutral	Knowledge, Magic, Trickery	Wizards, sorcerers, sages
Fharlanghn, God of Roads	Neutral	Luck, Protection, Travel	Bards, adventurers, merchants
Obad-Hai, God of Nature	Neutral	Air, Animal, Earth, Fire, Plant, Water	Druids, barbarians, rangers
Olidammara, God of Thieves	Chaotic neutral	Chaos, Luck, Trickery	Rogues, bards, thieves
Hextor, God of Tyranny	Lawful evil	Destruction, Evil, Law, War	Evil fighters, monks
Nerull, God of Death	Neutral evil	Death, Evil, Trickery	Evil necromancers, rogues
Vecna, God of Secrets	Neutral evil	Evil, Knowledge, Magic	Evil wizards, sorcerers, rogues, spies
Erythnul, God of Slaughter	Chaotic evil	Chaos, Evil, Trickery, War	Evil fighters, barbarians, rogues
Gruumsh, God of Orcs	Chaotic evil	Chaos, Evil, Strength, War	Half-orcs, orcs

other each day. If a domain spell is not on the Cleric Spells list, a cleric can only prepare it in his domain slot. Domain spells and granted powers are listed in Cleric Domains, page 162.

For example, Jozan is a cleric of Pelor. He chooses Good and Healing as his two domains. He gets both granted powers of his selected domains. The Good domain allows him to cast all spells identified by the good descriptor at +1 caster level (as if he were one level higher in experience as a cleric) as a granted power, and it gives him access to *protection from evil* as a domain spell. The Healing domain allows him to cast all healing subschool spells of the Conjuration school at +1 caster level as a granted power, and it gives him access to *cure light wounds* as a domain spell. When Jozan prepares his spells, he gets one 1st-level spell for being a 1st-level cleric, one 1st-level spell for having a high Wisdom (15), and one domain spell. The domain spell must be one of the two to which he has access, either *protection from evil* or *cure light wounds*.

Spontaneous Casting: Good clerics (and neutral clerics of good deities) can channel stored spell energy into healing spells that they haven't prepared ahead of time. The cleric can "lose" a prepared spell in order to cast any *cure* spell of the same level or lower (a *cure* spell is any spell with "cure" in its name). For example, a good cleric who has prepared *command* (a 1st-level spell) may lose *command* in order to cast *cure light wounds* (also a 1st-level spell). Clerics of good deities can cast *cure* spells in this way because they are especially proficient at wielding positive energy.

An evil cleric (or a neutral cleric of an evil deity), on the other hand, can't convert prepared spells to *cure* spells but can convert them to *inflict* spells (an *inflict* spell is one with "inflict" in the title). Such clerics are especially proficient at wielding negative energy.

A cleric who is neither good nor evil and whose deity is neither good nor evil can convert spells either to *cure* spells or to *inflict* spells (player's choice), depending on whether the cleric is more proficient at wielding positive or negative energy. Once the player makes this choice, it cannot be reversed. This choice also determines whether the neutral cleric turns or commands undead (see below). Exceptions: All lawful neutral clerics of Wee Jas convert spells to *inflict* spells, not *cure* spells. All clerics of St. Cuthbert and all nonevil clerics of Obad-Hai convert spells to *cure* spells, not *inflict* spells.

A cleric can't use spontaneous casting to convert domain spells into *cure* or *inflict* spells. These spells arise from the particular powers of the cleric's deity, not divine energy in general.

Chaotic, Evil, Good, and Lawful Spells: A cleric can't cast spells of an alignment opposed to his own or to his deity's. For example, a good cleric or a neutral cleric of a good deity cannot cast evil spells. Spells associated with the domains of Chaos, Evil, Good, and Law are identified as such on the "Level" line of the spell description.

Turn or Rebuke Undead: A good cleric (or a neutral cleric who worships a good deity) has the supernatural ability to turn undead, such as skeletons, zombies, ghosts, and vampires, forcing these unholy abominations to recoil from the channeled power of the god the cleric worships. Evil clerics (and neutral clerics who worship evil deities) can rebuke such creatures. Neutral clerics of neutral deities can do one or the other (player's choice), depending on whether the cleric is more proficient at wielding positive or negative energy. Once the player makes this choice, it cannot be reversed. This choice also determines whether the neutral cleric can cast spontaneous *cure* or *inflict* spells (see above). Exceptions: All lawful neutral clerics of Wee Jas rebuke undead rather than turning them. All clerics of St. Cuthbert and all non-evil clerics of Obad-Hai turn undead rather than rebuking them. (See Turn and Rebuke Undead, page 139.)

A cleric may attempt to turn or rebuke undead a number of times per day equal to three plus his Charisma modifier.

Extra Turning: As a feat, a cleric may take Extra Turning. This feat allows the cleric to turn undead four more times per day than

normal. A cleric can take this feat multiple times, gaining four extra daily turning attempts each time.

Bonus Languages: A cleric's list of bonus languages includes Celestial, Abyssal, and Infernal, in addition to the bonus languages available to the character because of his race (see Race and Languages, page 12, and the Speak Language skill, page 73). These are the languages of good, chaotic evil, and lawful evil outsiders, respectively.

Ex-Clerics

A cleric who grossly violates the code of conduct expected by his god (generally acting in ways opposed to the god's alignment or purposes) loses all spells and class features and cannot gain levels as a cleric of that god until he atones (see the *atonement* spell description, page 176).

Human Cleric Starting Package

Armor: Scale mail +4 AC, large wooden shield +2 AC, armor check penalty –6, speed 20 ft., 40 lb.

Weapons: Heavy mace (1d8, crit ×2, 12 lb., Medium-size, Bludgeoning).

Light crossbow (1d8, crit 19–20/×2, 80 ft., 6 lb., Small, Piercing).

Skill Selection: Pick a number of skills equal to 3 + Int modifier.

Skill	Ranks	Ability	Armor
Spellcraft	4	Int	
Concentration	4	Con	
Heal	4	Wis	
Knowledge (religion)	4	Int	
Diplomacy	4	Cha	
Gather Information (cc)	2	Cha	
Listen (cc)	2	Wis	

Feat: Scribe Scroll.

Bonus Feat: Alertness.

Deity/Domains: Pelor/Good and Healing.

Gear: Backpack with waterskin, one day's trail rations, bedroll, sack, and flint and steel. Case with 10 crossbow bolts. Wooden holy symbol: sun disc of Pelor. Three torches.

Gold: 1d4 gp.

Dwarven Cleric Starting Package

As human cleric, except

Armor: Speed 15 ft.

Weapons: Warhammer (1d8, crit ×3, 12 lb., Medium-size, Bludgeoning) instead of heavy mace.

Skill Selection: Pick a number of skills equal to 2 + Int modifier.

Feat: Martial Weapon Proficiency (warhammer).

Bonus Feat: None.

Deity/Domains: Moradin/Law and Strength.

Gear: Wooden holy symbol: hammer.

Elven Cleric Starting Package

As human cleric, except

Weapons: Longsword (1d8, crit 19–20/×2, 4 lb., Medium-size, Slashing) instead of heavy mace.

Shortbow (1d6, ×3 crit, 60 ft., 2 lb., Medium-size, Piercing) instead of crossbow.

Skill Selection: Pick a number of skills equal to 2 + Int modifier.

Bonus Feat: None.

Deity/Domains: Corellon Larethian/Protection and War.

Gear: Quiver of 20 arrows instead of case of bolts. Wooden holy symbol: crescent moon.

Gnome Cleric Starting Package

As human cleric, except

Armor: No shield, armor check penalty –4, speed 20 ft., 30 lb.

Weapons: Battleaxe (1d8, crit ×3, 7 lb., Medium-size, Slashing) instead of heavy mace.

Skill Selection: Pick a number of skills equal to 2 + Int modifier.

Feat: Martial Weapon Proficiency (battleaxe).

Bonus Feat: None.

Deity/Domains: Garl Glittergold/Good and Trickery.

Gear: Wooden holy symbol: gold nugget.

Gold: 3d4 gp.

Half-Elven Cleric Starting Package

As human cleric, except

Armor: Small wooden shield +1 AC instead of large wooden shield, armor check penalty –5, speed 20 ft., 35 lb.

Weapons: Longsword (1d8, crit 19–20/×2, 4 lb., Medium-size, Slashing) instead of heavy mace.

Skill Selection: Pick a number of skills equal to 2 + Int modifier.

Feat: Martial Weapon Proficiency (longsword).

Bonus Feat: None.

Deity/Domains: Ehlonna/Animal and Good.

Gear: Wooden holy symbol: unicorn horn.

Half-Orc Cleric Starting Package

As human cleric, except

Armor: no shield, armor check penalty –4, speed 20 ft., 30 lb.

Weapons: Shortspear (1d8, crit ×3, 20 ft., 5 lb., Large, Piercing) instead of heavy mace.

Heavy crossbow (1d10, crit 19–20/×2, 120 ft., 9 lb., Medium-size, Piercing) instead of light crossbow.

Skill Selection: Pick a number of skills equal to 2 + Int modifier.

Bonus Feat: None.

Deity/Domains: Gruumsh/Chaos and War.

Gear: Wooden holy symbol: staring eye.

Gold: 2d4 gp.

Halfling Cleric Starting Package

As human cleric, except

Armor: Speed 15 ft.

Weapons: Short sword (1d6, crit 19–20/×2, 3 lb., Small, Piercing) instead of heavy mace.

Skill Selection: Pick a number of skills equal to 2 + Int modifier.

Feat: Martial Weapon Proficiency (short sword).

Bonus Feat: None.

Deity/Domains: Yondalla/Law and Protection.

Gear: Wooden holy symbol: shield with cornucopia.

DRUID

The fury of a storm, the gentle strength of the morning sun, the cunning of the fox, the power of the bear—all these and more are at the druid's command. The druid however, claims no mastery over nature. That claim, she says, is the empty boast of a city dweller. The druid gains her power not by ruling nature but by being at one with it. To trespassers in a druid's sacred grove, to those who feel the druid's wrath, the distinction is overly fine.

Adventures: Druids adventure to gain knowledge, especially of animals and plants unfamiliar to them, and power. Sometimes, their superiors call on their services. Druids may also bring their power to bear against those who threaten what they love, which more often includes ancient stands of trees or trackless mountains than people. While druids accept that which is horrific or cruel in nature, they hate that which is unnatural, including aberrations (such as beholders and carrion crawlers) and undead (such as zombies and vampires). They sometimes lead raids against such creatures, especially when the creatures encroach on the druids' territory.

Characteristics: Druids cast divine spells much the same way clerics do, though they get their spells from the power of nature, not from gods. Their spells are oriented toward nature and animals.

In addition to spells, druids gain an increasing array of magical powers as they gain experience, including the ability to take the shapes of animals.

The weapons and armor of a druid are restricted by traditional oaths, not simply training. A druid could learn to use a two-handed sword, but using it would violate the druid's oath and suppress her druidic powers.

Druids avoid carrying much worked metal with them because it interferes with the pure and primal nature that they attempt to embody.

Alignment: Druids, in keeping with nature's ultimate indifference, must maintain at least some measure of dispassion. As such, they must be neutral in some way, if not true neutral. Just as nature encompasses dichotomies of life and death, beauty and horror, peace and violence, so two druids can manifest different or even opposite alignments (neutral good and neutral evil, for instance) and still be part of the druidic tradition.

Religion: Druids revere nature and gain their magical power from the forces of nature itself or from a nature deity. They usually pursue a mystic spirituality of transcendent union with nature rather than devotion to a divine entity. Still, some of them revere or at least respect either Obad-Hai, god of nature, or Ehlonna, goddess of the woodlands.

Background: Though their organization is invisible to most outsiders, who consider druids to be loners, druids are part of a society that spans the land, ignoring political borders. A prospective druid is inducted into this society through secret rituals, including tests that not all survive. Only after achieving some level of competence is the druid allowed to strike out on her own.

All druids are nominally members of the druidic society, though some are so isolated that they have never seen high-ranking members or participated in druidic gatherings. Still, all druids recognize each other as brothers and sisters. Like true creatures of the wilderness, however, druids sometimes compete with or even prey on each other.

A druid may be expected to perform services for higher-ranking druids, though proper payment is expected for these assignments. Likewise, a lower-ranking druid may appeal for aid from her higher-ranking brethren, for a fair price in coin or service.

Druids may live in small towns but always spend a good portion of their time in wild areas. Even large cities otherwise surrounded by cultivated land as far as the eye can see often have druid groves nearby—small, wild refuges where druids live and which they protect fiercely. Near coastal cities, the refuge is often a nearby island, where the druids can find the isolation they need.

Races: Elves and gnomes have an affinity for natural lands and are commonly druids. Humans and half-elves are also frequently druids, and druids are particularly common among savage humans. Dwarves, halflings, and half-orcs are rarely druids.

Few from among the brutal humanoids are inducted into druidic society, except that gnolls have a fair contingent of evil druids among them. Gnoll druids are accepted by druids of other races, if not welcomed.

Other Classes: Druids share with rangers and many barbarians a reverence for nature and a familiarity with natural lands. Druids dislike the paladin's devotion to abstract ideals instead of "the real world," they don't much understand the urban ways typical of a rogue, and they find arcane magic to be disruptive and slightly distasteful. Druids, however, are nothing if not accepting of diversity, and they take little offense at others, even those very different from them.

GAME RULE INFORMATION

Druids have the following game statistics.

Abilities: Wisdom determines how powerful a spell a druid can cast, how many spells the druid can cast per day, and how hard those spells are to resist. To cast a spell, a druid must have a Wisdom score of 10 + the spell's level. A druid gets bonus spells based on Wisdom. The Difficulty Class of a saving throw against a druid's spell is 10 + the spell's level + the druid's Wisdom modifier.

Since a druid wears light or medium armor, a high Dexterity improves her defensive ability.

Alignment: Neutral good, lawful neutral, neutral, chaotic neutral, or neutral evil.

Hit Die: d8.

Class Skills

The druid's class skills (and the key ability for each skill) are Animal Empathy (Cha, exclusive skill), Concentration (Con), Craft (Int), Diplomacy (Cha), Handle Animal (Cha), Heal (Wis), Intuit Direction (Wis), Knowledge (nature) (Int), Profession (Wis), Scry (Int, exclusive skill), Spellcraft (Int), Swim (Str), and Wilderness Lore (Wis). See Chapter 4: Skills for skill descriptions.

Skill Points at 1st Level: (4 + Int modifier) × 4.

Skill Points at Each Additional Level: 4 + Int modifier.

Class Features

All of the following are class features of the druid.

Weapon and Armor Proficiency: Druids are proficient with the following weapons: club, dagger, dart, longspear, quarterstaff, scimitar, sickle,

Vadania

shortspear, and sling. Their spiritual oaths prohibit them from using weapons other than these. They are proficient with light and medium armors but are prohibited from wearing metal armor (thus, they may wear only padded, leather, or hide armor). They are skilled with shields but must use only wooden ones. Note that armor check penalties for armor heavier than leather apply to the skills Balance, Climb, Escape Artist, Hide, Jump, Move Silently, Pick Pocket, and Tumble. Also, Swim checks suffer a –1 penalty for every 5 pounds of armor and equipment carried.

A druid who wears prohibited armor or wields a prohibited weapon is unable to use any of her magical powers while doing so and for 24 hours thereafter. (Note: A druid can use wooden items that have been altered by the *ironwood* spell so that they function as though they were steel. See the spell description, page 218.)

Spells: A druid casts divine spells according to Table 3–8: The Druid. A druid may prepare and cast any spell on the druid spell list (page 166) provided she can cast spells of that level. She prepares and casts spells the way a cleric does (though she cannot lose a prepared spell to cast a *cure* spell in its place). To prepare or cast a spell, a druid must have a Wisdom score of at least 10 + the spell's level. The Difficulty Class for a saving throw against a druid's spell is 10 + the spell's level + the druid's Wisdom modifier.

Bonus spells for druids are based on Wisdom (see Table 1–1: Ability Modifiers and Bonus Spells, page 8).

TABLE 3–8: THE DRUID

Level	Base Attack Bonus	Fort Save	Ref Save	Will Save	Special	Spells per Day									
						0	1	2	3	4	5	6	7	8	9
1	0	+2	+0	+2	Nature sense, animal companion	3	1	—	—	—	—	—	—	—	—
2	+1	+3	+0	+3	Woodland stride	4	2	—	—	—	—	—	—	—	—
3	+2	+3	+1	+3	Trackless step	4	2	1	—	—	—	—	—	—	—
4	+3	+4	+1	+4	Resist nature's lure	5	3	2	—	—	—	—	—	—	—
5	+3	+4	+1	+4	*Wild shape (1/day)*	5	3	2	1	—	—	—	—	—	—
6	+4	+5	+2	+5	*Wild shape (2/day)*	5	3	3	2	—	—	—	—	—	—
7	+5	+5	+2	+5	*Wild shape (3/day)*	6	4	3	2	1	—	—	—	—	—
8	+6/+1	+6	+2	+6	*Wild shape (Large)*	6	4	3	3	2	—	—	—	—	—
9	+6/+1	+6	+3	+6	Venom immunity	6	4	4	3	2	1	—	—	—	—
10	+7/+2	+7	+3	+7	*Wild shape (4/day)*	6	4	4	3	3	2	—	—	—	—
11	+8/+3	+7	+3	+7	*Wild shape (Tiny)*	6	5	4	4	3	2	1	—	—	—
12	+9/+4	+8	+4	+8	*Wild shape (dire)*	6	5	4	4	3	3	2	—	—	—
13	+9/+4	+8	+4	+8	A thousand faces	6	5	5	4	4	3	2	1	—	—
14	+10/+5	+9	+4	+9	*Wild shape (5/day)*	6	5	5	4	4	3	3	2	—	—
15	+11/+6/+1	+9	+5	+9	*Wild shape (Huge),* timeless body	6	5	5	4	4	4	3	2	1	—
16	+12/+7/+2	+10	+5	+10	*Wild shape (elemental 1/day)*	6	5	5	5	4	4	3	3	2	—
17	+12/+7/+2	+10	+5	+10		6	5	5	5	5	4	4	3	2	1
18	+13/+8/+3	+11	+6	+11	*Wild shape (6/day, elemental 3/day)*	6	5	5	5	5	4	4	3	3	2
19	+14/+9/+4	+11	+6	+11		6	5	5	5	5	5	4	4	3	3
20	+15/+10/+5	+12	+6	+12		6	5	5	5	5	5	4	4	4	4

Chaotic, Evil, Good, and Lawful Spells: A druid can't cast spells of an alignment opposed to her own. For example, a neutral good druid cannot cast evil spells. Spells associated with Chaos, Evil, Good, and Law are identified as such on the "Level" line of the spell description.

Bonus Languages: A druid may substitute Sylvan for one of the bonus languages available to her because of her race. In addition, a druid knows the Druidic language. This secret language is known only to druids, and druids are forbidden from teaching it to nondruids. Druidic has its own alphabet.

Nature Sense: A druid can identify plants and animals (their species and special traits) with perfect accuracy. She can whether water is safe to drink or dangerous (polluted, poisoned, or otherwise unfit for consumption).

Animal Companion: A 1st-level druid may begin play with an animal companion. This animal is one that the druid has befriended with the spell *animal friendship*. As such, it can have no more than 2 Hit Dice. A 1st-level druid may have more than one animal companion, provided the animals' total Hit Dice don't exceed 2. The druid can also cast *animal friendship* on other animals during play (see the spell description, page 173).

Woodland Stride: Starting at 2nd level, a druid may move through natural thorns, briars, overgrown areas, and similar terrain at her normal speed and without suffering damage or other impairment. However, thorns, briars, and overgrown areas that are enchanted or magically manipulated to impede motion still affect the druid.

Trackless Step: Starting at 3rd level, a druid leaves no trail in natural surroundings and cannot be tracked.

Resist Nature's Lure: Starting at 4th level, a druid gains a +4 bonus to saving throws against the spell-like abilities of feys (such as dryads, nymphs, and sprites).

Wild Shape: At 5th level, a druid gains the spell-like ability to *polymorph self* into a Small or Medium-size animal (but not a dire animal) and back again once per day (see the *polymorph self* spell, page 237). Unlike the standard use of the spell, however, the druid may only adopt one form. As stated in the spell description, the druid regains hit points as if she has rested for a day. Note: The creatures available include some giant animals but not unnatural beasts. The druid may *wild shape* into a dog or a giant lizard, for example, but not into an owlbear. The druid does not risk the standard penalty for being disoriented while in her *wild shape* (see the *polymorph other* spell, page 236).

The druid can use this ability more times per day at 6th, 7th, 10th, 14th, and 18th level, as noted on Table 3–8: The Druid. In addition, the druid gains the ability to take the shape of a Large animal at 8th level, a Tiny animal at 11th level, and a Huge animal at 15th level. At 12th level or higher, she can take the form of a dire animal.

At 16th level or higher, the druid may use *wild shape* to change into a Small, Medium-size, or Large air, earth, fire, or water elemental once per day. She gains all the elemental's special abilities when she does so. At 18th level, she can do this three times per day.

Venom Immunity: At 9th level, a druid gains immunity to all organic poisons, including monster poisons but not mineral poisons or poison gas.

A Thousand Faces: At 13th level, a druid gains the supernatural ability to change her appearance at will, as if using the spell *alter self* (page 172).

Timeless Body: After achieving 15th level, a druid no longer suffers ability penalties for aging (see Table 6–5: Aging Effects, page 93) and cannot be magically aged. Any penalties she may have already suffered, however, remain in place. Bonuses still accrue, and the druid still dies of old age when her time is up.

Ex-Druids

A druid who ceases to revere nature or who changes to a prohibited alignment loses all spells and druidic abilities and cannot gain levels as a druid until she atones (see the *atonement* spell description, page 176).

Half-Elven Druid Starting Package

Armor: Hide +3 AC, large wooden shield +2 AC, speed 30 ft., 35 lb., armor check penalty –5.

Weapons: Scimitar (1d6, crit 18–20/×2, 4 lb., Medium-size, Slashing).

Club (oaken cudgel): (1d6, crit ×2, 10 ft., 3 lb., Medium-size, Bludgeoning).

Sling (1d4, crit ×2, 50 ft., 0 lb., Small, Bludgeoning).

Skill Selection: Pick a number of skills equal to 4 + Int modifier.

Skill	Ranks	Ability	Armor
Spellcraft	4	Int	
Animal Empathy	4	Cha	
Concentration	4	Con	
Wilderness Lore	4	Wis	
Heal	4	Wis	
Handle Animal	4	Cha	
Knowledge (nature)	4	Int	
Listen (cc)	2	Wis	
Spot (cc)	2	Wis	

Feat: Scribe Scroll.

Gear: Backpack with waterskin, one day's trail rations, bedroll, sack, and flint and steel. Pouch with ten sling bullets. Holly and mistletoe. Three torches.

Animal Companion: Wolf (see the *Monster Manual* for details).

Gold: 1d6 gp.

Alternative Druid Starting Package

Same as half-elven druid, except

Race: Human, dwarf, elf, or half-orc.

Armor: Speed 20 ft. (dwarf only).

Skill Selection: Pick a number of skills equal to 5 + Int modifier (human only).

Bonus Feat: Alertness (human only).

Alternative Druid Starting Package

Same as half-elf druid, except

Race: Gnome or halfling.

Armor: Speed 20 ft.

Weapons: Sickle (1d6, crit ×2, 3 lb., Small, Slashing) instead of scimitar. Note: This druid uses her club two-handed.

Gold: 4d4 gp

FIGHTER

The questing knight, the conquering overlord, the king's champion, the elite foot soldier, the hardened mercenary, and the bandit king—all are fighters. Fighters can be stalwart defenders of those in need, cruel marauders, or gutsy adventurers. Some are among the land's best souls, willing to face death for the greater good. Others are among the worst, those who have no qualms about killing for private gain, or even for sport. Fighters who are not actively adventuring may be soldiers, guards, bodyguards, champions, or criminal enforcers. An adventuring fighter might call himself a warrior, a mercenary, a thug, or simply an adventurer.

Adventures: Most fighters see adventures, raids, and dangerous missions as their job. Some have patrons who pay them regularly. Others prefer to live like prospectors, taking great risks in hopes of the big haul. Some fighters are more civic-minded and use their combat skills to protect those in danger who cannot defend themselves. Whatever their initial motivations, however, fighters often wind up living for the thrill of combat and adventure.

Characteristics: Of all classes, fighters have the best all-around fighting capabilities (hence the name). Fighters are familiar with all the standard weapons and armors. In addition to general fighting prowess, each fighter develops particular specialties of his or her own. A given fighter may be especially capable with certain weapons, another trained to execute specific fancy maneuvers. As fighters gain experience, they get more opportunities to develop their fighting skills. Thanks to their focus on combat maneuvers, they can master the most difficult ones relatively quickly.

Alignment: Fighters may be of any alignment. Good fighters are often crusading types who seek out and fight evil. Lawful fighters may be champions who protect the land and its people. Chaotic fighters may be wandering mercenaries. Evil fighters tend to be bullies and petty villains who simply take what they want by brute force.

Religion: Fighters often worship Heironeous, god of valor; Kord, god of strength; St. Cuthbert, god of retribution; Hextor, god of tyranny; or Erythnul, god of slaughter. A fighter may style himself as a crusader in the service of his god, or he may just want someone to pray to before putting his life on the line yet another time.

Background: Fighters come to their profession in many ways. Most have had formal training in a noble's army or at least in the local militia. Some have trained in formal academies. Others are self-taught—unpolished but well tested. A fighter may have taken up the sword as a way to escape the limits of life on the farm, or he may be following a proud family tradition. Fighters share no special identity. They do not see themselves as a group or brotherhood. Those who hail from a particular academy, mercenary company, or lord's regiment, however, share a certain camaraderie.

Races: Human fighters are usually veterans of some military service, typically from more mundane parents. Dwarven fighters are commonly former members of the well-trained strike teams that protect the underground dwarven kingdoms. They are typically members of warrior families that can trace their lineages back for millennia, and they may have rivalries or alliances with other dwarven fighters depending on their lineages. Elven fighters are typically skilled with the longsword. They are proud of their ability at swordplay and eager to demonstrate or test it. Half-orc fighters are often self-taught outcasts who have achieved enough skill to earn recognition and something akin to respect. Gnome and halfling fighters usually stay in their own lands as part of the area militia rather than adventuring. Half-elves are rarely fighters, but they may take up swordplay in honor of the elven tradition.

Among the brutal humanoids, few can manage the discipline it takes to be a true fighter. The militaristic hobgoblins, however, produce quite a number of strong and skilled fighters.

Other Classes: The fighter excels in a straight fight, but he relies on others for magical support, healing, and scouting. On a team, it is his job to man the front lines, protect the other party members, and bring the tough opponents down. Fighters might not much understand the arcane ways of wizards or share the faith of clerics, but they recognize the value of teamwork.

Tordek

LOCKWOOD

GAME RULE INFORMATION

Fighters have the following game statistics.

Abilities: Strength is especially important for fighters because it improves their melee attack and damage rolls. Constitution is important for giving fighters lots of hit points, which they'll need in their many battles. Dexterity is important for fighters who want to be good archers or who want access to certain Dexterity-oriented feats, but the heavy armor that fighters usually wear reduces the benefit of a very high Dexterity.

Alignment: Any.

Hit Die: d10.

Class Skills

The fighter's class skills (and the key ability for each skill) are Climb (Str), Craft (Int), Handle Animal (Cha), Jump (Str), Ride (Dex), and Swim (Str). See Chapter 4: Skills for skill descriptions.

Skill Points at 1st Level: (2 + Int modifier) × 4.
Skill Points at Each Additional Level: 2 + Int modifier.

Class Features

All of the following are class features of the fighter.

Weapon and Armor Proficiency: The fighter is proficient in the use of all simple and martial weapons and all armor (heavy, medium, and light) and shields. Note that armor check penalties for armor heavier than leather apply to the skills Balance, Climb,

TABLE 3–9: THE FIGHTER

Level	Base Attack Bonus	Fort Save	Ref Save	Will Save	Special
1	+1	+2	+0	+0	Bonus feat
2	+2	+3	+0	+0	Bonus feat
3	+3	+3	+1	+1	
4	+4	+4	+1	+1	Bonus feat
5	+5	+4	+1	+1	
6	+6/+1	+5	+2	+2	Bonus feat
7	+7/+2	+5	+2	+2	
8	+8/+3	+6	+2	+2	Bonus feat
9	+9/+4	+6	+3	+3	
10	+10/+5	+7	+3	+3	Bonus feat
11	+11/+6/+1	+7	+3	+3	
12	+12/+7/+2	+8	+4	+4	Bonus feat
13	+13/+8/+3	+8	+4	+4	
14	+14/+9/+4	+9	+4	+4	Bonus feat
15	+15/+10/+5	+9	+5	+5	
16	+16/+11/+6/+1	+10	+5	+5	Bonus feat
17	+17/+12/+7/+2	+10	+5	+5	
18	+18/+13/+8/+3	+11	+6	+6	Bonus feat
19	+19/+14/+9/+4	+11	+6	+6	
20	+20/+15/+10/+5	+12	+6	+6	Bonus feat

Escape Artist, Hide, Jump, Move Silently, Pick Pocket, and Tumble. Also, Swim checks suffer a –1 penalty for every 5 pounds of armor and equipment carried.

Bonus Feats: At 1st level, the fighter gets a bonus feat in addition to the feat that any 1st-level character gets and the bonus feat granted to humans. The fighter gains an additional bonus feat at 2nd level and every two levels thereafter (4th, 6th, 8th, etc.). These bonus feats must be drawn from the following list: Ambidexterity, Blind-Fight, Combat Reflexes, Dodge (Mobility, Spring Attack), Exotic Weapon Proficiency*, Expertise (Improved Disarm, Improved Trip, Whirlwind Attack), Improved Critical*, Improved Initiative, Improved Unarmed Strike (Deflect Arrows, Stunning Fist), Mounted Combat (Mounted Archery, Trample, Ride-By Attack, Spirited Charge), Point Blank Shot (Far Shot, Precise Shot, Rapid Shot, Shot on the Run), Power Attack (Cleave, Improved Bull Rush, Sunder, Great Cleave), Quick Draw, Two-Weapon Fighting (Improved Two-Weapon Fighting), Weapon Finesse*, Weapon Focus*, Weapon Specialization*.

Some of the bonus feats available to a fighter cannot be acquired until the fighter has gained one or more prerequisite feats; these feats are listed parenthetically after the prerequisite feat. A fighter can select feats marked with an asterisk (*) more than once, but it must be for a different weapon each time. A fighter must still meet all prerequisites for a feat, including ability score and base attack bonus minimums. (See Chapter 5: Feats for descriptions of feats and their prerequisites.)

Important: These feats are in addition to the feat that a character of any class gets every three levels (as per Table 3–2: Experience and Level-Dependent Benefits). The fighter is not limited to the list given here when choosing those feats.

Weapon Specialization: On achieving 4th level or higher, as a feat the fighter (and only the fighter) may take Weapon Specialization. Weapon Specialization adds a +2 damage bonus with a chosen weapon. The fighter must have Weapon Focus with that weapon to take Weapon Specialization. If the weapon is a ranged weapon, the damage bonus only applies if the target is within 30 feet, because only at that range can the fighter strike precisely enough to hit more effectively. The fighter may take this feat as a bonus feat or as a regular one.

Dwarven Fighter Starting Package

Armor: Scale mail +4 AC, large wooden shield +2 AC, armor check penalty –6, speed 15 ft., 40 lb.

Weapons: Dwarven waraxe (1d10, crit ×3, 15 lb., Medium-size, Slashing).

Shortbow (1d6, crit ×3, 60 ft., 2 lb., Medium-size, Piercing).

Skill Selection: Pick a number of skills equal to 2 + Int modifier.

Skill	Ranks	Ability	Armor
Climb	4	Str	–6
Jump	4	Str	–6
Ride	4	Dex	
Swim	4	Str	–12*
Listen (cc)	2	Wis	
Search (cc)	2	Int	
Spot (cc)	2	Wis	

*–1 per 5 pounds of equipment.

Feat: Exotic Weapon Proficiency (dwarven waraxe).
Bonus Feat (Fighter): Weapon Focus (dwarven waraxe).
Gear: Backpack with waterskin, one day's trail rations, bedroll, sack, and flint and steel. Quiver with 20 arrows.
Gold: 4d4 gp.

Alternative Fighter Starting Package

Same as dwarven fighter, except
Race: Human, elf, half-elf, or half-orc.
Armor: Speed 20 ft. instead of 15 ft.

Weapons: Bastard sword (1d10, crit 19–20/×2, 10 lb., Medium-size, Slashing) instead of dwarven waraxe.
Skill Selection: Pick a number of skills equal to 3 + Int modifier (human only).

Skill	Ranks	Ability	Armor
Swim	4	Str	–11*

*–1 per 5 pounds of equipment.

Feat: Exotic Weapon Proficiency (bastard sword) instead of (dwarven waraxe).
Bonus Feat (Fighter): Weapon Focus (bastard sword) instead of Weapon Focus (dwarven waraxe).
Bonus Feat: Improved Initiative (human only).
Gold: 2d4 gp.

Alternative Fighter Starting Package

Same as dwarven fighter, except
Race: Gnome or halfling.
Weapons: Short sword (1d6, crit 19–20/×2, 3 lb., Small, Piercing) instead of waraxe.
Skill Selection: Pick a number of skills equal to 2 + Int modifier.

Skill	Ranks	Ability	Armor
Swim	4	Str	–5*

*–1 per 5 pounds of equipment.

Feat: Weapon Focus (short sword) instead of Exotic Weapon Proficiency (dwarven waraxe).
Bonus Feat (Fighter): If Dex 13 or higher, Dodge; if Dex 12 or less, Point Blank Shot instead.
Gold: 2d4×5 gp.

MONK

Dotted across the landscape are monasteries—small, walled cloisters inhabited by monks. These monks pursue personal perfection through action as well as contemplation. They train themselves to be versatile warriors skilled at fighting without weapons or armor. Monasteries headed by good masters serve as protectors of the people. Ready for battle even when barefoot and dressed in peasant clothes, monks are able to travel unnoticed among the populace, catching bandits, warlords, and corrupt nobles unawares. By contrast, monasteries headed by evil masters rule the surrounding lands through fear, virtually as an evil warlord's castle might. Evil monks make ideal spies, infiltrators, and assassins.

The individual monk, however, is unlikely to care passionately about championing commoners or amassing wealth. She cares for the perfection of her art and, thereby, her personal perfection. Her goal is to achieve a state that is, frankly, beyond the mortal realm.

Adventures: Monks approach adventures as if they were personal tests. While not prone to showing off, monks are willing to try their skills against whatever obstacles confront them. Monks are not greedy for material wealth, but they eagerly seek that which can help them perfect their art.

Characteristics: The key feature of the monk is her ability to fight unarmed and unarmored. Thanks to her rigorous training, she can strike as hard as if she were armed and strike faster than a warrior with a sword.

Though monks don't cast spells, they have a magic of their own. They channel a subtle energy, called *ki*, which allows them to perform amazing feats. The monk's best-known feat is her ability to stun an opponent with an unarmed blow. A monk also has a preternatural awareness of attacks. She can dodge an attack even if she is not consciously aware of it.

As the monk gains experience and power, her mundane and *ki*-oriented abilities grow, giving her more and more power over herself and, sometimes, over others.

Alignment: A monk's training requires strict discipline. Only those who are lawful at heart are capable of undertaking it.

Religion: A monk's training is her spiritual path. She is inner-directed, capable of a private, mystic connection to the spiritual world. She needs neither clerics nor gods. Certain lawful gods, however, may appeal to monks, and monks may meditate on the gods' likenesses and attempt to emulate their deeds. The three most likely candidates for a monk's devotion are Heironeous, god of valor; St. Cuthbert, god of retribution; and Hextor, god of tyranny.

Background: A monk typically trains in a monastery. Most monks were children when they joined the monastery, sent to live with the monks when their parents died, when there wasn't enough food in the family to keep them, or in return for some kindness that the monastery had performed for the family. Life in the monastery is so focused that by the time a monk sets off on her own, she feels little connection to her former family or village.

In larger cities, master monks have set up monk schools to teach their arts to those who are interested and worthy. The monks of these academies often see their rural cousins from the monasteries as backward.

A monk may feel a deep connection to her monastery or school, to the monk who taught her, to the lineage into which she was trained, or to all of these. Some monks, however, have no sense of connection other than to their own paths of personal development.

Monks recognize each other as a select group set apart from the rest of the populace. They may feel kinship, but they also love to compete with each other to see whose *ki* is strongest.

Races: Monasteries are mostly found among humans, who have incorporated them into their ever-evolving culture. Thus, many monks are humans (or half-orcs and half-elves who live among humans). Elves are capable of single-minded, long-term devotion to an interest, art, or discipline, and some of them leave the forests to become monks. The monk tradition is alien to dwarven and gnome culture, and halflings are typically too mobile to commit themselves to a monastery, so dwarves, gnomes, and halflings are very rarely monks.

The savage humanoids do not have the stable social structure that allows monk training, but the occasional orphaned or abandoned child from some humanoid tribe winds up in civilized monasteries or adopted by a wandering master. The evil subterranean elves known as the drow have a small but successful monk tradition.

Other Classes: Monks are sometimes distant from others because they have little in common with the motivations and skills of members of other classes. Monks recognize, however, that they work well with the support of others, and they prove themselves reliable companions.

GAME RULE INFORMATION

Monks have the following game statistics.

Abilities: Wisdom powers the monk's special offensive and defensive capabilities. Dexterity provides the unarmored monk with a better defense and with bonuses to some class skills. Strength helps a monk's unarmed combat ability.

Alignment: Any lawful.

Hit Die: d8.

Class Skills

The monk's class skills (and the key ability for each skill) are Balance (Dex), Climb (Str), Concentration (Con), Craft (Int), Diplomacy (Cha), Escape Artist (Dex), Hide (Dex), Jump (Str), Knowledge (arcana) (Int), Listen (Wis), Move Silently (Dex), Perform (Cha), Profession (Wis), Swim (Str), and Tumble (Dex). See Chapter 4: Skills for skill descriptions.

TABLE 3–10: THE MONK

Level	Base Attack Bonus	Fort Save	Ref Save	Will Save	Special	Unarmed Attack Bonus	Unarmed Damage*	AC Bonus**	Unarmored Speed***
1	0	+2	+2	+2	Unarmed Strike, stunning attack, evasion	+0	1d6	+0	30 ft.
2	+1	+3	+3	+3	Deflect Arrows feat	+1	1d6	+0	30 ft.
3	+2	+3	+3	+3	Still mind	+2	1d6	+0	40 ft.
4	+3	+4	+4	+4	Slow fall (20 ft.)	+3	1d8	+0	40 ft.
5	+3	+4	+4	+4	Purity of body	+3	1d8	+1	40 ft.
6	+4	+5	+5	+5	Slow fall (30 ft.), Improved Trip feat	+4/+1	1d8	+1	50 ft.
7	+5	+5	+5	+5	Wholeness of body, Leap of the clouds	+5/+2	1d8	+1	50 ft.
8	+6/+1	+6	+6	+6	Slow fall (50 ft.)	+6/+3	1d10	+1	50 ft.
9	+6/+1	+6	+6	+6	Improved evasion	+6/+3	1d10	+1	60 ft.
10	+7/+2	+7	+7	+7	*Ki* strike (+1)	+7/+4/+1	1d10	+2	60 ft.
11	+8/+3	+7	+7	+7	Diamond body	+8/+5/+2	1d10	+2	60 ft.
12	+9/+4	+8	+8	+8	*Abundant step*	+9/+6/+3	1d12	+2	70 ft.
13	+9/+4	+8	+8	+8	Diamond soul, *ki* strike (+2)	+9/+6/+3	1d12	+2	70 ft.
14	+10/+5	+9	+9	+9		+10/+7/+4/+1	1d12	+2	70 ft.
15	+11/+6/+1	+9	+9	+9	Quivering palm	+11/+8/+5/+2	1d12	+3	80 ft.
16	+12/+7/+2	+10	+10	+10	*Ki* strike (+3)	+12/+9/+6/+3	1d20	+3	80 ft.
17	+12/+7/+2	+10	+10	+10	Timeless body, tongue of the sun and moon	+12/+9/+6/+3	1d20	+3	80 ft.
18	+13/+8/+3	+11	+11	+11	Slow fall (any distance)	+13/+10/+7/+4/+1	1d20	+3	90 ft.
19	+14/+9/+4	+11	+11	+11	Empty body	+14/+11/+8/+5/+2	1d20	+3	90 ft.
20	+15/+10/+5	+12	+12	+12	Perfect self	+15/+12/+9/+6/+3	1d20	+4	90 ft.

*Small monks deal less damage (see Table 3–11: Small Monk Damage and Speed).

**This figure plus the monk's Wisdom modifier are added to the monk's AC (if this figure plus the monk's Wisdom modifier is not a positive number, do not add it). The AC bonus is 1/5 the monk's level.

***Small and dwarven monks are slower (see Table 3–11: Small Monk Damage and Speed).

Skill Points at 1st Level: (4 + Int modifier) × 4.
Skill Points at Each Additional Level: 4 + Int modifier.

Class Features

All of the following are class features of the monk.

Weapon and Armor Proficiency:
Monks are proficient with basic peasant weapons and special weapons whose use is part of monk training. The full list includes club, crossbow (light or heavy), dagger, handaxe, javelin, kama, nunchaku, quarterstaff, shuriken, siangham, and sling. (See Chapter 7: Equipment for descriptions of these weapons.)

Ember

A monk using a kama, nunchaku, or siangham can strike with her unarmed base attack, including her more favorable number of attacks per round (see below). Her damage, however, is standard for the weapon (1d6, crit ×2), not her unarmed damage. The weapon must be light, so a Small monk must use Tiny versions of these weapons in order to use the more favorable base attack.

Monks are not proficient with armor or shields, but they are highly trained at dodging blows, and they develop a "sixth sense" that lets them avoid even unanticipated attacks. A monk adds her Wisdom bonus (if any) to AC, in addition to her normal Dexterity modifier, and her AC improves as she gains levels. (Only add this extra AC bonus if the total of the monk's Wisdom modifier and the number in the "AC Bonus" column on Table 3–10 is a positive number.) The Wisdom bonus and the AC bonus represent a preternatural awareness of danger, and a monk does not lose either even in situations when she loses her Dexterity modifier due to being unprepared, ambushed, stunned, and so on. (Monks do lose these AC bonuses when immobilized.)

A monk's special skills all require freedom of movement. When wearing armor, a monk loses her AC bonus for Wisdom, AC bonus for class and level, favorable multiple unarmed attacks per round, and heightened movement. Furthermore, her special abilities all face the arcane spell failure chance that the armor type normally imposes. In addition, wearing armor heavier than leather imposes check penalties to the skills Balance, Climb, Escape Artist, Hide, Jump, Move Silently, Pick Pocket, and Tumble. Also, Swim checks suffer a –1 penalty for every 5 pounds of armor or equipment carried.

Unarmed Strike: Monks are highly trained in fighting unarmed, giving them considerable advantages when doing so. They deal more damage than normal, as shown on Table 3–10: The Monk. A monk fighting unarmed gains the benefits of the Improved Unarmed Strike feat and thus does not provoke attacks of opportunity from armed opponents that she attacks.

A monk's attacks may be with either fist interchangeably or even from elbows, knees, and feet. Making an off-hand attack makes no sense for a monk striking unarmed.

A monk fighting with a one-handed weapon can make an unarmed strike as an off-hand attack, but she suffers the standard penalties for two-weapon fighting (see Table 8–2: Two-Weapon Fighting Penalties, page 125). Likewise, a monk with a weapon (other than a special monk weapon) in her off hand gets an extra attack with that weapon but suffers the usual penalties for two-weapon fighting and can't strike with a flurry of blows (see below).

The unarmed damage on Table 3–10: The Monk is for Medium-size monks. Small monks deal less than stated damage with unarmed attacks (see Table 3–11: Small Monk Damage and Speed).

Flurry of Blows: The monk may strike with a flurry of blows at the expense of accuracy. When doing so, she may make one extra attack in a round at her highest base attack, but this attack and each other attack made that round suffer a –2 penalty apiece. For example, at 6th level, Ember gets two unarmed attacks at +7 and +4. If she executes a flurry of blows, she gets three attacks at +5, +5, and +2. This penalty applies for 1 round, so it affects attacks of opportunity the monk might make before her next action. The monk must use the full attack action (see page 124) to strike with a flurry of blows. A monk may also use the flurry of blows if armed with a special monk weapon (kama, nunchaku, or siangham). If armed with one such weapon, she makes the extra attack either with that weapon or unarmed. If armed with two such weapons, she uses one for the regular attack (or attacks) and the other for the extra attack. In any case, her damage bonus on the attack with her off hand is not reduced.

Usually, a monk's unarmed strikes deal normal damage rather than subdual damage (see Subdual Damage, page 134). However, she can choose to deal her damage as subdual damage when grappling (see Grapple, page 137).

LOCKWOOD

TABLE 3–11: SMALL MONK DAMAGE AND SPEED

Level	Damage	Speed	Level	Damage	Speed
1–2	1d4	20 ft.	9–11	1d8	40 ft.
3	1d4	25 ft.	12–14	1d10	45 ft.
4–5	1d6	25 ft.	15	1d10	55 ft.
6–7	1d6	35 ft.	16–17	2d6	55 ft.
8	1d8	35 ft.	18–20	2d6	60 ft.

Stunning Attack: A monk has the ability to stun a creature damaged by her unarmed attacks. The monk can use this ability once per round, but no more than once per level per day. The monk must declare she is using a stun attack before making the attack roll (thus, a missed attack roll ruins the attempt). A foe struck by the monk is forced to make a Fortitude saving throw (DC 10 + one-half the monk's level + Wisdom modifier), in addition to receiving normal damage. If the saving throw fails, the opponent is stunned for 1 round. A stunned character can't act and loses any Dexterity bonus to AC, while attackers get a +2 bonus on attack rolls against a stunned opponent. Constructs, oozes, plants, undead, incorporeal creatures, and creatures immune to critical hits cannot be stunned by the monk's stunning attack. The stunning attack is a supernatural ability.

Evasion: A monk can avoid even magical and unusual attacks with great agility. If a monk makes a successful Reflex saving throw against an attack that normally deals half damage on a successful save (such as a red dragon's fiery breath or a *fireball*), the monk instead takes no damage. Evasion can only be used if the monk is wearing light armor or no armor. It is an extraordinary ability.

Deflect Arrows: At 2nd level, a monk gains the Deflect Arrows feat (see page 81), even if she doesn't have the prerequisite Dexterity score.

Fast Movement: At 3rd level and higher, a monk moves faster than normal, as shown on Table 3–10: The Monk. A monk in armor (even light armor) or carrying a medium or heavy load loses this extra speed. A dwarf or a Small monk moves more slowly than a Medium-size monk (see Table 3–11: Small Monk Damage and Speed).

From 9th level on, the monk's running ability is actually a supernatural ability.

Still Mind: At 3rd level, a monk gains a +2 bonus to saving throws against spells and effects from the Enchantment school, since her meditation and training enable her to better resist mind-affecting attacks.

Slow Fall: At 4th level, a monk within arm's reach of a wall can use the wall to slow her descent. The monk takes damage as if the fall were 20 feet shorter than it actually is. Her ability to slow her fall (that is, to reduce the effective height of the fall when next to a wall) improves with her level until, at 18th level, the monk can use a nearby wall to slow her descent and fall any distance without harm. See the "Special" column on Table 3–10 for details.

Purity of Body: At 5th level, a monk gains control over her body's immune system. She gains immunity to all diseases except for magical diseases such as mummy rot and lycanthropy.

Improved Trip: At 6th level, a monk gains the Improved Trip feat (see page 83). She need not have taken the Expertise feat, normally a prerequisite, before this.

Wholeness of Body: At 7th level, a monk can cure her own wounds. She can cure up to twice her current level in hit points each day, and she can spread this healing out among several uses. Wholeness of body is a supernatural ability.

Leap of the Clouds: At 7th level or higher, a monk's jumping distance (vertical or horizontal) is not limited according to her height. (See the Jump skill description, page 70.)

Improved Evasion: At 9th level, a monk's evasion ability improves. She still takes no damage on a successful Reflex saving throw against attacks such as a dragon's breath weapon or a *fireball*, but henceforth she only takes half damage on a failed save.

Ki Strike: At 10th level, a monk's unarmed attack is empowered with *ki*. The unarmed strike damage from such an attack can deal damage to a creature with damage reduction, such as a wight, as if the blow were made with a weapon with a +1 enhancement bonus. *Ki* strike improves as the monk gains experience, allowing her unarmed strike at 13th level to deal damage against creatures with damage reduction as if it were made with a weapon with a +2 enhancement bonus, and at 16th level to deal damage against creatures with damage reduction as if it were made with a weapon with a +3 enhancement bonus. *Ki* strike is a supernatural ability.

Diamond Body: At 11th level, a monk is in such control of her own metabolism that she gains immunity to poison of all kinds. Diamond body is a supernatural ability.

Abundant Step: At 12th level, a monk can slip magically between spaces, as per the spell *dimension door*, once per day. This is a spell-like ability, and the monk's effective casting level is one-half her actual level (rounded down).

Diamond Soul: At 13th level, a monk gains spell resistance. Her spell resistance equals her level + 10. In order to affect the monk with a spell, a spellcaster must roll the monk's spell resistance or higher on 1d20 + the spellcaster's level. (See Spell Resistance, page 150.)

Quivering Palm: Starting at 15th level, a monk can use the quivering palm. This terrifying attack allows the monk to set up vibrations within the body of another creature that can then be fatal if the monk so desires.

The monk can use the quivering palm attack once a week, and she must announce her intent before making her attack roll. Constructs, oozes, plants, undead, incorporeal creatures, and creatures immune to critical hits cannot be affected. The monk must be of higher level than the target (or have more levels than the target's number of Hit Dice). If the monk strikes successfully and the target takes damage from the blow, the quivering palm attack succeeds. Thereafter the monk can choose to try to slay the victim at any later time within 1 day per level of the monk. The monk merely wills the target to die (a free action), and unless the target makes a Fortitude saving throw (DC 10 + one-half the monk's level + Wisdom modifier), it dies. If the saving throw is successful, the target is no longer in danger from that particular quivering palm attack (but may be affected by another one at a later time). Quivering palm is a supernatural ability.

Timeless Body: After achieving 17th level, a monk no longer suffers ability penalties for aging and cannot be magically aged. (Any penalties she may have already suffered remain in place.) Bonuses still accrue, and the monk still dies of old age when her time is up.

Tongue of the Sun and Moon: A monk of 17th level or above can speak with any living creature.

Empty Body: At 19th level or higher, a monk can assume an ethereal state for 1 round per level per day, as per the spell *etherealness*. The monk may go ethereal on a number of different occasions during any single day as long as the total number of rounds spent ethereal does not exceed her level. Empty body is a supernatural ability.

Perfect Self: At 20th level, a monk has tuned her body with skill and quasi-magical abilities to the point that she becomes a magical creature. She is forevermore treated as an outsider (extraplanar creature) rather than as a humanoid. For instance, *charm person* does not affect her. Additionally, the monk gains damage reduction 20/+1. This means that the monk ignores (instantly regenerates) the first 20 points of damage from any attack unless the damage is dealt by a weapon with a +1 enhancement bonus (or better), by a spell, or by a form of energy (fire, cold, etc.). As an outsider, a 20th-level monk is subject to spells that repel enchanted creatures, such as *protection from law.*

Ex-Monks

A monk who becomes nonlawful cannot gain new levels as a monk but retains all monk abilities.

Like a member of any other class, a monk may be a multiclass character, but monks face a special restriction. A monk who gains a new class or (if already multiclass) raises another class by a level may never again raise her monk level, though she retains all her monk abilities.

Human Monk Starting Package

Armor: None, speed 30 ft.

Weapons: Quarterstaff (1d6, crit ×2, 4 lb., Large, Bludgeoning). Sling (1d4, crit ×2, 50 ft., 0 lb., Small, Bludgeoning).

Skill Selection: Pick a number of skills equal to 5 + Int modifier.

Skill	Ranks	Ability	Armor
Listen	4	Wis	
Climb	4	Str	0
Move Silently	4	Dex	0
Tumble	4	Dex	0
Jump	4	Str	0
Escape Artist	4	Dex	0
Hide	4	Dex	0
Swim	4	Str	–4*
Balance	4	Dex	0

*–1 per 5 pounds of equipment.

Feat: If Dex 13 or higher, Dodge; if Dex 12 or less, Improved Initiative instead.

Bonus Feat: Skill Focus (Move Silently or other skill).

Gear: Backpack with waterskin, one day's trail rations, bedroll, sack, and flint and steel. Three torches. Pouch with 10 sling stones.

Gold: 2d4 gp.

Alternative Monk Starting Package

Same as human monk, except

    Race: Dwarf, elf, half-elf, or half-orc.

    Armor: Speed 20 ft. (dwarf only).

    Skill Selection: Pick a number of skills equal to 4 + Int modifier.

    Bonus Feat: None.

Alternative Monk Starting Package

Same as human monk, except

    Race: Gnome or halfling.

    Armor: Speed 20 ft.

    Weapons: Club (1d6, crit ×2, 10 ft., 3 lb., Bludgeoning) instead of quarterstaff.

    Skill Selection: Pick a number of skills equal to 4 + Int modifier.

Skill	Ranks	Ability	Armor
Swim	4	Str	−3*

*−1 per 5 pounds of equipment.

    Bonus Feat: None.

PALADIN

The compassion to pursue good, the will to uphold law, and the power to defeat evil—these are the three weapons of the paladin. Few have the purity and devotion that it takes to walk the paladin's path, but those few are rewarded with the power to protect, to heal, and to smite. In a land of scheming wizards, unholy priests, bloodthirsty dragons, and infernal fiends, the paladin is the final hope that cannot be extinguished.

Adventures: Paladins take their adventures seriously and have a penchant for referring to them as "quests." Even a mundane mission is, in the heart of the paladin, a personal test—an opportunity to demonstrate bravery, to develop martial skills, to learn tactics, and to find ways to do good. Still, the paladin really comes into her own when leading a mighty campaign against evil, not when merely looting ruins.

Characteristics: Divine power protects the paladin and gives her special powers. It wards off harm, protects her from disease, lets her heal herself, and guards her heart against fear. The paladin can also direct this power to help others, healing their wounds or curing diseases. Finally, the paladin can use this power to destroy evil. Even the least experienced paladin can detect evil, and more experienced paladins can smite evil foes and turn away undead. In addition, this power draws a mighty steed to the paladin and imbues that mount with strength, intelligence, and magical protection.

Alignment: Paladins must be lawful good, and they lose their divine powers if they deviate from that alignment. Additionally, paladins swear to follow a code of conduct that is in line with lawfulness and goodness.

Religion: Paladins need not devote themselves to a single deity. Devotion to righteousness is enough for most. Those who align themselves with particular religions prefer Heironeous, god of valor, over all others, but some paladins follow Pelor, the sun god. Paladins devoted to a god are scrupulous in observing religious duties and are welcome in every associated temple.

Background: No one ever chooses to be a paladin. Becoming a paladin is answering a call, accepting one's destiny. No one, no matter how diligent, can become a paladin through practice. The nature is either within one or not, and it is not possible to gain the paladin's nature by any act of will. It is possible to fail to recognize one's own potential, or to deny one's destiny. Some who are called to be paladins deny the call and pursue some other life instead.

Most paladins answer the call and begin training as adolescents. Typically, they become squires or assistants to experienced paladins, train for years, and finally set off on their own to further the causes of good and law. Other paladins, however, find their calling only later in life, after having pursued some other career. All paladins, regardless of background, recognize in each other an eternal bond that transcends culture, race, and even religion. Any two paladins, even from opposite sides of the world, consider themselves comrades.

Races: Humans, with their ambitious souls, make great paladins. Half-elves, who often have human ambition, may also find themselves called into service as paladins. Dwarves are sometimes paladins, but becoming a paladin may be hard on a dwarf because it means putting the duties of the paladin's life before duties to family, clan, and king. Elven paladins are few, and those few tend to follow quests that take them far and wide because their lawful bent puts them out of synch with life among the elves. Members of the other common races rarely hear the call to become paladins.

Among the savage humanoids, paladins are all but unheard of.

Other Classes: Even though paladins are in some ways set apart from others, they eagerly team up with those whose skills and capabilities complement their own. They work well with good and lawful clerics, and they appreciate working with those who are brave, honest, and committed to good. While they cannot abide evil acts by their companions, they are otherwise willing to work with a variety of people quite different from themselves. Charismatic, trustworthy, and well respected, the paladin makes a fine leader for a team.

GAME RULE INFORMATION

Paladins have the following game statistics.

Abilities: Charisma increases the paladin's healing, self-protective capabilities, and undead turning. Strength is important for a paladin because of its role in combat. A Wisdom score of 14 or higher is required to get access to the most powerful paladin spells, and a score of 11 or higher is required to cast any paladin spells at all.

Alhandra

Illus. by D. Martin / T. Lockwood

Alignment: Lawful good.

Hit Die: d10.

Class Skills

The paladin's class skills (and the key ability for each skill) are Concentration (Con), Craft (Int), Diplomacy (Cha), Handle Animal (Cha), Heal (Wis), Knowledge (religion) (Int), Profession (Wis), and Ride (Dex). See Chapter 4: Skills for skill descriptions.

Skill Points at 1st Level: (2 + Int modifier) × 4.

Skill Points at Each Additional Level: 2 + Int modifier.

Class Features

All of the following are class features of the paladin.

Weapon and Armor Proficiency: Paladins are proficient with all simple and martial weapons, with all types of armor (heavy, medium, and light), and with shields. Note that armor check penalties for armor heavier than leather apply to the skills Balance, Climb, Escape Artist, Hide, Jump, Move Silently, Pick Pocket, and Tumble. Also, Swim checks suffer a –1 penalty for every 5 pounds of armor and equipment carried.

Detect Evil: At will, the paladin can *detect evil* as a spell-like ability. This ability duplicates the effects of the spell *detect evil*.

Divine Grace: A paladin applies her Charisma modifier (if positive) as a bonus to all saving throws.

Lay on Hands: A paladin can heal wounds by touch. Each day she can cure a total number of hit points equal to her Charisma bonus (if any) times her level. For example, a 7th-level paladin with a 16 Charisma (+3 bonus) may cure up to 21 points of damage. The paladin can cure herself. She may choose to divide her curing among multiple recipients, and she doesn't have to use it all at once. *Lay on hands* is a spell-like ability whose use is a standard action.

Alternatively, the paladin can use any or all of these points to deal damage to undead creatures. Treat this attack just like a touch spell. The paladin decides how many cure points to use as damage after successfully touching the undead creature.

Divine Health: A paladin is immune to all diseases, including magical diseases such as mummy rot and lycanthropy.

Aura of Courage: Beginning at 2nd level, a paladin is immune to fear (magical or otherwise). Allies within 10 feet of the paladin gain a +4 morale bonus on saving throws against fear effects. Granting the morale bonus to allies is a supernatural ability.

Smite Evil: Once per day, a paladin of 2nd level or higher may attempt to smite evil with one normal melee attack. She adds her Charisma modifier (if positive) to her attack roll and deals 1 extra point of damage per level. For example, a 13th-level paladin armed with a longsword would deal 1d8+13 points of damage, plus any additional bonuses for high Strength or magical effects that normally apply. If the paladin accidentally smites a creature that is not evil, the smite has no effect but it is still used up for that day. Smite evil is a supernatural ability.

Remove Disease: Beginning at 3rd level, a paladin can *remove disease*, as per the spell *remove disease*, once per week. She can use this ability more often as she advances in levels (twice per week at 6th level, three times per week at 9th level, and so forth). *Remove disease* is a spell-like ability for paladins.

Turn Undead: When a paladin reaches 3rd level, she gains the supernatural ability to turn undead. She may use this ability a number of times per day equal to three plus her Charisma modifier. She turns undead as a cleric of two levels lower would. (See Turn and Rebuke Undead, page 139.)

Extra Turning: As a feat, a paladin may take Extra Turning. This feat allows the paladin to turn undead four more times per day than normal. A paladin can take this feat multiple times, gaining four extra daily turning attempts each time.

Spells: Beginning at 4th level, a paladin gains the ability to cast a small number of divine spells. To cast a spell, the paladin must have a Wisdom score of at least 10 + the spell's level, so a paladin with a Wisdom of 10 or lower cannot cast these spells. Paladin bonus spells are based on Wisdom, and saving throws against these spells have a Difficulty Class of 10 + spell level + Wisdom modifier. When the paladin gets 0 spells of a given level, such as 0 1st-level spells at 4th level, the paladin gets only bonus spells (as per Table 1–1: Ability Modifiers and Bonus Spells). A paladin without a bonus spell for that level cannot yet cast a spell of that level. The paladin's spell list appears on page 167. A paladin has access to any spell on the list and can freely choose which to prepare, just as a cleric can. A paladin prepares and casts spells just as a cleric does (though the paladin cannot use spontaneous casting to substitute a *cure* spell in place of a prepared spell).

TABLE 3–12: THE PALADIN

Level	Base Attack Bonus	Fort Save	Ref Save	Will Save	Special	Spells per Day			
						1	2	3	4
1	+1	+2	+0	+0	*Detect evil*, divine grace, *lay on hands*, divine health	—	—	—	—
2	+2	+3	+0	+0	Aura of courage, smite evil	—	—	—	—
3	+3	+3	+1	+1	*Remove disease*, turn undead	—	—	—	—
4	+4	+4	+1	+1		0	—	—	—
5	+5	+4	+1	+1	Special mount	0	—	—	—
6	+6/+1	+5	+2	+2	*Remove disease* 2/week	1	—	—	—
7	+7/+2	+5	+2	+2		1	—	—	—
8	+8/+3	+6	+2	+2		1	0	—	—
9	+9/+4	+6	+3	+3	*Remove disease* 3/week	1	0	—	—
10	+10/+5	+7	+3	+3		1	1	—	—
11	+11/+6/+1	+7	+3	+3		1	1	0	—
12	+12/+7/+2	+8	+4	+4	*Remove disease* 4/week	1	1	1	—
13	+13/+8/+3	+8	+4	+4		1	1	1	—
14	+14/+9/+4	+9	+4	+4		2	1	1	0
15	+15/+10/+5	+9	+5	+5	*Remove disease* 5/week	2	1	1	1
16	+16/+11/+6/+1	+10	+5	+5		2	2	1	1
17	+17/+12/+7/+2	+10	+5	+5		2	2	2	1
18	+18/+13/+8/+3	+11	+6	+6	*Remove disease* 6/week	3	2	2	1
19	+19/+14/+9/+4	+11	+6	+6		3	3	3	2
20	+20/+15/+10/+5	+12	+6	+6		3	3	3	3

Through 3rd level, a paladin has no caster level. Starting at 4th level, a paladin's caster level is one-half her class level.

Special Mount: Upon or after reaching 5th level, a paladin can call an unusually intelligent, strong, and loyal steed to serve her in her crusade against evil (see The Paladin's Mount sidebar). This mount is usually a heavy warhorse (for a Medium-size paladin) or a warpony (for a Small paladin).

Should the paladin's mount die, she may call for another one after a year and a day. The new mount has all the accumulated abilities due a mount of the paladin's level.

Code of Conduct: A paladin must be of lawful good alignment and loses all special class abilities if she ever willingly commits an act of evil. Additionally, a paladin's code requires that she respect legitimate authority, act with honor (not lying, not cheating, not using poison, etc.), help those who need help (provided they do not use the help for evil or chaotic ends), and punish those that harm or threaten innocents.

Associates: While she may adventure with characters of any good or neutral alignment, a paladin will never knowingly associate with evil characters. A paladin will not continue an association with someone who consistently offends her moral code. A paladin may only hire henchmen or accept followers who are lawful good.

x-Paladins

A paladin who ceases to be lawful good, who willfully commits an evil act, or who grossly violates the code of conduct loses all special abilities and spells, including the service of the paladin's warhorse. She also may not progress in levels as a paladin. She regains her abilities if she atones for her violations (see the *atonement* spell description, page 176), as appropriate.

Like a member of any other class, a paladin may be a multiclass character, but paladins face a special restriction. A paladin who gains a new class or (if already multiclass) raises another class by a level may never again raise her paladin level, though she retains all her paladin abilities. The path of the paladin requires a constant heart. Once you undertake the path, you must pursue it to the exclusion of all other careers. Once you have turned off the path, you may never return.

Human Paladin Starting Package

Armor: Scale mail +4 AC, large wooden shield +2 AC, armor check penalty –6, speed 20 ft., 40 lb.

Weapons: Longsword (1d8, crit 19–20/×2, 4 lb., Medium-size, Slashing).

Shortbow (1d6, ×3 crit, 60 ft., 2 lb., Medium-size, Piercing).

Skill Selection: Pick a number of skills equal to 3 + Int modifier.

Skill	Ranks	Ability	Armor
Heal	4	Wis	
Ride	4	Dex	
Diplomacy	4	Cha	
Spot (cc)	2	Wis	
Listen (cc)	2	Wis	
Climb (cc)	2	Str	–6
Search (cc)	2	Int	

Feat: Weapon Focus (longsword).

Bonus Feat: Improved Initiative.

THE PALADIN'S MOUNT

The paladin's mount is different from a standard animal of its type in many ways. The standard mount for a Medium-size paladin is a warhorse, and the standard mount for a Small paladin is a warpony (see the *Monster Manual* for warhorse and warpony basic statistics). Your DM may work with you to select another kind of mount, such as a riding dog. A paladin's mount is a magical beast, not an animal. It is superior to a normal mount of its kind and has special powers, as shown below:

Paladin Level	Bonus HD	Natural Armor	Str Adj.	Int	Special
5–7	+2	4	+1	6	Improved evasion, share spells, empathic link, share saving throws
8–10	+4	6	+2	7	
11–14	+6	8	+3	8	*Command* creatures of its kind
15–20	+8	10	+4	9	Spell resistance

Paladin Level: The level of the paladin. If the mount suffers a level drain, treat it as a mount of a lower-level paladin.

Bonus HD: These are extra eight-sided (d8) Hit Dice, each of which gains a Constitution modifier, as normal. Remember that extra Hit Dice improve the mount's base attack and base save bonuses.

Natural Armor: The number listed here is an improvement to the mount's AC. It represents the preternatural toughness of a paladin's mount.

Str Adj.: Add this figure to the mount's Strength score.

Int: The mount's Intelligence score.

Improved Evasion: If the mount is subjected to an attack that normally allows a Reflex saving throw for half damage, it takes no damage if it makes a successful saving throw and half damage even if the saving throw fails. Improved evasion is an extraordinary ability.

Share Spells: At the paladin's option, she may have any spell she casts on herself also affect her mount. The mount must be within 5 feet. If the spell has a duration other than instantaneous, the spell stops affecting the mount if it moves farther than 5 feet away and will not affect the mount again even if the mount returns to the paladin before the duration expires. Additionally, the paladin may cast a spell with a target of "You" on her mount (as a touch range spell) instead of on herself. The paladin and the mount can share spells even if the spells normally do not affect creatures of the mount's type (magical beast).

Empathic Link: The paladin has an empathic link with the mount out to a distance of up to one mile. The paladin cannot see through the mount's eyes, but they can communicate telepathically. Even intelligent mounts see the world differently from humans, so misunderstandings are always possible. This is a supernatural ability.

Because of the empathic link between the mount and the paladin, the paladin has the same connection to an item or place that the mount does, just as a master and his familiar (see Familiars, page 51).

Share Saving Throws: The mount uses its own base save or the paladin's, whichever is higher.

Command: The mount's *command* ability is a spell-like ability that it can use at will against other creatures of its kind (for warhorses and warponies, this includes donkeys, mules, and ponies) with fewer Hit Dice than it has itself. The mount can use this ability once per two levels of its paladin, and the ability functions just like the spell *command* (for purposes of this spell, the mount can make itself be understood by any normal animal of its kind). Since this is a spell-like ability, the mount must make a Concentration check (DC 21) if it's being ridden at the time (as in combat). If the check fails, the ability does not work that time, but it still counts against the mount's daily uses.

Spell Resistance: The mount's spell resistance equals the paladin's level + 5. To affect the mount with a spell, a spellcaster must make a caster level check (1d20 + caster level) at least equal to the mount's spell resistance.

Gear: Backpack with waterskin, one day's trail rations, bedroll, sack, flint and steel. Hooded lantern, three pints of oil. Quiver with 20 arrows. Wooden holy symbol: fist of Heironeous, god of valor.

Gold: 6d4 gp.

Alternative Paladin Starting Package

As human paladin, except

Race: Dwarf, elf, half-elf, or half-orc.

Armor: Speed 15 ft. (dwarf only).

Skill Selection: Pick a number of skills equal to 2 + Int modifier.

Bonus Feat: None.

Alternative Paladin Starting Package

As human paladin, except

Race: Gnome or halfling.

Armor: Speed 15 ft.

Weapons: Short sword (1d6, crit 19–20/×2, 3 lb., Small, Piercing) instead of longsword.

Skill Selection: Pick a number of skills equal to 2 + Int modifier.

Feat: Weapon Focus (short sword) instead of Weapon Focus (longsword).

Bonus Feat: None.

Gold: 8d4 gp.

RANGER

The forests are home to fierce and cunning creatures, such as bloodthirsty owlbears and malicious displacer beasts. But more cunning and powerful than these monsters is the ranger, a skilled hunter and stalker. He knows the woods as if they were his home (as indeed they are), and he knows his prey in deadly detail.

Soveliss

Adventures: Rangers often accept the role of protector, aiding those who live in or travel through the woods. In addition, they often carry grudges against certain types of creatures and look for opportunities to find and destroy them. Additionally, rangers may adventure for all the reasons that fighters do.

Characteristics: The ranger is proficient with all simple and martial weapons and capable in combat. His skills allow him to survive in the wilderness, to find his prey, and to avoid detection. He also has special knowledge of certain types of creatures. This knowledge makes him more capable of finding and defeating those foes. Finally, an experienced ranger has such a tie to nature that he can actually draw on natural power to cast divine spells, much as a druid does.

An experienced ranger often has one or more animal companions to aid him, thanks to his *animal friendship* spell.

Alignment: Rangers can be of any alignment. Most are good, and they are protectors of the wild areas. In this role, a ranger seeks out and destroys or drives off evil creatures that threaten the wilderness. Good rangers also protect those who travel through the wilderness, serving sometimes as guides and sometimes as unseen guardians. Rangers are also mostly chaotic, preferring to follow the ebb and flow of nature or of their own hearts instead of rigid rules. Evil rangers, though rare, are much to be feared. They revel in nature's thoughtless cruelty and seek to emulate her most fearsome predators. They gain divine spells just as good rangers do, for nature herself is indifferent to good and evil.

Religion: Though rangers gain their divine spells from the power of nature, like anyone else they may worship a chosen deity. Ehlonna, goddess of the woodlands, and Obad-Hai, god of nature, are the most common deities among them, though some rangers prefer more martial deities.

TABLE 3–13: THE RANGER

Level	Base Attack Bonus	Fort Save	Ref Save	Will Save	Special	1	2	3	4
1	+1	+2	+0	+0	Track, 1st favored enemy	—	—	—	—
2	+2	+3	+0	+0		—	—	—	—
3	+3	+3	+1	+1		—	—	—	—
4	+4	+4	+1	+1		0	—	—	—
5	+5	+4	+1	+1	2nd favored enemy	0	—	—	—
6	+6/+1	+5	+2	+2		1	—	—	—
7	+7/+2	+5	+2	+2		1	—	—	—
8	+8/+3	+6	+2	+2		1	0	—	—
9	+9/+4	+6	+3	+3		1	0	—	—
10	+10/+5	+7	+3	+3	3rd favored enemy	1	1	—	—
11	+11/+6/+1	+7	+3	+3		1	1	0	—
12	+12/+7/+2	+8	+4	+4		1	1	1	—
13	+13/+8/+3	+8	+4	+4		1	1	1	—
14	+14/+9/+4	+9	+4	+4		2	1	1	0
15	+15/+10/+5	+9	+5	+5	4th favored enemy	2	1	1	1
16	+16/+11/+6/+1	+10	+5	+5		2	2	1	1
17	+17/+12/+7/+2	+10	+5	+5		2	2	2	1
18	+18/+13/+8/+3	+11	+6	+6		3	2	2	1
19	+19/+14/+9/+4	+11	+6	+6		3	3	3	2
20	+20/+15/+10/+5	+12	+6	+6	5th favored enemy	3	3	3	3

Background: Some rangers gained their training as part of special military teams, but most learned their skills from solitary masters who accepted them as students and assistants. The rangers of a particular master may count themselves as cohorts, or they may be rivals for the status of "best student" and thus the rightful heir to their master's fame.

Races: Elves are commonly rangers. They are at home in the woods, and they have the grace to move stealthily. Half-elves who feel their elven parents' connection to the woods are also commonly rangers. Humans are often rangers as well, being adaptable enough to learn their way around the woods even if it doesn't come naturally. Half-orcs may find the life of a ranger more comfortable than life among cruel and taunting humans (or orcs). Gnome rangers are more common than gnome fighters, but still they tend to remain in their own lands rather than adventure among "the big people." Dwarf rangers are rare, but they can be quite effective. Instead of living in the surface wilderness, they are at home in the endless caverns beneath the earth. Here they hunt down and destroy the enemies of dwarvenkind with the relentless precision for which dwarves are known. Dwarf rangers are often known as "cavers." Halfling rangers are legendary—as in, you might hear stories about them but you'll probably never meet one.

Among the savage humanoids, only gnolls are commonly rangers, using their skills to slyly stalk their prey.

Classes: Rangers get along well with druids and to some extent with barbarians. They are known to bicker with paladins, mostly because they often share goals but differ in style, tactics, approach, philosophy, and esthetics. Since rangers don't much look to other people for support or friendship, they find it easy to tolerate people who are quite different from themselves, such as bookish wizards and preachy clerics. They just don't care enough to get upset about others' differences.

GAME RULE INFORMATION

Rangers have the following game statistics.

Abilities: Dexterity is important for a ranger because rangers tend to wear light armor and because several ranger skills are based on Dexterity. Strength is important for them because rangers frequently get involved in combat. Several ranger skills are based on Wisdom, and a Wisdom score of 14 or higher is required to get access to the most powerful ranger spells. A Wisdom score of 11 or higher is required to cast any ranger spells at all.

Alignment: Any.

Hit Die: d10.

Class Skills

The ranger's class skills (and the key ability for each skill) are Animal Empathy (Cha, exclusive skill), Climb (Str), Concentration (Con), Craft (Int), Handle Animal (Cha), Heal (Wis), Hide (Dex), Intuit Direction (Wis), Jump (Str), Knowledge (nature) (Int), Listen (Wis), Move Silently (Dex), Profession (Wis), Ride (Dex), Search (Int), Spot (Wis), Swim (Str), Use Rope (Dex), and Wilderness Lore (Wis). See Chapter 4: Skills for skill descriptions.

Skill Points at 1st Level: (4 + Int modifier) × 4.
Skill Points at Each Additional Level: 4 + Int modifier.

Class Features

All of the following are class features of the ranger.

Weapon and Armor Proficiency: A ranger is proficient with all simple and martial weapons, light armor, medium armor, and shields. Note that armor check penalties for armor heavier than leather apply to the skills Balance, Climb, Escape Artist, Hide, Jump, Move Silently, Pick Pocket, and Tumble. Also, Swim checks suffer a –1 penalty for every 5 pounds of armor and equipment carried. When wearing light armor or no armor, a ranger can fight with two weapons as if he had

the feats Ambidexterity and Two-Weapon Fighting. He loses this special bonus when fighting in medium or heavy armor, or when using a double-headed weapon (such as a double sword).

Spells: Beginning at 4th level, a ranger gains the ability to cast a small number of divine spells. To cast a spell, the ranger must have a Wisdom score of at least 10 + the spell's level, so a ranger with a Wisdom of 10 or lower cannot cast these spells. Ranger bonus spells are based on Wisdom, and saving throws against these spells have a Difficulty Class of 10 + spell level + Wisdom modifier. When the ranger gets 0 spells of a given level, such as 0 1st-level spells at 4th level, the ranger gets only bonus spells. A ranger without a bonus spell for that level (see Table 1–1: Ability Modifiers and Spells, page 8) cannot yet cast a spell of that level. The ranger's spell list appears on page 167. A ranger has access to any spell on the list and can freely choose which to prepare. A ranger prepares and casts spells just as a cleric does (though the ranger cannot use spontaneous casting to lose a spell and cast a *cure* or *inflict* spell in its place).

Through 3rd level, a ranger has no caster level. Starting at 4th level, a ranger's caster level is one-half his class level.

Track: A ranger gains Track (see page 85) as a bonus feat.

Favored Enemy: At 1st level, a ranger may select a type of creature (dragons, giants, goblinoids, undead, etc.) as a favored enemy. (A ranger can only select his own race as a favored enemy if he is evil.) Due to his extensive study of his foes and training in the proper techniques for combating them, the ranger gains a +1 bonus to Bluff, Listen, Sense Motive, Spot, and Wilderness Lore checks when using these skills against this type of creature. Likewise, he gets the same bonus to weapon damage rolls against creatures of this type. A ranger also gets the damage bonus with ranged weapons, but only against targets within 30 feet (the ranger cannot strike with deadly accuracy beyond that range). The bonus doesn't apply to damage against creatures that are immune to critical hits.

At 5th level and at every five levels thereafter (10th, 15th, and 20th level), the ranger may select a new favored enemy, and the bonus associated with every previously selected favored enemy goes up by +1. For example, a 15th-level ranger will have four favored enemies, with bonuses of +4, +3, +2, and +1.

Table 3–14: Ranger Favored Enemies lists possible categories for a ranger's favored enemy.

TABLE 3–14: RANGER FAVORED ENEMIES

Type	Examples
Aberrations	Beholders
Animals	Bears
Beasts	Owlbears
Constructs	Golems
Dragons	Black dragons
Elementals	Xorns
Fey	Dryads
Giants	Ogres
Humanoid type	*
Magical beasts	Displacer beasts
Oozes	Gelatinous cubes
Outsider type	*
Plants	Shambling mounds
Shapechangers	Werewolves
Undead	Zombies
Vermin	Giant spiders

*Rangers may not select "humanoid" or "outsider" as a favored enemy, but they may select a more narrowly defined type of humanoid (such as goblinoids, humans, or reptilian humanoids) or outsider (such as devils, efreet, or slaadi). See the *Monster Manual* for more information on types of creatures. A ranger can only select his own race as a favored enemy if he is evil.

Improved Two-Weapon Fighting: A ranger with a base attack bonus of at least +9 can choose to gain the Improved Two-Weapon

Fighting feat (see page 83) even if he does not have the other prerequisites for the feat. The ranger must be wearing light armor or no armor in order to use this benefit.

Elven Ranger Starting Package

Armor: Studded leather +3 AC, speed 30 ft., armor check penalty –1, 20 lb.

Weapons: Longsword (1d8, crit 19–20/×2, 4 lb., Medium-size, Slashing).

Short sword, off hand (1d6, crit 19–20/×2, 3 lb., Small, Piercing).

Note: When striking with both swords, the ranger is –2 with each attack. If the ranger has a Strength bonus, add only half of it to damage with the short sword, which is in the ranger's off hand.

Longbow (1d8, ×3 crit, 100 ft., 3 lb., Large, Piercing).

Skill Selection: Pick a number of skills equal to 4 + Int modifier.

Skill	Ranks	Ability	Armor
Wilderness Lore	4	Wis	
Animal Empathy	4	Cha	
Hide	4	Dex	–1
Move Silently	4	Wis	–1
Listen	4	Wis	
Spot	4	Wis	
Search	4	Int	
Heal	4	Wis	
Intuit Direction	4	Wis	

Feat: Point Blank Shot.

Favored Enemy: Magical beasts.

Gear: Backpack with waterskin, one day's trail rations, bedroll, sack, and flint and steel. Three torches. Quiver with 20 arrows.

Gold: 2d4 gp.

Alternative Ranger Starting Package

As elven ranger except

Race: Human, dwarf, half-elf, or half-orc.

Armor: Speed 20 ft. (dwarf only).

Skill Selection: Pick a number of skills equal to 5 + Int modifier (human only).

Bonus Feat: Skill Focus (Wilderness Lore or other skill) (human only).

Alternative Ranger Starting Package

As elven ranger except

Race: Gnome or halfling.

Armor: Speed 20 ft.

Weapons: Instead of longsword, short sword, and longbow: Short sword (1d6, crit 19–20/×2, 3 lb., Small, Piercing).

Dagger, off hand (1d4, crit 19–20/×2, 10 ft., 1 lb., Tiny, Piercing).

Note: When striking with both sword and dagger, the ranger is –2 with each attack.

Shortbow (1d6, ×3 crit, 60 ft., 2 lb., Medium-size, Piercing).

Favored Enemy: Reptilian humanoids instead of magical beasts (gnome only).

Gold: 5d4×5 gp.

ROGUE

Rogues share little in common with each other. Some are stealthy thieves. Others are silver-tongued tricksters. Still others are scouts, infiltrators, spies, diplomats, or thugs. What they share is versatility, adaptability, and resourcefulness. In general, rogues are skilled at getting what others don't want them to get: entrance into a locked treasure vault, safe passage past a deadly trap, secret battle plans, a guard's trust, or some random person's pocket money.

Adventures: Rogues adventure for the same reason they do most things: to get what they can get. Some are after loot, others experience. Some crave fame, others infamy. Quite a few also enjoy a challenge. Figuring out how to thwart a trap or avoid an alarm is great fun for many rogues.

Characteristics: Rogues are highly skilled, and they can concentrate in any of several types of skills. While not equal to members of many other classes in combat, a rogue knows how to hit where it hurts, and a rogue who can hit an opponent with a sneak attack can dish out a lot of damage.

Rogues have a sixth sense when it comes to avoiding danger. Experienced rogues develop nearly magical powers and skills as they master the arts of stealth, evasion, and sneak attacks. In addition, while not capable of casting spells on their own, rogues can "fake it" well enough to cast spells from scrolls, activate wands, and use just about any other magic item.

Alignment: Rogues follow opportunity, not ideals. They are more likely to be chaotic than lawful. Rogues, however, are a diverse bunch, and they may be of any alignment.

TABLE 3–15: THE ROGUE

Level	Base Attack Bonus	Fort Save	Ref Save	Will Save	Special
1	+0	+0	+2	+0	Sneak attack +1d6
2	+1	+0	+3	+0	Evasion
3	+2	+1	+3	+1	Uncanny dodge (Dex bonus to AC), sneak attack +2d6
4	+3	+1	+4	+1	
5	+3	+1	+4	+1	Sneak attack +3d6
6	+4	+2	+5	+2	Uncanny dodge (can't be flanked)
7	+5	+2	+5	+2	Sneak attack +4d6
8	+6/+1	+2	+6	+2	
9	+6/+1	+3	+6	+3	Sneak attack +5d6
10	+7/+2	+3	+7	+3	Special ability
11	+8/+3	+3	+7	+3	Uncanny dodge (+1 against traps), sneak attack +6d6
12	+9/+4	+4	+8	+4	
13	+9/+4	+4	+8	+4	Sneak attack +7d6, special ability
14	+10/+5	+4	+9	+4	Uncanny dodge (+2 against traps)
15	+11/+6/+1	+5	+9	+5	Sneak attack +8d6
16	+12/+7/+2	+5	+10	+5	Special ability
17	+12/+7/+2	+5	+10	+5	Uncanny dodge (+3 against traps), sneak attack +9d6
18	+13/+8/+3	+6	+11	+6	
19	+14/+9/+4	+6	+11	+6	Sneak attack +10d6, special ability
20	+15/+10/+5	+6	+12	+6	Uncanny dodge (+4 against traps)

Religion: Rogues most commonly worship Olidammara, god of thieves, though they are not renowned for their piety. Evil rogues might secretly worship Nerull, god of death, or Erythnul, god of slaughter. Since rogues are a diverse crew, however, many of them worship other deities, or none at all.

Background: Some rogues are officially inducted into an organized fellowship of rogues or "guild of thieves." Most, however, are self-taught or learned their skills from an independent mentor. Often, an experienced rogue needs an assistant for scams, second-story jobs, or just for watching her back. She recruits a likely youngster who then learns the skills of the trade on the job. Eventually, the trainee is ready to move on, perhaps because the mentor has run afoul of the law, or perhaps because the trainee has double-crossed her mentor and needs some "space."

Rogues do not see each other as fellows unless they happen to be members of the same guild or students of the same mentor. In fact, rogues trust other rogues less than they trust anyone else. They're no fools.

Races: Adaptable and often unprincipled, humans take to the rogue's life with ease. Halflings, elves, and half-elves, too, find themselves well suited to the demands of the career. Dwarf and gnome rogues, while less common, are renowned as experts with locks and traps. Half-orc rogues tend toward thuggery.

Rogues are common among brutal humanoids, especially goblins and bugbears. Rogues who learn their arts in savage lands, however, generally don't have experience with complex mechanisms such as traps and locks.

Other Classes: Rogues love and hate working with members of other classes. They excel when protected by warriors and supported by spellcasters. There are plenty of times, however, that they wish that everyone else was as quiet, guileful, and patient as a rogue. Rogues are particularly wary of paladins, either endeavoring to prove themselves useful or just avoiding them.

Lidda

GAME RULE INFORMATION

Rogues have the following game statistics.

Abilities: Dexterity affects many rogue skills and provides the lightly armored rogue extra protection. Intelligence and Wisdom are important for many of the rogue's skills. A high Intelligence score also gives the rogue extra skill points, which can be used to expand her repertoire.

Alignment: Any.

Hit Die: d6.

Class Skills

The rogue's class skills (and the key ability for each skill) are Appraise (Int), Balance (Dex), Bluff (Cha), Climb (Str), Craft (Int), Decipher Script (Int, exclusive skill), Diplomacy (Cha), Disable Device (Int), Disguise (Cha), Escape Artist (Dex), Forgery (Int), Gather Information (Cha), Hide (Dex), Innuendo (Wis), Intimidate (Cha), Intuit Direction (Wis), Jump (Str), Listen (Wis), Move Silently (Dex), Open Lock (Dex), Perform (Cha), Pick Pocket (Dex), Profession (Wis), Read Lips (Int, exclusive skill), Search (Int), Sense Motive (Wis), Spot (Wis), Swim (Str), Tumble (Dex), Use Magic

Device (Cha, exclusive skill), and Use Rope (Dex). See Chapter 4: Skills for skill descriptions.

Skill Points at 1st Level: (8 + Int modifier) × 4.
Skill Points at Each Additional Level: 8 + Int modifier.

Class Features

All of the following are class features of the rogue.

Weapon and Armor Proficiency: A rogue's weapon training focuses on weapons suitable for stealth and sneak attacks. Thus, all rogues are proficient with the crossbow (hand or light), dagger (any type), dart, light mace, sap, shortbow (normal and composite), and short sword. Medium-size rogues are also proficient with certain weapons that are too big for Small rogues to use and conceal easily: club, heavy crossbow, heavy mace, morningstar, quarterstaff, and rapier. Rogues are proficient with light armor but not with shields. Note that armor check penalties for armor heavier than leather apply to the skills Balance, Climb, Escape Artist, Hide, Jump, Move Silently, Pick Pocket, and Tumble. Also, Swim checks suffer a –1 penalty for every 5 pounds of armor, equipment, or loot carried.

Sneak Attack: If a rogue can catch an opponent when he is unable to defend himself effectively from her attack, she can strike a vital spot for extra damage. Basically, any time the rogue's target would be denied his Dexterity bonus to AC (whether he actually has a Dexterity bonus or not), or when the rogue flanks the target, the rogue's attack deals extra damage. The extra damage is +1d6 at 1st level and an additional 1d6 every two levels thereafter. Should the rogue score a critical hit with a sneak attack, this extra damage is not multiplied. (See Table 8–8: Attack Roll Modifiers, page 132, for combat situations in which the rogue flanks an opponent or the opponent loses his Dexterity bonus to AC.)

Ranged attacks can only count as sneak attacks if the target is within 30 feet. The rogue can't strike with deadly accuracy from beyond that range.

With a sap (blackjack) or an unarmed strike, the rogue can make a sneak attack that deals subdual damage instead of normal damage. She cannot use a weapon that deals normal damage to deal subdual damage in a sneak attack, not even with the usual –4 penalty, because she must make optimal use of her weapon in order to execute a sneak attack. (See Subdual Damage, page 134.)

A rogue can only sneak attack a living creature with a discernible anatomy—undead, constructs, oozes, plants, and incorporeal creatures lack vital areas to attack. Any creature that is immune to critical hits is also not vulnerable to sneak attacks. The rogue must be able to see the target well enough to pick out a vital spot and must be able to reach a vital spot. The rogue cannot sneak attack while striking a creature with concealment (see Table 8–10: Concealment, page 133) or striking the limbs of a creature whose vitals are beyond reach.

Traps: Rogues (and only rogues) can use the Search skill to locate traps when the task has a Difficulty Class higher than 20. Finding a nonmagical trap has a DC of at least 20, higher if it is well hidden. Finding a magic trap has a DC of 25 + the level of the spell used to create it.

Rogues (and only rogues) can use the Disable Device skill to disarm magic traps. A magic trap generally has a DC of 25 + the level of the spell used to create it.

A rogue who beats a trap's DC by 10 or more with a Disable Device check can generally study a trap, figure out how it works, and bypass it (with his party) without disarming it.

Evasion: At 2nd level, a rogue gains evasion. If exposed to any effect that normally allows a character to attempt a Reflex saving throw for half damage (such as a *fireball*), she takes no damage with a successful saving throw. Evasion can only be used if the rogue is wearing light armor or no armor. It is an extraordinary ability.

Uncanny Dodge: Starting at 3rd level, the rogue gains the extraordinary ability to react to danger before her senses would normally allow her to do so. At 3rd level and above, she retains her Dexterity bonus to AC (if any) regardless of being caught flat-footed or struck by an invisible attacker. (She still loses her Dexterity bonus to AC if immobilized.)

At 6th level, the rogue can no longer be flanked; she can react to opponents on opposite sides of her as easily as she can react to a single attacker. This defense denies other rogues the ability to use flank attacks to sneak attack her. The exception to this defense is that another rogue at least four levels higher than the character can flank her (and thus sneak attack her).

At 11th level, the rogue gains an intuitive sense that alerts her to danger from traps, giving her a +1 bonus to Reflex saves made to avoid traps and a +1 dodge bonus to AC against attacks by traps. At 14th level, these bonuses rise to +2. At 17th, they rise to +3, and at 20th they rise to +4.

Special Abilities: On achieving 10th level and every three levels thereafter (13th, 16th, and 19th), a rogue gets a special ability of her choice from among the following:

Crippling Strike: A rogue with this extraordinary ability can sneak attack opponents with such precision that her blows weaken and hamper them. When the rogue damages an opponent with a sneak attack, that character also takes 1 point of Strength damage. Ability points lost to damage return on their own at the rate of 1 point per day.

Defensive Roll: The rogue can roll with a potentially lethal blow to take less damage from it. Once per day, when a rogue would be reduced to 0 hit points or less by damage in combat (from a weapon or other blow, not a spell or special ability), the rogue can attempt to roll with the damage. She makes a Reflex saving throw (DC = damage dealt) and, if she's successful, she takes only half damage from the blow. She must be aware of the attack and able to react to

it in order to execute her defensive roll—if she is denied her Dexterity bonus to AC, she can't roll. Since this effect would not normally allow a character to make a Reflex save for half damage, the rogue's evasion ability does not apply to the defensive roll.

Improved Evasion: This ability works like evasion, except that while the rogue still takes no damage on a successful Reflex save against spells such as *fireball* or a breath weapon, she now takes only half damage on a failed save (the rogue's reflexes allow her to get out of harm's way with incredible speed).

Opportunist: Once per round, the rogue can make an attack of opportunity against an opponent who has just been struck for damage in melee by another character. This attack counts as the rogue's attacks of opportunity for that round. Even a rogue with the Combat Reflexes feat can't use the opportunist ability more than once per round.

Skill Mastery: The rogue selects a number of skills equal to 3 + her Intelligence modifier. When making a skill check with one of these skills, the rogue may take 10 even if stress and distractions would normally prevent her from doing so. She becomes so certain in her skill that she can use her skill reliably even under adverse conditions. The rogue may gain this special ability multiple times, selecting additional skills for it to apply to each time.

Slippery Mind: This extraordinary ability represents the rogue's ability to wriggle free from magical effects that would otherwise control or compel her. If a rogue with a slippery mind is affected by an enchantment and fails her saving throw, 1 round later she can attempt her saving throw again. She only gets this one extra chance to succeed at her saving throw.

Feat: A rogue may gain a feat in place of a special ability.

Halfling (or Gnome) Rogue Starting Package

Armor: Leather +2 AC, speed 20 ft., 15 lb.

Weapons: Short sword (1d6, crit 19–20/×2, 3 lb., Small, Piercing).

Light crossbow (1d8, crit 19–20/×2, 80 ft., 7 lb., Medium-size, Piercing).

Dagger. (1d4, crit 19–20/×2, 10 ft., 1 lb., Tiny, Piercing).

Skill Selection: Pick a number of skills equal to 8 + Int modifier.

Feat: Improved Initiative.

Gear: Backpack with waterskin, one day's trail rations, bedroll, sack, and flint and steel. Thieves' tools. Hooded lantern and three pints of oil. Case with 10 crossbow bolts.

Gold: 4d4 gp.

Alternative Rogue Starting Package

Same as halfling rogue, except

Race: Human, dwarf, elf, half-elf, or half-orc.

Armor: Speed 30 ft. (nondwarves only).

Weapons: Rapier (1d6, crit 18–20/×2, 3 lb., Small, Piercing) instead of short sword.

Shortbow (1d6, ×3 crit, 60 ft., 2 lb., Medium-size, Piercing) instead of crossbow.

Skill Selection: Pick a number of skills equal to 9 + Int modifier (human only).

Bonus Feat: Alertness (human only).

Gear: Quiver with 20 arrows instead of case of crossbow bolts.

Gold: 2d4 gp.

SORCERER

Sorcerers create magic the way a poet creates poems, with inborn talent honed by practice. They have no books, no mentors, no theories—just raw power that they direct at will.

Some sorcerers claim that the blood of dragons courses through their veins. It may even be true—it is common knowledge that certain powerful dragons can take humanoid form and even have humanoid lovers, and it's difficult to prove that a given sorcerer does *not* have a dragon ancestor. Sorcerers even often

Skill	Ranks	Ability	Armor
Move Silently	4	Dex	0
Hide	4	Dex	0
Climb	4	Str	0
Disable Device	4	Int	
Listen	4	Wis	
Open Lock	4	Dex	
Search	4	Int	
Spot	4	Wis	
Use Magic Device	4	Cha	
Pick Pocket	4	Dex	0
Decipher Script	4	Int	
Bluff	4	Cha	
Intimidate	4	Cha	

Table 3–16: The Sorcerer

	Base	Fort	Ref	Will		Spells per Day									
Level	Attack Bonus	Save	Save	Save	Special	0	1	2	3	4	5	6	7	8	9
1	+0	+0	+0	+2	Summon familiar	5	3	—	—	—	—	—	—	—	—
2	+1	+0	+0	+3		6	4	—	—	—	—	—	—	—	—
3	+1	+1	+1	+3		6	5	—	—	—	—	—	—	—	—
4	+2	+1	+1	+4		6	6	3	—	—	—	—	—	—	—
5	+2	+1	+1	+4		6	6	4	—	—	—	—	—	—	—
6	+3	+2	+2	+5		6	6	5	3	—	—	—	—	—	—
7	+3	+2	+2	+5		6	6	6	4	—	—	—	—	—	—
8	+4	+2	+2	+6		6	6	6	5	3	—	—	—	—	—
9	+4	+3	+3	+6		6	6	6	6	4	—	—	—	—	—
10	+5	+3	+3	+7		6	6	6	6	5	3	—	—	—	—
11	+5	+3	+3	+7		6	6	6	6	6	4	—	—	—	—
12	+6/+1	+4	+4	+8		6	6	6	6	6	5	3	—	—	—
13	+6/+1	+4	+4	+8		6	6	6	6	6	6	4	—	—	—
14	+7/+2	+4	+4	+9		6	6	6	6	6	6	5	3	—	—
15	+7/+2	+5	+5	+9		6	6	6	6	6	6	6	4	—	—
16	+8/+3	+5	+5	+10		6	6	6	6	6	6	6	5	3	—
17	+8/+3	+5	+5	+10		6	6	6	6	6	6	6	6	4	—
18	+9/+4	+6	+6	+11		6	6	6	6	6	6	6	6	5	3
19	+9/+4	+6	+6	+11		6	6	6	6	6	6	6	6	6	4
20	+10/+5	+6	+6	+12		6	6	6	6	6	6	6	6	6	6

have striking good looks, usually with a touch of the exotic that hints at an unusual heritage. Still, the claim that sorcerers are partially draconic is either an unsubstantiated boast on the part of certain sorcerers or envious gossip on the part of those who lack the sorcerer's gift.

Adventures: The typical sorcerer adventures in order to improve his abilities. Only by testing his limits can he expand them. A sorcerer's power is inborn, and part of his soul. Developing this power is a quest in itself for many sorcerers, regardless of how they wish to use their power.

Some good sorcerers are driven by the need to prove themselves. Marked as different by their power, they seek to win a place in society and to prove themselves to others. Evil sorcerers, however, also feel themselves set apart from others—apart and above. They adventure to gain power over those they look down on.

Characteristics: Sorcerers cast spells through innate power rather than through carefully trained skills. Their magic is intuitive rather than logical. They know fewer spells than wizards do and acquire powerful spells more slowly than wizards, but they can cast spells more often and have no need to select and prepare them ahead of time. Nor do sorcerers specialize in certain schools of magic the way wizards may.

Since sorcerers gain their powers without undergoing the years of rigorous study that wizards go through, they have more time to learn fighting skills. They are proficient with simple weapons.

Alignment: For a sorcerer, magic is an intuitive art, not a science. Sorcery favors the free, chaotic, creative spirit over the disciplined mind, so sorcerers tend slightly toward chaos over law.

Religion: Some sorcerers favor Boccob, god of magic, while others revere Wee Jas, goddess of death magic. However, many sorcerers follow some other deity, or none at all (wizards typically learn to follow Boccob or Wee Jas from their mentors, but most sorcerers are self-taught, having no master to induct them into a religion).

Background: Sorcerers develop rudimentary powers at puberty. Their first spells are incomplete, spontaneous, uncontrolled, and sometimes dangerous. A household with a budding sorcerer in it may be troubled by strange sounds or lights, creating the impression that the place is haunted. Eventually, the young sorcerer understands the power that he has been wielding unintentionally. From that point on, he can begin practicing and improving his powers.

Table 3–17: Sorcerer Spells Known

	Spells Known									
Level	0	1	2	3	4	5	6	7	8	9
1	4	2	—	—	—	—	—	—	—	—
2	5	2	—	—	—	—	—	—	—	—
3	5	3	—	—	—	—	—	—	—	—
4	6	3	1	—	—	—	—	—	—	—
5	6	4	2	—	—	—	—	—	—	—
6	7	4	2	1	—	—	—	—	—	—
7	7	5	3	2	—	—	—	—	—	—
8	8	5	3	2	1	—	—	—	—	—
9	8	5	4	3	2	—	—	—	—	—
10	9	5	4	3	2	1	—	—	—	—
11	9	5	5	4	3	2	—	—	—	—
12	9	5	5	4	3	2	1	—	—	—
13	9	5	5	4	4	3	2	—	—	—
14	9	5	5	4	4	3	2	1	—	—
15	9	5	5	4	4	4	3	2	—	—
16	9	5	5	4	4	4	3	2	1	—
17	9	5	5	4	4	4	3	3	2	—
18	9	5	5	4	4	4	3	3	2	1
19	9	5	5	4	4	4	3	3	3	2
20	9	5	5	4	4	4	3	3	3	3

Sometimes a sorcerer is fortunate enough to come under the care of an older, experienced sorcerer, someone to help him understand and use his new powers. More often, however, sorcerers are on their own, feared by erstwhile friends and misunderstood by family.

Sorcerers have no sense of identity as a group. Unlike wizards, they gain little by sharing their knowledge and have no strong incentive to work together.

Races: Most sorcerers are humans or half-elves. The innate talent for sorcery, however, is unpredictable, and it can show up in any of the common races.

Arcane spellcasters from savage lands or from among the brutal humanoids are more likely to be sorcerers than wizards. Kobolds are especially likely to be sorcerers, and they are fierce, if inarticulate, proponents of the "blood of the dragons" theory.

Other Classes: Sorcerers find they have the most in common with members of other self-taught classes, such as druids and rogues. They sometimes find themselves at odds with members of the more disciplined classes, such as paladins and monks. Since they cast the same spells as wizards but do so in a different way, they are sometimes competitive toward them.

Since sorcerers often have a powerful presence that gives them a way with people, they frequently serve as the "face" for an adventuring party, negotiating, bargaining, and speaking for others. The sorcerer's spells often help him sway others or gain information, so he makes an excellent spy or diplomat for an adventuring party.

GAME RULE INFORMATION
Sorcerers have the following game statistics.

Abilities: Charisma determines how powerful a spell a sorcerer can cast, how many spells the sorcerer can cast per day, and how hard those spells are to resist. To cast a spell, a sorcerer must have a Charisma score of 10 + the spell's level. A sorcerer gets bonus spells based on Charisma. The Difficulty Class of a saving throw against a sorcerer's spell is 10 + the spell's level + the sorcerer's Charisma modifier. Like a wizard, a sorcerer benefits from high Dexterity and Constitution scores.

Alignment: Any.

Hit Die: d4.

Class Skills
The sorcerer's class skills (and the key ability for each skill) are Alchemy (Int), Concentration (Con), Craft (Int), Knowledge (arcana) (Int), Profession (Wis), Scry (Int, exclusive skill), and Spellcraft (Int). See Chapter 4: Skills for skill descriptions.

Skill Points at 1st Level: (2 + Int modifier) × 4.

Skill Points at Each Additional Level: 2 + Int modifier.

Class Features
All of the following are class features of the sorcerer.

Weapon and Armor Proficiency: Sorcerers are proficient with all simple weapons. They are not proficient with any type of armor, nor with shields. Armor of any type interferes with a sorcerer's arcane gestures, which can cause his spells to fail (if those spells have somatic components). Note that armor check penalties for armor heavier than leather apply to the skills Balance, Climb, Escape Artist, Hide, Jump, Move Silently, Pick Pocket, and Tumble. Also, Swim checks suffer a –1 penalty for every 5 pounds of armor and equipment carried.

Spells: A sorcerer casts arcane spells, the same type of spells available to wizards. A sorcerer's selection of spells is extremely limited. Your sorcerer begins play knowing four 0-level spells (also called cantrips) and two 1st-level spells of your choice. At each level, the sorcerer gains one or more new spells, as indicated on Table 3–17: Sorcerer Spells Known. (Note: The number of spells a sorcerer knows is not affected by his Charisma bonus, if any; the numbers on Table 3–17 are fixed.) These spells can be common spells chosen from the sorcerer and wizard spell list (page 168), or they can be unusual spells that the sorcerer has gained some understanding of by study. For example, a sorcerer with a scroll or spellbook detailing an unusual arcane spell (one not on the sorcerer spell list) could select that spell as one of his new

Hennet

spells for achieving a new level, provided the spell is the right level. In any case, the sorcerer can't learn spells at a faster rate due to this means. It simply allows the sorcerer to occasionally select spells that aren't found on the sorcerer and wizard spell list.

A sorcerer is limited to casting a certain number of spells of each level per day, but he need not prepare his spells in advance. The number of spells he can cast per day is improved by his bonus spells, if any. For instance, at 1st level, the sorcerer Hennet can cast four 1st-level spells per day—three for being 1st level (see Table 3–16: The Sorcerer), plus one thanks to his high Charisma. However, he only knows two 1st-level spells: *magic missile* and *sleep* (see Table 3–17: Sorcerer Spells Known). In any given day, he can cast *magic missile* four times, cast *sleep* four times, or cast some combination of the two spells a total of four times. He does not have to decide ahead of time which spells he'll cast.

A sorcerer may use a higher-level slot to cast a lower-level spell if he so chooses. For example, if an 8th-level sorcerer has used up all of his 3rd-level spells slots for the day but wants to cast another one, he could use a 4th-level slot to do so. The spell is still treated as its actual level, not the level of the slot used to cast it.

To learn or cast a spell, a sorcerer must have a Charisma score of at least 10 + the spell's level. The Difficulty Class for saving throws against sorcerer spells is 10 + the spell's level + the sorcerer's Charisma modifier.

Familiar: A sorcerer can call a familiar. Doing so takes a day and uses up magical materials that cost 100 gp. A familiar is a magical, unusually tough, and intelligent version of a small animal (see the facing page). It is a magical beast, not an animal. The creature serves as a companion and servant.

The sorcerer chooses the type of familiar he gets. As the sorcerer increases in level, his familiar also increases in power.

If the familiar dies, or the sorcerer chooses to dismiss it, the sorcerer must attempt a Fortitude saving throw (DC 15). If the saving throw fails, the sorcerer loses 200 experience points per class level. A successful saving throw reduces the loss to half of that amount. However, a sorcerer's experience point total can never go below zero as the result of a familiar's demise. For example, Hennet is a 3rd-level sorcerer with 3,230 XP when his owl is killed by a bugbear. Hennet makes a successful saving throw, so he loses 300 XP, dropping him below 3,000 XP and back to 2nd level (the DUNGEON MASTER'S GUIDE has rules for losing levels). A slain or dismissed familiar cannot be replaced for a year and day. Slain familiars can be raised from the dead just as characters can be, but do not lose a level or a Constitution point when this happy event occurs.

Human Sorcerer Starting Package
Armor: None, speed 30 ft.

Weapons: Shortspear (1d8, crit ×3, 20 ft., 5 lb., Large, Piercing).
Light crossbow (1d8, crit 19–20/×2, 80 ft., 6 lb., Piercing).

Skill Selection: Pick a number of skills equal to 3 + Int modifier.

Skill	Ranks	Ability	Armor
Spellcraft	4	Int	
Concentration	4	Con	
Knowledge (arcana)	4	Int	
Gather Information (cc)	2	Cha	
Diplomacy (cc)	2	Cha	
Hide (cc)	2	Dex	0
Move Silently (cc)	2	Dex	0

Feat: Toughness.

Bonus Feat: Skill Focus (Spellcraft or other skill).

Spells Known: 0-level spells—*detect magic, ghost sound, light, read magic.*

1st-level spells—*magic missile, sleep.*

Gear: Backpack with waterskin, one day's trail rations, bedroll, sack, and flint and steel. Hooded lantern, 5 pints of oil. Spell component pouch. Case with 10 crossbow bolts.

Gold: 3d4 gp.

FAMILIARS

Familiars are magically linked to their masters. In some sense, the familiar and the master are practically one being. That's why, for example, the master can cast a personal range spell on a familiar even though normally he can only cast such a spell on himself. Familiars are similar to the normal creatures they resemble. However, some familiars have special abilities or grant special abilities to their master (a sorcerer or wizard), as given on Table 3–18: Familiars. These special abilities only apply when the master and familiar are within one mile of each other.

TABLE 3–18: FAMILIARS

Familiar	Special
Bat	—
Cat	Master gains a +2 bonus to Move Silently checks
Hawk	—
Owl	Has low-light vision; master gains a +2 bonus on Move Silently checks
Rat	Master gains a +2 bonus to Fortitude saves
Raven	Speaks one language
Snake (Tiny)	Poisonous bite
Toad	Master gains +2 to Constitution score
Weasel	Master gains a +2 bonus on Reflex saves

Familiar Basics: Use the basic statistics for a creature of its type, as given in the *Monster Manual*, but make these changes:

Hit Dice: Treat as the master's character level (for effects related to Hit Dice). Use the familiar's total if it is higher.

Hit Points: One-half the master's total, rounded down. For example, at 2nd level, Hennet has 9 hit points, so his familiar has 4.

Attacks: Use the master's base attack bonus. Use the familiar's Dexterity or Strength modifier, whichever is greater, to get the familiar's melee attack bonus with unarmed attacks. Damage equals that of a normal creature of that type.

Saving Throws: The familiar uses the master's base saving throw bonuses if they're better than the familiar's (Fortitude +2, Reflex +2, Will +0).

Skills: Use the normal skills for an animal of that type or the master's, whichever are better.

Familiar Ability Descriptions: All familiars have special abilities (or impart abilities to their masters) depending on the level of the master, as shown on Table 3–19. The abilities on Table 3–19 are cumulative.

Natural Armor: This number improves the familiar's AC. It represents a familiar's preternatural toughness.

Intelligence: The familiar's Intelligence score. Familiars are as smart as people (though not necessarily as smart as smart people).

Alertness: The presence of the familiar sharpens its master's senses. While the familiar is within arm's reach, the master gains Alertness.

Improved Evasion: If the familiar is subjected to an attack that normally allows a Reflex saving throw for half damage, the familiar takes no damage if it makes a successful saving throw and half damage even if the saving throw fails. Improved evasion is an extraordinary ability.

Share Spells: At the master's option, he may have any spell he casts on himself also affect his familiar. The familiar must be within 5 feet at the time. If the spell has a duration other than instantaneous, the spell stops affecting the familiar if it moves farther than 5 feet away. The spell's effect will not be restored even if the familiar returns to the master before the duration would otherwise have ended. Additionally, the master may cast a spell with a target of "You" on his familiar (as a Touch range spell) instead of on himself. The master and familiar can share spells even if the spells normally do not affect creatures of the familiar's type (magical beast).

Empathic Link: The master has an empathic link with the familiar out to a distance of up to one mile. The master cannot see through the familiar's eyes, but the two of them can communicate telepathically. Note that the low Intelligence of a low-level master's familiar limits what it is able to communicate or understand, and even intelligent familiars see the world differently from humans. This is a supernatural ability.

Because of the empathic link between the familiar and the master, the master has the same connection to an item or place that the familiar does. For instance, if his familiar has seen a room, a master can teleport into that room as if he has seen it too.

Touch: If the master is 3rd level or higher, the familiar can deliver touch spells for the master. When the master casts a touch spell, he can designate his familiar as the "toucher." (The master and the familiar have to be in contact at the time of casting.) The familiar can then deliver the touch spell just as the master could. As normal, if the master casts another spell, the touch spell dissipates.

Speak with Animals of Its Type: The familiar can communicate with animals of approximately the same type as itself (including dire variants): bats and rats with rodents, cats with felines, hawks and owls and ravens with birds, snakes with reptiles, toads with amphibians, weasels with creatures of the mustelidae family (weasels, minks, polecats, ermines, skunks, wolverines, and badgers). The communication is limited by the Intelligence of the conversing creatures.

Speak with Master: The familiar and master can communicate verbally as if they were using a common language. Other creatures do not understand the communication with out magical help.

Spell Resistance: If the master is 11th level or higher, the familiar gains spell resistance equal to the master's level + 5. If another spellcaster tries to affect someone else's familiar with a spell, that spellcaster must make a caster level check (1d20 + caster level) at least equal to the familiar's spell resistance.

Scry: If the master is 13th level or higher, the master may scry on the familiar (as if casting the spell *scrying*) once per day. This is a spell-like ability that requires no material components or focus.

TABLE 3–19: FAMILIAR SPECIAL ABILITIES

Master Class Level	Natural Armor	Int	Special
1–2	+1	6	Alertness, improved evasion, share spells, empathic link
3–4	+2	7	Touch
5–6	+3	8	Speak with master
7–8	+4	9	Speak with animals of its type
9–10	+5	10	
11–12	+6	11	Spell resistance
13–14	+7	12	*Scry* on familiar
15–16	+8	13	
17–18	+9	14	
19–20	+10	15	

Alternative Sorcerer Starting Package

As human sorcerer, except

Race: Dwarf, elf, half-elf, half-orc.
Armor: Speed 20 ft. (dwarf only).
Skill Selection: Pick a number of skills equal to 2 + Int modifier.
Bonus Feat: None.

Alternative Sorcerer Starting Package

As human sorcerer, except

Race: Gnome or halfling.
Armor: Speed 20 ft.
Weapons: Morningstar (1d8, crit ×2, 8 lb., Medium-size, Bludgeoning and Piercing) instead of shortspear.
Skill Selection: Pick a number of skills equal to 2 + Int modifier.
Bonus Feat: None.
Gold: 1d4 gp.

WIZARD

A few unintelligible words and a fleeting gesture carry more power than a battleaxe, when they are the words and gestures of a wizard. These simple acts make magic seem easy, but they only hint at the time the wizard must spend poring over her spellbook preparing each spell for casting, and the years before that spent in apprenticeship to learn the arts of magic.

Wizards depend on intensive study to create their magic. They examine musty old tomes, debate magical theory with their peers, and practice minor magics whenever they can. For a wizard, magic is not a talent but a difficult, rewarding art.

Adventures: Wizards conduct their adventures with caution and forethought. When prepared, they can use their spells to devastating effect. When caught by surprise, they are vulnerable. They seek knowledge, power, and the resources to conduct their studies. They may also have any of the noble or ignoble motivations that other adventurers have.

Mialee

Characteristics: The wizard's strength is her spells. Everything else is secondary. She learns new spells as she experiments and grows in experience, and she can also learn them from other wizards. In addition to learning new spells, over time a wizard learns to manipulate her spells so they go farther, work better, or are improved in some other way.

Some wizards prefer to specialize in a certain type of magic. Specialization makes a wizard more powerful in her chosen field, but prevents her from being able to cast some of the spells that lie outside her field. (See School Specialization, page 54.)

A wizard can call a familiar: a small, magical animal companion that serves her. For some wizards, their familiars are their only true friends.

Alignment: Overall, wizards show a slight tendency toward law over chaos because the study of magic rewards those who are disciplined. Illusionists and transmuters, however, are masters of deception and change, respectively. They favor chaos over law.

Religion: Wizards commonly revere Boccob, god of magic. Some, especially necromancers or simply more misanthropic wizards, prefer Wee Jas, goddess of magic and death. Evil necromancers are known to worship Nerull, god of death. Wizards in general, however, are more devoted to their studies than to their spiritual sides.

Background: Wizards recognize each other as comrades or rivals. Even wizards from very different cultures or magical traditions have much in common because they all conform to the universal laws of magic. Unlike fighters or rogues, wizards see themselves as members of a distinct, if diverse, group. In civilized lands where wizards study in academies, schools, or guilds, wizards also identify themselves and others according to

TABLE 3–20: THE WIZARD

Level	Base Attack Bonus	Fort Save	Ref Save	Will Save	Special	Spells per Day									
						0	1	2	3	4	5	6	7	8	9
1	+0	+0	+0	+2	Summon familiar, Scribe Scroll	3	1	—	—	—	—	—	—	—	—
2	+1	+0	+0	+3		4	2	—	—	—	—	—	—	—	—
3	+1	+1	+1	+3		4	2	1	—	—	—	—	—	—	—
4	+2	+1	+1	+4		4	3	2	—	—	—	—	—	—	—
5	+2	+1	+1	+4	Bonus feat	4	3	2	1	—	—	—	—	—	—
6	+3	+2	+2	+5		4	3	3	2	—	—	—	—	—	—
7	+3	+2	+2	+5		4	4	3	2	1	—	—	—	—	—
8	+4	+2	+2	+6		4	4	3	3	2	—	—	—	—	—
9	+4	+3	+3	+6		4	4	4	3	2	1	—	—	—	—
10	+5	+3	+3	+7	Bonus feat	4	4	4	3	3	2	—	—	—	—
11	+5	+3	+3	+7		4	4	4	4	3	2	1	—	—	—
12	+6/+1	+4	+4	+8		4	4	4	4	3	3	2	—	—	—
13	+6/+1	+4	+4	+8		4	4	4	4	4	3	2	1	—	—
14	+7/+2	+4	+4	+9		4	4	4	4	4	3	3	2	—	—
15	+7/+2	+5	+5	+9	Bonus feat	4	4	4	4	4	4	3	2	1	—
16	+8/+3	+5	+5	+10		4	4	4	4	4	4	3	3	2	—
17	+8/+3	+5	+5	+10		4	4	4	4	4	4	4	3	2	1
18	+9/+4	+6	+6	+11		4	4	4	4	4	4	4	3	3	2
19	+9/+4	+6	+6	+11		4	4	4	4	4	4	4	4	3	3
20	+10/+5	+6	+6	+12	Bonus feat	4	4	4	4	4	4	4	4	4	4

membership in these formal organizations. While a guild magician may look down her nose at a rustic wizard who learned his arts from a doddering hermit, she nevertheless can't deny the rustic's identity as a wizard.

Races: Humans take to magic for any of their varied reasons: curiosity, ambition, lust for power, or just personal inclination. Human wizards tend to be practical innovators, creating new spells or using old spells creatively.

Elves are fascinated by magic, and many of them become wizards for love of the art. Elven wizards see themselves as artists, and they hold magic in high regard as a wondrous mystery, as opposed to more pragmatic human wizards who see magic more as a set of tools or tricks.

Illusion magic comes so simply to gnomes that becoming an illusionist is just natural to brighter and more talented gnomes. Gnome wizards that don't specialize in the school of illusion are rare, but they don't suffer under any special stigma.

Half-elf wizards feel both the elf's attraction to magic and the human's drive to conquer and understand. Some of the most powerful wizards are half-elves.

Dwarf and halfling wizards are rare because their societies don't encourage the study of magic. Half-orc wizards are rare because few half-orcs have the brains necessary for wizardry.

Drow (evil, subterranean elves) are commonly wizards, but wizards are quite rare among the savage humanoids.

Other Classes: Wizards prefer to work with members of other classes. They love to cast their spells from behind strong fighters, to "magic up" rogues and send them out to scout, and to rely on the divine healing of clerics. They may find certain types, such as sorcerers, rogues, and bards, not quite serious enough, but they're not judgmental.

GAME RULE INFORMATION

Wizards have the following game statistics.

Abilities: Intelligence determines how powerful a spell a wizard can cast, how many spells she can cast, and how hard those spells are to resist. To cast a spell, a wizard must have an Intelligence score of 10 + the spell's level. In addition, a wizard gets bonus spells based on Intelligence. The Difficulty Class of a saving throw against a wizard's spell is 10 + the spell's level + the wizard's Intelligence modifier. High Dexterity is helpful for a wizard, who typically wears little or no armor, because it provides her with an Armor Class bonus. A good

Nebin [gnome illusionist]

Constitution gives a wizard extra hit points, a resource that she is otherwise very low on.

Alignment: Any.
Hit Die: d4.

Class Skills

The wizard's class skills (and the key ability for each skill) are Alchemy (Int), Concentration (Con), Craft (Int), Knowledge (all skills, taken individually) (Int), Profession (Wis), Scry (Int, exclusive skill), and Spellcraft (Int). See Chapter 4: Skills for skill descriptions.

Skill Points at 1st Level: (2 + Int modifier) × 4.

Skill Points at Each Additional Level: 2 + Int modifier.

Class Features

All of the following are class features of the wizard.

Weapon and Armor Proficiency: Wizards are skilled with the club, dagger, heavy crossbow, light crossbow, and quarterstaff. Wizards are not proficient with any type of armor nor with shields. Armor of any type interferes with a wizard's movements, which can cause her spells to fail (if those spells have somatic components). Note that armor check penalties for armor heavier than leather apply to the skills Balance, Climb, Escape Artist, Hide, Jump, Move Silently, Pick Pocket, and Tumble. Also, Swim checks suffer a −1 penalty for every 5 pounds of armor and equipment carried.

Spells: A wizard casts arcane spells. She is limited to a certain number of spells of each spell level per day, according to her class level. A wizard must prepare spells ahead of time by getting a good night's sleep and spending 1 hour studying her spellbook. While studying, the wizard decides which spells to prepare (see Preparing Wizard Spells, page 154). To learn, prepare, or cast a spell,

ARCANE SPELLS AND ARMOR

Wizards and sorcerers do not know how to wear armor effectively. They can wear armor anyway (though they'll be clumsy in it), and they can gain training in the proper use of armor (with the various Armor Proficiency feats—light, medium, and heavy—and the Shield Proficiency feat) or multiclass to add a class that grants them armor use (see Multiclass Characters later in this chapter). By contrast, bards do know how to wear light and medium armor effectively. However, they too wear heavier armor ineffectively and must either learn to wear heavier armor via the feat Armor Proficiency (heavy) or add a class (such as fighter) that grants them such Armor Proficiency as a class feature. Even if a wizard, sorcerer, or bard is wearing armor with which he or she is proficient, however, it might still interfere with his or her spells.

Characters have a difficult time casting most arcane spells while wearing armor (see Arcane Spells, page 154). The armor restricts the complicated gestures that they must make while casting any spell that has a somatic component (most do). To find the chance of arcane spell failure for a wizard, sorcerer, or bard wearing different types of armor, see Table 7–5: Armor, page 104.

If a spell doesn't have a somatic component, arcane spellcasters can cast it with no problem while wearing armor. Such spells can also be cast even if the caster's hands are bound or if he or she is being grappled (although Concentration checks still apply). Also, the metamagic feat Still Spell allows a spellcaster to prepare or cast a spell at one level higher than normal without the somatic component, which is a way of casting a spell while wearing armor without risking the chance of arcane spell failure. See Chapter 5: Feats for more about metamagic feats such as Still Spell.

a wizard must have an Intelligence score of at least 10 + the spell's level. A wizard's bonus spells are based on Intelligence (see Table 1–1: Ability Modifiers and Bonus Spells, page 8). The Difficulty Class for saving throws against wizard spells is 10 + the spell's level + the wizard's Intelligence modifier.

Unlike bards and sorcerers, wizards may know any number of spells (see Writing a New Spell into a Spellbook, page 155).

Bonus Languages: A wizard may substitute Draconic for one of the bonus languages available to the character because of her race (see Chapter 2: Races), since many ancient tomes of magic are written in Draconic and apprentice wizards often learn it as part of their studies.

Familiar: A wizard can summon a familiar in exactly the same manner as a sorcerer. See the sorcerer description and the accompanying Familiars sidebar for details.

Scribe Scroll: A wizard has the bonus item creation feat Scribe Scroll, enabling her to create magic scrolls (see the feat, page 84, and Magic Item Creation in the DUNGEON MASTER's Guide).

Bonus Feats: Every five levels, a wizard gains a bonus feat. This feat must be a metamagic feat, an item creation feat, or Spell Mastery (see below).

Note: these feats are in addition to those granted to every character by level regardless of class (see Table 3–2: Experience and Level-Dependent Benefits). Feats granted by overall character level (as opposed to class level), and the starting bonus feat for human characters, need not be metamagic or item creation feats.

Spellbooks: Wizards must study their spellbooks each day to prepare their spells (see Preparing Wizard Spells, page 154). A wizard cannot prepare any spell not recorded in her spellbook (except for read magic, which all wizards can prepare from memory). A wizard begins play with a spellbook containing all 0-level wizard spells plus three 1st-level spells of the player's choice. For each point of Intelligence bonus the wizard has (see Table 1–1: Ability Modifiers and Bonus Spells, page 8), the spellbook holds one additional 1st-level spell. Each time the wizard achieves a new level, she gains two new spells of any level or levels that she can cast (according to her new level). For example, when Mialee achieves 5th level, she can add two 3rd-level spells to her spellbook. The wizard can also add spells found in other wizards' spellbooks (see Adding Spells to a Wizard's Spellbook, page 155).

Spell Mastery: A wizard (and only a wizard) can take the special feat Spell Mastery. Each time the wizard takes this feat, choose a number of spells equal to the wizard's Intelligence modifier (they must be spells that the wizard already knows). From that point on, the wizard can prepare these spells without referring to a spellbook. The wizard is so intimately familiar with these spells that she doesn't need a spellbook to prepare them anymore.

Elven Wizard Starting Package

Armor: None, speed 30 ft.

Weapons: Quarterstaff (1d6, crit ×2, 4 lb., Large, Bludgeoning). Shortbow (1d6, crit ×3, 60 ft., 2 lb., Medium-size, Piercing).

Skill Selection: Pick a number of skills equal to 2 + Int modifier.

Feat: Toughness.

School Specialization: None.

Spellbook: All 0-level spells; plus *charm person*, *summon monster I*, and *sleep*; plus one of these spells of your choice per point of Intelligence bonus (if any): *cause fear*, *color spray*, *magic missile*, and *silent image*.

SCHOOL SPECIALIZATION

A school is one of eight groupings of spells, each defined by a common theme, such as illusion or necromancy. A wizard may specialize in one school of magic (see below). Specialization allows a wizard to cast extra spells from the chosen school, but the wizard then never learns to cast spells from one or more other schools. Essentially, the wizard gains exceptional mastery over a single school by neglecting the study of other schools. The more difficult a school is to master, the more one must give up in order to specialize in it. Some schools only require that a specialist give up one other school, while others might require the giving up of two or three. Spells of the school or schools that the specialist gives up are not available to her, and she can't even cast such spells from scrolls or wands. The wizard must choose whether to specialize and how at 1st level. She may not change her specialization later. The specialist can prepare one additional spell (of the school selected as a specialty) per spell level each day. The specialist gains a +2 bonus to Spellcraft checks to learn the spells of her chosen school (see Adding Spells to a Wizard's Spellbook, page 155).

The eight schools of arcane magic are Abjuration, Conjuration, Divination, Enchantment, Evocation, Illusion, Necromancy, and Transmutation. Spells that do not fall into any of these schools are called universal spells.

Abjuration: Spells that protect, block, or banish. An Abjuration specialist is called an abjurer. To become an abjurer, a wizard must select her prohibited school or schools from the following choices: (1) either Conjuration, Enchantment, Evocation, Illusion, or Transmutation; or (2) both Divination and Necromancy.

Conjuration: Spells that bring creatures or materials to the caster. A Conjuration specialist is called a conjurer. To become a conjurer, a wizard must select her prohibited school or schools from one of the following choices: (1) Evocation; (2) any two of the following three schools: Abjuration, Enchantment, and Illusion; (3) Transmutation; or (4) any three schools.

Divination: Spells that reveal information. A Divination specialist is called a diviner. To become a diviner, a wizard must select any other single school as her prohibited school.

Enchantment: Spells that imbue the recipient with some property or grant the caster power over another being. An Enchantment specialist is called an enchanter. To become an enchanter, a wizard must select her prohibited school or schools from the following choices: (1) either Abjuration, Conjuration, Evocation, Illusion, or Transmutation; or (2) both Divination and Necromancy.

Evocation: Spells that manipulate energy or create something from nothing. An Evocation specialist is called an evoker. To become an evoker, a wizard must select her prohibited school or schools from one of the following choices: (1) Conjuration; (2) any two of the following three schools: Abjuration, Enchantment, and Illusion; (3) Transmutation; or (4) any three schools.

Illusion: Spells that alter perception or create false images. An Illusion specialist is called an illusionist. To become an illusionist, a wizard must select her prohibited school or schools from the following choices: (1) either Abjuration, Conjuration, Enchantment, Evocation, or Transmutation; or (2) both Divination and Necromancy.

Necromancy: Spells that manipulate, create, or destroy life or life force. A Necromancy specialist is called a necromancer. To become a necromancer, a wizard must select any other single school as her prohibited school.

Transmutation: Spells that transform the recipient physically or change its properties in a more subtle way. A Transmutation specialist is called a transmuter. To become a transmuter, a wizard must select her prohibited school or schools from one of the following choices: (1) Conjuration; (2) Evocation; (2) any two of the following three schools: Abjuration, Enchantment, and Illusion; or (4) any three schools.

Universal: Not a school, but a category for spells all wizards can learn. A wizard cannot select universal as a specialty school or as a school to which she does not have access.

Skill	Ranks	Ability	Armor
Spellcraft	4	Int	
Concentration	4	Con	
Knowledge (arcana)	4	Int	
Hide (cc)	2	Dex	0
Move Silently (cc)	2	Dex	0
Search (cc)	2	Int	
Spot (cc)	2	Wis	

Gear: Backpack with waterskin, one day's trail rations, bedroll, sack, and flint and steel. Ten candles, map case, three pages of parchment, ink, inkpen. Spell component pouch, spellbook. Quiver with 20 arrows.

Gold: 3d6 gp.

Alternative Wizard Starting Package

As elven wizard, except

Race: Human, dwarf, half-elf, half-orc, or halfling.

Armor: Speed 20 ft. (dwarf and halfling only).

Weapons: Light crossbow (1d8, crit 19–20/×2, 80 ft., 6 lb., Piercing) instead of shortbow.

Weapons: Club (1d6, crit ×2, 10 ft., 3 lb., Bludgeoning) instead of quarterstaff (halfling only).

Skill Selection: Pick a number of skills equal to 3 + Int modifier (human only).

Bonus Feat: Skill Focus (Spellcraft or other skill) (human only).

Gear: Case with 10 bolts instead of quiver with 20 arrows.

Gold: 2d4.

Gnome Illusionist Starting Package

As elven wizard, except

Race: Gnome.

Armor: Speed 20 ft.

Weapons: Club (1d6, crit ×2, 10 ft., 3 lb., Bludgeoning) instead of quarterstaff.

Light crossbow (1d8, crit 19–20/×2, 80 ft., 6 lb., Piercing) instead of shortbow.

School Specialization: Illusion. Prohibited School: Enchantment.

Spellbook: All 0-level spells; plus *color spray, minor illusion,* and *summon monster I;* plus one of these spells of your choice per point of Intelligence bonus: *burning hands, cause fear, mage armor,* and *magic missile.*

Gear: Case with 10 bolts instead of quiver with 20 arrows.

Gold: 2d4 gp.

MULTICLASS CHARACTERS

A character may add new classes as he progresses in levels. The class abilities from a character's different classes add together to determine the multiclass character's total abilities. Multiclassing improves a character's versatility at the expense of focus.

HOW MULTICLASSING WORKS

Lidda, a 4th-level rogue, decides she wants to expand her repertoire by learning some wizardry. She locates a mentor who teaches her the ways of a wizard, and she spends a lot of time looking over the shoulder of Mialee, her party's wizard, while Mialee prepares her spells each morning. When Lidda amasses 10,000 XP, she becomes a 5th-level character. Instead of becoming a 5th-level rogue, however, she becomes a 4th-level rogue/1st-level wizard. Now, instead of gaining the benefits of attaining a new level as a rogue, she gains the benefits of becoming a 1st-level wizard. She gains a wizard's Hit Die (d4), a 1st-level wizard's +2 bonus on Will saves, and 4 skill points (2 for one wizard level and +2 for her Intelligence bonus for an ability score of 14) to be spent as a wizard. These benefits are added to the scores she already had as a rogue. Her base attack bonus, Reflex save, and Fortitude save do not increase because

these numbers are +0 for a 1st-level wizard. She gains a 1st-level wizard's beginning spellbook and spells per day. Her rogue skills and sneak attack capability, however, do not improve. She could spend some of her 4 skill points to improve her rogue skills, but, since they would be treated as cross-class skills for this purpose, these skill points would each only buy half a rank.

On reaching 15,000 XP, she becomes a 6th-level character. She decides she'd like to continue along the wizard path, so she increases her wizard level instead of her rogue level. Again she gains the wizard's benefits for attaining a new level rather than the rogue's. As a 2nd-level wizard, she gains another d4 Hit Die, her base attack and Will saves both go up by +1, she gains 4 skill points, and she can now prepare another 0-level spell and another 1st-level spell each day (as per Table 3–20: The Wizard). Additionally, as a 6th-level character overall she gets her third feat (as per Table 3–2: Experience and Level-Dependent Benefits).

At this point, Lidda is a 6th-level character: a 4th-level rogue/2nd-level wizard. She casts spells as a 2nd-level wizard does, and she sneak attacks as a 4th-level rogue. Her combat skill is a little better than a 4th-level rogue's would be, because she has learned something about fighting during her time as a wizard. (Her base attack bonus went up +1.) Her base Reflex save bonus is +4 (+4 from her rogue class and +0 from her wizard class), better than a 6th-level wizard's but not as good as a 6th-level rogue's. Her base Will save bonus is +4 (+1 from her rogue class and +3 from her wizard class), better than a 6th-level rogue's but not as good as a 6th-level wizard's.

At each new level, Lidda decides whether to increase her rogue level or her wizard level. Of course, if she really wants to have diverse abilities, she could even acquire a third class, maybe fighter.

CLASS AND LEVEL FEATURES

The abilities of a multiclass character are the sum of the abilities of each of the character's classes.

Level: "Character level" is the total level of the character. It derives from overall XP earned and is used to determine when feats and ability score boosts are gained, as per Table 3–2: Experience and Level-Dependent Benefits. "Class level" is the level of the character in a particular class, as per the individual class tables. For a single-class character, character level equals class level.

Hit Dice: The character gains Hit Dice from each class, with the resulting hit points added together.

Base Attack Bonus: Add the base attack bonuses for each class to get the character's base attack bonus. If the resulting value is +6 or higher, the character gets multiple attacks. Find the base attack value on Table 3–1: Base Save and Base Attack Bonuses to see how many additional attacks the character gets and at what bonuses. For instance, a 6th-level rogue/4th-level wizard would have a base attack bonus of +6 (+4 for the rogue class and +2 for the wizard class). A base attack bonus of +6 allows a second attack with a bonus of +1 (listed as +6/+1 on Table 3–1), even though neither the +4 from the rogue nor the +2 from the wizard normally allows an extra attack.

The monk is a special case because her additional unarmed attacks are better than her base attack bonus would suggest. For a multiclass monk fighting unarmed, the character must either use the additional attacks given for her monk levels (only) or the additional attacks that are standard for her combined base attack bonus, but not both. For instance, a 10th-level monk/7th-level wizard has a combined attack bonus of +10 (+7 for the monk class, +3 for the wizard class). Normally, this would give her an additional attack at +5 (+10/+5 on Table 3–1: Base Save and Base Attack Bonuses), but she can instead take the two additional unarmed attacks listed for a 10th-level monk, +4 and +1 (+7/+4/+1 on Table 3–10: The Monk).

Saving Throws: Add the base save bonuses for each class together. A 7th-level rogue/4th-level wizard gets +3 on Fortitude saving throws (+2 as a 7th-level rogue and +1 as a 4th-level wizard), +6 on Reflex saving throws (+5 and +1), and +6 on Will saving throws (+2 and +4).

Skills: The character retains and can access skills from all his or her classes. For purposes of calculating maximum ranks, a skill is a class skill if at least one of the character's classes has it as a class skill. The maximum rank for a class skill is 3 + the character level. For a 7th-level rogue/4th-level wizard (an 11th-level character), a rogue skill or wizard skill has a maximum rank of 14. For a cross-class skill, maximum rank is half the maximum for a class skill.

If a skill is unavailable to a class (that is, if it's an exclusive skill that a multiclass character's other class doesn't have access to), then levels in that class don't increase the multiclass character's maximum ranks. For instance, the 7th-level rogue/4th-level wizard would have a maximum rank of 10 in Use Magic Device, an exclusive class skill for rogues. The extra four levels in the wizard class do not increase the character's maximum rank with Use Magic Device. Likewise, the same character could have a maximum of 7 ranks in Scry, an exclusive skill for wizards.

Class Features: The character gets all class features of all classes but must also suffer the consequences of all special restrictions of all classes. (*Exception:* A character who acquires the barbarian class does not become illiterate.) Some class features don't work well with skills or class features of other classes. For example, although rogues are proficient with light armor, a rogue/wizard still suffers arcane spell failure chances if wearing armor.

In the special case of turning undead, both clerics and experienced paladins have the same ability. If the character's paladin is level 3 or higher, her effective turning level is her cleric level plus her paladin level minus 2. Thus, a 5th-level paladin/4th-level cleric turns undead like a 7th-level cleric.

In the special case of uncanny dodge, both experienced barbarians and experienced rogues have the same ability. A barbarian/rogue can treat her barbarian levels as rogue levels to determine how effective her uncanny dodge is.

Feats: For multiclass characters, feats are received every three character levels, regardless of individual class level (see Table 3–2: Experience and Level-Dependent Benefits).

Ability Increases: For multiclass characters, abilities are increased every four character levels, regardless of individual class level (see Table 3–2: Experience and Level-Dependent Benefits).

Spells: The character gains spells from all his or her classes. Thus, an experienced ranger/druid may have the spell *protection from elements* both as a ranger and as a druid. Since the spell's effect is based on the class level of the caster, the player must keep track of whether the character is preparing and casting *protection from elements* as a ranger or as a druid.

ADDING A SECOND CLASS

When a single-class character gains a level, he or she may choose to increase the level of his or her current class or pick up a new class at 1st level. The DM may restrict the choices available according to how he or she handles classes, skills, experience, and training. For instance, the character may need to find a tutor to teach him the ways of the new class. Additionally, the DM may require the player to declare what class his or her character is "working on" before he or she makes the jump to the next level, so the character has time to practice new skills. In this way, gaining the new class is the result of previous effort rather than a sudden development.

The character gains all the 1st-level base attack bonuses, base save bonuses, class skills, weapon proficiency, armor proficiency, spells, and other class features of the new class, as well as a Hit Die of the appropriate type. In addition, the character gets the new class's per-level skill points.

Picking up a new class is not exactly the same as starting a character in that class. Some of the benefits for a 1st-level character represent the advantage of training while young and fresh, with lots of time to practice. When picking up a new class, a character does not receive the following starting bonuses given to characters who begin their careers in that class:

- Maximum hit points from the first Hit Die.
- Quadruple the per-level skill points.
- Starting equipment.
- Starting gold.
- An animal companion (druid only).

ADVANCING A LEVEL

Each time a multiclass character achieves a new level, he or she either increases one of his or her current class levels by one or picks up a new class at 1st level.

When a multiclass character increases one of his or her classes by one level, he or she gets all the standard benefits that characters gets for achieving that level in that class: an extra Hit Die, possible bonuses in attacks and saving throws (depending on the class and the new level), possible new class features (as defined by the class), new spells, and new skill points.

Skill points are spent according to the class that the multiclass character just advanced in (see Table 4–1: Skill Points per Level, page 58). Skills purchased from Table 4–2: Skills are purchased at the cost appropriate for that class.

Rules for characters beyond 20th level (including multiclass characters beyond 20th level) will be covered in an upcoming rulebook.

EXPERIENCE FOR MULTICLASS CHARACTERS

Developing and maintaining skills and abilities in more than one class is demanding. Depending on the character's class levels and race, he or she might or might not suffer an XP penalty.

Even Levels: If your multiclass character's classes are nearly the same level (all within one level of each other), then he or she can balance the needs of his or her classes and suffers no penalty. For instance, a 4th-level wizard/3rd-level rogue suffers no penalty, nor does a 2nd-level fighter/2nd-level wizard/3rd-level rogue.

Uneven Levels: If any two of your multiclass character's classes are two or more levels apart, the strain of developing and maintaining different skills at different levels takes its toll. Your multiclass character suffers a –20% XP penalty for each class that is not within one level of his most experienced class. These penalties apply from the moment the character adds a class or raises a class's level too high. For instance, a 4th-level wizard/3rd-level rogue gets no penalty, but if that character raises his wizard level to 5th, then he would receive the –20% penalty from that point on until his levels were nearly even again.

Races and Multiclass XP: A racially favored class (see the individual race entries in Chapter 2: Races) does not count against the character for purposes of the –20% XP penalty. In such cases, calculate the XP penalty as if the character did not have that class. For instance, Bergwin is an 11th-level gnome character (a 9th-level rogue/2nd-level illusionist). He suffers no XP penalty because he has only one nonfavored class. (Illusionist is favored for gnomes.) Suppose he then achieves 12th level and adds 1st-level fighter to his classes, becoming a 9th-level rogue/2nd-level illusionist/1st-level fighter. He suffers a –20% XP penalty on future XP he earns because his fighter level is so much lower than his rogue level. Were he awarded 1,200 XP for an adventure, he would receive 80% of that amount, or 960 XP. If he rose to 13th level and picked up 1st level as a cleric, he would suffer a –40% XP penalty from then on.

When determining whether a multiclass character's classes are even, do not count the character's favored class. A dwarven 7th-level fighter/2nd-level cleric suffers no penalty, nor does he when he adds 1st-level rogue to his classes since his cleric and rogue classes are only one level apart. Note that in this case cleric counts as his highest class, not fighter, because fighter is favored for dwarves.

A human's or half-elf's highest-level class is always considered his or her favored class.

Illus. by A. Swekel

idda the rogue can walk quietly up to a door, put her ear to it, and hear the troglodyte priest on the other side casting a spell on his pet hell hound. If Jozan the cleric were to try the same thing, he'd make so much noise that the hell hound would hear him. He, however, could identify the spell that the evil priest is casting. Actions such as these rely on the skills that characters have (in this case, Move Silently, Listen, and Spellcraft).

SKILLS SUMMARY

Your skills represent a variety of abilities, and you get better at them as you go up in level.

Getting Skills: At each level, you get 2, 4, or 8 skill points that you use to buy skills. (Your Intelligence modifier adds to this number. Humans get 1 extra skill point at each level above 1st.) A 1st-level character gets four times this number. (Humans get 4 extra skill points at 1st level in addition to the standard initial amount for their class and Intelligence. These are added on at 1st level, not multiplied in.) If you buy a class skill (such as Listen for a rogue or Spellcraft for a cleric), you get 1 rank (equal to a +1 bonus) for each skill point. If you buy other classes' skills (cross-class skills), you get a half rank per skill point. Your maximum rank in a class skill is your level plus 3. Your maximum rank in a cross-class skill is half of this number (do not round up or down).

Using Skills: To make a skill check, roll:
1d20 + skill modifier
(Skill modifier = skill rank + ability modifier
+ miscellaneous modifiers)

This roll is made just like an attack roll or a saving throw. The higher the roll, the better. You're either trying to score a certain Difficulty Class (DC) or higher, or you're trying to beat another character's check. For instance, to sneak quietly past a guard, Lidda needs to beat the guard's Listen check with her own Move Silently check.

Skill rank is a number related to how many skill points a character has invested in a skill. Many skills can be used even if the character has no ranks in the skill; this is known as making an untrained skill check.

The ability modifier used in the skill check is the modifier for the skill's key ability (the ability most associated with the skill's use). The key ability of a skill is noted in its description and on Table 4–2: Skills.

Miscellaneous modifiers include racial bonuses and armor check penalties, among others.

HOW SKILLS WORK

This extended example shows how skills work. Detailed rules follow the example.

Devis's Skills at 1st Level: As a half-elven bard, Devis gets 4 skill points per level. Since his Intelligence score is 12, he gets +1 point per level, for a total of 5 skill points. As a 1st-level half-elven character, Devis gets four times this number, or 20 skill points. At 1st level, his maximum rank in a skill is 1 (his level) plus 3, or 4. With 20 points, he can increase to his maximum rank (max out) five class skills at 4 ranks each.

He chooses the skills Perform, Use Magic Device, Listen, Spellcraft, and Gather Information, each at 4 ranks. He can choose one type of performing for each rank he has in his Perform skill. The skill section on his character sheet looks like this:

Skill (cross-class?)	Skill Modifier		Ranks		Ability Modifier		Misc. Modifiers
Perform							
(epic, lute, melody, storytelling)	+6	=	4	+	+2	+	
Use Magic Device	+6	=	4	+	+2	+	
Listen	+4	=	4	+	−1	+	+1
Spellcraft	+5	=	4	+	+1	+	
Gather Information	+6	=	4	+	+2	+	

Listen is a Wisdom skill, so when Devis makes a Listen check he adds his 4 ranks, his −1 Wisdom penalty, and his +1 racial bonus together, for a skill modifier of +4. Spellcraft is an Intelligence skill, so when he makes a Spellcraft check he adds 4 for his rank and +1 for his Intelligence bonus, for a total skill modifier of +5. The other skills are all based on Charisma, so he gets his 4 ranks and his +2 Charisma bonus, for skill modifiers of +6. To make a Perform check, for example, Devis's player rolls 1d20+6.

Skills at 2nd Level: When Devis reaches 2nd level, he gets another 5 skill points, the same as he will each level after that (unless his Intelligence score goes up enough to increase his Intelligence bonus). He decides to use 1 skill point to increase his Perform (epic, lute, melody, storytelling) skill by 1 rank, raising his rank to 5 and his skill modifier up to +7. He chooses ballad as his new form of performance. He can't have more than 5 ranks in a class skill at 2nd level, so he can't raise Perform any higher. He uses the other 4 skill points to buy 2 ranks of Spot. (Spot is a cross-class skill for bards since it's not on the bard skill list, so his 4 skill points only buy 2 ranks.) Spot is a Wisdom skill, so Devis's −1 Wisdom penalty and his +1 racial bonus to Spot mean that he now gets a skill modifier of +2 on Spot checks. (He could use the Spot skill untrained, but without the ranks, he would just get his Wisdom penalty and racial bonus, which when added together result in a skill modifier of 0.)

These skills on his character sheet now look like this:

Skill (cross-class?)	Skill Modifier		Ranks		Ability Modifier		Misc. Modifiers
Perform	+7	=	5	+	+2	+	
Spot (cc)	+2	=	2	+	−1	+	+1

Skill Check: When Devis makes a skill check at 2nd level, his player rolls 1d20 and adds Devis's skill modifier (rank plus ability modifier plus any miscellaneous modifier). The higher the result, the better Devis does. On average, Devis will roll a 10 or 11 on the d20, so he will get a check result of 17 or 18 with his Perform checks. It's this total check result that matters, not the original roll. A result of 17 by a peasant with no pluses or minuses who rolls it naturally is the same as a result of 17 by Devis (10 on the d20 with +7 for his skill rank and Charisma modifier).

Opposed Check: Devis meets another bard (an NPC) on the road, and they set up an impromptu contest to see who is a better performer. Devis's player rolls 1d20+7 for his Perform check and gets a 22. The DM secretly makes a Perform check for the NPC bard, and the result is a 19. The DM tells Devis's player that the NPC bard was pretty good, but that most of the peasants assembled to watch preferred Devis's performance.

Check against a Difficulty Class (DC): Later, Devis gets the chance to play his lute for the cleric of Pelor who practically runs the town that he and his party are staying in. Devis is trying to win the cleric's favor. The DM secretly decides that this gruff cleric is hard to impress and sets the DC at 20. Devis's player rolls a 9 on 1d20 for a result of 16. This result would be enough to impress most people, but it is not enough to impress the cleric. The DM

tells the player that the cleric watches Devis's performance with disinterest.

Untrained Checks: Unsuccessful at winning the cleric's favor with song, Devis tries to sway her with words. He explains that he and his party are good people and that helping them would, in turn, help many others. Devis is trying to use the Diplomacy skill, which he doesn't have (he has 0 ranks in Diplomacy), so he doesn't get to add any ranks to his skill check, but he does get to add his +2 Charisma modifier. (Diplomacy is a Charisma skill.) The DM secretly sets the DC at 20, and Devis's player rolls 19 on the d20 for a result of 21. The cleric smiles and agrees to help Devis and his party.

ACQUIRING SKILL RANKS

Ranks indicate how much training or experience your character has with a given skill. Each of your skills has a rank, from 0 (for a skill in which your character has no training at all) to 23 (for the 20th-level character who has increased a skill to its maximum rank). When making a skill check, you add your skill ranks to the roll as part of the skill modifier, so the more ranks you have, the higher your skill check will be.

The class starting packages in Chapter 3 provide an easier way to select 1st-level skills, because they assume that you max out (increase to maximum rank) each skill you buy and because they provide a shorter list from which to choose. Although selecting skills from a starting package feels very different from buying them rank by rank, your character winds up with the same number of skill points spent no matter which way you select 1st-level skills.

The Skills paragraph on page 56 in Chapter 3: Classes covers the skill acquisition rules for multiclass characters.

ACQUIRING SKILLS AT 1ST LEVEL

Follow these two steps to pick skills for your 1st-level character:

1. Determine the number of skill points you get. This number depends on your class and Intelligence modifier, as shown on Table 4–1: Skill Points per Level. For example, Lidda is a beginning rogue with an Intelligence score of 14 (+2 Intelligence bonus). At the start of play, she has 40 skill points to spend (8 + 2 = 10, 10 × 4 = 40).
   - A character gets at least 4 skill points (1 × 4 = 4) even if he has an Intelligence penalty.
   - A human gets 4 extra skill points as a 1st-level character. A human character with the same class and Intelligence modifier as Lidda would have 44 skill points at the start of play.

2. Spend the skill points. Each skill point you spend on a class skill gets you 1 rank in that skill. Class skills are the skills found on

TABLE 4–1: SKILL POINTS PER LEVEL

Class	1st-level Skill Points*	Higher-level Skill Points**
Barbarian	(4 + Int modifier) × 4	4 + Int modifier
Bard	(4 + Int modifier) × 4	4 + Int modifier
Cleric	(2 + Int modifier) × 4	2 + Int modifier
Druid	(4 + Int modifier) × 4	4 + Int modifier
Fighter	(2 + Int modifier) × 4	2 + Int modifier
Monk	(4 + Int modifier) × 4	4 + Int modifier
Paladin	(2 + Int modifier) × 4	2 + Int modifier
Ranger	(4 + Int modifier) × 4	4 + Int modifier
Rogue	(8 + Int modifier) × 4	8 + Int modifier
Sorcerer	(2 + Int modifier) × 4	2 + Int modifier
Wizard	(2 + Int modifier) × 4	2 + Int modifier

*Humans add +4 to this total at 1st level.
**Humans add +1 each level.

your character's class skill list. Each skill point you spend on a cross-class skill gets your character a half rank in that skill. Cross-class skills are skills not found on your character's class skill list. (Half ranks do not improve your skill check, but two half ranks make 1 rank.) Your maximum rank in a class skill is 4. In a cross-class skill, it's 2. You will not be able to buy some skills because they are exclusive to certain classes.

- Table 4–2: Skills lists all the skills and indicates which are class skills, which are cross-class skills, and which are exclusive skills (those that can't be purchased except by certain classes).
- Spend all your skill points. You can't save them to spend later.

SKILLS AT HIGHER LEVELS

When you reach a new experience level, follow these steps to gain new skills and improve those you already have:

1. Determine the number of skill points you get. See Table 4–1: Skill Points per Level.
   - A character gets at least 1 skill point even if he has an Intelligence penalty.
   - A human gets 1 extra skill point per level.

2. You can improve any class skill that you've previously maxed out by 1 rank or any cross-class skill that you've previously maxed out by a half rank.

TABLE 4–2: SKILLS

Skill	Bbn	Brd	Clr	Drd	Ftr	Mnk	Pal	Rgr	Rog	Sor	Wiz	Untrained	Key Ability
Alchemy	·	●	·	·	·	·	·	·	·	●	●	No	Int
Animal Empathy	✗	✗	✗	●	✗	✗	✗	●	✗	✗	✗	No	Cha
Appraise	·	●	·	·	·	·	·	·	●	·	·	Yes	Int
Balance	·	●	·	·	·	●	·	·	●	·	·	Yes	Dex*
Bluff	·	●	·	·	·	·	·	·	●	·	·	Yes	Cha
Climb	●	●	·	·	●	●	·	●	●	·	·	Yes	Str*
Concentration	·	●	●	●	·	●	●	●	·	●	●	Yes	Con
Craft	●	●	●	●	●	●	●	●	●	●	●	Yes	Int
Decipher Script	✗	●	✗	✗	✗	✗	✗	✗	●	✗	✗	No	Int
Diplomacy	·	●	●	●	·	●	●	●	●	·	·	Yes	Cha
Disable Device	·	·	·	·	·	·	·	·	●	·	·	No	Int
Disguise	·	●	·	·	·	·	·	·	●	·	·	Yes	Cha
Escape Artist	·	●	·	·	·	●	·	·	●	·	·	Yes	Dex*
Forgery	·	·	·	·	·	·	·	·	●	·	·	Yes	Int
Gather Information	·	●	·	·	·	·	·	·	●	·	·	Yes	Cha
Handle Animal	●	·	·	●	●	·	●	●	·	·	·	No	Cha
Heal	·	·	●	●	·	·	●	●	·	·	·	Yes	Wis
Hide	·	·	·	·	·	●	·	●	●	·	·	Yes	Dex*
Innuendo	·	●	·	·	·	·	·	●	●	·	·	No	Wis
Intimidate	●	·	·	·	●	·	·	·	●	·	·	Yes	Cha
Intuit Direction	●	·	·	●	·	·	·	●	·	·	·	No	Wis
Jump	●	●	·	·	●	●	·	●	●	·	·	Yes	Str*
Knowledge (arcana)	·	●	●	·	·	●	·	·	·	●	●	No	Int
Knowledge (religion)	·	●	●	·	·	●	●	·	·	·	●	No	Int
Knowledge (nature)	·	●	·	●	·	·	·	●	·	·	●	No	Int
Knowledge (all skills**)	·	●	·	·	·	·	·	·	·	·	●	No	Int
Listen	●	●	·	●	·	●	·	●	●	·	·	Yes	Wis
Move Silently	·	·	·	·	·	●	·	●	●	·	·	Yes	Dex*
Open Lock	·	·	·	·	·	·	·	·	●	·	·	No	Dex
Perform	·	●	·	·	·	●	·	·	·	·	·	Yes	Cha
Pick Pocket	·	●	·	·	·	·	·	·	●	·	·	No	Dex*
Profession	·	●	●	●	·	●	●	●	●	●	●	No	Wis
Read Lips	✗	✗	✗	✗	✗	✗	✗	✗	●	✗	✗	No	Int
Ride	●	·	·	·	●	·	●	●	·	·	·	Yes	Dex
Scry	✗	●	●	●	✗	✗	✗	✗	✗	●	●	Yes	Int
Search	·	·	·	·	·	·	·	·	●	·	·	Yes	Int
Sense Motive	·	●	·	·	·	●	●	·	●	·	·	Yes	Wis
Speak Language	·	●	·	·	·	·	·	·	·	·	·	No	None
Spellcraft	·	●	●	●	·	·	·	·	·	●	●	No	Int
Spot	·	·	·	●	·	●	·	●	●	·	·	Yes	Wis
Swim	●	●	·	●	●	●	·	●	·	·	·	Yes	Str
Tumble	·	●	·	·	·	●	·	·	●	·	·	No	Dex*
Use Magic Device	✗	●	✗	✗	✗	✗	✗	✗	●	✗	✗	No	Cha
Use Rope	·	·	·	·	·	·	·	●	●	·	·	Yes	Dex
Wilderness Lore	●	·	·	●	·	·	·	●	·	·	·	Yes	Wis

● Class skill.
· Cross-class skill.
✗ You can't buy this skill because it is exclusive to another class.
* Your armor check penalty, if any, also applies.

**Bards and wizards buy all Knowledge skills as individual class skills.
Untrained: Yes: The skill can be used untrained. That is, a character can have 0 ranks in this skill but can make skill checks normally. No: You can't use the skill unless you have at least 1 rank.

3. If you have not maxed out a skill, you can spend extra skill points on it and increase its rank further.

First, find out what your maximum rank in the skill is. If it's a class skill, your maximum rank is your new level plus 3. If it's a cross-class skill, your maximum rank is half of that number (do not round up or down).

You may spend up to the number of skill points it takes to max out the skill (provided that you have that many skill points to spend).

4. If you want to pick up a new skill, you can spend up to your level plus 3 skill points on it. These skill points buy 1 rank each if the new skill is a class skill or a half rank each if it's a cross-class skill.

USING SKILLS

When you use a skill, you make a skill check to see how well you do. The higher the result on your skill check, the better you do. Based on the circumstances, your result must match or beat a particular number to use the skill successfully. The harder the task, the higher the number you need to roll.

A number of circumstances can affect your check. If you're free to work without distractions, you can make a careful attempt and avoid simple mistakes. If you have lots of time, you can try over and over again, assuring that you do your best. If others help you, you may succeed where otherwise you would fail.

SKILL CHECKS

A skill check takes into account your training (skill rank), natural talent (ability modifier), and luck (the die roll). It may also take into account your race's knack for doing certain things (racial bonus) or what armor you are wearing (armor check penalty), among other things. (For instance, a character who has the Skill Focus feat related to a certain skill gets a +2 bonus on all checks involving that skill; see page 85.)

To make a skill check, roll 1d20 and add your skill modifier for that skill. The skill modifier incorporates your rank with that skill, your ability modifier for that skill's key ability, and any other miscellaneous modifiers you have, including racial bonuses and any armor check penalty. The higher the result, the better. A natural 20 is not an automatic success, and a natural 1 is not an automatic failure (as is the case in the combat rules).

Difficulty Class

Some checks are made against a Difficulty Class (DC). The DC is a number set by the DM (using the skill rules as a guideline) that you must score as a result on your skill check to succeed. For example, climbing the outer wall of a ruined tower may have a DC of 15. To climb the wall, you must get a result of 15 or better on a Climb check. A Climb check is 1d20 plus Climb ranks (if any) plus Strength modifier plus any other modifiers.

Opposed Checks

Some skill checks are opposed checks. They are made against a randomized number, which is usually another character's skill check result. For example, to sneak up on a guard, you need to beat the guard's Listen check result with your Move Silently check result. You make a Move Silently check, and the DM makes a Listen check for the guard. Whoever gets the higher result wins the contest.

TABLE 4–3: EXAMPLE OPPOSED CHECKS

Task	Skill (Key Ability)	Opposing Skill (Key Ability)
Sneak up behind someone	Move Silently (Dex)	Listen (Wis)
Con someone	Bluff (Cha)	Sense Motive (Wis)
Hide from someone	Hide (Dex)	Spot (Wis)
Tie a prisoner securely	Use Rope (Dex)	Escape Artist (Dex)
Win a horserace	Ride (Dex)	Ride (Dex)
Pass as someone else	Disguise (Cha)	Spot (Wis)
Steal a coin pouch	Pick Pockets (Dex)	Spot (Wis)
Create a false map	Forgery (Int)	Forgery (Int)

For ties on opposed checks, the character with the higher key ability score wins. For instance, in a Move Silently against Listen check that results in a tie, the sneaker's Dexterity would be compared to the listener's Wisdom. If these scores are the same, flip a coin.

Retries

In general, you can try a skill check again if you fail, and can keep trying indefinitely. Some skills, however, have consequences of failure that must be taken into account. Some skills are virtually useless once a check has failed on an attempt to accomplish a particular task. For most skills, when a character has succeeded once at a given task, additional successes are meaningless.

For example, if Lidda the rogue misses an Open Lock check, she can try again and keep trying. If, however, a trap in the lock goes off if she misses an Open Lock check by 5 or more, then failing has its own penalties.

Similarly, if Lidda misses a Climb check, she can keep trying, but if she misses by 5 or more, she falls (after which she can get up and try again).

If Tordek has negative hit points and is dying, Lidda can make an untrained Heal check to stabilize him. If the check fails, Tordek probably loses another hit point, but Lidda can try again in the next round.

If a skill carries no penalties for failure, you can take 20 and assume that you go at it long enough to succeed eventually (see Checks without Rolls on the next page).

Untrained Skill Checks

Generally, if you attempt to use a skill you don't possess, you make a skill check as normal. Your skill modifier doesn't have your skill rank added in because you don't have any ranks in the skill. You do get other modifiers added into the skill modifier, though, such as the ability modifier for the skill's key ability.

Many skills can only be used if you are trained in the skill. If you don't have Spellcraft, for example, regardless of your class, ability scores, and experience level, you just don't know enough about magic even to attempt to identify a spell. Skills that cannot be used untrained are marked with a "No" in the "Untrained" column on Table 4–2: Skills.

For example, Krusk the barbarian's 4 ranks in Climb make his Climb check results 4 points higher than they otherwise would be, but even Devis the bard, with no Climb ranks, can make a Climb check. Devis only has a skill modifier of 0 (+1 for his Strength and –1 for his armor), but he can give it a try. However, Devis's ranks in Use Magic Device let him do something that he otherwise couldn't do at all, such as use a magic item as if he had a

ACCESS TO SKILLS

The rules assume that a character can find a way to learn any nonexclusive skill. For instance, if Jozan wants to learn Profession (sailor), nothing in the rules exists to stop him. However, the DM is in charge of the world, including decisions about where one can learn certain skills and where one can't. While Jozan is living in a desert, for example, the DM can decide that Jozan has no way of learning to be a sailor. It's up to the DM to say whether a character can learn a given skill in a given setting.

particular spell on his class spell list that he actually doesn't have. Krusk, with no ranks in the skill, can't make a Use Magic Device check even at a penalty.

Favorable and Unfavorable Conditions

Some situations may make a skill easier or harder to use, resulting in a bonus or penalty added into the skill modifier for the skill check or a change to the DC of the skill check. It's one thing for Krusk, with his Wilderness Lore skill, to hunt down enough food to eat while he's camping for the day in the middle of a rich forest, but foraging for food while traveling across barren desert is an entirely different matter.

The DM can alter the odds of success in four ways to take into account exceptional circumstances:

1. Give the skill user a +2 circumstance bonus to represent circumstances that improve performance, such as having the perfect tool for the job, getting help from another character (see Combining Skill Attempts on the next page), or possessing unusually accurate information.
2. Give the skill user a −2 circumstance penalty to represent conditions that hamper performance, such as being forced to use improvised tools or having misleading information.
3. Reduce the DC by 2 to represent circumstances that make the task easier, such as having a friendly audience or doing work that can be subpar.
4. Increase the DC by 2 to represent circumstances that make the task harder, such as having a hostile audience or doing work that must be flawless.

Conditions that affect your ability to perform the skill change your skill modifier. Conditions that modify how well you have to perform the skill to succeed change the DC. A bonus to your skill modifier and a reduction in the check's DC have the same result: they create a better chance that you will succeed. But they represent different circumstances, and sometimes that difference is important.

For example, Devis the bard wants to entertain a band of dwarves who are staying at the same inn where he and his party are staying. Before playing his lute, Devis listens to the dwarves' drinking songs so he can judge their mood. Doing so improves his performance, giving him a +2 to the skill modifier for his check. He rolls a 6 and adds +8 for his skill modifier (4 ranks, +2 Charisma modifier, and +2 for his impromptu research). His result is 14. The DM sets the DC at 15. The dwarves are in a good mood because they have recently won a skirmish with orc bandits, so the DM reduces the DC to 13. (Devis's performance isn't better just because the dwarves are in a good mood, so Devis doesn't get a bonus to add into his skill modifier. Instead, the DC goes down.) The leader of the dwarven band, however, has heard that a half-elf spy works for the bandits, and he's suspicious of Devis. The DC to entertain him is higher than normal: 17 instead of 15. Devis's skill check (14) is high enough to entertain the dwarves (DC 13) but not their leader (DC 17). The dwarves applaud Devis and offer to buy him drinks, but their leader eyes him suspiciously.

Time and Skill Checks

Using a skill might take a round, take no time, or take several rounds or even longer. Most skill uses are standard actions, move-equivalent actions, or full-round actions. Types of actions define how long activities take to perform within the framework of a combat round (6 seconds) and how movement is treated with respect to the activity (see Action Types, page 121). Some skill checks are instant and represent reactions to an event, or are included as part of an action. These skill checks are not actions. Other skill checks represent part of movement. The distance you jump when making a Jump check, for example, is part of your

movement. Some skills take more than a round to use, and the skill descriptions often specify how long these skills take to use.

Practically Impossible Tasks

Sometimes you want to do something that seems practically impossible. In general, to do something that's practically impossible requires that you have at least rank 10 in the skill and entails a penalty of −20 on your roll or +20 on the DC (which amounts to about the same thing).

Practically impossible tasks are hard to delineate ahead of time. They're the accomplishments that represent incredible, almost logic-defying skill and luck. Picking a lock by giving it a single, swift kick; swimming up a waterfall; or softening a demon's heart with a song are potential examples of practically impossible tasks.

The DM decides what is actually impossible and what is merely practically impossible. Just remember that characters with very high skill modifiers are capable of accomplishing incredible, almost unbelievable tasks, just as characters with very high combat bonuses are.

Extraordinary Success

If you have at least rank 10 in a skill and beat your DC by 20 or more on a normal skill check, you've completed the task impossibly well. For example, Devis the bard has reached 10th level and has rank 13 in Perform. He has increased his Charisma score by 2 points (once at 4th level and again at 8th level), so he now has an ability modifier of +3, giving him a total skill modifier of +16. He goes on stage in front of a receptive audience, so the DM assigns a DC of 15 to the skill check. Devis's player rolls a 19 on 1d20 and adds the +16 skill modifier for a result of 35—the audience likes the performance so much that Devis is considered a star, and from now on whenever he performs in front of this audience he can command and get twice the usual fee for his services.

Checks without Rolls

A skill check represents an attempt to accomplish some goal, usually with some sort of time pressure or distraction. Sometimes, though, you can use a skill under more favorable conditions and eliminate the luck factor.

Taking 10: When you are not in a rush and not being threatened or distracted, you may choose to take 10. Instead of rolling 1d20 for the skill check, calculate your result as if you had rolled a 10. For many routine tasks, taking 10 makes them automatically successful. Distractions or threats make it impossible for a character to take 10.

For example, Krusk the barbarian has a Climb skill modifier of +6 (4 ranks, +3 Strength modifier, −1 penalty for wearing studded leather armor). The steep, rocky slope he's climbing has a DC of 10. With a little care, he can take 10 and succeed automatically. But partway up the slope, a goblin scout begins pelting him with sling stones. Krusk needs to make a Climb check to get up to the goblin, and this time he can't simply take 10. If he rolls 4 or higher on 1d20, he succeeds.

Taking 20: When you have plenty of time (generally 2 minutes for a skill that can normally be checked in 1 round, one full-round action, or one standard action), and when the skill being attempted carries no penalties for failure, you can take 20. In other words, eventually you will get a 20 if you roll long enough. Instead of rolling 1d20 for the skill check, calculate your result as if you had rolled a 20. Taking 20 means you are trying until you get it right. Taking 20 takes about twenty times as long as making a single check would take.

For example, Krusk comes to a cliff face. He attempts to take 10, for a result of 16 (10 plus his +6 skill bonus), but the DC is 20, and the DM tells him that he fails to make progress up the cliff. (His check is at least high enough that he does not fall.) Krusk cannot take 20 because there is a penalty associated with failure (falling, in this case). He can try over and over, and eventually he may succeed, but he might fall one or more times in the process. Later, Krusk finds a cave in the cliff and searches it. The DM sees in the Search skill description that each 5-foot-square area takes a full-round action to search (and she secretly assigns a DC of 15 to the attempt). She estimates that the floors, walls, and ceiling of the cave make up about twenty 5-foot squares, so she tells Krusk's player that it takes 2 minutes to search the whole cave. Krusk's player gets a result of 12 on 1d20, adds no skill ranks because Krusk doesn't have the Search skill, and adds –1 because that's Krusk's Intelligence modifier. His roll fails. Now he declares that he is going to search the cavern high and low, taking as long as it takes. The DM takes the original time of 2 minutes and multiplies it by 20, for 40 minutes. That's how long it takes for Krusk to search the whole cave in exacting detail. Now Krusk's player treats his roll as if it were 20, for a result of 19. That's good enough to beat the DC of 15, and Krusk finds an old, bronze key discarded under a loose rock.

Ability Checks and Caster Level Checks: The normal take 10 rules apply for ability checks that are routine untrained skill checks (such as jumping but not disguising yourself) or when there is no skill associated with the check (such a breaking down a door). The normal take 20 rules apply to all ability checks. Neither rule applies to caster level checks (as when casting *dispel magic*).

COMBINING SKILL ATTEMPTS

When more than one character tries the same skill at the same time and for the same purpose, their efforts may overlap.

Individual Events

Often, several characters attempt some action and each succeeds or fails on her own.

For example, Krusk, the half-orc barbarian, and each of his friends needs to climb a slope if they're all to get to the top. Regardless of Krusk's roll, the other characters need successful checks, too. Every character makes a skill check.

Cooperation

Sometimes the individual PCs are essentially reacting to the same situation, but they can work together and help each other out. In this case, one character is considered the leader of the effort and makes a skill check while each helper makes a skill check against DC 10. (You can't take 10 on this check.) For each helper who succeeds, the leader gets a +2 circumstance bonus (as per the rule for favorable conditions). In many cases, a character's help won't be beneficial, or only a limited number of characters can help at once. The DM limits cooperation as she sees fit for the given conditions.

For instance, if Krusk has been badly wounded and is dying, Jozan can try a Heal check to keep him from losing more hit points. One other character can help Jozan. If the other character makes a Heal check against DC 10, then Jozan gets a +2 circumstance bonus on the Heal check he makes to help Krusk. The DM rules that two characters couldn't help Jozan at the same time because a third person would just get in the way.

Skill Synergy

It's also possible for a character to have two skills that work well together, such as someone with Handle Animal also having Animal Empathy. In general, having 5 or more ranks in one skill gives you a +2 synergy bonus on skill checks with its synergistic skills, as noted in the skill description.

ABILITY CHECKS

Sometimes you try to do something to which no specific skill really applies. In these cases, you make an ability check. An ability check is the roll of 1d20 plus the appropriate ability modifier. Essentially, you're making an untrained skill check. The DM assigns a Difficulty Class, or sets up an opposed check when two characters are engaged in a contest using one ability score or another. The initiative check in combat, for example, is essentially a Dexterity check. The character who rolls highest goes first.

In some cases, an action is a straight test of one's ability with no luck involved. Just as you wouldn't make a height check to see who is taller, you don't make a Strength check to see who is stronger. When two characters arm wrestle, for example, the stronger character simply wins. In the case of identical scores, flip a coin.

TABLE 4–4: EXAMPLE ABILITY CHECKS

Task	Key Ability
Breaking open a jammed or locked door	Strength
Threading a needle	Dexterity
Holding one's breath	Constitution
Navigating a maze	Intelligence
Remembering to lock a door	Wisdom
Getting oneself singled out in a crowd	Charisma

Breaking Open Doors: A common use of Strength is to break open doors. For example, Krusk approaches a locked door. He tries his Strength against it. He takes 10, adds +3 for his Strength, and gets a 13. The DM says that the door holds. (The player doesn't know that the door's DC is 15.) Krusk's player can keep making checks. He needs a roll of 12 or higher to get a result of 15 or higher. If he can devote sufficient time, he can take 20, for a total of 23, and plow through the door.

Larger and smaller creatures get size bonuses and size penalties on these checks: Fine –16, Diminutive –12, Tiny –8, Small –4, Large +4, Huge +8, Gargantuan +12, Colossal +16.

A portable ram (page 109) improves a character's chance of breaking open a door.

TABLE 4–5: EXAMPLE DOOR DCs

DC	Door
10 or lower	A door just about anyone can break open.
11 to 15	A door that a strong person could break with one try and an average person might break with one try.
13	Typical DC for a simple wooden door.
16 to 20	A door that almost anyone could break, given time.
18	Typical DC for a good wooden door.
21 to 25	A door that only a strong or very strong person has a hope of breaking, and probably not on the first try.
23	Typical DC for a strong wooden door.
25	Typical DC for an iron-barred wooden door.
26 or higher	A door that only an exceptionally strong person has a hope of breaking.
28	Typical DC for an iron door.
+5*	*Hold portal* (increases DC by 5).
+10*	*Arcane lock* (increases DC by 10).

*Not cumulative; if both apply, use the larger number.

SKILL DESCRIPTIONS

This section describes each skill, including common uses and typical modifiers. Characters can sometimes use skills for purposes other than those listed here. For example, you might be able to impress a bunch of alchemists by making an Alchemy check.

Here is the format for skill descriptions. Headings that do not apply to a particular skill are omitted in that skill's description.

SKILL NAME ([Key Ability]; Trained Only; Armor Check Penalty; [Class Name] Only)

The skill name line includes the following information:

Key Ability: The abbreviation of the ability whose modifier applies to the skill check. *Exception:* Speak Language has "None" listed as its key ability because the use of this skill does not require a check.

Trained Only: If "Trained Only" is included in the skill name line, you must have at least 1 rank in the skill to use it. If it is omitted, the skill can be used untrained (with a rank of 0). If any special notes apply to trained or untrained use, they are covered in the Special section (see below).

Armor Check Penalty: Apply any armor check penalty to skill checks for this skill.

[Class Name] Only: The skill is exclusive to a certain class or classes. No character not of these classes can take the skill. If omitted, the skill is not exclusive.

The skill name line is followed by a general description of what using the skill represents. After the description are three other types of information:

Check: What you can do with a successful skill check, how much time it takes to make a check, and the check's DC.

Retry: Any conditions that apply to successive attempts to use the skill successfully. If this paragraph is omitted, the skill can be retried without any inherent penalty other than consuming additional time.

Special: Any extra facts that apply to the skill, such as rules regarding untrained use, or if this skill has a synergistic relationship with other skills, or benefits that certain characters receive because of class or race.

ALCHEMY (Int; Trained Only)

Alchemists combine strange ingredients in secret ways to make marvelous substances.

Check: You can make alchemical items. Some items you can make are found in the item descriptions in Chapter 7: Equipment and listed on Table 7–9: Special and Superior Items. To determine how much time and material it takes to make an alchemical item, use the DCs listed below and the rules for making things found in the Craft skill description.

The DM may allow an alchemist to perform other tasks related to alchemy, such as identifying an unknown substance or a poison. Doing so takes 1 hour.

Task	DC	Notes
Identify substance	25	Costs 1 gp per attempt (or 20 gp to take 20)
Identify potion	25	Costs 1 gp per attempt (or 20 gp to take 20)
Make acid	15	See Craft skill
Identify poison (after casting *detect poison*)	20	See *detect poison* (page 193)
Make alchemist's fire, smokestick, or tindertwig	20	See Craft skill
Make antitoxin, sunrod, tanglefoot bag, or thunderstone	25	See Craft skill

Retry: Yes, but in the case of making items, each failure ruins the half the raw materials needed, and you have to pay half the raw material cost again. For identifying substances or potions, each failure consumes the cost per attempt.

Special: You must have alchemical equipment to make an item or identify it. If you are working in a city, you can buy what you need as part of the raw materials cost to make the item, but alchemical equipment is difficult or impossible to come by in some places. For identifying items, the cost represents additional supplies you must buy. Purchasing and maintaining an alchemist's lab (page 110) grants a +2 circumstance bonus to Alchemy checks (from the favorable condition of having the perfect tools for the job) but does not affect the cost of any items made using the skill.

Gnomes get a +2 racial bonus on Alchemy checks because a gnome's sensitive nose allows him to monitor alchemical processes by smell.

ANIMAL EMPATHY (Cha; Trained Only; Druid, Ranger Only)

Use this skill to keep a guard dog from barking at you, to get a wild bird to land on your outstretched hand, or to keep an owlbear calm while you back off.

Check: You can improve the attitude of an animal with a successful check. (Your DM has information in the *DMG* about attitudes, including the DCs to change them.) To use the skill, you and the animal must be able to study each other, noting each other's body language, vocalizations, and general demeanor. This means that you must be within 30 feet under normal conditions.

Generally, influencing an animal in this way takes 1 minute, but, as with influencing people, it might take more or less time.

This skill works on animals (such as bears and giant lizards). You can use it with a −4 penalty on beasts (such as owlbears) and magical beasts (such as blink dogs).

Retry: As with attempts to influence people, retries on the same animal generally don't work (or don't work any better), whether you have succeeded or not.

APPRAISE (Int)

Use this skill to tell an antique from old junk, a sword that's old and fancy from an elven heirloom, and high-quality jewelry from cheap stuff made to look good.

Check: You can appraise common or well-known objects within 10% of their value (DC 12). Failure means you estimate the value at 50% to 150% of actual value. The DM secretly rolls 2d6+3, multiplies by 10%, multiplies the actual value by that percentage, and tells you that value for the item. (For a common or well-known item, your chance of estimating the value within 10% is fairly high even if you fail the check—in such a case, you made a lucky guess.)

Rare or exotic items require a successful check against DC 15, 20, or higher. If successful, you estimate the value at 70% to 130% of its actual value. The DM secretly rolls 2d4+5, multiplies by 10%, multiplies the actual value by that percentage, and tells you that value for the item. Failure means you cannot estimate the item's value.

A magnifying glass (page 111) gives a +2 circumstance bonus to Appraise checks involving any item that is small or highly detailed, such as a gem. A merchant's scale (page 111) gives a +2 circumstance bonus to Appraise checks involving any items that are valued by weight, including anything made of precious metals. These bonuses stack.

Appraising an item takes 1 minute.

Retry: Not on the same object, regardless of success.

Special: If you are making the check untrained, for common items, failure means no estimate, and for rare items, success means an estimate of 50% to 150% (2d6+3 times 10%).

Dwarves have a +2 racial bonus on Appraise checks that are related to rare or exotic items because they are familiar with valuable items of all kinds (especially those made of stone or metal).

BALANCE (Dex; Armor Check Penalty)

You can keep your balance while walking on a tightrope, a narrow beam, a ledge, or an uneven floor.

Check: You can walk on a precarious surface as a move-equivalent action. A successful check lets you move at half your speed along the surface for 1 round. A failure means that you can't move for 1 round. A failure by 5 or more means that you fall. The difficulty varies with the surface:

Surface	DC	Surface	DC
7–12 inches wide	10	Uneven floor	10
2–6 inches wide	15	Surface angled	+5*
Less than 2 inches wide	20	Surface slippery	+5*
*Cumulative; if both apply, use both.			

Being Attacked while Walking a Tightrope: Attacks against you are made as if you were off balance: They gain a +2 attack bonus, and you lose your Dexterity bonus to AC, if any. If you have 5 or more ranks in Balance, then you can retain your Dexterity bonus to AC (if any) in the face of attacks. If you take damage, you must make a check again to stay on the tightrope.

Accelerated Movement: You try to can walk a precarious surface more quickly than normal. If you accept a –5 penalty, you can move your full speed as a move-equivalent action. (Moving twice your speed in a round requires two checks.)

Special: If you have 5 or more ranks in Tumble, you get a +2 synergy bonus on Balance checks.

BLUFF (Cha)

You can make the outrageous or the untrue seem plausible. The skill encompasses acting, conning, fast talking, misdirection, prevarication, and misleading body language. Use a bluff to sow temporary confusion, get someone to turn his head to look where you point, or simply look innocuous.

Check: A Bluff check is opposed by the target's Sense Motive check. Favorable and unfavorable circumstances weigh heavily on the outcome of a bluff. Two circumstances can weigh against you: The bluff is hard to believe, or the action that the target is to take goes against the target's self-interest, nature, personality, orders, etc. If it's important, the DM can distinguish between a bluff that fails because the target doesn't believe it and one that fails because it just asks too much of the target. For instance, if the target gets a +10 bonus because the bluff demands something risky of the target, and the Sense Motive check succeeds by 10 or less, then the target didn't so much see through the bluff as prove reluctant to go along with it. If the target succeeds by 11 or more, he has seen through the bluff (and would have done so even if it had not entailed any demand on him).

A successful Bluff check indicates that the target reacts as you wish, at least for a short time (usually 1 round or less) or believes something that you want him to believe. Bluff, however, is not a *suggestion* spell. For example, you could use a bluff to put someone off guard by telling him his shoes are untied. At best, such a bluff would make the target glance down at his shoes. It would not cause the target to ignore you and fiddle with his shoes.

A bluff requires interaction between the character and the target. Creatures unaware of the character cannot be bluffed. A bluff always takes at least 1 round (and is at least a full-round action) but can take much longer if you try something elaborate.

Feinting in Combat: You can also use Bluff to mislead an opponent in combat so that he can't dodge your attack effectively. Doing so is a miscellaneous standard action that does not draw an attack of opportunity. If you are successful, the next attack you make against the target does not

BLUFF CHECK

Example Circumstances	Sense Motive Modifier
The target wants to believe you.	–5
"These emeralds aren't stolen. I'm just desperate for coin right now, so I'm offering them to you cheap."	
The bluff is believable and doesn't affect the target much.	+0
"I don't know what you're talking about, sir. I'm just a simple peasant girl here for the fair."	
The bluff is a little hard to believe or puts the target at some risk.	+5
"You orcs want to fight? I'll take you all on myself. I don't need my friends' help. Just don't get your blood all over my new surcoat."	
The bluff is hard to believe or entails a large risk for the target.	+10
"This diadem doesn't belong to the duchess. It just looks like hers. Trust me, I wouldn't sell you jewelry that would get you hanged, would I?"	
The bluff is way out there; it's almost too incredible to consider.	+20
"You might find this hard to believe, but I'm actually a lammasu who's been polymorphed into halfling form by an evil sorcerer. You know we lammasu are trustworthy, so you can believe me."	

allow him to use his Dexterity bonus to Armor Class (if any). Feinting in this way against a nonhumanoid is difficult because it's harder to read a strange creature's body language; you suffer a –4 penalty. Against a creature of animal Intelligence (1 or 2) it's even harder; you suffer a –8 penalty. Against a nonintelligent creature, it's impossible.

Creating a Diversion to Hide: You can use Bluff to help you hide. A successful Bluff check can give you the momentary diversion you need to attempt a Hide check (page 69) while people are aware of you.

Retry: Generally, a failed Bluff check makes the target too suspicious for a bluffer to try another one in the same circumstances. For feinting in combat, you may retry freely.

Special: Having 5 or more ranks in Bluff gives you a +2 synergy bonus on Intimidate and Pick Pocket checks and a +2 synergy bonus on an Innuendo check to transmit a message. Also, if you have 5 or more ranks of Bluff, you get a +2 synergy bonus on Disguise checks when you know that you're being observed and you try to act in character.

A ranger gains a bonus on Bluff checks when using this skill against a favored enemy (page 45).

CLIMB
(Str; Armor Check Penalty)

Use this skill to scale a cliff, to get to the window on the second story of a wizard's tower, or to climb out of a pit after falling through a trapdoor.

Check: With each successful Climb check, you can advance up, down, or across a slope or a wall or other steep incline (or even a ceiling with handholds) one-half your speed as a miscellaneous full-round action.

Krusk helps Jozan climb the cliff.

You can move half that far, one-fourth of your speed, as a miscellaneous move-equivalent action. A slope is considered to be any incline of less than 60 degrees; a wall is any incline of 60 degrees or steeper.

A failed Climb check means that you make no progress, and a check that fails by 5 or more means that you fall from whatever height you have already attained.

A climber's kit (page 110) gives a +2 circumstance bonus to Climb checks.

The DC of the check depends on the conditions of the climb.

DC	Example Wall or Surface
0	A slope too steep to walk up. A knotted rope with a wall to brace against.
5	A rope with a wall to brace against, or a knotted rope, or a rope affected by the *rope trick* spell.
10	A surface with ledges to hold on to and stand on, such as a very rough wall or a ship's rigging.
15	Any surface with adequate handholds and footholds (natural or artificial), such as a very rough natural rock surface or a tree. An unknotted rope.
20	An uneven surface with some narrow handholds and footholds, such as a typical wall in a dungeon or ruins.
25	A rough surface, such as a natural rock wall or a brick wall.
25	Overhang or ceiling with handholds but no footholds.
—	A perfectly smooth, flat, vertical surface cannot be climbed.
–10*	Climbing a chimney (artificial or natural) or other location where one can brace against two opposite walls (reduces DC by 10).
–5*	Climbing a corner where you can brace against perpendicular walls (reduces DC by 5).
+5*	Surface is slippery (increases DC by 5).

*These modifiers are cumulative; use any that apply.

Since you can't move to avoid a blow while climbing, enemies can attack you as if you were stunned: An attacker gets a +2 bonus, and you lose any Dexterity bonus to Armor Class. You also can't use a shield.

Any time you take damage while climbing, make a Climb check against the DC of the slope or wall. Failure means you fall from your current height and sustain the appropriate falling damage. (The DUNGEON MASTER'S GUIDE has information on falling damage.)

Accelerated Climbing: You try to climb more quickly than normal. As a miscellaneous full-round action, you can attempt to cover your full speed in climbing distance, but you suffer a –5 penalty on Climb checks and you must make two checks each round. Each successful check allows you to climb a distance equal to one-half your speed. By accepting the –5 penalty, you can move this far as a move-equivalent action rather than as a full-round action.

Making Your Own Handholds and Footholds: You can make your own handholds and footholds by pounding pitons into a wall. Doing so takes 1 minute per piton, and one piton is needed per 3 feet. As with any surface with handholds and footholds, a wall with pitons in it has a DC of 15. In the same way, a climber with a hand-axe or similar implement can cut holds in an ice wall.

Catching Yourself When Falling: It's practically impossible to catch yourself on a wall while falling. Make a Climb check (DC = wall's DC + 20) to do so. A slope is a lot easier to catch yourself on (DC = slope's DC + 10).

Special: A character with 5 or more ranks in Use Rope gets a +2 synergy bonus on checks to climb a rope, a knotted rope, or a rope and wall combination.

Someone using a rope can haul a character upward (or lower the character) through sheer strength. Use double your maximum load (see Carrying Capacity, page 141) to determine how much a character can lift.

Halflings get a +2 racial bonus on Climb checks because they are agile and surefooted.

CONCENTRATION (Con)

You are particularly good at focusing your mind.

Check: You can make a Concentration check to cast a spell despite distractions, such as taking damage, getting hit by an unfriendly spell, and so on. You can also use this skill to maintain concentration in the face of other distractions or on other things besides spells, such as eavesdropping on a conversation despite distractions from other people.

The table below summarizes various types of distractions that cause you to make a Concentration check while casting a spell. "Spell level" refers to the level of the spell you're trying to cast. (See Concentration, page 151, for more information.)

DC	Distraction
10 + damage dealt + spell level	Injury or failed saving throw during the casting of a spell (for spells with a casting time of 1 full round or more) or injury by an attack of opportunity or readied attack made in response to the spell being cast (for spells with a casting time of 1 action). (See Distracting Spellcasters, page 134.)
10 + half of continuous damage last dealt + spell level	Suffering continuous damage (such as from *Melf's acid arrow*).
10 + damage dealt + spell level	Damaged by spell.
Distracting spell's save DC + spell level	Distracted by nondamaging spell. (If the spell allows no save, use the save DC it would have if it did allow a save.)
20 + spell level	Grappling or pinned. (Can only cast spells without somatic components and whose material component is in hand.)
10 + spell level	Vigorous motion (on a moving mount, bouncy wagon ride, small boat in rough water, belowdecks in a storm-tossed ship).
15 + spell level	Violent motion (galloping horse, very rough wagon ride, small boat in rapids, on deck of storm-tossed ship).
20 + spell level	Affected by *earthquake* spell.
5 + spell level	Weather is a high wind carrying blinding rain or sleet.
10 + spell level	Weather is wind-driven hail, dust, or debris.
Distracting spell's save DC + spell level	Weather caused by spell, such as *storm of vengeance* (same as distracted by nondamaging spell).
15 + spell level	Casting defensively (so as not to provoke attacks of opportunity).
15	Caster entangled by *animate rope* spell, *command plants* spell, *control plants* spell, *entangle* spell, *snare* spell, net, or tanglefoot bag.

Retry: Yes, though a success doesn't cancel the effects of a previous failure, which almost always is the loss of the spell being cast or the disruption of a spell being concentrated on.

Special: A character with the Combat Casting feat gets a +4 bonus to Concentration checks made to cast a spell while on the defensive (see page 125).

CRAFT (Int)

You are trained in a craft, trade, or art, such as armorsmithing, basketweaving, bookbinding, bowmaking, blacksmithing, calligraphy, carpentry, cobbling, gemcutting, leatherworking, locksmithing, painting, pottery, sculpture, shipmaking, stonemasonry, trapmaking, weaponsmithing, or weaving.

Craft is actually a number of separate skills. For instance, you could have the skill Craft (trapmaking). Your ranks in that skill don't affect any checks you happen to make for pottery or leatherworking, for example. You could have several Craft skills, each with its own ranks, each purchased as a separate skill.

A Craft skill is specifically focused on creating something; if it is not, it is a Profession (page 72).

Check: You can practice your trade and make a decent living, earning about half your check result in gold pieces per week of dedicated work. You know how to use the tools of your trade, how to perform the craft's daily tasks, how to supervise untrained helpers, and how to handle common problems. (Untrained laborers and assistants earn an average of 1 silver piece per day.)

However, the basic function of the Craft skill is to allow you to make an item of the appropriate type. The DC depends on the difficulty of the item created. The DC, your check results, and the price of the item determine how long it takes to make the item. The item's finished price also determines the cost of raw materials. (In the game world, it is the skill level required, the time required, and the raw materials required that determine an item's price. That's why the item's price and DC determine how long it takes to make the item and the cost of the raw materials.)

In some cases, the *fabricate* spell (page 202) can be used to achieve the results of a Craft check without your needing to make the check. However, you must make an appropriate Craft check when using the spell to make articles requiring a high degree of craftsmanship (jewelry, swords, glass, crystal, etc.).

A Craft check related to woodworking in conjunction with the casting of the *ironwood* spell (page 218) enables you to make wooden items that have the strength of steel.

When casting the spell *minor creation* (page 228), you must succeed at an appropriate Craft check to make a complex item, such as a Craft (bowmaking) check to make straight arrow shafts.

All crafts require artisan's tools (page 110) to give the best chance of success; if improvised tools are used instead, the check is made with a –2 circumstance penalty. On the other hand, masterwork artisan's tools provide a +2 circumstance bonus.

To determine how much time and money it takes to make an item:

1. Find the item's price in Chapter 7: Equipment or the Dungeon Master's Guide, or have the DM set the price for an item not listed. Put the price in silver pieces (1 gp = 10 sp).
2. Find the DC listed here or have the DM set one.
3. Pay one-third the item's price in raw materials.
4. Make a skill check representing one week's work.

If the check succeeds, multiply the check result by the DC. If the result × the DC equals the price of the item in sp, then you have completed the item. (If the result × the DC equals double or triple the price of the item in silver pieces, then you've completed the task in one-half or one-third the time, and so on.) If the result × the DC doesn't equal the price, then it represents progress you've made this week. Record the result and make a check for the next week. Each week you make more progress until your total reaches the price of the item in silver pieces.

If you fail the check, you make no progress this week. If you fail by 5 or more, you ruin half the raw materials and have to pay half the original raw material cost again.

Progress by the Day: You can make checks by the day instead of by the week, in which case your progress (result × DC) is in copper pieces instead of silver pieces.

Creating Masterwork Items: You can make a masterwork item (an item that conveys a bonus to its use through its exceptional craftsmanship, not through being magical). To create a masterwork version of an item on the table below, you create the masterwork component as if it were a separate item in addition to the standard item. The masterwork component has its own price (300 gp for a weapon or 150 gp for a suit of armor) and DC (20). Once both the standard component and the masterwork component are completed,

the masterwork item is finished. (Note: The price you pay for the masterwork component is one-third of the given amount, just as it is for the price in raw materials.)

Repairing Items: Generally, you can repair an item at the same DC that it takes to make it in the first place. The cost of repairing an item is one-fifth the item's price.

Item	Craft	DC
Armor, shield	Armorsmith	10 + AC bonus
Longbow, shortbow	Bowmaking	12
Composite longbow, composite shortbow	Bowmaking	15
Mighty bow	Bowmaking	15 +2/Str bonus
Crossbow	Weaponsmith	15
Simple melee or thrown weapon	Weaponsmith	12
Martial melee or thrown weapon	Weaponsmith	15
Exotic melee or thrown weapon	Weaponsmith	18
Very simple item (wooden spoon)	Varies	5
Typical item (iron pot)	Varies	10
High-quality item (bell)	Varies	15
Complex or superior item (lock)	Varies	20

Retry: Yes, but each time you miss by 5 or more, you ruin half the raw materials and have to pay half the original raw material cost again.

Special: Dwarves have a +2 racial bonus on Craft checks that are related to stone or metal, because dwarves are especially capable with stonework and metalwork.

DECIPHER SCRIPT
(Int; Trained Only; Bard, Rogue Only)
Use this skill to piece together the meaning of ancient runes carved into the wall of an abandoned temple, to get the gist of an intercepted letter written in the Infernal language, to follow the directions on a treasure map written in a forgotten alphabet, or to interpret the mysterious glyphs painted on a cave wall.

Check: You can decipher writing in an unfamiliar language or a message written in an incomplete or archaic form. The base DC is 20 for the simplest messages, 25 for standard texts, and 30 or higher for intricate, exotic, or very old writing.

If the check succeeds, you understand the general content of a piece of writing, reading about one single page of text (or its equivalent) in 1 minute. If the check fails, the DM makes a Wisdom check (DC 5) for you to see if you avoid drawing a false conclusion about the text. (Success means that you do not draw a false conclusion; failure means that you do.)

The DM secretly makes both the skill check and (if necessary) the Wisdom check so you can't tell whether the conclusion you draw is true or false.

Retry: No.

Special: If you have 5 or more ranks in Decipher Script, you get a +2 synergy bonus on Use Magic Device checks related to scrolls.

DIPLOMACY (Cha)
Use this skill to persuade the chamberlain to let you see the king, to negotiate peace between feuding barbarian tribes, or to convince the ogre mages that have captured you that they should ransom you back to your friends instead of twisting your limbs off one by one. Diplomacy includes etiquette, social grace, tact, subtlety, and a way with words. A skilled character knows the formal and informal rules of conduct, social expectations, proper forms of address, and so on. This skill represents the ability to give others the right impression of oneself, to negotiate effectively, and to influence others.

Check: You can change others' attitudes with a successful check. (The Dungeon Master's Guide has rules for influencing NPCs.) In negotiations, participants roll opposed Diplomacy checks to see who gains the advantage. Opposed checks also resolve cases when two advocates or diplomats plead opposite cases in a hearing before a third party.

Retry: Generally, retries do not work. Even if the initial check succeeds, the other character can only be persuaded so far, and a retry may do more harm than good. If the initial check fails, the other character has probably become more firmly committed to his position, and a retry is futile.

Special: Charisma checks to influence NPCs are generally untrained Diplomacy checks.

If you have 5 or more ranks in Bluff or Sense Motive, you get a +2 synergy bonus on Diplomacy checks. These bonuses stack.

DISABLE DEVICE (Int; Trained Only)

Use this skill to disarm a trap, jam a lock (in either the open or closed position), or rig a wagon wheel to fall off. You can examine a fairly simple or fairly small mechanical device and disable it. The effort requires at least a simple tool of the appropriate sort (a pick, pry bar, saw, file, etc.). Attempting a Disable Device check without a set of thieves' tools (page 111) carries a −2 circumstance penalty, even if a simple tool is employed. The use of masterwork thieves' tools enables you to make the check with a +2 circumstance bonus.

Check: The DM makes the Disable Device check so that you don't necessarily know whether you've succeeded. The amount of time needed to make a check and the DC for the check depend on how tricky the device is. Disabling a simple device takes 1 round (and is at least a full-round action). Intricate or complex devices require 2d4 rounds. You also can rig simple devices such as saddles or wagon wheels to work normally for a while and then fail or fall off some time later (usually after 1d4 rounds or minutes of use).

Disabling (or rigging or jamming) a fairly simple device has a DC of 10. More intricate and complex devices have a higher DC. The DM rolls the check. If the check succeeds, you disable the device. If the check fails by up to 4, you have failed but can try again. If you fail by 5 or more, something goes wrong. If it's a trap, you spring it. If it's some sort of sabotage, you think the device is disabled, but it still works normally.

Device	Time	DC*	Example
Simple	1 round	10	Jam a lock
Tricky	1d4 rounds	15	Sabotage a wagon wheel
Difficult	2d4 rounds	20	Disarm a trap, reset a trap
Wicked	2d4 rounds	25	Disarm a complex trap, cleverly sabotage a clockwork device

*If the character attempts to leave behind no trace of the tampering, add 5 to the DC.

Retry: Yes, though you must be aware that you have failed in order to try again.

Special: Rogues (and only rogues) can disarm magic traps. A magic trap generally has a DC of 25 + the level of the magic used to create it. For instance, disarming a trap set by the casting of *explosive runes* has a DC of 28 because *explosive runes* is a 3rd-level spell.

The spells *fire trap*, *glyph of warding*, *symbol*, and *teleportation circle* also create traps that a rogue can disarm with a Disable Device check. *Spike growth* and *spike stones*, however, create magic traps against which Disable Device checks do not succeed. See the individual spell descriptions in Chapter 11: Spells for details.

A rogue who beats a trap's DC by 10 or more can generally study a trap, figure out how it works, and bypass it (along with his companions) without disarming it.

DISGUISE (Cha)

Use this skill to change your appearance or someone else's. The effort requires at least a few props, some makeup, and 1d3 × 10 minutes of work. The use of a disguise kit (page 110) provides a +2 circumstance bonus to a Disguise check. A disguise can include an apparent change of height or weight of no more than one-tenth the original.

You can also impersonate people, either individuals or types, so that, for example, you might, with little or no actual disguise, make yourself seem like a traveler even if you're a local.

Check: Your Disguise check result determines how good the disguise is, and it is opposed by others' Spot check results. Make one Disguise check even if several people make Spot checks. The DM makes your Disguise check secretly so that you're not sure how good it is.

If you don't draw any attention to yourself, however, others do not get to make Spot checks. If you come to the attention of people who are suspicious (such as a guard who is watching commoners walking through a city gate), the DM can assume that such observers are taking 10 on their Spot checks.

The effectiveness of your disguise depends in part on how much you're attempting to change your appearance:

Disguise	Modifier
Minor details only	+5
Disguised as different sex	−2
Disguised as different race	−2
Disguised as different age category	−2*
Disguised as specific class	−2

*Per step of difference between character's actual age category and disguised age category (young [younger than adulthood], adulthood, middle age, old, venerable).

If you are impersonating a particular individual, those who know what that person looks like get a bonus on their Spot checks (and are automatically considered to be suspicious of you, so opposed checks are always invoked).

Familiarity	Bonus
Recognizes on sight	+4
Friends or associates	+6
Close friends	+8
Intimate	+10

Usually, an individual makes a check for detection immediately upon meeting you and each hour thereafter. If you casually meet many different creatures, each for a short time, check once per day or hour, using an average Spot bonus for the group. For example, if a character is trying to pass for a merchant at a bazaar, the DM can make one Spot check per hour for the people she encounters using a +1 bonus on the check to represent the average of the crowd (most people with no Spot ranks and a few with good Spot skills).

Retry: A character may try to redo a failed disguise, but once others know that a disguise was attempted they'll be more suspicious.

Special: If you have 5 or more ranks of Bluff, you get a +2 synergy bonus on Disguise checks when you know that you're being observed and you try to act in character.

Magic that alters the recipient's form, such as *alter self*, *change self*, *polymorph other*, or *shapechange*, grants the disguised individual a +10 bonus on her Disguise check (see the individual spell descriptions in Chapter 11: Spells). You must succeed at a Disguise check with a +10 bonus to duplicate the appearance of a specific individual using the *veil* spell. Divination magic that sees through illusions, such as *true seeing*, does not see through a mundane disguise, but can see through the magical component of a magically enhanced one.

You must make a Disguise check when you cast a *simulacrum* spell (page 252) to determine how good the likeness is.

ESCAPE ARTIST (Dex; Armor Check Penalty)

Use this skill to slip bonds or manacles, wriggle through tight spaces, or escape the grip of a monster that ensnares you, such as a roper.

Check: Making a check to escape from being bound up by ropes, manacles, or other restraints (except a grappler) requires 1 minute of work. Escaping a net or *entangle* spell is a full-round action. Squeezing through a tight space takes at least 1 minute, maybe longer, depending on how long the space is.

Restraint	DC
Ropes	Binder's Use Rope check at +20
Net, *animate rope* spell, *command plants* spell, *control plants* spell, or *entangle* spell	20
Snare spell	23
Manacles	30
Tight space	30
Masterwork manacles	35
Grappler	Grappler's grapple check

Ropes: Your Escape Artist check is opposed by the binder's Use Rope check. Since it's easier to tie someone up than to escape from being tied up, the binder gets a special +10 bonus on her check.

Manacles and Masterwork Manacles: Manacles have a DC set by their construction.

Net or Spell: Escaping from a net or an *animate rope, command plants, control plants,* or *entangle* spell is a full-round action.

Tight Space: This is the DC for getting through a space where one's head fits but one's shoulders don't. If the space is long, such as in a chimney, the DM may call for multiple checks. You can't fit through a space that your head does not fit through.

Grappler: You can make an Escape Artist check opposed by your enemy's grapple check to get out of a grapple or out of a pinned condition (so that you're just being grappled). Doing so is a standard action, so if you escape the grapple you can move in the same round. See "Wriggle Free" under Other Grappling Options, page 138.

Retry: You can make another check after a failed check if you're squeezing your way through a tight space, making multiple checks. If the situation permits, you can make additional checks or even take 20 as long as you're not being actively opposed.

Special: A character with 5 or more ranks of Use Rope gets a +2 synergy bonus on Escape Artist checks when escaping from rope bonds.

FORGERY (Int)

Use this skill to fake a written order from the duchess instructing a jailer to release prisoners, to create an authentic-looking treasure map, or to detect forgeries that others try to pass off.

Check: Forgery requires writing materials appropriate to the document being forged, enough light to write by, wax for seals (if appropriate), and some time. Forging a very short and simple document takes about 1 minute. Longer or more complex documents take 1d4 minutes per page. To forge a document on which the handwriting is not specific to a person (military orders, a government decree, a business ledger, or the like), the character needs only to have seen a similar document before and gains a +8 bonus on the roll. To forge a signature, an autograph of that person to copy is needed, and the character gains a +4 bonus on the roll. To forge a longer document written in the hand of some particular person, a large sample of that person's handwriting is needed.

The DM makes your check secretly so you're not sure how good your forgery is. As with Disguise, you don't even need to make a check until someone examines the work. This Forgery check is opposed by the person who examines the document to check its authenticity. That person makes a Forgery check opposed to the forger's. The reader gains bonuses or penalties to his or her check as described in the table below.

Condition	Reader's Check Modifier
Type of document unknown to reader	–2
Type of document somewhat known to reader	+0
Type of document well known to reader	+2
Handwriting not known to reader	–2
Handwriting somewhat known to reader	+0
Handwriting intimately known to reader	+2
Reader only casually reviews the document	–2

As with Bluff, a document that contradicts procedure, orders, or previous knowledge or one that requires sacrifice on the part of the person checking the document can increase that character's suspicion (and thus create favorable circumstances for the checker's opposing Forgery check).

Retry: Usually, no. A retry is never possible after a particular reader detects a particular forgery. But the document created by the forger might still fool someone else. The result of a Forgery check for a particular document must be used for every instance of a different reader examining the document. No reader can attempt to detect a particular forgery more than once; if that one opposed check goes in favor of the forger, then the reader can't try using his own skill again, even if he's suspicious about the document.

Special: To forge documents and detect forgeries, one must be able to read and write the language in question. (The skill is language-dependent.) Barbarians can't learn the Forgery skill unless they have learned to read and write.

GATHER INFORMATION (Cha)

Use this skill for making contacts in an area, finding out local gossip, rumormongering, and collecting general information.

Check: By succeeding at a skill check (DC 10), given an evening with a few gold pieces to use for making friends by buying drinks and such, you can get a general idea of what the major news items are in a city, assuming no obvious reasons exist why the information would be withheld (such as if you are an elf hanging out in an orc city, or if you can't speak the local language). The higher the check result, the better the information.

If you want to find out about a specific rumor ("Which way to the ruined temple of Erythnul?"), specific item ("What can you tell me about that pretty sword the captain of the guard walks around with?"), obtain a map, or do something else along those lines, the DC is 15 to 25 or higher.

Retry: Yes, but it takes an evening or so for each check, and characters may draw attention to themselves if they repeatedly pursue a certain type of information.

HANDLE ANIMAL (Cha; Trained Only)

Use this skill to drive a team of horses pulling a wagon over rough terrain, to teach a dog to guard, to raise an owlbear chick as a devoted pet, or to teach a tyrannosaur to "speak" on your command.

Check: The time required to get an effect and the DC depend on what you are trying to do.

Task	Time	DC
Handle a domestic animal	Varies	10
"Push" a domestic animal	Varies	15
Teach an animal tasks	2 months	15
Teach an animal unusual tasks	2 months	20
Rear a wild animal	1 year	15 + HD of animal
Rear a beast	1 year	20 + HD of beast
Train a wild animal	2 months	20 + HD of animal
Train a beast	2 months	25 + HD of beast

Time: For a task with a specific time frame, you must spend half this time (at the rate of 3 hours per day per animal being handled) working toward completion of the task before you make the skill check. If the check fails, you can't teach, rear, or train that animal. If the check succeeds, you must invest the remainder of the time before the teaching, rearing, or training is complete. If the time is interrupted or the task is not followed through to completion, any further attempts to teach, rear, or train the same animal automatically fail.

Handle a Domestic Animal: This means to command a trained dog, to drive beasts of labor, to tend to tired horses, and so forth.

"Push" a Domestic Animal: To push a domestic animal means to get more out of it than it usually gives, such as commanding a poorly trained dog or driving draft animals for extra effort.

Teach an Animal Tasks: This means to teach a domestic animal some tricks. You can train one type of animal per rank (chosen when the ranks are purchased) to obey commands and perform simple tricks. Animals commonly trained include dogs, horses, mules, oxen, falcons, and pigeons. You can work with up to three animals at one time, and you can teach them general tasks such as guarding, attacking, carrying riders, performing heavy labor, hunting and tracking, or fighting beside troops. An animal can be trained for one general purpose only.

Teach an Animal Unusual Tasks: This is similar to teaching an animal tasks, except that the tasks can be something unusual for that breed of animal, such as training a dog to be a riding animal. Alternatively, you can use this aspect of Handle Animal to train an animal to perform specialized tricks, such as teaching a horse to rear on command or come when whistled for or teaching a falcon to pluck objects from someone's grasp. Training a mount to *air walk* (page 172) counts as teaching it an unusual task.

You can teach simple tricks ("Sit," "Stay," etc.) to an animal that is the subject of an *animal friendship* spell without needing to make a skill check, but a complex trick, such as accepting a rider, requires the Handle Animal skill.

Rear a Wild Animal or a Beast: To rear an animal or beast means to raise a wild creature from infancy so that it is domesticated. A handler can rear up to three creatures of the same type at once. A successfully domesticated animal or beast can be taught tricks at the same time that it's being raised, or can be taught as a domesticated animal later.

Train a Wild Animal and *Train a Beast* mean train a wild creature to do certain tricks, but only at the character's command. The creature is still wild, though usually controllable.

Retry: For handling and pushing domestic animals, yes. For training and rearing, no.

Special: A character with 5 or more ranks of Animal Empathy gets a +2 synergy bonus on Handle Animal checks with animals. A character must have 9 or more ranks of Animal Empathy to get the same +2 synergy bonus on Handle Animal checks with beasts.

A character with 5 or more ranks of Handle Animal gets a +2 synergy bonus on Ride checks.

An untrained character can use a Charisma check to handle and push animals.

HEAL (Wis)

Use this skill to keep a badly wounded friend from dying, to help others recover faster from wounds, to keep your friend from succumbing to a wyvern's sting, or to treat disease.

Check: The DC and effect depend on the task you attempt.

Task	DC
First aid	15
Long-term care	15
Treat caltrop wound	15
Treat poison	Poison's DC
Treat disease	Disease's DC

First Aid: First aid usually means saving a dying character. If a character has negative hit points and is losing hit points (at 1 per round, 1 per hour, or 1 per day), you can make her stable. The character regains no hit points, but she does stop losing them. The check is a standard action. (See Dying, page 129.)

Long-term Care: Providing long-term care means treating a wounded person for a day or more. If successful, you let the patient recover hit points or ability score points (lost to temporary damage) at twice the normal rate: 2 hit points per level for each day of light activity, 3 hit points per level for each day of complete rest, and 2 ability score points per day. You can tend up to six patients at a time. You need a few items and supplies (bandages, salves, and so on) that are easy to come by in settled lands.

Giving long-term care counts as light activity for the healer. You cannot give long-term care to yourself.

A healer's kit (page 110) gives a +2 circumstance bonus to Heal checks.

Treat Wound from Caltrop, Spike Growth, or Spike Stones: A creature wounded by stepping on a caltrop has its speed reduced to one-half of normal. A successful Heal check removes this movement penalty. Treating a caltrop wound is a standard action.

A creature wounded by a *spike growth* or *spike stones* spell must succeed at a Reflex save or take injuries that slow his speed by one-third. Another character can remove this penalty by taking 10 minutes to dress the victim's injuries and succeeding at a Heal check against the spell's save DC.

Treat Poison: To treat poison means to tend a single character who has been poisoned and who is going to take more damage from the poison (or suffer some other effect). Every time the poisoned character makes a saving throw against the poison, you make a Heal check. The poisoned character uses your result in place of her saving throw if your Heal result is higher.

Treat Disease: To treat a disease means to tend a diseased character. Every time the diseased character makes a saving throw against disease effects, you make a Heal check. The diseased character uses your result in place of his or her saving throw if your Heal result is higher.

Special: If you have 5 or more ranks in Profession (herbalist), you get a +2 synergy bonus on Heal checks.

HIDE (Dex; Armor Check Penalty)

Use this skill to sink back into the shadows and proceed unseen, to approach a wizard's tower under cover of brush, or to tail someone through a busy street without being noticed.

Check: Your Hide check is opposed by the Spot check of anyone who might see you. You can move up to one-half your normal speed and hide at no penalty. At more than one-half and up to your full speed, you suffer a –5 penalty. It's practically impossible (–20 penalty) to hide while running or charging.

For example, Lidda has a speed of 20 feet. If she doesn't want to take a penalty on her Hide check, she can move only 10 feet as a move-equivalent action (and thus 20 feet in a round).

Larger and smaller creatures get size bonuses and size penalties on Hide checks: Fine +16, Diminutive +12, Tiny +8, Small +4, Large –4, Huge –8, Gargantuan –12, Colossal –16.

If people are observing you, even casually, you can't hide. You can run around a corner or something so that you're out of sight and then hide, but the others then know at least where you went. If your observers are momentarily distracted (as by a Bluff check; see below), though, you can attempt to hide. While the others turn their attention from you, you can attempt a Hide check if you can get to a hiding place of some kind. (As a general guideline, the hiding place has to be within 1 foot per rank you have in Hide.) This check, however, is at –10 because you have to move fast.

Creating a Diversion to Hide: You can use Bluff (page 64) to help you hide. A successful Bluff check can give you the momentary diversion you need to attempt a Hide check while people are aware of you.

INNUENDO (Wis; Trained Only)

You know how to give and understand secret messages while appearing to be speaking about other things. Two rogues, for example, might seem to be talking about bakery goods when they're really planning how to break into the evil wizard's laboratory.

Check: You can get a message across to another character with the Innuendo skill. The DC for a basic message is 10. The DC is 15 or 20 for complex messages, especially those that rely on getting across new information. Also, the character can try to discern the hidden message in a conversation between two other characters who are using this skill. The DC is the skill check of the character using Innuendo, and for each piece of information that the eavesdropper is missing, that character suffers a –2 penalty on the check. For example, if a character eavesdrops on people planning to assassinate a visiting diplomat, the eavesdropper suffers a –2 penalty if he doesn't know about the diplomat. Whether trying to send or intercept a message, a failure by 5 or more points means that some false information has been implied or inferred.

The DM makes your Innuendo check secretly so that you don't necessarily know whether you were successful.

Retry: Generally, retries are allowed when trying to send a message, but not when receiving or intercepting one. Each retry carries the chance of miscommunication.

Special: If you have 5 or more ranks in Bluff, you get a +2 synergy bonus on your check to transmit (but not receive) a message. If you have 5 or more ranks in Sense Motive, you get a +2 synergy bonus on your check to receive or intercept (but not transmit) a message.

INTIMIDATE (Cha)

Use this skill to get a bully to back down or to make a prisoner give you the information you want. Intimidation includes verbal threats and body language.

Check: You can change others' behavior with a successful check. The DC is typically 10 + the target's Hit Dice. Any bonuses that a target may have on saving throws against fear increase the DC.

Retry: Generally, retries do not work. Even if the initial check succeeds, the other character can only be intimidated so far, and a retry doesn't help. If the initial check fails, the other character has probably become more firmly resolved to resist the intimidator, and a retry is futile.

Special: If you have 5 or more ranks in Bluff , you get a +2 synergy bonus on Intimidate checks.

INTUIT DIRECTION (Wis; Trained Only)

You have an innate sense of direction.

Check: By concentrating for 1 minute, you can determine where true north lies in relation to yourself (DC 15). If the check fails, you cannot determine direction. On a natural roll of 1, you err and mistakenly identify a random direction as true north.

The DM makes your check secretly so that you don't know whether you rolled a successful result or a 1.

Retry: You can use Intuit Direction once per day. The roll represents how sensitive to direction you are that day.

Special: Untrained characters can't use an innate sense of direction, but they could determine direction by finding clues.

JUMP (Str; Armor Check Penalty)

Use this skill to leap over pits, vault low fences, or reach a tree's lowest branches.

Check: You jump a minimum distance plus an additional distance depending on the amount by which your Jump check result exceeds 10. The maximum distance of any jump is a function of your height.

Type of Jump	Minimum Distance	Additional Distance	Maximum Distance
Running jump*	5 ft.	+1 ft./1 point above 10	Height × 6
Standing jump	3 ft.	+1 ft./2 points above 10	Height × 2
Running high jump*	2 ft.	+1 ft./4 points above 10	Height × 1 1/2
Standing high jump	2 ft.	+1 ft./8 points above 10	Height
Jump back	1 ft.	+1 ft./8 points above 10	Height

*You must move 20 feet before jumping. A character can't take a running jump in heavy armor.

The distances listed are for characters with speeds of 30 feet. If you have a lower speed (from armor, encumbrance, or weight carried, for instance), reduce the distance jumped proportionally. If you have a higher speed (because you're a barbarian or an experienced monk, for instance), increase the distance jumped proportionally.

For example, Krusk the barbarian has a Jump skill modifier of +2 (no ranks, +3 Strength bonus, –1 armor check penalty) and a base speed of 40 feet. He attempts a running jump across a 10-foot wide chasm, and his player rolls an 11 for a result of 13. That's 3 over 10, so he clears 3 feet more than the minimum distance, or 8 feet. Also, his base speed is one-third higher than normal (40 feet instead of 30 feet), so his jumping distance is likewise one-third greater. Adding one-third of 8 feet to 8 feet yields another 2 feet, 8 inches, for a total of 10 feet, 8 inches. Krusk clears the chasm by 8 inches.

Distance moved by jumping is counted against maximum movement in a round normally. For example, Krusk runs 20 feet toward the chasm, leaps 10 feet over it, and then moves an additional 10 feet to be next to a hobgoblin. He can now attack the hobgoblin, since he can move 40 feet and make an attack in the same round.

If you intentionally jump down from a height, you might take less damage than if you just fall. If you succeed at a Jump check (DC 15), you take damage as if you had fallen 10 feet less than you actually did.

Special: If you have 5 or more ranks in Tumble, you get a +2 synergy bonus on Jump checks.

The spell *expeditious retreat* doubles both your speed and your maximum jumping distances. These increases count as enhancement bonuses.

The subject of a *jump* spell gets a +30 bonus on Jump checks and does not have the usual maximums for jumping distance. For leaps of maximum horizontal distance, the jump reaches its peak (one-fourth the horizontal distance) at the halfway point.

A character who has the Run feat and who makes a running jump increases the distance or height he clears by one-fourth, but not past the maximum.

Halflings get a +2 racial bonus on Jump checks because they are agile and athletic.

KNOWLEDGE (Int; Trained Only)

Like the Craft and Profession skills, Knowledge actually encompasses a number of unrelated skills. Knowledge represents a study of some body of lore, possibly an academic or even scientific discipline. Below are typical fields of study. With your DM's approval, you can invent new areas of knowledge.

- Arcana (ancient mysteries, magic traditions, arcane symbols, cryptic phrases)
- Architecture and engineering (buildings, aqueducts, bridges, fortifications)
- Geography (lands, terrain, climate, people, customs)
- History (royalty, wars, colonies, migrations, founding of cities)
- Local (legends, personalities, inhabitants, laws, and traditions)
- Nature (plants and animals, seasons and cycles, weather)

- Nobility and royalty (lineages, heraldry, customs, family trees, mottoes, personalities, laws)
- The planes (the Inner Planes, the Outer Planes, the Astral Plane, the Ethereal Plane, the planes' inhabitants, magic related to the planes)
- Religion (gods and goddesses, mythic history, ecclesiastic tradition, holy symbols)

Check: Answering a question within your field of study has a DC of 10 (for really easy questions), 15 (for basic questions), or 20 to 30 (for really tough questions).

Retry: No. The check represents what you know, and thinking about a topic a second time doesn't let you know something you never learned in the first place.

Special: An untrained Knowledge check is simply an Intelligence check. Without actual training, a character only knows common knowledge.

LISTEN (Wis)

Use this skill to hear approaching enemies, to detect someone sneaking up on you from behind, or to eavesdrop on someone else's conversation.

Check: Make a Listen check against a DC that reflects how quiet the noise is that you might hear or against an opposed Move Silently check.

The DM may make the Listen check so that you don't know whether not hearing anything means that nothing is there, or that you rolled low.

DC	Sound
0	People talking
5	A person in medium armor walking at a slow pace (10 ft./round) trying not to make noise.
10	An unarmored person walking at a slow pace (15 ft./round) trying not to make any noise.
15	A 1st-level rogue using Move Silently within 10 ft. of the listener
25	A cat stalking
30	An owl gliding in for a kill
+1	Per 10 ft. from the listener
+5	Through a door
+15	Through a stone wall

In the case of people trying to be quiet, the listed DCs could be replaced by Move Silently checks, in which case the listed DC would be the average result (or close to it). For instance, the "25" listed for a cat stalking means that a cat probably has about a +15 Move Silently skill modifier. (Assuming an average roll of 10 on 1d20, the skill check result would be 25.)

Retry: You can make a Listen check every time you have a chance to hear something in a reactive manner. As a full-round action, you may try to hear something you failed to hear previously.

Special: When several characters are listening to the same thing, the DM can make a single 1d20 roll and use it for all the listeners' skill checks.

The subject of a *hypnotism* spell suffers a –4 penalty on Listen checks.

The subject of a bard's *fascinate* ability suffers a –4 penalty on Listen checks.

A character with the Alertness feat gets a +2 synergy bonus on Listen checks.

A ranger gains a bonus on Listen checks when using this skill against a favored enemy (page 45).

Elves, gnomes, and halflings have a +2 racial bonus on Listen checks thanks to their keen ears.

Half-elves have a +1 racial bonus on Listen checks. Their hearing is good because of their elven heritage, but not as keen as that of a full elf.

MOVE SILENTLY (Dex; Armor Check Penalty)

You can use this skill to sneak up behind an enemy or to slink away without being noticed.

Check: Your Move Silently check is opposed by the Listen check of anyone who might hear you. You can move up to one-half your normal speed at no penalty. At more than one-half and up to your full speed, you suffer a –5 penalty. It's practically impossible (–20 penalty) to move silently while running or charging.

Special: The master of a cat familiar or an owl familiar (see Familiars, page 51) gains a +2 bonus on Move Silently checks.

Halflings get a +2 racial bonus on Move Silently checks because they are nimble.

OPEN LOCK (Dex; Trained Only)

You can pick padlocks, finesse combination locks, and solve puzzle locks. The effort requires at least a simple tool of the appropriate sort (a pick, pry bar, blank key, wire, etc.). Attempting an Open Lock check without a set of thieves' tools (page 111) carries a –2 circumstance penalty, even if a simple tool is employed. The use of masterwork thieves' tools enables you to make the check with a +2 circumstance bonus.

Check: Opening a lock entails 1 round of work and a successful check. (It is a full-round action.)

Lock	DC	Lock	DC
Very simple lock	20	Good lock	30
Average lock	25	Amazing lock	40

Special: Untrained characters cannot pick locks, but they might successfully force them open (see Breaking Items, page 136).

PERFORM (Cha)

You are skilled in several types of artistic expression and know how to put on a show. Possible Perform types include ballad, buffoonery, chant, comedy, dance, drama, drums, epic, flute, harp, juggling, limericks, lute, mandolin, melody, mime, ode, pan pipes, recorder, shalm, storytelling, and trumpet. (The DM may authorize other types.) You are capable of one form of performance per rank.

Check: You can impress audiences with your talent and skill.

DC	Performance
10	Routine performance. Trying to earn money by playing in public is essentially begging. You earn 1d10 cp/day.
15	Enjoyable performance. In a prosperous city, you can earn 1d10 sp/day.
20	Great performance. In a prosperous city, you can earn 3d10 sp/day. With time, you may be invited to join a professional troupe and may develop a regional reputation.
25	Memorable performance. In a prosperous city, you can earn 1d6 gp/day. With time, you may come to the attention of noble patrons and develop a national reputation.
30	Extraordinary performance. In a prosperous city, you can earn 3d6 gp/day. With time, you may draw attention from distant potential patrons or even from extraplanar beings.

A masterwork musical instrument (page 111) gives a +2 circumstance bonus to Perform checks that involve the use of the instrument.

Retry: Retries are allowed, but they don't negate previous failures, and an audience that has been unimpressed in the past is going to be prejudiced against future performances. (Increase the DC by 2 for each previous failure.)

Special: A bard must have at least 3 ranks in Perform to inspire courage in his allies, use his countersong ability, or use his *fascinate* ability. A bard needs 6 ranks in Perform to inspire competence,

9 ranks to use his suggestion ability, and 12 ranks to inspire greatness. See "Bardic Music" in the bard class description, page 28.

In addition to using the Perform skill, a character could entertain people with tumbling, tightrope walking, and spells (especially illusions).

PICK POCKET (Dex; Trained Only; Armor Check Penalty)

You can cut or lift a purse and hide it on your person, palm an unattended object, or perform some feat of legerdemain with an object no larger than a hat or a loaf of bread.

Check: A check against DC 10 lets you palm a coin-sized, unattended object. Minor feats of legerdemain, such as making a coin disappear, are also DC 10 unless an observer is determined to note where the item went.

When performing this skill under close observation, your skill check is opposed by the observer's Spot check. The observer's check doesn't prevent you from performing the action, just from doing it unnoticed.

If you try to take something from another creature, you must make a skill check against DC 20. The opponent makes a Spot check to detect the attempt. The opponent detects the attempt if her check result beats your check result, regardless of whether you got the item.

DC	Task
10	Palm a coin-sized object, make a coin disappear
20	Lift a small object from a person

Retry: A second Pick Pocket attempt against the same target, or when being watched by the same observer, has a DC +10 higher than the first skill check if the first check failed or if the attempt was noticed.

Special: If you have 5 or more ranks in Bluff, you get a +2 synergy bonus on Pick Pocket checks.

PROFESSION (Wis; Trained Only)

You are trained in a livelihood or a professional role, such as apothecary, boater, bookkeeper, brewer, cook, driver, farmer, fisher, guide, herbalist, herdsman, innkeeper, lumberjack, miller, miner, porter, rancher, sailor, scribe, siege engineer, stablehand, tanner, teamster, woodcutter, and so forth.

Like Craft, Profession is actually a number of separate skills. For instance, you could have the skill Profession (cook). Your ranks in that skill don't affect any checks you happen to make for milling or mining. You could have several Profession skills, each with its own ranks, each purchased as a separate skill.

While a Craft skill represents skill in creating or making an item, a Profession skill represents an aptitude in a vocation requiring a broader range of less specific knowledge. To draw a modern analogy, if an occupation is a service industry, it's probably a Profession skill. If it's in the manufacturing sector, it's probably a Craft skill.

Check: You can practice your trade and make a decent living, earning about half your check result in gold pieces per week of dedicated work. You know how to use the tools of your trade, how to perform the profession's daily tasks, how to supervise untrained helpers, and how to handle common problems. For example, a sailor knows how to tie several basic knots, how to tend and repair sails, and how to stand a deck watch at sea. The DM sets DCs for specialized tasks.

Retry: An attempt to use a Profession skill to earn an income cannot be retried. You are stuck with whatever weekly wage your check result brought you. (Another check may be made after a week to determine a new income for the next period of time.) An attempt to accomplish some specific task can usually be retried.

Special: Untrained laborers and assistants earn an average of 1 silver piece per day.

READ LIPS (Int; Trained Only; Rogue Only)

You can understand what others are saying by watching their lips.

Check: You must be within 30 feet of the speaker and be able to see her speak. You must be able to understand the speaker's language. (Use of this skill is language-dependent.) The base DC is 15, and it is higher for complex speech or an inarticulate speaker. You have to concentrate on reading lips for a full minute before making the skill check, and you can't perform some other action during this minute. You can move at half speed but not any faster, and you must maintain a line of sight to the lips being read. If the check succeeds, you can understand the general content of a minute's worth of speaking, but you usually still miss certain details.

If the check fails, you can't read the speaker's lips. If the check fails by 5 or more, you draw some incorrect conclusion about the speech.

The DM rolls your check so you don't know whether you succeeded or missed by 5.

Retry: The skill can be used once per minute.

RIDE (Dex)

You can ride a particular type of mount (usually a horse, but possibly a different mount). When you select this skill, choose the type of mount you are familiar with. For this purpose, "horses" includes mules, donkeys, and ponies. If you use the skill with a different mount (such as riding a giant lizard when you're used to riding horses), your rank is reduced by 2 (but not below 0). If you use this skill with a very different mount (such as riding a griffon when you're used to riding horses), your rank is reduced by 5 (but not below 0).

Check: Typical riding actions don't require checks. You can saddle, mount, ride, and dismount from a mount without a problem. Mounting or dismounting is a move-equivalent action. Some tasks require checks:

Riding Task	DC	Riding Task	DC
Guide with knees	5	Leap	15
Stay in saddle	5	Control mount in battle	20
Fight with warhorse	10	Fast mount or dismount	20*
Cover	15	*Armor check penalty applies.	
Soft fall	15		

Guide with Knees: You can react instantly to guide your mount with your knees so that you can use both hands in combat. Make the check at the start of your round. If you fail, you can only use one hand this round because you need to use the other to control your mount.

Stay in Saddle: You can react instantly to try to avoid falling when your mount rears or bolts unexpectedly or when you take damage.

Fight with Warhorse: If you direct your war-trained mount to attack in battle, you can still make your own attack or attacks normally.

Cover: You can react instantly to drop down and hang alongside your mount, using it as one-half cover. You can't attack or cast spells while using your mount as cover. If you fail, you don't get the cover benefit.

Soft Fall: You react instantly to try to take no damage when you fall off a mount, such as when it is killed or when it falls. If you fail, you take 1d6 points of falling damage.

Leap: You can get your mount to leap obstacles as part of its movement. Use your Ride skill modifier or the mount's Jump skill modifier (whichever is lower) to see how far the mount can jump. The DC (15) is what you need to roll to stay on the mount when it leaps.

Control Mount in Battle: As a move-equivalent action, you can attempt to control a light horse, pony, or heavy horse while in combat. If you fail, you can do nothing else that round. You do not need to roll for warhorses or warponies.

Fast Mount or Dismount: You can mount or dismount as a free action. If you fail the check, mounting or dismounting is a move-equivalent action. (You can't attempt a fast mount or dismount unless you can perform the mount or dismount as a move-equivalent action this round.)

Special: If you are riding bareback, you suffer a –5 penalty on Ride checks.

If you have 5 or more ranks in Handle Animal, you get a +2 synergy bonus to Ride checks.

If your mount has a military saddle (page 113), it gives a +2 circumstance bonus to Ride checks related to staying in the saddle.

The Ride skill is a prerequisite for the feats Mounted Combat, Mounted Archery, Trample, Ride-By Attack, and Spirited Charge. See the feat descriptions in Chapter 5: Feats for details.

SCRY (Int; Bard, Cleric, Druid, Sorcerer, Wizard Only)

Use this skill to spy on someone with a *scrying* spell or a *crystal ball* or to perform some divinations.

Check: You can't use this skill without some magical means to scry, such as the *scrying* spell, the *greater scrying* spell, the *vision* spell, or a *crystal ball*. Use of this skill is described in association with those spells and items. These items allow you to spy on others, and this skill just lets you do it better. This skill also improves your chance to notice when you're being scried, as detailed in the descriptions of the *arcane eye* and *detect scrying* spells.

Special: Although this skill is exclusive to certain classes, it can be used untrained. This means that a character with no ranks in Scry, and who is not allowed to buy ranks in this skill, can still make an Intelligence check to notice when he is being scried.

SEARCH (Int)

You can find secret doors, simple traps, hidden compartments, and other details not readily apparent. The Spot skill lets you notice something, such as a hiding rogue. The Search skill lets a character discern some small detail or irregularity through active effort.

Search does not allow you to find complex traps unless you are a rogue (see the "Special" section below).

Check: You generally must be within 10 feet of the object or surface to be searched. It takes 1 round to search a 5-foot-by-5-foot area or a volume of goods 5 feet on a side; doing so is a full-round action.

Task	DC
Ransack a chest full of junk to find a certain item	10
Notice a typical secret door or a simple trap	20
Find a difficult nonmagical trap not of stone (rogue only)*	21+
Find a magic trap (rogue only)*	25+
	spell level used to create
Notice a well-hidden secret door	30

*Even dwarves who are not rogues can use Search to do this if the trap is built into or out of stone.

Special: Elves get a +2 racial bonus on Search checks, and half-elves get a +1 racial bonus. An elf (but not a half-elf) who simply passes within 5 feet of a secret or concealed door can make a Search check to find that door.

Active Abjuration spells within 10 feet of each other for 24 hours or more create barely visible energy fluctuations. These fluctuations give characters a +4 bonus to Search checks to locate such Abjuration spells.

While anyone can use Search to find a trap whose DC is 20 or less, only a rogue can use Search to locate traps with higher DCs. (*Exception:* The spell *find traps* temporarily enables a cleric to use his Search skill as if he were a rogue.) Finding a nonmagical trap has a DC of at least 20, and the DC is higher if it is well hidden.

Finding a magic trap has a DC of 25 plus the level of the spell used to create it. Identifying the location of a *snare* spell has a DC of 23.

The spells *explosive runes, fire trap, glyph of warding, symbol,* and *teleportation circle* create magic traps that a rogue can find by making a Search check and then attempt to disarm by using Disable Device. *Spike growth* and *spike stones,* however, create magic traps that can be found using Search, but against which Disable Device checks do not succeed. See the individual spell descriptions in Chapter 11: Spells for details.

A dwarf, even one that is not a rogue, can use the Search skill to find a difficult trap (those with DCs above 20) if the trap is built into or out of stone. They gain a +2 racial bonus to do so from their stonecunning ability.

Special: A character who does not have the Track feat can use the Search skill to find tracks, but can only follow tracks if the DC is 10 or less. (See the Track feat, page 85.)

SENSE MOTIVE (Wis)

Use this skill to tell when someone is bluffing you. This skill represents sensitivity to the body language, speech habits, and mannerisms of others.

Check: A successful check allows you to avoid being bluffed (see the Bluff skill, page 64). You can also use the skill to tell when something is up (something odd is going on that you were unaware of) or to assess someone's trustworthiness. Trying to gain information with this skill takes at least 1 minute, and you could spend a whole evening trying to get a sense of the people around you.

Sense Motive Task	DC
Hunch	20
Sense enchantment	25

Hunch: This use of the skill essentially means making a gut assessment of the social situation. You can get the feeling from another's behavior that something is wrong, such as when you're talking to an impostor. Alternatively, you can get the feeling that someone is trustworthy.

Sense Enchantment: You can tell that someone's behavior is being influenced by an Enchantment effect (by definition, a mind-affecting effect), such as *charm person,* even if that person isn't aware of it herself.

Retry: No, though you may make a Sense Motive check for each bluff made on you.

Special: A ranger gains a bonus on Sense Motive checks when using this skill against a favored enemy (page 45).

SPEAK LANGUAGE (None; Trained Only)

The Speak Language skill doesn't work like a standard skill.

- You start at 1st level knowing one or two languages (according to your race) plus an additional number of languages equal to your Intelligence bonus. (See Chapter 2: Races.)
- Instead of buying a rank in Speak Language, you choose a new language that you can speak.
- You don't make Speak Language checks. You either know a language or you don't.
- A literate character (anyone but a barbarian) can read and write any language she speaks. Each language has an alphabet (though sometimes several spoken languages share a single alphabet).

Common languages and their alphabets are summarized in Table 4–6: Languages, on the next page.

Retry: Not applicable. (There are no Speak Language checks to fail.)

TABLE 4–6: LANGUAGES

Language	Typical Speakers	Alphabet
Abyssal	Demons, chaotic evil outsiders	Infernal
Aquan	Water-based creatures	Elven
Auran	Air-based creatures	Draconic
Celestial	Good outsiders	Celestial
Common	Humans, halflings, half-elves, half-orcs	Common
Draconic	Kobolds, troglodytes, lizardfolk, dragons	Draconic
Druidic	Druids (only)	Druidic
Dwarven	Dwarves	Dwarven
Elven	Elves	Elven
Gnome	Gnomes	Dwarven
Goblin	Goblins, hobgoblins, bugbears	Dwarven
Giant	Ettins, ogres, giants	Dwarven
Gnoll	Gnolls	Common
Halfling	Halflings	Common
Ignan	Fire-based creatures	Draconic
Infernal	Devils, lawful evil outsiders	Infernal
Orc	Orcs	Dwarven
Sylvan	Dryads, brownies, leprechauns	Elven
Terran	Xorn and other earth-based creatures	Dwarven
Undercommon	Drow, mind flayers	Elven

SPELLCRAFT (Int; Trained Only)

Use this skill to identify spells as they are cast or spells already in place.

Check: You can identify spells and magic effects.

DC	Task
13	When using *read magic*, identify a *glyph of warding*.
15 + spell level	Identify a spell being cast. (You must see or hear the spell's verbal or somatic components.) No retry.
15 + spell level	Learn a spell from a spellbook or scroll. (Wizard only.) No retry for that spell until you gain at least 1 rank in Spellcraft (even if you find another source to try to learn the spell from).
15 + spell level	Prepare a spell from a borrowed spellbook. (Wizard only.) One try per day.
15 + spell level	When casting *detect magic*, determine the school of magic involved in the aura of a single item or creature you can see. (If the aura is not a spell effect, the DC is 15 + half caster level.)
19	When using *read magic*, identify a *symbol*.
20 + spell level	Identify a spell that's already in place and in effect. (You must be able to see or detect the effects of the spell.) No retry.
20 + spell level	Identify materials created or shaped by magic, such as noting that an iron wall is the result of a *wall of iron* spell. No retry.
20 + spell level	Decipher a written spell (such as a scroll) without using *read magic*. One try per day.
20	Draw a diagram to augment casting *dimensional anchor* on a summoned creature. Takes 10 minutes. No retry. The DM makes this check.
30 or higher	Understand a strange or unique magical effect, such as the effects of a magic stream. No retry.

Additionally, certain spells allow you to gain information about magic provided that you make a Spellcraft check as detailed in the spell description (for example, see the *detect magic* spell, page 193).

Retry: See above.

Special: A specialist wizard gets a +2 bonus when dealing with a spell or effect from his specialized school. He suffers a –5 penalty when dealing with a spell or effect from a prohibited school (and some tasks, such as learning a prohibited spell, are just impossible).

If you have 5 or more ranks of Use Magic Device, you get a +2 synergy bonus to Spellcraft checks to decipher spells on scrolls.

SPOT (Wis)

Use this skill to notice bandits waiting in ambush, to see a rogue lurking in the shadows, or to see the giant centipede in the pile of trash.

Check: The Spot skill is used primarily to detect characters or creatures who are hiding. Typically, Spot is opposed by the Hide check of the creature trying not to be seen. Sometimes a creature isn't intentionally hiding but is still difficult to see, so a successful Spot check is necessary to notice it.

A Spot check result of greater than 20 can generally let you become aware of an invisible creature near you (though you can't actually see it).

Spot is also used to detect someone in disguise (see the Disguise skill, page 67).

Condition	Penalty
Per 10 feet of distance	–1
Spotter distracted	–5

Retry: You can make a Spot check every time you have the opportunity to notice something in a reactive manner. As a full-round action, you may attempt to spot something that you failed to spot previously.

Special: The subject of a *hypnotism* spell suffers a –4 penalty on Spot checks.

The target of a bard's *fascinate* ability suffers a –4 penalty on Spot checks.

A character with the Alertness feat gets a +2 synergy bonus on Spot checks.

A ranger gains a bonus on Spot checks when using this skill against a favored enemy (page 45).

Elves get a +2 racial bonus on Spot checks because of their keen senses.

Half-elves get a +1 racial bonus on Spot checks. Their senses are good, but not as keen as those of a full elf.

SWIM (Str)

Using this skill, a land-based creature can swim, dive, navigate underwater obstacles, and so on.

Check: A successful Swim check allows you to swim one-quarter of your speed as a move-equivalent action or one-half your speed as a full-round action. Roll once per round. If you fail, you make no progress through the water. If you fail by 5 or more, you go underwater and start to drown. The DUNGEON MASTER's Guide has rules for drowning.

If you are underwater (whether drowning or swimming underwater intentionally), you suffer a cumulative –1 penalty to your Swim check for each consecutive round you've been underwater.

The DC for the Swim check depends on the water:

Water	DC
Calm water	10
Rough water	15
Stormy water	20

Each hour that you swim, make a Swim check against DC 20 or take 1d6 points of subdual damage from fatigue.

Special: Instead of an armor check penalty, you suffer a penalty of –1 for each 5 pounds of gear you are carrying or wearing.

TUMBLE (Dex; Trained Only; Armor Check Penalty)

You can dive, roll, somersault, flip, and so on. You can't use this skill if your speed has been reduced by armor, excess equipment, or loot (see Table 9–2: Carrying Loads, page 142).

Check: You can land softly when you fall or tumble past opponents. You can also tumble to entertain an audience (as with the Perform skill).

DC	Task
15	Treat a fall as if it were 10 feet shorter when determining damage.
15	Tumble up to 20 feet (as part of normal movement), suffering no attacks of opportunity while doing so. Failure means you tumble 20 feet but suffer attacks of opportunity normally.
25	Tumble up to 20 feet (as part of normal movement), suffering no attacks of opportunity while doing so and moving through areas occupied by enemies (over, under, or around them). Failure means you tumble 20 feet and can move through enemy-occupied areas but suffer attacks of opportunity normally.

Retry: An audience, once it has judged a tumbler as uninteresting, is not receptive to repeat performances. You can try to reduce damage from a fall as an instant reaction once per fall. You can attempt to tumble as part of movement once per round.

Special: A character with 5 or more ranks in Tumble gains a +3 dodge AC bonus when executing the fight defensively standard or full-round action instead of a +2 dodge AC bonus (see Fighting Defensively, page 124).

A character with 5 or more ranks in Tumble gains a +6 dodge AC bonus when executing the total defense standard action instead of a +4 dodge AC bonus (see Total Defense, page 127).

If you have 5 or more ranks in Jump, you get a +2 synergy bonus on Tumble checks.

If you have 5 or more ranks in Tumble, you get a +2 synergy bonus on Balance checks.

USE MAGIC DEVICE (Cha; Trained Only; Bard, Rogue Only)

Use this skill to activate magic devices, including scrolls and wands, that otherwise you could not activate.

Check: You can use this skill to read a spell or to activate a magic item. This skill lets you use a magic item as if

Use Magic Device Task	DC
Decipher a written spell	25 + spell level
Emulate spell ability	20
Emulate class feature	20
Emulate ability score	25
Emulate race	25
Emulate alignment	30
Activate blindly	25

you had the spell ability or class features of another class, as if you were a different race, or as if you were a different alignment.

When you're attempting to activate a magic item using this skill, you do so as a standard action. (See Activate Magic Item, page 126, and the DUNGEON MASTER's Guide for discussions of how magic items are normally activated.) However, the checks you make to determine whether you are successful at emulating the desired factors to successfully perform the activation are instant. They take no time by themselves and are included in the activate magic item standard action.

You make emulation checks each time you activate a device such as a wand. If you are using the check to emulate an alignment or some other quality in an ongoing manner (such as to emulate neutral evil to prevent yourself from being damaged by a *book of vile darkness* you are carrying when you are not evil), you need to make the relevant emulation checks once per hour.

You must consciously choose what to emulate. That is, you have to know what you are trying to emulate when you make an emulation check.

Decipher a Written Spell: This works just like deciphering a written spell with the Spellcraft skill, except that the DC is 5 points higher.

Emulate Spell Ability: This use of the skill allows you to use a magic item as if you had a particular spell on your class spell list. To cast a spell from a scroll or use a wand, you have to have a particular spell on your class spell list. By using the skill this way, you can use such an

Illus by J. Foster

Lidda finds that using a magic device can be risky.

item as if you did have the spell on your class spell list. Your effective caster level is your result minus 20. (It's okay to have a caster level of 0.) For wands, it doesn't matter what caster level you are, but it does matter for scrolls. If your effective level is lower than the caster level, you may have a difficult time using a scroll successfully (see the DUNGEON MASTER'S *Guide* for more information on scrolls).

This skill does not let you cast the spell. It only lets you cast it from a scroll or wand as if the spell were on your class list. Note: If you are casting it from a scroll, you have to decipher it first.

Emulate Class Feature: Sometimes you need to use a class feature to activate a magic item. Your effective level in the emulated class equals your result minus 20. For example, Lidda finds a magic chalice that turns regular water into holy water when a cleric or experienced paladin channels positive energy into it as if turning undead. She attempts to activate the item by emulating the cleric's undead turning power. Her effective cleric level is her result minus 20. Since a cleric can turn undead at 1st level, she needs a result of 21 or higher on her Use Magic Device check.

This skill does not let you use the class feature of another class. It just lets you activate magic items as if you had the class feature.

If the class whose feature you are emulating has an alignment requirement, you must meet it, either honestly or by emulating an appropriate alignment as a separate check (see below).

Emulate Ability Score: To cast a spell from a scroll, you need a high ability score in the appropriate ability (Intelligence for wizard spells, Wisdom for divine spells, and Charisma for sorcerer or bard spells). Your effective ability score (appropriate to the class you're emulating when you try to cast the spell from the scroll) is your result minus 15. If you already have a high enough score in the appropriate ability, you don't need to make this check.

Emulate Race: Some magic items work only for certain races, or work better for those of certain races. You can use such an item as if you were a race of your choice. For example, Lidda, a halfling, could attempt to use a +3 *dwarven throwing hammer*. If she failed her Use Magic Device check, the hammer would work for her normally as a halfling, but if she succeeded, it would work for her as if she were a dwarf. You can emulate only one race at a time.

Emulate Alignment: Some magic items have positive or negative effects based on your alignment. You can use these items as if you were of an alignment of your choice. For example, the *book of vile darkness* damages nonevil characters who touch it. Lidda could emulate an evil alignment so she could handle the *book of vile darkness* safely. You can emulate only one alignment at a time.

Activate Blindly: Some magic items are activated by special words, thoughts, or actions. You can activate such items as if you were using the activation word, thought, or action even if you're not and even if you don't know it. You do have to use something equivalent. You have to speak, wave the item around, or otherwise attempt to get it to activate. You get a special +2 bonus if you've activated the item at least once before.

If you fail by 10 or more, you suffer a mishap. A mishap means that magical energy gets released but it doesn't do what you wanted it to do. The DM determines the result of a mishap, as with scroll mishaps. The default mishaps are that the item affects the wrong target or that uncontrolled magical energy gets released, dealing 2d6 points of damage to you. Note: This mishap is in addition to the chance for a mishap that you normally run when you cast a spell from a scroll and the spell's caster level is higher than your level.

Retry: Yes, but if you ever roll a natural 1 while attempting to activate an item and you fail, then you can't try to activate it again for a day.

Special: You cannot take 10 with this skill. Magic is too unpredictable for you to use this skill reliably.

If you have 5 or more ranks in Spellcraft, you get a +2 synergy bonus on Use Magic Device checks related to scrolls. If you have 5 or more ranks in Decipher Script, you get a +2 synergy bonus on Use Magic Device checks related to scrolls. These bonuses stack.

USE ROPE (Dex)

With this skill, you can make firm knots, undo tricky knots, and bind prisoners with ropes.

Check: Most tasks with a rope are relatively simple.

DC	Task
10	Tie a firm knot
15	Tie a special knot, such as one that slips, slides slowly, or loosens with a tug
15	Tie a rope around oneself one-handed
15	Splice two ropes together (takes 5 minutes)

When you bind another character with a rope, any Escape Artist check that the bound character makes is opposed by your Use Rope check. You get a special +10 bonus on the check because it is easier to bind someone than to escape from being tied up. You don't even make your Use Rope check until someone tries to escape.

Special: A silk rope (page 109) gives a +2 circumstance bonus on Use Rope checks. If you cast an *animate rope* spell on a rope, you get a +2 circumstance bonus to any Use Rope checks you make when using the rope. These bonuses stack.

If you have 5 or more ranks in Escape Artist, you get a +2 synergy bonus on checks to bind someone.

WILDERNESS LORE (Wis)

Use this skill to hunt wild game, guide a party safely through frozen wastelands, identify signs that owlbears live nearby, or avoid quicksand and other natural hazards.

Check: You can keep yourself and others safe and fed in the wild.

DC	Task
10	Get along in the wild. Move up to one-half your overland speed while hunting and foraging (no food or water supplies needed). You can provide food and water for one other person for every 2 points by which your check result exceeds 10.
15	Gain +2 on all Fortitude saves against severe weather while moving up to one-half your overland speed, or gain +4 if stationary. You may grant the same bonus to one other character for every 1 point by which the check result exceeds 15.
15	Avoid getting lost or avoid natural hazards, such as quicksand.

Retry: For getting along in the wild or for gaining the Fortitude save bonus, you make a check once every 24 hours. The result of that check applies until the next check is made. To avoid getting lost or avoid natural hazards, you make a check whenever the situation calls for one. Retries to avoid getting lost in a specific situation or to avoid a specific natural hazard are not allowed.

Special: If you have 5 or more ranks of Intuit Direction, you get a +2 synergy bonus on Wilderness Lore checks to avoid getting lost.

A ranger gains a bonus on Wilderness Lore checks when using this skill to gain information about a favored enemy (page 45).

FIG. B

Clock works
set off snares

Skill:

feat is a special feature that either gives your character a new capability or improves one he or she already has. For example, Lidda (a halfling rogue) chooses to start with the Improved Initiative feat at 1st level. That feat adds a +4 bonus to her initiative check results. At 3rd level (see Table 3–2: Experience and Level-Dependent Benefits, page 22), she gains a new feat and chooses Dodge. This feat allows her to avoid the attacks of an opponent she selects, improving her Armor Class against him.

Unlike a skill, a feat has no ranks. A character either has the feat or does not.

ACQUIRING FEATS

Unlike skills, feats are not bought with points. You simply choose them for your character. Each character gets one feat when the character is created. At 3rd level and every three levels thereafter (6th, 9th, 12th, 15th, and 18th), he or she gains another feat (see Table 3–2: Experience and Level-Dependent Benefits, page 22). For multiclass characters, the feats come according to total character level, regardless of individual class levels.

Additionally, fighters and wizards get extra class-related feats chosen from special lists (see Table 3–9: The Fighter, page 36, and Table 3–20: The Wizard, page 52). Humans also get a bonus feat at 1st level, chosen by the player from any feat for which his or her character qualifies.

PREREQUISITES

Some feats have prerequisites. You must have the listed ability score, feat, skill, or base attack bonus in order to select or use that feat. A character can gain a feat at the same level at which he or she gains the prerequisite. For example, at 3rd level, Krusk, the half-orc barbarian, could spend 1 skill point on the Ride skill (gaining his first rank in Ride) and select the Mounted Combat feat at the same time.

You can't use a feat if you've lost a prerequisite. For example, if your Strength drops below 13 because a *ray of enfeeblement* hits you, you can't use the Power Attack feat.

TYPES OF FEATS

Some feats are general, meaning that no special rules govern them as a group. Others are item creation feats, which allow spellcasters to create magic items of all sorts. A metamagic feat lets a spellcaster prepare and cast a spell with greater effect, albeit as if the spell were a higher level than it actually is. Special feats are available only to the specified class.

ITEM CREATION FEATS

Spellcasters can use their personal power to create lasting magic items. Doing so, however, is draining. A spellcaster must put a little of himself or herself into every magic item he or she creates.

An item creation feat lets a spellcaster create a magic item of a certain type. Regardless of the type of item, each item creation feat has certain features in common.

XP Cost: Power and energy that the spellcaster would normally have is expended when making a magic item. The XP cost equals 1/25 the cost of the

Acid spray is pumped by the clock works

Illus. by A. Swekel

item in gold pieces (see the DUNGEON MASTER's Guide for item costs). A character cannot spend so much XP that he or she loses a level. However, on gaining enough XP to achieve a new level, he or she can immediately expend XP on creating an item rather than keeping the XP to advance a level.

Raw Materials Cost: Creating a magic item requires costly components, most of which are consumed in the process. The cost of these materials equals half the cost of the item.

For example, at 12th level, Mialee the wizard gains the feat Forge Ring, and she creates a *ring of deflection +3*. The cost of the ring is 18,000 gp, so it costs her 720 XP plus 9,000 gp to make.

Using an item creation feat also requires access to a laboratory or magical workshop, special tools, and so on. A character generally has access to what he or she needs unless unusual circumstances apply (such as if she's traveling far from home).

Time: The time to create a magic item depends on the feat and the cost of the item. The minimum time is 1 day.

Item Cost: Brew Potion, Craft Wand, and Scribe Scroll create items that directly reproduce spell effects and whose power depends on their caster level. A spell from one of these items has the power it would have if cast by a spellcaster of that level. A *wand of fireball* at caster level 8, for example, would create *fireballs* that deal 8d6 damage and have a range of 720 feet. The price of these items (and thus the XP cost and the cost of the raw materials) depends on the caster level. The caster level must be high enough that the spellcaster creating the item can cast the spell at that level. To find the final price in each case, multiply the caster level by the spell level and then multiply the result by a constant:

Scrolls: Base price = spell level × caster level × 25 gp.

Potions: Base price = spell level × caster level × 50 gp.

Wands: Base price = spell level × caster level × 750 gp.

Extra Costs: Any potion, scroll, or wand that stores a spell with a costly material component or an XP cost also carries a commensurate cost. For potions and scrolls, the creator must expend the material component or pay the XP when creating the item. For a wand, the creator must expend fifty copies of the material component or pay fifty times the XP cost.

Some magic items similarly incur extra costs in material components or XP as noted in their descriptions. For example, a *ring of three wishes* costs 15,000 XP in addition to normal costs (as many XP as it costs to cast *wish* three times).

METAMAGIC FEATS

As a spellcaster's knowledge of magic grows, she can learn to cast spells in ways slightly different from how the spells were originally designed or learned. A spellcaster can learn to cast a spell without having to say its magic word, to cast a spell for greater effect, or even to cast it with nothing but a moment's thought. Preparing and casting a spell in such a way is harder than normal but, thanks to metamagic feats, at least it is possible.

For instance, at 3rd level, Mialee gains a feat, and she chooses Silent Spell, the metamagic feat that allows her to cast a spell without its verbal component. The cost of doing so, however, is that in preparing the spell, she must use up a spell slot one level higher than the spell actually is. If she prepares *charm person* as a silent spell, it takes up one of her 2nd-level slots. It is still, however, only a 1st-level spell. The DC for the Will save against her *charm person* spell, for example, does not go up. She cannot prepare a 2nd-level spell as a silent spell because she would have to prepare it as a 3rd-level spell, and she can't use 3rd-level spell slots until she reaches 5th level.

Wizards and Divine Spellcasters: Wizards and divine spellcasters (clerics, druids, paladins, and rangers) must prepare their spells in advance. It is during preparation that a wizard or divine spellcaster chooses which spells to prepare with metamagic feats (and thus taking up a higher-level spell slot than normal).

Sorcerers and Bards: Sorcerers and bards choose spells as they cast them. They can choose when they cast their spells whether to use metamagic feats to improve them. As with other spellcasters, the improved spell uses up a higher-level spell slot. For instance, a still *invisibility* spell cast by a bard counts against his allotment of 3rd-level spells as if the spell were 3rd level. Because the sorcerer or bard has not prepared the spell in a metamagic form in advance, he must do so on the spot. The sorcerer or bard, therefore, must take more time to cast a metamagic spell (one enhanced by a metamagic feat) than a regular spell. If its normal casting time is 1 action, casting a metamagic spell is a full-round action for a sorcerer or bard. For spells with a longer casting time, it takes an extra full-round action to cast the spell.

Spontaneous Casting and Metamagic Feats: Clerics spontaneously casting *cure* or *inflict* spells can cast metamagic versions of them. For instance, an 11th-level cleric can swap out a prepared 6th-level spell to cast an empowered *cure critical wounds*. Casting a 1-action metamagic spell spontaneously is a full-round action, and spells with longer casting times take an extra full-round action to cast.

Effects of Metamagic Feats on a Spell: In all ways, a metamagic spell operates at its original level even though it is prepared and cast as a higher-level spell. Saving throw modifications are not changed (unless stated otherwise in the feat description). The modifications made by these spells only apply to spells cast directly by the feat user. A spellcaster can't use a metamagic feat to alter a spell being cast from a wand, scroll, or other device.

Metamagic feats cannot be used for all spells. See the specific feat descriptions for the spells that a particular feat can't modify.

Multiple Metamagic Feats on a Spell: A spellcaster can use multiple metamagic feats on a single spell. Changes to its level are cumulative. A silent, still version of *charm person*, for example, would be prepared and cast as a 3rd-level spell.

Magic Items and Metamagic Spells: With the right item creation feat, you can store a metamagic spell in a scroll, potion, or wand. Level limits for potions and wands apply to the spell's higher, metamagic level. A character doesn't need the metamagic feat to activate an item storing a metamagic spell.

Counterspelling Metamagic Spells: Whether a spell has been enhanced by a metamagic feat does not affect its vulnerability to counterspelling or its ability to counterspell another spell. (See Counterspells, page 152.)

SPECIAL FEATS

These are feats available only to the specified class. Only clerics or paladins can take Extra Turning, only fighters can take Weapon Specialization, and only wizards can take Spell Mastery. These feats are described in the respective class entries for those classes in Chapter 3: Classes.

FEAT DESCRIPTIONS

Here is the format for feat descriptions.

FEAT NAME [Type of Feat]

Description of what the feat does or represents in plain language.

Prerequisite: A minimum ability score, another feat or feats, a minimum base attack, a skill, or a level that a character must have in order to acquire this feat. This entry is absent if a feat has no prerequisite. A feat may have more than one prerequisite.

Benefit: What the feat enables you (the character) to do.

Normal: What a character who does not have this feat is limited to or restricted from doing. If not having the feat causes no particular drawback, this entry is absent.

Special: Additional facts about the feat that may be helpful when you decide whether to acquire the feat.

TABLE 5–1: FEATS

General Feats	Prerequisite
Alertness	—
Ambidexterity	Dex 15+
Armor Proficiency (light)	—
Armor Proficiency (medium)	Armor Proficiency (light)
Armor Proficiency (heavy)	Armor Proficiency (light)
	Armor Proficiency (medium)
Blind-Fight	—
Combat Casting	—
Combat Reflexes	—
Dodge	Dex 13+
Mobility	Dex 13+
	Dodge
Spring Attack	Dex 13+
	Dodge
	Mobility
	Base attack bonus +4 or higher
Endurance	—
Exotic Weapon Proficiency*	Base attack bonus +1 or higher
Expertise	Int 13+
Improved Disarm	Int 13+
	Expertise
Improved Trip	Int 13+
	Expertise
Whirlwind Attack	Int 13+
	Expertise
	Dex 13+
	Dodge
	Mobility
	Base attack bonus +4 or higher
	Spring Attack
Great Fortitude	—
Improved Critical*	Proficient with weapon
	Base attack bonus +8 or higher
Improved Initiative	—
Improved Unarmed Strike	—
Deflect Arrows	Dex 13+
	Improved Unarmed Strike
Stunning Fist	Dex 13+
	Improved Unarmed Strike
	Wis 13+
	Base attack bonus +8 or higher
Iron Will	—
Leadership	Character Level 6th+
Lightning Reflexes	—
Martial Weapon Proficiency*	—
Mounted Combat	Ride skill
Mounted Archery	Ride skill
	Mounted Combat
Trample	Ride skill
	Mounted Combat
Ride-By Attack	Ride skill
	Mounted Combat
Spirited Charge	Ride skill
	Mounted Combat
	Ride-By Attack
Point Blank Shot	—
Far Shot	Point Blank Shot
Precise Shot	Point Blank Shot
Rapid Shot	Point Blank Shot
	Dex 13+
Shot on the Run	Point Blank Shot
	Dex 13+
	Dodge
	Mobility

General Feats (cont.)	Prerequisite
Power Attack	Str 13+
Cleave	Str 13+
	Power Attack
Improved Bull Rush	Str 13+
	Power Attack
Sunder	Str 13+
	Power Attack
Great Cleave	Str 13+
	Power Attack
	Cleave
	Base attack bonus +4 or higher
Quick Draw	Base attack bonus +1 or higher
Run	—
Shield Proficiency	—
Simple Weapon Proficiency	—
Skill Focus*	—
Spell Focus*	—
Spell Penetration	—
Toughness**	—
Track	—
Two-Weapon Fighting	—
Improved Two-Weapon Fighting	Two-Weapon Fighting
	Ambidexterity
	Base attack bonus +9 or higher
Weapon Finesse*	Proficient with weapon
	Base attack bonus +1 or higher
Weapon Focus*	Proficient with weapon
	Base attack bonus +1 or higher

Item Creation Feats	Prerequisite
Brew Potion	Spellcaster level 3rd+
Craft Magic Arms and Armor	Spellcaster level 5th+
Craft Rod	Spellcaster level 9th+
Craft Staff	Spellcaster level 12th+
Craft Wand	Spellcaster level 5th+
Craft Wondrous Item	Spellcaster level 3rd+
Forge Ring	Spellcaster level 12th+
Scribe Scroll	Spellcaster level 1st+

Metamagic Feats	Prerequisite
Empower Spell	—
Enlarge Spell	—
Extend Spell	—
Heighten Spell	—
Maximize Spell	—
Quicken Spell	—
Silent Spell	—
Still Spell	—

Special Feats†	Prerequisite
Extra Turning**	Cleric or paladin
Spell Mastery*	Wizard
Weapon Specialization*	Fighter level 4th+

*You can gain this feat multiple times. Its effects do not stack. Each time you take the feat, it applies to a new weapon, skill, school of magic, or selection of spells.

**You can gain this feat multiple times. Its effects stack.

†Special feats are described in the class descriptions for the classes that can select them in Chapter 4: Classes.

ALERTNESS [General]

You have finely tuned senses.

Benefit: You get a +2 bonus on all Listen checks and Spot checks.

Special: The master of a familiar (see page 51) gains the Alertness feat whenever the familiar is within arm's reach.

AMBIDEXTERITY [General]

You are equally adept at using either hand.

Prerequisite: Dex 15+.

Benefit: You ignore all penalties for using an off hand. You are neither left-handed nor right-handed.

Normal: Without this feat, a character who uses his or her off hand suffers a –4 penalty to attack rolls, ability checks, and skill checks. For example, a right-handed character wielding a weapon with her left hand suffers a –4 penalty to attack rolls with that weapon.

Special: This feat helps offset the penalty for fighting with two weapons. See the Two-Weapon Fighting feat, page 86, and Table 8–2: Two-Weapon Fighting Penalties, page 125.

A ranger wearing light armor or no armor can fight with two weapons as if he had the feats Ambidexterity and Two-Weapon Fighting.

ARMOR PROFICIENCY (HEAVY) [General]

You are proficient with heavy armor (see Table 7–5: Armor, page 104).

Prerequisites: Armor Proficiency (light), Armor Proficiency (medium).

Benefit: See Armor Proficiency (light).

Normal: See Armor Proficiency (light).

Special: Fighters, paladins, and clerics have this feat for free.

ARMOR PROFICIENCY (LIGHT) [General]

You are proficient with light armor (see Table 7–5: Armor, page 104).

Benefit: When you wear a type of armor with which you are proficient, the armor check penalty applies only to Balance, Climb, Escape Artist, Hide, Jump, Move Silently, Pick Pocket, and Tumble checks.

Normal: A character who is wearing armor with which she is not proficient suffers its armor check penalty on attack rolls and on all skill checks that involve moving, including Ride.

Special: All classes except wizards, sorcerers, and monks have this feat for free.

ARMOR PROFICIENCY (MEDIUM) [General]

You are proficient with medium armor (see Table 7–5: Armor, page 104).

Prerequisite: Armor Proficiency (light)

Benefit: See Armor Proficiency (light).

Normal: See Armor Proficiency (light).

Special: Fighters, barbarians, paladins, rangers, clerics, druids, and bards have this feat for free. Wizards, sorcerers, rogues, and monks do not.

BLIND-FIGHT [General]

You know how to fight in melee without being able to see your foes.

Benefit: In melee, every time you miss because of concealment, you can reroll your miss chance percentile roll one time to see if you actually hit (see Table 8–10: Concealment, page 133).

An invisible attacker gets no bonus to hit you in melee. That is, you don't lose your positive Dexterity bonus to Armor Class, and the attacker doesn't get the usual +2 bonus (see Table 8–8: Attack Roll Modifiers, page 132). The invisible attacker's bonuses do still apply for ranged attacks, however.

You suffer only half the usual penalty to speed for being unable to see. Darkness and poor visibility in general reduces your speed to three-quarters of normal, instead of one-half (see Table 9–4: Hampered Movement, page 143).

Normal: Regular attack roll modifiers for invisible attackers trying to hit you (see Table 8–8: Attack Roll Modifiers, page 132) apply, as does the speed reduction for darkness and poor visibility (see Table 9–4: Hampered Movement, page 143).

Special: The Blind-Fight feat is of no use against a character who is the subject of a *blink* spell (see the spell description, page 180, for details).

BREW POTION [Item Creation]

You can create potions, which carry spells within themselves. See the DUNGEON MASTER's Guide for rules on potions.

Prerequisite: Spellcaster level 3rd+.

Benefit: You can create a potion of any spell of 3rd level or lower that you know and that targets a creature or creatures. Brewing a potion takes 1 day. When you create a potion, you set the caster level. The caster level must be sufficient to cast the spell in question and no higher than your own level. The base price of a potion is its spell level multiplied by its caster level multiplied by 50 gp. To brew a potion, you must spend 1/25 of this base price in XP and use up raw materials costing half this base price.

When you create a potion, you make any choices that you would normally make when casting the spell. Whoever drinks the potion is the target of the spell.

Any potion that stores a spell with a costly material component or an XP cost also carries a commensurate cost. In addition to the costs derived from the base price, you must expend the material component or pay the XP when creating the potion.

CLEAVE [General]

You can follow through with powerful blows.

Prerequisites: Str 13+, Power Attack.

Benefit: If you deal a creature enough damage to make it drop (typically by dropping it to below 0 hit points, killing it, etc.), you get an immediate, extra melee attack against another creature in the immediate vicinity. You cannot take a 5-foot step before making this extra attack. The extra attack is with the same weapon and at the same bonus as the attack that dropped the previous creature. You can use this ability once per round.

Lidda dodges the ray of a spell cast by an evil cleric.

COMBAT CASTING [General]

You are adept at casting spells in combat.

Benefit: You get a +4 bonus to Concentration checks made to cast a spell while on the defensive (see Casting on the Defensive, page 125).

COMBAT REFLEXES [General]

You can respond quickly and repeatedly to opponents who let their defenses down.

Benefit: When foes leave themselves open, you may make a number of additional attacks of opportunity equal to your Dexterity modifier. For example, a character with a Dexterity of 15 can make a total of three attacks of opportunity in a round—the one attack of opportunity any character is entitled to, plus two more attacks because of his +2 Dexterity bonus. If four goblins move through the character's threatened area, he can make attacks of opportunity against three of the four. You still only make one attack of opportunity per enemy.

You may also make attacks of opportunity while flat-footed.

Normal: A character not capable of this feat can make only one attack of opportunity per round and can't make attacks of opportunity while flat-footed.

Special: A rogue with the Combat Reflexes feat still can only make one attack of opportunity in a round if he uses his opportunist ability (see page 48) to make that attack.

CRAFT MAGIC ARMS AND ARMOR [Item Creation]

You can create magic weapons, armor, and shields.

Prerequisite: Spellcaster level 5th+.

Benefit: You can create any magic weapon, armor, or shield whose prerequisites you meet. Enhancing a weapon, suit of armor, or shield takes 1 day for each 1,000 gp in the price of its magical features. To enhance a weapon, suit of armor, or shield, you must spend 1/25 of its features' total price in XP and use up raw materials costing half of this total price. See the DUNGEON MASTER's Guide for descriptions of magic weapons, armor, and shields, the prerequisites associated with each one, and prices of their features.

You can also mend a broken magic weapon, suit of armor, or shield if it is one that you could make. Doing so costs half the XP, half the raw materials, and half the time it would take to enchant that item in the first place.

The weapon, armor, or shield to be enhanced must be a masterwork item that you must provide. (Its cost is not included in the above cost.)

CRAFT ROD [Item Creation]

You can create magic rods, which have varied magical effects.

Prerequisite: Spellcaster level 9th+.

Benefit: You can create any rod whose prerequisites you meet. Crafting a rod takes 1 day for each 1,000 gp in its base price. To craft a rod, you must spend 1/25 of its base price in XP and use up raw materials costing half of its base price. See the DUNGEON MASTER's Guide for descriptions of rods, the prerequisites associated with each one, and their prices.

Some rods incur extra costs in material components or XP as noted in their descriptions. These costs are in addition to those derived from the rod's base price.

CRAFT STAFF [Item Creation]

You can create magic staffs, which have multiple magical effects.

Prerequisite: Spellcaster level 12th+.

Benefit: You can create any staff whose prerequisites you meet. Crafting a staff takes 1 day for each 1,000 gp in its base price. To craft a staff, you must spend 1/25 of its base price in XP and use up raw materials costing half of its base price. See the DUNGEON MASTER's Guide for descriptions of staffs, the prerequisites associated with each one, and their prices.

A newly created staff has 50 charges.

Some staffs incur extra costs in material components or XP as noted in their descriptions. These costs are in addition to those derived from the staff's base price.

CRAFT WAND [Item Creation]

You can create wands, which cast spells (see the DUNGEON MASTER's Guide for rules on wands).

Prerequisite: Spellcaster level 5th+.

Benefit: You can create a wand of any spell of 4th level or lower that you know. Crafting a wand takes 1 day for each 1,000 gp in its base price. The base price of a wand is its caster level multiplied by the spell level multiplied by 750 gp. To craft a wand, you must spend 1/25 of this base price in XP and use up raw materials costing half of this base price.

A newly created wand has 50 charges.

Any wand that stores a spell with a costly material component or an XP cost also carries a commensurate cost. In addition to the cost derived from the base cost, you must expend fifty copies of the material component or pay fifty times the XP cost.

CRAFT WONDROUS ITEM [Item Creation]

You can create miscellaneous magic items, such as *crystal balls* and *flying carpets*.

Prerequisite: Spellcaster level 3rd+.

Benefit: You can create any miscellaneous magic item whose prerequisites you meet. Enchanting a miscellaneous magic item takes 1 day for each 1,000 gp in its price. To enchant a miscellaneous magic item, the spellcaster must spend 1/25 of the item's price in XP and use up raw materials costing half of this price. See the DUNGEON MASTER's Guide for information on miscellaneous magic items.

You can also mend a broken miscellaneous magic item if it is one that you could make. Doing so costs half the XP, half the raw materials, and half the time it would take to enchant that item in the first place.

Some wondrous items incur extra costs in material components or XP as noted in their descriptions. These costs are in addition to those derived from the item's base price. You must pay such a cost to create an item or to mend a broken one.

DEFLECT ARROWS [General]

You can deflect incoming arrows, as well as crossbow bolts, spears, and other shot or thrown weapons.

Prerequisites: Dex 13+, Improved Unarmed Strike.

Benefit: You must have at least one hand free (holding nothing) to use this feat. Once per round when you would normally be hit with a ranged weapon, you may make a Reflex saving throw against a DC of 20 (if the ranged weapon has a magical bonus to attack, the DC increases by that amount). If you succeed, you deflect the weapon. You must be aware of the attack and not flat-footed. Attempting to deflect a ranged weapon doesn't count as an action. Exceptional ranged weapons, such as boulders hurled by giants or *Melf's acid arrows*, can't be deflected.

Special: A monk receives this feat for free at 2nd level, even if she does not have the prerequisite Dexterity score.

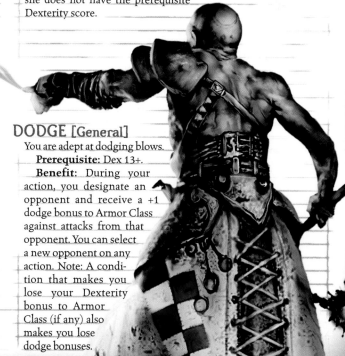

DODGE [General]

You are adept at dodging blows.

Prerequisite: Dex 13+.

Benefit: During your action, you designate an opponent and receive a +1 dodge bonus to Armor Class against attacks from that opponent. You can select a new opponent on any action. Note: A condition that makes you lose your Dexterity bonus to Armor Class (if any) also makes you lose dodge bonuses.

Illus by J. Foster

Also, dodge bonuses (such as this one and a dwarf's racial bonus to dodge giants) stack with each other, unlike most other types of bonuses.

EMPOWER SPELL [Metamagic]

You can cast spells to greater effect.

Benefit: All variable, numeric effects of an empowered spell are increased by one-half. An empowered spell deals half again as much damage as normal, cures half again as many hit points, affects half again as many targets, etc., as appropriate. For example, an empowered *magic missile* deals one and one-half times normal damage (roll 1d4+1 and multiply the result by 1.5 for each missile). Saving throws and opposed rolls (such as the one you make when you cast *dispel magic*) are not affected. Spells without random variables are not affected. An empowered spell uses up a spell slot two levels higher than the spell's actual level.

ENDURANCE [General]

You are capable of amazing feats of stamina.

Benefit: Whenever you make a check for performing a physical action that extends over a period of time (running, swimming, holding your breath, and so on), you get a +4 bonus to the check.

ENLARGE SPELL [Metamagic]

You can cast spells farther than normal.

Benefit: An enlarged spell has its range doubled. Spells whose ranges are not defined by distance do not have their ranges increased. A spell whose area or effect is determined by its range (such as *bless* or a cone spell) has the dimensions of its area or effect increased proportionally. An enlarged spell uses up a spell slot one level higher than the spell's actual level.

EXOTIC WEAPON PROFICIENCY [General]

Choose a type of exotic weapon, such as dire flail or shuriken (see Table 7–4: Weapons, page 99, for a list of exotic weapons). You understand how to use that type of exotic weapon in combat.

Prerequisite: Base attack bonus +1 or higher.

Benefit: You make attack rolls with the weapon normally.

Normal: A character who uses a weapon without being proficient with it suffers a –4 penalty on attack rolls.

Special: You can gain this feat multiple times. Each time you take the feat, it applies to a new weapon. Proficiency with the bastard sword or the dwarven waraxe has a prerequisite of Str 13+.

EXPERTISE [General]

You are trained at using your combat skill for defense as well as offense.

Prerequisite: Int 13+.

Benefit: When you use the attack action or full attack action in melee, you can take a penalty of as much as –5 on your attack and add the same number (up to +5) to your Armor Class. This number may not exceed your base attack bonus. The changes to attack rolls and Armor Class last until your next action. The bonus to your Armor Class is a dodge bonus.

Normal: A character not capable of the Expertise feat can fight defensively while using the attack or full attack action to take a –4 penalty on attacks and gain a +2 dodge bonus to Armor Class.

EXTEND SPELL [Metamagic]

You can cast spells that last longer than normal.

Benefit: An extended spell lasts twice as long as normal. Spells with a concentration, instantaneous, or permanent duration are not affected by this feat. An extended spell uses up a spell slot one level higher than the spell's actual level.

EXTRA TURNING [Special]

Extra Turning is available only to clerics and paladins. It is described in the Cleric section, on page 32, and the Paladin section, on page 42, in Chapter 3: Classes.

FAR SHOT [General]

You can get greater distance out of a ranged weapon.

Prerequisite: Point Blank Shot.

Benefit: When you use a projectile weapon, such as a bow, its range increment increases by one-half (multiply by 1.5). When you use a thrown weapon, its range increment is doubled.

FORGE RING [Item Creation]

You can create magic rings, which have varied magical effects.

Prerequisite: Spellcaster level 12th+.

Benefit: You can create any ring whose prerequisites you meet. Crafting a ring takes 1 day for each 1,000 gp in its base price. To craft a ring, you must spend 1/25 of its base price in XP and use up raw materials costing half of its base price. See the DUNGEON MASTER's *Guide* for descriptions of rings, the prerequisites associated with each one, and their prices.

You can also mend a broken ring if it is a ring that you could make. Doing so costs half the XP, half the raw materials, and half the time it would take to craft that ring in the first place.

Some magic rings incur extra costs in material components or XP as noted in their descriptions. For example, a *ring of three wishes* costs 15,000 XP in addition to costs derived from its base price (as much XP as it costs to cast *wish* three times). You must pay such a cost to create a ring or to mend a broken one.

GREAT CLEAVE [General]

You can wield a melee weapon with such power that you can strike multiple times when you fell your foes.

Prerequisites: Str 13+, Power Attack, Cleave, base attack bonus +4 or higher.

Benefit: As Cleave, except that you have no limit to the number of times you can use it per round.

GREAT FORTITUDE [General]

You are tougher than normal.

Benefit: You get a +2 bonus to all Fortitude saving throws.

HEIGHTEN SPELL [Metamagic]

You can cast a spell as if it were higher level than it actually is.

Benefit: A heightened spell has a higher spell level than normal (up to 9th level). Unlike other metamagic feats, Heighten Spell actually increases the effective level of the spell that it modifies. All effects dependent on spell level (such as saving throw DCs and ability to penetrate a *minor globe of invulnerability*) are calculated according to the heightened level. The heightened spell is as difficult to prepare and cast as a spell of its effective level. For example, a cleric could prepare *hold person* as a 4th-level spell (instead of a 2nd-level spell), and it would in all ways be treated as a 4th-level spell.

IMPROVED BULL RUSH [General]

You know how to push opponents back.

Prerequisites: Str 13+, Power Attack.

Benefit: When you perform a bull rush (see page 136), you do not draw an attack of opportunity from the defender.

IMPROVED CRITICAL [General]

Choose one type of weapon, such as longsword or greataxe. With that weapon, you know how to hit where it hurts.

Prerequisites: Proficient with weapon, base attack bonus +8 or higher.

Benefit: When using the weapon you selected, your threat range is doubled. For example, a longsword usually threatens a critical on a 19 or 20 (two numbers). If a character using a longsword has Improved Critical (longsword), the threat range becomes 17 through 20 (four numbers).

Note: "Keen" magic weapons also double their normal, nonmagical threat range. As with all doubled doublings, the result is triple. A magic longsword with a doubled threat range in the hands of a character with Improved Critical (longsword) would have a threat range of 15 through 20 (six numbers: 2 for being a longsword, +2 for being doubled once and +2 for being doubled a second time).

Special: You can gain this feat multiple times. The effects do not stack. Each time you take the feat, it applies to a new weapon.

IMPROVED DISARM [General]
You know how to disarm opponents in melee combat.

Prerequisites: Int 13+, Expertise.

Benefit: You do not suffer an attack of opportunity when you attempt to disarm an opponent, nor does the opponent have a chance to disarm you.

Normal: See the normal disarm rules, page 137.

IMPROVED INITIATIVE [General]
You can react more quickly than normal in a fight.

Benefit: You get a +4 bonus on initiative checks.

IMPROVED TRIP [General]
You are trained not only in tripping opponents but in following through with an attack.

Prerequisites: Int 13+, Expertise.

Benefit: If you trip an opponent in melee combat, you immediately get a melee attack against that opponent as if you hadn't used your attack for the trip attempt. For example, at 11th level, Tordek gets three attacks at base attack bonuses of +11, +6, and +1. In the current round, he attempts to trip his opponent. His first attempt fails (using up his first attack). His second attempt succeeds, and he immediately makes a melee attack against his opponent with a base attack of +6. Finally, he takes his last attack at +1.

Normal: See Trip, page 139.

Special: At 6th level, a monk gains the Improved Trip feat even if she does not have the Expertise feat.

IMPROVED TWO-WEAPON FIGHTING [General]
You are an expert in fighting two-handed.

Prerequisites: Two-Weapon Fighting, Ambidexterity, base attack bonus +9 or higher.

Benefit: In addition to the standard single extra attack you get with an off-hand weapon, you get a second attack with the off-hand weapon, albeit at a –5 penalty (see Table 8–2: Two-Weapon Fighting Penalties, page 125).

Normal: Without this feat, you can only get a single extra attack with an off-hand weapon.

Special: A ranger who meets only the base attack bonus prerequisite can gain this feat, but can only use it when wearing light armor or no armor.

IMPROVED UNARMED STRIKE [General]
You are skilled at fighting while unarmed.

Benefit: You are considered to be armed even when unarmed—that is, armed opponents do not get attacks of opportunity when you attack them while unarmed. However, you still get an opportunity attack against any opponent who makes an unarmed attack on you.

Special: A monk fighting unarmed automatically gains the benefit of this feat (see page 39).

IRON WILL [General]
You have a stronger will than normal.

Benefit: You get a +2 bonus to all Will saving throws.

LEADERSHIP [General]
Leadership is described in the DUNGEON MASTER's Guide.

LIGHTNING REFLEXES [General]
You have faster than normal reflexes.

Benefit: You get a +2 bonus to all Reflex saving throws.

MARTIAL WEAPON PROFICIENCY [General]
Choose a type of martial weapon, such as longbow (see Table 7–4: Weapons, pages 98–99, for a list of martial weapons). You understand how to use that type of martial weapon in combat.

Use this feat to expand the list of weapons you are proficient with beyond the basic list in the class description.

Benefit: You make attack rolls with the weapon normally.

Normal: A character who uses a weapon without being proficient with it suffers a –4 penalty on attack rolls.

Special: Barbarians, fighters, paladins, and rangers are proficient with all martial weapons.

You can gain this feat multiple times. Each time you take the feat, it applies to a new weapon.

A cleric whose deity's favored weapon is a martial weapon and who chooses War as one of his domains receives the Martial Weapon Proficiency feat related to that weapon for free, as well as the Weapon Focus feat related to that weapon.

A sorcerer or wizard who casts the spell *Tenser's transformation* on herself gains proficiency with all martial weapons for the duration of the spell.

MAXIMIZE SPELL [Metamagic]
You can cast spells to maximum effect.

Benefit: All variable, numeric effects of a maximized spell are maximized. A maximized spell deals maximum damage, cures the maximum number of hit points, affects the maximum number of targets, etc., as appropriate. For example, a maximized *fireball* deals 6 points of damage per caster level (up to 60 points of damage). Saving throws and opposed rolls (such as the one you make when you cast *dispel magic*) are not affected. Spells without random variables are not affected. A maximized spell uses up a spell slot three levels higher than the spell's actual level.

An empowered, maximized spell gains the separate benefits of each feat: the maximum result plus one-half the normally rolled result.

MOBILITY [General]
You are skilled at dodging past opponents and avoiding blows.

Prerequisites: Dex 13+, Dodge.

Benefit: You get a +4 dodge bonus to Armor Class against attacks of opportunity caused when you move out of or within a threatened area. Note: A condition that makes you lose your Dexterity bonus to Armor Class (if any) also makes you lose dodge bonuses. Also, dodge bonuses (such as this one and a dwarf's racial bonus to dodge giants) stack with each other, unlike most types of bonuses.

MOUNTED ARCHERY [General]
You are skilled at using ranged weapons from horseback.

Prerequisite: Ride skill, Mounted Combat.

Benefit: The penalty you suffer when using a ranged weapon from horseback is halved: –2 instead of –4 if your mount is taking a double move, and –4 instead of –8 if your mount is running. (See Mounted Combat, page 138.)

MOUNTED COMBAT [General]
You are skilled in mounted combat.

Prerequisite: Ride skill.

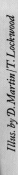

Illus. by D. Martin/T. Lockwood

Benefit: Once per round when your mount is hit in combat, you may make a Ride check to negate the hit. The hit is negated if your Ride check is greater than the attack roll (essentially, the Ride check becomes the mount's Armor Class if it's higher than the mount's regular AC).

POINT BLANK SHOT
[General]
You are skilled at making well-placed shots with ranged weapons at close range.

Benefit: You get a +1 bonus to attack and damage rolls with ranged weapons at ranges of up to 30 feet.

POWER ATTACK
[General]
You can make exceptionally powerful melee attacks.

Prerequisite: Str 13+.

Benefit: On your action, before making attack rolls for a round, you may choose to subtract a number from all melee attack rolls and add the same number to all melee damage rolls. This number may not exceed your base attack bonus. The penalty on attacks and bonus on damage apply until your next action.

PRECISE SHOT [General]
You are skilled at timing and aiming ranged attacks.

Prerequisite: Point Blank Shot.

Benefit: You can shoot or throw ranged weapons at an opponent engaged in melee without suffering the standard –4 penalty (see Shooting or Throwing into a Melee, page 124).

QUICK DRAW [General]
You can draw weapons with startling speed.

Prerequisite: Base attack bonus +1 or higher.

Benefit: You can draw a weapon as a free action instead of as a move-equivalent action.

QUICKEN SPELL
[Metamagic]
You can cast a spell with a moment's thought.

Benefit: Casting a quickened spell is a free action. You can perform another action, even casting another spell, in the same round as you cast a quickened spell. You may only cast one quickened spell per round. A spell whose casting time is more than 1 full round cannot be

Mialee casts a spell from a scroll she scribed.

quickened. A quickened spell uses up a spell slot four levels higher than the spell's actual level.

RAPID SHOT [General]
You can use ranged weapons with exceptional speed.

Prerequisites: Point Blank Shot, Dex 13+.

Benefit: You can get one extra attack per round with a ranged weapon. The attack is at your highest base attack bonus, but each attack (the extra one and the normal ones) suffers a –2 penalty. You must use the full attack action (see page 124) to use this feat.

RIDE-BY ATTACK
[General]
You are skilled at fast attack from horseback.

Prerequisites: Ride skill, Mounted Combat.

Benefit: When you are mounted and use the charge action, you may move and attack as with a standard charge and then move again (continuing the straight line of the charge). Your total movement for the round can't exceed double your mounted speed. You do not provoke an attack of opportunity from the opponent that you attack.

RUN [General]
You are fleet of foot.

Benefit: When running, you move five times your normal speed instead of four times the speed (see Run, page 127). If you make a running jump (see the Jump skill description, page 70), increase the distance or height you clear by one-fourth, but not past the maximum.

SCRIBE SCROLL
[Item Creation]
You can create scrolls, from which you or another a spellcaster can cast the scribed spells. See the DUNGEON MASTER's GUIDE for rules on scrolls.

Prerequisite: Spellcaster level 1st+.

Benefit: You can create a scroll of any spell that you know. Scribing a scroll takes 1 day for each 1,000 gp in its base price. The base price of a scroll is its spell level multiplied by its caster level multiplied by 25 gp. To scribe a scroll, you must spend 1/25 of this base price in XP and use up raw materials costing half of this base price.

Any scroll that stores a spell with a costly material component or an XP cost also carries a commensurate cost. In addition to the costs derived from the base price, you must expend the material component or pay the XP when scribing the scroll.

SHIELD PROFICIENCY [General]

You are proficient with shields.

Benefit: You can use a shield and suffer only the standard penalties (see Table 7–5: Armor, page 104).

Normal: A character who is using a shield with which he or she is not proficient suffers the shield's armor check penalty on attack rolls and on all skill rolls that involve moving, including Ride.

Special: Barbarians, bards, clerics, druids, fighters, paladins, and rangers have this feat for free. Monks, rogues, sorcerers, and wizards do not.

SHOT ON THE RUN [General]

You are highly trained in skirmish ranged weapon tactics.

Prerequisites: Point Blank Shot, Dex 13+, Dodge, Mobility.

Benefit: When using the attack action with a ranged weapon, you can move both before and after the attack, provided that your total distance moved is not greater than your speed.

SILENT SPELL [Metamagic]

You can cast spells silently.

Benefit: A silent spell can be cast with no verbal components. Spells without verbal components are not affected. A silent spell uses up a spell slot one level higher than the spell's actual level.

Special: Bard spells cannot be enhanced by this metamagic feat.

SIMPLE WEAPON PROFICIENCY [General]

You understand how to use all types of simple weapons in combat (see Table 7–4: Weapons, page 98, for a list of simple weapons).

Benefit: You make attack rolls with simple weapons normally.

Normal: A character who uses a weapon without being proficient with it suffers a –4 penalty on attack rolls.

Special: All characters except for druids, monks, rogues, and wizards are automatically proficient with all simple weapons.

A wizard who casts the spell *Tenser's transformation* on herself gains proficiency with all simple weapons for the duration of the spell.

SKILL FOCUS [General]

Choose a skill, such as Move Silently. You have a special knack with that skill.

Benefit: You get a +2 bonus on all skill checks with that skill.

Special: You can gain this feat multiple times. Its effects do not stack. Each time you take the feat, it applies to a new skill.

SPELL FOCUS [General]

Choose a school of magic, such as Illusion. Your spells of that school are more potent than normal.

Benefit: Add +2 to the Difficulty Class for all saving throws against spells from the school of magic you select to focus on.

Special: You can gain this feat multiple times. Its effects do not stack. Each time you take the feat, it applies to a new school of magic.

SPELL MASTERY [Special]

Spell Mastery is available only to wizards. It is described on page 54 in Chapter 3: Classes.

SPELL PENETRATION [General]

Your spells are especially potent, breaking through spell resistance more readily than normal.

Benefit: You get a +2 bonus to caster level checks (1d20+caster level) to beat a creature's spell resistance.

SPIRITED CHARGE [General]

You are trained at making a devastating mounted charge.

Prerequisites: Ride skill, Mounted Combat, Ride-By Attack.

Benefit: When mounted and using the charge action, you deal double damage with a melee weapon (or triple damage with a lance).

SPRING ATTACK [General]

You are trained in fast melee attacks and fancy footwork.

Prerequisites: Dex 13+, Dodge, Mobility, base attack bonus +4 or higher.

Benefit: When using the attack action with a melee weapon, you can move both before and after the attack, provided that your total distance moved is not greater than your speed. Moving in this way does not provoke an attack of opportunity from the defender you attack. You can't use this feat if you are in heavy armor.

STILL SPELL [Metamagic]

You can cast spells without gestures.

Benefit: A still spell can be cast with no somatic components. Spells without somatic components are not affected. A still spell uses up a spell slot one level higher than the spell's actual level.

STUNNING FIST [General]

You know how to strike opponents in vulnerable areas.

Prerequisites: Dex 13+, Improved Unarmed Strike, Wis 13+, base attack bonus +8 or higher.

Benefit: Declare that you are using the feat before you make your attack roll (thus, a missed attack roll ruins the attempt). It forces a foe damaged by your unarmed attack to make a Fortitude saving throw (DC 10 + one-half your level + Wis modifier), in addition to dealing damage normally. If the defender fails his saving throw, he is stunned for 1 round (until just before your next action). A stunned character can't act and loses any Dexterity bonus to Armor Class. Attackers get a +2 bonus on attack rolls against a stunned opponent. You may attempt a stunning attack once per day for every four levels you have attained, and no more than once per round.

SUNDER [General]

You are skilled at attacking others' weapons.

Prerequisites: Str 13+, Power Attack.

Benefit: When you strike at an opponent's weapon, you do not provoke an attack of opportunity (see Strike a Weapon, page 136).

TOUGHNESS [General]

You are tougher than normal.

Benefit: You gain +3 hit points.

Special: A character may gain this feat multiple times.

TRACK [General]

You can follow the trails of creatures and characters across most types of terrain.

Benefit: To find tracks or to follow them for one mile requires a Wilderness Lore check. You must make another Wilderness Lore check every time the tracks become difficult to follow, such as when other tracks cross them or when the tracks backtrack and diverge.

You move at half your normal speed (or at your normal speed with a –5 penalty on the check). The DC depends on the surface and the prevailing conditions:

Surface	DC	Surface	DC
Very soft	5	Firm	15
Soft	10	Hard	20

Very Soft Ground: Any surface (fresh snow, thick dust, wet mud) that holds deep, clear impressions of footprints.

Soft Ground: Any surface soft enough to yield to pressure, but firmer than wet mud or fresh snow, in which the creature leaves frequent but shallow footprints.

Firm Ground: Most normal outdoor surfaces (such as lawns, fields, woods, and the like) or exceptionally soft or dirty indoor surfaces (thick rugs, very dirty or dusty floors). The creature might leave some traces (broken branches, tufts of hair) but leaves only occasional or partial footprints.

Hard Ground: Any surface that doesn't hold footprints at all, such as bare rock or indoor floors. Most streambeds fall into this category, since any footprints left behind are obscured or washed away. The creature leaves only traces (scuff marks, displaced pebbles).

Condition	DC Modifier
Every three creatures in the group being tracked	−1
Size of creature or creatures being tracked:*	
Fine	+8
Diminutive	+4
Tiny	+2
Small	+1
Medium-size	0
Large	−1
Huge	−2
Gargantuan	−4
Colossal	−8
Every 24 hours since the trail was made	+1
Every hour of rain since the trail was made	+1
Fresh snow cover since the trail was made	+10
Poor visibility:**	
Overcast or moonless night	+6
Moonlight	+3
Fog or precipitation	+3
Tracked party hides trail (and moves at half speed)	+5

*For a group of mixed sizes, apply only the modifier for the largest size category.

**Apply only the largest modifier from this category.

If you fail a Wilderness Lore check, you can retry after 1 hour (outdoors) or 10 minutes (indoors) of searching.

Normal: A character without this feat can use the Search skill to find tracks, but can only follow tracks if the DC is 10 or less.

Special: A ranger receives Track as a bonus feat.

This feat does not allow you to find or follow the tracks of a subject of a *pass without trace* spell.

TRAMPLE [General]

You are trained in using your mount to knock down opponents.

Prerequisites: Ride skill, Mounted Combat.

Benefit: When you attempt to overrun an opponent while mounted, the target may not choose to avoid you. If you knock down the target, your mount may make one hoof attack against him or her, gaining the standard +4 bonus on attack rolls against prone targets. (See Overrun, page 139.)

TWO-WEAPON FIGHTING [General]

You can fight with a weapon in each hand. You can make one extra attack each round with the second weapon.

Benefit: Your penalties for fighting with two weapons are reduced by 2.

Normal: See Attacking with Two Weapons, page 124, and Table 8–2: Two-Weapon Fighting Penalties, page 125.

Special: The Ambidexterity feat reduces the attack penalty for the second weapon by 4.

A ranger wearing light armor or no armor can fight with two weapons as if he had the feats Ambidexterity and Two-Weapon Fighting.

WEAPON FINESSE [General]

You are especially skilled at using a certain weapon, one that can benefit as much from Dexterity as from Strength. Choose one light weapon. Alternatively, you can choose a rapier, provided you can use it in one hand, or a spiked chain, provided you're at least Medium-size.

Prerequisite: Proficient with weapon, base attack bonus +1 or higher.

Benefit: With the selected weapon, you may use your Dexterity modifier instead of your Strength modifier on attack rolls. Since you need your second hand for balance, if you carry a shield, apply the shield's armor check penalty to your attack rolls.

Special: You can gain this feat multiple times. Each time you take the feat, it applies to a new weapon.

WEAPON FOCUS [General]

Choose one type of weapon, such as greataxe. You are especially good at using this weapon. You can choose "unarmed strike" or "grapple" for your weapon for purposes of this feat. If you are a spellcaster, you can choose "ray," in which case you are especially good with rays, such as the one produced by the *ray of frost* spell.

Prerequisites: Proficient with weapon, base attack bonus +1 or higher.

Benefit: You add +1 to all attack rolls you make using the selected weapon.

Special: You can gain this feat multiple times. Its effects do not stack. Each time you take the feat, it applies to a new weapon.

A fighter must have Weapon Focus with a weapon to gain the Weapon Specialization feat for that weapon.

WEAPON SPECIALIZATION [Special]

Weapon Specialization is available only to fighters of 4th or higher level. See page 37.

WHIRLWIND ATTACK [General]

You can strike nearby opponents in an amazing, spinning attack.

Prerequisites: Int 13+, Expertise, Dex 13+, Dodge, Mobility, base attack bonus +4 or higher, Spring Attack.

Benefit: When you perform the full attack action, you can give up your regular attacks and instead make one melee attack at your full base attack bonus against each opponent within 5 feet.

Illus. by A. Swekel

Fig. A

Fig. B

Fig. C

Fig. D

Fig. E

Fig. F

hat does your character look like? How old is she? What sort of first impression does she make? When she prays, what deity or deities does she call on, if any? What led her to become an adventurer?

This chapter helps you establish your character's identity. These details make your character more lifelike, like a main character in a novel or a movie. For many players, the action lies here, in defining the character as a person to be roleplayed.

When you first play a character, it's fine to leave the details sketchy. As you play the character over time, you will get a better sense of who you want her to be. You will develop her details in much the way that an author develops a character over several drafts of a novel or over several novels in a series.

This chapter covers alignment (the character's place in the struggle between good and evil), religion (the character's deity or deities), vital statistics (name, gender, age, and so on), and personal description.

ALIGNMENT

In the temple of Pelor is an ancient tome. When the temple recruits adventurers for its most sensitive and important quests, each adventurer who wants to participate must kiss the book. Those who are evil in their hearts are blasted by holy power, and even those who are neither good nor evil are stunned. Only those who are good can kiss the tome without harm and are trusted with the temple's most important work. Good and evil are not philosophical concepts in the D&D game. They are the forces that define the cosmos.

Devils in human guise stalk the land, tempting people toward evil. Holy clerics use the power of good to protect worshipers. Devotees of evil gods bring ruin on innocents to win the favor of their deities, while trusting that rewards await them in the afterlife. Crusading paladins fearlessly confront evil-doers, knowing that this short life is nothing worth clinging to. Warlords turn to whichever supernatural power will help them conquer, and proxies for good and evil gods promise them rewards in return for the warlords' oaths of obedience.

A character's or creature's general moral and personal attitudes are represented by its alignment: lawful good, neutral good, chaotic good, lawful neutral, neutral, chaotic neutral, lawful evil, neutral evil, and chaotic evil. (See Table 6–1: Creature, Race, and Class Alignments to see which creatures, races, and classes favor which alignments.)

Choose an alignment for your character, using the character's race and class as a guide. Standard characters are good or neutral but not evil. Evil alignments are for villains and monsters.

Alignment is a tool for developing your character's identity. It is not a straitjacket for restricting your character. Each alignment represents a broad range of personality types or personal philosophies, so two lawful good characters can be quite different from each other. In addition, few people are completely consistent. A lawful good character may have a greedy streak, occasionally tempting him to take something or hoard something he has even if that's not the lawful or good thing to do. People are also not consistent from day to day. Good characters can lose their tempers, neutral characters can be inspired to perform noble acts, and so on.

EXAMPLES

OF HOLY SYMBOLS

Fig. K

Choosing an alignment for your character means stating your intent to play that character a certain way. If your character acts in a way more appropriate to another alignment, the DM may decide that your character's alignment has changed to match her actions.

TABLE 6–1: CREATURE, RACE, AND CLASS ALIGNMENTS

Lawful Good	Neutral Good	Chaotic Good
Archons	*Guardinals*	*Eladrins*
Gold dragons	Gnomes	Copper dragons
Lammasus		*Unicorns*
Dwarves		Elves
Paladins		Rangers

Lawful Neutral	Neutral	Chaotic Neutral
Monks	*Animals*	Half-elves
Wizards	Halflings	Half-orcs
	Humans	Barbarians
	Lizardfolk	Bards
	Druids	Rogues

Lawful Evil	Neutral Evil	Chaotic Evil
Devils	Drow	*Demons*
Blue dragons	Goblins	Red dragons
Beholders	Troglodytes	Vampires
Ogre mages		Bugbears
Hobgoblins		Gnolls
Kobolds		Ogres
		Orcs

Creatures and classes in *italic* are always the indicated alignment. Except for the paladin, they are born into that alignment. It is part of their nature. Usually, a creature with an inherent alignment has some connection (through ancestry, history, or magic) to the Outer Planes or is a magical beast.

For other creatures, races, and classes, the designated alignment is the typical or most common one. Normal sentient creatures can be of any alignment. They may have inherent tendencies toward a particular alignment, but individuals can vary from this norm. Depending on the type of creature, these tendencies may be stronger or weaker. For example, kobolds and beholders are usually lawful evil, but kobolds display more variation in alignment than beholders because their inherent alignment tendency isn't as strong. In addition to inborn tendencies, sentient creatures have cultural tendencies that usually reinforce inherent alignment tendencies. For example, orcs tend to be chaotic evil, and their culture tends to produce chaotic evil members. A human raised among orcs is more likely than normal to be chaotic evil, while an orc raised among humans is less likely to be so.

GOOD VS. EVIL

Good characters and creatures protect innocent life. Evil characters and creatures debase or destroy innocent life, whether for fun or profit.

"Good" implies altruism, respect for life, and a concern for the dignity of sentient beings. Good characters make personal sacrifices to help others.

"Evil" implies hurting, oppressing, and killing others. Some evil creatures simply have no compassion for others and kill without

qualms if doing so is convenient. Others actively pursue evil, killing for sport or out of duty to some evil deity or master.

People who are neutral with respect to good and evil have compunctions against killing the innocent but lack the commitment to make sacrifices to protect or help others. Neutral people are committed to others by personal relationships. A neutral person may sacrifice himself to protect his family or even his homeland, but he would not do so for strangers who are not related to him.

Being good or evil can be a conscious choice, as with the paladin who attempts to live up to her ideals or the evil cleric who causes pain and terror to emulate his god. For most people, though, being good or evil is an attitude that one recognizes but does not choose. Being neutral between good and evil usually represents a lack of commitment one way or the other, but for some it represents a positive commitment to a balanced view. While acknowledging that good and evil are objective states, not just opinions, these folk maintain that a balance between the two is the proper place for people, or at least for them.

Animals and other creatures incapable of moral action are neutral rather than good or evil. Even deadly vipers and tigers that eat people are neutral because they lack the capacity for morally right or wrong behavior.

LAW AND CHAOS

Lawful characters tell the truth, keep their word, respect authority, honor tradition, and judge those who fall short of their duties. Chaotic characters follow their consciences, resent being told what to do, favor new ideas over tradition, and do what they promise if they feel like it.

"Law" implies honor, trustworthiness, obedience to authority, and reliability. On the downside, lawfulness can include close-mindedness, reactionary adherence to tradition, judgmentalness, and a lack of adaptability. Those who consciously promote lawfulness say that only lawful behavior creates a society in which people can depend on each other and make the right decisions in full confidence that others will act as they should.

Regdar

"Chaos" implies freedom, adaptability, and flexibility. On the downside, chaos can include recklessness, resentment toward legitimate authority, arbitrary actions, and irresponsibility. Those who promote chaotic behavior say that only unfettered personal freedom allows people to express themselves fully and lets society benefit from the potential that its individuals have within them.

People who are neutral with respect to law and chaos have a normal respect for authority and feel neither a compulsion to obey nor to rebel. They are honest, but can be tempted into lying or deceiving others.

Devotion to law or chaos may be a conscious choice, but more often it is a personality trait that is recognized rather than being chosen. Neutrality with respect to law and chaos is usually simply a middle state, a state of not feeling compelled toward one side or the other. Some few neutrals, however, espouse neutrality as superior to law or chaos, regarding each as an extreme with its own blind spots and drawbacks.

Animals and other creatures incapable of moral action are neutral. Dogs may be obedient and cats free-spirited, but they do not have the moral capacity to be truly lawful or chaotic.

Illus. by T. Lockwood

THE NINE ALIGNMENTS

Nine distinct alignments define all the combinations of law vs. chaos and good vs. evil. Each description depicts the typical character of that alignment. Remember that individuals vary from this norm, and that a given character may act more or less in accord with her alignment from day to day. Use these descriptions as guidelines, not as scripts.

The first six alignments, lawful good through chaotic neutral, are the standard alignments for player characters. The three evil alignments are for monsters and villains.

Lawful Good, "Crusader": A lawful good character acts as a good person is expected or required to act. She combines a commitment to oppose evil with the discipline to fight relentlessly. She tells the truth, keeps her word, helps those in need, and speaks out against injustice. A lawful good character hates to see the guilty go unpunished. Alhandra, a paladin who fights evil without mercy and who protects the innocent without hesitation, is lawful good.

Lawful good is the best alignment you can be because it combines honor and compassion.

Neutral Good, "Benefactor": A neutral good character does the best that a good person can do. He is devoted to helping others. He works with kings and magistrates but does not feel beholden to them. Jozan, a cleric who helps others according to their needs, is neutral good.

The common phrase for neutral good is "true good."

Neutral good is the best alignment you can be because it means doing what is good without bias toward or against order.

Chaotic Good, "Rebel": A chaotic good character acts as his conscience directs him with little regard for what others expect of him. He makes his own way, but he's kind and benevolent. He believes in goodness and right but has little use for laws and regulations. He hates it when people try to intimidate others and tell them what to do. He follows his own moral compass, which, although good, may not agree with that of society. Soveliss, a ranger who waylays the evil baron's tax collectors, is chaotic good.

Chaotic good is the best alignment you can be because it combines a good heart with a free spirit.

Lawful Neutral, "Judge": A lawful neutral character acts as law, tradition, or a personal code directs her. Order and organization are paramount to her. She may believe in personal order and live by a code or standard, or she may believe in order for all and favor a strong, organized government. Ember, a monk who follows her discipline without being swayed by the demands of those in need nor by the temptations of evil, is lawful neutral.

The common phrase for lawful neutral is "true lawful."

Lawful neutral is the best alignment you can be because it means you are reliable and honorable without being a zealot.

Neutral, "Undecided": A neutral character does what seems to be a good idea. She doesn't feel strongly one way or the other when it comes to good vs. evil or law vs. chaos. Most neutrality is a lack of conviction or bias rather than a commitment to neutrality. Such a character thinks of good as better than evil. After all, she would rather have good neighbors and rulers than evil ones. Still, she's not personally committed to upholding good in any abstract or universal way. Mialee, a wizard who devotes herself to her art and is bored by the semantics of moral debate, is neutral.

Some neutral characters, on the other hand, commit themselves philosophically to neutrality. They see good, evil, law, and chaos as prejudices and dangerous extremes. They advocate the middle way of neutrality as the best, most balanced road in the long run.

The common phrase for neutral is "true neutral."

Neutral is the best alignment you can be because it means you act naturally, without prejudice or compulsion.

Chaotic Neutral, "Free Spirit": A chaotic neutral character follows his whims. He is an individualist first and last. He values his own liberty but doesn't strive to protect others' freedom. He avoids authority, resents restrictions, and challenges traditions. The chaotic neutral character does not intentionally disrupt organizations as part of a campaign of anarchy. To do so, he would have to be motivated either by good (and a desire to liberate others) or evil (and a desire to make those different from himself suffer). Devis, a bard who wanders the land living by his wits, is chaotic neutral.

The common phrase for chaotic neutral is "true chaotic."

Remember that the chaotic neutral character may be unpredictable, but his behavior is not totally random. He is not as likely to jump off a bridge as to cross it.

Chaotic neutral is the best alignment you can be because it represents true freedom both from society's restrictions and from a do-gooder's zeal.

Lawful Evil, "Dominator": A lawful evil villain methodically takes what he wants within the limits of his code of conduct without regard to whom it hurts. He cares about tradition, loyalty, and order, but not about freedom, dignity, or life. He plays by the rules, but without mercy or compassion. He is comfortable in a hierarchy and would like to rule, but he is willing to serve. He condemns others not according to their actions but according to race, religion, homeland, or social rank. He is loath to break laws or promises. This reluctance is partly because of his nature and partly because he depends on order to protect himself from those who oppose him on moral grounds. Some lawful evil villains have particular taboos, such as not killing in cold blood (but having underlings do it) or not letting children come to harm (if it can be helped). They imagine that these compunctions put them above unprincipled villains. The scheming baron who expands his power and exploits his people is lawful evil.

Some lawful evil people and creatures are committed to evil with a zeal like that of a crusader committed to good. Beyond being willing to hurt others for their own ends, they take pleasure in spreading evil as an end unto itself. They may also see doing evil as part of a duty to an evil deity or master.

Lawful evil is sometimes called "diabolical" because devils are the epitome of lawful evil.

Lawful evil is the most dangerous alignment because it represents methodical, intentional, and frequently successful evil.

Neutral Evil, "Malefactor": A neutral evil villain does whatever she can get away with. She is out for herself, pure and simple. She sheds no tears for those she kills, whether for profit, sport, or convenience. She has no love of order and holds no illusion that following laws, traditions, or codes would make her any better or more noble. On the other hand, she doesn't have the restless nature or love of conflict that a chaotic evil villain has. The criminal who robs and murders to get what she wants is neutral evil.

Some neutral evil villains hold up evil as an ideal, committing evil for its own sake. Most often, such villains are devoted to evil deities or secret societies.

Naull

Illus. by T. Lockwood

89

Illus. by S. Wood / T. Lockwood

The common phrase for neutral evil is "true evil."

Neutral evil is the most dangerous alignment because it represents pure evil without honor and without variation.

Chaotic Evil, "Destroyer": A chaotic evil character does whatever his greed, hatred, and lust for destruction drive him to do. He is hot-tempered, vicious, arbitrarily violent, and unpredictable. If simply out for whatever he can get, he is ruthless and brutal. If he is committed to the spread of evil and chaos, he is even worse. Thankfully, his plans are haphazard, and any groups he joins or forms are poorly organized. Typically, chaotic evil people can only be made to work together by force, and their leader lasts only as long as he can thwart attempts to topple or assassinate him. The demented sorcerer pursuing mad schemes of vengeance and havoc is chaotic evil.

Chaotic evil is sometimes called "demonic" because demons are the epitome of chaotic evil.

Chaotic evil is the most dangerous alignment because it represents the destruction not only of beauty and life but of the order on which beauty and life depend.

RELIGION

The gods are many. A few, such as Pelor, god of the sun, have grand temples that sponsor mighty processions through the streets on high holy days. Others, such as Erythnul, god of slaughter, have temples only in hidden places or evil lands. While the gods most strongly make their presence felt through their clerics, they also have lay followers who more or less attempt to live up to their deities' standards. The typical person has a deity whom he considers to be his patron. Still, it is only prudent to be respectful toward and even pray to other deities when the time is right. Before setting out on a journey, a follower of Pelor might leave a small sacrifice at a wayside shrine to Fharlanghn, god of roads, to improve his chances of having a safe

Eberk

journey. As long as one's own deity is not at odds with the others in such an act of piety, such simple practices are common. In times of tribulation, however, some people recite dark prayers to evil deities. Such prayers are best muttered under one's breath, lest others overhear.

Deities rule the various aspects of human existence: good and evil, law and chaos, life and death, knowledge and nature. In addition, various nonhuman races have racial deities of their own (see Table 6–2: Deities by Race). A character may not be a cleric of a racial deity unless he is of the right race, but he may worship such a deity and live according to that deity's guidance. For a deity who is not tied to a particular race (such as Pelor), a cleric's race is not an issue.

Deities of certain monster types are named in the *Monster Manual*. Many more deities than those described here or mentioned in the *Monster Manual* also exist.

Your character may or may not have a patron deity. If you want her to have one, consider first the deities most appropriate to her race, class, and alignment (see Table 6–2: Deities by Race and Table 6–3: Deities by Class). If a cleric selects a deity, which one she selects influences her character's capabilities. Players with cleric characters should read Deity, Domains, and Domain Spells, page 31, before picking a deity, though the information below describing the various gods and goddesses can help them make a decision.

DEITIES

Across the world, people and creatures worship a great number of varied deities. Those described here are the most common deities worshiped among the common races, by adventurers, and by villains. Each entry includes the deity's name, pronunciation, role, alignment, titles, and general description. These deities' holy (or unholy) symbols are shown accompanying their descriptions. (See Table 3–7: Deities, page 31, for a summary of the most common deities, their alignments, the domains they are associated with, and their typical worshipers.)

Boccob

The god of magic, Boccob (*bock*-obb), is neutral. His titles include the Uncaring, Lord of All Magics, and Archmage of the Deities. Boccob is a distant deity who promotes no special agenda in the world of mortals. As a god of magic and knowledge, he is worshiped by wizards, sorcerers, and sages. The domains he is associated with are Knowledge, Magic, and Trickery. The quarterstaff is his favored weapon.

Corellon Larethian

The god of elves, Corellon Larethian (*Core*-eh-lon lah-*reth*-ee-yen), is chaotic good. He is known as the Creator of the Elves, the Protector, Protector and Preserver of Life, and Ruler of All Elves. Corellon Larethian is the creator and protector of the elven race. He governs those things held in highest esteem among elves, such as magic, music, arts, crafts, poetry, and warfare. Elves, half-elves, and bards

Table 6–2: Deities by Race

Race	Deities
Human	By class and alignment
Dwarf	Moradin or by class and alignment
Elf	Corellon Larethian, Ehlonna, or by class and alignment
Gnome	Garl Glittergold, Ehlonna, or by class and alignment
Half-elf	Corellon Larethian, Ehlonna, or by class and alignment
Half-orc	Gruumsh or by class and alignment
Halfling	Yondalla, Ehlonna, or by class and alignment

Table 6–3: Deities by Class

Class	Deities (Alignment)
Fighters	Heironeous (LG), Kord (CG), St. Cuthbert (LN), Hextor (LE), Erythnul (CE)
Barbarians	Kord (CG), Obad-Hai (N), Erythnul (CE)
Paladins	Heironeous (LG)
Rangers	Ehlonna (NG), Obad-Hai (N)
Wizards	Wee Jas (LN), Boccob (N), Vecna (NE)
Illusionists	Boccob (N)
Necromancers	Wee Jas (LN), Nerull (NE)
Sorcerers	Wee Jas (LN), Boccob (N), Vecna (NE)
Clerics	Any
Druids	Obad-Hai (N)
Rogues	Olidammara (CN), Nerull (NE), Vecna (NE), Erythnul (CE)
Bards	Pelor (NG), Fharlanghn (N), Olidammara (CN)
Monks	Heironeous (LG), St. Cuthbert, (LN), Hextor (LE)

worship him. The domains he is associated with are Chaos, Good, Protection, and War. His favored weapon is the longsword. Gruumsh is his nemesis, and it is because of Corellon's battle prowess that Gruumsh is called "One-Eye."

Ehlonna

Ehlonna (eh-*loan*-nuh), goddess of the woodlands, is neutral good. Her most commonly encountered title is Ehlonna of the Forests. Ehlonna watches over all good people who live in the forest, love the woodlands, or make their livelihood there. She is pictured sometimes as an elf and sometimes as a human. She is especially close to elves, gnomes, half-elves, halflings, and brownies. She is also worshiped by rangers and some druids. The domains she is associated with are Animal, Good, Plant, and Sun. Her favored weapon is the longsword.

Erythnul

The god of slaughter, Erythnul (eh-*rith*-null), is chaotic evil. His title is the Many. Erythnul delights in panic and slaughter. In civilized lands, his followers (including evil fighters, barbarians, and rogues) form small, criminal cults. In savage lands, evil barbarians, gnolls, bugbears, ogres, and trolls commonly worship him. The domains he is associated with are Chaos, Evil, Trickery, and War. His favored weapon is a morningstar with a blunt stone head.

Fharlanghn

Fharlanghn (far-*lahng*-un), the god of roads, is neutral. His title is Dweller on the Horizon. Fharlanghn's wayside shrines are common on well-used roads, for he is the god of travel, roads, distance, and horizons. Bards, other wandering adventurers, and merchants favor Fharlanghn. The domains he is associated with are Luck, Protection, and Travel. The quarterstaff is his favored weapon.

Garl Glittergold

The god of gnomes, Garl Glittergold (garl *gliht*-er-gold), is neutral good. He is known as the Joker, the Watchful Protector, the Priceless Gem, and the Sparkling Wit. Garl Glittergold discovered the gnomes and led them into the world. Since then, he has been their protector. He governs humor, wit, gemcutting, and jewelrymaking. The domains he is associated with are Good, Protection, and Trickery. Garl's favored weapon is the battleaxe. He is renowned for the jokes and pranks he pulls on other deities, though not all his victims laugh off his jests. Garl once collapsed the cavern of Kurtulmak, the god of the kobolds. Since then, the two deities have been sworn enemies.

Gruumsh

Gruumsh (groomsh), god of orcs, is lawful evil. His titles are One-Eye and He-Who-Never-Sleeps. Gruumsh is the chief god of the orcs. He calls on his followers to be strong, to cull the weak from their numbers, and to take all the territory that Gruumsh thinks is rightfully theirs (which is almost everything). The domains he is associated with are Chaos, Evil, Strength, and War. Gruumsh's favored weapon is the spear. He harbors a special hatred for Corellon Larethian, Moradin, and their followers. In ages past, Corellon Larethian put out Gruumsh's left eye in a fight.

Heironeous

The god of valor, Heironeous (high-*roe*-nee-us), is lawful good. His title is the Invincible. Heironeous promotes justice, valor, chivalry, and honor. The domains he is associated with are Good, Law, and War. His favored weapon is the longsword, and he is worshiped by paladins, good fighters, and good monks. His archenemy is Hextor, his half-brother.

Hextor

The god of tyranny, Hextor (*heks*-tore), is lawful evil. His titles are Champion of Evil, Herald of Hell, and Scourge of Battle. Hextor is the six-armed god of war, conflict, and destruction. Hextor's worshipers include evil fighters and monks, and his favored weapon is the flail. The domains he is associated with are Destruction, Evil, Law, and War. He sends his followers to commit evil, and their special purpose is to overthrow the followers of Heironeous wherever they are found. Heironeous is Hextor's half-brother.

Kord

Kord (kord), god of strength, is chaotic good. He is known as the Brawler. Kord is the patron of athletes, especially wrestlers. His worshipers include good fighters, barbarians, and rogues. The domains he is associated with are Chaos, Good, Luck, and Strength. Kord's favored weapon is the greatsword.

Moradin

The god of dwarves, Moradin (*moar*-uh-din), is lawful good. His titles include the Soul Forger, Dwarffather, the All-Father, and the Creator. Moradin forged the first dwarves out of metal and gems and breathed life into them. He governs the arts and sciences of the dwarves: smithing, metalworking, engineering, and war. The domains he is associated with are Earth, Good, Law, and Protection. His favored weapon is the warhammer.

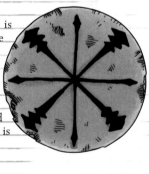

Illus. by S. Wood

Nerull

The god of death, Nerull (*nare*-ul), is neutral evil. He is known as the Reaper, the Foe of All Good, Hater of Life, Bringer of Darkness, King of All Gloom, and Reaper of Flesh. Nerull is the patron of those who seek the greatest evil for their own enjoyment or gain. The domains he is associated with are Death, Evil, and Trickery. His worshipers, who include evil necromancers and rogues, depict him as an almost skeletal cloaked figure who bears a scythe, his favored weapon.

Obad-Hai

Obad-Hai (*oh*-bod-*high*), god of nature, is neutral. He is known as the Shalm. Obad-Hai rules nature and the wilderness, and he is a friend to all who live in harmony with the natural world. Barbarians, rangers, and druids sometimes worship him. The domains he is associated with are Air, Animal, Earth, Fire, Plant, and Water. Because Obad-Hai strictly adheres to neutrality, he is a rival of Ehlonna. Obad-Hai plays a shalm (a double-reed woodwind musical instrument, also spelled "shawm") and takes his title from this instrument. His favored weapon is the quarterstaff.

Olidammara

The god of rogues, Olidammara (oh-*lih*-duh-*mar*-uh), is chaotic neutral. His title is the Laughing Rogue. Olidammara delights in wine, women, and song. He is a vagabond, a prankster, and a master of disguise. His temples are few, but many people are willing to raise a glass in his honor. Rogues and bards are frequently among his worshipers. The domains he is associated with are Chaos, Luck, and Trickery. The rapier is his favored weapon.

Pelor

Pelor (*pay*-lore), god of the sun, is neutral good. His title is the Shining One. Pelor is the creator of many good things, a supporter of those in need, and an adversary of all that is evil. He is the most commonly worshiped deity among ordinary humans, and his priests are well received wherever they go. Rangers and bards are found among his worshipers. The domains he is associated with are Good, Healing, Strength, and Sun. The mace is his favored weapon.

St. Cuthbert

The god of retribution, St. Cuthbert (saint *cuhth*-burt), is lawful neutral. He is known as St. Cuthbert of the Cudgel. St. Cuthbert exacts revenge and just punishment on those who transgress the law. Because evil creatures more commonly and flagrantly violate laws than good creatures do, St. Cuthbert favors good over evil, though he is not good himself. (His clerics cannot be evil.) The domains he is associated with are Destruction, Law, Protection, and Strength. His favored weapon is the mace.

Vecna

Vecna (*veck*-nuh), god of secrets, is neutral evil. He is known as the Maimed Lord, the Whispered One, and the Master of All That Is Secret and Hidden. Vecna rules that which is not meant to be known and that which people wish to keep secret. The domains he is associated with are Evil, Knowledge, and Magic. He usually appears as a lich who is missing his left hand and left eye. He lost his hand and eye in a fight with his traitorous lieutenant, Kas. Vecna's favored weapon is the dagger.

Wee Jas

Wee Jas (*wee* jass), goddess of death and magic, is lawful neutral. Her titles are Witch Goddess, Ruby Sorceress, Stern Lady, and Death's Guardian. Wee Jas is a demanding goddess who expects obedience from her followers. Her temples are few and far between, but she counts many powerful sorcerers and wizards (especially necromancers) among her worshipers. The domains she is associated with are Death, Law, and Magic. Her favored weapon is the dagger.

Yondalla

The goddess of halflings, Yondalla (yon-*dah*-lah), is lawful good. Her titles include the Protector and Provider, the Nurturing Matriarch, and the Blessed One. Yondalla is the creator and protector of the halfling race. She espouses harmony within the halfling race and stalwart defense against its enemies. Her followers hope to lead safe, prosperous lives by following her guidance. The domains she is associated with are Good, Law, and Protection. The short sword is her favored weapon.

VITAL STATISTICS

This section offers advice as you determine your character's name, gender, age, height, and weight. Start with some idea of your character's background and personality, and use that idea to help you add the details that bring your character to life.

NAME

Invent or choose a name that fits your character's race and class. Chapter 2: Races contains some examples of elven, dwarven, halfling, gnome, and orc names (and thus half-elf and half-orc names, too). A name is a great way for you to start thinking about your character's background. For instance, a dwarf's name might be the name of a great dwarven hero, and the dwarf may be striving to live up to her name. Alternatively, the name could be that of an infamous coward, and the character could be bent on proving that she is not like her namesake.

GENDER

Your character can be either male or female.

AGE

You can choose or randomly generate your character's age. If you choose it, it must be at least the minimum age for the character's race and class (see Table 6–4: Random Starting Ages). Your character's minimum starting age is her race's adulthood age plus the number of dice rolled for her class. For example, an elf ranger must be at least 116 years old (110 years plus 6 dice for rangers).

Alternatively, use Table 6–4: Random Starting Ages to determine how old your character is. An elf ranger's randomly generated starting age, for example, is 110+6d6 years.

As your character ages, her physical ability scores (Strength, Dexterity, and Constitution) decrease and her mental ability scores (Intelligence, Wisdom, and Charisma) increase. (See Table 6–5: Aging Effects.) The effects of each aging step are cumulative. However, any of a character's ability scores cannot be reduced below 1 in this way.

For example, when an elf reaches 175 years of age, his Strength, Dexterity, and Constitution scores each drop 1 point, while his Intelligence, Wisdom, and Charisma scores each increase 1 point. When he becomes 263 years old, his physical ability scores all drop an additional 2 points, while his mental ability scores increase by 1 again. So far he has lost a total of 3 points from his Strength, Constitution, and Dexterity scores and gained a total of 2 points to his Wisdom, Intelligence, and Charisma scores because of the effects of aging.

TABLE 6–4: RANDOM STARTING AGES

Race	Adulthood	Barbarian Rogue Sorcerer	Bard Fighter Paladin Ranger	Cleric Druid Monk Wizard
Human	15 years	+1d4	+1d6	+2d6
Dwarf	40 years	+3d6	+5d6	+7d6
Elf	110 years	+4d6	+6d6	+10d6
Gnome	40 years	+4d6	+6d6	+9d6
Half-elf	20 years	+1d6	+2d6	+3d6
Half-orc	14 years	+1d4	+1d6	+2d6
Halfling	20 years	+2d4	+3d6	+4d6

TABLE 6–5: AGING EFFECTS

Race	Middle Age*	Old**	Venerable†	Maximum Age
Human	35 years	53 years	70 years	+2d20 years
Dwarf	125 years	188 years	250 years	+2d% years
Elf	175 years	263 years	350 years	+4d% years
Gnome	100 years	150 years	200 years	+3d% years
Half-elf	62 years	93 years	125 years	+3d20 years
Half-orc	30 years	45 years	60 years	+2d10 years
Halfling	50 years	75 years	100 years	+5d20 years

*−1 to Str, Con, and Dex; +1 to Int, Wis, and Cha.
**−2 to Str, Con, and Dex; +1 to Int, Wis, and Cha.
†−3 to Str, Con, and Dex; +1 to Int, Wis, and Cha.

When a character becomes venerable, the DM secretly rolls her maximum age, which is the number from the Venerable column on Table 6–5: Aging Effects plus the modifier from the Maximum Age column on that table, and records the result, which the player does not know. When the character reaches her personal maximum age, she dies of old age at some time during the following year, as determined by the DM.

The maximum ages on Table 6–5: Aging Effects are for player characters. Most people in the world at large die from pestilence, accidents, infections, or violence before achieving the venerable age range.

HEIGHT AND WEIGHT

Choose your character's height and weight from the ranges mentioned in her race's description or from the ranges found on Table 6–6: Random Height and Weight. Think about what your character's abilities might say about her height and weight. If she is weak but agile, she may be thin. If she is strong and tough, she may be tall or just heavy.

Alternatively, roll randomly for your character's height and weight on Table 6–6: Random Height and Weight. The dice roll given in the Height Modifier column determines the character's extra height beyond the base height. That same number multiplied by the dice roll given in the Weight Modifier column determines the character's extra weight beyond the base weight. For example, Tordek (a dwarven man) stands 3′ 9″ tall plus 2d4″. Monte rolls 2d4 and gets 6, so Tordek stands 4′ 3″ tall. Then Monte uses that same roll, 6, and multiplies it by 2d6 pounds. His 2d6 roll is 9, so Tordek weighs an extra 54 pounds on top of his base 130 pounds, for a total of 184 pounds.

TABLE 6–6: RANDOM HEIGHT AND WEIGHT

Race	Base Height	Height Modifier	Base Weight	Weight Modifier
Human, man	4′10″	+2d10	120 lb.	× (2d4) lb.
Human, woman	4′ 5″	+2d10	85 lb.	× (2d4) lb.
Dwarf, man	3′ 9″	+2d4	130 lb.	× (2d6) lb.
Dwarf, woman	3′ 7″	+2d4	100 lb.	× (2d6) lb.
Elf, man	4′ 5″	+2d6	85 lb.	× (1d6) lb.
Elf, woman	4′ 5″	+2d6	80 lb.	× (1d6) lb.
Gnome, man	3′	+2d4	40 lb.	× 1 lb.
Gnome, woman	2′10″	+2d4	35 lb.	× 1 lb.
Half-elf, man	4′ 7″	+2d8	100 lb.	× (2d4) lb.
Half-elf, woman	4′ 5″	+2d8	80 lb.	× (2d4) lb.
Half-orc, man	4′10″	+2d10	130 lb.	× (2d4) lb.
Half-orc, woman	4′ 4″	+2d10	90 lb.	×(2d4) lb.
Halfling, man	2′ 8″	+2d4	30 lb.	× 1 lb.
Halfling, woman	2′ 6″	+2d4	25 lb.	× 1 lb.

LOOKS, PERSONALITY, AND BACKGROUND

You can detail your character to any degree you like. As you play the character, you will probably come up with more details you will want to add.

LOOKS

Decide what your character looks like using the descriptions of the various races in Chapter 2: Races as a starting point. Characters with high Charisma scores tend to be better-looking than those with low Charisma, though a character with high Charisma could have strange looks, giving him a sort of exotic beauty.

Your character can be right- or left-handed. (The Ambidexterity feat, page 80, allows her to use both hands equally well.)

Illus. by S. Wood

You can use your character's looks to tell something about her personality and background. For example:

- Krusk the half-orc is missing part of an ear and bears many scars that are the result of the violent life he led among the orcs that raised him. He keeps claws and fangs from beasts he has killed on a necklace.
- Alhandra the paladin has the hand of Heironeous branded on the inside of her forearm to show her devotion to him.
- Hennet the sorcerer wears an eclectic, makeshift outfit that is different from day to day, suggesting his chaotic nature.

PERSONALITY

Decide how your character acts, what she likes, what she wants out of life, what scares her, and what makes her angry. Race and alignment are good places to start when thinking about your character's personality, but they are bad places to stop. Make your lawful good dwarf (or whatever) different from every other lawful good dwarf.

A handy trick for making an interesting personality for your character is including some sort of conflict in her nature. For example, Tordek is lawful, but he's a little greedy, too. He may be tempted to steal if he can justify it to himself.

Your character's personality can change over time. Just because you decide some basic facts about your character's personality when you create the character doesn't mean you need to abide by those facts as if they were holy writ. Let your character grow and evolve the way real people do.

BACKGROUND

Decide what your character's life has been like up until now. Here are a few questions to get you thinking:

How did she decide to be an adventurer?

How did she acquire her class? A fighter, for example, might have been in the militia, she may come from a family of soldiers, she may have trained in a martial school, or she may be a self-taught warrior.

Where did she get her starting equipment from? Did she assemble it piece by piece over time? Was it a parting gift from a parent or mentor? Do any of her personal items have special significance to her?

What's the worst thing that's ever happened to her?

What's the best thing that's ever happened to her?

Does she stay in contact with her family? What do they think of her?

Kerwyn

CUSTOMIZING YOUR CHARACTER

The rules for creating your character provide a common ground for players, but you can tweak the rules to make your character unique. Any substantive changes, however, must be approved by the DM.

Race: The rules for a character of a given race apply to most but not all people of that race. For example, you could create a dwarf descended from dwarven outcasts who have been exiled from dwarven society. Your dwarf would have grown up among humans. He'd have the inborn qualities of a dwarf (better Constitution, worse Charisma, darkvision, and resistance to poison and spells) but not the cultural features (stonecunning, attack bonuses against goblinoids and orcs, dodge bonus against giants, bonuses to Appraise and Craft checks that relate to stone or metal, fighter as favored class, and perhaps even knowledge of the dwarven language). You could probably talk your DM into giving your character some special bonuses to balance the loss of the cultural features.

Class: Some classes already give you plenty of room to customize your character. With your DM's approval, however, you could change some of your class features. For instance, if you want a fighter who used to work for the thieves guild as an enforcer but who is now trying to become a legitimate bodyguard, he could be proficient only with the weapons and armor available to rogues, have 4 skill points per level instead of 2, and access to Innuendo and Bluff as class skills. Otherwise, he would be a regular fighter.

Skills and Feats: You can call your skills, feats, and class features whatever your character would call them. Lidda, the halfling rogue, talks about "footpaddin'" rather than about "moving silently," so her player writes "Footpaddin'" down on her character sheet to stand for the Move Silently skill. Ember, the monk, calls her Move Silently skill "Rice Paper Walk."

You might also think of other skills that your character ought to have. Your DM has guidelines (in the DUNGEON MASTER's *Guide*) for creating new skills.

Equipment: Your equipment can look the way you want it to look to match your character's style. One wizard's quarterstaff might be a plain, straight length of wood, while another wizard's is gnarled, twisted, and engraved with mystic runes.

Your character might have some items you don't see on the equipment list. Agree with your DM on what a new item would do and how much it would cost, and then your character can have it.

Sometimes you see a weapon in a movie or read about one in a book, and you want your character to use that weapon. If it's not on the weapon list in Chapter 7: Equipment, try to find a weapon on the list that seems equivalent. A katana (samurai sword), for example, is not on the weapon list, but you could equip your character with a katana and just treat it like a masterwork bastard sword.

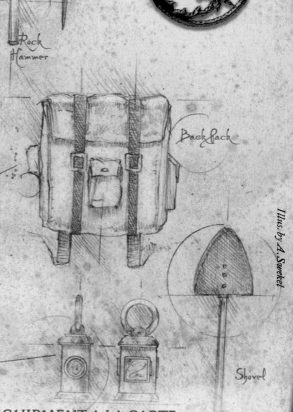

Illus. by A. Swekel

In the marketplace of a big city, armorsmiths and weapon-smiths offer a wide variety of arms and armor for those with the gold to buy them. Here you can find practical, sturdy swords and perhaps a few elven blades of exceptional quality. Alchemists sell acid, alchemist's fire, and smokesticks for those who want something flashier than a trusty blade. Wizards (or, more likely, their brokers) even sell magic scrolls, wands, weapons, and other items.

This chapter covers the mundane and exotic things that characters may want to purchase and how to go about doing so. (Magic items are covered in the DUNGEON MASTER's Guide.)

EQUIPPING A CHARACTER

A beginning character generally has enough wealth to start out with the basics: some weapons, some armor suitable to her class (if any), and some miscellaneous gear. As the character undertakes adventures and amasses loot, she can afford bigger and better gear. At first, however, her options are limited by her budget.

STARTING PACKAGES

Each class has a starting package that lists default equipment (as well as default skills, a default feat, etc.). If you equip your character with the default equipment, you can customize these packages a little by swapping in some equipment of your choice for listed equipment. Trades like this are fine as long as the value of the equipment you swap in isn't higher than the value of the equipment listed for the package.

EQUIPMENT A LA CARTE

If you don't want to take the standard package for a character of your class, you can instead purchase your weapons, armor, and miscellaneous equipment item by item. You begin with a random amount of money that is determined by your class, and you decide how to spend it (see Table 7–1: Random Starting Gold).

Note that buying beginning equipment this way is an abstraction. Your character doesn't walk into a store with handfuls of gold and buy every item one by one. Rather, these items may have come the character's way as gifts from family, equipment from patrons, gear granted during military service, swag gained through duplicity, and so on.

Assume your character owns at least one outfit of normal clothes. Pick any one of the following clothing outfits for free: artisan's outfit, entertainer's outfit, explorer's outfit, monk's outfit, peasant's outfit, scholar's outfit, or traveler's outfit. (See Clothing, page 111.)

TABLE 7–1: RANDOM STARTING GOLD

Class	Amount (gp)	Class	Amount (gp)
Barbarian	4d4 × 10	Paladin	6d4 × 10
Bard	4d4 × 10	Ranger	6d4 × 10
Cleric	5d4 × 10	Rogue	5d4 × 10
Druid	2d4 × 10	Sorcerer	3d4 × 10
Fighter	6d4 × 10	Wizard	3d4 × 10
Monk	5d4		

AVAILABILITY

All the items described in this chapter are assumed to be available to PCs with the wherewithal to buy them. Many of these items are very expensive and rare. You won't find them on the rack in a store by a town's main plaza. But a PC with the coin to buy an expensive item can usually connect with a seller and get what she wants. If you want to buy something not described in this chapter, the general rule is that you can buy anything that costs up to 3,000 gp. Buying more expensive items, such as +2 *longswords*, means either going to a big city where rare things are for sale, making a special deal with someone who makes or can provide the item, or paying a premium price to a merchant who makes a special effort to get you what you want.

Depending on where in the fantasy world you are, it might be possible to buy more expensive items without a problem, or it might be more difficult to do so. In a small town, for example, it's practically impossible to find someone who can make a suit of full plate armor for you. The DM determines what is and is not available depending on where you are and how he runs his world.

WEALTH AND MONEY

Adventurers are in the small group of people who regularly buy things with coins. Members of the peasantry trade mostly in goods, bartering for what they need and paying taxes in grain and cheese. Members of the nobility trade mostly in legal rights, such as the rights to a mine, a port, or farmland, or they trade in gold bars, measuring gold by the pound rather than by the coin.

COINS

The most common coin that adventurers use is the gold piece (gp). With a gold piece, you can buy a belt pouch, 50 feet of hempen rope, or a goat. A skilled (but not exceptional) artisan can earn a gold piece a day. The gold piece is the standard unit of measure for wealth. When merchants discuss deals that involve goods or services worth hundreds or thousands of gold pieces, the transactions don't usually involve the exchange of that many individual coins. Rather, the gold piece is a standard measure of value, and the actual exchange is in gold bars, letters of credit, or valuable goods.

The most prevalent coin among commoners is the silver piece (sp). A gold piece is worth 10 silver pieces. A silver piece buys a laborer's work for a day, a common lamp, or a poor meal of bread, baked turnips, onions, and water.

Each silver piece is worth 10 copper pieces (cp). With a single copper, you can buy a candle, a torch, or a piece of chalk. Coppers are common among laborers and beggars.

In addition to copper, silver, and gold coins, which people use daily, merchants also recognize platinum pieces (pp), which are each worth 10 gp. These coins are not in common circulation, but adventurers occasionally find them as part of ancient treasure hoards.

The standard coin weighs about a third of an ounce (fifty to the pound). It is the exact size of the coin pictured in the illustration on page 146.

TABLE 7–2: COINS

| | | Exchange Value | | |
	CP	SP	GP	PP
Copper piece (cp) =	1	1/10	1/100	1/1,000
Silver piece (sp) =	10	1	1/10	1/100
Gold piece (gp) =	100	10	1	1/10
Platinum piece (pp) =	1,000	100	10	1

WEALTH OTHER THAN COINS

Most wealth is not in coins. It is livestock, grain, land, rights to collect taxes, or rights to resources (such as a mine or a forest). Gems and jewelry also serve as portable wealth.

Trade

Guilds, nobles, and royalty regulate trade. Chartered companies are granted rights to dam rivers in order to provide power for mills, to conduct trade along certain routes, to send merchant ships to various ports, or to buy or sell specific goods. Guilds set prices for the goods or services that they control and determine who may or may not offer those goods and services. Merchants commonly exchange trade goods without using currency. Some trade goods are detailed on Table 7–3: Trade Goods.

TABLE 7–3: TRADE GOODS

Commodity	Cost	Commodity	Cost
Chicken, 1	2 cp	Ox, 1	15 gp
Cinnamon, 1 lb.	1 gp	Pig, 1	3 gp
Copper, 1 lb.	5 sp	Saffron or cloves, 1 lb.	15 gp
Cow, 1	10 gp	Salt, 1 lb.	5 gp
Dog, 1	25 gp	Sheep, 1	2 gp
Flour, 1 lb.	2 cp	Silk, 1 lb. (2 sq. yards)	20 gp
Ginger or pepper, 1 lb.	2 gp	Silver, 1 lb.	5 gp
Goat, 1	1 gp	Tea leaves, 1 lb.	2 sp
Gold, 1 lb.	50 gp	Tobacco, 1 lb.	5 sp
Iron, 1 lb.	1 sp	Wheat, 1 lb.	1 cp
Linen, 1 lb. (sq. yard)	4 gp		

SELLING LOOT

In general, you can sell something for half its listed price. Characters who want to upgrade to better armor or weaponry, for example, can sell their old equipment for half price.

Commodities are the exception to the half-price rule. A commodity, in this sense, is a valuable good that can be easily exchanged almost as if it were cash itself. Wheat, flour, cloth, and valuable metals are commodities, and merchants often trade in them directly without using currency (see Table 7–3: Trade Goods). Obviously, merchants can sell these goods for slightly more than they pay for them, but the difference is small enough that you don't have to worry about it.

WEAPONS

Your weapons help determine how capable you are in a variety of combat situations. See Table 7–4: Weapons for the list of weapons. See Table 7–10: Grenadelike Weapons for a summary of grenadelike weapons (acid, alchemist's fire, holy water, and so forth).

WEAPON CATEGORIES

Weapons are grouped into several interlocking sets of categories. These categories pertain to what skill is needed to be proficient in their use (simple, martial, and exotic), usefulness in close combat (melee) or at a distance (ranged, which includes both thrown and projectile), and weapon size (Tiny, Small, Medium-size, and Large).

Simple, Martial, and Exotic Weapons: Anybody but a druid, monk, rogue, or wizard is proficient with all simple weapons. Barbarians, fighters, paladins, and rangers are proficient with all simple and all martial weapons. Characters of other classes are proficient with an assortment of mainly simple weapons and possibly also some martial or even exotic weapons. If you use a weapon with which you are not proficient, you suffer a –4 penalty on attack rolls.

Melee and Ranged Weapons: Melee weapons are used for making melee attacks, though some of them can be thrown as well. Ranged weapons are thrown weapons or projectile weapons that are not effective in melee. You apply your Strength bonus to damage dealt by thrown weapons but not to damage dealt by projectile weapons (except for mighty composite shortbows or longbows).

Tiny, Small, Medium-Size, and Large Weapons: The size of a weapon compared to your size determines whether for you the weapon is light, one-handed, two-handed, or too large to use.

Light: If the weapon's size category is smaller than yours (such as a human using a Small weapon), then the weapon is light for you. Light weapons are easier to use in your off hand, and you can use them while grappling. You can use a light weapon in one hand. You get no special bonus when using it in two hands.

One-Handed: If the weapon's size category is the same as yours (such as a human using a rapier), then the weapon is one-handed for you. If you use a one-handed melee weapon two-handed, you can apply one and a half times your Strength bonus to damage (provided you have a bonus). Thrown weapons can only be thrown one-handed, and you receive your Strength bonus to damage.

Two-Handed: If the weapon's size category is one step larger than your own (such as a human using a greataxe), then the weapon is two-handed for you. You can use a two-handed melee weapon effectively in two hands, and when you deal damage with it, you add one and a half times your Strength bonus to damage (provided you have a bonus).

Thrown weapons can only be thrown one-handed. You can throw a thrown weapon with one hand even if it would be two-handed for you due to your size (such as a gnome throwing a javelin), but doing so counts as a full-round action because the weapon is bulkier and harder to handle than most thrown weapons. You receive your Strength bonus to damage.

You can use a two-handed projectile weapon (such as a bow or a crossbow) effectively in two hands. If you have a penalty for low Strength, apply it to damage rolls when you use a bow or a sling. You get no Strength bonus to damage with a projectile weapon unless it's a mighty composite shortbow or longbow (page 113).

Too Large to Use: If the weapon's size category is two or more steps larger than your own (such as a gnome trying to use a greatsword), the weapon is too large for you to use.

Unarmed Strikes: An unarmed strike is two size categories smaller than the character using it.

WEAPON QUALITIES

The weapon you use says something about who you are. You probably want both a melee weapon and a ranged weapon. If you can't afford both your melee weapon of choice and your ranged weapon of choice, decide which is more important to you.

What size of weapon you choose determines how you can choose to wield it (with one hand or two) and how much damage you deal with it. A two-handed weapon deals more damage than a one-handed weapon, but it keeps you from using a shield, so that's a trade-off. If you are Small, you need to choose smaller weapons.

Depending on your class, you are proficient with more or fewer weapons. If you see a weapon that you want to use but with which you're not proficient, you can become proficient with it by selecting the right feat. See Exotic Weapon Proficiency (page 82), Martial Weapon Proficiency (page 83), and Simple Weapon Proficiency (page 85).

A better weapon is usually more expensive than an inferior one, but more expensive doesn't always mean better. For instance, a rapier is more expensive than a longsword. For a dexterous rogue with the Weapon Finesse feat, a rapier is a terrific weapon. For a typical fighter, a longsword is better.

To choose your weapons, keep in mind these factors (given as column headings on Table 7–4: Weapons):

Cost: This is the weapon's cost in gold pieces (gp) or silver pieces (sp). The cost includes miscellaneous gear that goes with the weapon, such as a scabbard for a sword or a quiver for arrows.

Damage: The Damage column gives the damage you deal with a weapon when you score a hit. If the damage is designated "§," then the weapon deals subdual damage rather than normal damage (see Subdual Damage, page 134). If two damage ranges are given, such as "1d6/1d6" for the quarterstaff, then the weapon is a double weapon, and you can use a full attack full-round action to make one extra attack when using this weapon, as per the two-weapon rules

(see Attacking with Two Weapons, page 124). Use the second damage figure given for the extra attack.

Critical: The entry in this column notes how the weapon is used with the rules for critical hits. When you score a critical hit, you roll the damage with all modifiers two, three, or four times, as indicated by its critical multiplier, and add all the results together.

Exception: Bonus damage represented as extra dice, such as from a sneak attack or a flaming sword, is not multiplied when you score a critical hit.

×2: The weapon deals double damage on a critical hit.

×3: The weapon deals triple damage on a critical hit.

×3/×4: One head of this double weapon deals triple damage on a critical hit. The other head deals quadruple damage on a critical hit.

×4: The weapon deals quadruple damage on a critical hit.

19–20/×2: The weapon scores a threat (a possible critical hit) on a natural 19 or 20 (instead of just on a 20) and deals double damage on a critical hit. (The weapon has a threat range of 19–20.)

18–20/×2: The weapon scores a threat on a natural 18, 19, or 20 (instead of just on a 20) and deals double damage on a critical hit. (The weapon has a threat range of 18–20.)

Range Increment: Any attack at less than this distance is not penalized for range, so an arrow from a shortbow (range increment 60 feet) can strike at enemies up to 59 feet away with no penalty. However, each full range increment causes a cumulative –2 penalty to the attack roll. A shortbow archer firing at a target 200 feet away suffers a –6 attack penalty (because 200 feet is at least three range increments but not four increments). Thrown weapons, such as throwing axes, have a maximum range of five range increments. Projectile weapons, such as bows, can shoot up to ten increments.

Thrown Weapons: Daggers, clubs, halfspears, shortspears, darts, javelins, throwing axes, light hammers, tridents, shuriken, and nets are thrown weapons.

Projectile Weapons: Light crossbows, slings, heavy crossbows, shortbows, composite shortbows, longbows, composite longbows, hand crossbows, whips, and repeating crossbows are projectile weapons.

Improvised Thrown Weapons: Sometimes objects not crafted to be weapons get thrown: small rocks, small animals, vases, pitchers, and so forth. Because they are not designed for this use, all characters who use improvised thrown weapons are treated as not proficient with them and suffer a –4 penalty on their attack rolls. Improvised thrown weapons have a range increment of 10 feet. Their size and the damage they deal have to be adjudicated by the DM.

Weight: This column gives the weapon's weight.

Type: Weapons are classified according to types: bludgeoning, piercing, and slashing. Some monsters may be partially or wholly immune to attacks with some types of weapons. For example, a skeleton only takes half damage from slashing weapons and no damage from piercing weapons. If a weapon is of two types, a creature would have to be immune to both types of damage to have damage dealt by this weapon be ignored.

Special: Some weapons have special features, such as reach. See the weapon descriptions.

WEAPON DESCRIPTIONS

The weapons found on Table 7–4: Weapons are described below. Grenadelike weapons are summarized on Table 7–10: Grenadelike Weapons and described in the Special and Superior Items section later in this chapter.

Arrows: An arrow used as a melee weapon is Tiny and deals 1d4 points of piercing damage (×2 crit). Since it is not designed for this use, all characters are treated as not proficient with it and thus suffer a –4 penalty on their attack rolls. Arrows come in leather quivers that hold 20 arrows. An arrow that hits its target is destroyed; one that misses has a 50% chance to be destroyed or lost.

Axe, Throwing: A throwing axe is lighter than a handaxe and balanced for throwing. Gnome fighters often use throwing axes for both melee and ranged attacks.

TABLE 7–4: WEAPONS
SIMPLE WEAPONS—MELEE

Weapon	Cost	Damage	Critical	Range Increment	Weight	Type**
Unarmed Attacks						
Gauntlet	2 gp	*	*	—	2 lb.	Bludgeoning
Strike, unarmed (Medium-size being)	—	1d3§	×2	—	—	Bludgeoning
Strike, unarmed (Small being)	—	1d2§	×2	—	—	Bludgeoning
Tiny						
Dagger*	2 gp	1d4	19–20/×2	10 ft.	1 lb.	Piercing
Dagger, punching	2 gp	1d4	×3	—	2 lb.	Piercing
Gauntlet, spiked*	5 gp	1d4	×2	—	2 lb.	Piercing
Small						
Mace, light	5 gp	1d6	×2	—	6 lb.	Bludgeoning
Sickle	6 gp	1d6	×2	—	3 lb.	Slashing
Medium-size						
Club	—	1d6	×2	10 ft.	3 lb.	Bludgeoning
Halfspear[a]	1 gp	1d6	×3	20 ft.	3 lb.	Piercing
Mace, heavy	12 gp	1d8	×2	—	12 lb.	Bludgeoning
Morningstar	8 gp	1d8	×2	—	8 lb.	Bludgeoning and piercing
Large						
Quarterstaff*‡	—	1d6/1d6	×2	—	4 lb.	Bludgeoning
Shortspear[a]	2 gp	1d8	×3	20 ft.	5 lb.	Piercing

SIMPLE WEAPONS—RANGED

Weapon	Cost	Damage	Critical	Range Increment	Weight	Type**
Small						
Crossbow, light*	35 gp	1d8	19–20/×2	80 ft.	6 lb.	Piercing
Bolts, crossbow (10)*	1 gp	—	—	—	1 lb.	—
Dart	5 sp	1d4	×2	20 ft.	1/2 lb.	Piercing
Sling	—	1d4	×2	50 ft.	0 lb.	Bludgeoning
Bullets, sling (10)	1 sp	—	—	—	5 lb.	—
Medium-size						
Crossbow, heavy*	50 gp	1d10	19–20/×2	120 ft.	9 lb.	Piercing
Bolts, crossbow (10)*	1 gp	—	—	—	1 lb.	—
Javelin	1 gp	1d6	×2	30 ft.	2 lb.	Piercing

MARTIAL WEAPONS—MELEE

Weapon	Cost	Damage	Critical	Range Increment	Weight	Type**
Small						
Axe, throwing	8 gp	1d6	×2	10 ft.	4 lb.	Slashing
Hammer, light	1 gp	1d4	×2	20 ft.	2 lb.	Bludgeoning
Handaxe	6 gp	1d6	×3	—	5 lb.	Slashing
Lance, light*	6 gp	1d6	×3	—	5 lb.	Piercing
Pick, light*	4 gp	1d4	×4	—	4 lb.	Piercing
Sap	1 gp	1d6§	×2	—	3 lb.	Bludgeoning
Sword, short	10 gp	1d6	19–20/×2	—	3 lb.	Piercing
Medium-size						
Battleaxe	10 gp	1d8	×3	—	7 lb.	Slashing
Flail, light*	8 gp	1d8	×2	—	5 lb.	Bludgeoning
Lance, heavy*†	10 gp	1d8	×3	—	10 lb.	Piercing
Longsword	15 gp	1d8	19–20/×2	—	4 lb.	Slashing
Pick, heavy*	8 gp	1d6	×4	—	6 lb.	Piercing
Rapier*	20 gp	1d6	18–20/×2	—	3 lb.	Piercing
Scimitar	15 gp	1d6	18–20/×2	—	4 lb.	Slashing
Trident[a]	15 gp	1d8	×2	10 ft.	5 lb.	Piercing
Warhammer	12 gp	1d8	×3	—	8 lb.	Bludgeoning
Large						
Falchion	75 gp	2d4	18–20/×2	—	16 lb.	Slashing
Flail, heavy*	15 gp	1d10	19–20/×2	—	20 lb.	Bludgeoning
Glaive*†	8 gp	1d10	×3	—	15 lb.	Slashing
Greataxe	20 gp	1d12	×3	—	20 lb.	Slashing
Greatclub	5 gp	1d10	×2	—	10 lb.	Bludgeoning
Greatsword	50 gp	2d6	19–20/×2	—	15 lb.	Slashing
Guisarme*†	9 gp	2d4	×3	—	15 lb.	Slashing
Halberd*[a]	10 gp	1d10	×3	—	15 lb.	Piercing and slashing
Longspear*†[a]	5 gp	1d8	×3	—	9 lb.	Piercing
Ranseur*†	10 gp	2d4	×3	—	15 lb.	Piercing
Scythe	18 gp	2d4	×4	—	12 lb.	Piercing and slashing

TABLE 7–4: WEAPONS

MARTIAL WEAPONS—RANGED

Weapon	Cost	Damage	Critical	Range Increment	Weight	Type**
Medium-size						
Shortbow*	30 gp	1d6	×3	60 ft.	2 lb.	Piercing
Arrows (20)*	1 gp	—	—	—	3 lb.	—
Shortbow, composite*	75 gp	1d6	×3	70 ft.	2 lb.	Piercing
Arrows (20)*	1 gp	—	—	—	3 lb.	—
Large						
Longbow*	75 gp	1d8	×3	100 ft.	3 lb.	Piercing
Arrows (20)*	1 gp	—	—	—	3 lb.	—
Longbow, composite*	100 gp	1d8	×3	110 ft.	3 lb.	Piercing
Arrows (20)*	1 gp	—	—	—	3 lb.	—

EXOTIC WEAPONS—MELEE

Weapon	Cost	Damage	Critical	Range Increment	Weight	Type**
Tiny						
Kama, halfling*	2 gp	1d4	×2	—	1 lb.	Slashing
Kukri	8 gp	1d4	18–20/×2	—	3 lb.	Slashing
Nunchaku, halfling*	2 gp	1d4	×2	—	1 lb.	Bludgeoning
Siangham, halfling*	2 gp	1d4	×2	—	1 lb.	Piercing
Small						
Kama*	2 gp	1d6	×2	—	2 lb.	Slashing
Nunchaku*	2 gp	1d6	×2	—	2 lb.	Bludgeoning
Siangham*	3 gp	1d6	×2	—	1 lb.	Piercing
Medium-size						
Sword, bastard*	35 gp	1d10	19–20/×2	—	10 lb.	Slashing
Waraxe, dwarven*	30 gp	1d10	×3	—	15 lb.	Slashing
Hammer, gnome hooked*‡	20 gp	1d6/1d4	×3/×4	—	6 lb.	Bludgeoning and piercing
Large						
Axe, orc double*‡	60 gp	1d8/1d8	×3	—	25 lb.	Slashing
Chain, spiked*†	25 gp	2d4	×2	—	15 lb.	Piercing
Flail, dire*‡	90 gp	1d8/1d8	×2	—	20 lb.	Bludgeoning
Sword, two-bladed*‡	100 gp	1d8/1d8	19–20/×2	—	30 lb.	Slashing
Urgrosh, dwarven‡ª	50 gp	1d8/1d6	×3	—	15 lb.	Slashing and piercing

EXOTIC WEAPONS—RANGED

Weapon	Cost	Damage	Critical	Range Increment	Weight	Type**
Tiny						
Crossbow, hand*	100 gp	1d4	19–20/×2	30 ft.	3 lb.	Piercing
Bolts (10)*	1 gp	—	—	—	1 lb.	—
Shuriken*	1 gp	1	×2	10 ft.	1/10 lb.	Piercing
Small						
Whip*	1 gp	1d2§	×2	15 ft.*	2 lb.	Slashing
Medium-size						
Crossbow, repeating*	250 gp	1d8	19–20/×2	80 ft.	16 lb.	Piercing
Bolts (5)*	1 gp	—	—	—	1 lb.	—
Net*	20 gp	*	*	10 ft.*	10 lb.	*

*See the description of this weapon for special rules.
**When two types are given, the weapon is both types.
‡Double weapon.
§The weapon deals subdual damage rather than normal damage.

†Reach weapon.
ª If you use a ready action to set this weapon against a charge, you deal double damage if you score a hit against a charging character.

Axe, Orc Double: An orc double axe is a double weapon. You can fight with it as if fighting with two weapons, but if you do, you incur all the normal attack penalties associated with fighting with two weapons, as if you were wielding a one-handed weapon and a light weapon (see Attacking with Two Weapons, page 124). A creature using a double weapon in one hand, such as an ogre using an orc double axe, can't use it as a double weapon.

Battleaxe: The battleaxe is the most common melee weapon among dwarves.

Bolts: A crossbow bolt used as a melee weapon is Tiny and deals 1d4 points of piercing damage (×2 crit). Since it is not designed for this use, all characters are treated as not proficient with it and thus suffer a –4 penalty on their attack rolls. Bolts come in wooden cases that hold 10 bolts. A bolt that hits its target is destroyed; one that misses has a 50% chance to be destroyed or lost.

Bullets, Sling: Bullets are lead spheres, much heavier than stones of the same size. They come in a leather pouch that holds 10 bullets. A bullet that hits its target is destroyed; one that misses has a 50% chance to be destroyed or lost.

Chain, Spiked: A spiked chain has reach. You can strike opponents 10 feet away with it. In addition, unlike other weapons with reach, you can use it against an adjacent foe.

Because the chain can wrap around an enemy's leg or other limb, you can make trip attacks with it. If you are tripped during your own trip attempt, you can drop the chain to avoid being tripped.

When using a spiked chain, you get a +2 bonus on your opposed attack roll when attempting to disarm an opponent (including the roll to avoid being disarmed if you fail to disarm your opponent).

You can use the Weapon Finesse feat (see page 86) to apply your Dexterity modifier instead of your Strength modifier to attack rolls with a spiked chain.

Club: A wooden club is so easy to find and fashion that it has no cost.

Crossbow, Hand: This exotic weapon is common among rogues and others who favor stealth over power. You can draw a hand crossbow back by hand. Loading a hand crossbow is a move-equivalent action that provokes attacks of opportunity.

Crossbow, Heavy: A heavy crossbow requires two hands to use effectively, regardless of the user's size. You draw a heavy crossbow back by turning a small winch. Loading a heavy crossbow is a full-round action that provokes attacks of opportunity.

A Medium-size or larger character can shoot, but not load, a heavy crossbow with one hand at a –4 penalty. A Medium-size or larger character can shoot a heavy crossbow with each hand at a –6 penalty, plus the usual –4 penalty for the off-hand attack (–6 primary hand/–10 off hand). The Two-Weapon Fighting feat does not reduce these penalties because it represents skill with melee weapons, not ranged weapons. The Ambidexterity feat lets someone avoid the –4 off-hand penalty (–6 primary hand/–6 off hand).

Crossbow, Light: A light crossbow requires two hands to use, regardless of the user's size. You draw a light crossbow back by pulling a lever. Loading a light crossbow is a move-equivalent action that provokes attacks of opportunity.

A Small or larger character can shoot, but not load, a light crossbow with one hand at a –4 penalty. A Small or larger character can shoot a light crossbow with each hand as noted for heavy crossbows, above.

Crossbow, Repeating: The repeating crossbow holds five crossbow bolts. While it holds bolts, you can shoot the crossbow according to your normal number of attacks without reloading. Loading a new case of five bolts is a full-round action that provokes attacks of opportunity.

Dagger: The dagger is a common secondary weapon. You can use the Weapon Finesse feat (see page 86) to apply your Dexterity modifier instead of your Strength modifier to attack rolls with a dagger.

Dagger, Punching: This dagger puts the full force of the wielder's punch behind it, making it capable of deadly strikes.

Dart: A dart is the size of a large arrow and has a weighted head. Essentially, it is a small javelin.

Falchion: This sword, which is essentially a two-handed scimitar, has a curve that gives it an effectively keener edge.

Flail, Dire: A dire flail is a double weapon. You can fight with it as if fighting with two weapons, but if you do, you incur all the normal attack penalties associated with fighting with two weapons, as if you were using a one-handed weapon and a light weapon (see Attacking with Two Weapons, page 124). A creature using a double weapon in one hand, such as an ogre using a dire flail, can't use it as a double weapon.

With a dire flail, you get a +2 bonus on your opposed attack roll when attempting to disarm an enemy (including the opposed attack roll to avoid being disarmed if you fail to disarm your enemy).

You can also use this weapon to make trip attacks. If you are tripped during your own trip attempt, you can drop the dire flail to avoid being tripped.

Flail, Heavy or Light: With a flail, you get a +2 bonus on your opposed attack roll when attempting to disarm an enemy (including the roll to avoid being disarmed if you fail to disarm your enemy).

You can also use this weapon to make trip attacks. If you are tripped during your own trip attempt, you can drop the flail to avoid being tripped.

Gauntlet: These metal gloves protect your hands and let you deal normal damage with unarmed strikes rather than subdual damage. A strike with a gauntlet is otherwise considered an unarmed attack. The cost and weight given are for a single gauntlet. Medium and heavy armors (except breastplate) come with gauntlets.

Gauntlet, Spiked: Your opponent cannot use a disarm action to disarm you of spiked gauntlets. The cost and weight given are for a

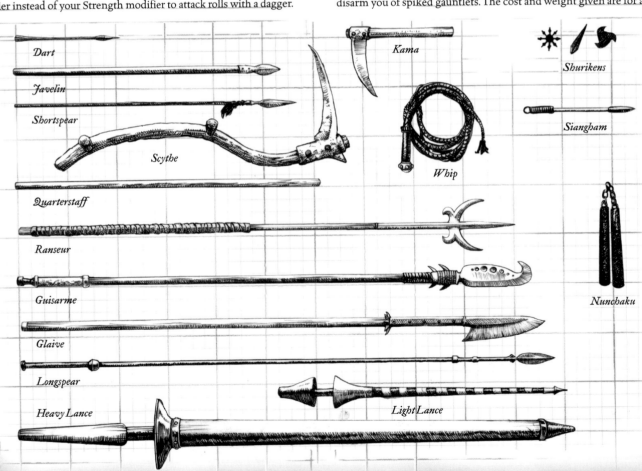

Dart

Javelin

Shortspear

Scythe

Quarterstaff

Ranseur

Guisarme

Glaive

Longspear

Heavy Lance

Kama

Whip

Light Lance

Shurikens

Siangham

Nunchaku

single gauntlet. An attack with a spiked gauntlet is considered an armed attack.

Glaive: A glaive has reach. You can strike opponents 10 feet away with it, but you can't use it against an adjacent foe.

Greataxe: This big, heavy axe is a favorite of barbarians or anybody else who wants the capability to deal out incredible damage.

Greatclub: A greatclub is a two-handed version of a regular club. It is often studded with nails or spikes or ringed by bands of iron.

Greatsword: Adventurers recognize the greatsword as one of the best melee weapons available. It's reliable and powerful.

Guisarme: A guisarme has reach. You can strike opponents 10 feet away with it, but you can't use it against an adjacent foe.

Because of the guisarme's curved blade, you can also use it to make trip attacks. If you are tripped during your own trip attempt, you can drop the guisarme to avoid being tripped.

Halberd: Normally, you strike with the halberd's axe head, but the spike on the end is useful against charging opponents.

Because of the hook on the back of the halberd, you can use it to make trip attacks. If you are tripped during your own trip attempt, you can drop the halberd to avoid being tripped.

Halfspear: The halfspear is small enough for a Small character to use it.

Hammer, Gnome Hooked: A gnome hooked hammer is a double weapon. You can fight with it as if fighting with two weapons, but if you do, you incur all the normal attack penalties associated with fighting with two weapons, as if you were using a one-handed weapon and a light weapon (see Attacking with Two Weapons, page 124). A creature using a double weapon in one hand, such as a human using a gnome hooked hammer, can't use it as a double weapon. The hammer's blunt head is a bludgeoning weapon that deals 1d6 points of damage (×3 crit). Its hook is a piercing weapon that deals 1d4 points of damage (×4 crit). You can use either head as the primary weapon head. The other head is the off-hand weapon.

Hammer, Light: This is a small sledge light enough to throw. It is favored by dwarves.

Handaxe: Dwarves favor these axes as off-hand weapons.

Javelin: This weapon is a light, flexible spear intended for throwing. You can use it in melee, but not well. Since it is not designed for melee, all characters are treated as not proficient with it and thus suffer −4 on their melee attack rolls.

Kama or Halfling Kama: A monk using a kama can strike with her unarmed base attack, including her more favorable number of attacks per round, along with other applicable attack modifiers. The halfling kama is for Small monks.

Kukri: This heavy, curved dagger has its sharp edge on the inside of the curve.

Lance, Heavy or Light: A lance deals double damage when used from the back of a charging mount. A heavy lance has reach. You can strike opponents 10 feet away with it, but you can't use it against an adjacent foe. Light lances are primarily for Small riders.

Longbow: You need at least two hands to use a bow, regardless of its size. This bow is too big to use while you are mounted.

Longbow, Composite: You need at least two hands to use a bow, regardless of its size. You must be at least Medium-size to use this bow while mounted. Composite bows are made from laminated horn, wood, or bone and built with a recurve, meaning that the bow remains bow-shaped even when unstrung. They can be made with especially heavy pulls to take advantage of a character's above-average Strength (see Mighty Composite Longbow or Shortbow, page 113).

Longspear: A longspear has reach. You can strike opponents 10 feet away with it, but you can't use it against an adjacent foe.

Longsword: This classic, straight blade is the weapon of knighthood and valor. It is the favored weapon of paladins.

Mace, Heavy or Light: A mace is made of metal, even the haft, making it quite heavy and very hard to break.

Illus. by L. Grant-West

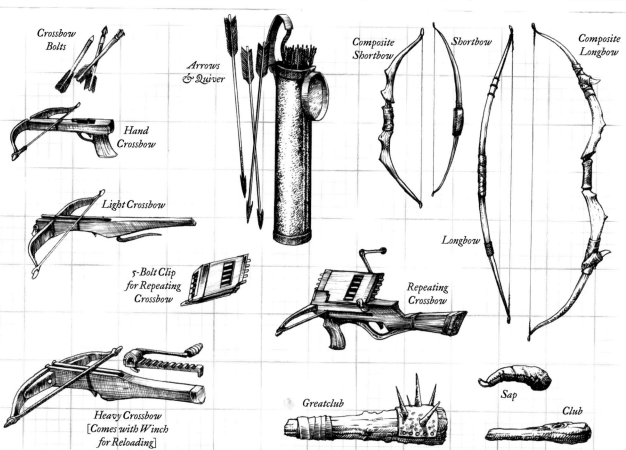

Crossbow Bolts

Hand Crossbow

Light Crossbow

5-Bolt Clip for Repeating Crossbow

Heavy Crossbow [Comes with Winch for Reloading]

Arrows & Quiver

Greatclub

Repeating Crossbow

Composite Shortbow

Shortbow

Composite Longbow

Longbow

Sap

Club

Morningstar: This simple weapon combines the impact of a club with the piercing force of spikes.

Net: A fighting net has small barbs in the weave and a trailing rope to control netted opponents. You use it to entangle opponents.

When you throw a net, you make a ranged touch attack against your target. A net's maximum range is 10 feet, and you suffer no range penalties to throw it even to its maximum range. If you hit, the target is entangled. An entangled creature suffers –2 on attack rolls and a –4 penalty on effective Dexterity. The entangled creature can only move at half speed and cannot charge or run. If you control the trailing rope by succeeding at an opposed Strength check while holding it, the entangled creature can only move within the limits that the rope allows. If the entangled creature attempts to cast a spell, it must succeed at a Concentration check (DC 15) or be unable to cast the spell.

The entangled creature can escape with an Escape Artist check (DC 20) that is a full-round action. The net has 5 hit points and can be burst with a Strength check (DC 25, also a full-round action).

A net is only useful against creatures between Tiny and Large size, inclusive.

A net must be folded to be thrown effectively. The first time you throw your net in a fight, you make a normal ranged touch attack roll. After the net is unfolded, you suffer a –4 penalty on attack rolls with it. It takes 2 rounds for a proficient user to fold a net and twice that long for a nonproficient one to do so.

Nunchaku or Halfling Nunchaku: A monk using a nunchaku fights with her unarmed base attack, including her more favorable number of attacks per round, along with other applicable attack modifiers. The halfling nunchaku is for Small monks.

Pick, Heavy or Light: A pick is designed to concentrate its force on a small, penetrating point. A light or heavy pick resembles a miner's pick but is specifically designed for war.

Quarterstaff: This is the favored weapon of travelers, peasants, merchants, and wizards. You can strike with either end, allowing you to take full advantage of openings in your opponent's defenses.

A quarterstaff is a double weapon. You can fight with it as if fighting with two weapons, but if you do, you incur all the normal attack penalties associated with fighting with two weapons as if you are using a one-handed weapon and a light weapon (see Attacking with Two Weapons, page 124). A creature using a double weapon in one hand, such as a Large creature using a quarterstaff, can't use it as a double weapon.

Ranseur: A ranseur has reach. You can strike opponents 10 feet away with it, but you can't use it against an adjacent foe.

With a ranseur, you get a +2 bonus on your opposed attack rolls when attempting to disarm an opponent (including the roll to avoid being disarmed if you fail to disarm your opponent).

Rapier: You can use the Weapon Finesse feat (see page 86) to apply your Dexterity modifier instead of your Strength modifier to attack rolls with a rapier.

Sap: A sap comes in handy when you want to knock an opponent out instead of killing him.

Scimitar: The curve on this blade makes the weapon's edge effectively sharper.

Scythe: While it resembles the standard farm implement of the same name, this scythe is balanced and strengthened for war. The design of the scythe focuses tremendous force on the sharp point as well as allowing devastating slashes with the blade edge.

Shortbow: You need at least two hands to use a bow, regardless of its size. A character who is Medium-size or larger can use this bow while mounted.

Shortbow, Composite: You need at least two hands to use a bow, regardless of its size. A character who is Small or larger can use this bow while mounted. Composite bows are made from

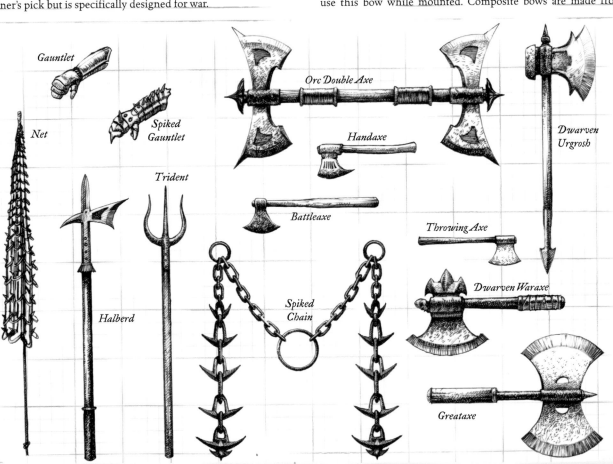

Gauntlet

Net

Spiked Gauntlet

Orc Double Axe

Handaxe

Dwarven Urgrosh

Trident

Battleaxe

Throwing Axe

Halberd

Spiked Chain

Dwarven Waraxe

Gre ataxe

laminated horn, wood, or bone and built with a recurve, meaning that the bow remains bow-shaped even when unstrung. They can be made with especially heavy pulls to take advantage of a character's above-average Strength (see Mighty Composite Longbow or Shortbow, page 113).

Shortspear: Because a shortspear is not as long as a longspear, it can be thrown.

Shuriken: You can throw up to three shuriken per attack (all at the same target). Do not apply your Strength modifier to damage with shuriken. They are too small to carry the extra force that a strong character can usually impart to a thrown weapon.

Siangham or Halfling Siangham: A monk using a siangham fights with her unarmed base attack, including her more favorable number of attacks per round, along with other applicable attack modifiers. The halfling siangham is for Small monks.

Sickle: This weapon is like a farmer's sickle, but it is strengthened for use as a weapon. It is favored by druids or by anyone who wants a weapon that might be overlooked by guards.

Sling: The sling hurls lead bullets. It's not as easy to use as the crossbow nor as powerful as a bow, but it's cheap, and easy to improvise from common materials. Druids and halflings favor slings.

You can hurl ordinary stones with a sling, but stones are not as dense or as round as bullets, so you deal only 1d3 points of damage and suffer a –1 penalty on attack rolls.

Strike, Unarmed: A Medium-size character deals 1d3 points of subdual damage with an unarmed strike, which may be a punch, kick, head butt, or other type of attack. A Small character deals 1d2 points of subdual damage. The damage from an unarmed strike is considered weapon damage for the purposes of effects that give you a bonus to weapon damage.

You can use the Weapon Finesse feat (see page 86) to apply your Dexterity modifier instead of your Strength modifier to attack rolls with an unarmed strike.

Sword, Bastard: A bastard sword is too large to use in one hand without special training; thus, it is an exotic weapon. A Medium-size character can use a bastard sword two-handed as a martial weapon, or a Large creature can use it one-handed in the same way. Bastard swords are also known as hand-and-a-half swords.

Sword, Short: This sword is popular as an off-hand weapon or as a primary weapon for Small characters.

Sword, Two-Bladed: A two-bladed sword is a double weapon. You can fight with it as if fighting with two weapons, but if you do, you incur all the normal attack penalties associated with fighting with two weapons as if you were using a one-handed weapon and a light weapon (see Attacking with Two Weapons, page 124). A creature using a double weapon in one hand, such as an ogre using a two-bladed sword, can't use it as a double weapon.

Trident: This three-tined piercing weapon can be thrown just as a halfspear or shortspear can be, but its range increment is shorter because it's not as aerodynamic as those other weapons.

Urgrosh, Dwarven: A dwarven urgrosh is a double weapon. You can fight with it as if fighting with two weapons, but if you do, you incur all the normal attack penalties associated with fighting with two weapons as if you were using a one-handed weapon and a light weapon (see Attacking with Two Weapons, page 124). A creature using a double weapon in one hand, such as an ogre using a dwarven urgrosh, can't use it as a double weapon. The urgrosh's axe head is a slashing weapon that deals 1d8 points of damage. Its spear head is a piercing weapon that deals 1d6 points of damage. You can use either head as the primary weapon head. The other is the off-hand weapon.

If you use an urgrosh against a charging character, the spear head is the part of the weapon that does damage.

An urgrosh is also called a spear-axe.

Waraxe, Dwarven: A dwarven waraxe is too large to use in one hand without special training; thus, it is an exotic weapon. A

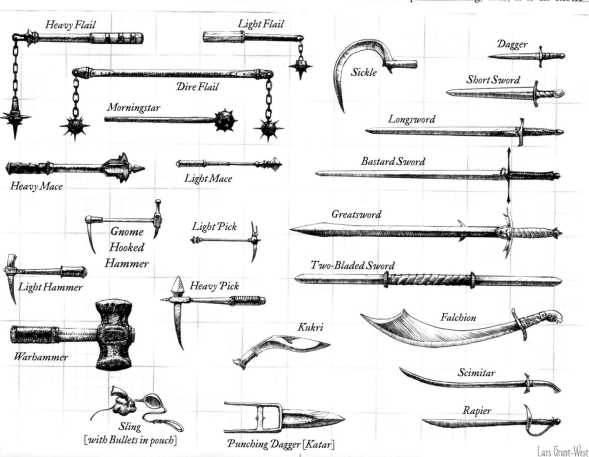

Heavy Flail — *Light Flail* — *Dire Flail* — *Morningstar* — *Heavy Mace* — *Light Mace* — *Gnome Hooked Hammer* — *Light Pick* — *Light Hammer* — *Heavy Pick* — *Warhammer* — *Sling [with Bullets in pouch]* — *Punching Dagger [Katar]* — *Kukri* — *Sickle* — *Dagger* — *Short Sword* — *Longsword* — *Bastard Sword* — *Greatsword* — *Two-Bladed Sword* — *Falchion* — *Scimitar* — *Rapier*

Lars Grant-West

Medium-size character can use a dwarven waraxe two-handed as a martial weapon, or a Large creature can use it one-handed in the same way.

Warhammer: This weapon, favored by dwarves, is a one-handed sledge or maul with a large, heavy head.

Whip: The whip deals subdual damage. It deals no damage to any creature with even a +1 armor bonus or at least a +3 natural armor bonus. Although you keep it in hand, treat it as a projectile weapon with a maximum range of 15 feet and no range penalties.

Because the whip can wrap around an enemy's leg or other limb, you can make trip attacks with it. If you are tripped during your own trip attempt, you can drop the whip to avoid being tripped.

When using a whip, you get a +2 bonus on your opposed attack roll when attempting to disarm an opponent (including the roll to keep from being disarmed if you fail to disarm your opponent).

ARMOR

Your armor protects you in combat, but it can also slow you down. See Table 7–5: Armor for the list of armors. The information given on this table is for Medium-size creatures. The time it takes to get into or out of armor depends on its type (see Table 7–6: Donning Armor).

ARMOR QUALITIES

What armor you wear isn't the only fashion statement you can make, but it's a big one. In addition, depending on your class, you may be proficient in the use of all, some, or no armors, including shields. To wear heavier armor effectively, you can select the Armor Proficiency feats (page 80), but most classes are proficient in the armors that work best for them. When choosing armor, keep in mind these factors (see Table 7–5: Armor):

Cost: The cost of the armor.

Armor Bonus: The protective value of the armor. Bonuses from armor and a shield stack. This bonus is an armor bonus, so it does not stack with other effects that increase your armor bonus, such as the *mage armor* spell or *bracers of armor*.

Maximum Dex Bonus: This number is the maximum Dexterity bonus to AC that this type of armor allows. Heavier armors limit your mobility, reducing your ability to dodge blows. For example, chainmail permits a maximum Dexterity bonus of +2. A character with a Dexterity score of 18 normally gains a +4 bonus to his AC, but if he's wearing chainmail, his bonus drops to +2. His final Armor Class would be 17 (10 + 5 + 2 = 17), assuming he has no other modifiers. (The +5 is the chainmail and the +2 is his maximum Dexterity bonus.)

Even if your Dexterity bonus drops to 0, you are not considered to have lost your Dexterity bonus. For example, a rogue can't sneak attack you just because you're wearing half-plate.

Shields: Shields do not affect your maximum Dexterity bonus.

Armor Check Penalty: Anything heavier than leather hurts your ability to use some of your skills. Some characters don't much care, but others do. The barbarian, in particular, faces a trade-off between heavier armor and better skill checks.

Skills: The armor check penalty number is the armor check penalty you apply to certain skill checks. If you're wearing any armor heavier than leather, you can't climb, sneak, or tumble as well as you would if you weren't wearing such heavy armor. This penalty applies to Balance, Climb, Escape Artist, Hide, Jump, Move Silently, Pick Pockets, and Tumble checks. Swim checks face a similar penalty based on the weight of the gear you are carrying and wearing.

Shields: If you are wearing armor and using a shield, both armor check penalties apply.

Nonproficient with Armor Worn: If you wear armor with which you are not proficient, you suffer the armor's armor check penalty on attack rolls and on all skill rolls that involve moving, including Ride.

TABLE 7–5: ARMOR

Armor	Cost	Armor Bonus	Maximum Dex Bonus	Armor Check Penalty	Arcane Spell Failure	Speed (30 ft.)	Speed (20 ft.)	Weight‡
Light armor								
Padded	5 gp	+1	+8	0	5%	30 ft.	20 ft.	10 lb.
Leather	10 gp	+2	+6	0	10%	30 ft.	20 ft.	15 lb.
Studded leather	25 gp	+3	+5	−1	15%	30 ft.	20 ft.	20 lb.
Chain shirt	100 gp	+4	+4	−2	20%	30 ft.	20 ft.	25 lb.
Medium armor								
Hide	15 gp	+3	+4	−3	20%	20 ft.	15 ft.	25 lb.
Scale mail	50 gp	+4	+3	−4	25%	20 ft.	15 ft.	30 lb.
Chainmail	150 gp	+5	+2	−5	30%	20 ft.	15 ft.	40 lb.
Breastplate	200 gp	+5	+3	−4	25%	20 ft.	15 ft.	30 lb.
Heavy armor								
Splint mail	200 gp	+6	+0	−7	40%	20 ft.*	15 ft.*	45 lb.
Banded mail	250 gp	+6	+1	−6	35%	20 ft.*	15 ft.*	35 lb.
Half-plate	600 gp	+7	+0	−7	40%	20 ft.*	15 ft.*	50 lb.
Full plate	1,500 gp	+8	+1	−6	35%	20 ft.*	15 ft.*	50 lb.
Shields								
Buckler	15 gp	+1	—	−1	5%	—	—	5 lb.
Shield, small, wooden	3 gp	+1	—	−1	5%	—	—	5 lb.
Shield, small, steel	9 gp	+1	—	−1	5%	—	—	6 lb.
Shield, large, wooden	7 gp	+2	—	−2	15%	—	—	10 lb.
Shield, large, steel	20 gp	+2	—	−2	15%	—	—	15 lb.
Shield, tower	30 gp	**	—	−10	50%	—	—	45 lb.
Extras								
Armor spikes	+50 gp	—	—	—	—	—	—	+10 lb.
Gauntlet, locked†	8 gp	—	—	Special	—	—	—	+5 lb.
Shield spikes	+10 gp	—	—	—	—	—	—	+5 lb.

*When running in heavy armor, you move only triple your speed, not quadruple.
**The tower shield grants you cover. See the description.
†Cannot cast spells with somatic components while worn.
‡Armor fitted for Small characters weighs half as much.

Sleeping in Armor: If you sleep in a suit of armor with an armor check penalty of –5 or worse, you are automatically fatigued the next day. You suffer a –2 penalty on Strength and Dexterity, and you can't charge or run.

Arcane Spell Failure: Armor interferes with the gestures that you need to make to cast an arcane spell. Arcane spellcasters face the possibility of arcane spell failure if they're wearing armor, so wizards and sorcerers usually don't wear armor. Bards have a hard choice because they're more likely to get into combat than wizards and they cast fewer spells, so getting some armor makes more sense for them than it does for a wizard.

Casting an Arcane Spell in Armor: When you cast an arcane spell while wearing armor, you often must make an arcane spell failure roll. The number in the Arcane Spell Failure column on Table 7–5: Armor is the chance that the spell fails and is ruined. If the spell lacks a somatic (S) component, however, you can cast it without making the arcane spell failure roll.

Shields: If you are wearing armor and using a shield, add the two numbers together to get a single arcane spell failure chance.

Speed: Medium and heavy armor slows you down. It's better to be slow and alive than to be quick and dead, but don't neglect to give speed some thought. The number on Table 7–5: Armor is your speed while wearing the armor. Humans, elves, half-elves, and half-orcs have an unencumbered speed of 30 feet. They use the first column. Dwarves, gnomes, and halflings have an unencumbered speed of 20 feet. They use the second column.

Shields: Shields do not affect your speed.

Weight: The weight of the armor. Armor fitted for Small characters weighs half as much.

GETTING INTO AND OUT OF ARMOR

The time required to don armor depends on its type (see Table 7–6: Donning Armor).

Don: This column records how long it takes you to put the armor on. (One minute is 10 rounds.)

Don Hastily: This column records how long it takes you to put the armor on in a hurry. Hastily donned armor has an armor check penalty and armor bonus each 1 point worse than normal. For example, if Tordek donned his scale mail hastily, it would take him 1 minute (10 rounds), the armor would provide only a +3 bonus to his AC (instead of +4), and his armor check penalty would be –5 (instead of –4).

Remove: This column records how long it takes you to get the armor off (especially important to know if you are suddenly submerged; see the drowning rules in the DUNGEON MASTER'S *Guide*).

TABLE 7–6: DONNING ARMOR

Armor Type	Don	Don Hastily	Remove
Padded, leather, hide, studded leather, or chain shirt	1 minute	5 rounds	1 minute*
Breastplate, scale mail, chainmail, banded mail, or splint mail	4 minutes*	1 minute	1 minute*
Half-plate or full plate	4 minutes**	4 minutes*	1d4+1 minutes*

*If you have some help, cut this time in half. A single character doing nothing else can help one or two adjacent characters. Two characters can't help each other don armor at the same time.

**You must have help to don this armor. Without help, you can only don it hastily.

ARMOR FOR UNUSUAL CREATURES

The information on Table 7–5: Armor is for Medium-size creatures. Armor for Tiny or smaller creatures costs half as much as that for Medium-size creatures (provided you can find an armorsmith who can even make it), provides half as much protection, and weighs one-tenth or less as much. Armor for Large characters costs double and weighs twice as much, and for Huge creatures it costs quadruple and weighs five times as much. Armor for even larger creatures must be specially made and has no standard price or weight.

Armor for a nonhumanoid creature costs twice as much as the same armor for a humanoid.

ARMOR DESCRIPTIONS

The types of armor found on Table 7–5: Armor are described below (in alphabetical order).

Armor Spikes: You can have spikes added to your armor. They allow you to deal 1d6 points of piercing damage (×2 crit) with a successful grapple attack. The spikes count as a martial weapon. If you are not proficient with them, you suffer a –4 penalty on grapple checks when you try to use them. You can also make a regular melee attack (or off-hand attack) with the spikes, and they count as a light weapon in this case.

An enhancement bonus on a suit of armor does not improve the spikes' effectiveness, but the spikes can be made into magic weapons in their own right.

Banded Mail: This armor is made of overlapping strips of metal sewn to a backing of leather and chainmail. The strips cover vulnerable areas, while the chain and leather protect the joints and provide freedom of movement. Straps and buckles distribute the weight evenly. It includes gauntlets.

Breastplate: A breastplate covers your front and your back. It comes with a helmet and matching greaves (plates to cover your lower legs). A light suit or skirt of studded leather beneath the breastplate protects your limbs without restricting movement much.

Buckler: This small metal shield is strapped to your forearm, allowing you to wear it and still use your hand. You can use a bow or crossbow without penalty. You can also use an off-hand weapon, but you suffer a –1 penalty on attack rolls because of the extra weight on your arm. This penalty stacks with those for fighting with your off hand and, if appropriate, for fighting with two weapons. In any case, if you use a weapon in your off-hand, you don't get the buckler's AC bonus for the rest of the round.

You can't effectively bash someone with a buckler.

Chain Shirt: A shirt of chainmail protects your torso while leaving your limbs free and mobile. A layer of quilted fabric underneath it prevents chafing and cushions the impact of blows. It comes with a steel cap.

Chainmail: This armor is made of interlocking metal rings. It includes a layer of quilted fabric underneath it to prevent chafing and to cushion the impact of blows. Several layers of mail are hung over vital areas. Most of the armor's weight hangs from the shoulders, making chainmail uncomfortable to wear for long periods of time. It includes gauntlets.

Full Plate: This armor consists of shaped and fitted metal plates riveted and interlocked to cover the entire body. It includes gauntlets, heavy leather boots, and a visored helmet. You wear a thick layer of padding underneath it (included). Buckles and straps distribute the weight over the body, so full plate hampers movement less than splint mail even though splint is lighter. Each suit of full plate must be individually fitted to its owner by a master armorsmith, although a captured suit can be resized to fit a new owner at a cost of 200 to 800 (2d4 × 100) gold pieces.

Full plate is also known as field plate.

Gauntlet, Locked: This armored gauntlet has small chains and braces that allow the wearer to attach her weapon so that it cannot be dropped easily. It adds a +10 bonus to any roll to keep from being disarmed in combat. Removing a weapon from a locked gauntlet or attaching a weapon to a locked gauntlet is a full-round action that provokes attacks of opportunity. The price given is for a single locked gauntlet. The weight given only applies if you're wearing a breastplate, light armor, or no armor. Otherwise, the locked gauntlet replaces a gauntlet you already have as part of the armor.

While the gauntlet is locked, you can't use the hand wearing it for casting spells or employing skills. (You can still cast spells with somatic (S) components provided your other hand is free.)

Like a normal gauntlet, a locked gauntlet lets you deal normal damage rather than subdual damage with an unarmed strike.

Half-Plate: This armor is a combination of chainmail with metal plates (breastplate, epaulettes, elbow guards, gauntlets, tasses, and greaves) covering vital areas. Buckles and straps hold the whole suit together and distribute the weight, but the armor still hangs more loosely than full plate. It includes gauntlets.

Hide: This armor is prepared from multiple layers of leather and animal hides. It is stiff and hard to move in. Druids, who only wear nonmetallic armor, favor hide.

Leather: The breastplate and shoulder protectors of this armor are made of leather that has been stiffened by boiling in oil. The rest of the armor is softer and more flexible leather.

Padded: Padded armor features quilted layers of cloth and batting. It gets hot quickly and can become foul with sweat, grime, lice, and fleas.

Scale Mail: This is a coat and leggings (and perhaps a separate skirt) of leather covered with overlapping pieces of metal, much like the scales of a fish. It includes gauntlets.

Shield, Large or Small, Wooden or Steel: You strap a shield to your forearm and grip it with your hand.

Small Shield: A small shield's light weight lets you carry other items in that hand (although you cannot use weapons).

Large Shield: A large shield is too heavy for you to use your shield hand for anything else.

Wooden or Steel: Wooden and steel shields offer the same basic protection, though they respond differently to special attacks (such as *warp wood* and *heat metal*).

Shield Bash Attacks: You can bash an opponent with a shield, using it as an off-hand weapon. A Medium-size character deals 1d4 points of damage (×2 crit) with a large shield or 1d3 (×2 crit) with a small one. (You cannot bash with a tower shield.) A Small character deals 1d3 points of damage (×2 crit) with a large shield or 1d2 (×2 crit) with a small one. Used this way, the shield is a martial bludgeoning weapon. For purposes of attack penalties, treat a shield as a light weapon. If you use your shield as a weapon, you lose its AC bonus until your next action (usually until the next round).

Shield Spikes: When added to your shield, these spikes turn it into a martial piercing weapon that deals 1d6 points of damage (×2 crit) no matter whether the shield is small or large. You can't put spikes on a buckler or a tower shield. Otherwise, attacking with a spiked shield is like a shield bash attack (see above).

Shield, Tower: This massive wooden shield is nearly as tall as the wielder. Basically, it is a portable wall meant to provide cover. It can provide up to total cover, depending on how far you come out from behind it. A tower shield, however, does not provide cover against targeted spells; a spellcaster can cast a spell on you by targeting the shield you are holding. You cannot bash with a tower shield.

Splint Mail: This armor is made of narrow vertical strips of metal riveted to a backing of leather that is worn over cloth padding. Flexible chainmail protects the joints. It includes gauntlets.

Studded Leather: This armor is made from tough but flexible leather (not hardened leather as with normal leather armor) reinforced with close-set metal rivets.

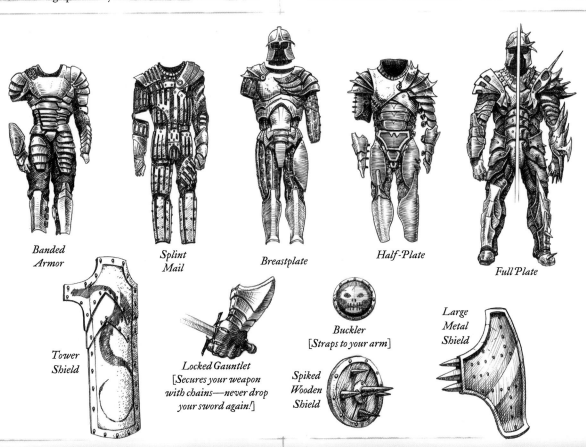

Banded Armor

Splint Mail

Breastplate

Half-Plate

Full Plate

Tower Shield

Locked Gauntlet [Secures your weapon with chains—never drop your sword again!]

Spiked Wooden Shield

Buckler [Straps to your arm]

Large Metal Shield

GOODS AND SERVICES

Weights for all the items listed on Table 7–7: Goods and Services are their filled weights (except where otherwise designated).

ADVENTURING GEAR

Adventurers face all sorts of challenges and difficulties, and the right gear can make the difference between a successful adventure and failure. Most of this gear is basic equipment that might come in handy regardless of your skills or class.

For objects with hardness and hit points, see Strike an Object, page 135.

Backpack: A leather pack carried on the back, typically with straps to secure it.

Bedroll: Adventurers never know where they're going to sleep, and bedrolls help them get better sleep in haylofts or on the cold ground. A bedroll is bedding and a blanket thin enough to be rolled up and tied. In an emergency, it can double as a stretcher.

Blanket, Winter: A thick, quilted, wool blanket.

Caltrops: Caltrops resemble large metal jacks with sharpened points rather than balls on the ends of their arms. They are essentially iron spikes designed so that one point is always facing up. You scatter them on the ground in the hope that your enemies step on them or are at least forced to slow down to avoid them. One bag of caltrops (the 2-pound unit listed on Table 7–7: Goods and Services) covers an area 5 feet square. Each time a creature moves into an area covered by caltrops (or spends a round fighting while standing in such an area), the creature may step on one. The caltrops make an attack roll (base attack bonus +0) against the creature. For this attack, the creature's shield, armor, and deflection bonus do not count. (Deflection averts blows as they approach you, but it does not prevent you from touching something dangerous.) If the creature is wearing shoes or other footwear, it gets a +2 armor bonus to AC. If the caltrops succeed at the attack, the creature has stepped on one. The caltrop deals 1 point of damage, and the creature's speed is reduced by one-half because its foot is wounded. This movement penalty lasts for 1 day, until the creature is successfully treated with the Heal skill (DC 15), or until it receives at least 1 point of magical curing. A charging or running creature must immediately stop if it steps on a caltrop. Any creature moving at half speed or slower can pick its way through a bed of caltrops with no trouble.

The DM judges the effectiveness of caltrops against unusual opponents. A giant centipede, for example, can scramble among the caltrops with no chance of hurting itself, and a fire giant wearing fire-giant-size boots is immune to normal-size caltrops. (They just get stuck in the soles of his boots.)

Candle: A candle clearly illuminates a 5-foot radius and burns for 1 hour.

Case, Map or Scroll: A capped leather or tin tube for holding rolled pieces of parchment or paper.

Chain: Chain has a hardness of 10 and 5 hit points. It can be burst with a Strength check (DC 26).

Crowbar: An iron bar for levering things open.

Flask: A ceramic, glass, or metal container fitted with a tight stopper. It holds 1 pint of liquid.

Flint and Steel: Striking the steel and flint together creates sparks. By knocking sparks into tinder, you can create a small flame. Lighting a torch with flint and steel is a full-round action, and lighting any other fire with them takes at least that long.

Grappling Hook: Tied to the end of a rope, the hook can secure the rope to battlements, windows, tree limbs, and so forth.

Hammer: A one-handed hammer with an iron head that is useful for pounding pitons into a wall.

Ink: This is black ink. You can buy ink in other colors, but it costs twice as much.

Padded Armor

Leather Armor [Available Plain or Studded]

Hide Armor

Scale Mail

Chainmail

Chain Shirt

Close-Up of Chainmail

Close-Up of Scale Mail

Lars Grant-West

Inkpen: A wooden stick with a special tip on the end. The tip draws ink in when dipped in a vial and leaves an ink trail when drawn across a surface.

Jug, Clay: A basic ceramic jug fitted with a stopper. It holds 1 gallon of liquid.

Ladder, 10-foot: A straight, simple wooden ladder.

Lamp, Common: A lamp clearly illuminates things in a 15-foot radius and burns for 6 hours on a pint of oil. It burns with a more

even flame than a torch, but, unlike a lantern, it uses an open flame and it can spill easily, making it too dangerous for most adventuring. You can carry a lamp in one hand.

Lantern, Bullseye: A bullseye lantern has only a single shutter, with its other sides being highly polished inside to reflect the light in a single direction. It illuminates a cone 60 feet long and 20 feet wide at the end, and it burns for 6 hours on a pint of oil. You can carry a lantern in one hand.

TABLE 7–7: GOODS AND SERVICES

ADVENTURING GEAR

Item	Cost	Weight
Backpack (empty)	2 gp	2 lb.†
Barrel (empty)	2 gp	30 lb.
Basket (empty)	4 sp	1 lb.
Bedroll	1 sp	5 lb.†
Bell	1 gp	*
Blanket, winter	5 sp	3 lb.†
Block and tackle	5 gp	5 lb.
Bottle, wine, glass	2 gp	*
Bucket (empty)	5 sp	2 lb.
Caltrops	1 gp	2 lb.
Candle	1 cp	*
Canvas (sq. yd.)	1 sp	1 lb.
Case, map or scroll	1 gp	1/2 lb.
Chain (10 ft.)	30 gp	2 lb.
Chalk, 1 piece	1 cp	*
Chest (empty)	2 gp	25 lb.
Crowbar	2 gp	5 lb.
Firewood (per day)	1 cp	20 lb.
Fishhook	1 sp	*
Fishing net, 25 sq. ft.	4 gp	5 lb.
Flask	3 cp	*
Flint and steel	1 gp	*
Grappling hook	1 gp	4 lb.
Hammer	5 sp	2 lb.
Ink (1 oz. vial)	8 gp	*
Inkpen	1 sp	*
Jug, clay	3 cp	9 lb.
Ladder, 10-foot	5 cp	20 lb.
Lamp, common	1 sp	1 lb.
Lantern, bullseye	12 gp	3 lb.
Lantern, hooded	7 gp	2 lb.
Lock‡		1 lb.
Very simple	20 gp	1 lb.
Average	40 gp	1 lb.
Good	80 gp	1 lb.
Amazing	150 gp	1 lb.
Manacles	15 gp	2 lb.
Manacles, masterwork	50 gp	2 lb.
Mirror, small steel	10 gp	1/2 lb.
Mug/tankard, clay	2 cp	1 lb.
Oil (1-pint flask)	1 sp	1 lb.
Paper (sheet)	4 sp	*
Parchment (sheet)	2 sp	*
Pick, miner's	3 gp	10 lb.
Pitcher, clay	2 cp	5 lb.
Piton	1 sp	1/2 lb.
Pole, 10-foot	2 sp	8 lb.
Pot, iron	5 sp	10 lb.
Pouch, belt	1 gp	3 lb.†
Ram, portable	10 gp	20 lb.
Rations, trail (per day)	5 sp	1 lb.†
Rope, hemp (50 ft.)	1 gp	10 lb.
Rope, silk (50 ft.)	10 gp	5 lb.
Sack (empty)	1 sp	1/2 lb.†

Item	Cost	Weight
Sealing wax	1 gp	1 lb.
Sewing needle	5 sp	*
Signal whistle	8 sp	**
Signet ring‡	5 gp	*
Sledge	1 gp	10 lb.
Soap (per lb.)	5 sp	1 lb.
Spade or shovel	2 gp	8 lb.
Spyglass	1,000 gp	1 lb.
Tent	10 gp	20 lb.†
Torch	1 cp	1 lb.
Vial, ink or potion	1 gp	*
Waterskin	1 gp	4 lb.†
Whetstone	2 cp	1 lb.

CLASS TOOLS AND SKILL KITS

Item	Cost	Weight
Alchemist's lab‡	500 gp	40 lb.
Artisan's tools‡	5 gp	5 lb.
Artisan's tools, masterwork‡	55 gp	5 lb.
Climber's kit	80 gp	5 lb.†
Disguise kit	50 gp	8 lb.†
Healer's kit	50 gp	1 lb.
Holly and mistletoe	—	*
Holy symbol, wooden	1 gp	**
Holy symbol, silver	25 gp	1 lb.
Hourglass	25 gp	1 lb.
Magnifying glass‡	100 gp	*
Musical instrument, common	5 gp	3 lb.†
Musical instrument, masterwork	100 gp	3 lb.†
Scale, merchant's‡	2 gp	1 lb.
Spell component pouch	5 gp	3 lb.†
Spellbook, wizard's (blank)	15 gp	3 lb.†
Thieves' tools	30 gp	1 lb.
Thieves' tools, masterwork	100 gp	2 lb.
Water clock‡	1,000 gp	200 lb.

CLOTHING

Item	Cost	Weight
Artisan's outfit	1 gp	4 lb.†
Cleric's vestments	5 gp	6 lb.†
Cold weather outfit	8 gp	7 lb.†
Courtier's outfit	30 gp	6 lb.†
Entertainer's outfit	3 gp	4 lb.†
Explorer's outfit	10 gp	8 lb.†
Monk's outfit	5 gp	2 lb.†
Noble's outfit	75 gp	10 lb.†
Peasant's outfit	1 sp	2 lb.†
Royal outfit	200 gp	15 lb.†
Scholar's outfit	5 gp	6 lb.†
Traveler's outfit	1 gp	5 lb.†

FOOD, DRINK, AND LODGING

Item	Cost	Weight
Ale		
Gallon	2 sp	8 lb.
Mug	4 cp	1 lb.
Banquet (per person)	10 gp	—
Bread, per loaf	2 cp	1/2 lb.
Cheese, hunk of	1 sp	1/2 lb.
Inn stay (per day)‡		
Good	2 gp	
Common	5 sp	
Poor	2 sp	
Meals (per day)‡		
Good	5 sp	
Common	3 sp	
Poor	1 sp	
Meat, chunk of	3 sp	1/2 lb.
Rations, trail (per day)	5 sp	1 lb.†
Wine		
Common (pitcher)	2 sp	6 lb.
Fine (bottle)	10 gp	1 1/2 lb.

MOUNTS AND RELATED GEAR

Item	Cost	Weight
Barding		
Medium-size creature	×2	×1
Large creature	×4	×2
Bit and bridle	2 gp	1 lb.
Cart	15 gp	200 lb.
Dog, riding	150 gp	—
Donkey or mule	8 gp	—
Feed (per day)	5 cp	10 lb.
Horse		
Horse, heavy	200 gp	
Horse, light	75 gp	
Pony	30 gp	
Warhorse, heavy	400 gp	
Warhorse, light	150 gp	
Warpony	100 gp	
Saddle		
Military	20 gp	30 lb.
Pack	5 gp	15 lb.
Riding	10 gp	25 lb.
Saddle, Exotic		
Military	60 gp	40 lb.
Pack	15 gp	20 lb.
Riding	30 gp	30 lb.
Saddlebags	4 gp	8 lb.
Sled	20 gp	300 lb.
Stabling (per day)	5 sp	—
Wagon	35 gp	400 lb.

*No weight worth noting.

**Ten of these items together weigh 1 pound.

†These items weigh one-quarter this amount when made for Small characters. Containers for Small characters also carry one-quarter the normal amount.

‡See description.

Lantern, Hooded: A hooded lantern is a standard lantern with shuttered or hinged sides. You can carry a lantern in one hand. It clearly illuminates a 30-foot radius and burns for 6 hours on a pint of oil.

Lock: A lock is worked with a large, bulky key. The DC to open this kind of lock with the Open Locks skill depends on the lock's quality: very simple (DC 20), average (DC 25), good (DC 30), amazingly good (DC 40).

Manacles and Manacles, Masterwork: These manacles can bind a Medium-size creature. The manacled character can use the Escape Artist skill to slip free (DC 30, or DC 35 for masterwork manacles). To break the manacles requires success at a Strength check (DC 26, or DC 28 for masterwork manacles). Manacles have a hardness of 10 and 10 hit points. Most manacles have locks; add the cost of the lock you want to the cost of the manacles.

For the same price, one can buy manacles for Small creatures. For Large creatures, manacles cost ten times this amount, and for Huge creatures, one hundred times this amount. Gargantuan, Colossal, Tiny, Diminutive, and Fine creatures can only be held by specially made manacles.

Mirror, Small Steel: A polished steel mirror is handy when you want to look around corners, signal friends with reflected sunlight, keep an eye on a medusa, make sure that you look good enough to present yourself to the queen, or examine wounds that you've received on hard-to-see parts of your body.

Oil: A pint of oil burns for 6 hours in a lantern. You can use a flask of oil as a grenadelike weapon (see Table 7–10: Grenadelike Weapons, page 114, and Grenadelike Weapon Attacks, page 138). Use the rules for alchemist's fire, except that it takes a full-round action to prepare a flask with a fuse. Once it is thrown, there is only a 50% chance that the flask ignites successfully.

You can pour a pint of oil on the ground to cover an area 5 feet square (provided the surface is smooth). If lit, the oil burns for 2 rounds and deals 1d3 points of damage to each creature in the area.

Paper: A white sheet of paper made from cloth fibers.

Parchment: Goat hide or sheepskin prepared for writing on.

Piton: When a wall doesn't offer you handholds and footholds, you can make your own. A piton is a steel spike with an eye through which you can loop a rope. (See the Climb skill, page 64).

Pole, 10-foot: When you suspect a trap, you'd rather put the end of your 10-foot pole through a hole in a wall than your hand.

Pouch, Belt: This leather pouch straps to your belt. It's good for holding things that you may need in a hurry, such as potions.

Ram, Portable: This iron-shod wooden beam is the perfect tool for battering down doors. Not only does it give you a +2 circumstance bonus on your Strength check to break open a door, but it allows a second person to help you without having to roll, adding another +2 to your check (see Breaking Open Doors, page 62).

Rations, Trail: Trail rations are compact, dry, high-energy foods suitable for travel, such as jerky, dried fruit, hardtack, and nuts.

Rope, Hemp: This rope has 2 hit points and can be burst with a successful Strength check (DC 23).

Rope, Silk: This rope has 4 hit points and can be burst with a successful Strength check (DC 24). It is so supple that it adds a +2 circumstance bonus to Use Rope checks.

Sack: A drawstring sack made of burlap or a similar material.

Signet Ring: Your signet ring has a unique design carved into it. When you press this ring into warm sealing wax, you leave an identifying mark.

Sledge: A two-handed, iron-headed hammer that is good for smashing open treasure chests.

Spyglass: Objects viewed through a spyglass are magnified to twice their size.

Tent: This simple tent sleeps two.

Torch: A wooden rod capped with twisted flax soaked in tallow or a similar item. A torch clearly illuminates a 20-foot radius and burns for 1 hour.

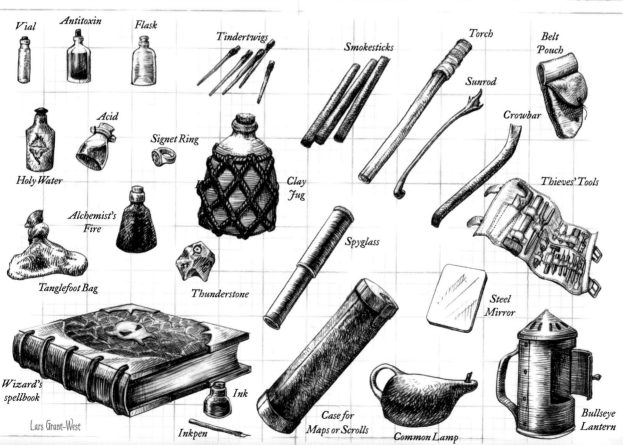

Vial   *Antitoxin*   *Flask*   *Tindertwigs*   *Smokesticks*   *Torch*   *Belt Pouch*

Sunrod

Acid   *Signet Ring*   *Crowbar*

Holy Water   *Clay Jug*   *Thieves' Tools*

Alchemist's Fire

Spyglass

Tanglefoot Bag   *Thunderstone*   *Steel Mirror*

Wizard's spellbook   *Ink*

Lars Grant-West

Inkpen   *Case for Maps or Scrolls*   *Common Lamp*   *Bullseye Lantern*

TABLE 7–8: CONTAINERS AND CARRIERS
HAULING VEHICLES

Item	Cost	Weight‡	Holds or Carries
Cart	15 gp	200 lb.	1/2 ton
Sled	20 gp	300 lb.	1 ton
Wagon	35 gp	400 lb.	2 tons

DRY GOODS

Item	Cost	Weight‡	Holds or Carries
Backpack	2 gp	2 lb.†	1 cu. ft.
Barrel	2 gp	30 lb.	10 cu. ft.
Basket	4 sp	1 lb.	2 cu ft.
Bucket	5 sp	2 lb.	1 cu. ft.
Chest	2 gp	25 lb.	2 cu. ft.
Pouch, belt	1 gp	1/2 lb.†	1/5 cu. ft.
Sack	1 sp	1/2 lb.†	1 cu. ft.
Saddlebags	4 gp	8 lb.	5 cu. ft.
Spell component pouch	5 gp	1/4 lb.†	1/8 cu. ft.

LIQUIDS

Item	Cost	Weight‡	Holds or Carries
Bottle, wine, glass	2 gp	*	1 1/2 pint
Flask	3 cp	*	1 pint
Jug, clay	3 cp	1 lb.	1 gallon
Mug/tankard, clay	2 cp	*	1 pint
Pitcher, clay	2 cp	1 lb.	1/2 gallon
Pot, iron	5 sp	2 lb.	1 gallon
Vial, ink or potion	1 gp	*	1 ounce
Waterskin	1 gp	*	1/2 gallon

*No weight worth noting.
†These items weigh one-quarter this amount and carry one-quarter the normal amount when made for Small characters.
‡Empty weight.

Vial: A ceramic, glass, or metal vial fitted with a tight stopper. The stoppered container usually is no more than 1 inch wide and 3 inches high. It holds 1 ounce of liquid.

Waterskin: A leather pouch with a narrow neck that is used for holding water.

CLASS TOOLS AND SKILL KITS

This equipment is particularly useful if you have certain skills or are of a certain class.

Alchemist's Lab: This includes beakers, bottles, mixing and measuring equipment and a miscellany of chemicals and substances. This is the perfect tool for the job and so adds a +2 circumstance bonus to Alchemy checks, but it has no bearing on the costs related to the Alchemy skill (see the Alchemy skill, page 63). Without this lab, a character with the Alchemy skill is assumed to have enough tools to use the skill but not enough to get the +2 bonus that the lab provides.

Artisan's Tools: This is the set of special tools needed for any craft. Without these tools, you have to use improvised tools (–2 penalty on your Craft check) if you can do the job at all.

Artisan's Tools, Masterwork: As artisan's tools, but these are the perfect tools for the job, so you get a +2 circumstance bonus on your Craft check.

Climber's Kit: Special pitons, boot tips, gloves, and a harness that aids in all sorts of climbing. This is the perfect tool for climbing and gives you a +2 circumstance bonus to Climb checks.

Disguise Kit: A bag containing cosmetics, hair dye, and small physical props. This is the perfect tool for disguise and adds a +2 circumstance bonus to Disguise checks. It's exhausted after ten uses.

Healer's Kit: This kit is full of herbs, salves, bandages and other useful materials. It is the perfect tool for anyone attempting a Heal check. It adds a +2 circumstance bonus to the check. It's exhausted after ten uses.

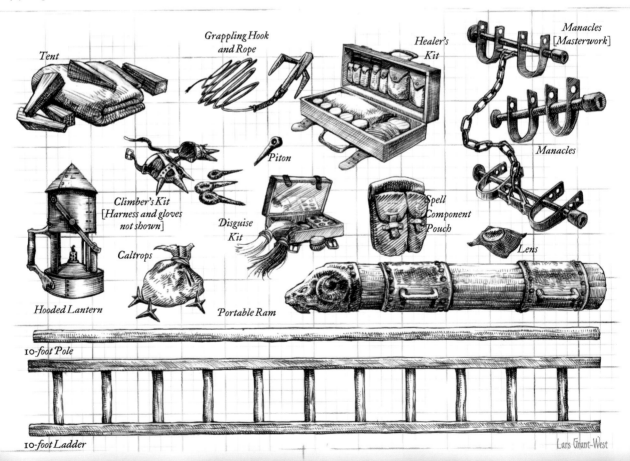

Tent

Grappling Hook and Rope

Healer's Kit

Manacles [Masterwork]

Piton

Manacles

Climber's Kit [Harness and gloves not shown]

Disguise Kit

Spell Component Pouch

Lens

Caltrops

Hooded Lantern

Portable Ram

10-foot Pole

10-foot Ladder

Lars Grant-West

Holly and Mistletoe: Sprigs of holly and mistletoe are used by druids as the default divine focus for druid spells. Holly and mistletoe plants are easily found in wooded areas by druids, and sprigs from them are harvested essentially for free.

Holy Symbol, Silver or Wooden: A holy symbol focuses positive energy. Clerics use them as the focuses for their spells and as tools for turning undead. Each religion has its own holy symbol, and a sun symbol is the default holy symbol for clerics not associated with any particular religion.

A silver holy symbol works no better than a wooden one, but it serves as a mark of status for the wielder.

Unholy Symbols: An unholy symbol is like a holy symbol except that it focuses negative energy and is used by evil clerics (or by neutral clerics who want to cast evil spells or command undead). A skull is the default unholy symbol for clerics not associated with any particular religion.

Magnifying Glass: This simple lens allows a closer look at small objects. It is useful as a substitute for flint, steel, and tinder when starting fires (though it takes light as bright as direct sunlight to focus, tinder to light, and at least a full-round action to light a fire with a magnifying glass). It grants you a +2 circumstance bonus on Appraise checks involving any item that is small or highly detailed, such as a gem.

Musical Instrument, Common or Masterwork: Popular instruments include fifes, recorders, lutes, mandolins, and shalms. A masterwork instrument is of superior make. It adds a +2 circumstance bonus to Perform checks and serves as a mark of status.

Scale, Merchant's: This scale includes a small balance and pans and a suitable assortment of weights. A scale grants you a +2 circumstance bonus to Appraise checks involving items that are valued by weight, including anything made of precious metals.

Spell Component Pouch: A small, watertight leather belt pouch with many small compartments. A spellcaster with a spell component pouch is assumed to have all the material components and focuses she needs except those that have a listed cost, divine focuses, or focuses that wouldn't fit in a pouch (such as the natural pool that a druid needs to look into to cast *scrying*).

Spellbook, Wizard's (Blank): A large, leatherbound book that serves as a wizard's reference. A spellbook has 100 pages of parchment, and each spell takes up two pages per level (one page for 0-level spells). See Arcane Spells, page 154.

Thieves' Tools: These are the tools you need to use the Disable Device and Open Lock skills. The kit includes one or more skeleton keys, long metal picks and pries, a long-nosed clamp, a small hand saw, and a small wedge and hammer. Without these tools, you have to improvise tools, and you suffer a −2 circumstance penalty on your Disable Device and Open Locks checks.

Thieves' Tools, Masterwork: This kit contains extra tools and tools of better make, granting you a +2 circumstance bonus on Disable Device and Open Lock checks.

Water Clock: This large, bulky contrivance gives the time accurate to within half an hour per day since it was last set. It requires a source of water, and it must be kept still because it marks time by the regulated flow of droplets of water. It is primarily an amusement for the wealthy and a tool for the student of arcane lore. Most people have no way to tell exact time, and there's little point in knowing that it is 2:30 P.M. if nobody else does.

CLOTHING

Different characters may want different outfits for various occasions. A beginning character is assumed to have an artisan's, entertainer's, explorer's, monk's, peasant's, scholar's, or traveler's outfit. This first outfit is free of cost and does not count against the amount of weight a character can carry.

Artisan's Outfit: A shirt with buttons, a skirt or pants with a drawstring, shoes, and perhaps a cap or hat. This outfit may include a belt or a leather or cloth apron for carrying tools.

Cleric's Vestments: Ecclesiastical clothes for performing priestly functions, not for adventuring.

Cold Weather Outfit: A wool coat, linen shirt, wool cap, heavy cloak, thick pants or skirt, and boots. When wearing a cold weather

Cart—Can be pulled by a single horse, donkey, or mule. Comes with harness.

Sled—For use on snow and ice. Can be pulled by a single horse, donkey, or mule. Comes with harness.

Wagon—Best for heavier loads. Requires two horses. Comes with harness.

Lars Grant-West

outfit, add a +5 circumstance bonus to Fortitude saving throws against exposure to cold weather (see the DUNGEON MASTER's Guide for information on cold dangers).

Courtier's Outfit: Fancy, tailored clothes in whatever fashion happens to be the current style in the courts of the nobles. Anyone trying to influence nobles or courtiers while wearing street dress will have a hard time of it. Without jewelry (costing perhaps an additional 50 gp), you look like an out-of-place commoner.

Entertainer's Outfit: A set of flashy, perhaps even gaudy, clothes for entertaining. While the outfit looks whimsical, its practical design lets you tumble, dance, walk a tightrope, or just run (if the audience turns ugly).

Explorer's Outfit: This is a full set of clothes for someone who never knows what to expect. It includes sturdy boots, leather breeches or a skirt, a belt, a shirt (perhaps with a vest or jacket), gloves, and a cloak. Rather than a leather skirt, a leather overtunic may be worn instead over a cloth skirt. The clothes have plenty of pockets (especially the cloak). The outfit also includes any extra items you might need, such as a scarf or a wide-brimmed hat.

Monk's Outfit: This simple outfit includes sandals, loose breeches, and a loose shirt, and is all bound together with sashes. Though it looks casual, the outfit is designed to give you maximum mobility, and it's made of high-quality fabric. You can hide small weapons in pockets hidden in the folds, and the sashes are strong enough to serve as short ropes. Depending on your style, the outfit may be decorated with designs that indicate your lineage or philosophical outlook.

Noble's Outfit: This set of clothes is designed specifically to be expensive and to show it. Precious metals and gems are worked into the clothing. To fit into the noble crowd, every would-be noble also needs a signet ring (see Adventuring Gear above) and jewelry (worth at least 100 gp, or at least appearing to be worth that much).

And it would be advisable to not show up to a ball in the same noble's outfit twice.

Peasant's Outfit: A loose shirt and baggy breeches, or a loose shirt and skirt or overdress. Cloth wrappings are used for shoes.

Royal Outfit: This is just the clothes, not the royal scepter, crown, ring, and other accoutrements. Royal clothes are ostentatious, with gems, gold, silk, and fur in abundance.

Scholar's Outfit: A robe, a belt, a cap, soft shoes, and possibly a cloak.

Traveler's Outfit: Boots, a wool skirt or breeches, a sturdy belt, a shirt (perhaps with a vest or jacket), and an ample cloak with a hood.

FOOD, DRINK, AND LODGING

Many travelers are lodged by guilds, churches, family, or nobility. Adventurers, however, typically pay for hospitality.

Inn: Poor accommodations at an inn amount to a place on the floor near the hearth, plus the use of a blanket if the innkeeper likes you and you're not worried about fleas. Common accommodations are a place on a raised, heated floor, the use of a blanket and a pillow, and the presence of a higher class of company. Good accommodations are a small, private room with one bed, some amenities, and a covered chamber pot in the corner.

Meals: Poor meals might be composed of bread, baked turnips, onions, and water. Common meals might consist of bread, chicken stew (easy on the chicken), carrots, and watered-down ale or wine. Good meals might be composed of bread and pastries, beef, peas, and ale or wine.

Rations, Trail: See Adventuring Gear, above.

MOUNTS AND RELATED GEAR

Horses and other mounts let you travel faster and more easily.

Barding, Medium-Size Creature and Large Creature: Barding is simply some type of armor covering the head, neck, chest, body,

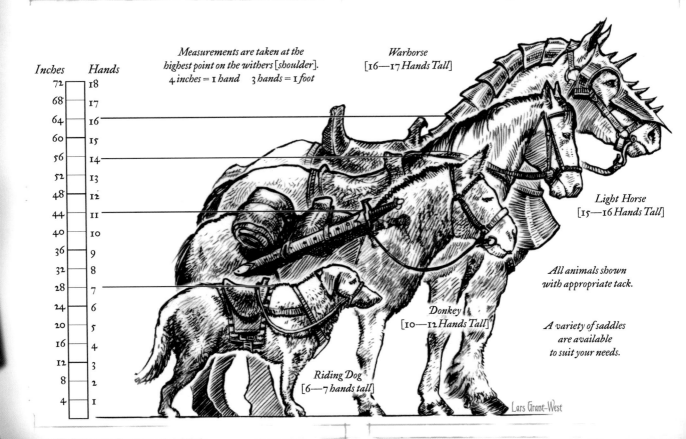

Measurements are taken at the highest point on the withers [shoulder].
4 inches = 1 hand   3 hands = 1 foot

Inches	Hands
72	18
68	17
64	16
60	15
56	14
52	13
48	12
44	11
40	10
36	9
32	8
28	7
24	6
20	5
16	4
12	3
8	2
4	1

Warhorse [16—17 Hands Tall]

Light Horse [15—16 Hands Tall]

All animals shown with appropriate tack.

Donkey [10—12 Hands Tall]

A variety of saddles are available to suit your needs.

Riding Dog [6—7 hands tall]

Lars Grant-West

and possibly legs of a horse. Heavier types provide better protection at the expense of lower speed. Barding comes in most of the types found on Table 7–5: Armor. As with any nonhumanoid Large creature, a horse's armor costs four times what a human's (a humanoid Medium-size creature's) armor costs and also weighs twice as much as the armor found on Table 7–5: Armor (see Armor for Unusual Creatures, page 105). (If the barding is for a pony, which is Medium-size, the cost is only double, and the weight is the same.)

Medium or heavy barding slows mounts:

	Speed		
Barding	**(40 ft.)**	**(50 ft.)**	**(60 ft.)**
Medium	30 ft.	35 ft.	40 ft.
Heavy	30 ft.*	35 ft.*	40 ft.*

*A mount wearing heavy armor moves at only triple normal rate when running instead of quadruple.

Flying mounts can't fly in medium or heavy barding.

Barded animals require special attention. You must take care to prevent chafing and sores caused by the armor. The armor must be removed at night and ideally should not be put on the mount except to prepare for a battle. Removing and fitting barding takes five times as long as the figures given on Table 7–6: Donning Armor. Barded animals cannot be used to carry any load other than the rider and normal saddlebags. Because of this, a mounted warrior often leads a second mount for carrying gear and supplies.

Cart: A two-wheeled vehicle drawn by a single horse (or other beast of burden). It comes with a harness.

Dog, Riding: This Medium-size dog is specially trained to carry a Small humanoid rider (and not a dwarf). It is brave in combat like a warhorse. You take no damage when you fall from a riding dog. (See the *Monster Manual* for more information on riding dogs.)

Donkey or Mule: The best pack animal around, a donkey or mule is stolid in the face of danger, hardy, sure-footed, and capable of carrying heavy loads over vast distances. Unlike horses, they're willing (though not eager) to enter dungeons and other strange or threatening places. (See the *Monster Manual* for more information on donkeys and mules.)

Feed: Horses, donkeys, mules, and ponies can graze to sustain themselves, but providing feed for them (such as oats) is much better because it provides a more concentrated form of energy, especially if the animal is exerting itself. If you have a riding dog, you have to feed it at least some meat, which may cost more or less than the given amount.

Horse: The horse is the best all-around work animal and mount in common use. A horse (other than a pony) is suitable as a mount for a human, elf, half-elf, or half-orc. A pony is smaller than a horse. A pony is a suitable mount for a dwarf, gnome, or halfling. (See the *Monster Manual* for more information on horses and ponies.)

Warhorses and warponies can be ridden easily into combat. Light horses, ponies, and heavy horses are hard to control in combat (see Mounted Combat, page 138, and the Ride skill, page 72).

Saddle, Exotic: An exotic saddle is like a normal saddle of the same type except that it is designed for an unusual mount, such as a pegasus. Exotic saddles come in military, pack, and riding styles.

Saddle, Military: A military saddle braces the rider, adding a +2 circumstance bonus to Ride checks related to staying in the saddle. If you're knocked unconscious while in a military saddle, you have a 75% chance to stay in the saddle (compared to 50% for a riding saddle).

Saddle, Pack: A pack saddle holds gear and supplies, not a rider. A pack saddle holds as much gear as the mount can carry. (The *Monster Manual* has notes on how much mounts can carry.)

Saddle, Riding: The standard riding saddle supports a rider.

Sled: This is a wagon on runners for moving through snow and over ice. In general, two horses (or other beasts of burden) draw it. It comes with the harness needed to pull it.

Stabling: Includes a stable, feed, and grooming.

Wagon: This is a four-wheeled, open vehicle for transporting heavy loads. In general, two horses (or other beasts of burden) draw it. It comes with the harness needed to pull it.

SPECIAL AND SUPERIOR ITEMS

In addition to the mundane and typical items found on other equipment lists, adventurers with enough gold can buy special or superior items. An item's price is a good indication of its rarity.

Prices for the items described here are given on Table 7–9: Special and Superior Items.

Acid: You can throw a flask of acid as a grenadelike weapon (see Table 7–10: Grenadelike Weapons, page 114, and Grenadelike Weapon Attacks, page 138).

Alchemist's Fire: Alchemist's fire is a sticky, adhesive substance that ignites when exposed to air. You can throw a flask of alchemist's fire as a grenadelike weapon (see Table 7–10: Grenadelike Weapons, page 114, and Grenadelike Weapon Attacks, page 138).

On the round following a direct hit, the target takes an additional 1d6 points of damage. The target can take a full-round action to attempt to extinguish the flames before taking this additional damage. It takes a successful Reflex saving throw (DC 15) to extinguish the flames. Rolling on the ground allows the character a +2 bonus. Leaping into a lake or magically extinguishing the flames automatically smothers the flames.

Antitoxin: If you drink antitoxin, you get a +5 alchemical bonus on all Fortitude saving throws against poison for 1 hour.

Armor or Shield, Masterwork: These well-made items function like the normal versions except that their armor check penalties are reduced by 1.

Arrow, Bolt, or Bullet, Masterwork: A masterwork projectile functions like a normal projectile of the same type except that it is so aerodynamically sound you get a +1 bonus on attack rolls when you use it. This bonus stacks with any bonus you might get by using a masterwork bow, crossbow, or sling. The projectile is damaged (effectively destroyed) when it is used.

Arrow, Bolt, or Bullet, Silvered: A silvered projectile functions like a normal projectile, except that some creatures that resist damage from normal weapons, such as werewolves, can be hurt by silvered weapons.

Dagger, Silvered: A silvered dagger functions as a normal dagger, except that some creatures that resist damage from normal weapons, such as werewolves, can be hurt by silvered weapons.

Holy Water: Holy water damages undead and evil outsiders almost as if it were acid. Typically, a flask of holy water deals 2d4 points of damage to an undead creature or an evil outsider on a direct hit or 1 point of damage if it splashes such a creature. Also, holy water is considered blessed, which means it has special effects on certain creatures. A flask of holy water can be thrown as a grenadelike weapon (see Table 7–10: Grenadelike Weapons, page 114, and Grenadelike Weapon Attacks, page 138). A flask breaks if thrown against the body of a corporeal creature, but against an incorporeal creature, the flask must be opened and the holy water poured out onto it. Thus, you can only douse an incorporeal creature with holy water if you are adjacent to it. Doing so is a ranged touch attack that does not provoke attacks of opportunity.

Temples to good deities sell holy water at cost (making no profit) because they are happy to supply people with what they need to battle evil.

Mighty Composite Longbow or Shortbow: A mighty bow is a composite bow made with an especially heavy pull to allow a strong archer to take advantage of an above-average Strength. The mighty bow allows you to add your Strength bonus to damage up to the maximum bonus listed. For example, Tordek has a +2

TABLE 7–9: SPECIAL AND SUPERIOR ITEMS

Weapon or Armor	Cost
Weapon, masterwork	+300 gp*
Arrow, bolt, or bullet, silvered	1 gp
Arrow, bolt, or bullet, masterwork	7 gp
Mighty composite shortbow	
(+1 Str bonus)	150 gp
(+2 Str bonus)	225 gp
Mighty composite longbow	
(+1 Str bonus)	200 gp
(+2 Str bonus)	300 gp
(+3 Str bonus)	400 gp
(+4 Str bonus)	500 gp
Dagger, silvered	10 gp
Armor or shield, masterwork	+150 gp*

Special Substances and Items	Cost
Acid (flask)	10 gp
Alchemist's fire (flask)	20 gp
Antitoxin (vial)	50 gp
Holy water (flask)	25 gp
Smokestick	20 gp
Sunrod	2 gp
Tanglefoot bag	50 gp
Thunderstone	30 gp
Tindertwig	1 gp

Miscellaneous	Cost
Tool, masterwork	+50 gp*

Spells	Cost**
0-level	Caster level × 5 gp
1st-level	Caster level × 10 gp
2nd-level	Caster level × 20 gp
3rd-level	Caster level × 30 gp
4th-level	Caster level × 40 gp
5th-level	Caster level × 50 gp
6th-level	Caster level × 60 gp
7th-level	Caster level × 70 gp
8th-level	Caster level × 80 gp
9th-level	Caster level × 90 gp

*Plus the cost of the normal item. For example, a masterwork bastard sword costs 335 gp. Double weapons cost double (+600 gp).

**See description for additional costs. If the additional costs put the item's total cost above 3,000 gp, that item is not generally available.

Strength bonus. With a regular composite shortbow, he gets no modifier to damage. For 150 gp, he can buy a mighty composite shortbow (+1), which lets him add +1 to the damage. For 225 gp, he can buy one that lets him add his entire +2 bonus. Even if he paid 400 gp for a mighty composite longbow (+3), he would still only get +2 to damage. The bow can't grant him a higher bonus than he already has.

Smokestick: This alchemically treated wooden stick instantly creates thick, opaque smoke when ignited. The smoke fills a 10-foot cube. The stick is consumed after 1 round, and the smoke dissipates naturally.

Spell: This is how much it costs to get a spellcaster to cast a spell for you. This cost assumes that you can go to the spellcaster and have the spell cast at her convenience. If you want to bring the spellcaster somewhere to cast a spell, such as into a dungeon to cast *knock* on a secret door that you can't open, you need to negotiate with the spellcaster, and the default answer is "no."

The cost listed is for a spell with no cost for a material component or focus component and no XP cost. If the spell includes a material component, add the cost of the component to the cost of the spell. If the spell requires a focus component (other than a divine focus), add 1/10 the cost of the focus to the cost of the spell. If the spell requires an XP cost, add 5 gp per XP lost. For instance, to get a 9th-level cleric to cast *commune* for you, you need to pay 450 gp for a 5th-level spell at caster level 9, plus 500 gp for the 100 XP loss that the caster suffers, for a total of 950 gp.

Because you must get an actual spellcaster to cast a spell for you and can't rely on a neutral broker, money is not always sufficient to get a spell cast. If the spellcaster is opposed to you on religious, moral, or political grounds, you may not be able to get the spell you want for any price.

Sunrod: This 1-foot-long, gold-tipped, iron rod glows brightly when struck. It clearly illuminates a 30-foot radius and glows for 6 hours, after which the gold tip is burned out and worthless.

Tanglefoot Bag: You can throw this round leather bag full of alchemical goo as a grenadelike weapon (see Table 7–10: Grenade-like Weapons, on this page, and Grenadelike Weapon Attacks, page 138). When you throw the bag against a creature (as a ranged touch attack), the bag comes apart and the goo bursts out, entangling the target and then becoming tough and resilient on exposure to air. An entangled creature suffers a –2 penalty to attack rolls and a –4 penalty to effective Dexterity. The entangled character must make a Reflex save (DC 15) or be glued to the floor, unable to move. Even with a successful save, it can only move at half speed.

A character who is glued to the floor can break free with a successful Strength check (DC 27) or by dealing 15 points of damage to the goo with a slashing weapon. A character trying to scrape goo off himself, or another character assisting, does not need to make an attack roll; hitting the goo is automatic, after which the character who hit makes a damage roll to see how much of the goo he happened to scrape off. Once free, a character can move at half speed. A character capable of spellcasting who is bound by the goo must make a Concentration check (DC 15) to cast a spell. The goo becomes brittle and fragile after 10 minutes.

Thunderstone: You can throw this stone as a grenadelike weapon (see Table 7–10: Grenadelike Weapons, on this page, and Grenadelike Weapon Attacks, page 138). When it strikes a hard surface (or is struck hard), it creates a deafening bang (a sonic attack). Creatures within a 10-foot radius must make Fortitude saves (DC 15) or be deafened. Deaf creatures, in addition to the obvious effects, suffer a –4 penalty on initiative and a 20% chance to miscast and lose any spell with a verbal (V) component that they try to cast.

Tindertwig: The alchemical substance on the end of this small, wooden stick ignites when struck against a rough surface. Creating a flame with a tindertwig is much faster than creating a flame with flint and steel (or a magnifying glass) and tinder. Lighting a torch with a tindertwig is a standard action (rather than a full-round action), and lighting any other fire with one takes at least a standard action.

Tool, Masterwork: This well-made item is the perfect tool for the job and adds a +2 circumstance bonus to a related skill check (if any). Some examples of this sort of item are on Table 7–7: Goods and Services, such as masterwork artisan's tools, masterwork thieves' tools, disguise kit, climber's kit, healer's kit, and masterwork musical instrument. This entry covers just about anything else. Bonuses provided by multiple masterwork items used toward the same skill check do not stack, so masterwork pitons and a masterwork climber's kit do not provide a +4 bonus if used together on a Climb check.

Weapon, Masterwork: These well-made weapons add a +1 bonus to attack rolls. Prices for these items are given on Table 7–9: Special and Superior Items. A masterwork weapon's bonus to attack does not stack with an enhancement bonus to attack.

TABLE 7–10: GRENADELIKE WEAPONS

Weapon*	Cost	Damage Direct Hit	Splash	Range Increment	Weight
Acid (flask)	10 gp	1d6	1 pt**	10 ft.	1 1/4 lb.
Alchemist's fire (flask)	20 gp	1d6	1 pt**	10 ft.	1 1/4 lb.
Holy water (flask)	25 gp	2d4	1 pt**	10 ft.	1 1/4 lb.
Tanglefoot bag	50 gp	Entangles	—	10 ft.	4 lb.
Thunderstone	30 gp	Sonic attack	—	20 ft.	1 lb.

*Grenadelike weapons require no proficiency to use. See text for full details on using these weapons.

**Grenadelike weapons deal splash damage to all creatures within 5 feet of where they land.

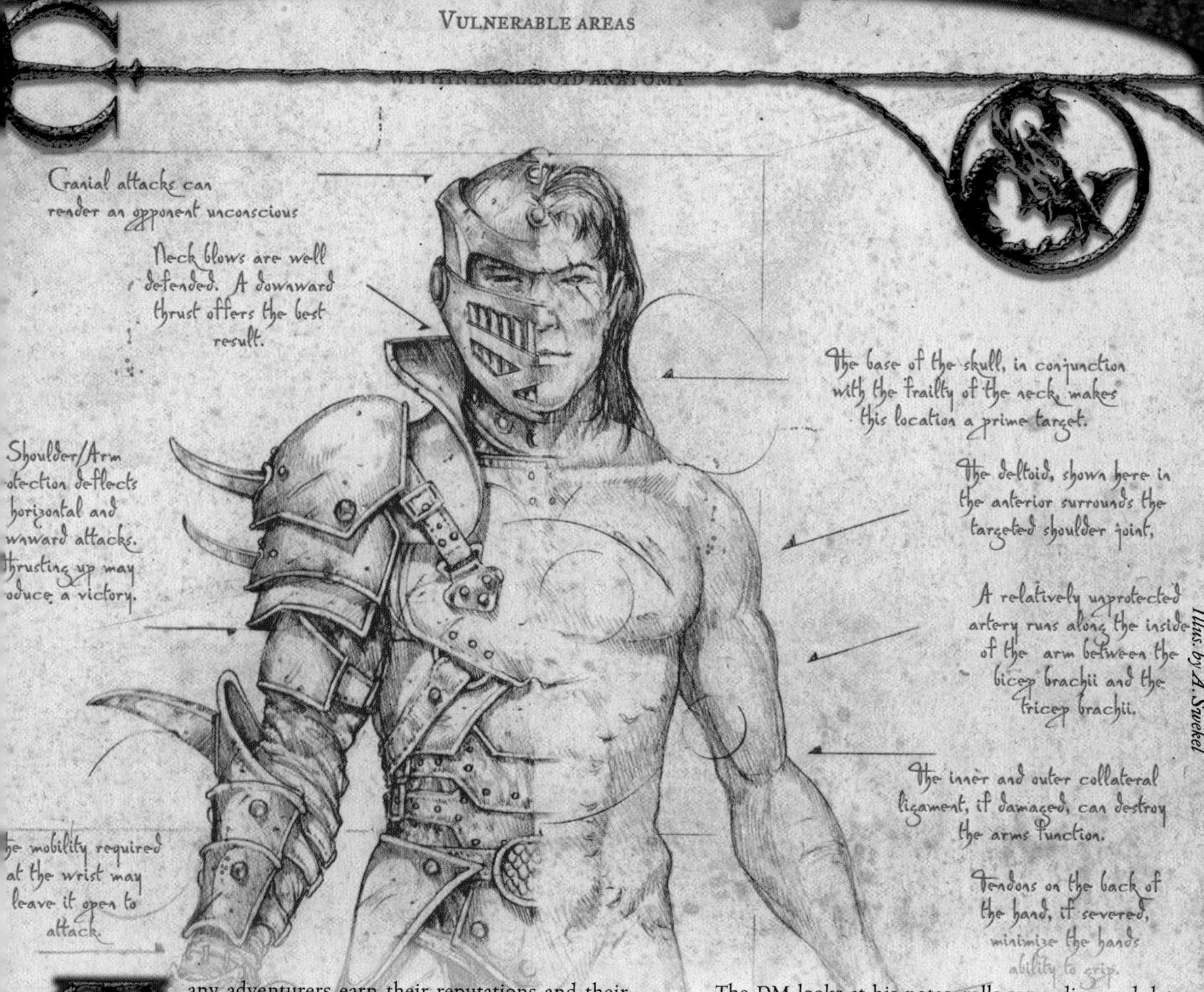

Cranial attacks can render an opponent unconscious

Neck blows are well defended. A downward thrust offers the best result.

Shoulder/Arm protection deflects horizontal and upward attacks. Thrusting up may produce a victory.

The base of the skull, in conjunction with the frailty of the neck, makes this location a prime target.

The deltoid, shown here in the anterior surrounds the targeted shoulder joint.

A relatively unprotected artery runs along the inside of the arm between the bicep brachii and the tricep brachii.

The inner and outer collateral ligament, if damaged, can destroy the arms function.

Tendons on the back of the hand, if severed, minimise the hands ability to grip.

The mobility required at the wrist may leave it open to attack.

Illus. by A. Swekel

Many adventurers earn their reputations and their wealth by defeating horrible monsters in combat. Opportunities for battle abound for those who are not held back by fear or good sense. Undead creatures lurk in ancient crypts, displacer beasts hole up in haunted ruins, and hordes of scaly troglodytes make their homes deep in dark caverns. While more mundane villains, such as goblin bandits, use spears and swords, the more exotic creatures wield an array of extraordinary weapons against adventurers, from the troglodytes' stench to the dragon's deadly breath.

This chapter details the combat rules, starting with an example, then covering the basics, and finally some of the more unusual combat strategies that characters can employ. Many special abilities and forms of damage that affect combat are also covered in the DUNGEON MASTER'S GUIDE.

HOW COMBAT WORKS

This extended example of combat demonstrates the most commonly used combat rules.

SETUP

Tordek, the dwarven fighter; Mialee, the elven wizard; Jozan, the human cleric of Pelor; and Lidda, the halfling rogue, are in a 10-foot-wide dungeon corridor at a door. Tordek is making Strength checks to try to break it down. The DM asks the players to tell him where their characters are. Tordek is in front of the door. Lidda and Jozan are to either side of it, and Mialee is behind Jozan. The players are playing with miniatures, so they arrange their miniatures in a line: Lidda, Tordek, Jozan, and Mialee.

The DM looks at his notes, rolls some dice, and determines that a gang of four orc marauders has arrived, having heard Tordek banging against the door. The orcs have come around the corner at a T-shaped intersection at the end of the corridor. They're 50 feet away from the door, so they're 40 feet away from Mialee, 45 feet away from Jozan, 50 feet away from Tordek, and 55 feet away from Lidda.

The orcs know that the adventurers are there. The DM needs to know who among the adventurers is aware of the orcs. Those who are caught unaware will be surprised. The DM asks each player to make a Listen check (DC 9). Jozan and Lidda succeed. Tordek and Mialee fail.

SURPRISE ROUND

During the surprise round, only the characters who are aware of their enemies can act, and each takes only a partial action. The orcs, Jozan, and Lidda all act during the surprise round.

The DM asks Jozan's and Lidda's players to make initiative checks. Jozan's initiative modifier is −1 (the same as his Dexterity penalty). Lidda's is +7 (+3 for her Dexterity bonus and +4 for her Improved Initiative). They get 7 and 19 as their initiative results. The DM rolls for all four orcs (+0) and gets a result of 11. The order of battle during the surprise round is Lidda first, followed by the orcs, followed by Jozan.

The DM calls on Lidda's player. Lidda recognizes the bloody eye symbols painted on the orcs' shields: The symbol identifies them as marauders. She steps to one side to get a clear line of sight past her friends and shoots a crossbow bolt at one of the orcs.

Lidda's attack bonus with a crossbow is +4 (+0 base attack bonus, +3 Dexterity bonus, +1 size bonus). The orc is 55 feet away, well under the light crossbow's range increment of 80 feet. Lidda therefore suffers no range penalty. Even though the orc is flat-footed, Lidda can't sneak attack it because it is more than 30 feet away.

Lidda's player rolls a 17 for an attack result of 21, well over the orc's AC of 16. She rolls 1d8 for damage and gets a 3. The orcs have 4 hit points each, so the wounded orc has 1 hit point left. "He staggers," says the DM, "but he doesn't fall."

Then it is the orcs' turn. Two orcs have javelins, and they throw them. The DM decides that the two javelins head toward Mialee, 40 feet away. Javelins have a range increment of 30 feet. The targets are located more than one range increment and less than two range increments away, for a range penalty of −2. So, the orcs have a −2 attack penalty with their javelins (+0 base attack bonus, +0 Dexterity bonus, +0 size bonus, −2 range penalty).

Mialee's AC is usually 13 (due to a +3 Dexterity bonus), but she can't use her Dexterity bonus while she's flat-footed, so her AC right now is 10. Rolling for the orcs, the DM gets an 18 and a 13 for results of 16 and 11. That means both javelins aimed at her hit. The orcs deal 1d6+2 points of damage with their javelins (1d6 for the javelin, +2 Strength bonus), so the DM rolls 2d6+4 and gets a result of 12 points of damage. Mialee is knocked from 7 hit points to −5. She falls to the stone floor, unconscious and dying.

Then Jozan takes his action. He is next to Mialee already. He reaches down and casts *cure minor wounds* on her. Her hit points rise to −4, and she is no longer dying. (If he had not cured her, she would probably have lost another hit point at the end of the round.)

With that, the surprise round ends.

FIRST REGULAR ROUND

The DM asks Tordek's player to make an initiative check because he's the only conscious character who hasn't done so. He gets a 14, so he goes after Lidda and before the orcs. The order of battle is: Lidda, Tordek, orcs, Jozan. (Mialee is unconscious and can't take an action.)

On her turn, Lidda fires another crossbow bolt, but she misses. She drops her crossbow and switches to her short sword (rather than reloading her crossbow).

Then Tordek moves 15 feet to get between the orcs and Mialee. (The orcs are 50 feet away from him, too far for him to reach them and attack, even with a charge.) The corridor is too wide (10 feet) for him to keep the orcs from getting past him, but he will at least get an attack of opportunity on any single orc that tries it.

On their action, the orcs are 35 feet away from Tordek. That's within charging range. (They can charge 40 feet.) The two orcs with battleaxes in hand charge and attack. In a 10-foot-wide corridor, only two can fight side by side. The other two in the back ready their axes and wait to get in. One orc could try to move past Tordek so another orc could get at him, but then Tordek would get an attack of opportunity on the first orc.

The orcs have a +4 attack bonus on their attack rolls with their battleaxes (+0 base attack bonus, +2 Strength bonus, +2 charge bonus). Tordek's AC is 17 (+4 armor bonus, +2 shield bonus, +1 Dexterity bonus), and neither charging orc hits him. "Their battleaxes clang against your shield and armor," says the DM, "and you can feel the strength behind their blows, but you're not hurt."

Jozan casts *cure light wounds* (his 1st-level domain spell) on Mialee. That spell restores 1d8+2 hit points to Mialee, but Jozan's player rolls a 1 for a result of only 3 hit points cured. Mialee's hit points rise to −1, but that's not enough to get her back on her feet.

SECOND REGULAR ROUND

Lidda steps in next to Tordek and thrusts with her short sword at the orc she wounded with the crossbow bolt. Her attack bonus is +0, and she misses even though the orc's AC is penalized by −2 because he charged in the previous round.

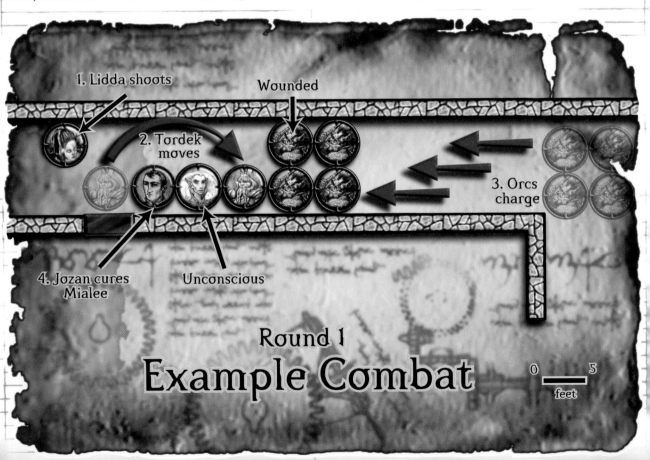

1. Lidda shoots
Wounded
2. Tordek moves
3. Orcs charge
4. Jozan cures Mialee
Unconscious

Round 1
Example Combat

0   5
feet

Combat Basics

ROUNDS

Combat is broken up into rounds. Each round, each combatant gets to do something. A round represents 6 seconds in the game world.

INITIATIVE

Before the first round, each player makes an initiative check for her character. The DM makes initiative checks for the monsters or foes. An initiative check is a Dexterity check (1d20+Dexterity modifier). Characters act in order from highest initiative result to lowest, with the check applying to all rounds of the combat (unless a combatant takes an action that changes her initiative).

ATTACKS

You can move and make a single attack. Making a ranged attack provokes attacks of opportunity from threatening enemies (see below).

Attack Roll

To score a hit that deals damage on your attack roll, you must roll the target's Armor Class (AC) or better.

Melee Attack Roll: 1d20 + base attack bonus + Strength modifier + size modifier = AC hit

Ranged Attack Roll: 1d20 + base attack bonus + Dexterity modifier + size modifier + range penalty = AC hit

Damage

If you score a hit, roll damage and deduct it from the target's current hit points. Add your Strength modifier to damage from melee and thrown weapons. If you have a Strength penalty (not a bonus), add it to damage from bows and slings (but not crossbows). If you're using a weapon in your off hand, add half your Strength modifier (if it's a bonus). If you're wielding a weapon with both hands, add one and a half times your Strength modifier to the damage (if it's a bonus).

Armor Class (AC)

A character's Armor Class (AC) is the result you need to get on your attack roll to hit that character in combat.

Armor Class: 10 + armor bonus + shield bonus + Dexterity modifier + size modifier

Hit Points

Hit points represent how much damage a character can take before falling unconscious or dying.

Attack Options

When attacking, you have several basic options:

Attack: You can move and make a single attack, or attack and move.

Charge: When making a charge, you move in a straight line for up to double your speed and then make one attack with a +2 charge bonus on the attack roll. You suffer a –2 charge penalty to your AC until your next action.

Full Attack: Some characters can strike more than once each melee round, but only when making a full attack. Other than taking a 5-foot step, you can't move when you make a full attack.

SPELLS

You can move and cast a single 1-action spell. Casting a spell provokes attacks of opportunity from threatening enemies (see below).

SAVING THROWS

When you are subject to an unusual or magical attack, you generally get a saving throw to negate or reduce its effect. To succeed at a saving throw, you roll a result equal to or higher than its Difficulty Class. Saving throws come in three kinds: Fortitude, Reflex, and Will.

Fortitude Saving Throw: 1d20 + base save bonus + Constitution modifier

Reflex Saving Throw: 1d20 + base save bonus + Dexterity modifier

Will Saving Throw: 1d20 + base save bonus + Wisdom modifier

MOVEMENT

Each character has a speed measured in feet. You can move that distance as well as attack or cast a 1-action spell, and you can move before or after attacking or casting.

You can also make a double move, which lets you move double your speed, or a run, which lets you move quadruple your speed.

When you move in or away from an area that an enemy threatens, you provoke an attack of opportunity (see below) from that enemy.

Exceptions to these conditions for attacks of opportunity due to moving in or away from a threatened area include the following:

- If all that you do is move (but not run) during your turn, the space (generally about 5 feet across) that you start out in is not considered threatened, and therefore enemies do not get attacks of opportunity for you moving from that space. If you move into another threatened space, however, enemies get attacks of opportunity for you leaving it.
- If your entire move for the round is 5 feet (a 5-foot step), enemies do not get attacks of opportunity for you moving.

ATTACKS OF OPPORTUNITY

You threaten the area next to you, even when it's not your action. An enemy that takes certain actions while in a threatened area provokes an attack of opportunity from you. An attack of opportunity is a single attack, and you can only make one per round. Actions that provoke attacks of opportunity include moving (except as noted above in the Movement section), casting a spell, and attacking with a ranged weapon.

DEATH, DYING, AND HEALING

Your hit points represent how much damage you can take before being disabled, knocked unconscious, or killed.

0 Hit Points: If your hit points drop to 0, you are disabled. You can only take partial actions, and you take 1 point of damage after completing an action.

–1 to –9 Hit Points: If your hit points drop to from –1 to –9 hit points, you're unconscious and dying, and you lose 1 hit point per round. Each round, before losing that hit point, you have a 10% chance to stabilize. While stabilized, you're still unconscious. Each hour you have a 10% chance to regain consciousness, and if you don't, you lose 1 hit point instead.

–10 Hit Points: If your hit points fall to –10 or below, you're dead.

Healing: You can stop a dying character's loss of hit points with a successful Heal check (DC 15) or with even 1 point of magical healing. If healing raises a character's hit points to 1 or more, he can resume acting as normal.

MINIATURES

When you use miniatures to keep track of where the characters and monsters are, use a scale of 1 inch = 5 feet.

Tordek swings his dwarven waraxe at the orc in front of him. His attack bonus is +4 (+1 base attack bonus, +2 Strength bonus, +1 Weapon Focus bonus). He hits the orc (whose AC is also penalized) and deals 2d4+2 points of damage. His total is 7, which is enough to take the orc out.

Another orc marauder steps over the body of his fallen comrade and swings his battleaxe at Tordek. He hits and deals 1d8+2 points of damage (1d8 for a battleaxe, +2 Strength bonus). Tordek sustains 7 points of damage, and his hit points drop to 6. He's now hurt badly enough that one more hit could easily drop him.

The orc that Lidda tried to stab curses her for hitting him with a crossbow bolt, swings his battleaxe at her, misses, and curses again.

Jozan, worried that the team could lose its fighter, drops her prepared *bless* spell to spontaneously cast *cure light wounds* on Tordek. Jozan's player rolls a 7, for a result of 8 hit points cured. Tordek is now healed back to his original 13 hit points (he only needed 7 of the 8 points of curing).

THIRD REGULAR ROUND

Lidda moves back away from the orc to let Jozan step in. Since Lidda is taking a double move (doing nothing but moving), and since she moves directly away from the orcs, the orcs don't get to make attacks of opportunity against her.

Tordek's player rolls a natural 20 on his attack roll. That's a threat (a possible critical hit). He makes a critical roll (1d20 + his total attack bonus), and the result is 17. Since that would hit the orc, Tordek's hit is a critical hit. Dwarven waraxes deal 1d10 points of damage on a normal hit and ×3 damage on critical hits, so Tordek's player rolls 3d10. He gets a result of 19 points of damage, which is more than enough to kill the orc instantly.

The last orc steps in to attack Tordek. He swings and misses. The orc that had been attacking Lidda also attacks Tordek and misses.

Jozan steps in next to Tordek with his heavy mace, hits the orc that Lidda had wounded, and downs it.

Now only one orc is left, and he's 10 feet away from Tordek and Jozan.

FOURTH REGULAR ROUND

Lidda darts between Tordek and Jozan and swings at the orc, but she misses.

Tordek moves up and swings but also misses.

The orc takes a double move and moves 25 feet back to the T-shaped intersection and 15 feet around the corner. Since this action involved only movement and the orc moved away from Tordek and Lidda without entering another area threatened by them, they do not get attacks of opportunity against him.

Jozan and Lidda each can run as fast as the orc. They might be able to catch him. But Tordek can't keep up, and Mialee is still unconscious, so they let him go.

COMBAT SEQUENCE

As seen in the example, combat is cyclical. (Everybody acts in turn in a regular cycle.) Generally, combat runs in the following way:

1. Each combatant starts the battle flat-footed. Once a combatant acts, she or he is no longer flat-footed.
2. The DM determines which characters are aware of their opponents at the start of the battle. If some but not all of the combatants are aware of their opponents, a surprise round happens before regular rounds begin. The combatants who are aware of the opponents can act in the surprise round, so they roll for initiative. In initiative order (highest to lowest), combatants who started the battle aware of their opponents each take a partial action during the surprise round. Combatants who were unaware do not get to act in the surprise round. If no one or everyone starts the battle aware, there is no surprise round.
3. Combatants who have not yet rolled initiative do so. All combatants are now ready to begin their first regular round.
4. Combatants act in initiative order.
5. When everyone has had a turn, the combatant with the highest initiative acts again, and steps 4 and 5 repeat until combat ends.

COMBAT STATISTICS

Several fundamental statistics determine how well you do in combat. This section summarizes these statistics, and the following sections detail how to use them.

ATTACK ROLL

When you make an attack roll, you roll a d20 and add your attack bonus. If your result equals the target's AC or better, you hit and deal damage. Lots of modifiers affect the attack roll, such as a +1 bonus if you have Weapon Focus with that weapon, a +1 bonus if you're using a masterwork weapon, a +1 morale bonus if you're the recipient of a *bless* spell, a +2 bonus if your opponent is stunned, and so forth.

ATTACK BONUS

Your attack bonus with a melee weapon is:

Base attack bonus + Strength modifier + size modifier

With a ranged weapon, your attack bonus is:

Base attack bonus + Dexterity modifier + size modifier + range penalty

Strength Modifier: Strength helps you swing a weapon harder and faster, so your Strength modifier applies to melee attack rolls.

Dexterity Modifier: Since Dexterity measures coordination and steadiness, your Dexterity modifier applies to attacks with ranged weapons.

Size Modifier: The smaller you are, the bigger other creatures are relative to you. A human is a big target to a halfling, just as an ogre is a big target to a human. Since this same size modifier applies to AC, two creatures of the same size strike each other normally, regardless of what size they actually are. Size modifiers are as follows: Colossal –8, Gargantuan –4, Huge –2, Large –1, Medium-size +0, Small +1, Tiny +2, Diminutive +4, Fine +8.

Range Penalty: The range penalty with a ranged weapon depends on what weapon you're using and how far away the target is. All ranged weapons have a range increment, such as 10 feet for a thrown dagger or 120 feet for a heavy crossbow (see Table 7–4: Weapons, pages 98–99). Any attack from a distance of less than one range increment is not penalized for range, so an arrow from a shortbow (range increment 60 feet) can strike at enemies up to 59 feet away with no penalty. However, each full range increment causes a cumulative –2 penalty to the attack roll. A shortbow archer firing at a target 200 feet away suffers a –6 attack penalty (because 200 feet is at least three range increments but not four increments). Thrown weapons, such as throwing axes, have a maximum range of five range increments. Projectile weapons, such as bows, can shoot up to ten increments.

DAMAGE

When you hit with a weapon, you deal damage according to the type of weapon (see Table 7–4: Weapons, pages 98–99). Unarmed strikes and the natural physical attack forms of creatures are considered to deal weapon damage for the purposes of effects that give you a bonus to weapon damage.

Minimum Weapon Damage: If penalties to damage bring the damage result below 1, a hit still deals 1 point of damage.

Strength Bonus: When you hit with a weapon, you also add your Strength modifier to damage with melee and thrown weapons. If you have a Strength penalty (not a bonus), apply it to damage you deal with bows and slings. Apply neither a Strength bonus nor a Strength penalty to damage from a crossbow. If you have a Strength bonus (not a penalty), you sometimes add more than or less than the bonus:

Off-Hand Weapon: When you deal damage with a weapon in your off hand, you add only one-half of your Strength bonus.

Wielding a Weapon Two-Handed: When you deal damage with a weapon that you are wielding two-handed, you add one and one half times your Strength bonus. Light weapons don't get this higher Strength bonus when used two-handed (see Tiny, Small, Medium-size, and Large Weapons, page 96).

Multiplying Damage: Sometimes you multiply damage by some factor, such as when you score a critical hit. Roll the damage (with all modifiers) multiple times and total the results. Note: When you multiply damage more than once, each multiplier works off the original, unmultiplied damage (see Multiplying, page 275).

Exception: Bonus damage represented as extra dice, such as from a sneak attack or a flaming sword, is not multiplied when you score a critical hit.

For example, Krusk the half-orc barbarian gets a +3 bonus to damage when using a longsword, a +4 bonus to damage when using a greataxe (two-handed), and a +1 bonus to damage when using a weapon in his off hand. His critical multiplier with a greataxe is ×3, so if he scored a critical hit, he would roll 1d12+4 points of damage three times (the same as rolling 3d12+12).

Ability Score Damage: Certain creatures and magical effects can cause temporary ability damage (a reduction to an ability score). The DUNGEON MASTER's *Guide* has details on ability damage.

ARMOR CLASS (AC)

Your Armor Class (AC) represents how hard it is for opponents to land a solid, damaging blow on you. It's the attack roll result that an opponent needs to achieve to hit you. The average, unarmored peasant has an AC of 10. Your AC is is equal to the following:

10 + armor bonus + shield bonus + Dexterity modifier + size modifier

Armor and Shield Bonuses: Your armor and shield each provide a bonus to your AC. This bonus represents their ability to protect you from blows.

Dexterity Modifier: If your Dexterity is high, you are particularly adept at dodging blows. If your Dexterity is low, you are particularly inept at it. That's why you apply your Dexterity modifier to your AC.

Note that armor limits your Dexterity bonus, so if you're wearing armor you might not be able to apply your whole Dexterity bonus to your AC (see Table 7–5: Armor, page 104).

Sometimes you can't use your Dexterity bonus (if you have one). The AC bonus you get for a high Dexterity represents your ability to dodge incoming attacks. If you can't react to a blow, you can't use your Dexterity bonus on AC. (If you don't have a Dexterity bonus, nothing happens.) You lose your Dexterity bonus when, for example, an invisible opponent attacks you, you're hanging on for dear life to the face of a crumbling cliff high above a river of lava, or you're caught flat-footed at the beginning of a combat.

Size Modifier: The bigger a creature is, the easier it is to hit in combat. The smaller it is, the harder it is to hit. Since this same modifier applies to attack rolls, a halfling, for example, doesn't have a hard time hitting another halfling. Size modifiers are as follows: Colossal –8, Gargantuan –4, Huge –2, Large –1, Medium-size +0, Small +1, Tiny +2, Diminutive +4, Fine +8.

Other Modifiers: Many other factors add to your AC:

Dodge Feat: The Dodge feat (page 81) improves your AC by +1 against a single opponent.

Enhancement Bonuses: Enhancement effects make your armor better (+1 *chainmail*, +2 *large shield*, etc.).

Deflection Bonus: Magical deflection effects ward off attacks and improve your AC.

Natural Armor: Natural armor improves your AC. (Members of the common races don't have natural armor, which usually consists of scales, fur, or layers of huge muscles. You might get natural armor from a magic item or from the druid spell *barkskin*.)

Dodge Bonuses: Some other AC bonuses represent actively avoiding blows, such as the dwarf's AC bonus against giants or the AC bonus for fighting defensively. These bonuses are called dodge bonuses. Any situation that denies you your Dexterity bonus also denies you dodge bonuses. (Wearing armor, however, does not limit these bonuses the way it limits a Dexterity bonus to AC.) Unlike most sorts of bonuses, dodge bonuses stack with each other. A dwarf's +4 AC bonus against giants and his +2 AC bonus for fighting defensively combine to give him a +6 bonus.

Touch Attacks: Some attacks disregard armor, including shields and natural armor. For example, a wizard's touch with a *shocking grasp* spell hurts you regardless of what armor you're wearing or how thick your skin happens to be. In these cases, the attacker makes a touch attack roll (either a ranged touch attack roll or a melee touch attack roll). The attacker makes her attack roll as normal, but your AC does not include any armor bonus, shield bonus, or natural armor bonus. Your size modifier, Dexterity modifier, and deflection bonus (if any) all apply normally. For example, if a sorcerer tries to touch Tordek with a *shocking grasp* spell, Tordek gets his +1 Dexterity bonus, but not his +4 armor bonus for his scale mail or his +2 shield bonus for his large wooden shield. His AC is only 11 against a touch attack.

HIT POINTS

Your hit points tell you how much punishment you can take before dropping. Your hit points are based on your class and level and are modified by your Constitution modifier. Most monsters' hit points are based on their type, though some monsters have class and level, too. (Watch out for the medusa sorcerers.)

When your hit point total reaches 0, you're disabled. When it reaches –1, you're dying. When it gets to –10, your problems are over—you're dead (see Injury and Death, page 127).

SPEED

Your speed tells you how far you can move in a round and still do something, such as attack or cast a spell. Your speed depends mostly on your race and what armor you're wearing.

Dwarves, gnomes, and halflings move 20 feet, or 15 feet when wearing medium or heavy armor.

Humans, elves, half-elves, and half-orcs move 30 feet, or 20 feet when wearing medium or heavy armor.

If you take a double move action in a round, you can move up to double your normal speed. If you run all out, you can move up to quadruple your normal speed (or triple if you are in heavy armor).

SAVING THROWS

As an adventurer, you have more to worry about than taking damage. You also have to face the petrifying gaze of the medusa, the wyvern's lethal venom, and the harpy's compelling song. Luckily, a tough adventurer can survive these threats, too.

Generally, when you are subject to an unusual or magical attack, you get a saving throw to avoid or reduce the effect. Like an attack roll, a saving throw is a d20 roll plus a bonus based on your class, level, and an ability score. Your saving throw bonus is:

Base save bonus + ability modifier

Saving Throw Types: The three different kinds of saving throws are these:

Fortitude: These saves measure your ability to stand up to massive physical punishment or attacks against your vitality and health such as poison, paralysis, and magic that causes instant death. Apply your Constitution modifier to your Fortitude saving throws. Fortitude saves can be made against attacks or effects such as poison, disease, paralysis, petrification, energy drain, *destruction*, and *disintegrate*.

Reflex: These saves test your ability to dodge massive attacks such as a wizard's *fireball* or the lethal breath of a dragon. Apply your Dexterity modifier to your Reflex saving throws. Reflex saves can be made against attacks or effects such as pit traps, catching on fire, *fireball*, *lightning bolt*, and red dragon breath.

Will: These saves reflect your resistance to mental influence and domination as well as many magical effects. Apply your Wisdom modifier to your Will saving throws. Will saves can be made against attacks or effects such as *charm person*, *hold person*, *polymorph other*, and most illusion spells.

Saving Throw Difficulty Class: The DC for a save is determined by the attack itself. Two examples: A Medium-size monstrous centipede's poison allows a Fortitude save against DC 11. An ancient red dragon's fiery breath allows a Reflex save against DC 35.

INITIATIVE

Each round, each combatant gets to do something. The combatants' initiative checks determine the order in which they act, from highest to lowest. As adventurers say, "Striking first is good, but striking last is better."

Initiative Checks: At the start of a battle, each combatant makes a single initiative check. An initiative check is a Dexterity check. The DM finds out what order characters are acting in, counting down from highest result to lowest, and each character acts in turn, with the check applying to all rounds of the combat (unless a character takes an action that results in her initiative changing; see Special Initiative Actions, page 133). Usually, the DM writes the names of the characters down in initiative order so that on subsequent rounds he can move quickly from one character to the next. If two or more combatants have the same initiative check result, the combatants who are tied go in order of Dexterity (highest first). If there is still a tie, flip a coin.

Monster Initiative: Typically, the DM makes a single initiative check for the monsters. That way, each player gets a turn each round and the DM also gets one turn. At the DM's option, however, he can make separate initiative checks for different groups of monsters or even for individual creatures. For instance, the DM may make one initiative check for an evil cleric of Nerull and another check for all seven of her zombie guards.

Flat-Footed: At the start of a battle, before you have had a chance to act (specifically, before your first regular turn in the initiative order), you are flat-footed. You can't use your Dexterity bonus to AC (if any) while flat-footed. (This fact can be very bad for you if you're attacked by rogues.) Barbarians' and rogues' uncanny dodge extraordinary ability allows them to avoid losing their Dexterity bonus to AC due to being flat-footed. A flat-footed character can't make attacks of opportunity.

SURPRISE

When a combat starts, if you were not aware of your enemies and they were aware of you, you're surprised.

How Surprise Works

Lidda is "footpaddin'" 40 feet in advance of her companions as they walk down a dungeon corridor. She hears something coming her group's way from around a corner ahead of her, and her companions don't hear it. Before she can raise a hand to signal her companions, a troll comes around the corner. The troll and Lidda's friends are surprised, but Lidda is not. She gets a free partial action before anyone else can do anything, and she lets loose a bolt from her light crossbow. Since the troll is surprised, it does not get its +2 Dexterity bonus to AC. Lidda's bolt strikes home. Because the monster was denied its Dexterity bonus to AC and the troll is within 30 feet of her, Lidda's sneak attack ability kicks in. She rolls 1d8+1d6 for damage instead of just 1d8, and deals 11 points of damage on the troll. With that, the surprise round ends and the first regular round begins. If Lidda's initiative result is better than the troll's, she gets to act again before it does (and it will still be flat-footed).

Awareness and Surprise

Sometimes all the combatants on a side are aware of the enemies, sometimes none are, sometimes only some of them are. Sometimes a few combatants on each side are aware and the other combatants on each side are unaware.

Determining Awareness: The DM determines who is aware of whom at the start of a battle. She may call for Listen checks, Spot checks, or other checks to see how aware the PCs are of the enemy. Some example situations:

- The party (including Tordek, a fighter, and Jozan, a cleric, clanging along in metal armor) comes to a door in a dungeon. The DM knows that the displacer beasts on the other side of the door hear the party. Lidda listens at the door, hears guttural snarling, and tells the rest of the party about it. Tordek breaks the door open. Both sides are aware; neither is surprised. The characters and displacer beasts make initiative checks, and the battle begins.

- The party is exploring a ruined armory, looking through the rusted weapons for anything of value. Kobolds lurking in hiding places are waiting for the right time to strike. Jozan spots one of the kobolds, and the kobolds let out a shriek and charge. The kobolds and Jozan each get a partial action during the surprise round. Kobolds that are close enough can charge adventurers and attack them. Others can move to try to put themselves in advantageous positions or shoot arrows at the flat-footed party members. Jozan can cast a spell, attack, or take some other action. After the surprise round, the first regular round begins.

- The party is advancing down a dark corridor, using *light* spells to light the way. At the end of the corridor is a kobold sorcerer who does not want to be disturbed, and she angrily casts a *lightning bolt*. That's the surprise round. After the *lightning bolt*, the first regular round begins, and the party is in a tough spot, since they still can't see who attacked them.

The Surprise Round: If some but not all of the combatants are aware of their opponents, a

Lidda surprises . . .

surprise round happens before regular rounds begin. The combatants who are aware of the opponents can act in the surprise round, so they roll for initiative. In initiative order (highest to lowest), combatants who started the battle aware of their opponents each take a partial action during the surprise round (see Partial Actions, page 127). If no one or everyone is surprised, a surprise round does not occur.

Unaware Combatants: Combatants who are unaware at the start of battle do not get to act in the surprise round. Unaware combatants are still flat-footed because they have not acted yet. Because of this, they lose any Dexterity bonus to AC.

ACTIONS IN COMBAT

The fundamental actions of moving, attacking, and casting spells cover most of what you want to do in a battle. They're all described here. Other, more specialized options are touched on in Table 8–4: Miscellaneous Actions, page 128, and covered later in Special Initiative Actions, page 133, and Special Attacks and Damage, page 134.

THE COMBAT ROUND

Each round represents about 6 seconds in the game world. In the real world, a round is an opportunity for each character involved in a combat to take an action. Anything a person could reasonably do in 6 seconds, your character can do in 1 round. The most common combat actions that can be performed in 1 round— attacking, casting a spell, moving, charging, and others—are described in detail on the following pages.

Each round begins with the character with the highest initiative result and then proceeds, in order, from there. Each round uses the same initiative order. When a character's turn comes up in the initiative sequence, that character performs his entire round's worth of actions. (For exceptions, see Attacks of Opportunity, page 122, and Special Initiative Actions, page 133.)

… and sneak attacks a troll.

For almost all purposes, there is no relevance to the end of a round or the beginning of a round. The term "round" works like the word "month." A month can mean either a calendar month or a span of time from a day in one month to the same day the next month. In the same way, a round can be a segment of game time starting with the first character to act and ending with the last, but it usually means a span of time from one round to the same initiative number (initiative count) in the next round. Effects that last a certain number of rounds end just before the same initiative count that they began on. For instance, a monk acts at initiative count 15. The monk's stunning attack stuns a creature for 1 round. The stun lasts through initiative count 16 in the next round, not until the end of the current round. On initiative count 15 in the next round, the stun effect ends.

ACTION TYPES

What type an action is essentially tells you how long the action takes to perform (within the framework of the 6-second combat round) and how movement is treated.

Standard Action: A standard action allows you to do something and move your speed during a combat round. You can move before or after performing the activity of the action. Doing this action takes the same time as casting a 1-action spell in terms of what else

you can do in the round. For instance, you can move and dismiss a spell or move and use the Heal skill to help a dying friend. You can also perform as many free actions (see below) as your DM allows.

Full-Round Action: A full-round action consumes all your effort during a round. The only movement you can take during a full-round action is a 5-foot step before, during, or after the action. You can also perform free actions (see below) as your DM allows.

Some full-round actions do not allow you to take a 5-foot step.

Move-Equivalent Action: Move-equivalent actions take the place of movement in a standard action or take the place of an entire partial action. Taking such an action counts as moving your speed. For instance, Tordek can use the attack action to move 15 feet and attack once, or to stand up from prone (a move-equivalent action) and attack once. He could also use the double move action to stand up from prone and move 15 feet. He could even use a double move action to stand up from prone and retrieve a stored item (both move-equivalent actions).

If you move no actual distance in a round (commonly because you have swapped your move for one or more move-equivalent actions), you can take one 5-foot step either before, during, or after the action. For example, if Tordek is on the ground, he can stand up (a move-equivalent action), move 5 feet (his 5-foot step), and attack.

Free Action: Free actions consume a very small amount of time and effort, and over the span of the round, their impact is so minor that they are considered free. You can perform one or more free actions while taking another action normally. However, the DM puts reasonable limits on what you can really do for free. For instance, calling out to your friends for help is free. Reciting your clan's war history, however, takes several minutes.

Not an Action: Some activities are not even considered free actions. They literally don't take any time at all to do and are considered an inherent part of doing something else. For instance, using the Use Magic Device skill (page 75) to emulate different class features while trying to activate a device is not an action, it is part of the activate magic item action.

Partial Action: Usually, you don't elect to take a partial action; the condition you are in or a decision you have made (usually the ready action) mandates its use. (You can elect to take a partial action as an extra action in some situations, such as when you're affected by a *haste* spell.) A partial action is like a standard action, except that you can't do as much. As a general rule, you can do as much with a partial action as you could with a standard action minus a move. Thus, you can attack once as a partial action or move your speed, but you can't both move and attack unless you are performing a partial charge action. Typically, you may take a 5-foot step as part of a partial action. You take a partial action instead of a standard action for a variety of reasons, including during a surprise

Illus. by J. Foster

round; when you have readied a partial action; and when you are disabled, staggered, *slowed*, or otherwise hampered. See Partial Actions, page 127.

ATTACKS OF OPPORTUNITY

The melee rules assume that combatants are actively avoiding attacks. A player doesn't have to declare anything special for her character to be on the defensive. Even if a character's figure is just standing there on the tabletop like a piece of lead, you can be sure that if some orc with a battleaxe attacks the character, she is weaving, dodging, and even threatening the orc with a weapon to keep the orc a little worried for his own hide.

Sometimes, however, a combatant in a melee lets her guard down, and she is not on the defensive as usual. In this case, combatants near her can take advantage of her lapse in defense to attack her for free. These attacks are called attacks of opportunity.

Threatened Area: You threaten the area into which you can make a melee attack, even when it is not your action. Generally, that's everything within 5 feet of you in any direction. An enemy that takes certain actions while in a threatened area provokes an attack of opportunity from you.

Provoking an Attack of Opportunity: If you move within or out of a threatened area, you usually provoke an attack of opportunity. If all you do is move (not run) during your turn, the space that you start out in is not considered threatened, and therefore enemies do not get attacks of opportunity against you when you move from that space. If you move into another threatened space, enemies do get attacks of opportunity for your leaving the first threatened space. In addition, if your entire move for the round is 5 feet (a 5-foot step), enemies do not get attacks of opportunity for your moving.

Some actions themselves provoke attacks of opportunity, including casting a spell and attacking with a ranged weapon. Table 8–1: Fundamental Actions in Combat; Table 8–4: Miscellaneous Actions;

and Table 8–3: Partial Actions note many of the actions that provoke attacks of opportunity.

Making an Attack of Opportunity: An attack of opportunity is a single melee attack, and you can only make one per round. You do not have to make an attack of opportunity if you don't want to.

An experienced character gets additional regular melee attacks (by using the full attack action), but at a lower attack bonus. You make your attack of opportunity, however, at your normal attack bonus—even if you've already attacked this round.

Combat Reflexes and Additional Attacks of Opportunity: If you have the Combat Reflexes feat (page 80), you can add your Dexterity modifier to the number of attacks of opportunity you can make between actions. (This feat does not, however, let you make more than one attack for a given opportunity.) All these attacks are at your normal attack bonus. You do not suffer reductions to your attack bonus for making multiple attacks of opportunity.

ATTACK ACTIONS

These are the most common, straightforward actions that a character or creature might take to attack. More specialized attack actions are mentioned in Miscellaneous Actions, page 127, and covered in Special Attacks and Damage, page 134.

Attack

The attack action is a standard action. You can move and then make a single attack, or attack and then move.

TABLE 8–1: FUNDAMENTAL ACTIONS IN COMBAT

Action	Move	Attack of Opportunity*
Attack Actions		
Attack (melee)	Yes	No
Attack (ranged)	Yes	Yes
Attack (unarmed)	Yes	Maybe
Charge	×2 (special)†	No
Full attack	5-ft. step	No
Magic Actions		
Cast a spell		
1-action spell	Yes	Yes
Full-round spell	5-ft. step	Yes
Concentrate to maintain	Yes	No
Activate magic item	Yes	Maybe
Use special ability		
Use spell-like ability	Usually**	Yes
Use supernatural ability	Usually**	No
Use extraordinary ability††	Usually**	No
Movement-Only Actions		
Double move	×2	Maybe
Run	×4	Yes
Miscellaneous Actions	Maybe	Maybe

×2: You can move twice your normal speed.

×4: You can move quadruple your normal speed.

*Regardless of the action, if you move within or out of a threatened area, you usually provoke an attack of opportunity. This column indicates whether the action itself, not moving, provokes an attack of opportunity.

**You can move unless the action is defined as a full-round action, in which case you normally get a 5-foot step.

†You can move up to twice your normal speed, but only before the attack, not after. You must move at least 10 feet, and the entire move must be in a straight line.

††Most extraordinary abilities aren't actions. This applies to those that are.

Tordek threatens the spaces occupied by Rats #1 #2, & #3, but not #4. Rats #1 and #3 are flanking him, but #2 is not.

Rat #1

Rat #2

Rat #3

Rat #4

5 feet

Tordek

Threatened Area and Flanking

Melee Attacks: With a normal melee weapon, you can strike any enemy within 5 feet. (Enemies within 5 feet are considered adjacent to you.) Some melee weapons have reach, as indicated in their descriptions in Chapter 7: Equipment. You can strike opponents 10 feet away with a reach weapon, but you cannot strike adjacent foes (those within 5 feet).

Ranged Attacks: With a ranged weapon, you can shoot or throw at any target that is within the ranged weapon's maximum range and in line of sight. A target is in line of sight if no obstructions are between you and the target. The maximum range for a thrown weapon is five range increments. For projectile weapons, it is ten range increments. Some ranged weapons have shorter maximum ranges, as specified in their descriptions.

Unarmed Attacks: Unarmed attacks are covered in Unarmed Attacks, page 140, and Subdual Damage, page 134.

Attack Rolls: An attack roll represents your attempts to strike your opponent, including feints and wild swings. It does not represent a single swing of the sword, for example. Rather, it simply indicates whether, over perhaps several attempts, you managed to connect solidly.

Your attack roll is 1d20 + your attack bonus with the weapon you're using. If the result is at least as high as the target's AC, you hit and deal damage.

Automatic Misses and Hits: A natural 1 (the d20 comes up 1) on the attack roll is always a miss. A natural 20 (the d20 comes up 20) is always a hit. A natural 20 is also a threat—a possible critical hit (see Critical Hits, below).

Damage Rolls: If the attack roll result equals or exceeds the target's AC, the attack is successful, and you deal damage. Roll the appropriate damage for your weapon (see Table 7–4: Weapons, pages 98–99). Damage is deducted from the target's current hit points. If the opponent's hit points drop to 0 or less, he's in bad shape (see Injury and Death, page 127).

Critical Hits: When you make an attack roll and get a natural 20 (the d20 shows 20), you hit regardless of your target's AC, and you have scored a threat. The hit might be a critical hit (or "crit"). To find out if it's a critical hit, you immediately make a critical roll—another attack roll with all the same modifiers as the attack roll you just made. If the critical roll also results in a hit against the target's AC, your original hit is a critical hit. (The critical roll just needs to hit to give you a crit. It doesn't need to come up 20 again.) If the critical roll is a miss, then your hit is just a regular hit.

A critical hit means that you roll your damage more than once, with all your usual bonuses, and add the rolls together to get total damage. Unless otherwise specified, the threat range for a critical hit on an attack roll is 20, and the multiplier is ×2. (See Increased Threat Range and Increased Critical Multiplier, below.)

Exception: Bonus damage represented as extra dice, such as from a sneak attack or a flaming sword, is not multiplied when you score a critical hit.

Increased Threat Range: Sometimes your threat range is greater than 20. That is, you can score a threat on a lower number. Longswords, for instance, give you a threat on a natural attack roll of 19 or 20. In such cases, a roll below 20 is not an automatic hit. Any attack roll that doesn't result in a hit is not a threat.

Increased Critical Multiplier: Some weapons, such as battleaxes and arrows, deal better than double damage with a critical hit. See Table 7–4: Weapons and the "Critical" section of Weapon Qualities, page 97.

Spells and Critical Hits: A spell that requires an attack roll, such as *shocking grasp* or *Melf's acid arrow,* can score a critical hit. A spell attack that requires no attack roll, such as *lightning bolt,* cannot score a critical hit.

Multiple Attacks: A character with more than one attack per round must use the full attack action in order to get more than one attack.

Lidda suffers a -4 penalty because this orc is in melee with Jozan. Jozan also provides it with a +4 cover bonus to AC, and if Lidda misses by 1 to 4 points, she might hit him instead of the orc.

0   5
feet

This orc has one-half cover (+4 AC).

Lidda can shoot this orc but she suffers a -4 penalty because it is in melee with Jozan.

Lidda has a line of sight to this orc.

Ranged Weapon Attacks

Illus. by T. Lockwood

Shooting or Throwing into a Melee: If you shoot or throw a ranged weapon at a target that is engaged in melee with an ally, you suffer a –4 penalty on your attack roll because you have to aim carefully to avoid hitting your ally. Two characters are engaged in melee if they are enemies of each other and either threatens the other. (A *held*, unconscious, or otherwise immobilized character is not considered engaged unless he is actually being attacked.)

If your target (or the part of your target you're aiming at, if it's a big target) is at least 10 feet away from the nearest ally, you can avoid the –4 penalty, even if the creature you're aiming at is engaged in melee with an ally.

Precise Shot: If you have the Precise Shot feat (page 84), you don't suffer this penalty.

Fighting Defensively: You can choose to fight defensively when taking the attack action. If you do so, you take a –4 penalty on all attacks in a round to gain a +2 dodge bonus to AC for the same round.

Charge

Charging is a special standard action that allows you to move more than your speed and attack during the action. However, it carries tight restrictions on how you can move.

Movement during a Charge: You must move before your attack, not after. You must move at least 10 feet and may move up to double your speed. All movement must be in a straight line, with no backing up allowed. You must stop as soon as you are within striking range of your target. You can't run past him and attack from another direction.

Attacking: After moving, you may make a single melee attack. Since you can use the momentum of the charge in your favor, you get a +2 bonus on the attack roll. Since a charge is impossible without a bit of recklessness, you also suffer a –2 penalty to your AC for 1 round.

Even if you have extra attacks, such as from having a high enough base attack bonus or from using multiple weapons, you only get to make one attack during a charge.

Lances and Charge Attacks: A lance deals double damage if employed by a mounted character in a charge.

Weapons Readied against a Charge: Spears, tridents, and certain other piercing weapons deal double damage when readied (set) and used against a charging character (see Table 7–4: Weapons, pages 98–99, and Ready, page 134).

Full Attack

If you get more than one attack per action because your base attack bonus is high enough, because you fight with two weapons, because you're using a double weapon, or for some special reason (such as a feat or a magic item), you must use the full attack action to get your additional attacks. You do not need to specify the targets of your attacks ahead of time. You can see how the earlier attacks turn out before assigning the later ones.

Full attack is a full-round action. Because of this, the only movement you can take during a full attack is a 5-foot step. You may take the step before, after, or between your attacks.

If you get multiple attacks based on your base attack bonus, you must make the attacks in order from highest bonus to lowest. If you are using two weapons, you can strike with either weapon first. If you are using a double weapon, you can strike with either part of the weapon first.

Deciding between an Attack or a Full Attack Action: After your first attack, if you have not yet taken a 5-foot step, you can decide to move instead of making your remaining attacks. Essentially, you can decide whether to take the normal attack action or the full attack action depending on how the first attack turns out.

Fighting Defensively: You can choose to fight defensively when taking the full attack action. If you do so, you take a –4 penalty on all attacks in a round to gain a +2 dodge bonus to AC for the same round.

Attacking with Two Weapons: If you wield a second weapon in your off hand, you can get one extra attack per round with that weapon. Fighting in this way is very hard, however, and you suffer a –6 penalty with your regular attack or attacks with your primary hand and a –10 penalty to the attack with your off hand. You can reduce these stiff penalties in three ways:

This dragon finds Tordek hard to swallow.

- If your off-hand weapon is light, the penalties are reduced by 2 each. A light weapon is one that's smaller than a weapon you could use in one hand. Its size category is smaller than yours. (An unarmed strike is always considered light.) A short sword is light to a human and a dagger is light to a gnome.
- The Ambidexterity feat reduces the off-hand penalty by 4.
- The Two-Weapon Fighting feat reduces both penalties by 2.

Table 8–2: Two-Weapon Fighting Penalties summarizes the interaction of all these factors.

Double Weapons: You can use a double weapon to make an extra attack as if you were fighting with two weapons. The penalties apply as if the off-hand weapon were light.

TABLE 8–2: TWO-WEAPON FIGHTING PENALTIES

Circumstances	Primary Hand	Off Hand
Normal penalties	–6	–10
Off-hand weapon is light	–4	–8
Ambidexterity feat	–6	–6
Two-Weapon Fighting feat	–4	–8
Off-hand weapon is light and Ambidexterity feat	–4	–4
Off-hand weapon is light and Two-Weapon Fighting feat	–2	–6
Ambidexterity feat and Two-Weapon Fighting feat	–4	–4
Off-hand weapon is light, Ambidexterity feat and Two-Weapon Fighting feat	–2	–2

MAGIC ACTIONS

These are the most common, straightforward actions involving the use of magic. Less commonly used magic actions are touched on in Table 8–4: Miscellaneous Actions (page 128), Turn and Rebuke Undead (page 139), and the descriptions of the Concentration skill in Chapter 4: Skills (page 65) and in Chapter 10: Magic (page 151).

Cast a Spell

Casting a spell with a casting time of 1 action is a standard action. You can move and then cast the spell, or cast the spell and then move. Casting a spell with a casting time of 1 full round is a full-round action. You can take a 5-foot step before, during, or after casting such a spell, but cannot otherwise move. See Chapter 10: Magic for details on casting spells, their effects, saving throws, and so on.

Note: You retain your Dexterity bonus to AC while casting.

Spell Components: To cast a spell with a verbal (V) component, you must speak in a firm voice. If you're gagged or in the area of a *silence* spell, you can't cast such a spell. A spellcaster who has been deafened has a 20% chance to spoil any spell he tries to cast if that spell has a verbal component.

To cast a spell with a somatic (S) component, you must gesture freely with at least one hand. You can't cast a spell of this type while bound, grappled, or with both your hands full or occupied (swimming, clinging to a cliff, etc.).

To cast a spell with a material (M), focus (F), or divine focus (DF) component, you have to have the proper materials, as described by the spell. Unless these materials are elaborate, such as the 2-foot-by-4-foot mirror that a wizard needs to cast *scrying*, preparing these materials is a free action. For material components and focuses whose costs are not listed, you can assume that you have them if you have your spell component pouch.

Some powerful spells have an experience point (XP) component and entail an experience point cost to you. No spell, not even *restoration*, can restore the lost XP. You cannot spend so much XP that you lose a level, so you cannot cast the spell unless you have enough XP to spare. However, you may, on gaining enough XP to achieve a new level, immediately spend the XP on casting the spell rather than keeping it to advance a level. The XP are expended when you cast the spell, whether or not the casting succeeds.

Concentration: You must concentrate to cast a spell. If you can't concentrate, such as because hundreds of malignant insects are biting off little pieces of your skin all over your body (see the *summon swarm* spell, page 261), you can't cast a spell. If you start casting a spell but something interferes with your concentration, such as an ogre taking the opportunity to hit you with its 40-pound club (successfully hitting you with his attack of opportunity), you must make a Concentration check or lose the spell. The check's DC depends on what is threatening your concentration (see the Concentration skill, page 65, and Concentration, page 151). If you fail, the spell fizzles with no effect. If you prepare spells (as a wizard, cleric, druid, paladin, or ranger does), it is lost from preparation. If you cast at will (as a sorcerer or bard does), it counts against your daily limit of spells even though you did not cast it successfully.

Concentrating to Maintain a Spell: Some spells require continued concentration to keep them going. Concentrating to maintain a spell is a standard action that doesn't provoke an attack of opportunity. Anything that could break your concentration when casting a spell can keep you from concentrating to maintain a spell. If your concentration breaks, the spell ends.

Casting Time: Most spells have a casting time of 1 action. These spells you can cast as a standard action. A spell cast in this manner immediately takes effect.

A few spells have a casting time of 1 full round or even longer. A spell that takes 1 full round to cast is a full-round action, and it comes into effect just before the beginning of your turn in the round after you began casting the spell. You then act normally after the spell is completed. A spell that takes 1 minute to cast comes into effect just before your turn 1 minute later (and for each of those 10 rounds, you are casting a spell as a full-round action).

When you begin a spell that takes a full round or longer to cast, you must continue the invocations, gestures, and concentration from one round to just before your turn in the next round (at least). If you lose concentration after starting the spell and before it is complete, you lose the spell.

Attacks of Opportunity: Generally, if you cast a spell, you provoke attacks of opportunity from threatening enemies. If you take damage from an attack of opportunity, you must make a Concentration check (DC 10 + points of damage taken) or lose the spell.

Casting on the Defensive: You may attempt to cast a spell while on the defensive. This option means casting the spell while paying attention to threats and avoiding blows. In this case, you are no more vulnerable to attack than you would be if you were just standing there, so casting a spell while on the defensive does not provoke an attack of opportunity. It does, however, require a Concentration check (DC 15 + spell level) to pull off. Failure means that you lose the spell.

Touch Spells in Combat: Many spells have a range of "Touch." To use these spells, you cast the spell and then touch the subject, either in the same round or any time later. In the same round that you cast the spell, you may also touch (or attempt to touch) the target. You may take your move before casting the spell, after touching the target, or between casting the spell and touching the target. You can automatically touch one friend or use the spell on yourself, but to touch an opponent, you must succeed at an attack.

Touch Attacks: Since you need only touch your enemy, you make a touch attack instead of a regular attack. Touching an opponent with a touch spell is considered to be an armed attack and therefore does not provoke attacks of opportunity when it is discharged on an armed opponent. The touch spell provides you with a credible threat that the defender is obliged to take into account just as if it were a weapon. However, the act of casting a spell does provoke an attack of opportunity, so you may want to cast the spell and then move to the target instead of vice versa. Touch attacks come in two types: melee touch attacks (for touches made with, say, your hand) and ranged touch attacks (for touches made with magic rays, for example). You can score critical hits with either type of attack. Your opponent's AC against a touch attack does not include any armor bonus, shield bonus, or natural armor bonus. His size modifier, Dexterity modifier, and deflection bonus (if any) all apply normally.

Holding the Charge: If you don't discharge the spell on the round you cast the spell, you can hold the discharge of the spell (hold the charge) indefinitely. You can continue to make touch attacks round after round. You can touch one friend as a standard action or up to six friends as a full-round action. If you touch anything or anyone while holding a charge, even unintentionally, the spell discharges. If you cast another spell, the touch spell dissipates.

Activate Magic Item

Many magic items don't need to be activated—magic weapons, magic armor, *gauntlets of dexterity*, and so forth. However, certain magic items need to be activated, especially potions, scrolls, wands, rods, and staffs. Activating a magic item is a standard action (unless the item description indicates otherwise).

Spell Completion Items: Activating a spell completion item, such as a scroll, is the equivalent of casting a spell. It requires concentration and provokes attacks of opportunity. You lose the spell if your concentration is broken, and you can attempt to activate the item while on the defensive, as with a spell (see Casting on the Defensive, above).

Spell Trigger, Command Word, or Use-Activated Items: Activating a spell trigger, command word, or use-activated item does not require concentration and does not provoke attacks of opportunity. The *Dungeon Master's Guide* has much more information on magic items.

Use Special Ability

Using a special ability is usually an action, but whether it is a standard action, a full-round action, or not an action at all is defined by the ability. See Special Abilities, page 158.

Spell-Like Abilities: Using a spell-like ability (such as a paladin's laying on of hands) works like casting a spell in that it requires concentration and provokes attacks of opportunity. Spell-like abilities can be disrupted. If your concentration is broken, the attempt to use the ability fails, but the attempt counts as if you had used the ability (for example, it counts against your daily limit if you have one). The casting time of a spell-like ability is 1 action, making its use a standard action, unless the ability description notes otherwise.

Using a Spell-Like Ability on the Defensive: You may attempt to use a spell-like ability on the defensive, just as with a spell. If the Concentration check (DC 15) fails, you can't use the ability, but the attempt counts as if you had used the ability (for example, it counts against your daily limit if you have one, or it uses up at least 1 point of increment of its daily complement, such as in laying on hands).

Supernatural Abilities: Using a supernatural ability (such as a cleric's turn undead or rebuke undead ability) is usually a standard action (unless defined otherwise by the ability description). Its use cannot be disrupted, does not require concentration, and does not provoke attacks of opportunity.

Extraordinary Abilities: Using an extraordinary ability (such as a barbarian's uncanny dodge ability) is usually not an action because most extraordinary abilities automatically happen in a reactive fashion. Those extraordinary abilities that are actions are usually standard actions that cannot be disrupted, do not require concentration, and do not provoke attacks of opportunity. The descriptions of these abilities note any exceptions to these general rules.

MOVEMENT-ONLY ACTIONS

Sometimes you just want to cover ground as quickly as possible or put as much distance as you can between yourself and an opponent. The actions covered here are actions during which you devote your efforts only to moving during a round. Less commonly used movement actions, including many move-equivalent actions, are covered in Miscellaneous Actions (see the next page) and Table 8–4: Miscellaneous Actions.

Double Move

You can move up to double your speed as a special standard action. You do not get to move your speed in addition to this as in a normal standard action, however. Essentially, the double move action already counts the move of a standard action. It's a "move and a move," thus a double move.

As with any other move, if you move within or out of a threatened area, you provoke an attack of opportunity from the threatening enemy. However, since all you do when you take a double move action is to move, the space where you begin your move is not considered threatened, and therefore enemies do not get attacks of opportunity for your moving from that space. If you move into another threatened space, enemies get attacks of opportunity for your leaving the first threatened space.

For example, an orc marauder is fighting Tordek and Lidda in a hallway. Tordek and Lidda are side by side. Using the double move action, the orc flees directly away from them. Since all the orc does is move during his turn, the space where he starts (about 5 feet across) is not threatened, so Tordek and Lidda don't get attacks of opportunity against him. If, on the other hand, the orc were between Tordek and Lidda, the space where the marauder started would not be threatened, but no matter which direction he moved, he would enter another threatened space, since both Tordek and Lidda threaten 5-foot areas around themselves. The marauder would have to move away from Tordek (and thus into a space still threatened by Lidda) or away from Lidda (and thus into a space still threatened by Tordek). Whichever character he did not move away from would get an attack of opportunity against the orc as he moved out of the threatened space that he entered. If he moved to either side, he would be moving into a space threatened by both opponents, so each would get an attack of opportunity against him.

SPEEDING UP COMBAT

You can use a couple of tricks to make combat run faster.

Attack and Damage: Roll your attack die and damage die (or dice) at the same time. If you miss, you can ignore the damage, but if you hit, your friends don't have to wait for you to make a second roll for damage.

Multiple Attacks: Use dice of different colors so you can make your attack rolls all at once instead of one at a time. Designate which attack is which color before you roll.

Roll Ahead of Time: Once you know who you are attacking and how, make your attack rolls before it is your turn so you have the results ready when your turn comes around. (Get your DM's okay before you roll ahead of time. Some DMs like to watch the players' attack rolls.)

Dice as Counters: Use dice to keep track of how many rounds a short-duration magical effect has been active. Each round, turn the die to the next number until the effect ends.

Concealment Rolls: If you know what your chance to miss is because of your target's concealment, you can roll it along with your attack roll. If the concealment roll indicates a miss, just ignore the attack roll.

Prep Initiative: Have your DM roll the characters' and creatures' initiative checks ahead of time and prepare the order of battle. That way when a battle starts you can skip the initiative checks and get right to the action.

Miniatures: Use miniatures to show the relative positions of the combatants. It's a lot faster to place a miniature where you want your character to be than to explain (and remember) where your character is relative to everyone else.

A double move represents a hustle, which for an unencumbered human is about six miles per hour.

Run

You can run as a full-round action. (You do not get a 5-foot step.) When you run, you can move up to four times your normal speed in a straight line (or three times your speed if you're in heavy armor). You lose any Dexterity bonus to AC since you can't avoid attacks.

You can run for a number of rounds equal to your Constitution score, but after that, you must succeed at a Constitution check (DC 10) to continue running. You must check again each round in which you continue to run, and the DC of this check increases by 1 for each check you have made. When you fail this check, you must stop running. A character who has run to his limit must rest for 1 minute (10 rounds) before running again. During a rest period, the character can move no faster than a normal move.

A run represents a speed of about twelve miles per hour for an unencumbered human.

PARTIAL ACTIONS

Usually you don't take a partial action because you elect to, but rather because you are required to. (You can elect to take a partial action as an extra action in some situations, such as when you're affected by a *haste* spell.) Partial actions are like standard actions, except that you can't do as much with a partial action as you can with a standard action.

As a general rule, you can do as much with a partial action as you could with a standard action minus a move. Thus, you can attack once as a partial action *or* move your speed, but you can't both move and attack. If an action is normally a full-round action, sometimes you can still do it as a partial action, and sometimes to complete it you need to use the start full-round action action and complete the action in the following round with another partial action (see Start Full-Round Action, below). Typically, you may take a 5-foot step as part of a partial action.

Actions that take more than a round typically take twice as long to perform when you must take partial actions to accomplish them. Thus, a spell that normally takes 1 minute to cast would instead take 2 minutes.

When to Use Partial Actions: You take partial actions instead of standard actions for a variety of reasons, including:

- It is a surprise round instead of a regular round.
- You readied a partial action (see Ready, page 134).
- You are disabled, *slowed*, staggered, or otherwise hampered.

Start Full-Round Action: The start full-round action partial action lets you start undertaking a miscellaneous full-round action (such as those listed on Table 8–4: Miscellaneous Actions), which you can complete on the following round (even with a partial action). For instance, if you are limited to partial actions, you can shoot a heavy crossbow every 3 rounds: 2 rounds to load it and 1 round to shoot it.

MISCELLANEOUS ACTIONS

Some actions don't fit neatly into the above categories. Some of these options are actions that take the place of or are variations on the actions described in Attack Actions, Magic Actions, and Movement-Only Actions. For actions not covered below, the DM lets you know how long such an action takes to perform and whether doing so provokes attacks of opportunity from threatening enemies. The variant and special attacks mentioned here are covered in Special Attacks and Damage, page 134.

Total Defense

You can simply defend yourself and move during a round as a standard action. You don't attack or perform any other activity other

than moving your speed, but you get a +4 dodge bonus on your AC for 1 round. Your AC improves at the start of this action, so it helps you against any attacks of opportunity you suffer while moving.

Use Feat

Certain feats, such as Whirlwind Attack, let you take special actions in combat. Others are not actions themselves, but they give you a bonus when attempting something you can already do, such as Improved Disarm. Some feats, such as item creation feats, are not meant to be used within the framework of combat. The individual feat descriptions tell you what you need to know about them.

INJURY AND DEATH

Your hit points measure how hard you are to kill. While exotic monsters have a number of special ways to hurt, harm, or kill you, usually you just take damage and lose hit points. The damage from each successful attack and each fight accumulates, dropping your hit point total to 0 or below. Then you're in trouble. Luckily, you also have a number of ways to regain hit points. If you have a few days to rest, you can recover lost hit points on your own, and divine magic includes a number of spells for restoring lost hit points.

LOSS OF HIT POINTS

The most common way that your character gets hurt is to take damage and lose hit points, whether from an orc's battleaxe, a

TABLE 8–3: PARTIAL ACTIONS

Partial Actions	Move	Attack of Opportunity*
Attack Partial Actions		
Attack (melee)	5-ft. step	No
Attack (ranged)	5-ft. step	Yes
Attack (unarmed)	5-ft. step	Maybe
Partial charge	Yes (special)†	No
Magic Partial Actions		
Cast a spell‡	5-ft. step	Yes
Activate magic item	5-ft. step	Maybe
Use special ability‡	5-ft. step	Maybe
Concentrate to maintain a spell	5-ft. step	No
Dismiss a spell	5-ft. step	No
Movement-Only Partial Actions		
Single move	Yes	No
Partial run	×2	Yes
Miscellaneous Partial Actions**	5-ft. step	Maybe
Special Partial Action		
Start full-round action	No	Maybe

*Regardless of the action, if you move within or out of a threatened area, you usually provoke an attack of opportunity. This column indicates whether the action itself (not the moving) provokes an attack of opportunity.

†You must move in a straight line before attacking and must move at least 10 feet.

‡Unless doing so is a full-round action, in which case you could start a full-round action and then finish it the next round with a cast a spell action. Spells that take longer than 1 full round to cast take twice as long to cast.

**Those actions on Table 8–4: Miscellaneous Actions defined as standard or move-equivalent actions. Most allow a 5-foot step, though actions that are variant charge actions follow the move for partial charge.

TABLE 8–4: MISCELLANEOUS ACTIONS

No Action	Attack of Opportunity*
Delay	No

Free Actions	
Cast a quickened spell (page 84) or *feather fall* spell (page 203)	No
Cease concentration on a spell	No
Prepare spell components to cast a spell**	No
Direct *Bigby's clenched fist* spell (page 178), *rainbow pattern* spell (page 241), or *shield* spell (page 251)	No
Attack with *eyebite* spell (page 202)	No
Change form (*shapechange*)	No
Dismiss *tree shape* spell (page 267)	No
Drop an item	No
Drop to the floor	No
Speak	No
Make Spellcraft check on counterspell attempt (page 152)	No

Move-Equivalent Actions	
Climb (one-quarter your speed)	No
Draw a weapon†	No
Sheathe a weapon	Yes
Ready a shield†	No
Loose a shield†	No
Open a door	No
Pick up an item	Yes
Retrieve a stored item	Yes
Move a heavy object	Yes
Stand up from prone	No
Load a hand crossbow	Yes
Load a light crossbow	Yes
Control a frightened mount	Yes
Mount a horse or dismount	No
Direct the movement of a *flaming sphere* spell (page 206) or the recipient of a *levitate* spell (page 222)	No

Standard Actions	
Ready (triggers a partial action)	No
Concentrate to maintain or redirect a spell	No
Dismiss a spell	No
Aid another	No
Bull rush (charge)	No
Bull rush (attack)	No
Change form (shapeshifter)	No
Use touch spell on self (page 151)	No
Escape a grapple (page 138)	No
Evoke *sunbeam* spell (page 261)	No
Feint (see Bluff, page 64)	No
Issue command to animated rope	No
Overrun (charge)	No

Standard Actions (cont.)	Attack of Opportunity*
Heal a dying friend (page 69)	Yes
Light a torch with a tindertwig (page 114)	Yes
Use a skill that takes 1 action	Usually
Rebuke undead (use special ability)	No
Turn undead (use special ability)	No
Strike a weapon (attack)	Yes
Strike an object (attack)	Maybe††
Total defense	No

Full-Round Actions	
Climb (one-half your speed)	No
Use a skill that takes 1 round	Usually
Coup de grace (page 133)	Yes
Light a torch	Yes
Change form (*polymorph self*)	Yes
Extinguish flames	No
Load a heavy crossbow	Yes
Load a repeating crossbow	Yes
Lock or unlock weapon in locked gauntlet	Yes
Prepare to throw oil (page 109)	Yes
Throw a two-handed weapon with one hand (page 97)	Yes
Transport (*tree stride* spell, page 267)	No
Use touch spell on up to six friends (page 151)	Yes
Refocus (no move)	No
Escape from a net (page 102), *entangle* spell (page 200), *Otiluke's freezing sphere* (page 233), etc.	Yes

Action Type Varies	
Disarm‡	Yes
Grapple‡	Yes
Trip an opponent‡	No
Use feat‡‡	Varies

*Regardless of the action, if you move within or out of a threatened area, you usually provoke an attack of opportunity. This column indicates whether the action itself (not the moving) provokes an attack of opportunity.

**Unless the component is an extremely large or awkward item (DM's call).

†If you have a base attack bonus of +1 or higher, you can combine one of these actions with a regular move. If you have the Two-Weapon Fighting feat, you can draw two light or one-handed weapons in the time it would normally take you to draw one.

††If the object is being held, carried, or worn by a creature, yes. If not, no.

‡These attack forms substitute for a melee attack, not an action. As melee attacks, they can be used once in an attack or charge action, one or more times in a full attack action, or even as an attack of opportunity.

‡‡The description of a feat defines its effect.

---

wizard's *lightning bolt*, or a fall into molten lava. You record your character's hit point total on your character sheet. As your character takes damage, you subtract that damage from your hit points, leaving you with your current hit points. Current hit points go down when you take damage and go back up when you recover.

What Hit Points Represent: Hit points mean two things in the game world: the ability to take physical punishment and keep going, and the ability to turn a serious blow into a less serious one. A 10th-level fighter who has taken 50 points of damage is not as badly hurt as a 10th-level wizard who has taken that much damage. Indeed, unless the wizard has a high Constitution score, she's probably dead or dying, while the fighter is battered but otherwise

doing fine. Why the difference? Partly because the fighter is better at rolling with the punches, protecting vital areas, and dodging just enough that a blow that would be fatal only wounds him. Partly because he's tough as nails. He can take damage that would drop a horse and still swing his sword with deadly effect. For some characters, hit points may represent divine favor or inner power. When a paladin survives a *fireball*, you will be hard pressed to convince bystanders that she doesn't have the favor of some higher power.

A 10th-level fighter who has taken 50 points of damage may be about as physically hurt as a 10th-level wizard who has taken 30 points of damage, the 1st-level fighter who has taken 5 points of damage, or the 1st-level wizard who has taken 3. Details at this level, however, don't affect how the dice roll. When picturing a scene, just remember that 50 points of damage means different things to different people.

Damaging Helpless Defenders: Even if you have lots of hit points, however, a dagger through the eye is a dagger through the eye. When a character can't avoid damage or deflect blows somehow, when he's really helpless, he's in trouble (see Helpless Defenders, page 133).

Effects of Hit Point Damage: Damage gives you scars, bangs up your armor, and gets blood on your surcoat, but it doesn't slow you down until your current hit points reach 0 or lower.

At 0 hit points, you're disabled (see below).

At from –1 to –9 hit points, you're dying (see below).

At –10 or lower, you're dead (see below).

Massive Damage: If you ever sustain damage so massive that a single attack deals 50 points of damage or more and it doesn't kill you outright, you must make a Fortitude save (DC 15). If this saving throw fails, you die regardless of your current hit points. This amount of damage represents a single trauma so major that it has a chance to kill even the toughest creature. If, however, you take 50 points of damage from multiple attacks, none of which dealt 50 or more points itself, the massive damage rule does not apply.

DISABLED (0 HIT POINTS)

When your current hit points drop to exactly 0, you're disabled. You're not unconscious, but you're close to it. You can only take a partial action each round, and if you perform any strenuous activity, you take 1 point of damage after the completing the act. Strenuous activities include running, attacking, casting a spell, or using any ability that requires physical exertion or mental concentration. Unless your activity increased your hit points, you are now at –1 hit points, and you're dying.

Healing that raises you above 0 makes you fully functional again, just as if you'd never been reduced to 0 or less. A spellcaster retains the spellcasting capability she had before dropping to 0 hit points.

You can also become disabled when recovering from dying. In this case, it's a step up along the road to recovery, and you can have fewer than 0 hit points (see Stable Characters and Recovery, below).

DYING (–1 TO –9 HIT POINTS)

When your character's current hit points drop to between –1 and –9 inclusive, he's dying.

He immediately falls unconscious and can take no actions.

At the end of each round (starting with the round in which the character dropped below 0), roll d% to see whether he stabilizes. He has a 10% chance to become stable. If he doesn't, he loses 1 hit point.

If the character's hit points drop to –10 (or lower), he's dead.

You can keep a dying character from losing any more hit points and make him stable with a successful Heal check (DC 15).

If any sort of healing cures the dying character of even 1 point of damage, he stops losing hit points and becomes stable.

Healing that raises the dying character's hit points to 0 makes him conscious and disabled. Healing that raises his hit points to 1 or more makes him fully functional again, just as if he'd never been reduced to 0 or less. A spellcaster retains the spellcasting capability she had before dropping below 0 hit points.

DEAD (–10 HIT POINTS OR LOWER)

When your character's current hit points drop to –10 or lower, or if he takes massive damage (see above), he's dead. A character can also die from taking ability damage or suffering an ability drain that reduces his Constitution to 0. When a character dies, his soul immediately departs. Getting it back into the body is a major hassle (see Bringing Back the Dead, page 153).

STABLE CHARACTERS AND RECOVERY

A stable character who has been tended by a healer or who has been magically healed eventually regains consciousness and recovers hit points naturally. If the character has no one to tend him, however, his life is still in danger, and he may yet slip away.

Recovering with Help: An hour after a tended, dying character becomes stable, roll d%. He has a 10% chance of becoming conscious, at which point he is disabled (as if he had 0 hit points). If he remains unconscious, he has the same chance to revive and become disabled every hour. Even if unconscious, he recovers hit points naturally. He is back to normal when his hit points rise to 1 or higher.

Recovering without Help: A severely wounded character left alone usually dies. He has a small chance, however, of recovering on his own. Even if he seems as though he's pulling through, he can still finally succumb to his wounds hours or days after originally taking damage.

A character who stabilizes on his own (by making the 10% roll while dying) and who has no one to tend for him still loses hit points, just at a slower rate. He has a 10% chance each hour of becoming conscious. Each time he misses his hourly roll to become conscious, he loses 1 hit point. He also does not recover hit points through natural healing.

Even once he becomes conscious and is disabled, an unaided character still does not recover hit points naturally. Instead, each day he has a 10% chance to start recovering hit points naturally (starting with that day); otherwise, he loses 1 hit point.

Once an unaided character starts recovering hit points naturally, he is no longer in danger of losing hit points (even if his current hit point total is negative).

HEALING

After taking damage, you can recover hit points through natural healing (over the course of days) or through magical healing (nearly instantly). In any case, you can't regain hit points past your hit point total.

Natural Healing: You recover 1 hit point per character level per day of rest. For example, a 5th-level fighter recovers 5 hit points per day of rest. You may engage in light, nonstrenuous travel or activity, but any combat or spellcasting prevents you from healing that day.

If you undergo complete bed rest (doing nothing for an entire day), you recover one and one half times your character level in hit points. A 5th-level fighter recovers 7 hit points per day of bed rest.

Higher-level characters recover lost hit points faster than lower-level characters because they're tougher, and also because a given number of lost hit points represents a lighter wound for a higher-level character. A 5th-level fighter who has lost 10 hit points isn't seriously wounded, but a 1st-level fighter who has taken 10 points of damage is.

Magical Healing: Various abilities and spells, such as a cleric's *cure* spells or a paladin's lay on hands ability, can give you back hit points. Each use of the spell or ability restores a different amount of hit points.

Healing Limits: You can never get back more hit points than you lost. Magical healing won't raise your current hit points higher than your hit point total.

Healing Ability Damage: Temporary ability damage returns at the rate of 1 point per day of rest (light activity, no combat or spellcasting). Complete bed rest restores 2 points per day.

TEMPORARY HIT POINTS

Certain effects, such as the *aid* spell, give a character temporary hit points. When a character gains temporary hit points, note his current hit points. When the temporary hit points go away, such as at the end of the *aid* spell, the character's hit points drop to that score. If the character's hit points are already below that score at that time, all the temporary hit points have already been lost and the character's hit point score does not drop.

When temporary hit points are lost, they cannot be restored as real hit points can be, even by magic.

For example, Jozan casts *aid* on Tordek. Tordek (now a 3rd-level fighter) normally has 30 hit points, but he's wounded and only has 26. Jozan rolls 1d8 for *aid*'s temporary hit points and gets a 6. Tordek's current hit points rise (temporarily) to 32. A little while later, Tordek takes 3 points of damage from an arrow shot, leaving him with 29 hit points. When the *aid* spell ends, his current hit points drop back down to 26.

Increases in Constitution Score and Current Hit Points: Note that an increase in a character's Constitution score, even a temporary one, can give him more hit points (an effective hit point increase), but these are not temporary hit points. They can be restored, such as with *cure light wounds*, and they are not lost first as temporary hit points are. For example, Krusk (now a 3rd-level barbarian) gains +4 to his Constitution score and +6 hit points when he rages, raising his hit points from 31 to 37. If Krusk takes damage dropping him to 32 hit points, Jozan can cure those lost points and get him back to 37. If Krusk is so wounded at the end of his rage that he only has 5 hit points left, then when he loses his 6 extra hit points, he drops to –1 hit points and starts dying.

MOVEMENT AND POSITION

Few characters in a fight are likely to stand still for long. Enemies appear and charge the party. The heroes reply, advancing to take on new foes after they down their first opponents. Wizards remain outside the fight, looking for the best place to use their magic. Rogues quietly skirt the fracas seeking a straggler or an unwary opponent to strike with a sneak attack. Finally, if the fight is lost, most characters find it to their advantage to remove themselves from the vicinity. Movement is just as important as attack skill and armor in gaining the upper hand on the battlefield.

Movement and position are most easily handled by using miniature figures to represent the characters and their opponents. The standard scale equates 1 inch on the tabletop to 5 feet in the game world. Whenever possible, use units of 5 feet for movement and position. Calculating distance more precisely than that is more trouble than it's worth. The DUNGEON MASTER'S Guide has guidelines for using a tabletop grid to regulate movement, position, and related issues.

TABLE 8–5: STANDARD SCALE

One inch = 5 feet
"Next to" or "adjacent" = 1 inch (5 feet) away
30 mm figure = A human-size creature
A human-size creature occupies an area 1 inch (5 feet) across
One round = 6 seconds

TACTICAL MOVEMENT

Where you can move, how long it takes you to get there, and whether you're vulnerable to attacks of opportunity while you're moving are key questions in combat.

How Far Can Your Character Move?

Your speed is determined by your race and your armor (see Table 8–6: Tactical Speed). Your speed while unarmored is sometimes called your base speed.

Encumbrance: A character encumbered by carrying a large amount of gear, treasure (you wish), or fallen comrades (more likely) may move slower than normal (see Carrying Capacity, page 141).

Movement in Combat: Generally, you can move your speed in a round and still do something, such as swing an axe or cast a spell. If you do nothing but move, you can move double your rate. If you flat-out run, you can move quadruple your rate. If you do something that requires a full round, such as attacking more than once, you can only take a 5-foot step. Some specific actions don't allow you to move at

all. See Action Types, page 121; Table 8–1: Fundamental Actions in Combat; Table 8–3: Partial Actions; and Table 8–4: Miscellaneous Actions to see how far you can move with each action.

Class and Movement: A barbarian has a +10 foot bonus to his speed (unless he's wearing heavy armor). Experienced monks also have higher speed (unless they're wearing armor of any sort).

TABLE 8–6: TACTICAL SPEED

Race	No Armor or Light Armor	Medium or Heavy Armor
Human, elf, half-elf, half-orc	30 ft.	20 ft.
Dwarf, halfling, gnome	20 ft.	15 ft.

Passing Through

Sometimes you can pass through an area occupied by another character or creature.

Friendly Creature: You can move through an area occupied by a friendly character.

Unfriendly Creature Not an Obstacle: You can also move through an area occupied by an unfriendly character who doesn't present an obstacle, such as one who is dead, unconscious, bound, *held*, stunned, or just cowering.

Charging: As part of a charge, you can attempt to move through an area occupied by a resisting enemy (see Overrun, page 139).

Tumbling: A trained character can attempt to tumble through an area occupied by an enemy. (See the Tumble skill, page 75.)

Very Small Creature: A Fine, Diminutive, or Tiny creature can move into or through an occupied area. The creature provokes an attack of opportunity when doing so (as normal).

Area Occupied by Creature Three Sizes Larger or Smaller: Any creature can move through an area occupied by a creature three size categories larger than it is. A gnome (Small), for example, can run between the legs of a hill giant (Huge).

A big creature can move through an area occupied by a creature three size categories smaller than it is. A hill giant, for example, can step over a gnome.

Designated Exceptions: Some creatures break the above rules. For example, a gelatinous cube fills the area it occupies to a height of 10 feet. A creature can't move through an area occupied by a cube, even with the Tumble skill or similar special abilities.

FLANKING

If you are making a melee attack against a creature, and an ally directly opposite you is threatening the creature, you and your ally flank the creature. You gain a +2 flanking bonus on your attack roll. A rogue in this position can also sneak attack the target. The ally must be on the other side of the defender, so that the defender is directly between you.

GANGING UP

Typically, up to eight opponents can gang up on a single target, provided they have room to maneuver freely. If the defender can fight side by side with allies, back into a corner, fight through a doorway, or otherwise protect himself, attackers can't gang up in this way.

Picture the eight attackers as evenly spaced out surrounding the defender. The defender can reduce the opportunity for attackers to gang up based on how much of the area around himself he can block off. Backed against a wall, a creature only allows five attackers to get at him. If he's backed into a corner, only three attackers can get at him at a time. If the defender is standing in a doorway, the creature in front of him can attack normally, and one attacker on either side can attack as well, but the defender benefits from one-half cover (see Cover, page 132). If the defender is fighting in a 5-foot-wide corridor, only one attacker can get at him (unless attackers are coming at him from both directions).

The above rules are for Medium-size and Small creatures fighting with nonreach weapons. Larger creatures present room for more attackers to get at them (see below), and combatants with reach weapons can get at defenders more easily, though they cannot attack adjacent defenders.

TABLE 8–7: CREATURE SIZE AND SCALE

Creature Size	Example Creature	Natural Reach	Face*
Fine	Fly	0	1/2 ft. × 1/2 ft.
Diminutive	Toad	0	1 ft. × 1 ft.
Tiny	Cat	0	2-1/2 ft. × 2-1/2 ft.
Small	Halfling	5 ft.	5 ft. × 5 ft.
Medium-size	Human	5 ft.	5 ft. × 5 ft.
Large (tall)**	Hill giant	10 ft.	5 ft. × 5 ft.
Large (long)**	Horse	5 ft.	5 ft. × 10 ft.
Huge (tall)**	Cloud giant	15 ft.	10 ft. × 10 ft.
Huge (long)**	Bulette	10 ft.	10 ft. × 20 ft.
	Retriever	10 ft.	15 ft. × 15 ft.
Gargantuan (tall)**	50-ft. animated statue	20 ft.	20 ft. × 20 ft.
Gargantuan (long)**	Kraken	10 ft.†	20 ft. × 40 ft.
	Purple worm (coiled)	15 ft.	30 ft. × 30 ft.
Colossal (tall)*	The tarrasque	25 ft.	40 ft. × 40 ft.
Colossal (long)*	Great red wyrm	15 ft.	40 ft. × 80 ft.

*Listed width by length.
**Tall creatures are upright. Long creatures are primarily horizontal. Big, long creatures may be in any of several shapes. See the *Monster Manual* for details.
†Bite attack.

BIG AND LITTLE CREATURES IN COMBAT

Creatures smaller than Small or bigger than Medium-size have special rules relating to position. (The DUNGEON MASTER'S *Guide* also has rules for using a grid to regulate combatants' sizes and faces.) These rules concern the creatures' "faces," or sides, and their reach.

Face: "Face" is how wide a face a creature presents in combat. This width determines how many creatures can fight side by side in a 10-foot-wide corridor, and

Creature Size Categories

Tiny Small Medium Large Huge Gargantuan Colossal

how many opponents can attack a creature at the same time. A face is essentially the border between the square or rectangular space that a creature occupies and the space next to it. These faces are abstract, not "front, back, left, and right," because combatants are constantly moving and turning in battle. Unless a creature is immobile, it practically doesn't have a front or a left side—at least not one you can locate on the tabletop.

Natural Reach: Natural reach is how far the creature can reach when it fights. It threatens the area within that distance from itself.

Big Creatures: Big creatures (long, Large creatures plus Huge, Gargantuan, and Colossal creatures) take up more space on the battlefield than a Medium-size human does. More combatants can attack them because more combatants can crowd around them. As a rule of thumb, assume that one Small or Medium-size combatant can get to each 5-foot length of the creature and four more combatants can fit into the "corners" where one side meets another. (This rule is why you can get eight people around a Medium-size creature at once: One fits on each 5-foot face, and one fits on each corner.)

For example, a bulette has a 10-foot face instead of the 5-foot face typical of Medium-size creatures. If you had enough characters, they could surround the bulette with twelve combatants: two along each face and four more in the corners.

Unlike a reach weapon, a creature with greater than normal natural reach (more than 5 feet) can still strike at creatures next to it. A creature with greater natural reach usually gets an attack of opportunity against you if you approach it, because you enter and move within its threatened area before you can attack it. (This does not apply if you take a 5-foot step.)

Large or Bigger Creatures with Reach Weapons: Large or bigger creatures with reach weapons can strike out to double their natural reach but can't strike at their natural reach or less. For example, an ogre with an ogre-sized longspear could strike at 15 or 20 feet but not at 5 or 10 feet.

Very Small Creatures: Very small creatures (Fine, Diminutive, and Tiny) have no effective natural reach. They have to enter or be in your area to attack you. Since they have to pass through your threatened area to get to you, you get attacks of opportunity against them. You can attack into your own area if you need to, so you can attack them normally. Since they have no natural reach, they do not threaten the area around them. You can move past them without provoking attacks of opportunity.

Bigger Creatures Attacking Smaller Creatures: Big and small creatures can attack a defender in different numbers. Hill giants occupy a space 10 feet wide. Only four of them could surround a Medium-size creature because each giant would take up a side or face as well as a corner.

COMBAT MODIFIERS

Sometimes you just have to go toe-to-toe in a fight, but you can usually gain some advantage by seeking a better position, either offensively or defensively. This section covers the rules for when you can line up a particularly good attack or are forced to make a disadvantageous one.

FAVORABLE AND UNFAVORABLE CONDITIONS

Depending on the situation, you may gain bonuses or suffer penalties on your attack roll. Your DM judges what bonuses and penalties apply, using Table 8–8: Attack Roll Modifiers as a guide.

COVER

One of the best defenses available is cover. By taking cover behind a tree, a ruined wall, the side of a wagon, or the battlements of a castle, you can protect yourself from attacks, especially ranged attacks.

TABLE 8–8: ATTACK ROLL MODIFIERS

Circumstance	Melee	Ranged
Attacker flanking defender*	+2	—
Attacker on higher ground	+1	+0
Attacker prone	–4	**
Attacker invisible	+2†	+2†
Defender sitting or kneeling	+2	–2
Defender prone	+4	–4
Defender stunned, cowering, or off balance	+2†	+2†
Defender climbing (cannot use shield)	+2†	+2†
Defender surprised or flat-footed	+0†	+0†
Defender running	+0†	–2†
Defender grappling (attacker not)	+0†	+0†††
Defender pinned	+4†	–4†
Defender has cover	See Cover	
Defender concealed or invisible	See Concealment	
Defender helpless (such as paralyzed, sleeping, or bound)	See Helpless Defenders	

*You flank a defender when you have an ally on the opposite side of the defender threatening him. Rogues can sneak attack defenders that they flank.

**Most ranged weapons can't be used while the attacker is prone, but you can use a crossbow while prone.

†The defender loses any Dexterity bonus to AC.

††Roll randomly to see which grappling combatant you strike. That defender loses any Dexterity bonus to AC.

Cover provides a bonus to your AC. The more cover you have, the bigger the bonus. In a melee, if you have cover against an opponent, that opponent probably has cover against you, too. With ranged weapons, however, it's easy to have better cover than your opponent. Indeed, that's what arrow slits in castle walls are all about.

The DM may impose other penalties or restrictions to attacks depending on the details of the cover. For example, to strike effectively through a narrow opening, you need to use a long piercing weapon, such as an arrow or a spear. A battleaxe or a pick isn't going to get through an arrow slit to the person standing behind it.

Cover and Attacks of Opportunity: An attacker can't execute an attack of opportunity against a character with one-half or better cover.

Cover and Reach Weapons: If you're using a reach weapon, a character standing between you and your target provides cover to your target. Generally, if both of the other creatures are the same size, the one in the back has one-half cover (+4 AC). If you hit the creature providing cover, it takes no damage because you strike it with the haft of your weapon.

Degree of Cover: Cover is assessed in subjective measurements of how much protection it offers you. Your DM determines the value of cover. This measure is not a strict mathematical calculation because you gain more value from covering the parts of your body that are more likely to be struck. If the bottom half of your body is covered (as when a human stands behind a 3-foot wall), that only gives you one-quarter cover. If one side or the other of your body is covered, as when you're partly behind a corner, you get one-half cover.

Table 8–9: Cover gives examples of various situations that usually produce certain degrees of cover. These examples might not hold true in exceptional circumstances. For example, a 3-foot wall might provide a human one-half cover in melee against kobolds, who have a hard time striking a human's upper body, but the same wall might grant a human no cover in melee against a giant.

Cover AC Bonus: Table 8–9: Cover lists the AC bonuses for different degrees of cover. Add the relevant number to your AC. This cover bonus overlaps (does not stack) with certain other bonuses. For example, kneeling gives you a +2 bonus to your AC against ranged weapons. Kneeling behind a low wall could change your cover from one-quarter (+2) to three-quarters (+7). You would not get the +2 kneeling bonus on top of the cover bonus.

TABLE 8–9: COVER

Degree of Cover	Example	Cover AC Bonus	Cover Reflex Save Bonus
One-quarter	A human standing behind a 3-ft. high wall	+2	+1
One-half	Fighting from around a corner or a tree; standing at an open window; behind a creature of same size	+4	+2
Three-quarters	Peering around a corner or a tree	+7	+3
Nine-tenths	Standing at an arrow slit; behind a door that's slightly ajar	+10	+4*
Total	On the other side of a solid wall	—	—

*Half damage if save is failed; no damage if successful.

Cover Reflex Save Bonus: Table 8–9: Cover lists the Reflex save bonuses for different degrees of cover. Add this bonus to Reflex saves against attacks that affect an area, such as a red dragon's breath or a *fireball*. For nine-tenths cover, you also effectively have improved evasion. These bonuses, however, only apply to attacks that originate or spread out from a point on the other side of the cover.

Striking the Cover Instead of a Missed Target: If it ever becomes important to know whether the cover was actually struck by an incoming attack that misses the intended target, the DM should determine if the attack roll would have hit the protected target without the cover. If the attack roll falls within a range low enough to miss the target with cover but high enough to strike the target if there had been no cover, the object used for cover was struck. This can be particularly important to know in cases where a character uses another creature as cover. In such a case, if the cover is struck and the attack roll exceeds the AC of the covering creature, the covering creature takes the damage intended for the target.

If the covering creature has a Dexterity bonus to AC or a dodge bonus, and this bonus keeps the covering creature from being hit, then the original target is hit instead. The covering creature has dodged out of the way and didn't provide cover after all. A covering creature can choose not to apply his Dexterity bonus to AC and/or his dodge bonus, if his intent is to try to take the damage in order to keep the covered character from being hit.

CONCEALMENT

Besides cover, another way to avoid attacks is to make it hard for opponents to know where you are. Concealment includes all circumstances where nothing physically blocks a blow or shot but where something interferes with an attacker's accuracy.

Concealment: Concealment is subjectively measured as to how well concealed the defender is. Examples of what might qualify as concealment of various degrees are given on Table 8–10: Concealment. Concealment always depends on the point of view of the attacker. Total darkness, for example, is meaningless to a creature with darkvision. Moderate darkness doesn't hamper a creature with low-light vision, and near total darkness is only one-half concealment for such a creature.

Concealment Miss Chance: Concealment gives the subject of a successful attack a chance that the attacker missed because of the concealment. If the attacker hits, the defender must make a miss chance percentile roll to avoid being struck. (Actually, it doesn't matter who makes the roll or whether it's rolled before or after the attack roll. To save time, you can first make the roll that's most likely to result in a miss, so that you're less likely to have to make two rolls, or you can just make both rolls at the same time.) When multiple concealment conditions apply to a defender (behind dense foliage, near total darkness, and a *blur* spell, for example), use the one that would produce the highest miss chance. Do not add the miss chances together.

TABLE 8–10: CONCEALMENT

Concealment	Example	Miss Chance
One-quarter	Light fog; moderate darkness; light foliage	10%
One-half	*Blur* spell; dense fog at 5 ft. (such as *obscuring mist*)	20%
Three-quarters	Dense foliage	30%
Nine-tenths	Near total darkness	40%
Total	*Invisibility*; attacker blind; total darkness; dense fog at 10 ft.	50% and must guess target's location

HELPLESS DEFENDERS

A helpless foe—one who is bound, *held*, sleeping, paralyzed, unconscious, or otherwise at your mercy—is an easy target.

Regular Attack: A melee attack against a helpless character gets a +4 circumstance bonus on the attack roll. A ranged attack gets no special bonus. A helpless defender (naturally) can't use any Dexterity bonus to AC. In fact, his Dexterity score is treated as if it were 0 and his Dexterity modifier to AC as if it were −5 (and a rogue can sneak attack him).

Coup de Grace: As a full-round action, you can use a melee weapon to deliver a coup de grace to a helpless foe. You can also use a bow or crossbow, provided you are adjacent to the target. You automatically hit and score a critical hit. If the defender survives the damage, he still must make a Fortitude save (DC 10 + damage dealt) or die.

It's overkill, but a rogue also gets her extra sneak attack damage against a helpless foe when delivering a coup de grace.

Delivering a coup de grace provokes attacks of opportunity from threatening foes because it involves focused concentration and methodical action.

You can't deliver a coup de grace against a creature that is immune to critical hits, such as a golem.

SPECIAL INITIATIVE ACTIONS

Usually you act as soon as you can in combat, but sometimes you want to act later, at a better time, or in response to the actions of someone else.

DELAY

By choosing to delay, you take no action and then act normally at whatever initiative point you decide to act. When you delay, you voluntarily reduce your own initiative result for the rest of the combat. When your new, lower initiative count comes up later in the same round, you can act normally. You can specify this new initiative result or just wait until some time later in the round and act then, thus fixing your new initiative count at that point.

Delaying is useful if you need to see what your friends or enemies are going to do before deciding what to do yourself. You cannot, however, interrupt anyone's action with a delayed action (as you can with a readied action). The price you pay is lost initiative. You never get back the time you spend waiting to see what's going to happen.

For example, Lidda and Tordek both want to get past an ogre who is guarding a troglodyte cleric. Lidda's initiative count is 22, but she delays. She knows that if she passed the ogre, she would provoke an attack of opportunity. On count 14, the cleric creates a *spiritual weapon* (a toothy maw) to attack Tordek. On count 8, the ogre readies to attack anyone who comes in range. On count 6, Tordek charges past the ogre. The ogre gets one strike (for being ready) and a second one (an attack of opportunity because Tordek moved in his threatened area). Tordek shrugs it off, reaches the cleric, and makes a single attack. Now, on count 5, Lidda acts. She too charges past the ogre, which can't get an attack of opportunity against her because it has already taken an attack of opportunity this round. For the rest of the battle, Lidda acts on initiative count 5.

Delaying Limits: A character can only voluntarily lower her initiative to −10 minus her initiative bonus. When the initiative count reaches −10 minus a delaying character's initiative bonus, that character must act or forfeit any action that round.

Multiple Characters Delaying: If multiple characters are delaying, the one with the highest initiative bonus (or highest Dexterity, in case of a tie) has the advantage. If two or more delaying characters both want to act on the same initiative count, the one with the highest bonus gets to go first. If two or more delaying characters are trying to go after the other, the one with the highest initiative bonus gets to go last.

For instance, Lidda and an elf stranger run across each other in a back alley in a big city. Lidda's initiative count is 17, higher than the elf's. She doesn't want to commit to attacking, fleeing, or parleying, so she delays, intending to act after the elf acts. The elf's initiative count is 12. He delays, too. The initiative count drops down, and neither character acts. (If there were other characters in the encounter, they would act on their initiative counts.) Finally, the count reaches −17, Lidda's limit (thanks to her +7 initiative bonus), and the elf still hasn't acted. Lidda has to choose, and the elf (who apparently has a higher initiative bonus) will get to respond. "Well met," says Lidda, crossing her fingers.

READY

The ready action lets you prepare to take an action later, after your turn is over but before your next one has begun. Readying is a standard action, so you can move as well. It does not provoke an attack of opportunity (though the action that you ready might do so).

How Readying Works: Mialee, the wizard, and her friends are fighting hobgoblin bandits. On initiative count 14, Mialee specifies that she is going to cast *charm person* on the first hobgoblin to come within 25 feet. On count 10, Tordek, the fighter, moves next to Mialee and readies an attack so that he can strike any foe that comes into the area he threatens. On 7, the hobgoblins charge. As soon as the lead hobgoblin is within 25 feet of Mialee, she casts *charm person* on him, but he succeeds at his Will save and is not affected. Tordek swings at and drops the first hobgoblin to reach him. Other hobgoblins, however, reach him and attack him. From this point on, Mialee and Tordek act on initiative count 7 (and before the hobgoblins).

Readying an Action: Only partial actions can be readied. To do so, specify the partial action you will take and the conditions under which you will take it. Then, any time before your next

action, you may take the readied partial action in response to those conditions. The partial action comes before the action that triggers it. For the rest of the fight, your initiative result is the count on which you took the readied action, and you act immediately ahead of the character whose action triggered your readied action.

Initiative Consequences of Readying: Your initiative result becomes the count on which you took the readied action. If you come to your next action and have not yet performed your readied action, you don't get to take the readied action (though you can ready the same action again). If you take your readied action in the next round, before your regular turn comes up, your initiative rises to that new point in the order of battle, and you do not get your regular action that round.

Distracting Spellcasters: You can ready an attack against a spellcaster with the trigger "if she starts casting a spell." If you succeed in damaging the spellcaster or otherwise distracting her, she may lose the spell she was trying to cast (as determined by her Concentration check result).

Readying to Counterspell: You may ready a counterspell against a spellcaster (often with the trigger "if she starts casting a spell"). In this case, when the spellcaster starts a spell, you get a chance to identify it with a Spellcraft check (DC 15 + spell level). If you do, and if you can cast that same spell (are able to cast it and have it prepared, if you prepare spells), you can cast the spell as a counterspell and automatically ruin the other spellcaster's spell. Counterspelling works even if one spell is divine and the other arcane.

A spellcaster can use *dispel magic* (page 196) to counterspell another spellcaster, but it doesn't always work.

Readying a Weapon against a Charge: You can ready certain piercing weapons, setting them to receive charges (see Table 7–4: Weapons, pages 98–99). A readied weapon of this type deals double damage if you score a hit with it against a charging character.

REFOCUS

Refocus is a full-round action during which you cannot move. A character can choose to do nothing for an entire round and refocus his thoughts as he gets his bearings and appraises the situation. The effect is that on the following rounds of the combat, the character moves up in the initiative count and is positioned as though he had rolled a 20 on his initiative check. Other modifiers (such as for Dexterity and for the Improved Initiative feat) also apply to this roll of 20 when determining the initiative check result.

SPECIAL ATTACKS AND DAMAGE

This section covers subdual damage, unarmed attacks, grappling, throwing grenadelike weapons that "splash" (such as acid), attacking objects (such as trying to destroy an opponent's shield or hacking apart a locked treasure chest), turning or rebuking undead (for clerics and paladins), and an assortment of other special attacks.

SUBDUAL DAMAGE

Sometimes you get roughed up or weakened, such as by getting clocked in a fistfight or tired out by a forced march. This sort of stress won't kill you, but it can knock you out or make you faint.

Nonlethal damage is subdual damage. If you take sufficient subdual damage, you fall unconscious, but you don't die. Subdual damage goes away much faster than standard damage.

How Subdual Damage Works: Tordek, the dwarven fighter, gets into a fistfight in a tavern with two rowdy half-orcs who taunted him by tugging on his beard. They exchange blows, and Tordek takes 4 points of subdual damage. He has 13 hit points, so 4 points of subdual damage doesn't bother him. He lands a lucky blow for 4 points of damage, enough to stagger one of the half-orcs (who each have 4 hit points). His next blow knocks the half-orc unconscious (its subdual damage exceeds its current hit points), but Tordek takes another 5 points of subdual damage, putting his total at 9. When Tordek turns on the second half-orc, the scoundrel snatches up a dagger and stabs Tordek for 5 points of damage (normal damage, not subdual damage). That drops Tordek's hit points to 8. Now that Tordek's subdual damage (9) is higher than his current hit points (8), he is knocked out. He still has 8 hit points, and he's not dying, but he's unconscious. The half-orc with the dagger beats feet before the city watch comes by.

Jozan, the human cleric, hears the commotion and comes to see what's happening. He casts *cure light wounds* on his unconscious friend, curing 4 points of damage. That raises Tordek's hit points back to 12 and simultaneously reduces his subdual damage from 9 to 5. Now that his hit points are higher than his subdual damage, he comes to, with vengeance in his eyes.

Dealing Subdual Damage: Certain attacks deal subdual damage, such as a normal human's unarmed strike (a punch, kick, or head butt). Other stresses, such as heat or exhaustion, also deal subdual damage. When you take subdual damage, keep a running total of how much you've accumulated. *Do not deduct the subdual damage number from your current hit points.* It is not "real" damage. Instead, when your subdual damage equals your current hit points, you're staggered, and when it exceeds your current hit points, you go unconscious. It doesn't matter whether the subdual damage equals or exceeds your current hit points because the subdual damage has gone up or because your current hit points have gone down.

Subdual Damage with a Weapon that Deals Normal Damage: You can use a melee weapon that deals normal damage to deal subdual damage instead, but you suffer a –4 penalty on your attack roll because you have to use the flat of the blade, strike in nonvital areas, or check your swing.

Normal Damage with a Weapon that Deals Subdual Damage: You can use a weapon that deals subdual damage, including an unarmed strike, to deal normal damage instead, but you suffer a –4 penalty on your attack roll because you have to strike only in the most vulnerable areas to cause normal damage.

Staggered and Unconscious: When your subdual damage exactly equals your current hit points, you're staggered. You're so badly weakened or roughed up that you can only take a partial action each round. You cease being staggered when your hit points exceed your subdual damage again.

When your subdual damage exceeds your current hit points, you fall to the floor unconscious. While unconscious, you are helpless (see Helpless Defenders, page 133).

Each full minute that you're unconscious, you have a 10% chance to wake up and be staggered until your hit points exceed your subdual damage again. Nothing bad happens to you if you miss this roll.

Spellcasters who are rendered unconscious retain any spellcasting ability they had before going unconscious.

Healing Subdual Damage: You heal subdual damage at the rate of 1 hit point per hour per character level. For example, a 7th-level wizard heals 7 points of subdual damage each hour until all the subdual damage is gone.

When a spell or a magical power cures hit point damage, it also removes an equal amount of subdual damage, if any.

ID ANOTHER

In combat, you can help a friend attack or defend by distracting or interfering with an opponent. If you're in position to attack an opponent with which a friend of yours is engaged in melee combat, you can attempt to aid your friend as a standard action. You make an attack roll against AC 10. If you succeed, your friend gains either a +2 circumstance bonus to attack that opponent or a +2 circumstance bonus to AC against that opponent (your choice).

You can also use this action to help a friend in other ways, such as when he is affected by a *hypnotism* spell (page 215) or a *sleep* spell (page 252).

ATTACK AN OBJECT

Sometimes you need to attack or break an object, such as when you want to smash a statue, strike a foe's weapon, or break open a door.

Strike an Object

Objects are easier to hit than creatures because they usually don't move, but many are tough enough to shrug off some damage from each blow.

How Striking an Object Works: Lidda, a rogue, can't pick the lock on the big treasure chest that Mialee, the elf, just found behind a secret door, so Krusk, the barbarian, volunteers to open it "the half-orc way." He chops at it with his greataxe, dealing 10 points of damage. The chest, made of wood, has a hardness of 5, so the chest only takes 5 points of damage. The wood is 1 inch thick, so it had 10 hit points. Now it has 5. Krusk has gouged the wood but not yet broken the chest open. On his second attack, he deals 4 points of damage. That's lower than the chest's hardness, so the chest takes no damage—a glancing blow. His third blow, however, deals 12 points of damage (which means the chest takes 7), and the chest breaks open. Unbeknownst to the adventurers, however, the racket that Krusk just made has alerted a nearby ogre to their presence, and he's now shuffling down the corridor to investigate.

Object Armor Classes and Bonuses to Attack: Objects are harder or easier to hit depending on several factors:

Inanimate, Immobile Objects: Attacking an inanimate, immobile object not in use by a creature does not provoke an attack of opportunity. An inanimate, immobile object has an AC of 10 + its Dexterity modifier (–5 for no Dexterity) + its size modifier. Immobile objects, such as a lantern hanging from the ceiling, are easy to hit. With a melee weapon, you get a +4 bonus on your attack roll. If you take a full-round action to line up a shot (as with the coup de grace against a helpless foe), you get an automatic hit with a melee weapon and a +5 attack bonus with a ranged weapon. (Objects, however, are immune to critical hits.)

Animated Objects: Animated objects count as creatures for AC purposes (see the *Monster Manual*).

Opponents' Weapons and Shields: Attacking these objects is covered in Strike a Weapon, below.

Held, Carried, or Worn Objects: Attacking a held, carried, or worn object provokes an attack of opportunity. Objects that are held, carried, or worn by a creature, such as an evil sorcerer's wand, are harder to hit. The object uses the creature's Dexterity modifier (not its own –5) and any magic deflection bonus to AC the creature may have. You don't get any special bonus for attacking the object. If it's in the creature's hand (or tentacle, or whatever), it gets a +5 AC bonus because the creature can move it quickly out of harm's way.

Damage to Objects: The amount of damage that an object can withstand depends on what it's made out of and how big it is. Weapon damage is rolled normally against objects.

Immunities: Inanimate objects are immune to critical hits. Objects are immune to subdual damage. Animated objects are immune to critical hits because they are constructs.

Ranged Weapon Damage: Objects take half damage from ranged weapons (except for siege engines and the like). Divide the damage by 2 before applying the object's hardness.

Energy Attacks: Objects take half damage from acid, fire, and lightning attacks. Divide the damage by 2 before applying the hardness. Cold attacks deal one-quarter damage to objects. Sonic attacks deal full damage to objects.

Ineffective Weapons: The DM may determine that certain weapons just can't deal damage effectively to certain objects. For example, you will have a hard time chopping down a door by shooting arrows at it or cutting a rope with a club.

Vulnerability to Certain Attacks: The DM may rule that certain attacks are especially successful against some objects. For example, it's easy to light a curtain on fire or rip up a scroll.

TABLE 8–11: SIZE AND AC OF OBJECTS

Size (Example)	AC Modifier	Size (Example)	AC Modifier
Colossal (broad side of a barn)	–8	Medium-size (barrel)	+0
		Small (chair)	+1
Gigantic (narrow side of a barn)	–4	Tiny (tome)	+2
		Diminutive (scroll)	+4
Huge (wagon)	–2	Fine (potion in a vial)	+8
Large (big door)	–1		

Hardness: Each object has hardness—a number that represents how well it resists damage. Whenever an object takes damage, subtract its hardness from the damage. Only damage in excess of its hardness is deducted from the object's hit points (see Table 8–12: Substance Hardness and Hit Points; Table 8–14: Object Hardness and Hit Points; and Table 8–13: Common Weapon and Shield Hardness and Hit Points).

Hit Points: An object's hit point total depends on what it is made of and how big it is (see Table 8–12, Table 8–13, and Table 8–14). When an object's hit points reach 0, it's ruined.

Very large objects have separate hit point totals for different sections. For example, you can attack and ruin a wagon wheel without destroying the whole wagon.

Saving Throws: Nonmagical, unattended items never make saving throws. They are considered to have failed their saving throws, so they always are affected by (for instance) a *disintegrate* spell. An item attended by a character (being grasped, touched, or worn) receives a saving throw just as if the character herself were making the saving throw.

Magic items always get saving throws. A magic item's Fortitude, Reflex, and Will save bonuses are equal to 2 + one-half its caster level. Attended magic items either make saving throws as their owner or use their own saving throws, whichever are better. (Caster levels of magic items are covered in the DUNGEON MASTER's Guide.)

Strike a Weapon

You can use a melee attack with a slashing weapon to strike a weapon or shield that your opponent is holding. The attacking weapon must be no more than one size category smaller than the weapon attacked. (Treat a buckler as Small, a small shield as Medium-size, a large shield as Large, and a tower shield as Huge.) Doing so provokes an attack of opportunity from the opponent because you are diverting your attention from him to his armaments. Then you and the defender make opposed attack rolls. If you win, you have landed a good blow against the defender's weapon or shield. Roll damage and deal it to the weapon or shield (see Strike an Object, above).

Magic Weapons and Shields: The attacker cannot damage a magic weapon or shield that has an enhancement bonus unless his own weapon has at least as high an enhancement bonus as the weapon or shield struck. Each +1 of enhancement bonus also adds 1 to the weapon's or shield's hardness and hit points. If your shield has a +2 enhancement bonus, you add 2 to its hardness and to its hit points.

TABLE 8–12: SUBSTANCE HARDNESS AND HIT POINTS

Substance	Hardness	Hit Points
Paper	0	2/inch of thickness
Rope	0	2/inch of thickness
Glass	1	1/inch of thickness
Ice	0	3/inch of thickness
Wood	5	10/inch of thickness
Stone	8	15/inch of thickness
Iron	10	30/inch of thickness
Mithral	15	30/inch of thickness
Adamantite	20	40/inch of thickness

Breaking Items

When you try to break something with sudden force rather than by dealing regular damage, use a Strength check to see whether you succeed. The DC depends more on the construction of the item than on the material. For instance, an iron door with a weak lock can be forced open much more easily than it can be hacked down.

If an item has lost half or more of its hit points, the DC to break it drops by 2.

BULL RUSH

You can bull rush as an attack action or a charge action. When you bull rush, you attempt to push an opponent straight back instead of attacking him. You can only bull rush an opponent who is one size category larger than you, the same size, or smaller.

Initiating a Bull Rush: First, you move into the defender's space. Moving in this way provokes an attack of opportunity from each foe that threatens you, probably including the defender. Any attack of opportunity made by anyone other than the defender against you during a bull rush has a 25% chance of accidentally targeting the defender instead, and any attack of opportunity by anyone other than you against the defender likewise has a 25% chance of accidentally targeting you. (When someone makes an attack of opportunity, she makes the attack roll and then rolls to see whether the attack went astray.)

TABLE 8–13: COMMON WEAPON AND SHIELD HARDNESS AND HIT POINTS

Weapon	Example	Hardness	HP
Tiny blade	Dagger	10	1
Small blade	Short sword	10	2
Medium-size blade	Longsword	10	5
Large blade	Greatsword	10	10
Small metal-hafted weapon	Light mace	10	10
Medium-size metal-hafted weapon	Heavy mace	10	25
Small hafted weapon	Handaxe	5	2
Medium-size hafted weapon	Battleaxe	5	5
Large hafted weapon	Greataxe	5	10
Huge club	Ogre's club	5	60
Buckler	—	10	5
Small wooden shield	—	5	10
Large wooden shield	—	5	15
Small steel shield	—	10	10
Large steel shield	—	10	20
Tower shield	—	5	20

TABLE 8–14: DCs TO BREAK OR BURST ITEMS

Strength Check to:	DC	Strength Check to:	DC
Break down simple door	13	Bend iron bars	24
Break down good door	18	Break down barred door	25
Break down strong door	23	Burst chain bonds	26
Burst rope bonds	23	Break down iron door	28

TABLE 8–15: OBJECT HARDNESS AND HIT POINTS

Object	Hardness	Hit Points	Break DC
Rope (1 inch diam.)	0	2	23
Simple wooden door	5	10	13
Spear	5	2	14
Small chest	5	1	17
Good wooden door	5	15	18
Treasure chest	5	15	23
Strong wooden door	5	20	23
Masonry wall (1 ft. thick)	8	90	35
Hewn stone (3 ft. thick)	8	540	50
Chain	10	5	26
Manacles	10	10	26
Masterwork manacles	10	10	28
Iron door (2 in. thick)	10	60	28

Second, you and the defender make opposed Strength checks. You each add a +4 bonus for each size category you are above Medium-size or a –4 penalty for each size category you are below Medium-size. You get a +2 charge bonus if you were charging. The defender gets a +4 stability bonus if he has more than two legs or is otherwise exceptionally stable.

Bull Rush Results: If you beat the defender, you push him back 5 feet. If you wish to move with the defender, you can push him back up to a distance of an additional 1 foot for each point by which you exceed the defender's check result. You can't, however, exceed your normal movement limit. (Note: The defender provokes attacks of opportunity if he is moved. So do you, if you move with him. The two of you do not provoke attacks of opportunity from each other as a result of this movement.)

If you fail to beat the defender's Strength check, you move 5 feet straight back to where you were before you moved into his space. If that space is occupied, you fall prone in that space (see Table 8–8: Attack Roll Modifiers).

DISARM

As a melee attack, you may make a disarm attempt. In doing so, you provoke an attack of opportunity from the defender. Then you and the defender make opposed attack rolls with your respective weapons. If the weapons are different sizes, the combatant with the larger weapon gets a bonus on the attack roll of +4 per difference in size category. If the defender is using a weapon in two hands, he gets an additional +4 bonus. If you beat the defender, the defender is disarmed. If you attempted the disarm action unarmed, you now have the weapon. Otherwise, it's on the ground at the defender's feet. If you fail, then the defender may immediately react and make an attempt to disarm you with the same sort of opposed melee attack roll.

Note: A defender wearing spiked gauntlets (page 100) can't be relieved of the gauntlets by a disarm action. A defender using a weapon attached to a locked gauntlet (page 106) gets a +10 bonus to any disarm attempt made by an opponent.

GRAPPLE

Grappling means wrestling and struggling hand-to-hand. It's tricky to perform, but sometimes you want to pin foes instead of killing them, and sometimes you have no choice in the matter. For monsters, grappling can mean trapping you in a toothy maw (the purple worm's favorite tactic) or holding you down so it can chew you up (the dire lion's trick).

Grapple Checks

Repeatedly in a grapple, you need to make opposed grapple checks against an opponent. A grapple check is something like a melee attack roll. Your attack bonus on a grapple check is:

Base attack bonus + Strength modifier + special size modifier

Special Size Modifier: The special size modifier for a grapple check is as follows: Colossal +16, Gargantuan +12, Huge +8, Large +4, Medium-size +0, Small –4, Tiny –8, Diminutive –12, Fine –16. Use this number in place of the normal size modifier you use when making an attack roll.

Starting a Grapple

To start a grapple, you first need to grab and hold your target. Attempting to start a grapple is the equivalent of making a melee attack. If you get multiple attacks in a round, you can attempt to start a grapple multiple times (at successively lower base attack bonuses). A monk can use his unarmed attack rate of attacks per round while grappling.

Attack of Opportunity: You provoke an attack of opportunity from the target you are trying to grapple. If the attack of opportunity deals you damage, you fail to start the grapple. (Certain monsters that grapple do not provoke attacks of opportunity when they attempt to start a grapple.)

Grab: You make a melee touch attack to grab the target. If you fail to hit the target, you fail to start the grapple.

Hold: Make an opposed grapple check. If you succeed, you have started the grapple, and you deal damage to the target as if with an unarmed strike.

If you lose, you fail to start the grapple. You automatically lose an attempt to hold if the target is two or more size categories larger than you are (but you can still make an attempt to grab such a target, if that's all you want to do).

Move In: To maintain the grapple, you must move into the target's space. Moving, as normal, provokes attacks of opportunity from threatening enemies, but not from your target.

Grappling: You and your target are now grappling.

Joining a Grapple

If your target is already grappling someone else, then you can use an attack to start a grapple, as above, except that the target doesn't get an attack of opportunity against you, and your grab automatically succeeds. You still have to make a successful opposed grapple check to deal damage and move in to be part of the grapple.

If You're Grappling

When you are grappling (regardless of who started the grapple), you can make an opposed grapple check as an attack. If you win, you can do the following:

Damage Your Opponent: You deal damage as with an unarmed strike (1d3 points for Medium-size attackers or 1d2 points for Small attackers, plus Strength modifiers). If you want to deal normal damage, you suffer a –4 penalty on your grapple check.

Exception: Monks deal more damage on an unarmed strike than other characters, and the damage is normal. However, they can choose to deal their damage as subdual damage when grappling without paying the usual –4 penalty for changing normal damage to subdual damage (see Dealing Subdual Damage, page 135).

Pin: You hold your opponent immobile for 1 round. (If you get multiple attacks, you can use subsequent attacks to damage your opponent. You can't use a weapon on a pinned character or attempt to damage or pin a second opponent while holding a pin on the first.) While you're pinned, opponents other than the one pinning you get a +4 bonus on attack rolls against you (but you're not helpless).

Break Another's Pin: You can break the hold that an opponent has over an ally.

Escape: You can escape the grapple. You can take whatever movement you get. If more than one opponent is grappling you, your grapple check result has to beat all their check results to escape. (Opponents don't have to try to hold you if they don't want to.)

If You're Pinned

When an opponent has pinned you, you are held immobile (but not helpless) for 1 round. You can make an opposed grapple check as a melee attack. If you win, you escape the pin, but you're still grappling.

Other Grappling Options

In addition to making opposed grapple checks, you have a few other options while grappling.

Weapons: You can attack with a light weapon while grappling (but not while pinned or pinning). You can't attack with two weapons while grappling.

Spells: You can attempt to cast a spell while grappling or even while pinned, provided its casting time is no more than 1 action, it has no somatic (S) components, and you have in hand any material components or focuses you might need. Any spell that requires precise and careful action, such as drawing a circle with powdered silver for *protection from evil*, is impossible to cast while grappling or being pinned. If the spell is one that you can cast while grappling, you still have to make a Concentration check (DC 20 + spell level) or lose the spell.

Wriggle Free: You can make an Escape Artist check (opposed by your opponent's grapple check) to get out of a grapple or out of being pinned (so that you're just being grappled). Doing so counts as a standard action; if you escape a grapple, you can also move in the same round.

Multiple Grapplers

Several combatants can be in a single grapple. Up to four combatants can grapple a single opponent in a given round. Creatures that are one size category smaller than you count for half, creatures that are one size category larger than you count double, and creatures two or more size categories larger count quadruple. For example, if you're Medium-size, eight goblins (Small), four orcs (Medium-size), two ogres (Large), or a single hill giant (Huge) could grapple you. In the same way, four goblins (counting as two opponents) plus one ogre (counting as two opponents) could grapple you.

Additional enemies can aid their friends with the aid another action (page 135).

Grappling Consequences

While you're grappling, your ability to attack others and defend yourself is limited.

No Threatened Area: You don't threaten any area while grappling.

No Dexterity Bonus: You lose your Dexterity bonus to AC (if you have one) against opponents you aren't grappling. (You can still use it against opponents you are grappling.)

GRENADELIKE WEAPON ATTACKS

A grenadelike weapon is one that "splashes." It has a broad enough effect that it can hurt characters just by landing close to them.

Grenadelike
Weapons

8 1 2

7 3

6 4
5

Direction of Throw

Grenadelike weapons include flasks of acid and of alchemist's fire. Attacks with grenadelike weapons are ranged touch attack rolls. Direct hits deal direct hit damage. (Grenadelike weapon damage is covered on Table 7–10: Grenadelike Weapons, page 114.)

If you miss your target, roll 1d6 to see how many feet away from the target the weapon lands. Add +1 foot for every range increment of distance that you threw the weapon. Then roll 1d8 to determine the direction in which the object deviated: 1 means long, 2 means long and to the right, 3 right, 4 short and right, 5 short, 6, short and left, 7 left, 8 long and left.

Once you know where the weapon landed, it deals splash damage (see Table 7–10: Grenadelike Weapons, page 114) to all creatures within 5 feet.

MOUNTED COMBAT

Riding a horse into battle gives you several advantages, provided you have the right horse and the right skills (see the Ride skill, page 72, and the Mounted Combat feat, page 83).

Horses in Combat: Warhorses and warponies serve readily as combat steeds. Light horses, ponies, and heavy horses, however, are frightened by combat. If you don't dismount, you must make a Ride check (DC 20) each round as a move-equivalent action just to control such a horse. If you succeed, you can perform a partial action after the move-equivalent action. If you fail this Ride check, it is considered to have been a full-round action (which means you can't do anything else until your next turn).

Your mount acts on your initiative as you direct it. You move at its speed, but the mount uses its action to move.

A horse (not a pony) is a long, Large creature (see Big and Little Creatures in Combat, page 131). It takes up more space on the battlefield than you do. A horse takes up a 5-foot-by-10-foot space, and you take up a space 5 feet across. For simplicity, assume that you occupy the back part of the horse.

Combat while Mounted: With a successful Ride check (DC 5), you can guide your mount with your knees so as to use both hands to attack or defend yourself while mounted.

If your mount moves more than 5 feet, you can only make a partial melee attack. Essentially, you have to wait until the mount gets to your enemy before attacking, so you can't make a full attack.

When you attack a Medium-size or smaller creature that is on foot, you get the +1 bonus on melee attacks for being on higher ground.

When charging on horseback, you deal double damage with a lance.

You can use ranged weapons while your mount is taking a double move, but at a –4 penalty on the attack roll. You can use ranged weapons while your mount is running (quadruple speed), at a –8 penalty. In either case, you make the attack roll when your mount has completed half its movement. You can even exercise the full attack action while your mount is moving. Likewise, you can take move-equivalent actions normally (you are not using your personal move for much else), so that, for instance, you can load and fire a light crossbow in a round while your mount is moving.

Casting Spells while Mounted: You can cast a spell normally if your mount moves up to a normal move (its speed) either before or after you cast. If you have your mount move both before and after you cast a spell, then you're casting the spell while the mount is moving, and you have to make a Concentration check due to the vigorous motion (DC 10 + spell level) or lose the spell. If the mount is running (quadruple speed), you can cast a spell when your mount has moved up to twice its speed, but your Concentration check is more difficult due to the violent motion (DC 15 + spell level).

If Your Mount Is Dropped in Battle: If your mount falls while you're riding it, you have to succeed at a Ride check (DC 15) to make a soft fall. If the check fails, you take 1d6 points of damage.

If You Are Dropped: If you are knocked unconscious, you have a 50% chance to stay in the saddle (or 75% if you're in a military saddle). Otherwise you fall and take 1d6 points of damage. Without you to guide it, the horse avoids combat.

OVERRUN

You can try to overrun as part of a charge action. You can only overrun an opponent who is one size category larger than you, the same size, or smaller. You can make only one overrun attempt per action.

An overrun takes place during the movement portion of a charge. With an overrun, you attempt to plow past or over your opponent (and move through his area).

First, you must move at least 10 feet in a straight line into the defender's space (provoking attacks of opportunity normally).

Then the defender chooses either to avoid you or to block you. If he avoids you, you keep moving. (You can always move through the space occupied by someone who lets you by.) If he blocks you, make a trip attack against him (see Trip, below). If you succeed in tripping your opponent, you can continue your charge in a straight line as normal.

If you fail and are tripped in turn, you are prone in the defender's space (see Table 8–8: Attack Roll Modifiers). If you fail but are not tripped, you have to move 5 feet back the way you came. If that space is occupied, you fall prone in that space.

TRIP

You can try to trip an opponent as a melee attack. You can only trip an opponent who is one size category larger than you, the same size, or smaller.

Making a Trip Attack: Make a melee attack as a melee touch attack. If the attack succeeds, make a Strength check opposed by the defender's Dexterity or Strength check (whichever ability score has the higher modifier). A combatant gets a +4 bonus for every size category he is larger than Medium-size or a –4 penalty for every size category he is smaller. The defender gets a +4 stability bonus on his check if he has more than two legs or is otherwise more stable than a normal humanoid. If you win, you trip the defender. If you lose, the defender may immediately react and make a Strength check opposed by your Dexterity or Strength check to try to trip you.

Being Tripped (Prone): A tripped character is prone (see Table 8–8: Attack Roll Modifiers). Standing up from prone is a move-equivalent action.

Tripping a Mounted Opponent: You may make a trip attack against a mounted opponent. The defender may use his Ride skill in place of his Dexterity or Strength check. If you succeed, you pull the rider from his mount.

TURN AND REBUKE UNDEAD

Good clerics and paladins and some neutral clerics can channel positive energy, which drives off (turns) or destroys undead. Evil clerics and some neutral clerics

can channel negative energy, which awes (rebukes), controls (commands), or bolsters undead.

How Turning Works

Jozan, the cleric, and his friends confront a pack of seven ghouls led by a ghast. Calling on the goodness and power of Pelor, Jozan raises his sun disk and attempts to drive the undead away.

First, his player, Skip, makes a turning check (1d20 + Charisma modifier) to see what the most powerful undead creature is that Jozan can turn in this action. His result is 9, so he can only turn undead that have less Hit Dice than he has levels. Jozan is 3rd level, so he can turn creatures with 2 Hit Dice (such as ghouls) or 1 Hit Die (such as skeletons) but nothing with more Hit Dice (such as a ghast). He does not have twice as many levels as either the ghouls or ghasts, so he will not destroy any of them.

Next, Skip rolls his turning damage (2d6 + Jozan's level + Charisma modifier) to see how many total Hit Dice of creatures he can turn. His result is 11. That's enough to turn away the five closest ghouls (accounting for 10 HD out of the maximum of 11). That leaves two ghouls and the ghast. (The extra HD of turning is wasted, because there are no undead present with 1 Hit Die.)

On Jozan's second round, he attempts to turn undead again. This time, his turning check result is 21—enough to turn undead creatures of up to 6 HD. His turning damage roll, however, is only 7, so he can only turn 7 HD worth of creatures. He turns the two nearest undead (2-HD ghouls), but the remaining 3 HD of turning isn't enough to turn the 4-HD ghast.

Turning Checks

Turning undead is a supernatural ability that a cleric can perform as a standard action. It does not provoke attacks of opportunity. You must present your holy symbol to turn undead. Turning is considered an attack.

Times per Day: You may attempt to turn undead a number of times per day equal to 3 + your Charisma modifier. This number can be increased by the Extra Turning feat (page 32).

Range: You turn the closest turnable undead first, and you can't turn undead that are more than 60 feet away or that have total cover relative to you.

Turning Check: The first thing you do is roll a turning check to see how powerful an undead creature you can turn. This is a Charisma check (1d20 + your Charisma modifier). Table 8–16: Turning Undead gives you the Hit Dice of the most powerful undead you can affect, relative to your level. With a given turning attempt, you

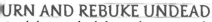

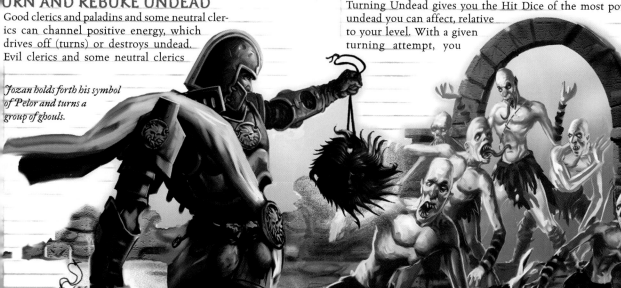

Jozan holds forth his symbol of Pelor and turns a group of ghouls.

can turn no undead creature whose Hit Dice exceed the result on this table.

Turning Damage: If your roll on Table 8–16: Turning Undead is high enough to let you turn at least some of the undead within 60 feet, roll 2d6 + your cleric level + your Charisma modifier for turning damage. That's how many total Hit Dice of undead you can turn.

If your Charisma score is average or low, it's possible (but unusual) to roll fewer Hit Dice turned than indicated on Table 8–16: Turning Undead. In this case, you may not have the power to turn even a single undead creature. For instance, a 1st-level cleric with an average Charisma score could get a turning check result of 19 (cleric's level +3, or 4 HD), which is enough to turn a wight, but then roll only 3 on his turning damage roll—not enough to turn that wight after all.

You may skip over already turned undead that are still within range, so that you do not waste your turning capacity on them.

Effect and Duration of Turning: Turned undead flee you by the best and fastest means available to them. They flee for 10 rounds (1 minute). If they cannot flee, they cower (giving any attack rolls against them a +2 bonus). If you approach within 10 feet of them, however, they overcome being turned and act normally. (You can stand within 10 feet without breaking the turning effect. You just can't approach them.) You can attack them with ranged attacks (from at least 10 feet away), and others can attack them in any fashion, without breaking the turning effect.

Destroying Undead: If you have twice as many levels (or more) as the undead have Hit Dice, you destroy any that you would normally turn.

Table 8–16: Turning Undead

Turning Check Result	Most Powerful Undead Affected (Maximum Hit Dice)
Up to 0	Cleric's level – 4
1–3	Cleric's level – 3
4–6	Cleric's level – 2
7–9	Cleric's level – 1
10–12	Cleric's level
13–15	Cleric's level + 1
16–18	Cleric's level + 2
19–21	Cleric's level + 3
22+	Cleric's level + 4

Evil Clerics and Undead

Evil clerics channel negative energy to rebuke (awe) or command (control) undead rather than channeling positive energy to turn or destroy them. An evil cleric makes the equivalent of a turning check. Undead that would be turned are rebuked instead, and those that would be destroyed are commanded.

Rebuked: A rebuked undead creature cowers as if in awe. (Attack rolls against the creature get a +2 bonus.) The effect lasts 10 rounds.

Commanded: A commanded undead creature is under the mental control of the evil cleric. The cleric must take a standard action to give mental orders to a commanded undead. At any one time, the cleric may command any number of undead whose total Hit Dice do not exceed his level. He may voluntarily relinquish command on any commanded undead creature or creatures in order to command new ones.

Alternatively, an evil cleric may command a single undead creature with more Hit Dice than he has levels, but he must concentrate continuously to do so (as in concentrating to maintain a spell), and he can command no other undead at the same time.

Dispelling Turning: An evil cleric may channel negative energy to dispel a good cleric's turning effect. The evil cleric makes a turning check as if attempting to rebuke the undead. If the turning check result is equal to or greater than the turning check result that the good cleric scored when turning the undead, then the

undead are no longer turned. The evil cleric rolls turning damage of 2d6 + cleric level + Charisma modifier to see how many Hit Dice worth of undead he can affect in this way (as if he were rebuking them).

Bolstering Undead: An evil cleric may also bolster undead creatures against turning in advance. He makes a turning check as if attempting to rebuke the undead, but the Hit Dice result on Table 8–16: Turning Undead becomes the undead creatures' effective Hit Dice as far as turning is concerned (provided the result is higher than the creatures' actual Hit Dice). The bolstering lasts 10 rounds.

Neutral Clerics and Undead

A neutral cleric (one who is neither good nor evil) can either turn undead but not rebuke them, or rebuke undead but not turn them. When you create a neutral cleric, decide which effect he has on undead. That is the effect he has from then on. Essentially, the neutral cleric has the turning abilities either of a good cleric or of an evil one. Some deities specify what effect their neutral clerics must have on undead.

Even if a cleric is neutral, channeling positive energy is a good act and channeling negative energy is evil.

Paladins and Undead

Paladins can turn undead as if they were clerics of two levels lower than they actually are. That means a paladin can't turn undead until 3rd level, at which point she turns undead as if she were a 1st-level cleric.

Other Uses for Energy

Positive or negative energy may have uses other than affecting undead. For example, a holy site might be guarded by a magic door that opens for any good cleric who can make a turning check high enough to affect a 3-HD undead and that shatters for an evil cleric who can make a similar check.

UNARMED ATTACKS

Striking for damage with punches, kicks, and head butts is like attacking with a weapon, except for the following:

Attacks of Opportunity: Attacking unarmed provokes an attack of opportunity from the character you attack, provided she is armed. The attack of opportunity comes before your attack. An unarmed attack does not provoke attacks of opportunity from other foes, as shooting a bow does, nor does it provoke an attack of opportunity from an unarmed foe. You provoke the attack of opportunity because you have to bring your body close to your opponent.

"Armed" Unarmed Attacks: Sometimes a character or creature attacks unarmed but still counts as armed. A monk, a character with the Improved Unarmed Strike feat (page 83), a spellcaster delivering a touch attack spell, and a creature with claws, fangs, and similar natural physical weapons all count as armed. Note that being armed counts for both offense and defense. Not only does a monk not provoke an attack of opportunity when attacking an armed foe, but you provoke an attack of opportunity from a monk if you make an unarmed attack against her.

Unarmed Strike Damage: An unarmed strike from a Medium-size character deals 1d3 points of damage (with your Strength modifier, as normal). A Small character's unarmed strike deals 1d2 points of damage. All damage is subdual damage. Unarmed strikes count as light weapons (for purposes of two-weapon attack penalties and so on).

Dealing Normal Damage: You can specify that your unarmed strike will deal normal damage before you make your attack roll, but you suffer a –4 penalty on your attack roll because you have to strike a particularly vulnerable spot to deal normal damage.

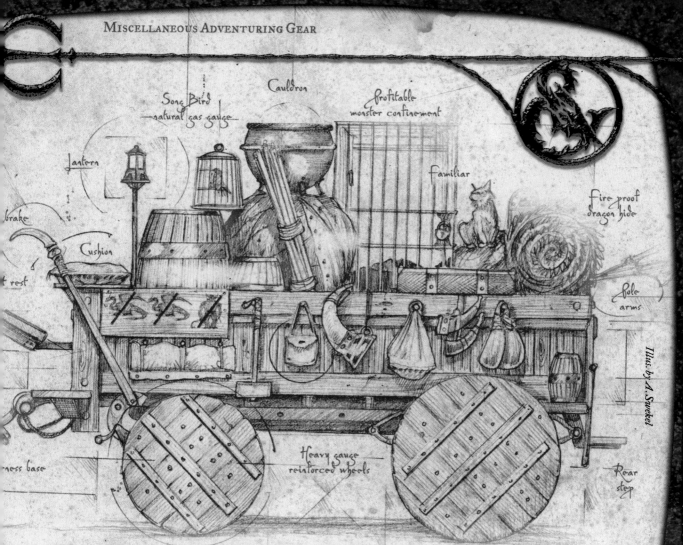

Song Bird
natural gas gauge

Cauldron

profitable
monster confinement

Lantern

Familiar

Fire-proof
dragon hide

brake

Cushion

Pole
arms

rest

ness base

Heavy gauge
reinforced wheels

Rear
step

Illus. by A. Swekel

Hand
brake

BOTTOM VIEW

Jozan, Lidda, Mialee, and Tordek prepare for an expedition into the mountains, following an old map that they found in a ruined temple. They ride their horses out into the wilderness, find the cavern marked on the map, and descend into dark chambers that have never been touched by light. There they meet strange and dangerous creatures and recover gems, gold, and magic items. When they have taken enough damage and used enough spells that further exploration would be too dangerous, and when the treasure they're carrying is weighing them down, they return to the light of day, mount their steeds, and ride home. There they divvy up the treasure that they have captured, including a magic shield that Jozan and Tordek both want. The adventurers each reflect on what they have learned from the expedition, confident that every challenge they have faced makes them stronger, individually and as a team.

This chapter covers carrying capacity and encumbrance, movement overland and through adventure sites, exploration, treasure, and experience.

CARRYING CAPACITY

Encumbrance rules determine how much a character's armor and equipment slow him or her down. Encumbrance comes in two parts: encumbrance by armor and encumbrance by total weight.

Encumbrance by Armor: Your armor (as shown on Table 7–5: Armor) defines your maximum Dexterity bonus to AC, your armor check penalty, your speed, and how fast you move when you run. Unless your character is weak or carrying a lot of gear, that's all you need to know. The extra gear your character carries, such as weapons and rope, won't slow your character down any more than his or her armor already does.

If your character is weak or carrying a lot of gear, however, then you'll need to calculate encumbrance by weight. Doing so is most important when your character is trying to carry some heavy object, such as a treasure chest.

Weight: If you want to determine whether your character's gear is heavy enough to slow him or her down (more than the armor already does), total the weight of all his or her armor, weapons, and gear. Compare this total to the character's Strength on Table 9–1: Carrying Capacity. Depending on how the weight compares to your carrying capacity, you will be carrying a light, medium, or heavy load. Like armor, your load gives you a maximum Dexterity bonus to AC, a check penalty (which works like an armor check penalty), speed, and run factor, as shown on Table 9–2: Carrying Loads. Carrying a light load does not encumber a character.

If you are wearing armor, use the worse figure (from armor or from weight) for each category. Do not stack the penalties.

For example, Tordek the dwarf is wearing scale mail. As shown by Table 7–5: Armor, it cuts his maximum Dexterity bonus to AC down to +3, gives him a –4 armor check penalty, and cuts his speed to 15 feet. The total weight of his gear, including armor, is 71 1/2 pounds. With a Strength of 15, his maximum carrying capacity (maximum load) is 200 pounds. A medium load for him is is 67 pounds or more, and a heavy load is 134 pounds or more, so he is carrying a medium load . Looking at the medium load line on Table 9–2: Carrying Loads, Monte sees that these figures are all as good or better than the penalties that Tordek is already incurring for wearing scale mail, so he incurs no extra encumbrance penalties.

Mialee has a Strength of 10, and she's carrying 28 pounds of gear. Her light load capacity is 33, so she's carrying a light load (no penalties). She finds 500 gold pieces (weighing 10 pounds) and adds it to her load, so now she's carrying a medium load. Doing so reduces her speed from 30 feet to 20 feet, gives her a –3 check penalty, and sets her maximum Dexterity bonus to AC at +3 (which is okay with her, since that's her Dexterity bonus anyway).

Then Mialee is knocked unconscious in a fight, and Tordek wants to carry her out of the dungeon. She weighs 104 pounds, and her gear weighs 28 pounds (or 38 pounds with the gold), so Tordek can't quite manage to carry her and her gear. (It would put him over his 200 pounds maximum load.) Jozan takes her gear (and the gold), Tordek hoists Mialee onto his shoulders, and now he's carrying 175 1/2 pounds. He can manage it, but it's a heavy load. His maximum Dexterity bonus to AC drops to +1, his check penalty increases from –4 (the armor check penalty for scale mail) to –6 (the check penalty for a heavy load), and now he runs at ×3 speed instead of ×4.

Lifting and Dragging: A character can lift up to the maximum load over his or her head.

A character can lift up to double the maximum load off the ground, but he or she can only stagger around with it. While overloaded in this way, the character loses any Dexterity bonus to AC and can only move 5 feet per round (as a full-round action).

A character can generally push or drag along the ground up to five times the maximum load. Favorable conditions (smooth ground, dragging a slick object) can double these numbers, and bad circumstances (broken ground, pushing an object that snags) can reduce them to one-half or less.

Bigger and Smaller Creatures: The figures on Table 9–1: Carrying Capacity are for Medium-size creatures. Larger creatures can carry more weight depending on size category: Large (×2), Huge (×4), Gargantuan (×8), and Colossal (×16). Smaller creatures can carry less weight depending on size category: Small (3/4), Tiny (1/2), Diminutive (1/4), and Fine (1/8). Thus, a human with a Strength score magically boosted to equal that of a giant would still have a harder time lifting, say, a horse or a boulder than a giant would.

For example, Mialee, an elf with 10 Strength, can carry up to 100 pounds. Lidda, a halfling with 10 Strength, can only carry 75 pounds.

Tremendous Strength: For Strength scores not listed, determine the carrying capacity this way. Find the Strength score between 20 and 29 that has the same ones digit as the creature's Strength score. Multiply the figures by four if the creature's Strength is in the 30s, 16 if it's in the 40s, 64 if it's in the 50s, and so on. For example, a cloud giant with a 35 Strength can carry four times what a creature with a 25 Strength can carry, or 3,200 pounds, multiplied by eight because the cloud giant is Gargantuan, for a grand total of 25,600 pounds.

MOVEMENT

Characters spend a lot of time getting from one place to another. If your character needs to reach the evil tower, he might choose to walk along the road, hire a boat to row him along the river, or cut cross-country on horseback. He can climb trees to get a better look at his surroundings, scale mountains, or ford streams.

The DM moderates the pace of a game session, so he or she determines when movement is so important that it's worth measuring. During casual scenes, you usually won't have to worry about movement rates. If your character has come to a new city and takes a stroll to get a feel for the place, no one needs to know exactly how many rounds or minutes the circuit takes.

There are three movement scales in the game:

- Tactical, for combat, measured in feet per round.
- Local, for exploring an area, measured in feet per minute.
- Overland, for getting from place to place, measured in miles per hour or day.

Modes of Movement: While moving at the different movement scales, creatures generally walk, hustle, or run.

Walk: A walk represents unhurried but purposeful movement at three miles per hour for an unencumbered human.

Hustle: A hustle is a jog that is movement at about six miles per hour for an unencumbered human. The double move action represents a hustle.

Run (×3): Moving three times your standard speed is a running pace for a character in heavy armor. It is moving about six miles per hour for a human in full plate.

Run (×4): Moving four times your standard speed is a running pace for a character in light, medium, or no armor. It is moving about twelve miles per hour for an unencumbered human, or eight miles per hour for a human in chainmail.

Hampered Movement: Obstructions, bad surface conditions, or poor visibility can hamper movement. The DM determines the category that a specific condition falls into (see Table 9–4: Hampered Movement). When movement is hampered, multiply the standard distance by the movement penalty (a fraction) to determine the distance covered. For example, a character who could normally cover 40 feet with a double move (hustle) can only cover 30 feet if moving through undergrowth.

If more than one condition applies, multiply the normal distance covered by all movement penalty fractions that apply. For

TABLE 9–1: CARRYING CAPACITY

Strength	Light Load	Medium Load	Heavy Load
1 Str	up to 3 lb.	4–6 lb.	7–10 lb.
2 Str	up to 6 lb.	7–13 lb.	14–20 lb.
3 Str	up to 10 lb.	11–20 lb.	21–30 lb.
4 Str	up to 13 lb.	14–26 lb.	27–40 lb.
5 Str	up to 16 lb.	17–33 lb.	34–50 lb.
6 Str	up to 20 lb.	21–40 lb.	41–60 lb.
7 Str	up to 23 lb.	24–46 lb.	47–70 lb.
8 Str	up to 26 lb.	27–53 lb.	54–80 lb.
9 Str	up to 30 lb.	31–60 lb.	61–90 lb.
10 Str	up to 33 lb.	34–66 lb.	67–100 lb.
11 Str	up to 38 lb.	39–76 lb.	77–115 lb.
12 Str	up to 43 lb.	44–86 lb.	87–130 lb.
13 Str	up to 50 lb.	51–100 lb.	101–150 lb.
14 Str	up to 58 lb.	59–116 lb.	117–175 lb.
15 Str	up to 66 lb.	67–133 lb.	134–200 lb.
16 Str	up to 76 lb.	77–153 lb.	154–230 lb.
17 Str	up to 86 lb.	87–173 lb.	174–260 lb.
18 Str	up to 100 lb.	101–200 lb.	201–300 lb.
19 Str	up to 116 lb.	117–233 lb.	234–350 lb.
20 Str	up to 133 lb.	134–266 lb.	267–400 lb.
21 Str	up to 153 lb.	154–306 lb.	307–460 lb.
22 Str	up to 173 lb.	174–346 lb.	347–520 lb.
23 Str	up to 200 lb.	201–400 lb.	401–600 lb.
24 Str	up to 233 lb.	234–466 lb.	467–700 lb.
25 Str	up to 266 lb.	267–533 lb.	534–800 lb.
26 Str	up to 306 lb.	307–613 lb.	614–920 lb.
27 Str	up to 346 lb.	347–693 lb.	694–1,040 lb.
28 Str	up to 400 lb.	401–800 lb.	801–1,200 lb.
29 Str	up to 466 lb.	467–933 lb.	934–1,400 lb.
+10 Str	×4	×4	×4

TABLE 9–2: CARRYING LOADS

Load	Max Dex	Check Penalty	Speed (30 ft.)	(20 ft.)	Run
Medium	+3	–3	20 ft.	15 ft.	×4
Heavy	+1	–6	20 ft.	15 ft.	×3

TABLE 9–3: MOVEMENT AND DISTANCE

	Speed			
	15 feet	20 feet	30 feet	40 feet
One Round (Tactical)				
Walk	15 ft.	20 ft.	30 ft.	40 ft.
Hustle	30 ft.	40 ft.	60 ft.	80 ft.
Run (×3)	45 ft.	60 ft.	90 ft.	120 ft.
Run (×4)	60 ft.	80 ft.	120 ft.	160 ft.
One Minute (Local)				
Walk	150 ft.	200 ft.	300 ft.	400 ft.
Hustle	300 ft.	400 ft.	600 ft.	800 ft.
Run (×3)	450 ft.	600 ft.	900 ft.	1,200 ft.
Run (×4)	600 ft.	800 ft.	1,200 ft.	1,600 ft.
One Hour (Overland)				
Walk	1 1/2 miles	2 miles	3 miles	4 miles
Hustle	3 miles	4 miles	6 miles	8 miles
Run	—	—	—	—
One Day (Overland)				
Walk	12 miles	16 miles	24 miles	32 miles
Hustle	—	—	—	—
Run	—	—	—	—

TABLE 9–4: HAMPERED MOVEMENT

Condition	Example	Movement Penalty
Obstruction		
Moderate	Undergrowth	× 3/4
Heavy	Thick undergrowth	× 1/2
Surface		
Bad	Steep slope or mud	× 1/2
Very bad	Deep snow	× 1/4
Poor visibility	Darkness or fog	× 1/2

instance, a character who could normally cover 60 feet with a double move (hustle) could only cover 15 feet moving through thick undergrowth in fog (one-quarter as far as normal).

TACTICAL MOVEMENT

Use tactical speed for combat, as detailed in Chapter 8: Combat. Characters generally don't walk during combat: They hustle or run. A character who moves his or her speed and takes some action, such as attacking or casting a spell, is hustling for about half the round and doing something else the other half.

LOCAL MOVEMENT

Characters exploring an area use local movement, measured in minutes.

Walk: A character can walk without a problem on the local scale.

Hustle: A character can hustle without a problem on the local scale. See Overland Movement, below, for movement measured in hours.

Run: A character with a Constitution score of 9 or higher can run for a minute without a problem. Generally, a character can run for about a minute or two before having to rest for a minute (see Run, page 127).

OVERLAND MOVEMENT

Characters covering long distances cross-country use overland movement. Overland movement is measured in hours or days. A day represents 8 hours of actual travel time. For rowed watercraft, a day represents 10 hours of rowing. For a sailing ship, it represents 24 hours.

Walk: You can walk 8 hours in a day of travel without a problem. Walking for longer than that can wear you out (see Forced March, below).

Hustle: You can hustle for 1 hour without a problem. Hustling for a second hour in between sleep cycles causes you 1 point of subdual damage, and each additional hour causes twice the damage taken during the previous hour.

Run: You can't run for an extended period of time. Attempts to run and rest in cycles effectively work out to a hustle.

Terrain: The terrain through which you travel affects how much distance you can cover in an hour or a day (see Table 9–5: Terrain and Overland Movement). Travel is quickest on a highway, followed by on a road (or trail), and least quick through trackless terrain. A highway is a straight, major, paved road. A road is typically a dirt track. A trail is like a road, except that it allows only single-file travel and does not benefit a party traveling with vehicles. Trackless terrain is a wild area with no paths.

Forced March: In a day of normal walking, you walk for 8 hours. You spend the rest of daylight time making and breaking camp, resting, and eating.

You can walk for more than 8 hours in a day by making a forced march. For each hour of marching beyond 8 hours, you make a Constitution check (DC 10 + 1 per extra hour). If the check fails, you take 1d6 points of subdual damage. You can't recover this subdual damage normally until you halt and rest for at least 4 hours. It's possible for a character to march into unconsciousness by pushing himself or herself too hard.

TABLE 9–5: TERRAIN AND OVERLAND MOVEMENT

Terrain	Highway	Road	Trackless
Plains	×1	×1	×1
Scrub, rough	×1	×1	×3/4
Forest	×1	×1	×1/2
Jungle	×1	×3/4	×1/4
Swamp	×1	×3/4	×1/2
Hills	×1	×3/4	×1/2
Mountains	×3/4	×1/2	×1/4
Sandy desert	×1	—	×1/2

TABLE 9–6: MOUNTS AND VEHICLES

Mount/Vehicle	Per Hour	Per Day
Mount (carrying load)		
Light horse or light warhorse	6 miles	48 miles
Light horse (101–300 lb.)	4 miles	32 miles
Light warhorse (134–400 lb.)	4 miles	32 miles
Heavy horse	5 miles	40 miles
Heavy horse (134–400 lb.)	3 1/2 miles	28 miles
Heavy warhorse	4 miles	32 miles
Heavy warhorse (174–520 lb.)	3 miles	24 miles
Pony or warpony	4 miles	32 miles
Pony (44–130 lb.)	3 miles	24 miles
Warpony (51–150 lb.)	3 miles	24 miles
Donkey or mule	3 miles	24 miles
Mule (94–280 lb.)	2 miles	16 miles
Cart or wagon	2 miles	16 miles
Ship		
Raft or barge (poled or towed)*	1/2 mile	5 miles
Keelboat (rowed)*	1 mile	10 miles
Rowboat	1 1/2 miles	15 miles
Sailing ship (sailed)	2 miles	48 miles
Warship (sailed and rowed)	2 1/2 miles	60 miles
Longship (sailed and rowed)	3 miles	72 miles
Galley (rowed and sailed)	4 miles	96 miles

*Rafts, barges, and keelboats are used on lakes and rivers. If going downstream, add the speed of the current (typically 3 mph) to the speed of the vehicle. In addition to 10 hours of being rowed, the vehicle can also float an additional 14 hours, if someone can guide it, so add an additional 42 miles to the daily distance traveled. These vehicles can't be rowed against any significant current, but they can be pulled upstream by draft animals on the shores.

Mounted Movement: A horse bearing a rider can move at a hustle. The damage it takes, however, is normal damage, not subdual damage. It can also be force-marched, but its Constitution checks automatically fail, and, again, the damage it takes is normal damage.

See Table 9–6: Mounts and Vehicles for mounted speeds and speeds for vehicles pulled by draft animals.

Waterborne Movement: See Table 9–6: Mounts and Vehicles for speeds for water vehicles.

EXPLORATION

Adventurers spend time exploring dark caverns, cursed ruins, catacombs, and other dangerous and forbidding areas. A little careful forethought can help the characters in their adventures.

PREPARATIONS

Characters should have the supplies they need for their adventures: arrows, food, water, torches, bedrolls, or whatever is needed for the task at hand. Rope, chains, crowbars, and other tools can come in handy, too. Characters should have ranged weapons, if possible, for combats in which they can't close with the enemy (or don't want to). Horses are useful for overland journeys, while sure-footed pack donkeys and mules can be handy for exploring ruins and dungeons.

VISION AND LIGHT

Characters need a way to see in the dark, dangerous places where they often find adventures. Dwarves and half-orcs have darkvision, but everyone else needs light to see by. Typically, adventurers bring along torches or lanterns, and spellcasters have spells that can create light. See Table 9–7: Light Sources for the radius that a light source illuminates and how long it lasts.

Characters with low-light vision (elves, gnomes, and half-elves) can see objects twice as far away as the given radius. Characters with darkvision (dwarves and half-orcs) can see lit areas normally as well as dark areas within 60 feet.

MARCHING ORDER

The characters in a party need to decide what their marching order is. Marching order is the relative position of the characters to each other while they are moving (who is in front of or next to whom,

TABLE 9–7: LIGHT SOURCES

Object	Light	Duration
Candle	5 ft.	1 hr.
Lamp, common	15 ft.	6 hr./pint
Lantern, bullseye	60-ft. cone*	6 hr./pint
Lantern, hooded	30 ft.	6 hr./pint
Sunrod	30 ft.	6 hr.
Torch	20 ft.	1 hr.

Spell	Light	Duration
Continual flame	20 ft.	Permanent
Dancing lights (torches)	20 ft. (each)	1 min.
Daylight	60 ft.	30 min.
Light	20 ft.	10 min.

*A cone 60 feet long and 20 feet wide at the far end.

for instance). If you're using miniatures, arrange them on the table to represent the PCs' relative locations. You can change the marching order as the party enters different areas, as characters get wounded, or at other times for some reason.

In a marching order, the sturdiest characters, such as barbarians, fighters, and paladins, usually go in front. Wizards, sorcerers, and bards often find a place in the middle or back, where they are protected from direct attack. Clerics and druids are good choices for rear guard. They're tough enough to withstand a rear attack, and they're important enough as healers that it's risky to put them in the front line. Rogues, rangers, and monks might serve as stealthy scouts, though they have to be careful if they're away from the safety of the party.

If the characters are close together, they can protect each other, but they're more vulnerable to spells that way, so sometimes it pays to spread out a little.

EXPERIENCE AND LEVELS

Experience points (XP) measure how much your character has learned and how much he or she has grown in personal power. Your character earns XP by defeating monsters and other opponents. The DM assigns XP to the characters at the end of each adventure based on what they have accomplished. Characters accumulate XP from adventure to adventure. When a character earns

---

HOW PLAYERS CAN HELP

Here are a few ways in which you can help the game go more smoothly.

Mapping: Someone should keep a map of places you explore so that you know where you've been and where you have yet to explore. The responsibility for mapping can be rotated from person to person, if more than one player likes to do this sort of thing, but as a rule the same person should be the mapper throughout a single playing session.

A map is most useful and most important when the characters are in a dungeon setting—an environment with lots of corridors, doors, and rooms that would be almost impossible to navigate through without a record of what parts the characters have already explored.

To make a map, you start with a blank sheet of paper (graph paper is best) and draw the floor plan of the dungeon as you and your group discover it and the Dungeon Master describes what you're seeing. For example, when the characters come to a new, empty room, the DM might say, "The door you have opened leads east into a room twenty-five feet wide and thirty feet deep. The door is in the middle of the room's west wall, and you can see two other doors: one in the north wall near the corner with the east wall, and one in the east wall about five feet south of the middle." Or, if it's easier for you to visualize, the DM might express the information this way: "From the north edge of the door, the wall goes two squares north, six squares east, five squares south, back

six squares west, and then north back to the door. There's a door on the sixth square of the north wall and on the fourth square of the east wall."

Party Notes: It often pays to keep notes: names of NPCs the party has met, treasure the party has won, secrets the characters have learned, and so forth. The Dungeon Master might keep track of all this information for his or her own benefit, but even so it can be handy for you to jot down facts that might be needed later—at the least, doing this prevents you from having to ask the Dungeon Master, "What was the name of that old man we met in the woods last week?" You might also use this sort of information to make a connection between two seemingly unrelated facts—you can look back through your notes and discover that the birthmark on the arm of the old man (which you noted when you first encountered him) is the same as the birthmark said to be borne by the long-lost heir to the throne (which you just found out about).

Character Notes: You should keep track of hit points, spells, and other characteristics about your character that change during an adventure on scratch paper. Between playing sessions, you might decide to write some of this information directly on your character sheet—but don't worry about updating the sheet constantly. For instance, it would be tedious (and could make a mess of the sheet) if you erased your character's current hit points and wrote in a new number every time he or she took damage.

enough XP, he or she attains a new character level (see Table 3–2: Experience and Level-Dependent Benefits, page 22).

Advancing a Level: When your character's XP total reaches at least the minimum XP needed for a new character level (see Table 3–2: Experience and Level-Dependent Benefits, page 22), she goes up a level. For example, when Tordek obtains 1,000 or more XP, he becomes a 2nd-level character. After that, once he accumulates a total of 3,000 XP or higher, he reaches 3rd level. Going up a level provides the character with several immediate benefits (see below).

A character can only advance one level at a time. If, for some extraordinary reason, a character gains enough XP to advance two or more levels at once, he or she instead advances one level and gains just enough XP to be 1 XP short of the next level. For example, if Tordek has 5,000 XP (1,000 points short of 4th level) and gains 6,000 more, normally that would put him at 11,000—enough for 5th level. Instead, he only attains 4th level, and his XP total is 9,999.

Training and Practice: Characters spend time between adventures training, studying, or otherwise practicing their skills. This work consolidates what they learn on adventures and keeps them in top form. If, for some reason, a character can't practice or train for an extended time, the DM may reduce XP awards or even cause him or her to lose experience points.

LEVEL ADVANCEMENT

Each character class has a table that shows how the class features and statistics increase as a member of that class advances in level. When your character achieves a new level, make these changes:

1. **Choose Class:** Most characters have only one class, and when such a character achieves a new level, it is a new level in that class. If your character has more than one class or wants to acquire a new class, however, you choose which class goes up one level. The other class or classes stay at the previous level. (See Multiclass Characters, page 55.)

2. **Base Attack Bonus:** The base attack bonus for fighters, barbarians, rangers, and paladins increases by +1 every level. The base attack bonus for other characters increases at a slower rate. If your character's base attack bonus changes, record it on your character sheet.

3. **Base Save Bonuses:** Like base attack bonuses, base save bonuses improve at varying rates as characters increase in level. Check your character's base save bonuses to see if any of them have increased by +1. Some base save bonuses increase at every even-numbered level; others increase at every level divisible by three.

4. **Skill Points:** Each character gains skill points to spend on skills as detailed in the class section. For class skills, each skill point buys 1 rank, and a character's maximum rank in the skill is his or her level plus 3. For cross-class skills, each skill point only buys a half rank, and the maximum rank in the skill is one-half that of class skills (don't round up or down). See Table 3–2: Experience and Level-Dependent Benefits, page 22.

If you have been maxing out a skill (putting as many skill points into it as possible), you don't have to worry about calculating your maximum rank with it. At each new level, you can always assign 1 skill point—and just 1—to any skill that you're maxing out. (If it's a cross-class skill, this point buys half a rank.)

Your character's Intelligence modifier affects the number of skill points he or she gets at each level (see Table 1–1: Ability Modifiers and Bonus Spells, page 8). This rule represents an intelligent character's ability to learn faster over time (and the slower rate for dim-witted characters), so use the Intelligence score that your character had during his or her previous level. If he or she was *feebleminded* for a short time during the previous level, that doesn't reduce the number of skill points he or she acquires. Likewise, wearing a *headband of intellect* for a short time doesn't grant him or her extra skill points. Only a change in Intelligence that was constant (or very nearly constant) over the previous level affects how many skill points were acquired during that level.

5. **Ability Score:** If your character has just attained 4th, 8th, 12th, 16th, or 20th level, raise one of his or her ability scores by 1 point.

Illus. by J. Foster

Lidda savors the rewards of opening the treasure chest.

Illus. by L. Grant-West

(It's okay for a score to go above 18.) For a multiclass character, it is the overall character level, not the class level, that counts.

If your character's Constitution modifier increases by +1 (see Table 1–1: Ability Modifiers and Bonus Spells, page 8), add +1 to his or her hit point total for every character level lower than the one just attained. For example, if you raise your character's Constitution from 11 to 12 at 4th level, he or she gets +3 hit points. Add these points before rolling for hit points (the next step).

6. **Hit Points:** Roll a Hit Die, add your character's Constitution modifier, and add the total roll to his or her total hit points. Even if he or she has a Constitution penalty and the roll was so low as to yield a result of 0 or fewer hit points, always add at least 1 hit point upon gaining a new level.

7. **Feats:** Upon reaching 3rd level and every third level thereafter (6th, 9th, 12th, 15th, and 18th), you gain one feat of your choice (see Table 5–1: Feats, page 79). As with ability score increases, for multiclass characters it is the overall character level, not the class level, that determines when a character gets a new feat.

8. **Spells:** Spellcasting characters gain the ability to cast more spells as they advance in levels. Each spellcasting class has a "Spells per Day" section on its class table that shows how many spells of a given level a character can cast. See your character's class description in Chapter 3: Classes for details.

9. **Class Features:** Check the table for your class in Chapter 3: Classes for new capabilities you may receive. Many characters gain special attacks or new special powers as they advance in levels.

TREASURE

When characters undertake adventures, they usually end up with some amount of silver, gold, gems, or other treasure. These rewards might be ancient treasures that they have unearthed, the hoards of the villains they have conquered, or pay from a patron who hired the characters to go on the adventure.

Splitting Treasure: Split treasure evenly among the characters who participated. Some characters may be of higher level than others, or some characters might happen to have done more on a particular adventure than others did, but the simplest, fastest, and best policy is to split treasure up evenly.

Special Items: While gems can be cashed in for gold pieces and the coins split evenly among adventurers, some treasures can't be split up so easily. Magic items, for instance, can be sold, but only for half of what they would cost, so it's usually better for characters to keep them. When a character gets a magic item, count half its cost against his or her share of the treasure. For instance, if Jozan, Lidda, Mialee, and Tordek split a treasure of 5,000 gp and a *+1 large steel shield*, the group would count the magic shield as worth 500 gp, roughly half the price someone would have to pay to buy one. Since the treasure is worth 5,500 gp altogether, three characters would each get 1,375 gp, and the fourth character (probably Tordek or Jozan) would get the shield (valued at 500 gp) plus 875 gp in coin.

If more than one character wants a single item, they can bid for it. For example, Jozan and Tordek both want the shield, so they bid over how much they're each willing to "pay" for it. Tordek wins the bid at 800 gp. That means the total treasure is 5,800 gp. Mialee, Jozan, and Lidda each get 1,450 gp, and Tordek gets the shield (800 gp) plus 650 gp.

A character can only bid as much as his share of the treasure would amount to, unless he has extra gold pieces or treasure to

back up the bid. For example, if Tordek had no other treasure from earlier adventures, the most he could bid for the magic shield is 1,250 gp—he would get the shield, and the other three characters would split the 5,000 gp.

If no one is willing to take a special item, the party members should sell it (for half its cost, as listed in the DUNGEON MASTER'S Guide, if they can find a buyer) and split the gold evenly.

Costs: Sometimes characters incur costs on adventures. A character turned to stone by a basilisk may need a *break enchantment* spell cast on him, and it costs at least 450 gp to pay a cleric to cast that spell. (See Table 7–9: Special and Superior Items, page 114. A cleric must be at least 9th level to cast *break enchantment*, which is a 5th-level spell). The default policy is to pay these costs out of the treasure found on the adventure, as a sort of "adventurer's insurance," and then to split whatever's left.

Party Fund: The party may also want to have a pool of money that they can use to buy things that benefit the whole group, such as *potions of healing* or holy water.

Amassing Wealth: When you and your friends have split up the treasure, record your character's share on your character sheet. Soon, you'll have enough gold to buy better weapons and equipment, even magic items.

Gold piece [exact size]

OTHER REWARDS

The other rewards that characters can earn, and there are many, depend more on the characters' actions and the style of campaign that the DM is running. They bear mention, but the rules cannot define them. These rewards develop naturally in the campaign.

REPUTATION

You can't put it in the bank, but many characters enjoy and even pursue fame and notoriety. Someone who seeks a reputation should wear distinctive clothes or armor, should treat bards well, and might even want to invent a personal symbol for signet rings, surcoats, banners, and other forms of display.

FOLLOWERS

When others hear of the characters, they may offer their services as followers. Followers may be apprentices, admirers, henchmen, students, or sidekicks.

If a character stands for some cause, he or she may win followers to the cause as well as personal followers.

LAND

A character (or a party) might gain land through force of arms or be granted a tract of land by a powerful figure. Land brings in revenues appropriate to the type of land (such as taxes on harvests in arable land), and it provides a place for a character (or party) to build a stronghold of some type. In addition to being a base and a safe place, a stronghold can serve as a church, a monastery, a wizards' school, or some other purpose, as the master of the stronghold wishes.

In most settled lands, it is impossible to own land (legally) without some sort of noble or royal title. A character granted land is given at least a nominal title to go with it. Characters who seize a villain's fortress merely have squatter's rights until the rightful owner (assuming it's not the villain!) confirms their prize.

TITLES AND HONORS

High priests, nobles, and royals often acknowledge the services of powerful characters by granting them honors and titles. These awards sometimes come with gifts of gold or land, memberships in elite orders, or with medals, signet rings, diadems, and other symbolic items.

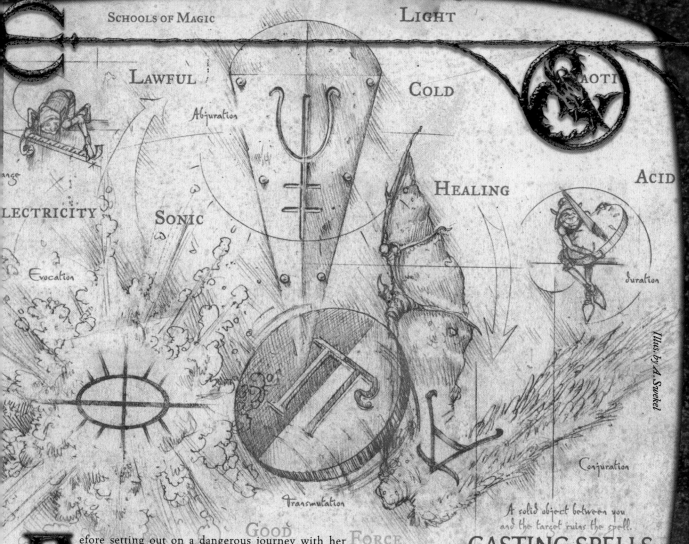

SCHOOLS OF MAGIC

LIGHT

LAWFUL

COLD

CHAOTI

Abjuration

ACID

HEALING

ange

LECTRICITY

SONIC

duration

Evocation

Conjuration

A solid object between you
and the target ruins the spell.

Transmutation

Illus by A. Swekel

GOOD

FORCE

efore setting out on a dangerous journey with her
companions, Mialee, now an accomplished wizard, sits
in her study and opens her spellbook. First she pages
through it, selecting the spells that she thinks will be
most useful on her adventure. When she has chosen the
spells she wants (which could mean choosing the same spell
more than once), she meditates on the pages that describe each
one. The arcane symbols, which she has penned by hand, would
be nonsense to anyone else, but they unlock power from her
mind. As she concentrates, she all but finishes casting each spell
that she prepares. Each spell now lacks only its final triggering
symbol. When she closes the book, her mind is full of spells,
each of which she can complete at will in a brief time. With a
few magical words and gestures, she can win a stranger's friendship, disappear from sight, throw fireballs, or transform an
enemy into a toad.

Spells come in two types: arcane and divine. Wizards, sorcerers, and bards cast arcane spells. Clerics, druids, experienced
paladins, and experienced rangers cast divine spells. Characters
of different classes have different ways of learning and preparing
their spells, but when it comes to casting them, the spells are
very much alike.

Cutting across the categories of arcane and divine spells are
the eight schools of magic. These schools represent the different
ways spells take effect. This chapter describes the differences
among the eight schools of magic. In addition, it provides an
overview of the spell description format combined with an
extensive discussion of how spells work, discusses what
happens when magical effects combine, and explains the differences between certain kinds of special abilities, some of which
are magical.

CASTING SPELLS

Bards, clerics, druids, experienced paladins, experienced
rangers, sorcerers, and wizards all cast spells. Whether the
spells are arcane or divine, and whether the character
prepares them in advance or chooses them on the spot,
casting a spell works the same way.

HOW DOES SPELLCASTING WORK?

Spells work in different ways depending on the type of
spell you're casting. Here are four basic examples.

Charm Person: Tordek is trying to bully some captured
goblin bandits into revealing the whereabouts of their
camp when Mialee casts *charm person* on one of them.
The DM rolls a Will saving throw for him against
Mialee's DC of 13 for her 1st-level spells, and he fails.
Mialee is 1st level, so for the next hour the goblin
regards her as his good friend, and she gets the information out of him.

Summon Monster I: Lidda is fighting a hobgoblin,
and Mialee casts *summon monster I* to conjure a
celestial hound. She can have the hound materialize in any location that she can see within 25 feet,
so she places the creature on the opposite side of
the hobgoblin from Lidda. Flanked, the hobgoblin suffers a sneak attack from Lidda, strikes back
at Lidda and misses, and then is brought down by
the hound (which acts on Mialee's next turn). At the
end of its turn, the hound disappears because the
spell that conjured it lasts only 1 round for a 1st-
level caster.

FEAR

Burning Hands: Nebin, the gnome illusionist, wants to cast *burning hands* on some kobolds, and he wants to hit as many of them as he can. He moves to a spot that puts three kobolds within 10 feet of him, but none next to him, where they might strike him during casting. He chooses a direction and casts his spell. A semicircle of magical flame shoots out 10 feet, catching the three kobolds in its area. Nebin's player rolls 1d4 to see how much damage each kobold takes. He gets a 3. The DM makes a Reflex save (DC 13 for one of Nebin's 1st-level spells) for each kobold, and only one succeeds. The other two take 3 points of damage each and drop. The lucky one takes half damage (1 point) and survives.

CASTING A SPELL

Casting a spell can be a straightforward process, as when Jozan casts *cure light wounds* to remove some of the damage that Tordek has taken, or it can be complicated, as when Jozan is attempting to aim an *insect plague* by ear at a group of nagas who have hidden themselves in a *deeper darkness* spell, all while avoiding the attacks of the naga's troglodyte servants.

Choosing a Spell

First choose which spell to cast. A cleric, druid, experienced paladin, experienced ranger, or wizard selects from among spells prepared earlier in the day and not yet cast (see Preparing Wizard Spells, page 154, and Preparing Divine Spells, page 156). A bard or sorcerer can select any spell he knows, provided the character is capable of casting spells of that level or higher.

To cast a spell, you must be able to speak (if the spell has a verbal component), gesture (if it has a somatic component), and manipulate the material components or focus (if any). Additionally, you must concentrate to cast a spell—and it's hard to concentrate in the heat of battle. (See below for details.)

If a spell has multiple versions, you choose which version to use when you cast it. You don't have to prepare (or learn, in the case of a bard or sorcerer) a specific version of the spell. For example, *endure elements* protects a creature from fire, cold, or other attack forms. You choose when you cast the spell which element it will protect the subject from.

Once you've cast a prepared spell, you can't cast it again until you prepare it again. (If you've prepared multiple copies of a single spell, you can cast each copy once.) If you're a bard or sorcerer, casting a spell counts against your daily limit for spells of that level, but you can cast the same spell again if you haven't reached your limit.

Spell Slots: The various character class tables in Chapter 3: Classes show how many spells of each level a character can cast per day. You always have the option to fill a higher-level spell slot with a lower-level spell. For example, a 7th-level wizard has at least one 4th-level spell slot and two 3rd-level spell slots (see Table 3–20: The Wizard, page 52). However, the character could choose to memorize three 3rd-level spells instead, filling the 4th-level slot with a lower-level spell. Note that a spellcaster who lacks a high enough ability score to cast spells that would otherwise be his or her due still gets the slots but must fill them with spells of lower level. For example, a 9th-level wizard who has an Intelligence of only 14

cannot cast a 5th-level spell but can prepare an extra lower-level spell in its place and store it in the 5th-level spell slot.

Casting Time

You can cast a spell with a casting time of 1 action as a standard action, just like making an attack (see Cast a Spell, page 125).

A spell that takes 1 full round to cast is a full-round action. It comes into effect just before the beginning of your turn in the round after you began casting the spell. You then act normally after the spell is completed. A spell that takes 1 minute to cast comes into effect just before your turn 1 minute later (and for each of those 10 rounds, you are casting a spell as a full-round action).

You must make all pertinent decisions about a spell (range, target, area, effect, version, etc.) when you begin casting. For example, when casting a *summon monster* spell, you need to decide where you want the monster to appear.

Range

A spell's range indicates how far from you it can reach, as defined on the Range line of the spell description. A spell's range is the maximum distance from you that the spell's effect can occur, as well as the maximum distance at which you can designate the spell's point of origin. If any portion of the spell's area would extend beyond the range, that area is wasted. Standard ranges include:

Personal: The spell affects only you.

Touch: You must touch a creature or object to affect it.

Close: The spell can reach up to 25 feet away from you. The maximum range increases by 5 feet for every two full caster levels.

Medium: The spell can reach up to 100 feet + 10 feet per caster level.

Long: The spell can reach up to 400 feet + 40 feet per caster level.

Unlimited: The spell can reach anywhere on the same plane of existence.

Range Expressed in Feet: Some spells have no standard range category, just a range expressed in feet.

Aiming a Spell

You must make some choice about whom the spell is to affect or where the effect is to originate, depending on the type of spell.

Target or Targets: Some spells, such as *charm person*, have a target or targets. You cast these spells directly on creatures or objects, as defined by the spell itself. You must be able to see or touch the target, and you must specifically choose that target. For example, you can't fire a *magic missile* spell (which always hits its target) into a group of bandits with the instruction to strike "the leader." To strike the leader, you must be able to identify and see the leader (or guess which is the leader and get lucky). However, you do not have to select your target until the moment you finish casting the spell.

If you cast a targeted spell on the wrong sort of target, such as casting *charm person* on a dog, the spell has no effect.

If the target of a spell is yourself ("Target: You"), you do not receive a saving throw, and spell resistance does not apply. The Saving Throw and Spell Resistance lines are omitted from such spells.

WHAT IS A SPELL?

A spell is a one-time magical effect. Most spellcasting characters—wizards, clerics, druids, paladins, and rangers—prepare their spells in advance and use them when the time is right. Preparing a spell requires careful reading from a spellbook (for wizards) or devout prayers or meditation (for divine spellcasters). In either case, preparing a spell means casting the first and lengthiest part of it. Only the very end of the

spell, its trigger, remains to be activated. After preparing a spell, the character carries it, nearly cast, in his or her mind, ready for use. To use a spell, the character completes casting it. Spellcasting might require a few special words, specific gestures, a specific item, or any combination of the three. Even though most of the spell was essentially cast ahead of time during the preparation, this final action is known as "casting" the spell.

Effect: Some spells, such as *summon monster* spells, create or summon things rather than affecting things that are already present. You must designate the location where these things are to appear, either by seeing it or defining it (such as "The *insect plague* will appear 20 feet into the area of darkness that the nagas are hiding in"). Range determines how far away an effect can appear, but if the effect is mobile (a summoned monster, for instance) it can move regardless of the spell's range.

Ray: Some effects are rays, such as in the spell *ray of enfeeblement*. You aim a ray as if using a ranged weapon, though typically you make a ranged touch attack rather than a normal ranged attack. As with a ranged weapon, you can fire into the dark or at an invisible creature and hope you hit something. You don't have to see the creature you're trying to hit, as you do with a targeted spell. Intervening creatures and obstacles, however, can block your line of sight or provide cover for the creature you're aiming at.

If a ray spell has a duration, it's the duration of the effect that the ray causes, not the length of time the ray itself persists.

Spread: Some effects, notably clouds and fogs, spread out from a point of origin to a distance described in the spell. The effect can extend around corners and into areas that you can't see. Figure distance by actual distance traveled, taking into account turns the spell effect takes. You must designate the point of origin for such an effect but need not have line of effect to all portions of the effect (see below). Example: *obscuring mist*.

Area: Some spells affect an area. You select where the spell starts, but otherwise you don't control which creatures or objects the spell affects. Sometimes a spell describes a specially defined area, but usually an area falls into one of the categories below.

Burst: As with an effect, you select the spell's point of origin. The spell bursts out from this point, affecting whatever it catches in its area. For instance, if you designate a four-way intersection of corridors to be the point of origin of a *dispel magic* spell, the spell bursts out

in all four directions, possibly catching creatures that you can't see because they're around the corner from you.

A burst spell has a radius that indicates how far from the point of origin the spell's effect extends.

Cone: When you cast a spell with a cone area, the cone shoots away from you in the direction you designate. A cone starts as a point directly before you, and it widens out as it goes. A cone's width at a given distance from you equals that distance. Its far end is as wide as the effect is long. (A 25-foot-long cone is 10 feet wide at 10 feet of its length and 25 wide at its far end.) Example: *cone of cold*.

Creatures: Some spells affect creatures directly (like a targeted spell), but they affect creatures in an area of some kind rather than individual creatures you select. The area might be a burst (such as *sleep*), a cone (such as *fear*), or some other shape.

Many spells affect "living creatures," which means all creatures other than constructs and undead. *Sleep*, for instance, affects living creatures. If you cast *sleep* in the midst of gnolls and skeletons, the *sleep* spell ignores the skeletons and affects the gnolls. The skeletons do not count against the creatures affected.

Cylinder: As with a burst, you select the spell's point of origin. This point is the center of a horizontal circle, and the spell shoots down from the circle, filling a cylinder. Example: *flame strike*.

Emanation: Some spells, such as *silence*, have an area like a burst except that the effect continues to radiate from the point of origin for the duration of the spell.

Objects: Some spells affect objects within an area you select (as above, but affecting objects instead of creatures).

Spread: Some spells spread out like a burst but can turn corners. You select the point of origin, and the spell spreads out a given distance in all directions. Figure distance by actual distance traveled, taking into account turns the spell effect takes. Example: *fireball*.

Spell Area

Holy smite is a 20-foot burst. Jozan's spell can affect even creatures he can't see. In this case #2, #3, and #6 are affected.

With *magic missile*, Mialee can strike up to five creatures, no two of which can be more than 15 feet apart. She does not have a line of effect to #1, and #5 is too far away from #2 and #3.

feet
0   10

Other: A spell can have a unique area, as defined in its description.

(S) Shapeable: If an Area or Effect entry ends with "(S)," you can shape the spell. A shaped effect or area can have no dimension smaller than 10 feet. Many effects or areas are given as cubes to make it easy to model irregular shapes. Three-dimensional volumes are most often needed to define aerial or underwater effects and areas.

Line of Effect: A line of effect is a straight, unblocked path that indicates what a spell can affect. A line of effect is canceled by a solid barrier. It's like line of sight for ranged weapons, except it's not blocked by fog, darkness, and other factors that limit normal sight.

You must have a clear line of effect to any target that you cast a spell on or to any space in which you wish to create an effect (such as conjuring a monster). You must have a clear line of effect to the point of origin of any spell you cast, such as the central point of a *fireball*. For bursts, cones, cylinders, and emanating spells, the spell only affects areas, creatures, or objects to which it has line of effect from its origin (a burst's point, a cone's starting point, a cylinder's circle, or an emanating spell's point of origin).

An otherwise solid barrier with a hole of at least 1 square foot through it does not block a spell's line of effect. Such an opening makes a 5-foot length of wall no longer considered a barrier for purposes of a spell's line of effect (though the rest of the wall farther from the hole can still block the spell).

Saving Throw

Most harmful spells allow an affected creature to make a saving throw to avoid some or all of the effect. The Saving Throw line in a spell description defines which type of saving throw the spell allows and describes how saving throws against the spell work.

Negates: This term means that the spell has no effect on an affected creature that makes a successful saving throw.

Partial: The spell causes an effect on its subject, such as death. A successful saving throw means that some lesser effect occurs (such as being dealt damage rather than being killed).

Half: The spell deals damage, and a successful saving throw halves the damage taken (round down).

None: No saving throw is allowed.

Disbelief: A successful save lets the subject ignore the effect.

(Object): The spell can be cast on objects, which receive saving throws only if they are magical or if they are attended (held, worn, grasped, etc.) by a creature resisting the spell, in which case the object gets the creature's saving throw bonus unless its own bonus is greater. (This notation does not mean that a spell can only be cast on objects. Some spells of this sort can be cast on creatures or objects.) A magic item's saving throw bonuses are each equal to 2 + one-half its caster level.

(Harmless): The spell is usually beneficial, not harmful, but a targeted creature can attempt a saving throw if it wishes.

Saving Throw Difficulty Class: A saving throw against your spell has a DC of 10 + the level of the spell + your bonus for the relevant ability (Intelligence for a wizard, Charisma for a sorcerer or bard, Wisdom for a cleric, druid, paladin, or ranger). A spell's level can vary depending on your class. For example, *fire trap* is a 2nd-level spell for a druid but a 4th-level spell for a sorcerer or wizard. Always use the spell level applicable to your class.

Succeeding at a Saving Throw: A creature that successfully saves against a spell without obvious physical effects feels a hostile force or a tingle, but cannot deduce the exact nature of the attack. For example, if you secretly cast *charm person* on a character and his saving throw succeeds, he knows that someone used magic against him, but he can't tell what you were trying to do. Likewise, if a creature's saving throw succeeds against a targeted spell, such as *charm person*, you sense that the spell has failed. You do not sense when creatures succeed at saving throws against effect and area spells.

Voluntarily Giving Up a Saving Throw: A creature can voluntarily forego a saving throw and willingly accept a spell's result. Even a character with a special resistance to magic (for example, an elf's resistance to sleep effects) can suppress this if he or she wants to.

Items Surviving after a Saving Throw: Unless the descriptive text for the spell specifies otherwise, all items carried and worn are assumed to survive a magical attack. If a character rolls a natural 1 on his saving throw, however, an exposed item is harmed (if the attack can harm objects). The four items nearest the top on Table 10–1: Items Affected by Magical Attacks are the most likely to be struck. Determine which four objects are most likely to be struck and roll randomly among them. The randomly determined item must make a saving throw against the attack form and take whatever damage the attack deals (see Strike an Object, page 135). For instance Tordek is hit by a *lightning bolt*, and gets a natural 1 on his saving throw. The items most likely to have been affected are his shield, his armor, his waraxe, and his stowed shortbow. (He doesn't have a magic helmet or cloak, so those entries are skipped.)

If an item is not carried or worn and is not magical, it does not get a saving throw. It simply is dealt the appropriate damage. Magic item saving throws are covered in the *Dungeon Master's Guide*.

Table 10–1: Items Affected by Magical Attacks

Order*	Item
1st	Shield
2nd	Armor
3rd	Magic helmet
4th	Item in hand (including weapon, wand, etc.)
5th	Magic cloak
6th	Stowed or sheathed weapon
7th	Magic bracers
8th	Magic clothing
9th	Magic jewelry (including rings)
10th	Anything else

*In order of most likely to least likely to be affected.

Spell Resistance

Spell resistance is a special defensive ability. If your spell is being resisted by a creature with spell resistance, you must make a caster level check (1d20 + caster level) at least equal to the creature's spell resistance rating for the spell to affect that creature. The defender's spell resistance rating is like an AC against magical attacks. The *Dungeon Master's Guide* has more details on spell resistance.

The Spell Resistance line and descriptive text of a spell tell you if spell resistance protects creatures from it. In many cases, SR applies only when a resistant creature is targeted by the spell, not when a resistant creature encounters a spell that is already in place.

The terms "Object" and "Harmless" mean the same thing as for saving throws. A creature with spell resistance must voluntarily drop the resistance in order to receive the effects of a spell noted as Harmless without the caster level check described above.

The Spell's Result

Once you know which creatures (or objects or areas) are affected, and whether those creatures have made successful saving throws (if any), you can apply whatever results a spell entails.

Many spells affect particular sorts of creatures. *Repel vermin* keeps "vermin" away, and *calm animals* can calm down "animals, beasts, and magical beasts." These terms, and terms like them, refer to specific creature types that are given for each creature in the *Monster Manual*.

Duration

Once you've determined who's affected and how, you need to know for how long. A spell's Duration line tells you how long the magical energy of the spell lasts.

Timed Durations: Many durations are measured in rounds, minutes, hours, or some other increment. When the time is up, the magic goes away and the spell ends. If a spell's duration is variable, such as for *power word, stun* or *control weather*, the DM rolls it secretly.

Instantaneous: The spell energy comes and goes the instant the spell is cast, though the consequences of the spell might be long-lasting. For example, a *cure light wounds* spell lasts only an instant, but the healing it bestows never runs out or goes away.

Permanent: The energy remains as long as the effect does. This means the spell is vulnerable to *dispel magic*. Example: *secret page*.

Concentration: The spell lasts as long as you concentrate on it. Concentrating to maintain a spell is a standard action that doesn't provoke attacks of opportunity. Anything that could break your concentration when casting a spell can also break your concentration while you're maintaining one, causing the spell to end (see Concentration, below). You can't cast a spell while concentrating on another one. Sometimes a spell lasts for a short time after you cease concentrating. For example, the spell *hypnotic pattern* has a duration of "Concentration + 2 rounds." In these cases, the spell keeps going for the stated length of time after you stop concentrating. Otherwise, you must concentrate to maintain the spell, but you can't maintain it for more than a stated duration in any event.

Subjects, Effects, and Areas: If the spell affects creatures directly (for example, *charm person* or *sleep*), the result travels with the subjects for the spell's duration. If the spell creates an effect, the effect lasts for the duration. The effect might move (such as a summoned monster chasing your enemies) or remain still. Such effects can be destroyed prior to when their durations end (such as *fog cloud* being dispersed by wind). If the spell affects an area, such as *silence* does, then the spell stays with that area for the spell's duration. Creatures become subject to the spell when they enter the area and become no longer subject to it when they leave.

Touch Spells and Holding the Charge: If you don't discharge a touch spell on the round you cast the spell, you can hold the discharge of the spell (hold the charge) indefinitely. You can make touch attacks round after round. You can touch one friend (or yourself) as a standard action or up to six friends as a full-round action. If you touch anything with your hand while holding a charge, the spell discharges. If you cast another spell, the touch spell dissipates.

Discharge: A few spells last for a set duration or until triggered or discharged. For instance, *magic mouth* waits until triggered, and the spell ends once the mouth has said its message.

(D): If the Duration line ends with "(D)," you can dismiss the spell at will. You must be within range of the spell's effect and must speak words of dismissal, which are usually a modified form of the spell's verbal component. If the spell has no verbal component, you dismiss the spell with a gesture. Dismissing a spell is a standard action that does not provoke attacks of opportunity. A spell that depends on concentration is dismissible by its very nature, and dismissing it does not require an action (since all you have to do to end the spell is to stop concentrating).

COMPONENTS

As mentioned above, a spell's components are what you must do or possess to cast it. A spell's Components line includes abbreviations that tell you what type of components it has. Specifics for material, focus, and XP components are given at the end of the descriptive text. Usually you don't worry about components, but when you can't use a component for some reason or when a material or focus component is expensive, then they count.

V (Verbal): A verbal component is a spoken incantation. To provide a verbal component, you must be able to speak in a strong voice. A *silence* spell or a gag spoils the incantation (and thus the spell). A spellcaster who has been deafened has a 20% chance to spoil any spell he tries to cast if that spell has a verbal component.

S (Somatic): A somatic component is a measured and precise movement of the hand or some other part of the body. You must have at least one hand free to provide a somatic component.

M (Material): A material component is a physical substance or object that is annihilated by the spell energies in the casting process. Unless a cost is given for a material component, the cost is negligible. Don't bother to keep track of material components with negligible cost. Assume you have all you need as long as you have your spell component pouch.

F (Focus): A focus component is a prop of some sort. Unlike a material component, a focus is not consumed when the spell is cast and can be reused. As with material components, the cost for a focus is negligible unless a specific price is listed. Assume that focus components of negligible cost are in your spell component pouch.

DF (Divine Focus): A divine focus component is an item of spiritual significance. The divine focus for a cleric or a paladin is a holy symbol appropriate to the character's faith. For an evil cleric, the divine focus is an unholy symbol. The default divine focus for a druid or a ranger is a sprig of mistletoe or some holly.

If the Components line includes F/DF or M/DF, the arcane version of the spell has a focus component or a material component and the divine version has a divine focus component.

XP (XP Cost): Some powerful spells (*wish, commune, miracle*) entail an experience point (XP) cost to you. No spell, not even *restoration*, can restore the lost XP. You cannot spend so much XP that you lose a level, so you cannot cast the spell unless you have enough XP to spare. However, you may, on gaining enough XP to attain a new level, use the XP for casting a spell rather than keeping the XP and advancing a level. The XP are treated just like a material component—expended when you cast the spell, whether or not the casting succeeds.

CONCENTRATION

To cast a spell, you must concentrate. If something interrupts your concentration while you're casting, you must make a Concentration check or lose the spell. The more distracting the interruption and the higher the level of the spell you are trying to cast, the higher the DC is. (The DC depends partly on the spell level because more powerful spells require more mental effort.) If you fail the check, you lose the spell just as if you had cast it to no effect.

Injury: Getting hurt or being affected by hostile magic while trying to cast a spell can break your concentration and ruin a spell. If while trying to cast a spell you take damage, fail a saving throw, or are otherwise successfully assaulted, you must make a Concentration check. The DC is 10 + points of damage taken + the level of the spell you're casting. If you fail the check, you lose the spell without effect. The interrupting event strikes during spellcasting if it comes between when you start and complete a spell (for a spell with a casting time of 1 full round or more) or if it comes in response to your casting the spell (such as an attack of opportunity provoked by the spell or a contingent attack, such as a readied action).

If you are taking continuous damage, such as from *Melf's acid arrow*, half the damage is considered to take place while you are casting a spell. You must make a Concentration check (DC 10 + one-half the damage that the continuous source last dealt + the level of the spell you're casting). If the last damage dealt was the last damage that the effect could deal (such as the last round of a *Melf's acid arrow*), then the damage is over, and it does not distract you. Repeated damage, such as from a *spiritual weapon*, does not count as continuous damage.

Spell: If you are affected by a spell while attempting to cast a spell of your own, you must make a Concentration check or lose the spell you are casting. If the spell affecting you deals damage, the DC is 10 + points of damage + the level of the spell you're casting. If the spell interferes with you or distracts you in some other way, the DC is the spell's saving throw DC + the level of the spell you're casting. For spells with no saving throw, it's the DC that the spell's saving throw would have if it did allow a saving throw.

Grappling or Pinned: The only spells you can cast while grappling or pinned are those without somatic components and whose material components (if any) you have in hand. Even so, you must make a Concentration check (DC 20 + the level of the spell you're casting) or lose the spell.

Vigorous Motion: If you are riding on a moving mount, taking a bouncy ride in a wagon, on a small boat in rough water, belowdecks in a storm-tossed ship, or simply being jostled in a similar fashion, you must make a Concentration check (DC 10 + the level of the spell you're casting) or lose the spell.

Violent Motion: If you are on a galloping horse, taking a very rough ride in a wagon, on a small boat in rapids or in a storm, on deck in a storm-tossed ship, or being tossed roughly about in a similar fashion, you must make a Concentration check (DC 15 + the level of the spell you're casting) or lose the spell.

Violent Weather: If you are in a high wind carrying blinding rain or sleet, the DC is 5 + the level of the spell you're casting. If you are in wind-driven hail, dust, or debris, the DC is 10 + the level of the spell you're casting. You lose the spell if you fail the Concentration check. If the weather is caused by a spell, use the rules in the Spell subsection above.

Casting Defensively: If you want to cast a spell without provoking any attacks of opportunity, you need to dodge and weave. You must make a Concentration check (DC 15 + the level of the spell you're casting) to succeed. You lose the spell if you fail.

Entangled: If you want to cast a spell while entangled in a net or by a tanglefoot bag (page 114) or affected by a spell with similar effects (*animate rope, command plants, control plants, entangle,* or *snare*), you must make a Concentration check (DC 15) to cast the spell. You lose the spell if you fail.

COUNTERSPELLS

It is possible to cast any spell as a counterspell. By doing so, you are using the spell's energy to disrupt the casting of the same spell by another character. Counterspelling works even if one spell is divine and the other arcane.

How Counterspells Work: To use a counterspell, you must select an opponent as the target of the counterspell. You do this by choosing the ready action (page 134). In doing so, you elect to wait to complete your action until your opponent tries to cast a spell. (You may still move your speed, since ready is a standard action.)

If the target of your counterspell tries to cast a spell, make a Spellcraft check (DC 15 + the spell's level). This check is a free action. If the check succeeds, you correctly identify the opponent's spell and can attempt to counter it. (If the check fails, you can't do either of these things.)

To complete the action, you must cast the correct spell. As a general rule, a spell can only counter itself. For example, a *fireball* spell is effective as a counter to another *fireball* spell, but not to any other spell, no matter how similar. *Fireball* cannot counter *delayed blast fireball* or vice versa. If you are able to cast the same spell and have it prepared (if you prepare spells), you cast it, altering it slightly to create a counterspell effect. If the target is within range, both spells automatically negate each other with no other results.

Counterspelling Metamagic Spells: Metamagic feats are not taken into account when determining whether a spell can be countered. For example, a normal *fireball* can counter a maximized *fireball* (that is, a *fireball* that has been enhanced by the metamagic feat Maximize Spell) and vice versa.

Specific Exceptions: Some spells specifically counter each other, especially when they have diametrically opposed effects. For example, you can counter a *haste* spell with a *slow* spell as well as with another *haste* spell, or *reduce* with *enlarge.*

***Dispel Magic* as a Counterspell:** You can use *dispel magic* to counterspell another spellcaster, and you don't need to identify the spell he or she is casting. However, *dispel magic* doesn't always work as a counterspell (see *dispel magic,* page 196).

CASTER LEVEL

A spell's power often depends on its caster level, which is generally equal to your class level. For example, a *fireball* deals 1d6 points of damage per caster level (to a maximum of 10d6), so a 10th-level wizard can cast a more powerful *fireball* than a 5th-level wizard can.

You can cast a spell at a lower caster level than normal, but the caster level must be high enough for you to cast the spell in question, and all level-dependent features must be based on the same caster level. For example, at 10th level, Mialee can cast a *fireball* to a range of 800 feet for 10d6 points of damage. If she wishes, she can cast a *fireball* that deals less damage by casting the spell at a lower caster level, but she must reduce the range according to the selected caster level, and she can't cast *fireball* with a caster level lower than 5th (the minimum level required for a wizard to cast *fireball*). Hennet, a sorcerer, can't cast a *fireball* with a caster level lower than 6th (the minimum level required for a sorcerer to cast *fireball*).

SPELL FAILURE

If you ever try to cast a spell in conditions where the characteristics of the spell (range, area, etc.) cannot be made to conform, the casting fails and the spell is wasted. For example, if you cast *charm person* on a dog (even a dog polymorphed into a human), the spell fails because a dog is the wrong sort of target for the spell.

Spells also fail if your concentration is broken (see Concentration, page 151) and might fail if you're wearing armor while casting a spell with somatic components (see Table 7–5: Armor, page 104).

SPECIAL SPELL EFFECTS

Many special spell effects are handled according to the school of the spells in question. For example, illusory figments all have certain effects in common (see Schools of Magic, page 156). Certain other special spell features are found across spell schools.

Attacks: Some spells refer to attacking. For instance, *invisibility* is dispelled if you attack anyone or anything while under its effects. All offensive combat actions, even those that don't damage opponents, such as disarm and bull rush, are attacks. Attempts to turn or rebuke undead count as attacks. All spells that opponents resist with saving throws, that deal damage, or that otherwise harm or hamper subjects are attacks. *Summon monster I* and similar spells are not attacks because such spells bring combatants to you, but the spells themselves don't harm anyone.

Bonus Types: Many spells give their subjects bonuses on ability scores, Armor Class, attacks, and other attributes. Each bonus has a type that indicates how the spell grants the bonus. For example, *mage armor* grants an armor bonus to AC, indicating that the spell creates a tangible barrier around you. *Shield of faith*, on the other hand, grants a deflection bonus to AC, which makes attacks veer off. (Bonus types are covered in detail in the DUNGEON MASTER's *Guide.*) The important aspect of bonus types is that two bonuses of the same type don't generally stack. With the exception of dodge bonuses, most circumstance bonuses, and bonuses granted by a suit of armor and a shield used in conjunction by a creature, only the better bonus works (see Combining Magical Effects, page 153). The same principle applies to penalties—a character suffering two or more penalties of the same type applies only the worst one.

Descriptors: Some spells have descriptors indicating something about how the spell functions. For example, *charm person* is a mind-affecting spell (as noted in the line beneath the spell name). Most of these descriptors have no game effect by themselves, but they govern how the spell interacts with other spells, with special abilities, with unusual creatures, with alignment, and so on. For instance, the bard's countersong supernatural ability (page 28) only works against language-dependent or sonic spells.

The descriptors are acid, chaotic, cold, darkness, death, electricity, evil, fear, fire, force, good, language-dependent, lawful, light, mind-affecting, sonic, and teleportation.

A language-dependent spell uses intelligible language as a medium. For instance, a cleric's *command* spell fails if the target can't understand what the cleric says, either because she doesn't understand the language the cleric is speaking or because background noise prevents her from hearing what the cleric says.

Bringing Back the Dead: Several spells have the power to restore slain characters to life. Divine spells are better at reviving the dead than arcane spells are.

When a living creature dies, its soul departs the body, leaves the Material Plane, travels through the Astral Plane, and goes to abide on the plane where the creature's deity resides. If the creature did not worship a deity, its soul departs to the plane corresponding to its alignment. Bringing someone back from the dead means retrieving his or her soul and returning it to his or her body.

Level Loss: The passage from life to death and back again is a wrenching journey for a being's soul. Consequently, any creature brought back to life usually loses one level of experience. The character's new XP total is midway between the minimum needed for his or her new level and the minimum needed for the next one. If the character was 1st level, he or she loses 1 point of Constitution instead of losing a level. This level loss or Constitution loss cannot be repaired by any mortal spell, even *wish* or *miracle*. Still, the revived character can improve his or her Constitution normally (at 4th, 8th, 12th, 16th, and 20th level) and earn experience by further adventuring to regain the lost level.

Preventing Revivification: Enemies can take steps to make it more difficult for a character to be returned from the dead. Keeping the body prevents others from using *raise dead* or *resurrection* to restore the slain character to life. Casting *trap the soul* prevents any sort of revivification unless the soul is first released.

Revivification Against One's Will: A soul cannot be returned to life if it does not wish to be. A soul knows the name, alignment, and patron deity (if any) of the character attempting to revive it and may refuse to return on that basis. For example, if Alhandra the paladin is slain and her archenemy, a high priest of Nerull, god of death, grabs her body, Alhandra probably does not wish to be raised from the dead by him. Any attempts he makes to revive her automatically fail.

If the evil cleric wants to revive Alhandra to interrogate her, he needs to find some way to trick her soul, such as duping a good cleric into raising her and then capturing her once she's alive again.

Jozan brings a friend back from the dead.

COMBINING MAGICAL EFFECTS

Spells or magical effects usually work as described, no matter how many other spells or magical effects happen to be operating in the same area or on the same recipient. Except in special cases, a spell does not affect the way another spell operates. Whenever a spell has a specific effect on other spells, the spell description explains the effect. Several other general rules apply when spells or magical effects operate in the same place:

Stacking Effects: Spells that give bonuses or penalties to attack rolls, damage rolls, saving throws, and other attributes usually do not stack with themselves. For example, two *bless* spells don't give recipients twice the benefits of one *bless*. Both *bless* spells, however, continue to act simultaneously, and if one ends first, the other one continues to operate for the remainder of its duration. Likewise, two *haste* spells do not make a creature doubly fast.

More generally, two bonuses of the same type don't stack even if they come from different spells (or from effects other than spells). For example, the enhancement bonus to Strength from a *bull's strength* spell and the enhancement bonus to Strength from a *divine power* spell don't stack. You use whichever bonus gives you the better Strength score. In the same way, a *belt of giant strength* gives you an enhancement bonus to Strength, which does not stack with the bonus you get from a *bull's strength* spell.

Different Bonus Names: The bonuses or penalties from two different spells do stack, however, if the effects are of different types. For example, *bless* provides a +1 morale bonus on saves against fear effects, and *protection from evil* provides a +2 resistance bonus to saving throws against spells cast by evil creatures. A character under the influence of a *bless* spell and a *protection from evil* spell gets a +1 bonus against all fear effects, a +2 bonus against spells cast by evil beings, and a +3 bonus against *fear* spells cast by evil creatures.

A bonus that isn't named (just a "+2 bonus" rather than a "+2 resistance bonus") stacks with any named bonus or any other unnamed one.

Same Effect More than Once in Different Strengths: In cases when two or more identical spells are operating in the same area, but at different strengths, only the best one applies. For example, if a character adds 3 to his Strength score from a *bull's strength* spell and then receives a second *bull's strength* spell that adds 5 to his Strength score, the character receives only the 5. Both spells are still operating on the character, however. If one *bull's strength* spell is dispelled or its duration runs out, the other *bull's strength* spell takes over (assuming its duration has not yet expired).

Same Effect with Differing Results: The same spell can sometimes produce varying effects if applied to the same recipient more than once. For example, a series of *polymorph other* spells might turn a creature into a mouse, a lion, and then a snail. In this case, the last spell in the series trumps the others. None of the previous spells are actually removed or dispelled, but their effects become irrelevant while the final spell in the series lasts.

One Effect Makes Another Irrelevant: Sometimes, one spell can render a later spell irrelevant. For example, if a wizard is using a *polymorph self* spell to take the shape of an eagle, a *polymorph other* spell could change the wizard into a goldfish. The *polymorph self* spell is not negated, however, and since the *polymorph other* spell has no effect on the recipient's mind, the wizard could use the *polymorph self* effect to resume the form of an eagle (or any other form the spell allows) whenever he or she desires. If a creature using a *polymorph self* effect is petrified by a *flesh to stone* spell, however, it becomes a mindless, inert statue, and the *polymorph self* effect cannot help it escape.

Multiple Mental Control Effects: Sometimes magical effects that establish mental control render each other irrelevant. For example, a *hold person* effect renders any other form of mental control irrelevant because it robs the *held* character of the ability to move. Mental controls that don't remove the recipient's ability to act usually do not interfere with each other. For example, a person who has received a *geas/quest* spell can also be subjected to a *charm person* spell. The *charmed* person remains committed to fulfilling the quest, however, and resists any order that interferes with the quest. In this case, the *geas/quest* spell doesn't negate the *charm person* but reduces its effectiveness (just as nonmagical devotion to a quest would). If a creature is under the mental control of two or more creatures, it tends to obey each to the best of its ability (and to the extent of the control each effect allows). If the controlled creature receives conflicting orders simultaneously, the competing controllers must make opposed Charisma checks to determine which one the creature obeys.

Spells with Opposite Effects: Spells that have opposite effects apply normally, with all bonuses, penalties, or changes accruing in the order that they apply. For example, if a creature 6 feet tall is polymorphed into a 9-foot-tall ogre and then receives a *reduce* spell that makes it shrink by 50%, it becomes 4 1/2 feet tall. Some spells negate or counter each other completely. For example, a *slow* spell negates a *haste* spell and vice versa. This is a special effect that is noted in a spell's description.

Instantaneous Effects: Two or more magical effects with instantaneous durations work cumulatively when they affect the same object, place, or creature. For example, when two *fireballs* strike the same creature, the creature must attempt a saving throw against each *fireball* and takes damage from each according to the saving throws' results. If the same creature receives two *cure light wounds* spells in a later round, both work normally.

ARCANE SPELLS

Wizards, sorcerers, and bards cast arcane spells. Arcane spells involve the direct manipulation of mystic energies. These manipulations require natural talent (in the case of sorcerers), long study (in the case of wizards), or both (in the case of bards). Compared to divine spells, arcane spells are more likely to produce dramatic results, such as flight, explosions, or transformations. What arcane spells do poorly is heal wounds.

PREPARING WIZARD SPELLS

Before setting out on an adventure with her companions, Mialee (at 1st level) pores over her spellbook and prepares two 1st-level spells (one for being a 1st-level wizard and an additional one as her 1st-level bonus spell for Intelligence 15) and three 0-level spells. (Arcane spellcasters often call their 0-level spells "cantrips.") From the spells in her spellbook, she chooses *charm person, sleep, detect magic* (twice), and *light*. While traveling, she and her party are attacked by gnoll raiders, and she casts her *sleep* spell. After she and her companions have dispatched the gnolls, she casts *detect magic* to see whether any of the gnolls' items are enchanted. (They're not.) The party then camps for the night in the wilderness. Come morning, Mialee can once again prepare spells from her spellbook. She already has *charm person, detect magic* (once), and *light* prepared from the day before. She chooses to abandon her *light* spell and then prepare *sleep, detect magic,* and *ghost sound.* It takes her a little over half an hour to prepare these spells because they represent a little over half of her daily capacity.

A wizard's level limits the number of spells she can prepare and cast (see Table 3–20: The Wizard, page 52). A wizard's high Intelligence score (see Table 1–1: Ability Modifiers and Bonus Spells, page 8) might allow her to prepare a few extra spells. She can prepare the same spell more than once, but each preparation counts as one spell toward her daily limit. Preparing arcane spells is an arduous mental task. To do so, the wizard must have an Intelligence score of at least 10 plus the spell's level.

Rest: To prepare her daily spells, a wizard must have a clear mind. To clear her mind, the wizard must first sleep for 8 hours. The character does not have to slumber for every minute of the time, but she must refrain from movement, combat, spellcasting, skill use, conversation, or any other fairly demanding physical or mental task during the rest period. If the wizard's rest is interrupted, each interruption adds 1 hour to the total amount of time she has to rest in order to clear her mind, and the wizard must have at least 1 hour of rest immediately prior to preparing her spells. If the character does not need to sleep for some reason, she still must have 8 hours of restful calm before preparing any spells. For example, elven wizards need 8 hours of rest to clear their minds even though they need only 4 hours of trance to refresh their bodies (so they could trance for 4 hours and rest for 4 hours and then prepare spells).

Recent Casting Limit/Rest Interruptions: If a wizard has cast spells recently, the drain on her resources reduces her capacity to prepare new spells. When she prepares spells for the coming day, all spells she has cast within the last 8 hours count against her daily limit. If Mialee can normally cast two 1st-level spells a day, but she had to cast *magic missile* during the night, she can only prepare one 1st-level spell the next day.

Preparation Environment: To prepare any spell, the wizard must have enough peace, quiet, and comfort to allow for proper concentration. The wizard's surroundings need not be luxurious, but they must be free from overt distractions, such as combat raging nearby or other loud noises. Exposure to inclement weather prevents the necessary concentration, as does any injury or failed saving throw the character might suffer while studying. Wizards also must have access to their spellbooks to study from and sufficient light to read them by. One major exception: A wizard can prepare a *read magic* spell even without a spellbook. A great portion of a wizard's initial training goes into mastering this minor but vital feat of magic.

Spell Preparation Time: After resting, a wizard must study her spellbook to prepare any spells that day. If the character wants to prepare all her spells, the process takes 1 hour. Preparing some smaller portion of her daily capacity takes a proportionally smaller amount of time, but always at least 15 minutes, the minimum time required to achieve the proper mental state.

Spell Selection and Preparation: Until she prepares spells from her spellbook, the only spells a wizard has available to cast are the ones that she already had prepared from the previous day and has not yet used. During the study period, a wizard chooses which spells to prepare. The act of preparing a spell is actually the first step in casting it. A spell is designed in such a way that it has an interruption point near its end. This allows a wizard to cast most of the spell ahead of time and finish the spell when it's needed, even if the character is under considerable pressure. The wizard's spellbook serves as a guide to the mental exercises the wizard must perform to create the spell's effect. If a wizard already has spells prepared (from the previous day) that she has not cast, she can abandon some or all of them to make room for new spells.

When preparing spells for the day, the wizard can leave some spell slots open. Later during that day, the wizard can repeat the preparation process as often as she likes, time and circumstances permitting. During these extra sessions of preparation, a wizard can fill these unused spell slots. She cannot, however, abandon a previously prepared spell to replace it with another one or fill a slot that is empty because she has cast a spell in the meantime. That sort of preparation requires a mind fresh from rest. Like the first session of the day, this preparation takes at least 15 minutes, and it takes longer if the wizard prepares more than one-quarter of her spells.

Prepared Spell Retention: Once a wizard prepares a spell, it remains in her mind as a nearly cast spell until she uses the prescribed components to complete and trigger it (or until she abandons it). Upon casting, the spell's energy is expended and purged from the character, leaving her feeling a little tired. Certain other events, such as the effects of magic items or special attacks from monsters, can wipe a prepared spell from a character's mind.

Death and Prepared Spell Retention: If the character dies, all spells stored in her mind are wiped away. Potent magic (such as *raise dead, resurrection,* or *true resurrection*) can recover the lost energy when it recovers the character.

ARCANE MAGICAL WRITINGS

To record an arcane spell in written form, a character uses complex notation that describes the magical forces involved in the spell. The notation constitutes a universal arcane language that wizards have discovered, not invented. The writer uses the same system no matter what her native language or culture. However, each character uses the system in her own way. Another person's magical writing remains incomprehensible to even the most powerful wizard until she takes time to study and decipher it.

To decipher an arcane magical writing (such as a single spell in written form in another's spellbook or on a scroll), a character must make a successful Spellcraft check (DC 20 + the spell's level). If the skill check fails, the character cannot attempt to read that particular spell until the next day. A *read magic* spell automatically deciphers a magical writing without a skill check. If the person who created the magical writing is on hand to help the reader, success is also automatic.

Once a character deciphers a particular magical writing, she does not need to decipher it again. Deciphering a magical writing allows the reader to identify the spell and gives some idea of its effects (as explained in the spell description). If the magical writing was a scroll and the reader can cast arcane spells, she can attempt to use the scroll (see the information on scrolls in the *Dungeon Master's Guide*).

Wizard Spells and Borrowed Spellbooks

A wizard can use a borrowed spellbook to prepare a spell she already knows and has recorded in her own spellbook, but preparation success is not assured. First, the wizard must decipher the writing in the book (see Arcane Magical Writings, above). Once a spell from another spellcaster's book is deciphered, the reader must make a successful Spellcraft check (DC 15 + spell's level) to prepare the spell. If the check succeeds, the wizard can prepare the spell. She must repeat the check to prepare the spell again, no matter how many times she has prepared the spell before. If the check fails, she cannot try to prepare the spell from the same source again until the next day. (However, as explained above, she does not need to repeat a check to decipher the writing.)

Adding Spells to a Wizard's Spellbook

Wizards can add new spells to their spellbooks through several methods. If a wizard has chosen to specialize in a school of magic, she can learn spells only from schools she can cast.

Spells Gained at a New Level: Wizards perform a certain amount of spell research between adventures. Each time a wizard achieves a new level, she gains two spells of her choice to add to her spellbook. These spells represent the results of her research. The two free spells must be of levels the wizard can cast. If she has chosen to specialize in a school of magic, one of the two free spells must be from the wizard's specialty school.

Spells Copied from Another's Spellbook or a Scroll: A wizard can also add spells to her book whenever she encounters a new spell on a magic scroll or in another wizard's spellbook. No matter what the spell's source, the character must first decipher the magical writing (see Arcane Magical Writings, above). Next, the wizard must spend a day studying the spell. At the end of the day, the character must make a Spellcraft check (DC 15 + spell's level). A wizard who has specialized in a school of spells gains a +2 bonus to the check if the new spell is from her specialty school. She cannot, however, learn any spells from her prohibited schools.

If the check succeeds, the wizard understands the spell and can copy it into her spellbook (see Writing a New Spell into a Spellbook, below). The process leaves a spellbook that was copied from unharmed, but a spell successfully copied from a magic scroll disappears from the scroll.

If the check fails, the wizard cannot understand the spell and cannot attempt to learn it again even if she studies it from another source until she gains another rank in Spellcraft. If the check fails, the character cannot copy the spell from another's spellbook, and the spell does not vanish from the scroll.

Independent Research: A wizard also can research a spell independently, duplicating an existing spell or creating an entirely new one. The *Dungeon Master's Guide* has information on this topic.

Writing a New Spell into a Spellbook

Once a wizard understands a new spell, she can record it into her spellbook.

Time: The process requires 1 day plus 1 additional day per spell level. Zero-level spells require 1 day.

Space in the Spellbook: A spell takes up 2 pages of the spellbook per spell level (so a 2nd-level spell takes 4 pages, a 5th-level spell takes 10 pages, and so forth). A 0-level spell (cantrip) takes but a single page. A spellbook has 100 pages.

Materials and Costs: Materials for writing the spell (special quills, inks, and other supplies) cost 100 gp per page.

Note that a wizard does not have to pay these costs in time or gold for the spells she gains for free at each new level. The wizard adds these to her spellbook as part of her ongoing research.

Replacing and Copying Spellbooks

A wizard can use the procedure for learning a spell to reconstruct a lost spellbook. If she already has a particular spell prepared, she can write it directly into a new book at a cost of 100 gp per page (as noted in Writing a New Spell into a Spellbook). The process wipes the prepared spell from her mind, just as casting it would. If she does not have the spell prepared, she can prepare it from a borrowed spellbook and then write it into a new book.

Duplicating an existing spellbook uses the same procedure as replacing it, except that the task is much easier. The time requirement and cost per page are halved.

SORCERERS AND BARDS

Sorcerers and bards cast arcane spells, but they do not have spellbooks and do not prepare spells. A sorcerer's or bard's level limits the number of spells he can cast (see these class descriptions in Chapter 3: Classes). A sorcerer's or bard's high Charisma score (see Table 1–1: Ability Modifiers and Bonus Spells, page 8) might allow him to cast a few extra spells. Members of either class must have a Charisma score of at least 10 + a spell's level to cast the spell.

Daily Readying of Spells: Each day, sorcerers and bards must focus their minds on the task of casting their spells. A sorcerer or bard needs 8 hours of rest (just like a wizard), after which he spends 15 minutes concentrating. A bard must sing or play an instrument of some kind while concentrating. During this period, the sorcerer or bard readies his mind to cast his daily allotment of spells. Without such a period to refresh himself, the character does not regain the spell slots he used up the day before.

For example, at 7th level, Devis the bard can cast one 3rd-level spell (a bonus spell due to his 16 Charisma). If he casts his 3rd-level spell, he can't use it again until the next day—after he readies his spells for the day.

Recent Casting Limit: As with wizards, any spells cast within the last 8 hours count against the sorcerer's or bard's daily limit.

Adding Spells to a Sorcerer's or Bard's Repertoire: Sorcerers and bards gain spells each time they attain new experience levels and never gain spells any other way. When you gain a new level, consult Table 3–5: Bard Spells Known or Table 3–17: Sorcerer Spells Known to learn how many spells from the appropriate spell list in Chapter 11: Spells you now know. With the DM's permission, sorcerers and bards can also select the spells they gain from new and unusual spells that they have gained some understanding of (see Spells in the sorcerer description, page 50).

For instance, when Hennet the sorcerer becomes 2nd level, he gains an additional 0-level spell. He can pick that spell from the 0-level spells on the sorcerer and wizard spell list, or he might have learned an unusual spell from an arcane scroll or spellbook.

DIVINE SPELLS

Clerics, druids, experienced paladins, and experienced rangers can cast divine spells. Unlike arcane spells, divine spells draw power from a divine source. Clerics gain spell power from deities or from divine forces. The divine force of nature powers druid and ranger spells. The divine forces of law and good power paladin spells. Divine spells tend to be less flashy, destructive, and disruptive than arcane spells. What they do better than arcane spells is heal.

PREPARING DIVINE SPELLS

Divine spellcasters prepare their spells in largely the same manner as wizards, but with a few differences. The relevant ability for divine spells is Wisdom. To prepare a divine spell, a character must have a Wisdom score of 10 + the spell's level. For example, a cleric or druid must have a Wisdom score of at least 10 to prepare a 0-level spell and a Wisdom score of 11 to prepare a 1st-level spell. (Divine spellcasters often call their 0-level spells "orisons.") Likewise, bonus spells are based on Wisdom. Other differences include:

Time of Day: A divine spellcaster chooses and prepares spells ahead of time, just as a wizard does. However, divine spellcasters do not require a period of rest to prepare spells. Instead, the character chooses a particular part of the day to pray and receive spells. The time usually is associated with some daily event. Dawn, dusk, noon, or midnight are common choices. Some deities set the time or impose other special conditions for granting spells to their clerics. If some event prevents the character from praying at the proper time, he must do so as soon as possible. If the character does not stop to pray for spells at the first opportunity, he must wait until the next day to prepare spells.

Spell Selection and Preparation: A divine spellcaster selects and prepares spells ahead of time through prayer and meditation at a particular time of day. The time required to prepare spells is the same as for a wizard (1 hour), as is the requirement for a relatively peaceful environment in which to perform the preparation. A divine spellcaster does not have to prepare all his spells at once. However, the character's mind is only considered fresh during his first daily spell preparation, so he cannot fill a slot that is empty because he has cast a spell or abandoned a previously prepared spell. However, he can

spontaneously cast *cure* or *inflict* spells in place of certain prepared spells (see Spontaneous Casting of *Cure* and *Inflict* Spells, below).

Divine spellcasters do not require spellbooks. However, a character's spell selection is limited to the spells on the list for his class (see Chapter 11: Spells). Clerics, druids, paladins, and rangers have separate spell lists. Clerics also have access to two domains determined during their character creation. Each domain gives a cleric access to a domain spell at each spell level, as well as a special granted power. With access to two domain spells at each given spell level—one from each of his two domains—a cleric must prepare, as an extra domain spell, one or the other each day for each level of spell he can cast. (The extra domain spell is the "+1" that appears as part of the cleric's Spells per Day figure on Table 3–6: The Cleric, page 30.) If a domain spell is not on the Cleric Spells List, it can only be prepared in a domain slot.

Recent Casting Limit: As with arcane spells, at the time of preparation any spells cast within the previous 8 hours count against the number of spells that can be prepared.

Spontaneous Casting of *Cure* and *Inflict* Spells: A good cleric (or a cleric of a good deity) can spontaneously cast a *cure* spell in place of a prepared spell of the same level or higher, but not in place of an extra domain spell. An evil cleric (or a cleric of an evil deity) can spontaneously cast an *inflict* spell in place of a prepared nondomain spell of the same level or higher. Each neutral cleric of a neutral deity either spontaneously casts *cure* spells like a good cleric or *inflict* spells like an evil one, depending on which option the player chooses when creating the character. The divine energy of the spell that the *cure* or *inflict* spell substitutes for is converted into the *cure* or *inflict* spell as if that spell had been prepared all along.

DIVINE MAGICAL WRITINGS

Divine spells can be written down and deciphered just as arcane spells can (see Arcane Magical Writings, above). Any character with the Spellcraft skill can attempt to decipher the divine magical writing and identify it. However, only characters who have the spell in question (in its divine form) on their class-based spell lists can cast a divine spell from a scroll.

NEW DIVINE SPELLS

Divine spellcasters most frequently gain new spells in one of the following two ways:

Spells Gained at a New Level: Characters who can cast divine spells undertake a certain amount of study of divine magic between adventures. Each time a character receives a new level of divine spells, he learns new spells from that level automatically.

Independent Research: The character also can research a spell independently, much as an arcane spellcaster can. (The DUNGEON MASTER's Guide has information on this topic.) Only the creator of such a spell can prepare and cast it, unless he decides to share it with others. Some such creators share their research with their churches, but others do not. The character can create a magic scroll (provided he has the Scribe Scroll feat) or write a special text similar to a spellbook to contain spells he has independently researched. Other divine spellcasters who find the spell in written form can learn to cast it, provided they are of sufficient level to do so and are of the same class as the creator. The process requires deciphering the writing (see Arcane Magical Writings, above).

SCHOOLS OF MAGIC

Almost every spell belongs to one of eight schools of magic. A school of magic is a group of related spells that work in similar ways. A small number of spells (*detect magic*, *read magic*, and *wish*, among others) are universal, belonging to no school.

ABJURATION

Abjurations are protective spells. They create physical or magical barriers, negate magical or physical abilities, harm trespassers, or even banish the subject to another plane of existence. Representative spells include *protection from evil*, *dispel magic*, *antimagic field*, and *banishment*.

If more than one abjuration spell is active within 10 feet of another for 24 hours or more, the magical fields interfere with each other and create barely visible energy fluctuations. The DC to find such spells with the Search skill drops by 4.

If an abjuration creates a barrier that keeps certain types of creatures at bay, the barrier cannot be used to push away those creatures. If you force the barrier against such a creature, you feel a discernible pressure against the barrier. If you continue to apply pressure, you break the spell.

CONJURATION

Conjurations bring manifestations of objects, creatures, or some form of energy to you (summoning), actually transport creatures from another plane of existence to your plane (calling), heal (healing), or create such objects or effects on the spot (creation). Creatures you conjure usually, but not always, obey your commands. Representative spells include the various *summon monster* spells, *cure light wounds*, *raise dead*, *wall of iron*, and the *power word* spells.

A creature or object brought into being or transported to your location by a conjuration spell cannot appear inside another creature or object, nor can it appear floating in an empty space. It must arrive in an open location on a surface capable of supporting it. The creature or object must appear within the spell's range, but it does not have to remain within the range.

Calling: The spell fully transports a creature from another plane to the plane you are on. The spell grants the creature the one-time ability to return to its plane of origin, although the spell may limit the circumstances under which this is possible. Creatures who are called actually die when they are killed; they do not disappear and reform, as do those brought by a summoning spell (see below). The duration of a calling spell is instantaneous, which means that the called creature can't be dispelled.

Spells that call powerful extraplanar creatures (most notably the *lesser planar binding*, *planar binding*, and *greater planar binding* spells) are most useful when the conjurer has a magical trap to hold the summoned creature. The simplest type of trap is a *magic circle* spell (*magic circle against chaos*, *magic circle against evil*, etc.). When focused inward, a *magic circle* spell binds a called creature for a maximum of 24 hours per caster level, provided that you cast the spell that calls the creature within 1 round of casting the *magic circle*. A *magic circle* leaves much to be desired as a trap, however. If the circle of powdered silver laid down in the process of spellcasting is broken, the effect immediately ends. The trapped creature can do nothing that disturbs the circle, directly or indirectly, but other creatures can. If the called creature has spell resistance, it can test the trap once a day. If you fail to overcome the spell resistance, the creature breaks free, destroying the circle. A creature capable of any form of dimensional travel (*astral projection*, *blink*, *dimension door*, *etherealness*, *gate*, *maze*, *plane shift*, *shadow walk*, *teleport*, and similar abilities) can simply leave the circle through that means. You can prevent the creature's extradimensional escape by casting a *dimensional anchor* spell on it, but you must cast the spell before the creature acts. If successful, the *anchor* effect lasts as long as the *magic circle* does. The creature cannot reach across the *magic circle*, but its ranged attacks (ranged weapons, spells, magical abilities, etc.) can. The creature can attack any target it can reach with its ranged attacks except for the circle itself.

You can use a special diagram (a two-dimensional bounded figure with no gaps along its circumference, augmented with various magical sigils) to make the trap more secure. Drawing the diagram by hand takes 10 minutes and requires a Spellcraft check (DC 20). The DM makes this check secretly. If the check fails, the diagram is ineffective. You can take 10 (see page 61) when drawing the diagram if you are under no particular time pressure to complete the task. This also takes 10 full minutes. If time is no factor at all, and you devote 3 hours and 20 minutes to the task, you can take 20. A successful diagram allows you to cast a *dimensional anchor* spell on the trap during the round before casting any summoning spell. The *anchor* holds any called creatures in the diagram for 24 hours per caster level. A creature cannot use its spell resistance against a trap prepared with a diagram, and none of its abilities or attacks can cross the diagram. If the creature tries a Charisma check to break free of the trap (see the *lesser planar binding*, *planar binding*, and *greater planar binding* spells), the DC increases by 5. The creature is immediately released if anything disturbs the diagram—even a straw laid across it. However, the creature cannot disturb the diagram itself either directly or indirectly, as noted above.

Creation: The spell manipulates matter to create an object or creature in the place the spellcaster designates (subject to the limits noted above for conjurations). If the spell has a duration other than instantaneous, magic holds the creation together, and when the spell ends or is dispelled, the conjured creature or object vanishes without a trace. If the spell has an instantaneous duration, the created object or creature is merely assembled through magic. It lasts indefinitely and does not depend on magic for its existence.

Healing: Certain divine conjurations heal creatures or even bring them back to life. These include *cure* spells, which good clerics can cast spontaneously.

Summoning: The spell instantly brings a creature or object to a place you designate. When the spell ends or is dispelled, a summoned creature is instantly sent back to where it came from, but a summoned object is not sent back unless the spell description specifically indicates this. A summoned creature also goes away if it is killed or dropped to 0 hit points. It is not really dead. It takes 24 hours for the creature to reform, during which time it can't be summoned again.

When the spell that summoned a creature ends and the creature disappears, all the spells it has cast end (if they haven't already). A summoned creature cannot use any innate summoning abilities it may have, and it refuses to cast any spells or use any spell-like abilities that would cost it XP.

DIVINATION

Divination spells enable you to learn secrets long forgotten, to predict the future, to find hidden things, and to foil deceptive spells. Representative spells include *identify*, *detect thoughts*, *clairaudience/clairvoyance*, and *true seeing*.

Many divination spells have cone-shaped areas (see page 149). These move with you and extend in the direction you look. The cone defines the area that you can sweep each round. If you study the same area for multiple rounds, you can often gain additional information, as noted in the descriptive text for the spell.

ENCHANTMENT

Enchantment spells affect the minds of others, influencing or controlling their behavior. Representative spells include *charm person*, *suggestion*, and *domination*.

All enchantments are mind-affecting spells. Two types of enchantment spells grant you influence over a subject creature:

Charm: The spell changes the way the subject views you, typically making the subject see you as a good friend.

Compulsion: The spell forces the subject to act in some manner or changes the way her mind works. Some spells determine the subject's actions (or the effects on the subject), some allow you to determine the subject's actions when you cast the spell, and others give you ongoing control over the subject.

EVOCATION

Evocation spells manipulate energy or tap an unseen source of power to produce a desired end. In effect, they create something out of nothing. Many of these spells produce spectacular effects, and evocation spells can deal large amounts of damage. Representative spells include *magic missile*, *fireball*, and *lightning bolt*.

ILLUSION

Illusion spells deceive the senses or minds of others. They cause people to see things that are not there, not see things that are there, hear phantom noises, or remember things that never happened. Representative illusions include *silent image*, *invisibility*, and *veil*. Illusions come in five types: figments, glamers, patterns, phantasms, and shadows.

Figment: A figment spell creates a false sensation. Those who perceive the figment perceive the same thing, not their own slightly different versions of the figment. (It is not a personalized mental impression.) Figments cannot make something seem to be something else. A figment that includes audible effects cannot duplicate intelligible speech unless the spell description specifically says it can. If intelligible speech is possible, it must be in a language you can speak. If you try to duplicate a language you cannot speak, the image produces gibberish. Likewise, you cannot make a visual copy of something unless you know what it looks like.

Because figments and glamers (see below) are unreal, they cannot produce real effects the way that other types of illusions can. They cannot cause damage to objects or creatures, support weight, provide nutrition, illuminate darkness, or provide protection from the elements. Consequently, these spells are useful for confounding or delaying foes, but useless for attacking them directly. For example, it is possible to use a *silent image* spell to create an illusory cottage, but the cottage offers no protection from rain. A clever caster, however, can take pains to make the place look old and decrepit, so that the rain falling on the occupants seems to fall from a leaky roof.

Glamer: A glamer spell changes a subject's sensory qualities, making it look, feel, taste, smell, or sound like something else, or even seem to disappear.

Pattern: Like a figment, a pattern spell creates an image that others can see, but a pattern also affects the minds of those who see it or are caught in it. All patterns are mind-affecting spells.

Phantasm: A phantasm spell creates a mental image that usually only the caster and the subject (or subjects) of the spell can perceive. This impression is totally in the minds of the subjects. It is a personalized mental impression. (It's all in their heads and not a fake picture or something that they actually see.) Third parties viewing or studying the scene don't notice the phantasm at all. All phantasms are mind-affecting spells.

Shadow: A shadow spell creates something that is partially real (quasi-real). The caster weaves it from extradimensional energies. Such illusions can have real effects. If a creature takes damage from a shadow illusion, that damage is real.

Saving Throws and Illusions (Disbelief): Creatures encountering an illusion effect usually do not receive saving throws to recognize it as illusory until they study it carefully or interact with it in some fashion. For example, if a party encounters a section of illusory floor, the character in the lead would receive a saving throw if she stopped and studied the floor or if she probed the floor. Likewise, if an illusory giant attacks a character, the character receives a saving throw because he is interacting with the giant.

A successful saving throw against an illusion reveals it to be false, but a figment or phantasm remains as a translucent outline. For example, a character making a successful saving throw against a figment of an illusory section of floor knows the "floor" isn't safe to walk on and can see what lies below (light permitting), but he can still note where the figment lies.

A failed saving throw indicates that a character fails to notice something is amiss. A character faced with incontrovertible proof that an illusion isn't real needs no saving throw. A character who falls through a section of illusory floor into a pit knows something is amiss, as does a character who spends a few rounds poking at the same illusion. If any viewer successfully disbelieves an illusion and communicates this fact to other viewers, each such viewer gains a saving throw with a +4 bonus.

NECROMANCY

Necromancy spells manipulate the power of death. Spells involving undead creatures make up a large part of this school. Representative spells include *cause fear*, *animate dead*, and *finger of death*.

TRANSMUTATION

Transmutation spells change the properties of some creature, thing, or condition. A transmutation usually changes only one property at a time, but it can be any property. Representative spells include *enlarge*, *reduce*, *polymorph other*, and *shapechange*.

SPECIAL ABILITIES

Medusas, dryads, harpies, and other magical creatures can create magical effects without being spellcasters. Characters using magic wands, rods, and other enchanted items can also create magical effects. These effects come in two types: spell-like and supernatural. Additionally, members of certain classes and certain creatures can use special abilities that aren't magical. These abilities are called extraordinary or natural.

Spell-Like Abilities: A dryad's *charm person* effect and a devil's *teleport* ability are spell-like abilities. Usually, a spell-like ability works just like the spell of that name. A few spell-like abilities are unique; these are explained in the text where they are described.

Spell-like abilities have no verbal, somatic, or material components. The user activates them mentally. Armor never affects a spell-like ability's use, even if the ability resembles an arcane spell with a somatic component. A spell-like ability has a casting time of 1 action unless noted otherwise in the ability or spell description. In all other ways, a spell-like ability functions just like a spell.

Spell-like abilities are subject to spell resistance and to being dispelled by *dispel magic*. They do not function in areas where magic is suppressed or negated (such as an *antimagic field*). Spell-like abilities cannot be used to counter spell, nor can they be counterspelled.

Some creatures are actually sorcerers of a sort. They cast arcane spells as sorcerers do, including using components. In fact, an individual creature (such as some dragons) could have some spell-like abilities and cast other spells as a sorcerer.

Supernatural Abilities: A dragon's fiery breath, a medusa's petrifying gaze, a spectre's energy draining, and a cleric's use of positive or negative energy to turn or rebuke undead are supernatural abilities. These abilities cannot be disrupted in combat, as spells can, and generally do not provoke attacks of opportunity (except as noted in their descriptions). Supernatural abilities are not subject to spell resistance or to being dispelled by *dispel magic*. However, supernatural abilities still do not function in areas where magic is suppressed or negated (such as an *antimagic field*).

Extraordinary Abilities: A rogue's evasion ability and a troll's ability to regenerate are extraordinary abilities. These abilities cannot be disrupted in combat, as spells can, and generally do not provoke attacks of opportunity (exceptions noted). Effects or areas that negate or disrupt magic have no effect on extraordinary abilities. They are not subject to dispelling, and they function normally in an *antimagic field*. Indeed, they do not qualify as magical, though they may break the laws of physics.

Natural Abilities: Things a creature can do that aren't extraordinary, supernatural, or spell-like are natural abilities, such as a bird's ability to fly.

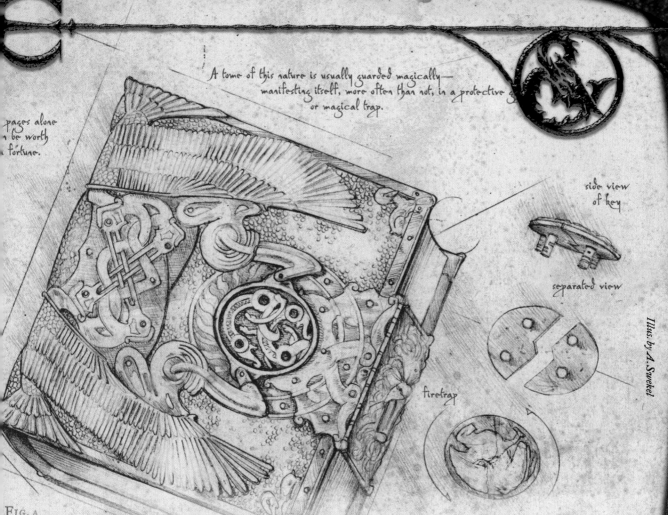

A tome of this nature is usually guarded magically—manifesting itself, more often than not, in a protective g... or magical trap.

pages alone ... be worth ... a fortune.

side view of key

separated view

firetrap

Illus. by A. Swekel

FIG. A

This chapter begins with the spell lists of the spellcasting classes and the domain lists. The rest of the chapter contains spell descriptions in alphabetical order by spell name.

Spell Chains: Some spells reference other spells that they are based upon. Only information in a spell later in the spell chain that is different from the base spell is covered in the spell being described. Header entries and other information that are the same as the base spell are not repeated.

Hit Dice: The term "Hit Dice" is used synonymously with "character levels" for effects that affect a number of Hit Dice of creatures. (Creatures with only Hit Dice from their race, not classes, have character levels equal to their Hit Dice.)

Caster Level: A spell's power often depends on caster level, which is the caster's class level. Creatures with no classes have a caster level equal to their Hit Dice unless otherwise specified. The word "level" in the spell lists always refers to caster level.

Creatures and Characters: "Creatures" and "characters" are used synonymously in the spell descriptions.

BARD SPELLS

0-LEVEL BARD SPELLS (CANTRIPS)

Dancing Lights. Figment torches or other lights.
Daze. Creature loses next action.
Detect Magic. Detects spells and magic items within 60 ft.
Flare. Dazzles one creature (–1 attack).
Ghost Sound. Figment sounds.
Light. Object shines like a torch.
Mage Hand. 5-pound telekinesis.
Mending. Makes minor repairs on an object.

Open/Close. Opens or closes small or light things.
Prestidigitation. Performs minor tricks.
Read Magic. Read scrolls and spellbooks.
Resistance. Subject gains +1 on saving throws.

1st-LEVEL BARD SPELLS

Alarm. Wards an area for 2 hours/level.
Cause Fear. One creature flees for 1d4 rounds.
Charm Person. Makes one person your friend.
Cure Light Wounds. Cures 1d8 +1/level damage (max +5).
Detect Secret Doors. Reveals hidden doors within 60 ft.
Erase. Mundane or magical writing vanishes.
Expeditious Retreat. Doubles your speed.
Feather Fall. Objects or creatures fall slowly.
Grease. Makes 10-ft. square or one object slippery.
Hypnotism. Fascinates 2d4 HD of creatures.
Identify. Determines single feature of magic item.
Mage Armor. Gives subject +4 armor bonus.
Magic Weapon. Weapon gains +1 bonus.
Message. Whispered conversation at distance.
Protection from Chaos/Evil/Good/Law. +2 AC and saves, counter mind control, hedge out elementals and outsiders.
Silent Image. Creates minor illusion of your design.
Sleep. Put 2d4 HD of creatures into comatose slumber.
Summon Monster I. Calls outsider to fight for you.
Unseen Servant. Creates invisible force that obeys your commands.
Ventriloquism. Throws voice for 1 min./level.

View of Spine

Opened properly, the book can be a library into itself— as well as a vast archive of archaic knowledge.

2nd-LEVEL BARD SPELLS

Animal Trance. Fascinates 2d6 HD of animals.
Blindness/Deafness. Makes subject blind or deaf.
Blur. Attacks miss subject 20% of the time.
Bull's Strength. Subject gains 1d4+1 Str for 1 hr./level.
Cat's Grace. Subject gains 1d4+1 Dex for 1 hr./level.
Cure Moderate Wounds. Cures 2d8 +1/level damage (max +10).
Darkness. 20-ft. radius of supernatural darkness.
Daylight. 60-ft. radius of bright light.
Delay Poison. Stops poison from harming subject for 1 hour/level.
Detect Thoughts. Allows "listening" to surface thoughts.
Enthrall. Captivates all within 100 ft. + 10 ft./level.
Glitterdust. Blinds creatures, outlines invisible creatures.
Hold Person. Holds one person helpless for 1 round/level.
Hypnotic Pattern. Fascinates 2d4+1 HD/level of creatures.
Invisibility. Subject is invisible for 10 min./level or until it attacks.
Levitate. Subject moves up and down at your direction.
Locate Object. Senses direction toward object (specific or type).
Magic Mouth. Speaks once when triggered.
Minor Image. As *silent image*, plus some sound.
Mirror Image. Creates decoy duplicates of you (1d4 +1/three levels, max 8).
Misdirection. Misleads divinations for one creature or object.
Obscure Object. Masks object against divination.
Pyrotechnics. Turns fire into blinding light or choking smoke.
Scare. Panics creatures up to 5 HD (15-ft. radius).
See Invisibility. Reveals invisible creatures or objects.
Shatter. Sonic vibration damages objects or crystalline creatures.
Silence. Negates sound in 15-ft. radius.
Sound Burst. Deals 1d8 sonic damage to subjects; may stun them.
Suggestion. Compels subject to follow stated course of action.
Summon Monster II. Calls outsider to fight for you.
Summon Swarm. Summons swarm of small crawling or flying creatures.
Tasha's Hideous Laughter. Subject loses actions for 1d3 rounds.
Tongues. Speak any language.
Undetectable Alignment. Conceals alignment for 24 hours.
Whispering Wind. Sends a short message one mile/level.

3rd-LEVEL BARD SPELLS

Bestow Curse. –6 to an ability; –4 on attacks, saves, and checks; or 50% chance of losing each action.
Blink. You randomly vanish and reappear for 1 round/level.
Charm Monster. Makes monster believe it is your ally.
Clairaudience/Clairvoyance. Hear or see at a distance for 1 min./level.
Confusion. Makes subject behave oddly for 1 round/level.
Cure Serious Wounds. Cures 3d8 +1/level damage (max +15).
Dispel Magic. Cancels magical spells and effects.
Displacement. Attacks miss subject 50%.
Emotion. Arouses strong emotion in subject.
Fear. Subjects within cone flee for 1 round/level.
Gaseous Form. Subject becomes insubstantial and can fly slowly.
Greater Magic Weapon. +1 bonus/three levels (max +5).
Gust of Wind. Blows away or knocks down smaller creatures.
Haste. Extra partial action and +4 AC.
Illusory Script. Only intended reader can decipher.
Invisibility Sphere. Makes everyone within 10 ft. invisible.
Keen Edge. Doubles normal weapon's threat range.
Leomund's Tiny Hut. Creates shelter for 10 creatures.
Lesser Geas. Commands subject of 7 HD or less.
Magic Circle against Chaos/Evil/Good/ Law. As *protection* spells, but 10-ft. radius and 10 min./level.
Major Image. As *silent image*, plus sound, smell and thermal effects.
Phantom Steed. Magical horse appears for 1 hour/level.
Remove Curse. Frees object or person from curse.
Remove Disease. Cures all diseases affecting subject.

Scrying. Spies on subject from a distance.
Sculpt Sound. Creates new sounds or changes existing ones.
Sepia Snake Sigil. Creates text symbol that immobilizes reader.
Slow. One subject/level takes only partial actions, –2 AC, –2 melee rolls.
Summon Monster III. Calls outsider to fight for you.
Wind Wall. Deflects arrows, smaller creatures, and gases.

4th-LEVEL BARD SPELLS

Break Enchantment. Frees subjects from enchantments, alterations, curses, and petrification.
Cure Critical Wounds. Cures 4d8 +1/level damage (max +20).
Detect Scrying. Alerts you of magical eavesdropping.
Dimension Door. Teleports you and up to 500 lb.
Dismissal. Forces a creature to return to native plane.
Dominate Person. Controls humanoid telepathically.
Hallucinatory Terrain. Makes one type of terrain appear like another (field into forest, etc.).
Hold Monster. As *hold person*, but any creature.
Improved Invisibility. As *invisibility*, but subject can attack and stay invisible.
Legend Lore. Learn tales about a person, place, or thing.
Leomund's Secure Shelter. Creates sturdy cottage.
Locate Creature. Indicates direction to familiar creature.
Modify Memory. Changes 5 minutes of subject's memories.
Neutralize Poison. Detoxifies venom in or on subject.
Rainbow Pattern. Lights prevent 24 HD of creatures from attacking or moving away.
Shout. Deafens all within cone and deals 2d6 damage.
Summon Monster IV. Calls outsider to fight for you.

5th-LEVEL BARD SPELLS

Contact Other Plane. Ask question of extraplanar entity.
Control Water. Raises, lowers, or parts bodies of water.
Dream. Sends message to anyone sleeping.
False Vision. Fools scrying with an illusion.
Greater Dispelling. As *dispel magic*, but +20 on check.
Healing Circle. Cures 1d8 +1/level damage in all directions.
Mind Fog. Subjects in fog get –10 Wis, Will checks.
Mirage Arcana. As *hallucinatory terrain*, plus structures.
Mislead. Turns you invisible and creates illusory double.
Nightmare. Sends vision dealing 1d10 damage, fatigue.
Persistent Image. As *major image*, but no concentration required.
Summon Monster V. Calls outsider to fight for you.

6th-LEVEL BARD SPELLS

Control Weather. Changes weather in local area.
Eyebite. *Charm, fear, sicken* or *sleep* one subject.
Geas/Quest. As *lesser geas*, plus it affects any creature.
Greater Scrying. As *scrying*, but faster and longer.
Mass Haste. As *haste*, affects one/level subjects.
Mass Suggestion. As *suggestion*, plus one/level subjects.
Permanent Image. Includes sight, sound, and smell.
Plane Shift. Up to eight subjects travel to another plane.
Programmed Image. As *major image*, plus triggered by event.
Project Image. Illusory double can talk and cast spells.
Repulsion. Creatures can't approach you.
Summon Monster VI. Calls outsider to fight for you.
Veil. Changes appearance of group of creatures.

CLERIC SPELLS

0-LEVEL CLERIC SPELLS (Orisons)

Create Water. Creates 2 gallons/level of pure water.
Cure Minor Wounds. Cures 1 point of damage.
Detect Magic. Detects spells and magic items within 60 ft.

Detect Poison. Detects poison in one creature or small object.
Guidance. +1 on one roll, save, or check.
Inflict Minor Wounds. Touch attack, 1 point of damage.
Light. Object shines like a torch.
Mending. Makes minor repairs on an object.
Purify Food and Drink. Purifies 1 cu. ft./level of food or water.
Read Magic. Read scrolls and spellbooks.
Resistance. Subject gains +1 on saving throws.
Virtue. Subject gains 1 temporary hp.

st-LEVEL CLERIC SPELLS

Bane. Enemies suffer −1 attack, −1 on saves against fear.
Bless. Allies gain +1 attack and +1 on saves against fear.
Bless Water. Makes holy water.
Cause Fear. One creature flees for 1d4 rounds.
Command. One subject obeys one-word command for 1 round.
Comprehend Languages. Understand all spoken and written languages.
Cure Light Wounds. Cures 1d8 +1/level damage (max +5).
Curse Water. Makes unholy water.
Deathwatch. Sees how wounded subjects within 30 ft. are.
Detect Chaos/Evil/Good/Law. Reveals creatures, spells, or objects.
Detect Undead. Reveals undead within 60 ft.
Divine Favor. You gain attack, damage bonus, +1/three levels.
Doom. One subject suffers −2 on attacks, damage, saves, and checks.
Endure Elements. Ignores 5 damage/round from one energy type.
Entropic Shield. Ranged attacks against you suffer 20% miss chance.
Inflict Light Wounds. Touch, 1d8 +1/level damage (max +5).
Invisibility to Undead. Undead can't perceive one subject/level.
Magic Stone. Three stones gain +1 attack, deal 1d6+1 damage.
Magic Weapon. Weapon gains +1 bonus.
Obscuring Mist. Fog surrounds you.
Protection from Chaos/Evil/Good/Law. +2 AC and saves, counter mind control, hedge out elementals and outsiders.
Random Action. One creature acts randomly for one round.
Remove Fear. +4 on saves against fear for one subject +1/four levels.
Sanctuary. Opponents can't attack you, and you can't attack.
Shield of Faith. Aura grants +2 or higher deflection bonus.
Summon Monster I. Calls outsider to fight for you.

nd-LEVEL CLERIC SPELLS

Aid. +1 attack, +1 on saves against fear, 1d8 temporary hit points.
Animal Messenger. Sends a Tiny animal to a specific place.
Augury. Learns whether an action will be good or bad.
Bull's Strength. Subject gains 1d4+1 Str for 1 hr./level.
Calm Emotions. Calms 1d6 subjects/level, negating emotion effects.
Consecrate. Fills area with positive energy, making undead weaker.
Cure Moderate Wounds. Cures 2d8 +1/level damage (max +10).
Darkness. 20-ft. radius of supernatural darkness.
Death Knell. Kills dying creature; you gain 1d8 temporary hp, +2 Str, and +1 level.
Delay Poison. Stops poison from harming subject for 1 hour/level.
Desecrate. Fills area with negative energy, making undead stronger.
Endurance. Gain 1d4+1 Con for 1 hr./level.
Enthrall. Captivates all within 100 ft. + 10 ft./level.
Find Traps. Notice traps as a rogue does.
Gentle Repose. Preserves one corpse.
Hold Person. Holds one person helpless; 1 round/level.
Inflict Moderate Wounds. Touch attack, 2d8 +1/level damage (max +10).
Lesser Restoration. Dispels magic ability penalty or repairs 1d4 ability damage.
Make Whole. Repairs an object.
Remove Paralysis. Frees one or more creatures from paralysis, *hold*, or *slow*.
Resist Elements. Ignores 12 damage/round from one energy type.

Shatter. Sonic vibration damages objects or crystalline creatures.
Shield Other. You take half of subject's damage.
Silence. Negates sound in 15-ft. radius.
Sound Burst. Deals 1d8 sonic damage to subjects; may stun them.
Speak with Animals. You can communicate with natural animals.
Spiritual Weapon. Magical weapon attacks on its own.
Summon Monster II. Calls outsider to fight for you.
Undetectable Alignment. Conceals alignment for 24 hours.
Zone of Truth. Subjects within range cannot lie.

3rd-LEVEL CLERIC SPELLS

Animate Dead. Creates undead skeletons and zombies.
Bestow Curse. −6 to an ability; −4 on attacks, saves, and checks; or 50% chance of losing each action.
Blindness/Deafness. Makes subject blind or deaf.
Contagion. Infects subject with chosen disease.
Continual Flame. Makes a permanent, heatless torch.
Create Food and Water. Feeds three humans (or one horse)/level.
Cure Serious Wounds. Cures 3d8 +1/level damage (max +15).
Daylight. 60-ft. radius of bright light.
Deeper Darkness. Object sheds absolute darkness in 60-ft. radius.
Dispel Magic. Cancels magical spells and effects.
Glyph of Warding. Inscription harms those who pass it.
Helping Hand. Ghostly hand leads subject to you.
Inflict Serious Wounds. Touch attack, 3d8 +1/level damage (max +15).
Invisibility Purge. Dispels invisibility within 5 ft./level.
Locate Object. Senses direction toward object (specific or type).
Magic Circle against Chaos/Evil/Good/Law. As *protection* spells, but 10-ft. radius and 10 min./level.
Magic Vestment. Armor or shield gains +1 enhancement/three levels.
Meld into Stone. You and your gear merge with stone.
Negative Energy Protection. Subject resists level and ability drains.
Obscure Object. Masks object against divination.
Prayer. Allies gain +1 on most rolls, and enemies suffer −1.
Protection from Elements. Absorb 12 damage/level from one kind of energy.
Remove Blindness/Deafness. Cures normal or magical conditions.
Remove Curse. Frees object or person from curse.
Remove Disease. Cures all diseases affecting subject.
Searing Light. Ray deals 1d8/two levels, more against undead.
Speak with Dead. Corpse answers one question/two levels.
Speak with Plants. You can talk to normal plants and plant creatures.
Stone Shape. Sculpts stone into any form.
Summon Monster III. Calls outsider to fight for you.
Water Breathing. Subjects can breathe underwater.
Water Walk. Subject treads on water as if solid.
Wind Wall. Deflects arrows, smaller creatures, and gases.

4th-LEVEL CLERIC SPELLS

Air Walk. Subject treads on air as if solid (climb at 45-degree angle).
Control Water. Raises, lowers, or parts bodies of water.
Cure Critical Wounds. Cures 4d8 +1/level damage (max +20).
Death Ward. Grants immunity to death spells and effects.
Dimensional Anchor. Bars extradimensional movement.
Discern Lies. Reveals deliberate falsehoods.
Dismissal. Forces a creature to return to native plane.
Divination. Provides useful advice for specific proposed actions.
Divine Power. You gain attack bonus, 18 Str, and 1 hp/level.
Freedom of Movement. Subject moves normally despite impediments.
Giant Vermin. Turns insects into giant vermin.
Greater Magic Weapon. +1 bonus/three levels (max +5).
Imbue with Spell Ability. Transfer spells to subject.
Inflict Critical Wounds. Touch attack, 4d8 +1/level damage (max +20).

Lesser Planar Ally. Exchange services with an 8 HD outsider.

Neutralize Poison. Detoxifies venom in or on subject.

Poison. Touch deals 1d10 Con damage, repeats in 1 min.

Repel Vermin. Insects stay 10 ft. away.

Restoration. Restores level and ability score drains.

Sending. Delivers short message anywhere, instantly.

Spell Immunity. Subject is immune to one spell/four levels.

Status. Monitors condition, position of allies.

Summon Monster IV. Calls outsider to fight for you.

Tongues. Speak any language.

5th-LEVEL CLERIC SPELLS

Atonement. Removes burden of misdeeds from subject.

Break Enchantment. Frees subjects from enchantments, alterations, curses, and petrification.

Circle of Doom. Deals 1d8 +1/level damage in all directions.

Commune. Deity answers one yes-or-no question/level.

Dispel Chaos/Evil/Good/Law. +4 bonus against attacks.

Ethereal Jaunt. You become ethereal for 1 round/level.

Flame Strike. Smites foes with divine fire (1d6/level).

Greater Command. As *command*, but affects one subject/level.

Hallow. Designates location as holy.

Healing Circle. Cures 1d8 +1/level damage in all directions.

Insect Plague. Insect horde limits vision, inflicts damage, and weak creatures flee.

Mark of Justice. Designates action that will trigger *curse* on subject.

Plane Shift. Up to eight subjects travel to another plane.

Raise Dead. Restores life to subject who died up to 1 day/level ago.

Righteous Might. Your size increases, and you gain +4 Str.

Scrying. Spies on subject from a distance.

Slay Living. Touch attack kills subject.

Spell Resistance. Subject gains +12 +1/level SR.

Summon Monster V. Calls outsider to fight for you.

True Seeing. See all things as they really are.

Unhallow. Designates location as unholy.

Wall of Stone. 20 hp/four levels; can be shaped.

6th-LEVEL CLERIC SPELLS

Animate Objects. Objects attack your foes.

Antilife Shell. 10-ft. field hedges out living creatures.

Banishment. Banishes 2 HD/level extraplanar creatures.

Blade Barrier. Blades encircling you deal 1d6 damage/level.

Create Undead. Ghouls, shadows, ghasts, wights, or wraiths.

Etherealness. Travel to Ethereal Plane with companions.

Find the Path. Shows most direct way to a location.

Forbiddance. Denies area to creatures of another alignment.

Geas/Quest. As *lesser geas*, plus it affects any creature.

Greater Dispelling. As *dispel magic*, but up to +20 on check.

Greater Glyph of Warding. As *glyph of warding*, but up to 10d8 damage or 6th-level spell.

Harm. Subject loses all but 1d4 hp.

Heal. Cures all damage, diseases, and mental conditions.

Heroes' Feast. Food for one creature/level cures and *blesses*.

Planar Ally. As *lesser planar ally*, but up to 16 HD.

Summon Monster VI. Calls outsider to fight for you.

Wind Walk. You and your allies turn vaporous and travel fast.

Word of Recall. Teleports you back to designated place.

7th-LEVEL CLERIC SPELLS

Blasphemy. Kills, paralyzes, weakens, or dazes nonevil subjects.

Control Weather. Changes weather in local area.

Destruction. Kills subject and destroys remains.

Dictum. Kills, paralyzes, weakens, or dazes nonlawful subjects.

Greater Restoration. As *restoration*, plus restores all levels and ability scores.

Greater Scrying. As *scrying*, but faster and longer.

Holy Word. Kills, paralyzes, weakens, or dazes nongood subjects.

Refuge. Alters item to transport its possessor to you.

Regenerate. Subject's severed limbs grow back.

Repulsion. Creatures can't approach you.

Resurrection. Fully restore dead subject.

Summon Monster VII. Calls outsider to fight for you.

Word of Chaos. Kills, confuses, stuns, or deafens nonchaotic subjects.

8th-LEVEL CLERIC SPELLS

Antimagic Field. Negates magic within 10 ft.

Cloak of Chaos. +4 AC, +4 resistance, and SR 25 against lawful spells.

Create Greater Undead. Mummies, spectres, vampires, or ghosts.

Discern Location. Exact location of creature or object.

Earthquake. Intense tremor shakes 5-ft./level radius.

Fire Storm. Deals 1d6 fire damage/level.

Greater Planar Ally. As *lesser planar ally*, but up to 24 HD.

Holy Aura. +4 AC, +4 resistance, and SR 25 against evil spells.

Mass Heal. As *heal*, but with several subjects.

Shield of Law. +4 AC, +4 resistance, and SR 25 against chaotic spells.

Summon Monster VIII. Calls outsider to fight for you.

Symbol. Triggered runes have array of effects.

Unholy Aura. +4 AC, +4 resistance, and SR 25 against good spells.

9th-LEVEL CLERIC SPELLS

Astral Projection. Projects you and companions into Astral Plane.

Energy Drain. Subject gains 2d4 negative levels.

Gate. Connects two planes for travel or summoning.

Implosion. Kills one creature/round.

Miracle. Requests a deity's intercession.

Soul Bind. Traps newly dead soul to prevent *resurrection*.

Storm of Vengeance. Storm rains acid, lightning, and hail.

Summon Monster IX. Calls outsider to fight for you.

True Resurrection. As *resurrection*, plus remains aren't needed.

CLERIC DOMAINS

Air Domain

Deities: Obad-Hai.

Granted Powers: Turn or destroy earth creatures as a good cleric turns undead. Rebuke or command air creatures as an evil cleric rebukes undead. Use these abilities a total number of times per day equal to 3 + your Charisma modifier.

Air Domain Spells

1 **Obscuring Mist.** Fog surrounds you.
2 **Wind Wall.** Deflects arrows, smaller creatures, and gases.
3 **Gaseous Form.** Subject becomes insubstantial and can fly slowly.
4 **Air Walk.** Subject treads on air as if solid (climb at 45-degree angle).
5 **Control Winds.** Change wind direction and speed.
6 **Chain Lightning.** 1d6 damage/level; secondary bolts.
7 **Control Weather.** Changes weather in local area.
8 **Whirlwind.** Cyclone inflicts damage and can pick up creatures.
9 **Elemental Swarm.*** Summons 2d4 Large, 1d4 Huge elementals.

*Cast as an air spell only.

Animal Domain

Deities: Ehlonna, Obad-Hai.

Granted Powers: You cast *animal friendship* once per day. Knowledge (nature) is a class skill.

Animal Domain Spells

1 **Calm Animals.** Calms 2d4 +1/level HD of animals, beasts, and magical beasts.

2 **Hold Animal.** Hold one animal helpless; 1 round/level.
3 **Dominate Animal.** Subject animal obeys silent mental commands.
4 **Repel Vermin.** Insects stay 10 ft. away.
5 **Commune with Nature.** Learn about terrain for one mile/level.
6 **Antilife Shell.** 10-ft. field hedges out living creatures.
7 **Animal Shapes.** One ally/level *polymorphs* into chosen animal.
8 **Creeping Doom.** Carpet of insects attacks at your command.
9 **Shapechange.** Transforms you into any creature, and change forms once per round.

Chaos Domain

Deities: Corellon Larethian, Erythnul, Gruumsh, Kord, Olidammara.
Granted Power: You cast chaos spells at +1 caster level.

Chaos Domain Spells

1 **Protection from Law.** +2 AC and saves, counter mind control, hedge out elementals and outsiders.
2 **Shatter.** Sonic vibration damages objects or crystalline creatures.
3 **Magic Circle against Law.** As *protection* spells, but 10-ft. radius and 10 min./level.
4 **Chaos Hammer.** Damages and staggers lawful creatures.
5 **Dispel Law.** +4 bonus against attacks by lawful creatures.
6 **Animate Objects.** Objects attack your foes.
7 **Word of Chaos.** Kills, confuses, stuns, or deafens nonchaotic subjects.
8 **Cloak of Chaos.** +4 AC, +4 resistance, SR 25 against lawful spells.
9 **Summon Monster IX.*** Calls outsider to fight for you.
*Cast as a chaos spell only.

Death Domain

Deities: Nerull, Wee Jas.
Granted Power: You may use a death touch once per day. Your death touch is a spell-like ability that is a death effect. You must succeed at a melee touch attack against a living creature (using the rules for touch spells). When you touch, roll 1d6 per your cleric level. If the total at least equals the creature's current hit points, it dies.

Death Domain Spells

1 **Cause Fear.** One creature flees for 1d4 rounds.
2 **Death Knell.** Kill dying creature and gain 1d8 temp. hp, +2 Str, and +1 caster level.
3 **Animate Dead.** Creates undead skeletons and zombies.
4 **Death Ward.** Grants immunity to death spells and effects.
5 **Slay Living.** Touch attack kills subject.
6 **Create Undead.** Ghouls, shadows, ghasts, wights, or wraiths.
7 **Destruction.** Kills subject and destroys remains.
8 **Create Greater Undead.** Mummies, spectres, vampires, or ghosts.
9 **Wail of the Banshee.** Kills one creature/level.

Destruction Domain

Deities: St. Cuthbert, Hextor.
Granted Power: You gain the smite power, the supernatural ability to make a single melee attack with a +4 attack bonus and a damage bonus equal to your cleric level (if you hit). You must declare the smite before making the attack. It is usable once per day.

Destruction Domain Spells

1 **Inflict Light Wounds.** Touch attack, 1d8 +1/level damage (max +5).
2 **Shatter.** Sonic vibration damages objects or crystalline creatures.
3 **Contagion.** Infects subject with chosen disease.
4 **Inflict Critical Wounds.** Touch attack, 4d8 +1/level damage (max +20).
5 **Circle of Doom.** Deals 1d8 +1/level damage in all directions.
6 **Harm.** Subject loses all but 1d4 hp.

7 **Disintegrate.** Makes one creature or object vanish.
8 **Earthquake.** Intense tremor shakes 5-ft./level radius.
9 **Implosion.** Kills one creature/round.

Earth Domain

Deities: Moradin, Obad-Hai.
Granted Power: Turn or destroy air creatures as a good cleric turns undead. Rebuke or command earth creatures as an evil cleric rebukes undead. Use these abilities a total number of times per day equal to 3 + your Charisma modifier.

Earth Domain Spells

1 **Magic Stone.** Three stones become +1 projectiles, 1d6+1 damage.
2 **Soften Earth and Stone.** Turns stone to clay or dirt to sand or mud.
3 **Stone Shape.** Sculpts stone into any form.
4 **Spike Stones.** Creatures in area take 1d8 damage, may be *slowed*.
5 **Wall of Stone.** 20 hp/four levels; can be shaped.
6 **Stoneskin.** Stops blows, cuts, stabs, and slashes.
7 **Earthquake.** Intense tremor shakes 5-ft./level radius.
8 **Iron Body.** Your body becomes living iron.
9 **Elemental Swarm.*** Summons 2d4 Large, 1d4 Huge elementals.
*Cast as an earth spell only.

Evil Domain

Deities: Erythnul, Gruumsh, Hextor, Nerull, Vecna.
Granted Power: You cast evil spells at +1 caster level.

Evil Domain Spells

1 **Protection from Good.** +2 AC and saves, counter mind control, hedge out elementals and outsiders.
2 **Desecrate.** Fills area with negative energy, making undead stronger.
3 **Magic Circle against Good.** As *protection* spells, but 10-ft. radius and 10 min./level.
4 **Unholy Blight.** Damages and sickens good creatures.
5 **Dispel Good.** +4 bonus against attacks by good creatures.
6 **Create Undead.** Ghouls, shadows, ghasts, wights, or wraiths.
7 **Blasphemy.** Kills, paralyzes, weakens, or dazes nonevil subjects.
8 **Unholy Aura.** +4 AC, +4 resistance, SR 25 against good spells.
9 **Summon Monster IX.*** Calls outsider to fight for you.
*Cast as an evil spell only.

Fire Domain

Deity: Obad-Hai.
Granted Power: Turn or destroy water creatures as a good cleric turns undead. Rebuke or command fire creatures as an evil cleric rebukes undead. Use these abilities a total number of times per day equal to 3 + your Charisma modifier.

Fire Domain Spells

1 **Burning Hands.** 1d4 fire damage/level (max 5d4).
2 **Produce Flame.** 1d4 +1/two levels damage, touch or thrown.
3 **Resist Elements.*** Ignore first 12 damage from one energy type each round.
4 **Wall of Fire.** Deals 2d4 fire damage out to 10 ft. and 1d4 out to 20 ft. Passing through wall deals 2d6 +1/level.
5 **Fire Shield.** Creatures attacking you take fire damage; you're protected from heat or cold.
6 **Fire Seeds.** Acorns and berries become grenades and bombs.
7 **Fire Storm.** Deals 1d6 fire damage/level.
8 **Incendiary Cloud.** Cloud deals 4d6 fire damage/round.
9 **Elemental Swarm.**** Summons 2d4 Large, 1d4 Huge elementals.
*Resist cold or fire only.
**Cast as a fire spell only.

Good Domain

Deities: Corellon Larethian, Ehlonna, Garl Glittergold, Heironeous, Kord, Moradin, Pelor, Yondalla.

Granted Power: You cast good spells at +1 caster level.

Good Domain Spells

1 **Protection from Evil.** +2 AC and saves, counter mind control, hedge out elementals and outsiders.
2 **Aid.** +1 attack, +1 on saves against fear, 1d6 temporary hit points.
3 **Magic Circle against Evil.** As *protection* spells, but 10-ft. radius and 10 min./level.
4 **Holy Smite.** Damages and blinds evil creatures.
5 **Dispel Evil.** +4 bonus against attacks by evil creatures.
6 **Blade Barrier.** Blades encircling you deal 1d6 damage/level.
7 **Holy Word.** Kills, paralyzes, weakens, or dazes nongood subjects.
8 **Holy Aura.** +4 AC, +4 resistance, and SR 25 against evil spells.
9 **Summon Monster IX.*** Calls outsider to fight for you.

*Cast as a good spell only.

Healing Domain

Deity: Pelor.

Granted Power: You cast healing spells at +1 caster level.

Healing Domain Spells

1 **Cure Light Wounds.** Cures 1d8 +1/level damage (max +5).
2 **Cure Moderate Wounds.** Cures 2d8 +1/level damage (max +10).
3 **Cure Serious Wounds.** Cures 3d8 +1/level damage (max +15).
4 **Cure Critical Wounds.** Cures 4d8 +1/level damage (max +20).
5 **Healing Circle.** Cures 1d8 +1/level damage in all directions.
6 **Heal.** Cures all damage, diseases, and mental conditions.
7 **Regenerate.** Subject's severed limbs grow back.
8 **Mass Heal.** As *heal*, but with several subjects.
9 **True Resurrection.** As *resurrection*, plus remains aren't needed.

Knowledge Domain

Deities: Boccob, Vecna.

Granted Power: All Knowledge skills are class skills. You cast divinations at +1 caster level.

Knowledge Domain Spells

1 **Detect Secret Doors.** Reveals hidden doors within 60 ft.
2 **Detect Thoughts.** Allows "listening" to surface thoughts.
3 **Clairaudience/Clairvoyance.** Hear or see at a distance for 1 min./level.
4 **Divination.** Provides useful advice on to specific proposed actions.
5 **True Seeing.** See all things as they really are.
6 **Find the Path.** Shows most direct way to a location.
7 **Legend Lore.** Learn tales about a person, place, or thing.
8 **Discern Location.** Exact location of creature or object.
9 **Foresight.** "Sixth sense" warns of impending danger.

Law Domain

Deities: St. Cuthbert, Heironeous, Hextor, Moradin, Wee Jas, Yondalla.

Granted Power: You cast law spells at +1 caster level.

Law Domain Spells

1 **Protection from Chaos.** +2 AC and saves, counter mind control, hedge out elementals and outsiders.
2 **Calm Emotions.** Calms 1d6 creatures/level, negating emotion effects.
3 **Magic Circle against Chaos.** As *protection* spells, but 10-ft. radius and 10 min./level.
4 **Order's Wrath.** Damages and dazes chaotic creatures.
5 **Dispel Chaos.** +4 bonus against attacks by chaotic creatures.

6 **Hold Monster.** As *hold person*, but any creature.
7 **Dictum.** Kills, paralyzes, weakens, or dazes nonlawful subjects.
8 **Shield of Law.** +4 AC, +4 resistance, and SR 25 against chaotic spells.
9 **Summon Monster IX.*** Calls outsider to fight for you.

*Cast as a law spell only.

Luck Domain

Deities: Fharlanghn, Kord, Olidammara.

Granted Power: You gain the power of good fortune, which is usable once per day. This extraordinary ability allows you to reroll one roll that you have just made. You must take the result of the reroll, even if it's worse than the original roll.

Luck Domain Spells

1 **Entropic Shield.** Ranged attacks against you suffer 20% miss chance.
2 **Aid.** +1 attack, +1 against fear, 1d8 temporary hit points.
3 **Protection from Elements.** Absorb 12 damage/level from one kind of energy.
4 **Freedom of Movement.** Subject moves normally despite impediments.
5 **Break Enchantment.** Frees subjects from enchantments, alterations, curses, and petrification.
6 **Mislead.** Turns you invisible and creates illusory double.
7 **Spell Turning.** Reflect 1d4+6 spell levels back at caster.
8 **Holy Aura.** +4 AC, +4 resistance, and SR 25 against evil spells.
9 **Miracle.** Requests a deity's intercession.

Magic Domain

Deities: Boccob, Vecna, Wee Jas.

Granted Power: Use scrolls, wands, and other devices with spell completion or spell trigger activation as a wizard of one-half your cleric level (at least 1st level). For the purpose of using a scroll or other magic device, if you are also a wizard, actual wizard levels and these effective wizard levels stack.

Magic Domain Spells

1 **Nystul's Undetectable Aura.** Masks magic item's aura.
2 **Identify.** Determines single feature of magic item.
3 **Dispel Magic.** Cancels magical spells and effects.
4 **Imbue with Spell Ability.** Transfer spells to subject.
5 **Spell Resistance.** Subject gains +12 +1/level SR.
6 **Antimagic Field.** Negates magic within 10 ft.
7 **Spell Turning.** Reflect 1d4+6 spell levels back at caster.
8 **Protection from Spells.** Confers +8 resistance bonus.
9 **Mordenkainen's Disjunction.** Dispels magic, disenchants magic items.

Plant Domain

Deities: Ehlonna, Obad-Hai.

Granted Powers: Rebuke or command plant creatures as an evil cleric rebukes or commands undead. Use these abilities a total number of times per day equal to 3 + your Charisma modifier. Knowledge (nature) is a class skill.

Plant Domain Spells

1 **Entangle.** Plants entangle everyone in 40-ft.-radius circle.
2 **Barkskin.** Grants +3 natural armor bonus (or higher).
3 **Plant Growth.** Grows vegetation, improves crops.
4 **Control Plants.** Talk to and control plants & fungi.
5 **Wall of Thorns.** Thorns damage anyone who tries to pass.
6 **Repel Wood.** Pushes away wooden objects.
7 **Changestaff.** Your staff becomes a treant on command.
8 **Command Plants.** Plants animate and vegetation entangles.
9 **Shambler.** Summons 1d4+2 shambling mounds to fight for you.

Protection Domain

Deities: Corellon Larethian, St. Cuthbert, Fharlanghn, Garl Glittergold, Moradin, Yondalla.

Granted Power: You can generate a *protective ward*, a spell-like ability to grant someone you touch a resistance bonus on her next saving throw equal to your level. Activating this power is a standard action. The *protective ward* is an abjuration effect with a duration of 1 hour that is usable once per day.

Protection Domain Spells

1 **Sanctuary.** Opponents can't attack you, and you can't attack.
2 **Shield Other.** You take half of subject's damage.
3 **Protection from Elements.** Absorb 12 damage/level from one kind of energy.
4 **Spell Immunity.** Subject is immune to one spell/four levels.
5 **Spell Resistance.** Subject gains +12 +1/level SR.
6 **Antimagic Field.** Negates magic within 10 ft.
7 **Repulsion.** Creatures can't approach you.
8 **Mind Blank.** Subject is immune to mental/emotional magic and scrying.
9 **Prismatic Sphere.** As *prismatic wall*, but surrounds on all sides.

Strength Domain

Deities: St. Cuthbert, Gruumsh, Kord, Pelor.

Granted Power: You can perform a feat of strength, which is the supernatural ability to gain an enhancement bonus to Strength equal to your level. Activating the power is a free action, the power lasts 1 round, and it's usable once per day.

Strength Domain Spells

1 **Endure Elements.** Ignores 5 damage/round from one energy type.
2 **Bull's Strength.** Subject gains 1d4+1 Str for 1 hr./level.
3 **Magic Vestment.** Armor or shield gains +1 enhancement/three level.
4 **Spell Immunity.** Subject is immune to one spell/four levels.
5 **Righteous Might.** Your size increases, and you gain +4 Str.
6 **Stoneskin.** Stops blows, cuts, stabs, and slashes.
7 **Bigby's Grasping Hand.** Hand provides cover, pushes, or grapples.
8 **Bigby's Clenched Fist.** Large hand attacks your foes.
9 **Bigby's Crushing Hand.** As *Bigby's grasping hand*, but stronger.

Sun Domain

Deities: Ehlonna, Pelor.

Granted Power: Once per day, you can perform a greater turning against undead in place of a regular turning (or rebuking) attempt. The greater turning is like a normal turning (or rebuking) attempt except that the undead creatures that would be turned (or rebuked or commanded) are destroyed instead.

Sun Domain Spells

1 **Endure Elements.*** Ignores 5 damage/round from one energy type.
2 **Heat Metal.** Make metal so hot it damages those that touch it.
3 **Searing Light.** Ray deals 1d8/two levels, more against undead.
4 **Fire Shield.** Creatures attacking you take fire damage; you're protected from heat or cold.
5 **Flame Strike.** Smite foes with divine fire (1d8/level).
6 **Fire Seeds.** Acorns and berries become grenades and bombs.
7 **Sunbeam.** Beam blinds and deals 3d6 damage.
8 **Sunburst.** Blinds all within 10 ft., deals 3d6 damage.
9 **Prismatic Sphere.** As *prismatic wall*, but surrounds on all sides.
*Endure cold or fire only.

Travel Domain

Deities: Fharlanghn.

Granted Powers: For a total of 1 round per your cleric level per day, you can act normally regardless of magical effects that impede movement (similar to the effect of the spell *freedom of movement*). This effect occurs automatically as soon as it applies, lasts until it runs out or is no longer needed, and can operate multiple times per day (up to the total daily limit of rounds). This is a spell-like ability. Wilderness Lore is a class skill.

Travel Domain Spells

1 **Expeditious Retreat.** Doubles your speed.
2 **Locate Object.** Senses direction toward object (specific or type).
3 **Fly.** Subject flies at speed of 90.
4 **Dimension Door.** Teleports you and up to 500 lb.
5 **Teleport.** Instantly transports you anywhere.
6 **Find the Path.** Shows most direct way to a location.
7 **Teleport without Error.** As *teleport*, but no off-target arrival.
8 **Phase Door.** Invisible passage through wood or stone.
9 **Astral Projection.** Projects you and companions into Astral Plane.

Trickery Domain

Deities: Boccob, Erythnul, Garl Glittergold, Olidammara, Nerull.

Granted Power: Bluff, Disguise, and Hide are class skills.

Trickery Domain Spells

1 **Change Self.** Change own appearance.
2 **Invisibility.** Subject invisible 10 min./level or until it attacks.
3 **Nondetection.** Hides subject from divination, scrying.
4 **Confusion.** Makes subjects behave oddly for 1 round/level.
5 **False Vision.** Fools scrying with an illusion.
6 **Mislead.** Turns you invisible and creates illusory double.
7 **Screen.** Illusion hides area from vision, scrying.
8 **Polymorph Any Object.** Changes any subject into anything else.
9 **Time Stop.** You act freely for 1d4+1 rounds.

War Domain

Deities: Corellon Larethian, Erythnul, Gruumsh, Heironeous, Hextor.

Granted Power: Free Martial Weapon Proficiency (if necessary) and Weapon Focus with the deity's favored weapon.

War Deity	Favored Weapon
Corellon Larethian	Longsword
Erythnul	Morningstar
Gruumsh	Spear (halfspear, shortspear, or longspear)
Hextor	Flail (light or heavy)
Heironeous	Longsword

War Domain Spells

1 **Magic Weapon.** Weapon gains +1 bonus.
2 **Spiritual Weapon.** Magical weapon attacks on its own..
3 **Magic Vestment.** Armor or shield gains +1 enhancement/three levels.
4 **Divine Power.** You gain attack bonus, 18 Str, and 1 hp/level.
5 **Flame Strike.** Smite foes with divine fire (1d6 damage/level).
6 **Blade Barrier.** Blades encircling you deal 1d6 damage/level.
7 **Power Word, Stun.** Stuns creature with up to 150 hp.
8 **Power Word, Blind.** Blinds 200 hp worth of creatures.
9 **Power Word, Kill.** Kills one tough subject or many weak ones.

Water Domain

Deity: Obad-Hai.

Granted Power: Turn or destroy fire creatures as a good cleric turns undead. Rebuke or command water creatures as an evil cleric rebukes undead. Use these abilities a total number of times per day equal to 3 + your Charisma modifier.

Water Domain Spells

1. **Obscuring Mist.** Fog surrounds you.
2. **Fog Cloud.** Fog obscures vision.
3. **Water Breathing.** Subjects can breathe underwater.
4. **Control Water.** Raise, lower, or part bodies of water.
5. **Ice Storm.** Hail deals 5d6 damage in cylinder 40 ft. across.
6. **Cone of Cold.** 1d6 cold damage/level.
7. **Acid Fog.** Fog deals acid damage.
8. **Horrid Wilting.** Deals 1d8 damage/level within 30 ft.
9. **Elemental Swarm.*** Summons 2d4 Large, 1d4 Huge elementals.

*Cast as a water spell only.

DRUID SPELLS

0-LEVEL DRUID SPELLS (Orisons)

Create Water. Creates 2 gallons/level of pure water.
Cure Minor Wounds. Cures 1 point of damage.
Detect Magic. Detects spells and magic items within 60 ft..
Detect Poison. Detects poison in one creature or small object.
Flare. Dazzles one creature (–1 attack).
Guidance. +1 on one roll, throw, or check.
Know Direction. You discern north.
Light. Object shines like a torch.
Mending. Makes minor repairs on an object.
Purify Food and Drink. Purifies 1 cu. ft./level of food or water.
Read Magic. Read scrolls and spellbooks.
Resistance. Subject gains +1 on saving throws.
Virtue. Subject gains 1 temporary hp.

1st-LEVEL DRUID SPELLS

Animal Friendship. Gains permanent animal companions.
Calm Animals. Calms 2d4 +1/level HD of animals, beasts, and magical beasts.
Cure Light Wounds. Cures 1d8 +1/level damage (max +5).
Detect Animals or Plants. Detects species of animals or plants.
Detect Snares and Pits. Reveals natural or primitive traps.
Endure Elements. Ignores 5 damage/round from one energy type.
Entangle. Plants entangle everyone in 40-ft.-radius circle.
Faerie Fire. Outlines subjects with light, canceling *blur*, concealment, etc.
Goodberry. 2d4 berries each cure 1 hp (max 8 hp/24 hours).
Invisibility to Animals. Animals can't perceive one subject/level.
Magic Fang. One natural weapon of subject creature gets +1 bonus to attack and damage.
Obscuring Mist. Fog surrounds you.
Pass without Trace. One subject/level leaves no tracks.
Shillelagh. Cudgel or quarterstaff becomes +1 weapon (1d10 damage) for 1 minute/level.
Summon Nature's Ally I. Calls creature to fight.

2nd-LEVEL DRUID SPELLS

Animal Messenger. Sends a Tiny animal to a specific place.
Animal Trance. Fascinates 2d6 HD of animals.
Barkskin. Grants +3 natural armor bonus (or higher).
Charm Person or Animal. Makes one person or animal your friend.
Chill Metal. Cold metal damages those who touch it.
Delay Poison. Stops poison from harming subject for 1 hour/level.
Fire Trap. Opened object deals 1d4 +1/level damage.
Flame Blade. Touch attack deals 1d8 +1/two levels damage.
Flaming Sphere. Rolling ball of fire, 2d6 damage, lasts 1 round/level.
Heat Metal. Hot metal damages those who touch it.
Hold Animal. Holds one animal helpless; 1 round/level.
Lesser Restoration. Dispels magic ability penalty or repairs 1d4 ability damage.
Produce Flame. 1d4 +1/two levels damage, touch or thrown.

Resist Elements. Ignores first 12 damage from one energy type each round.
Soften Earth and Stone. Turns stone to clay or dirt to sand or mud.
Speak with Animals. You can communicate with natural animals.
Summon Nature's Ally II. Calls creature to fight.
Summon Swarm. Summons swarm of small crawling or flying creatures.
Tree Shape. You look exactly like a tree for 1 hour/level.
Warp Wood. Bends wood (shaft, handle, door, plank).
Wood Shape. Rearranges wooden objects to suit you.

3rd-LEVEL DRUID SPELLS

Call Lightning. Directs lightning bolts (1d10/level) during storms.
Contagion. Infects subject with chosen disease.
Cure Moderate Wounds. Cures 2d8 +1/level damage (max +10).
Diminish Plants. Reduces size or blights growth of normal plants.
Dominate Animal. Subject animal obeys silent mental commands.
Greater Magic Fang. One natural weapon of subject creature gets +1 bonus to attack and damage per three caster levels (max +5).
Meld into Stone. You and your gear merge with stone.
Neutralize Poison. Detoxifies venom in or on subject.
Plant Growth. Grows vegetation, improves crops.
Poison. Touch deals 1d10 Con damage, repeats in 1 min.
Protection from Elements. Absorb 12 damage/level from one kind of energy.
Remove Disease. Cures all diseases affecting subject.
Snare. Creates a magical booby trap.
Speak with Plants. You can talk to normal plants and plant creatures.
Spike Growth. Creatures in area take 1d4 damage, may be *slowed*.
Stone Shape. Sculpts stone into any form.
Summon Nature's Ally III. Calls creature to fight.
Water Breathing. Subjects can breathe underwater.

4th-LEVEL DRUID SPELLS

Antiplant Shell. Keeps animated plants at bay.
Control Plants. Talk to and control plants & fungi.
Cure Serious Wounds. Cures 3d8 +1/level damage (max +15).
Dispel Magic. Cancels magical spells and effects.
Flame Strike. Smites foes with divine fire (1d6/level).
Freedom of Movement. Subject moves normally despite impediments.
Giant Vermin. Turns insects into giant vermin.
Quench. Extinguishes nonmagical fires or one magic item.
Reincarnate. Brings dead subject back in a random body.
Repel Vermin. Insects stay 10 ft. away.
Rusting Grasp. Your touch corrodes iron and alloys.
Scrying. Spies on subject from a distance.
Sleet Storm. Hampers vision and movement.
Spike Stones. Creatures in area take 1d8 damage, may be *slowed*.
Summon Nature's Ally IV. Calls creature to fight.

5th-LEVEL DRUID SPELLS

Animal Growth. One animal/two levels doubles in size, HD.
Atonement. Removes burden of misdeeds from subject.
Awaken. Animal or tree gains human intellect.
Commune with Nature. Learn about terrain for one mile/level.
Control Winds. Change wind direction and speed.
Cure Critical Wounds. Cures 4d8 +1/level damage (max +20).
Death Ward. Grants immunity to all death spells and effects.
Hallow. Designates location as holy.
Ice Storm. Hail deals 5d6 damage in cylinder 40 ft. across.
Insect Plague. Insect horde limits vision, inflicts damage, and weak creatures flee.
Summon Nature's Ally V. Calls creature to fight.
Transmute Mud to Rock. Transforms two 10-ft. cubes/level.
Transmute Rock to Mud. Transforms two 10-ft. cubes/level.

Tree Stride. Step from one tree to another far away.

Unhallow. Designates location as unholy.

Wall of Fire. Deals 2d4 fire damage out to 10 ft. and 1d4 out to 20 ft. Passing through wall deals 2d6 +1/level.

Wall of Thorns. Thorns damage anyone who tries to pass.

th-LEVEL DRUID SPELLS

Antilife Shell. 10-ft. field hedges out living creatures.

Find the Path. Shows most direct way to a location.

Fire Seeds. Acorns and berries become grenades and bombs.

Greater Dispelling. As *dispel magic*, but +20 on check.

Healing Circle. Cures 1d8 +1/level damage in all directions.

Ironwood. Magical wood is strong as steel.

Liveoak. Oak becomes treant guardian.

Repel Wood. Pushes away wooden objects.

Spellstaff. Stores one spell in wooden quarterstaff.

Stone Tell. Talk to natural or worked stone.

Summon Nature's Ally VI. Calls creature to fight.

Transport via Plants. Move instantly from one plant to another of the same species.

Wall of Stone. 20 hp/four levels; can be shaped.

th-LEVEL DRUID SPELLS

Changestaff. Your staff becomes a treant on command.

Control Weather. Changes weather in local area.

Creeping Doom. Carpet of insects attacks at your command.

Fire Storm. Deals 1d6 fire damage/level.

Greater Scrying. As *scrying*, but faster and longer.

Harm. Subject loses all but 1d4 hp.

Heal. Cures all damage, diseases, and mental conditions.

Summon Nature's Ally VII. Calls creature to fight.

Sunbeam. Beam blinds and deals 3d6 damage.

Transmute Metal to Wood. Metal within 40 ft. becomes wood.

True Seeing. See all things as they really are.

Wind Walk. You and your allies turn vaporous and travel fast.

th-LEVEL DRUID SPELLS

Animal Shapes. One ally/level *polymorphs* into chosen animal.

Command Plants. Plants animate and vegetation entangles.

Finger of Death. Kills one subject.

Repel Metal or Stone. Pushes away metal and stone.

Reverse Gravity. Objects and creatures fall upward.

Summon Nature's Ally VIII. Calls creature to fight.

Sunburst. Blinds all within 10 ft., deals 3d6 damage.

Whirlwind. Cyclone inflicts damage and can pick up creatures.

Word of Recall. Teleports you back to designated place.

th-LEVEL DRUID SPELLS

Antipathy. Object or location affected by spell repels certain creatures.

Earthquake. Intense tremor shakes 5-ft./level radius.

Elemental Swarm. Summons 2d4 Large, 1d4 Huge elementals.

Foresight. "Sixth sense" warns of impending danger.

Mass Heal. As *heal*, but with several subjects.

Shambler. Summons 1d4+2 shambling mounds to fight for you.

Shapechange. Transforms you into any creature, and change forms once per round.

Summon Nature's Ally IX. Calls creature to fight.

Sympathy. Object or location attracts certain creatures.

PALADIN SPELLS

t-LEVEL PALADIN SPELLS

Bless. Allies gain +1 attack and +1 on saves against fear.

Bless Water. Makes holy water.

Bless Weapon. Weapon gains +1 bonus.

Create Water. Creates 2 gallons/level of pure water.

Cure Light Wounds. Cures 1d8 +1/level damage (max +5).

Detect Poison. Detects poison in one creature or small object.

Detect Undead. Reveals undead within 60 ft.

Divine Favor. You gain attack, damage bonus, +1/three levels.

Endure Elements. Ignores 5 damage/round from one energy type.

Magic Weapon. Weapon gains +1 bonus.

Protection from Evil. +2 AC and saves, counter mind control, hedge out elementals and outsiders.

Read Magic. Read scrolls and spellbooks.

Resistance. Subject gains +1 on saving throws.

Virtue. Subject gains 1 temporary hp.

2nd-LEVEL PALADIN SPELLS

Delay Poison. Stops poison from harming subject for 1 hour/level.

Remove Paralysis. Frees one or more creatures from paralysis, *hold* or *slow*.

Resist Elements. Ignores 12 damage/round from one energy type.

Shield Other. You take half of subject's damage.

Undetectable Alignment. Conceals alignment for 24 hours.

3rd-LEVEL PALADIN SPELLS

Cure Moderate Wounds. Cures 2d8 +1/level (max +10).

Discern Lies. Reveals deliberate falsehoods.

Dispel Magic. Cancels magical spells and effects.

Greater Magic Weapon. +1 bonus/three levels (max +5).

Heal Mount. As *heal* on warhorse or other mount.

Magic Circle against Evil. As *protection* spells, but 10-ft. radius and 10 min./level.

Prayer. Allies gain +1 on most rolls, enemies suffer −1.

Remove Blindness/Deafness. Cures normal or magical conditions.

4th-LEVEL PALADIN SPELLS

Cure Serious Wounds. Cures 3d8 +1/level (max +15*).

Death Ward. Grants immunity to death spells and effects.

Dispel Evil. +4 bonus against attacks by evil creatures.

Freedom of Movement. Subject moves normally despite impediments.

Holy Sword. Weapon becomes +5, does double damage against evil.

Neutralize Poison. Detoxifies venom in or on subject.

*Paladin's maximum effective caster level is 10.

RANGER SPELLS

1st-LEVEL RANGER SPELLS

Alarm. Wards an area for 2 hours/level.

Animal Friendship. Gains permanent animal companions.

Delay Poison. Stops poison from harming subject for 1 hour/level.

Detect Animals or Plants. Detects species of animals or plants.

Detect Snares and Pits. Reveals natural or primitive traps.

Entangle. Plants entangle everyone in 40-ft.-radius circle.

Magic Fang. One natural weapon of subject creature gets +1 bonus to attack and damage.

Pass without Trace. One subject/level leaves no tracks.

Read Magic. Read scrolls and spellbooks.

Resist Elements. Ignores first 12 damage from one energy type each round.

Speak with Animals. You can communicate with natural animals.

Summon Nature's Ally I. Calls animal to fight for you.

2nd-LEVEL RANGER SPELLS

Animal Messenger. Sends a Tiny animal to a specific place.

Cure Light Wounds. Cures 1d8 +1/level damage (max +5).

Detect Chaos/Evil/Good/Law. Reveals creatures, spells, or objects.

Hold Animal. Holds one animal helpless; 1 round/level.

Protection from Elements. Absorb 12 damage/level from one kind of energy.

Sleep. Put 2d4 HD of creatures into comatose slumber.
Snare. Creates a magical booby trap.
Speak with Plants. You can talk to normal plants and plant creatures.
Summon Nature's Ally II. Calls animal to fight for you.

3rd-LEVEL RANGER SPELLS

Control Plants. Talk to and control plants & fungi.
Diminish Plants. Reduces size or blights growth of normal plants.
Greater Magic Fang. One natural weapon of subject creature gets +1 bonus to attack and damage per three caster levels (max +5).
Neutralize Poison. Detoxifies venom in or on subject.
Plant Growth. Grows vegetation, improves crops.
Remove Disease. Cures all diseases affecting subject.
Summon Nature's Ally III. Calls animal to fight for you.
Tree Shape. You look exactly like a tree for 1 hour/level.
Water Walk. Subject treads on water as if solid.

4th-LEVEL RANGER SPELLS

Cure Serious Wounds. Cures 3d8 +1/level damage (max +15).
Freedom of Movement . Subject moves normally despite impediments.
Nondetection. Hides subject from divination, scrying.
Polymorph Self. You assume a new form.
Summon Nature's Ally IV. Calls animal to fight for you.
Tree Stride. Step from one tree to another far away.
Wind Wall. Deflects arrows, smaller creatures, and gases.

SORCERER AND WIZARD SPELLS

0-LEVEL SORCERER AND WIZARD SPELLS (Cantrips)

Abjur   **Resistance**. Subject gains +1 on saving throws.
Conj   **Ray of Frost**. Ray deals 1d3 cold damage.
Div   **Detect Poison**. Detects poison in one creature or small object.
Ench   **Daze**. Creature loses next action.
Evoc   **Flare**. Dazzles one creature (–1 attack).
   Light. Object shines like a torch.
Illus   **Dancing Lights**. Figment torches or other lights.
   Ghost Sound. Figment sounds.
Necro   **Disrupt Undead**. Deals 1d6 damage to one undead.
Trans   **Mage Hand**. 5-pound telekinesis.
   Mending. Makes minor repairs on an object.
   Open/Close. Opens or closes small or light things.
Univ   **Arcane Mark**. Inscribes a personal rune (visible or invisible).
   Detect Magic. Detects spells and magic items within 60 ft.
   Prestidigitation. Performs minor tricks.
   Read Magic. Read scrolls and spellbooks.

1st-LEVEL SORCERER AND WIZARD SPELLS

Abjur   **Alarm**. Wards an area for 2 hours/level.
   Endure Elements. Ignores 5 damage/round from one energy type.
   Hold Portal. Holds door shut.
   Protection from Chaos/Evil/Good/Law. +2 AC and saves, counter mind control, hedge out elementals and outsiders.
   Shield. Invisible disc gives cover and blocks *magic missiles*.
Conj   **Grease**. Makes 10-ft. square or one object slippery.
   Mage Armor. Gives subject +4 armor bonus.
   Mount. Summons riding horse for 2 hr./level.
   Obscuring Mist. Fog surrounds you.
   Summon Monster I. Calls outsider to fight for you.

Unseen Servant. Creates invisible force that obeys your commands.
Div   **Comprehend Languages**. Understands all spoken and written languages.
   Detect Secret Doors. Reveals hidden doors within 60 ft.
   Detect Undead. Reveals undead within 60 ft.
   Identify. Determines single feature of magic item.
   True Strike. Adds +20 bonus to your next attack roll.
Ench   **Charm Person**. Makes one person your friend.
   Hypnotism. Fascinates 2d4 HD of creatures.
   Sleep. Put 2d4 HD of creatures into comatose slumber.
Evoc   **Magic Missile**. 1d4+1 damage; +1 missile/two levels above 1st (max +5).
   Tenser's Floating Disk. 3-ft.-diameter horizontal disk that holds 100 lb./level.
Illus   **Change Self**. Changes your appearance.
   Color Spray. Knocks unconscious, blinds, or stuns 1d6 weak creatures.
   Nystul's Magical Aura. Grants object false magic aura.
   Nystul's Undetectable Aura. Masks magic item's aura.
   Silent Image. Creates minor illusion of your design.
   Ventriloquism. Throws voice for 1 min./level.
Necro   **Cause Fear**. One creature flees for 1d4 rounds.
   Chill Touch. 1 touch/level deals 1d6 damage and possibly 1 Str damage.
   Ray of Enfeeblement. Ray reduces Str by 1d6 points +1 point/two levels.
Trans   **Animate Rope**. Makes a rope move at your command.
   Burning Hands. 1d4 fire damage/level (max: 5d4).
   Enlarge. Object or creature grows +10%/level (max +50%).
   Erase. Mundane or magical writing vanishes.
   Expeditious Retreat. Doubles your speed.
   Feather Fall. Objects or creatures fall slowly.
   Jump. Subject gets +30 on Jump checks.
   Magic Weapon. Weapon gains +1 bonus.
   Message. Whispered conversation at distance.
   Reduce. Object or creature shrinks 10%/level (max 50%).
   Shocking Grasp. Touch delivers 1d8 +1/level electricity.
   Spider Climb. Grants ability to walk on walls and ceilings.

2ND-LEVEL SORCERER AND WIZARD SPELLS

Abjur   **Arcane Lock**. Magically locks a portal or chest.
   Obscure Object. Masks object against divination.
   Protection from Arrows. Subject immune to most ranged attacks.
   Resist Elements. Ignores 12 damage/round from one energy type.
Conj   **Fog Cloud**. Fog obscures vision.
   Glitterdust. Blinds creatures, outlines invisible creatures.
   Melf's Acid Arrow. Ranged touch attack; 2d4 damage for 1 round + 1 round/three levels.
   Summon Monster II. Calls outsider to fight for you.
   Summon Swarm. Summons swarm of small crawling or flying creatures.
   Web. Fills 10-ft. cube/level with sticky spider webs.
Div   **Detect Thoughts**. Allows "listening" to surface thoughts.
   Locate Object. Senses direction toward object (specific or type).
   See Invisibility. Reveals invisible creatures or objects.
Ench   **Tasha's Hideous Laughter**. Subject loses actions for 1d3 rounds.
Evoc   **Darkness**. 20-ft. radius of supernatural darkness.
   Daylight. 60-ft. radius of bright light.
   Flaming Sphere. Rolling ball of fire, 2d6 damage, lasts 1 round/level.
   Shatter. Sonic vibration damages objects or crystalline creatures.

Illus **Blur**. Attacks miss subject 20% of the time.

Continual Flame. Makes a permanent, heatless torch.

Hypnotic Pattern. Fascinates 2d4+1 HD/level of creatures.

Invisibility. Subject is invisible for 10 min./level or until it attacks.

Leomund's Trap. Makes item seem trapped.

Magic Mouth. Speaks once when triggered.

Minor Image. As *silent image*, plus some sound.

Mirror Image. Creates decoy duplicates of you (1d4 +1/three levels, max 8).

Misdirection. Misleads divinations for one creature or object.

Necro **Ghoul Touch**. Paralyzes one subject, who exudes stench (−2 penalty) nearby.

Scare. Panics creatures up to 5 HD (15-ft. radius).

Spectral Hand. Creates disembodied glowing hand to deliver touch attacks.

Trans **Alter Self**. As *change self*, plus more drastic changes.

Blindness/Deafness. Makes subject blind or deaf.

Bull's Strength. Subject gains 1d4+1 Str for 1 hr./level.

Cat's Grace. Subject gains 1d4+1 Dex for 1 hr./level.

Darkvision. See 60 ft. in total darkness.

Endurance. Gain 1d4+1 Con for 1 hr./level.

Knock. Opens locked or magically sealed door.

Levitate. Subject moves up and down at your direction.

Pyrotechnics. Turns fire into blinding light or choking smoke.

Rope Trick. Up to eight creatures hide in extradimensional space.

Whispering Wind. Sends a short message one mile/level.

rd-LEVEL SORCERER AND WIZARD SPELLS

Abjur **Dispel Magic**. Cancels magical spells and effects.

Explosive Runes. Deals 6d6 damage when read.

Magic Circle against Chaos/Evil/Good/Law. As *protection* spells, but 10-ft. radius and 10 min./level.

Nondetection. Hides subject from divination, scrying.

Protection from Elements. Absorb 12 damage/level from one kind of energy.

Conj **Flame Arrow**. Shoots flaming projectiles (extra damage) or fiery bolts (4d6 damage).

Phantom Steed. Magical horse appears for 1 hour/level.

Sepia Snake Sigil. Creates text symbol that immobilizes reader.

Sleet Storm. Hampers vision and movement.

Stinking Cloud. Nauseating vapors, 1 round/level.

Summon Monster III. Calls outsider to fight for you.

Div **Clairaudience/Clairvoyance**. Hear or see at a distance for 1 min./level.

Tongues. Speak any language.

Ench **Hold Person**. Holds one person helpless; 1 round/level.

Suggestion. Compels subject to follow stated course of action.

Evoc **Fireball**. 1d6 damage per level, 20-ft. radius.

Gust of Wind. Blows away or knocks down smaller creatures.

Leomund's Tiny Hut. Creates shelter for 10 creatures.

Lightning Bolt. Electricity deals 1d6 damage/level.

Wind Wall. Deflects arrows, smaller creatures, and gases.

Illus **Displacement**. Attacks miss subject 50%.

Illusory Script. Only intended reader can decipher.

Invisibility Sphere. Makes everyone within 10 ft. invisible.

Major Image. As *silent image*, plus sound, smell and thermal effects.

Necro **Gentle Repose**. Preserves one corpse.

Halt Undead. Immobilizes undead for 1 round/level.

Vampiric Touch. Touch deals 1d6/two caster levels; caster gains damage as hp.

Trans **Blink**. You randomly vanish and reappear for 1 round/level.

Fly. Subject flies at speed of 90.

Gaseous Form. Subject becomes insubstantial and can fly slowly.

Greater Magic Weapon. +1/three levels (max +5).

Haste. Extra partial action and +4 AC.

Keen Edge. Doubles normal weapon's threat range.

Secret Page. Changes one page to hide its real content.

Shrink Item. Object shrinks to one-twelfth size.

Slow. One subject/level takes only partial actions, −2 AC, −2 melee rolls.

Water Breathing. Subjects can breathe underwater.

4th-LEVEL SORCERER AND WIZARD SPELLS

Abjur **Dimensional Anchor**. Bars extradimensional movement.

Fire Trap. Opened object deals 1d4 +1/level damage.

Minor Globe of Invulnerability. Stops 1st- through 3rd-level spell effects.

Remove Curse. Frees object or person from curse.

Stoneskin. Stops blows, cuts, stabs, and slashes.

Conj **Evard's Black Tentacles**. 1d4 +1/level tentacles grapple randomly within 15 ft.

Leomund's Secure Shelter. Creates sturdy cottage.

Minor Creation. Creates one cloth or wood object.

Solid Fog. Blocks vision and slows movement.

Summon Monster IV. Calls outsider to fight for you.

Div **Arcane Eye**. Invisible floating eye moves 30 ft./round.

Detect Scrying. Alerts you of magical eavesdropping.

Locate Creature. Indicates direction to familiar creature.

Scrying. Spies on subject from a distance.

Ench **Charm Monster**. Makes monster believe it is your ally.

Confusion. Makes subject behave oddly for 1 round/level.

Emotion. Arouses strong emotion in subject.

Lesser Geas. Commands subject of 7 HD or less.

Evoc **Fire Shield**. Creatures attacking you take fire damage; you're protected from heat or cold.

Ice Storm. Hail deals 5d6 damage in cylinder 40 ft. across.

Otiluke's Resilient Sphere. Force globe protects but traps one subject.

Shout. Deafens all within cone and deals 2d6 damage.

Wall of Fire. Deals 2d4 fire damage out to 10 ft. and 1d4 out to 20 ft. Passing through wall deals 2d6 +1/level.

Wall of Ice. *Ice plane* creates wall with 15 hp +1/level, or *hemisphere* can trap creatures inside.

Illus **Hallucinatory Terrain**. Makes one type of terrain appear like another (field into forest, etc.).

Illusory Wall. Wall, floor, or ceiling looks real, but anything can pass through.

Improved Invisibility. As *invisibility*, but subject can attack and stay invisible.

Phantasmal Killer. Fearsome illusion kills subject or deals 3d6 damage.

Rainbow Pattern. Lights prevent 24 HD of creatures from attacking or moving away.

Shadow Conjuration. Mimics conjuring below 4th level.

Necro **Contagion**. Infects subject with chosen disease.

Enervation. Subject gains 1d4 negative levels.

Fear. Subjects within cone flee for 1 round/level.

Trans **Bestow Curse**. −6 to an ability; −4 on attacks, saves, and checks; or 50% chance of losing each action.

Dimension Door. Teleports you and up to 500 lb.

Polymorph Other. Gives one subject a new form.

Polymorph Self. You assume a new form.

Rary's Mnemonic Enhancer. Prepares extra spells or retains one just cast. *Wizard only.*

5th-LEVEL SORCERER AND WIZARD SPELLS

Abjur **Dismissal**. Forces a creature to return to native plane.
Conj **Cloudkill**. Kills 3 HD or less; 4–6 HD save or die.
Leomund's Secret Chest. Hides expensive chest on Ethereal Plane; you retrieve it at will.
Lesser Planar Binding. Traps outsider until it performs a task.
Major Creation. As *minor creation*, plus stone and metal.
Mordenkainen's Faithful Hound. Phantom dog can guard, attack.
Summon Monster V. Calls outsider to fight for you.
Wall of Iron. 30 hp/four levels; can topple onto foes.
Wall of Stone. 20 hp/four levels; can be shaped.
Div **Contact Other Plane**. Ask question of extraplanar entity.
Prying Eyes. 1d4 floating eyes +1/level scout for you.
Rary's Telepathic Bond. Link lets allies communicate.
Ench **Dominate Person**. Controls humanoid telepathically.
Feeblemind. Subject's Int drops to 1.
Hold Monster. As *hold person*, but any creature.
Mind Fog. Subjects in fog get –10 Wis, Will checks.
Evoc **Bigby's Interposing Hand**. Hand provides 90% cover against one opponent.
Cone of Cold. 1d6 cold damage/level.
Sending. Delivers short message anywhere, instantly.
Wall of Force. Wall is immune to damage.
Illus **Dream**. Sends message to anyone sleeping.
False Vision. Fools scrying with an illusion.
Greater Shadow Conjuration. As *shadow conjuration*, but up to 4th level and 40% real.
Mirage Arcana. As *hallucinatory terrain*, plus structures.
Nightmare. Sends vision dealing 1d10 damage, fatigue.
Persistent Image. As *major image*, but no concentration required.
Seeming. Changes appearance of one person/two levels.
Shadow Evocation. Mimics evocation less than 5th level.
Necro **Animate Dead**. Creates undead skeletons and zombies.
Magic Jar. Enables possession of another creature.
Trans **Animal Growth**. One animal/two levels doubles in size, HD.
Fabricate. Transforms raw materials into finished items.
Passwall. Breaches walls 1 ft. thick/level.
Stone Shape. Sculpts stone into any form.
Telekinesis. Lifts or moves 25 lb./level at long range.
Teleport. Instantly transports you anywhere.
Transmute Mud to Rock. Transforms two 10-ft. cubes/level.
Transmute Rock to Mud. Transforms two 10-ft. cubes/level.
Univ **Permanency**. Makes certain spells permanent; costs XP.

6th-LEVEL SORCERER AND WIZARD SPELLS

Abjur **Antimagic Field**. Negates magic within 10 ft.
Globe of Invulnerability. As *minor globe*, plus 4th level.
Greater Dispelling. As *dispel magic*, but +20 on check.
Guards and Wards. Array of magic effects protect area.
Repulsion. Creatures can't approach you.
Conj **Acid Fog**. Fog deals acid damage.
Planar Binding. As *lesser planar binding*, but up to 16 HD.
Summon Monster VI. Calls outsider to fight for you.
Div **Analyze Dweomer**. Reveals magical aspects of subject.
Legend Lore. Learn tales about a person, place, or thing.
True Seeing. See all things as they really are.
Ench **Geas/Quest**. As *lesser geas*, plus it affects any creature.
Mass Suggestion. As *suggestion*, plus one/level subjects.
Evoc **Bigby's Forceful Hand**. Hand pushes creatures away.
Chain Lightning. 1d6 damage/level; secondary bolts.
Contingency. Sets trigger condition for another spell.
Otiluke's Freezing Sphere. Freezes water or deals cold damage.
Illus **Greater Shadow Evocation**. As *shadow evocation*, but up to 5th level.

Mislead. Turns you invisible and creates illusory double.
Permanent Image. Includes sight, sound, and smell.
Programmed Image. As *major image*, plus triggered by event.
Project Image. Illusory double can talk and cast spells.
Shades. As *shadow conjuration*, but up to 5th level and 60% real.
Veil. Changes appearance of group of creatures.
Necro **Circle of Death**. Kills 1d4 HD/level.
Trans **Control Water**. Raises, lowers, or parts bodies of water.
Control Weather. Changes weather in local area.
Disintegrate. Makes one creature or object vanish.
Eyebite. *Charm, fear, sicken* or *sleep* one subject.
Flesh to Stone. Turns subject creature into statue.
Mass Haste. As *haste*, affects one/level subjects.
Mordenkainen's Lucubration. Recalls spell of 5th level or less. *Wizard only*.
Move Earth. Digs trenches and build hills.
Stone to Flesh. Restores petrified creature.
Tenser's Transformation. You gain combat bonuses.

7th-LEVEL SORCERER AND WIZARD SPELLS

Abjur **Banishment**. Banishes 2 HD/level extraplanar creatures.
Sequester. Subject is invisible to sight and scrying.
Spell Turning. Reflect 1d4+6 spell levels back at caster.
Conj **Drawmij's Instant Summons**. Prepared object appears in your hand.
Mordenkainen's Magnificent Mansion. Door leads to extradimensional mansion.
Phase Door. Invisible passage through wood or stone.
Power Word, Stun. Stuns creature with up to 150 hp.
Summon Monster VII. Calls outsider to fight for you.
Div **Greater Scrying**. As *scrying*, but faster and longer.
Vision. As *legend lore*, but quicker and strenuous.
Ench **Insanity**. Subject suffers continuous *confusion*.
Evoc **Bigby's Grasping Hand**. Hand provides cover, pushes, or grapples.
Delayed Blast Fireball. 1d8 fire damage/level; you can delay blast for 5 rounds.
Forcecage. Cube of force imprisons all inside.
Mordenkainen's Sword. Floating magic blade strikes opponents.
Prismatic Spray. Rays hit subjects with variety of effects.
Illus **Mass Invisibility**. As *invisibility*, but affects all in range.
Shadow Walk. Step into shadow to travel rapidly.
Simulacrum. Creates partially real double of a creature.
Necro **Control Undead**. Undead don't attack you while under your command.
Finger of Death. Kills one subject.
Trans **Ethereal Jaunt**. You become ethereal for 1 round/level.
Plane Shift. Up to eight subjects travel to another plane.
Reverse Gravity. Objects and creatures fall upward.
Statue. Subject can become a statue at will.
Teleport without Error. As *teleport*, but no off-target arrival.
Vanish. As *teleport*, but affects a touched object.
Univ **Limited Wish**. Alters reality—within spell limits.

8th-LEVEL SORCERER AND WIZARD SPELLS

Abjur **Mind Blank**. Subject is immune to mental/emotional magic and scrying.
Prismatic Wall. Wall's colors have array of effects.
Protection from Spells. Confers +8 resistance bonus.
Conj **Greater Planar Binding**. As *lesser planar binding*, but up to 24 HD.
Incendiary Cloud. Cloud deals 4d6 fire damage/round.
Maze. Traps subject in extradimensional maze.
Power Word, Blind. Blinds 200 hp worth of creatures.
Summon Monster VIII. Calls outsider to fight for you.

Div **Trap the Soul**. Imprisons subject within gem.
Div **Discern Location**. Exact location of creature or object.
Ench **Antipathy**. Object or location affected by spell repels certain creatures.
Binding. Array of techniques to imprison a creature.
Demand. As *sending*, plus you can send *suggestion*.
Mass Charm. As *charm monster*, but all within 30 ft.
Otto's Irresistible Dance. Forces subject to dance.
Sympathy. Object or location attracts certain creatures.
Evoc **Bigby's Clenched Fist**. Large hand attacks your foes.
Otiluke's Telekinetic Sphere. As *Otiluke's resilient sphere*, but you move sphere telekinetically.
Sunburst. Blinds all within 10 ft., deals 3d6 damage.
Illus **Screen**. Illusion hides area from vision, scrying.
Necro **Clone**. Duplicate awakens when original dies.
Horrid Wilting. Deals 1d8 damage/level within 30 ft.
Trans **Etherealness**. Travel to Ethereal Plane with companions.
Iron Body. Your body becomes living iron.
Polymorph Any Object. Changes any subject into anything else.
Univ **Symbol**. Triggered runes have array of effects.

th-LEVEL SORCERER AND WIZARD SPELLS

Abjur **Freedom**. Releases creature suffering *imprisonment*.
Imprisonment. Entombs subject beneath the earth.
Mordenkainen's Disjunction. Dispels magic, disenchants magic items.
Prismatic Sphere. As *prismatic wall*, but surrounds on all sides.
Conj **Gate**. Connects two planes for travel or summoning.
Power Word, Kill. Kills one tough subject or many weak ones.
Summon Monster IX. Calls outsider to fight for you.
Div **Foresight**. "Sixth sense" warns of impending danger.
Ench **Dominate Monster**. As *dominate person*, but any creature.
Evoc **Bigby's Crushing Hand**. As *Bigby's interposing hand*, but stronger.
Meteor Swarm. Deals 24d6 fire damage, plus bursts.
Illus **Weird**. As *phantasmal killer*, but affects all within 30 ft.
Necro **Astral Projection**. Projects you and companions into Astral Plane.
Energy Drain. Subject gains 2d4 negative levels.
Soul Bind. Traps newly dead soul to prevent *resurrection*.
Wail of the Banshee. Kills one creature/level.
Trans **Refuge**. Alters item to transport its possessor to you.
Shapechange. Transforms you into any creature, and change forms once per round.
Teleportation Circle. Circle teleports any creature inside to designated spot.
Temporal Stasis. Puts subject into suspended animation.
Time Stop. You act freely for 1d4+1 rounds.
Univ **Wish**. As *limited wish*, but with fewer limits.

SPELL FORMAT

Each spell description follows the same format. This section discusses that format and some of the fine points of how spells work.

AME

This is the name by which the spell is generally known. Spells might be known by other names in some locales, and spellcasters often have different names for their spells, such as "sand of slumber" instead of *sleep*.

CHOOL, SUBSCHOOL, AND DESCRIPTORS

This is the school to which the spell belongs. "Universal" refers to a spell that belongs to no school. If the spell is a subtype within a school, the subschool is given here (in parentheses). See Schools of Magic, page 156.

Any descriptors that apply are given here [in brackets]. See Special Spell Effects, page 152.

Schools: Abjuration, Conjuration, Divination, Enchantment, Evocation, Illusion, Necromancy, and Transmutation.

Subschools: *Conjuration:* creation, healing, and summoning; *Enchantment:* charm and compulsion; *Illusion:* figment, glamer, pattern, phantasm, and shadow.

Descriptors: Acid, chaotic, cold, darkness, death, electricity, evil, fear, fire, force, good, language-dependent, lawful, light, mind-affecting, sonic, and teleportation.

LEVEL

This is the relative power level of the spell, ranging from 0 level through 1st level up to 9th level. This entry includes an abbreviation for each class that can cast this spell. The "Level" entry also indicates if a spell is a domain spell and, if so, what its level is. A spell's level affects the DC for any save allowed against the spell.

For example, the level entry for *hold person* is "Brd 3, Clr 2, Sor/Wiz 3." That means it is a 3rd-level spell for bards, a 2nd-level spell for clerics, and a 3rd-level spell for sorcerers and wizards. The entry for *magic vestment* is "Clr 3, Strength 3." That means it is a 3rd-level spell for clerics and the 3rd-level Strength domain spell.

Class Abbreviations: Brd (bard), Clr (cleric), Drd (druid), Pal (paladin), Rgr (ranger), Sor (sorcerer), Wiz (wizard).

Domains: Air, Animal, Chaos, Death, Destruction, Earth, Evil, Fire, Good, Healing, Knowledge, Law, Luck, Magic, Plant, Protection, Strength, Sun, Travel, Trickery, War, and Water.

COMPONENTS

This entry indicates what you must have or do to cast the spell. If the necessary components are not present, the casting fails. Spells can have verbal (V), somatic (S), material (M), focus (F), divine focus (DF), or experience point cost (XP) components, or any combination thereof. See Components, page 151.

CASTING TIME

The time required to cast a spell. See Casting Time, page 148.

RANGE

The maximum distance from you at which the spell can affect a target. See Range, page 148.

TARGET OR TARGETS/EFFECT/AREA

This entry lists the number of creatures, dimensions, volume, weight, and so on, that the spell affects. The entry starts with one of three headings: "Target," "Effect," or "Area." See Aiming a Spell, page 148. If the target of a spell is "You," you do not receive a saving throw, and spell resistance does not apply. The saving throw and spell resistance headings are omitted from such spells.

DURATION

How long the spell lasts. See Duration, page 150.

SAVING THROW

Whether a spell allows a saving throw, what type of saving throw it is, and the effect of a successful save. See Saving Throw, page 150.

SPELL RESISTANCE

Whether spell resistance (SR), a special defensive ability, resists this spell. See Spell Resistance, page 150.

DESCRIPTIVE TEXT

This portion of the spell description details what the spell does and how it works. If one of the previous portions of the description included "(see text)," this is where the explanation is found. (If the spell you're reading about is part of a spell chain, you might have to refer to a different spell for the "(see text)" information.)

SPELLS

The spells herein are presented in alphabetical order.

Acid Fog

Conjuration (Creation) [Acid]
Level: Sor/Wiz 6, Water 7
Components: V, S, M/DF
Casting Time: 1 action
Range: Medium (100 ft. + 10 ft./level)
Effect: Fog spreads 30 ft., 20 ft. high
Duration: 1 round/level
Saving Throw: None
Spell Resistance: Yes

Acid fog creates a billowing mass of misty vapors similar to a *solid fog* spell. In addition to slowing creatures down and obscuring sight, this spell's vapors are highly acidic. Each round, starting when you cast the spell, the fog deals 2d6 points of acid damage to creatures and objects within it.

Arcane Material Components: A pinch of dried, powdered peas combined with powdered animal hoof.

Aid

Enchantment (Compulsion)
[Mind-Affecting]
Level: Clr 2, Good 2, Luck 2
Components: V, S, DF
Casting Time: 1 action
Range: Touch
Target: Living creature touched
Duration: 1 minute/level
Saving Throw: None
Spell Resistance: Yes (harmless)

Aid is almost like a *bless* and a proactive *cure light wounds* spell rolled into one. The subject is encouraged just as with *bless* (+1 morale bonus to attack rolls and saves against fear effects), plus it gains 1d8 temporary hit points (see page 129).

Air Walk

Transmutation
Level: Air 4, Clr 4
Components: V, S, DF
Casting Time: 1 action
Range: Touch
Target: Creature (Gargantuan or smaller) touched
Duration: 10 minutes/level
Saving Throw: None
Spell Resistance: Yes (harmless)

The transmuted creature can tread on air as if walking on solid ground. Moving upward is similar to walking up a hill. The maximum upward or downward angle possible is 45 degrees, at a rate equal to one-half the creature's normal speed.

A strong wind (21+ mph) can push an air walker along or hold her back. At the end of her turn each round, the wind blows her 5 feet for each 5 miles per hour of wind speed. The creature can, at the DM's option, be subject to additional penalties in exceptionally strong or turbulent winds, such as loss of control over movement or suffering physical damage from being buffeted about.

You can cast *air walk* on a specially trained mount so it can be ridden through the air. You train a mount to *air walk* with the Handle Animal skill (*air walking* counts as an unusual task; see page 68).

Alarm

Abjuration
Level: Brd 1, Rgr 1, Sor/Wiz 1
Components: V, S, F/DF
Casting Time: 1 action
Range: Close (25 ft. + 5 ft./2 levels)
Area: 25-ft.-radius emanation centered on a point in space
Duration: 2 hours/level (D)
Saving Throw: None
Spell Resistance: No

Alarm sounds a mental or audible alarm each time a creature of Tiny or larger size enters the warded area or touches it. A creature who speaks the password (determined by you at the time of casting) does not set off the *alarm.* You decide at the time of casting whether the alarm will be mental or audible.

Mental Alarm: A mental *alarm* alerts you (and only you) so long as you remain within a mile of the warded area. You note a single mental "ping" that awakens you from normal sleep but does not otherwise disturb concentration. A *silence* spell has no effect on a mental *alarm.*

Audible Alarm: An audible *alarm* produces the sound of a hand bell, and anyone within 60 feet of the warded area can hear it clearly. Reduce the distance by 10 feet for each interposing closed door and by 20 feet for each substantial interposing wall. In quiet conditions, the ringing can be heard faintly up to 180 feet away. The ringing lasts for 1 round. Creatures within a *silence* spell cannot hear the ringing.

Ethereal or astral creatures do not trigger the *alarm* unless the intruder becomes material while in the warded area.

Arcane Focus: A tiny bell and a piece of very fine silver wire.

Alter Self

Transmutation
Level: Sor/Wiz 2
Components: V, S
Casting Time: 1 action
Range: Personal
Target: You
Duration: 10 minutes/level (D)

You can alter your appearance and form—including clothing and equipment—to appear taller or shorter, thin, fat, or in between. The assumed form must be corporeal. Your body can undergo a limited physical transmutation, including adding or subtracting one or two limbs, and your weight can be changed up to one-half. If the form selected has wings, you can fly at a speed of 30 feet with poor maneuverability (The *DUNGEON MASTER's Guide* has information on maneuverability.) If the form has gills, you can breathe underwater.

Your attack rolls, natural armor bonus, and saves do not change. The spell does not confer special abilities, attack forms, defenses, ability scores, or mannerisms of the chosen form. Once the new form is chosen, it remains for the duration of the spell. If you are slain, you automatically return to your normal form.

If you use this spell to create a disguise, you get a +10 bonus on your Disguise check.

Analyze Dweomer

Divination
Level: Sor/Wiz 6
Components: V, S, F
Casting Time: 8 hours
Range: Close (25 ft. + 5 ft./2 levels)
Target: One object or creature
Duration: 1 round/level (D)
Saving Throw: See text
Spell Resistance: No

You discern spells and magical properties present in a creature or object. One property, spell, or power is revealed each round, from lowest level (or weakest power) to highest (or strongest). For each spell or power, you make a caster level check (1d20 + caster level). If the result is equal to or higher than the spell's or power's caster level, you identify it. Otherwise, you fail to identify that spell or power, and you can check for the next one next round.

Analyze dweomer does not function when used on an artifact (see the *DUNGEON MASTER's Guide* for details on artifacts).

After you analyze one object or creature, the spell ends, even if its duration has not expired yet. Casting this spell is physically taxing; you must make a Fortitude save (DC 21) when the spell ends or be exhausted and unable to do anything but rest for the next 1d8 hours. While this spell is most frequently used in the comfort and safety of your laboratory, you could also cast *analyze dweomer* to study the magic seals and barriers on a portal or to determine just how a companion has been cursed.

Focus: A tiny lens of ruby or sapphire set in a small golden loop. The gemstone must be worth at least 1,500 gp.

Animal Friendship
Enchantment (Charm) [Mind-Affecting]
Level: Drd 1, Rgr 1
Components: V, S, M
Casting Time: 1 action
Range: Close (25 ft. + 5 ft./2 levels)
Target: One animal
Duration: Instantaneous
Saving Throw: Will negates
Spell Resistance: Yes

You win the loyalty of an animal, provided that your heart is true. The spell functions only if you actually wish to be the animal's friend. If you are not willing to treat the animal as a friend (for example, you intend to eat it, or to use it to set off traps), the spell fails. An animal's loyalty, once gained, is natural (not magical) and lasting.

You can teach the befriended animal three specific tricks or tasks for each point of Intelligence it possesses. Typical tasks are coming when called, rolling over on command, fetching, or shaking hands. They cannot be complex (complex tricks, such as accepting a rider, require the Handle Animal skill; see page 68).

At any one time, you can have only a certain number of animals befriended to you. You can have animal friends whose Hit Dice total no more than twice your caster level. For example, a 3rd-level druid could use the spell to win the friendship of an animal of 6 HD or less, and a 5th-level ranger could use it to win the friendship of an animal of 4 HD or less. You may dismiss animal friends to enable you to befriend new ones.

Material Component: A piece of food the animal likes.

Animal Growth
Transmutation
Level: Drd 5, Sor/Wiz 5
Components: V, S
Casting Time: 1 action
Range: Medium (100 ft. + 10 ft./level)
Targets: Up to one animal/two levels, no two of which can be more than 30 ft. apart
Duration: 1 minute/level
Saving Throw: None
Spell Resistance: Yes

&A number of animals grow to twice their normal size. This doubles each animal's height, length, and width, increasing its weight by a factor of eight. This increase in size has a number of effects:

Hit Dice: The creature's HD double, doubling the creature's base attack bonus and increasing its saves accordingly.

Size: The creature's size increases one step. This increase reduces its AC (according to the new size), reduces its attack bonus (according to the new size), affects its ability to grapple (page 137), and so on.

The creature gains an enlargement bonus to Strength and Constitution scores, and its damage with natural attacks increases. This spell does not affect Colossal creatures.

For details on how the characteristics of an enlarged animal change, see the *Monster Manual.*

When the spell ends, the creature's hit points return to normal, and all damage the creature has taken while enlarged is divided by 2.

The spell gives you no special means of command or influence over the enlarged animals.

Animal Messenger
Enchantment (Compulsion) [Mind-Affecting]
Level: Clr 2, Drd 2, Rgr 2
Components: V, S, M
Casting Time: 1 action
Range: Close (25 ft. + 5 ft./2 levels)
Target: One Tiny animal
Duration: 1 day/level
Saving Throw: None
Spell Resistance: Yes

You compel a Tiny animal to go to a spot you designate. The most common use for this spell is to get the animal to carry a message to your allies. The animal cannot be one tamed or trained by someone else.

Using some type of food desirable to the animal as a lure, you call the animal to you. It advances and awaits your bidding. You can mentally impress on the animal a certain place well known to you or an obvious landmark (such as the peak of a distant mountain or mouth of a nearby river). The directions must be simple, because the animal depends on your knowledge and can't find a destination on its own. You can attach some small item or note to the messenger. The animal then goes to the designated location and waits there until the duration of the spell expires, whereupon it resumes its normal activities.

During this period of waiting, the messenger allows others to approach it and remove any scroll or token it carries. Note that unless the intended recipient of a message is expecting a messenger in the form of a bird or other small animal, the carrier may be ignored. The intended recipient of a message gains no special ability to communicate with the animal or read any attached message (if it's in a language she doesn't know, for example).

The spell works only on animals with an Intelligence score of 1 or 2.

Material Component: A morsel of food the animal likes.

Animal Shapes
Transmutation
Level: Animal 7, Drd 8
Components: V, S, DF

Casting Time: 1 action
Range: Close (25 ft. + 5 ft./2 levels)
Targets: One willing creature/level, all within 30 ft. of each other
Duration: 1 hour/level (D)
Saving Throw: None (see text)
Spell Resistance: Yes (harmless)

As *polymorph other,* except you polymorph up to one willing creature per level into an animal of your choice; the spell has no effect on unwilling creatures. Recipients remain in the animal form until the spell expires or you dismiss the spell for all recipients. In addition, an individual subject may choose to resume her normal form (as a full-round action); doing so ends the spell for her and her alone.

The allowed size of the animal form depends on your level:

Caster Level	Allowed Sizes
Up to 16th	Small or Medium-size
17th–19th	Tiny through Large
20th	Diminutive through Huge

Creatures polymorphed by this spell don't suffer the disorientation penalty that those transformed by *polymorph other* often do.

Animal Trance
Enchantment (Compulsion) [Mind-Affecting, Sonic]
Level: Brd 2, Drd 2
Components: V, S
Casting Time: 1 action
Range: Close (25 ft. + 5 ft./2 levels)
Targets: Animals, beasts, or magical beasts of Intelligence 1 or 2
Duration: Concentration
Saving Throw: Will negates (see text)
Spell Resistance: Yes

Your swaying motions and music (or singing, or chanting) compel animals, beasts, and magical beasts to do nothing but watch you. Only creatures with Intelligence scores of 1 or 2 can be affected by this spell. Roll 2d6 to determine the total number of HD that you entrance. The closest targets are selected first until no more targets within range can be affected. For example, if Vadania affects 7 HD worth of animals and there are several 2-HD wolves within close range, only the three closest wolves are affected.

Animals trained to attack or guard, beasts, and magical beasts are allowed saving throws; animals not trained to attack or guard are not. An entranced creature can be struck (with a +2 bonus to the attack roll, as if it were stunned), but it then recovers from the compulsion and is no longer affected by the spell.

Animate Dead

Necromancy [Evil]
Level: Clr 3, Death 3, Sor/Wiz 5
Components: V, S, M
Casting Time: 1 action
Range: Touch
Targets: One or more corpses touched
Duration: Instantaneous
Saving Throw: None
Spell Resistance: No

This spell turns the bones or bodies of dead creatures into undead skeletons or zombies that follow your spoken commands. The skeletons or zombies can follow you, or can remain in an area and attack any creature (or just a specific type of creature) entering the place. The undead remain animated until they are destroyed. (A destroyed skeleton or zombie can't be animated again.)

Regardless of the type of undead, you can't create more HD of undead than you have caster levels with a single casting of *animate dead*.

The undead you create remain under your control indefinitely. No matter how many times you use this spell, however, you can control only 2 HD worth of undead creatures per caster level. If you exceed this number, all the newly created creatures fall under your control, and any excess undead from previous castings become uncontrolled (you choose which creatures are released). If you are a cleric, any undead you might command by virtue of your power to command or rebuke undead do not count toward the limit.

Skeletons: A skeleton can be created only from a mostly intact corpse or skeleton. The corpse must have bones (so purple worm skeletons are not allowed). If a skeleton is made from a corpse, the flesh falls off the bones. The statistics for a skeleton depend on its size; they do not depend on what abilities the creature may have had while alive. See the *Monster Manual* for details.

Zombies: A zombie can be created only from a mostly intact corpse. The creature must have a true anatomy (so gelatinous cube zombies are not allowed). The statistics for a zombie depend on its size, not on what abilities the creature may have had while alive. See the *Monster Manual*.

Material Component: You must place a black onyx gem worth at least 50 gp into the mouth or eye socket of each corpse. The magic of the spell turns these gems into worthless, burned-out shells.

Animate Objects

Transmutation
Level: Chaos 6, Clr 6
Components: V, S
Casting Time: 1 action
Range: Medium (100 ft. + 10 ft./level)
Target: Objects or matter, 1 cu. ft./level
Duration: 1 round/level
Saving Throw: None
Spell Resistance: No

You imbue inanimate objects with mobility and a semblance of life. The animated object, or objects, then attack whomever or whatever you initially designate. The animated object can be of any nonmagical material—wood, metal, stone, fabric, leather, ceramic, glass, etc. You can also animate masses of raw matter, such as water, a rock from a wall or a rock on the ground, as long as the volume of material does not exceed 1 cubic foot per caster level.

Animate dead created these skeletons.

Statistics for animated objects are found in the *Monster Manual*.

The spell cannot animate objects carried or worn by a creature.

Animate Rope

Transmutation
Level: Sor/Wiz 1
Components: V, S
Casting Time: 1 action
Range: Medium (100 ft. + 10 ft./level)
Target: One ropelike object, length up to 50 ft. + 5 ft./level

Duration: 1 round/level
Saving Throw: None
Spell Resistance: No

You can animate a nonliving ropelike object, including string, yarn, cord, line, rope, or even a cable. The maximum length assumes a rope with a 1-inch diameter. Reduce the total length by 50% for every additional inch of thickness, and increase the length by 50% for each reduction of the rope's width by half. The possible commands are "Coil" (form a neat, coiled stack), "Coil and knot," "Loop," "Loop and knot," "Tie and knot," and the opposites of all of the above ("Uncoil," etc.). One command can be given each round as a standard action.

The rope can enwrap only a creature or an object within 1 foot of it—it does not snake outward—so it must be thrown near the intended target. Doing so requires a successful ranged touch attack roll. The rope has a range increment of 10 feet. A typical rope has 2 hit points, AC 10, and can be burst with a Strength check (DC 23). The rope does not deal damage of any type, but it can be used as a trip line or to entangle a single opponent who fails a Reflex saving throw. An *entangled* creature suffers a −2 penalty to attack rolls and a −4 penalty to effective Dexterity. If the rope can anchor itself to an immobile object, the *entangled* creature cannot move. Otherwise, it can move at half speed but can't run or charge. A creature capable of spellcasting that is bound by this spell must make a Concentration check (DC 15) to cast a spell. An *entangled* creature can slip free with an Escape Artist check (DC 20).

The rope itself, and any knots tied in it, are not magical.

This spell grants a +2 bonus to any Use Rope checks you make when using the transmuted rope.

Antilife Shell

Abjuration
Level: Animal 6, Clr 6, Drd 6
Components: V, S, DF
Casting Time: 1 full round
Range: 10 ft.

Area: 10-ft.-radius emanation, centered on you
Duration: 10 minutes/level (D)
Saving Throw: None
Spell Resistance: Yes

You bring into being a mobile, hemispherical energy field that prevents the entrance of most sorts of living creatures. The effect hedges out animals, aberrations, beasts, magical beasts, dragons, fey, giants, humanoids, monstrous humanoids, oozes, plants, shapechangers, and vermin, but not constructs, elementals, outsiders, or undead. (See the *Monster Manual* for an explanation of creature types.)

Note: This spell may be used only defensively, not aggressively; forcing an abjuration barrier against creatures whom the spell keeps at bay collapses the barrier (see page 157).

Antimagic Field

Abjuration
Level: Clr 8, Magic 6, Protection 6, Sor/Wiz 6
Components: V, S, M/DF
Casting Time: 1 action
Range: 10 ft.
Area: 10-ft.-radius emanation, centered on you
Duration: 10 minutes/level (D)
Saving Throw: None
Spell Resistance: See text

An invisible barrier surrounds you and moves with you. The space within this barrier is impervious to most magical effects, including spells, spell-like abilities, and supernatural abilities. Likewise, it prevents the functioning of any magic items or spells within its confines.

An *antimagic field* suppresses any spell or magical effect used within, brought into, or cast into the area, but does not dispel it. A *hasted* creature, for example, is not *hasted* while inside the field, but the spell resumes functioning when it leaves the field. Time spent within an *antimagic field* counts against the suppressed spell's duration.

Golems and other magical constructs, elementals, outsiders, and corporeal undead, still function in an antimagic area (though the antimagic area suppresses their supernatural, spell-like, and spell abilities normally). If such creatures are summoned or conjured, however, see below.

Summoned or conjured creatures of any type and incorporeal undead wink out if they enter an antimagic field. They reappear in the same spot once the field goes away. Time spent winked out counts normally against the duration of the conjuration that's maintaining the creature. If you cast *antimagic field* in an area

occupied by a conjured creature who has spell resistance, you must make a caster level check (1d20 + caster level) against the creature's SR to make it wink out. (The effects of instantaneous conjurations, such as *create water*, are not affected by the *antimagic field* because the conjuration itself is no longer in effect, only its result.)

Normal creatures (a normally encountered troll rather than a conjured one, for instance) can enter the area, as can normal missiles. Furthermore, while a magic sword does not function magically within the area, it is still a sword (and a masterwork sword at that). The spell has no effect on constructs that are imbued with magic during their creation process and are thereafter self-supporting (unless they have been summoned, in which case they are treated like any other summoned creatures). Undead and outsiders are likewise unaffected unless summoned. These creatures' spell-like or supernatural abilities, however, may be temporarily nullified by the field.

Dispel magic does not remove the field. Two or more *antimagic fields* sharing any of the same space have no effect on each other. Certain spells, such as *wall of force*, *prismatic sphere*, and *prismatic wall* remain unaffected by *antimagic field* (see the individual spell descriptions). Artifacts and creatures of demigod or higher status are unaffected by mortal magic such as this.

Note: Should you be larger than the area enclosed by the barrier, any part of your person that lies outside the barrier is unaffected by the field.

Arcane Material Component: A pinch of powdered iron or iron filings.

Antipathy

Enchantment (Compulsion)
   [Mind-Affecting]
Level: Drd 9, Sor/Wiz 8
Components: V, S, M/DF
Casting Time: 1 hour
Range: Close (25 ft. + 5 ft./2 levels)
Target: One location (up to a 10-ft. cube/level) or one object
Duration: 2 hours/level
Saving Throw: Will partial
Spell Resistance: Yes

You cause an object or location to emanate magical vibrations that repel either a specific type of intelligent creature or creatures of a particular alignment, as defined by you. The particular type of creature to be affected must be named specifically—for example, red dragons, hill giants, wererats, lammasu, cloakers, or vampires. Larger groups, such as "goblinoids," are not specific enough. Likewise, the specific alignment must be named—for example,

chaotic evil, chaotic good, lawful neutral, or true neutral.

Creatures of the designated type or alignment feel an overpowering urge to leave the area or to avoid the affected item. A compulsion forces them to abandon the area or item, shunning it and never willingly returning to it while the spell is in effect. A creature who makes a successful saving throw can stay in the area or touch the item, but feels very uncomfortable doing so. This distracting discomfort reduces the creature's Dexterity score by 4 points.

Antipathy counters and dispels *sympathy*. This spell cannot be cast upon living creatures.

Arcane Material Component: A lump of alum soaked in vinegar.

Antiplant Shell

Abjuration
Level: Drd 4
Components: V, S, DF
Casting Time: 1 action
Range: 10 ft.
Area: 10-ft.-radius emanation, centered on you
Duration: 10 minutes/level (D)
Saving Throw: None
Spell Resistance: Yes

The *antiplant shell* spell creates an invisible, mobile barrier that keeps all creatures within the shell protected from attacks by plant creatures or animated plants. As with many abjuration spells, forcing the barrier against creatures whom the spell keeps at bay strains and collapses the field (see page 157).

Arcane Eye

Divination
Level: Sor/Wiz 4
Components: V, S, M
Casting Time: 10 minutes
Range: Unlimited
Effect: Magical sensor
Duration: 1 minute/level
Saving Throw: None
Spell Resistance: No

You create an invisible magical sensor that sends you visual information. The *arcane eye* travels at 30 feet per round (300 feet per minute) if viewing an area ahead as a human would (primarily looking at the floor) or 10 feet per round (100 feet per minute) if examining the ceiling and walls as well as the floor ahead. The *arcane eye* sees exactly as you would see if you were there. The *arcane eye* can travel in any direction as long as the spell lasts. Solid barriers prevent the passage of an *arcane eye*, although it can pass through a space no smaller than a small mouse hole (1 inch in diameter).

You must concentrate to use the eye. If you do not concentrate, the eye is inert until you again concentrate. The powers of the eye cannot be enhanced by other spells or items (though you can use magic to improve your own eyesight). You are subject to any gaze attack met by the eye. A successful *dispel magic* cast on you or the eye ends the spell. With respect to blindness, magical darkness, and other phenomena that affect vision, the *arcane eye* is considered an independent sensory organ of yours. (For example, it is not blinded if your normal eyes are blinded.)

Any creature with Intelligence 12 or higher can notice the *arcane eye* by making a Scry check or an Intelligence check (DC 20). Spells such as *detect scrying* can also detect the eye.

Material Component: A bit of bat fur.

Arcane Lock

Abjuration
Level: Sor/Wiz 2
Components: V, S, M
Casting Time: 1 action
Range: Touch
Target: The door, chest, or portal touched, up to 30 sq. ft./level in size
Duration: Permanent
Saving Throw: None
Spell Resistance: No

An *arcane lock* spell cast upon a door, chest, or portal magically locks it. You can freely pass your own lock without affecting it; otherwise, a door or object secured with *arcane lock* can be opened only by breaking in or by a successful *dispel magic* or *knock* spell. Add +10 to the normal DC to break open a door or portal affected by this spell. Note that a *knock* spell does not remove an *arcane lock*. It only suppresses it for 10 minutes.

Material Component: Gold dust worth 25 gp.

Arcane Mark

Universal
Level: Sor/Wiz 0
Components: V, S
Casting Time: 1 action
Range: Touch
Effect: One personal rune or mark, all of which must fit within 1 ft. square
Duration: Permanent
Saving Throw: None
Spell Resistance: No

This spell allows you to inscribe your personal rune or mark, which can be no taller than 6 inches in height and consist of no more than six characters. The writing can be visible or invisible. An *arcane mark* spell enables you to etch the rune upon any substance (even stone or metal) without harm to the material upon which the mark is

placed. If an invisible mark is made, a *detect magic* spell causes it to glow and be visible (though not necessarily understandable). *See invisibility, true seeing,* a *gem of seeing,* or a *robe of eyes* likewise allows their users to see an invisible *arcane mark.* A *read magic* spell reveals the words, if any. The mark cannot be dispelled, but it can be removed by the caster or by an *erase* spell. If cast on a living being, normal wear gradually causes the mark to fade in about a month.

Arcane mark must be cast on an object prior to casting *Drawmij's instant summons* on the same object (see that spell description for details).

Astral Projection

Necromancy
Level: Clr 9, Sor/Wiz 9, Travel 9
Components: V, S, M
Casting Time: 30 minutes
Range: Touch
Targets: You plus one additional creature touched per two levels
Duration: See text
Saving Throw: None
Spell Resistance: Yes

Freeing your spirit from your physical body, this spell allows you to project an astral body into another plane altogether. You can bring the astral forms of other creatures with you, provided the creatures are linked in a circle with you at the time of the casting. These fellow travelers are dependent upon you and must accompany you at all times. If something happens to you during the journey, the companions are stranded wherever you left them.

You project your astral self into the Astral Plane, leaving your physical body behind on the Material Plane in a state of suspended animation. The spell projects an astral copy of you and all you wear or carry onto the Astral Plane. Since the Astral Plane touches upon other planes, you can travel astrally to any of these other planes as you will. You then leave the Astral Plane, forming a new physical body (and equipment) on the plane of existence you have chosen to enter.

When on the Astral Plane or another plane, your astral body is connected at all times to your material body by a silvery cord. If the cord is broken, you are killed, astrally and materially. Luckily, very few things can destroy a silver cord. When a second body is formed on a different plane, the incorporeal silvery cord remains invisibly attached to the new body. If the second body or the astral form is slain, the cord simply returns to your body where it rests on the Material Plane, reviving it from its state of suspended animation. Although astral projections are able to function on the Astral Plane, their actions affect only creatures existing on

the Astral Plane; a physical body must be materialized on other planes.

You and your companions may travel through the Astral Plane indefinitely. Your bodies simply wait behind in a state of suspended animation until you choose to return your spirits to their physical bodies. The spell lasts until you desire to end it, or until it is terminated by some outside means, such as *dispel magic* cast upon either the physical body or the astral form, or the destruction of your body back on the Material Plane (which kills you).

Material Components: A jacinth worth at least 1,000 gp, plus a silver bar worth 5 gp for each person to be affected.

Atonement

Abjuration
Level: Clr 5, Drd 5
Components: V, S, M, F, DF, XP
Casting Time: 1 hour
Range: Touch
Target: Living creature touched
Duration: Instantaneous
Saving Throw: None
Spell Resistance: Yes

This spell removes the burden of evil acts or misdeeds from the subject. The creature seeking atonement must be truly repentant and desirous of setting right its misdeeds. If the atoning creature committed the evil act unwittingly or under some form of compulsion, *atonement* operates normally at no cost to you. However, in the case of a creature atoning for deliberate misdeeds and acts of knowing and willful nature, you must intercede with your deity at the cost of 500 experience points in order to expunge the subject's burden. Naturally, many casters first assign a subject of this sort a quest (see *geas/quest*) or similar penance to determine if the creature is truly contrite before casting the *atonement* spell on its behalf.

Atonement may be cast for one of several purposes, depending on the version selected:

Reverse Magical Alignment Change: If a creature has had its alignment magically changed, *atonement* returns its alignment to its original status at no cost in experience points.

Restore Class: A paladin who has lost her class features due to unwillingly or unwittingly committing an evil act may have her paladinhood restored to her by this spell. Note: A paladin who willingly and deliberately commits an evil act can never regain her paladinhood.

Restore Cleric or Druid Spell Powers: A cleric or druid who has lost his ability to cast spells because he incurred the anger of his deity may regain his spell powers by seeking *atonement* from another cleric of the same deity or another druid. If the transgression was intentional, the casting cleric loses 500 XP for his intercession. If the transgression was unintentional, he does not lose XP.

Redemption or Temptation: You may cast this spell upon a creature of an opposing alignment in order to offer it a chance to change its alignment to match yours. The prospective subject must be present for the entire casting process. Upon completion of the spell, the subject freely chooses whether it retains its original alignment or acquiesces to your offer and changes to your alignment. No duress, compulsion, or magical influence can force the subject to take advantage of the opportunity offered if it is unwilling to abandon its old alignment. This use of the spell does not work on outsiders (or any creature incapable of changing its alignment naturally).

Note: Normally, changing alignment is up to the player (for PCs) or the DM (NPCs). This use of *atonement* simply offers a believable way for a character to change her alignment drastically, suddenly, and definitively.

Material Component: Burning incense.

Focus: In addition to your holy symbol or normal divine focus, you need a set of prayer beads (or other prayer device, such as a prayer wheel or prayer book) worth at least 500 gp.

XP Cost: When cast for the benefit of creatures whose guilt was the result of deliberate acts, the cost to you is 500 XP per casting (see above).

Augury

Divination
Level: Clr 2
Components: V, S, F
Casting Time: 1 action
Range: Personal
Target: You
Duration: Instantaneous

An *augury* can tell you whether a particular action will bring good or bad results for you in the immediate future. For example, if a party is considering destroying a weird seal that closes a portal, an *augury* might determine whether it's a good idea.

The base chance for receiving a meaningful reply is 70% + 1% per caster level; the DM makes the roll secretly. The DM may determine that the question is so straightforward that a successful result is automatic, or so vague as to have no chance of success. If the augury succeeds, you get one of four results:

- "Weal" (if the action will probably bring good results).
- "Woe" (for bad results).
- "Weal and woe" (for both).

- "Nothing" (for actions that don't have especially good or bad results).

If the spell fails, you get the "nothing" result. A cleric who gets the "nothing" result has no way to tell whether it resulted from a failed or successful augury.

The augury can see into the future only about half an hour, so anything that might happen after that does not affect the augury. Thus, it might miss the long-term consequences of the contemplated action. All *auguries* cast by the same person about the same topic within half an hour use the same dice result as the first *augury*.

Focus: A set of marked sticks, bones, or similar tokens of at least 25 gp value.

Awaken

Transmutation
Level: Drd 5
Components: V, S, F, XP
Casting Time: One day
Range: Touch
Target: Animal or tree touched
Duration: Instantaneous
Saving Throw: Will negates
Spell Resistance: Yes

You awaken a tree or animal to humanlike sentience. To succeed, you must make a Will save (DC 10 + the target's HD, or the HD the tree will have once awakened).

The awakened animal or tree is friendly toward you. You have no special empathy or connection with a creature you awaken, although it serves you in specific tasks or endeavors if you communicate your desires to it.

An awakened tree has characteristics as if it were an animated object (see the *Monster Manual*), except that its Intelligence, Wisdom, and Charisma scores are all 3d6. Awakened plants gain the ability to move their limbs, roots, vines, creepers, etc., and have senses similar to a human's.

An awakened animal gets 3d6 Intelligence, +1d3 Charisma, and +2 HD.

An awakened tree or animal can speak one language that you know, plus one additional language that you know per point of Intelligence bonus (if any).

XP Cost: 250 XP.

Bane

Enchantment (Compulsion)
[Mind-Affecting]
Level: Clr 1
Components: V, S, DF
Casting Time: 1 action
Range: 50 ft.
Area: All enemies within 50 ft.
Duration: 1 minute/level
Saving Throw: Will negates
Spell Resistance: Yes

Bane fills your enemies with fear and doubt. They suffer a –1 morale penalty on their attack rolls and a –1 morale penalty on saving throws against fear effects.

Bane counters and dispels *bless*.

Banishment

Abjuration
Level: Clr 6, Sor/Wiz 7
Components: V, S, F
Casting Time: 1 action
Range: Close (25 ft. + 5 ft./2 levels)
Targets: One or more extraplanar creatures, no two of which can be more than 30 ft. apart
Duration: Instantaneous
Saving Throw: Will negates
Spell Resistance: Yes

A *banishment* spell is a more powerful version of the *dismissal* spell. It enables you to force extraplanar creatures out of your home plane. Up to 2 HD of creatures per caster level can be banished. To target a creature, you must present at least one object or substance that it hates, fears, or otherwise opposes. For each such object or substance, you gain +1 on your caster level check to overcome the target's SR (if any) and +2 on the saving throw DC. For example, if this spell were cast on a demon that hated light and was vulnerable to holy water and iron weapons, you might use iron, holy water, and a torch in the spell. The three items would add +3 to your check to overcome the demon's SR and add +6 to the spell's DC.

At the DM's option, certain rare items might work twice as well (each providing +2 against SR and +4 on the spell's DC).

Barkskin

Transmutation
Level: Drd 2, Plant 2
Components: V, S, DF
Casting Time: 1 action
Range: Touch
Target: Living creature touched
Duration: 10 minutes/level
Saving Throw: None
Spell Resistance: Yes (harmless)

Barkskin makes a creature's skin as tough as bark. The effect grants a +3 natural armor bonus to AC. This bonus increases to +4 at 6th level and to +5 at 12th level and up.

Since the AC bonus is a natural armor bonus, it does not stack with any natural armor the subject may already have.

Bestow Curse

Transmutation
Level: Brd 3, Clr 3, Sor/Wiz 4
Components: V, S
Casting Time: 1 action
Range: Touch
Target: Creature touched

Duration: Permanent
Saving Throw: Will negates
Spell Resistance: Yes

You place a curse on the creature touched. You choose one of the three following effects, depending on the version selected:

- –6 effective decrease to an ability score (minimum 1).
- –4 enhancement penalty on attack rolls, saving throws, ability checks, and skill checks.
- Each turn, the target has a 50% chance to act normally; otherwise, he takes no action.

You may also invent your own curse, but it should be no more powerful than those listed above, and the DM has final say on the curse's effect.

The *curse* cannot be dispelled, but it can be removed with a *break enchantment*, *limited wish*, *miracle*, *remove curse*, or *wish* spell.

Bestow curse counters *remove curse*.

Bigby's Clenched Fist
Evocation
Level: Sor/Wiz 8, Strength 8
Components: V, S, F/DF

As *Bigby's interposing hand*, except it moves and attacks as directed by you. (You direct it as a free action.) The floating hand can move up to 60 feet and can attack in the same round. Since this hand is directed by you, its ability to notice or attack invisible or concealed creatures is no better than yours.

The hand attacks once per round, and its attack bonus equals your level + your Intelligence, Wisdom, or Charisma modifier (for a wizard, cleric, or sorcerer, respectively), +11 for the hand's Strength score (33), –1 for being Large. The hand's damage is 1d8+12, and any creature struck must make a Fortitude save (against this spell's save DC) or be stunned for 1 round. A stunned creature can't act and loses any Dexterity bonus to AC. Attackers gain +2 bonuses to attack it.

Clerics who cast this spell name it for their deities—*Pelor's clenched fist*, for example.

Arcane Focus: A leather glove and a small device (similar to brass knuckles) consisting of four rings joined in a slightly curved line, which must be slipped onto the four fingers of the caster's dominant hand. The device must be fashioned of an alloy of copper and zinc.

Bigby's Crushing Hand
Evocation
Level: Sor/Wiz 9, Strength 9
Components: V, S, M, F/DF

As *Bigby's interposing hand*, except the hand can interpose itself, push, or crush one opponent that you select.

The *crushing hand* can interpose itself as *Bigby's interposing hand* does, or it can bull rush an opponent as *Bigby's forceful hand* does, but at +18 on the Strength check.

The *crushing hand* can grapple an opponent as *Bigby's grasping hand* does, but with a +12 bonus for the hand's Strength score (35). The hand deals 2d6+12 points of grapple damage (normal, not subdual).

Clerics who cast this spell name it for their deities—*St. Cuthbert's crushing hand*, for example.

Arcane Material Component: The shell of an egg.

Arcane Focus: A glove of snakeskin.

Bigby's Forceful Hand
Evocation
Level: Sor/Wiz 6
Components: V, S, F

Bigby's crushing hand grabs a beholder.

As *Bigby's interposing hand*, except the forceful hand pursues and pushes away the opponent that you designate. Treat this as a bull rush with a +14 bonus on the Strength check (+8 for Strength 27, +4 for being Large, and +2 for charging bonus, which it always gets). The hand always

moves with the opponent to push him back the full distance allowed, and it has no speed limit.

A very strong creature could not push the hand out of its way (because the hand would instantly reposition itself between the creature and you), but it could push the hand up against you by successfully bull rushing the hand.

Focus: A sturdy glove made of leather or heavy cloth.

Bigby's Grasping Hand
Evocation
Level: Sor/Wiz 7, Strength 7
Components: V, S, F/DF

As *Bigby's interposing hand*, except the hand can also grapple one opponent that you select. The *grasping hand* gets one grappling attack per round. Its attack bonus to make contact is your level + your Intelligence, Wisdom, or Charisma modifier (for wizards, clerics, and sorcerers, respectively), +10 for the hand's Strength score (31), –1 for being Large. Its grapple check is this same figure, except with +4 for being Large instead of –1. It holds but does not harm creatures it grapples.

The *grasping hand* can also bull rush an opponent as *Bigby's forceful hand* does, but at +16 on the Strength check, or interpose itself as *Bigby's interposing hand* does.

Clerics who cast this spell name it for their deities—*Kord's grasping hand*, for example.

Arcane Focus: A leather glove.

Bigby's Interposing Hand
Evocation
Level: Sor/Wiz 5
Components: V, S, F
Casting Time: 1 action
Range: Medium (100 ft. + 10 ft./level)
Effect: 10-ft. hand
Duration: 1 round/level (D)
Saving Throw: None
Spell Resistance: Yes

Bigby's interposing hand creates a Large magic hand that appears between you and one opponent. This floating, disembodied hand then moves to remain between the two, regardless of where you move or how the opponent tries to get around it, providing nine-tenths cover (+10 AC) for you against that opponent. Nothing can fool the hand—it sticks with the selected opponent in spite of darkness, *invisibility*, *polymorphing*, or any other attempt to hide or disguise himself. The hand does not pursue an opponent, however.

A *Bigby's hand* is 10 feet long and about that wide with its fingers outstretched. It has as many hit points as you when undamaged, and its AC is 20 (−1 size, +11 natural). It takes damage as a normal creature, but most magical effects that don't cause damage do not affect it. The hand cannot push through a *wall of force* or enter an *antimagic field*. It suffers the full effects of a *prismatic wall* or *prismatic sphere*. The hand makes saving throws as its caster. *Disintegrate* or a successful *dispel magic* destroys the hand.

Any creature weighing less than 2,000 pounds trying to push past the hand is slowed to half its normal speed. If the opponent weighs more than 2,000 pounds, the hand cannot reduce its speed but still affects the opponent's attacks.

By concentrating (as a standard action), you can designate a new opponent for the hand.

Focus: A soft glove.

Binding

Enchantment (Compulsion)
[Mind-Affecting]
Level: Sor/Wiz 8
Components: V, S, M
Casting Time: One minute
Range: Close (25 ft. + 5 ft./2 levels)
Target: One living creature
Duration: See text (D)
Saving Throw: Will negates (see text)
Spell Resistance: Yes

A *binding* spell creates a magical restraint to hold a creature. The target only gets an initial saving throw if its HD is equal to at least half your caster level.

You may have up to six assistants help you with the spell. For each assistant who casts *suggestion*, your caster level for this casting of the spell increases by +1. For each assistant who casts *dominate animal*, *dominate person*, or *dominate monster*, your effective level increases by a number equal to one-third that assistant's level (provided the target is appropriate for the spell). All the assistants must join in chanting the spell (see the details on the spell's verbal component, below). Your caster level determines whether the target gets an initial Will saving throw and how long the *binding* lasts. All *binding* durations are dismissible.

The *binding* spell has six versions. Choose one of the following versions when you cast the spell.

Chaining: The subject is confined by restraints that generate an *antipathy* spell affecting all creatures who approach the subject, except you. Duration is one year per caster level. The subject of this form of *binding* is confined to the spot it occupied when it received the spell.

Slumber: Brings a comatose sleep upon the subject for up to one year per caster level. The subject does not need to eat or drink while *slumbering*, nor does it age.

This form of *binding* is more difficult to cast than *chaining*, making it slightly easier to resist. Reduce the spell's save DC by 1.

Bound Slumber: A combination of *chaining* and *slumber* that lasts for up to one month per caster level. Reduce save DC by 2.

Hedged Prison: The subject is transported to or otherwise brought within a confined area (such as a labyrinth) from which it cannot wander by any means. The spell is permanent. Reduce save DC by 3.

Metamorphosis: The subject assumes gaseous form, except for its head or face. It is held harmless in a jar or other container, which may be transparent (your choice). The creature remains aware of its surroundings and can speak, but cannot leave the container, attack, or use any of its powers or abilities. The *binding* is permanent. The subject does not need to breathe, eat, or drink while *metamorphosed*, nor does it age. Reduce save DC by 4.

Minimus Containment: The subject is shrunk to a height of 1 inch or even less and held within some gem or similar object or jar. The *binding* is permanent. The subject does not need to breathe, eat, or drink while *contained*, nor does it age. Reduce save DC by 4.

Regardless of the version of *binding* you cast, you can specify triggering conditions that end the spell and release the creature whenever they occur. These can be as simple or elaborate as you desire (but the DM must agree that the condition is reasonable and has a likelihood of coming to pass). The conditions can be based on a creature's name, identity, or alignment but otherwise must be based on observable actions or qualities. Intangibles such as level, class, HD, or hit points don't qualify. For example, a *bound* creature can be released when a lawful good creature approaches, but not when a paladin approaches. Once the spell is cast, its triggering conditions cannot be changed. Setting a release condition increases the save DC (assuming a saving throw is allowed) by +2 and increases the cost of the spell's material components by one-half (see below).

In the case of the first three versions of *binding* (those with limited durations), you may cast additional *binding* spells to prolong the effect (the durations overlap). If you do so, the target gets a saving throw at the end of the first spell's duration (even if your caster level was high enough to disallow an initial saving throw). If the creature succeeds at this save, all the *binding* spells it has received are broken.

Components: The components for a *binding* spell vary according to the version of the spell, but they include a continuous chanting utterance read from the scroll or book page giving the spell, somatic gestures, and materials appropriate to the form of *binding*. These include such items as

miniature chains of special metals (silver for lycanthropes, etc.), soporific herbs of the rarest sort (for *slumber* bindings), a bell jar of the finest crystal, and so on.

In addition to the specially made props suited to the specific type of *binding* (cost 500 gp), the spell requires opals worth at least 500 gp for each HD of the target and a vellum depiction or carved statuette of the subject to be captured.

Blade Barrier

Evocation
Level: Clr 6, Good 6, War 6
Components: V, S
Casting Time: 1 full round
Range: Medium (100 ft. + 10 ft./level)
Effect: Spinning disk of blades, up to 30-ft. radius
Duration: 10 minutes/level
Saving Throw: Reflex negates (see text)
Spell Resistance: Yes

This spell creates a spinning disk of razor-sharp blades. These whirl and flash around a central point, creating an immobile, circular barrier. Any creature passing through the *blade barrier* takes 1d6 points of slashing damage per caster level (maximum 20d6). The plane of rotation of the blades can be horizontal, vertical, or slanted.

Creatures within the *blade barrier* when it is invoked take the damage as well. They can negate the damage with a successful Reflex saving throw, provided they can and do physically leave the area of the blades by the shortest possible route. Once the barrier is in place, anything entering or passing through the blades automatically takes damage.

A *blade barrier* serves as one-half cover (+4 AC) for anyone beyond it.

Blasphemy

Evocation [Evil, Sonic]
Level: Clr 7, Evil 7
Components: V
Casting Time: 1 action
Range: 30 ft.
Area: Creatures in a 30-ft.-radius spread centered on you
Duration: Instantaneous
Saving Throw: None
Spell Resistance: Yes

Uttering *blasphemy* creates two effects.

If you are on your home plane, nonevil extraplanar creatures within the area are instantly banished back to their home planes. Creatures so banished cannot return for at least 1 day. This effect takes place regardless of whether the creatures hear the *blasphemy*.

Creatures native to your plane who hear the *blasphemy* and are not evil suffer the following ill effects:

HD	Effect
12 or more	Dazed
Less than 12	Weakened, dazed
Less than 8	Paralyzed, weakened, dazed
Less than 4	Killed

The effects are cumulative.

Dazed: The creature is dazed and can take no actions for 1 round (but defends itself normally).

Weakened: The creature's Strength score decreases by 2d6 points for 2d4 rounds.

Paralyzed: The creature is paralyzed and helpless for 1d10 minutes, unable to move or act in any way.

Killed: Living creatures die. Undead creatures are destroyed.

Bless

Enchantment (Compulsion)
[Mind-Affecting]
Level: Clr 1, Pal 1
Components: V, S, DF
Casting Time: 1 action
Range: 50 ft.
Area: All allies within 50 ft.
Duration: 1 minute/level
Saving Throw: None
Spell Resistance: Yes (harmless)

Bless fills your allies with courage. They gain a morale bonus of +1 on their attack rolls and a morale bonus of +1 on saving throws against fear effects.

Bless counters and dispels *bane*.

Bless Water

Transmutation [Good]
Level: Clr 1, Pal 1
Components: V, S, M
Casting Time: 1 minute
Range: Touch
Target: Flask of water touched
Duration: Instantaneous
Saving Throw: Will negates (object)
Spell Resistance: Yes (object)

This transmutation imbues a flask (1 pint) of water with positive energy, turning it into holy water (page 113). Holy water is considered blessed, which means it has special effects on certain creatures.

Material Component: 5 pounds of powdered silver (worth 25 gp).

Bless Weapon

Transmutation
Level: Pal 1
Components: V, S
Casting Time: 1 action
Range: Touch
Target: Weapon touched
Duration: 1 minute/level
Saving Throw: None
Spell Resistance: No

This transmutation makes a weapon strike true against evil foes. All critical rolls against evil foes are automatically successful (so every threat is a critical hit). The weapon negates the damage reduction of evil creatures and is capable of striking evil incorporeal creatures as if it had a +1 enhancement bonus. Also, the weapon is considered blessed, which means it has special effects on certain creatures. Individual arrows or bolts can be transmuted, but affected projectile weapons (such as bows) don't confer the benefit to the projectiles they shoot.

This transmutation can't affect any weapon that already has a magical effect related to critical hits, such as a keen weapon or a vorpal sword.

Blindness/Deafness

Transmutation
Level: Brd 2, Clr 3, Sor/Wiz 2
Components: V
Casting Time: 1 action
Range: Medium (100 ft. + 10 ft./level)
Target: One living creature
Duration: Permanent (D)
Saving Throw: Fortitude negates
Spell Resistance: Yes

The subject becomes blinded or deafened, as you choose. In addition to the obvious effects, a blinded creature suffers a 50% miss chance in combat (all opponents have full concealment), loses any Dexterity bonus to AC, grants a +2 bonus to attackers' attack rolls (they are effectively invisible), moves at half speed, and suffers a –4 penalty on most Strength- and Dexterity-based skills. A deafened character, in addition to the obvious effects, suffers a –4 penalty on initiative and a 20% chance to miscast and lose any spell with a verbal (V) component that he tries to cast.

The *DUNGEON MASTER's Guide* has more details on the effects of blindness and deafness.

Blink

Transmutation
Level: Brd 3, Sor/Wiz 3
Components: V, S
Casting Time: 1 action
Range: Personal
Target: You
Duration: 1 round/level (D)

Like a blink dog, you "blink" back and forth between the Material and the Ethereal planes. You look as though you're winking in and out of reality very quickly and at random.

Blinking has several effects:

Physical attacks suffer a 50% miss chance, and the Blind-Fight feat doesn't help (since the *blinker* is ethereal and not merely invisible). If the attack is capable of striking ethereal or incorporeal creatures, the miss chance is only 20% (for one-half concealment). If the attacker can see invisible creatures, the miss chance is also only 20%. If the attacker can both see and strike ethereal creatures, he suffers no penalty. Likewise, your own attacks suffer a 20% miss chance, since you sometimes go ethereal just as you are about to strike.

Individually targeted spells have a 50% chance to fail against you while *blinking* unless your attacker can target invisible, ethereal creatures. Likewise, your own spells have a 20% chance to activate just as you go ethereal, in which case they typically do not affect the Material Plane.

While *blinking*, you take only half damage from area attacks (or full damage from those that extend onto the Ethereal Plane). You strike as an invisible creature (+2 attack), denying your target any Dexterity bonus to AC. You suffer only half damage from falling, since you fall only while you are material.

While *blinking*, you can step through (but not see through) solid objects. For each 5 feet of solid material you walk through, there's a 50% chance that you become material, with regrettable consequences (see below). You can move only at three-quarters speed: Movement on the Ethereal Plane is at half speed, and you spend about half your time there and half your time material.

Since you spend about half your time on the Ethereal Plane, you can see and even attack ethereal creatures. You interact with ethereal creatures roughly the same way you interact with material ones. For instance, your spells against ethereal creatures are 20% likely to activate just as you go material and be lost.

Note: An ethereal creature is invisible, incorporeal, and capable of moving in any direction, even up or down (albeit at normal speed). As an incorporeal creature, you can move through solid objects, including living creatures. An ethereal creature can see and hear the Material Plane, but everything looks gray and insubstantial. Sight and hearing on the Material Plane are limited to 60 feet. Force effects (such as *magic missile* and *wall of force*) and abjurations affect you normally. Their effects extend onto the Ethereal Plane from the Material Plane, but not vice versa. An ethereal creature can't attack material creatures, and spells you cast while ethereal affect only other ethereal things. Certain material creatures or objects have attacks or effects that work on the Ethereal Plane (such as the basilisk and its gaze attack). Treat other ethereal creatures and ethereal objects as normally material. An ethereal creature who becomes material while in a material object is shunted off to the nearest open space and takes 1d6 points of damage per 5 feet so traveled.

The subject of a blur spell.

Blur

Illusion (Glamer)
Level: Brd 2, Sor/Wiz 2
Components: V
Casting Time: 1 action
Range: Touch
Target: Creature touched
Duration: 1 minute/level
Saving Throw: Will negates (harmless)
Spell Resistance: Yes (harmless)

The subject's outline appears blurred, shifting and wavering. This distortion grants the subject one-half concealment (20% miss chance).

A *see invisibility* spell does not counteract the *blur* effect, but a *true seeing* spell does.

Note: Opponents who cannot see the subject ignore the spell's effect (though fighting an unseen opponent carries penalties of its own; see page 132).

Break Enchantment

Abjuration
Level: Brd 4, Clr 5, Luck 5
Components: V, S
Casting Time: 1 minute
Range: Close (25 ft. + 5 ft./2 levels)
Target or Targets: Up to one creature per level, all within 30 ft. of each other
Duration: Instantaneous

Saving Throw: See text
Spell Resistance: No

This dispelling spell frees creatures from enchantments, transmutations, curses, and petrification (as well as other magical transformations). *Break enchantment* can reverse even an instantaneous effect, such as *flesh to stone*. For each such effect, you make a check of 1d20 + caster level (maximum +15) against a DC of 11 + caster level of the effect. Success means that the creature is free of the spell, curse, or effect. For cursed magic items, the DC is 25.

If the spell is one that, as a special property, cannot be dispelled by *dispel magic*, *break enchantment* works only if that spell is 5th level or lower. For instance, *bestow curse* cannot be dispelled by *dispel magic*, but *break enchantment* can dispel it.

If the effect comes from some permanent magic item, such as a cursed sword, *break enchantment* does not remove the curse from the item but merely frees the victim from the item's effects, leaving the item cursed. For example, a cursed item can change the alignment of its user. *Break enchantment* allows the victim to be rid of the item (and negates the alignment change), but the item's curse is intact and affects the next person to pick up the item (even if it's the *break enchantment* recipient).

Bull's Strength

Transmutation
Level: Brd 2, Clr 2, Sor/Wiz 2, Strength 2
Components: V, S, M/DF
Casting Time: 1 action
Range: Touch
Target: Creature touched
Duration: 1 hour/level
Saving Throw: Will negates (harmless)
Spell Resistance: Yes (harmless)

The subject becomes stronger. The spell grants an enhancement bonus to Strength of 1d4+1 points, adding the usual benefits to melee attack rolls, melee damage rolls, and other uses of the Strength modifier.

Arcane Material Component: A few hairs, or a pinch of dung, from a bull.

Burning Hands

Transmutation [Fire]
Level: Fire 1, Sor/Wiz 1
Components: V, S
Casting Time: 1 action
Range: 10 ft.
Area: Semicircular burst of flames 10 ft. long, centered on your hands
Duration: Instantaneous
Saving Throw: Reflex half
Spell Resistance: Yes

A thin sheet of searing flame shoots from your outspread fingertips. You must hold

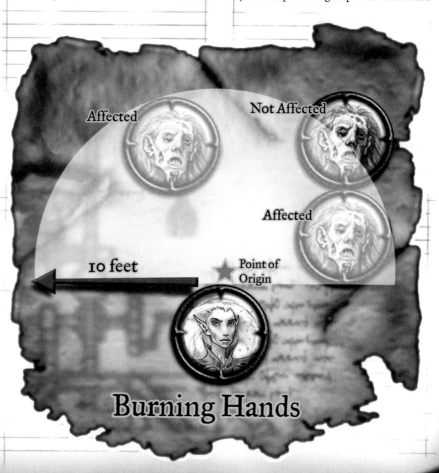

Burning Hands

Illus. by D. Martin

your hands with your thumbs touching and your fingers spread. The sheet of flame is about as thick as your thumbs. Any creature in the area of the flames takes 1d4 points of fire damage per your caster level (maximum 5d4). Flammable materials such as cloth, paper, parchment, and thin wood burn if the flames touch them. A character can extinguish burning items as a full-round action.

Call Lightning

Evocation [Electricity]
Level: Drd 3
Components: V, S
Casting Time: 10 minutes, plus 1 action per bolt called
Range: Long (400 ft. + 40 ft./level)
Effect: See text
Duration: 10 minutes/level
Saving Throw: Reflex half
Spell Resistance: Yes

To cast *call lightning*, you must be in a stormy area—a rain shower, clouds and wind, hot and cloudy conditions, or even a tornado (including a whirlwind formed by a djinn or air elemental of 7 HD or more). You are then able to evoke bolts of lightning as long as you remain in the stormy area. (The spell ends if you leave the stormy area.) You can call down one bolt every 10 minutes. You need not call a bolt of lightning immediately—other actions, even spellcasting, can be performed. However, you must use a standard action (concentrating on the spell) to call each bolt. A bolt causes 1d10 points of electrical damage per caster level (maximum 10d10).

The bolt of lightning flashes down in a vertical stroke at whatever target point you choose, within range (measured from your position at the time). The bolt takes the shortest possible unobstructed path between a nearby cloud and the target. Any creature within a 10-foot radius of the path or the point where the lightning strikes is affected.

This spell can be used only outdoors. It does not function indoors, underground, or underwater.

Calm Animals

Enchantment (Compulsion)
   [Mind-Affecting]
Level: Animal 1, Drd 1
Components: V, S
Casting Time: 1 action
Range: Close (25 ft. + 5 ft./2 levels)
Targets: Animals, beasts, or magical beasts with Intelligence 1 or 2 within 30 ft. of each other
Duration: 1 minute/level
Saving Throw: Will negates (see text)
Spell Resistance: Yes

This spell soothes and quiets animals, beasts, and magical beasts, rendering them docile and harmless. Only creatures with Intelligence scores of 1 or 2 can be affected by this spell. All the subjects must be of the same species and within a 30-foot sphere. Roll 2d4 + caster level to determine the total number of HD affected. Animals trained to attack or guard, dire animals, beasts, and magical beasts are allowed saving throws. Animals not trained to attack or guard are not. (A druid could calm a normal bear or wolf with little trouble, but it's more difficult to affect a winter wolf, a bulette, or a trained guard dog.)

The affected creatures remain where they are and do not attack or flee. They are not helpless and defend themselves normally if attacked. Any threat (fire, a hungry predator, an imminent attack) breaks the spell on the threatened creatures.

Calm Emotions

Enchantment (Compulsion)
   [Mind-Affecting]
Level: Clr 2, Law 2
Components: V, S, DF
Casting Time: 1 action
Range: Medium (100 ft. + 10 ft./level)
Targets: 1d6 creatures/level, all of whom must be within 30 ft. of each other
Duration: Concentration, up to 1 round/level (D)
Saving Throw: Will negates
Spell Resistance: Yes

This spell calms agitated creatures. You have no control over the affected creatures, but this spell can stop raging creatures from fighting or joyous ones from reveling. Creatures so affected cannot take violent actions (although they can defend themselves) or do anything destructive, except to protect themselves. Any aggressive action or life-threatening damage against *calmed* creatures immediately breaks the spell on the threatened creatures.

This spell automatically suppresses (but does not dispel) mind-affecting spells such as *bless, confusion, emotion,* and *fear,* as well as negating a bard's ability to inspire courage or a barbarian's rage. While the *calm emotions* spell lasts, a suppressed spell has no effect. When the *calm emotions* spell ends, the original spell takes hold of the creature again, provided its duration has not expired in the meantime.

Cat's Grace

Transmutation
Level: Brd 2, Sor/Wiz 2
Components: V, S, M
Casting Time: 1 action
Range: Touch
Target: Creature touched
Duration: 1 hour/level
Saving Throw: None
Spell Resistance: Yes

The transmuted creature becomes more graceful, agile, and coordinated. The spell grants an enhancement bonus to Dexterity of 1d4+1 points, adding the usual benefits to AC, Reflex saves, and other uses of the Dexterity modifier.

Material Component: A pinch of cat fur.

Cause Fear

Necromancy [Fear, Mind-Affecting]
Level: Brd 1, Clr 1, Death 1, Sor/Wiz 1
Components: V, S
Casting Time: 1 action
Range: Close (25 ft. + 5 ft./2 levels)
Target: One living creature
Duration: 1d4 rounds
Saving Throw: Will negates
Spell Resistance: Yes

The affected creature becomes frightened. It suffers a –2 morale penalty on attack rolls, weapon damage rolls, and saving throws. It flees from you as well as it can. If unable to flee, the creature may fight. Creatures with 6 or more Hit Dice are immune. *Cause fear* counters *remove fear.*

Note: Mind-affecting spells do not affect nonintelligent creatures, and fear spells do not affect undead.

Chain Lightning

Evocation [Electricity]
Level: Air 6, Sor/Wiz 6
Components: V, S, F
Casting Time: 1 action
Range: Long (400 ft. + 40 ft./level)
Targets: One primary target plus one secondary target/level (each must be within 30 ft. of the primary target)
Duration: Instantaneous
Saving Throw: Reflex half
Spell Resistance: Yes

This spell creates an electrical discharge that begins as a single stroke commencing from your fingertips. Unlike *lightning bolt,* *chain lightning* strikes one object or creature initially, then arcs to other targets.

The bolt deals 1d6 points of electricity damage per caster level (maximum 20d6) on the primary target. After the bolt strikes, lightning can arc to as many secondary targets as you have levels. The secondary bolts each strike one target and deal half as many dice of damage as the primary (rounded down). For example, a 19th-level caster generates a primary bolt (19d6 points of damage) and up to nineteen secondary bolts (9d6 points of damage each). All subjects can attempt Reflex saving throws for half damage. You choose secondary targets as you like, but they must all be within 30 feet of the primary target, and no target can be struck more than once. You can choose to affect fewer secondary targets than the maximum (to avoid allies in the area, for example).

Focus: A bit of fur; a piece of amber, glass, or a crystal rod; and one silver pin for each of your caster levels.

Change Self

Illusion (Glamer)
Level: Sor/Wiz 1, Trickery 1
Components: V, S
Casting Time: 1 action
Range: Personal
Target: You
Duration: 10 minutes/level (D)

You make yourself—including clothing, armor, weapons, and equipment—look different. You can seem 1 foot shorter or taller, thin, fat, or in between. You cannot change your body type. For example, a human caster could look human, humanoid, or like any other generally human-shaped bipedal creature. Otherwise, the extent of the apparent change is up to you. You could add or obscure a minor feature, such as a mole or a beard, or look like an entirely different person.

The spell does not provide the abilities or mannerisms of the chosen form. It does not alter the perceived tactile (touch) or audible (sound) properties of you or your equipment. A battleaxe made to look like a dagger still functions as a battleaxe.

If you use this spell to create a disguise, you get a +10 bonus on the Disguise check.

Note: Creatures get Will saves to recognize the glamer as an illusion if they interact with it (such as by touching you and having that not match what they see, in this case of this spell).

Changestaff

Transmutation
Level: Drd 7, Plant 7
Components: V, S, F
Casting Time: 1 full round
Range: Touch
Target: Your touched staff
Duration: 1 hour/level (D)
Saving Throw: None
Spell Resistance: No

You change a specially prepared quarter-staff into a Huge treantlike creature, about 24 feet tall. When you plant the end of the staff in the ground and speak a special command to conclude the casting of the spell, your staff turns into a creature who looks and fights just like a treant. The staff-treant defends you and obeys any spoken commands. However, it is by no means a true treant; it cannot converse with actual treants or control trees. If the staff-treant is reduced to 0 hit points or less, it crumbles

to powder and the staff is destroyed. Otherwise, the staff can be used as the focus for another casting of the spell. The staff-treant is always at full strength when created, despite any wounds it may have suffered the last time it appeared.

Focus: The quarterstaff, which must be specially prepared. The staff must be a sound limb cut from an ash, oak, or yew, then cured, shaped, carved, and polished (a process taking 28 days). You cannot adventure or engage in other strenuous activity during the shaping and carving of the staff.

Chaos Hammer

Evocation [Chaotic]
Level: Chaos 4
Components: V, S
Casting Time: 1 action
Range: Medium (100 ft. + 10 ft./level)
Area: 20-ft.-radius burst
Duration: Instantaneous
Saving Throw: Will half (see text)
Spell Resistance: Yes

You unleash chaotic power to smite your enemies. The power takes the form of a multicolored explosion of leaping, ricocheting energy. Only lawful and neutral (not chaotic) creatures are harmed by the spell.

The spell deals 1d8 points of damage per two caster levels (maximum 5d8) to lawful creatures and staggers them for 1d6 rounds. A staggered character can take only partial actions. A successful Will save reduces the damage by half and negates the stagger effect.

The spell deals only half damage against creatures who are neither lawful nor chaotic, and they are not staggered. They can reduce the damage by half again (down to one-quarter of the roll) with a successful Will save.

Charm Monster

Enchantment (Charm) [Mind-Affecting]
Level: Brd 3, Sor/Wiz 4
Target: One living creature
Duration: 1 day/level

As *charm person*, except that the spell is not restricted by creature type or size.

Charm Person

Enchantment (Charm) [Mind-Affecting]
Level: Brd 1, Sor/Wiz 1
Components: V, S
Casting Time: 1 action
Range: Close (25 ft. + 5 ft./2 levels)
Target: One person
Duration: 1 hour/level
Saving Throw: Will negates
Spell Resistance: Yes

This charm makes a humanoid of Medium-size or smaller regard you as his trusted

friend and ally. If the creature is currently being threatened or attacked by you or your allies, however, he receives a +5 bonus on his saving throw.

The spell does not enable you to control the *charmed* person as if he were an automaton, but he perceives your words and actions in the most favorable way. You can try to give the subject orders, but you must win an opposed Charisma check to convince him to do anything he wouldn't ordinarily do. (Retries not allowed.) A *charmed* person never obeys suicidal or obviously harmful orders, but he might believe you if you assured him that the only chance to save your life is for him to hold back an onrushing red dragon for "just a few seconds." Any act by you or your apparent allies that threatens the *charmed* person breaks the spell. Note also that you must speak the person's language to communicate your commands, or else be good at pantomiming.

Charm Person or Animal

Enchantment (Charm) [Mind-Affecting]
Level: Drd 2
Target: One person or animal

As *charm person*, except that it can also affect an animal. When in doubt about whether something is an "animal" as defined by the spell, check the *Monster Manual*.

Chill Metal

Transmutation [Cold]
Level: Drd 2
Components: V, S, DF
Casting Time: 1 action
Range: Close (25 ft. + 5 ft./2 levels)
Target: Metal equipment of one creature/ two levels, no two of which can be more than 30 ft. apart; or 25 lb. of metal/ level, none of which can be more than 30 ft. away from any of the rest
Duration: 7 rounds
Saving Throw: Will negates (object)
Spell Resistance: Yes (object)

Chill metal makes metal extremely cold. Unattended, nonmagical metal gets no saving throw. Enchanted metal is allowed a saving throw against the spell. (Magic items' saving throws are covered in the *Dungeon Master's Guide*.) An item in a creature's possession uses the creature's saving throw (unless its own is higher).

A creature takes cold damage if its equipment is chilled. It takes full damage if its armor is affected or if it's holding, touching, wearing, or carrying metal weighing one-fifth of its weight. The creature takes minimum damage (1 point or 2 points; see the table) if it's not wearing metal armor and the metal that it's carrying weighs less than one-fifth of its weight.

On the first round of the spell, the metal becomes very chilly and uncomfortable to touch but deals no damage (this is also the effect on the last round of the spell's duration). During the second (and also the next-to-last) round, icy coldness causes pain and damage. In the third, fourth, and fifth rounds, the metal is freezing cold, causing more damage, as shown below:

	Metal	
Round	Temperature	Damage
1	Cold	None
2	Icy	1d4 points
3–5	Freezing	2d4 points
6	Icy	1d4 points
7	Cold	None

Any heat intense enough to damage the creature negates cold damage from the spell (and vice versa) on a point-for-point basis. For example, if the damage roll from a *chill metal* spell indicates 5 points of cold damage and the creature plunges through a *wall of fire* in the same round and takes 8 points of fire damage, it winds up taking no chill damage and only 3 points of fire damage. Underwater, *chill metal* deals no damage, but ice immediately forms around the affected metal, making it more buoyant.

Chill metal counters and dispels *heat metal*.

Chill Touch

Necromancy
Level: Sor/Wiz 1
Components: V, S
Casting Time: 1 action
Range: Touch
Targets: Creature or creatures touched (up to one/level)
Duration: Instantaneous
Saving Throw: Fortitude partial
Spell Resistance: Yes

A touch from your hand, which glows with blue energy, disrupts the life force of living creatures. Each touch channels negative energy that deals 1d6 points of damage and possibly also 1 point of temporary Strength damage. (A successful Fortitude saving throw negates the Strength damage.) You can use this melee touch attack up to one time per level.

The spell has a special effect on undead creatures. Undead touched by you suffer no damage or Strength loss, but they must make successful Will saving throws or flee as if panicked for 1d4 rounds +1 round per caster level.

Circle of Death

Necromancy [Death]
Level: Sor/Wiz 6
Components: V, S, M
Casting Time: 1 action
Range: Medium (100 ft. + 10 ft./level)
Area: Several living creatures within a 50-ft.-radius burst
Duration: Instantaneous
Saving Throw: Fortitude negates
Spell Resistance: Yes

A *circle of death* snuffs out the life forces of living creatures, killing them instantly.

The spell slays 1d4 HD worth of living creatures per caster level (maximum 20d4). Creatures with the fewest HD are affected first; among creatures with equal HD, those who are closest to the point of origin of the burst are affected first. No creature with 9 or more HD is affected, and HD that are not sufficient to affect a creature are wasted.

Material Component: The powder of a crushed black pearl with a minimum value of 500 gp.

Circle of Doom

Necromancy
Level: Clr 5, Destruction 5
Components: V, S
Casting Time: 1 action
Range: 20 ft.
Area: All living enemies and undead creatures within a 20-ft.-radius burst centered on you
Duration: Instantaneous
Saving Throw: Fortitude half
Spell Resistance: Yes

Negative energy bursts in all directions from the point of origin, dealing 1d8 points of damage +1 point per caster level (maximum +20) to nearby living enemies.

Like *inflict* spells, *circle of doom* cures undead in its area rather than harming them.

Clairaudience/Clairvoyance

Divination
Level: Brd 3, Knowledge 3, Sor/Wiz 3
Components: V, S, F/DF
Casting Time: 1 action
Range: See text
Effect: Magical sensor
Duration: 1 minute/level (D)
Saving Throw: None
Spell Resistance: No

Clairaudience/clairvoyance enables you to concentrate upon some locale and hear or see (your choice) almost as if you were there. Distance is not a factor, but the locale must be known—a place familiar to you or an obvious one (such as behind a door, around a corner, or in a grove of trees). The spell does not allow magically enhanced senses to work through it. If the chosen locale is magically dark, you see nothing. If it is naturally pitch black, you can see in a 10-foot radius around the center of the spell's effect. Lead sheeting or

magical protection (such as *antimagic field*, *mind blank*, or *nondetection*) blocks the spell, and you sense that the spell is so blocked. The spell creates an invisible sensor, similar to that created by a *scrying* spell, that can be dispelled. The spell functions only on the plane of existence you are currently occupying.

Arcane Focus: A small horn (for hearing) or a glass eye (for seeing).

Cloak of Chaos

Abjuration [Chaotic]
Level: Chaos 8, Clr 8
Components: V, S, F
Casting Time: 1 action
Range: 20 ft.
Targets: One creature/level in a 20-ft.-radius burst centered on you
Duration: 1 round/level (D)
Saving Throw: See text
Spell Resistance: Yes (harmless)

A random pattern of color surrounds the subjects, protecting them from attacks, granting them resistance to spells cast by lawful creatures, and confusing lawful creatures when they strike the subjects. This abjuration has four effects:

First, the warded creatures gain a +4 deflection bonus to AC and a +4 resistance bonus to saves. Unlike *protection from law*, this benefit applies against all attacks, not just against attacks by lawful creatures.

Second, the warded creatures gain SR 25 against lawful spells and spells cast by lawful creatures.

Third, the abjuration blocks possession and mental influence, just as *protection from law* does.

Finally, if a lawful creature succeeds with a melee attack against a warded creature, the offending attacker is confused for 1 round (Will save negates, as *confusion*, but against the save DC of *cloak of chaos*).

Focus: A tiny reliquary containing some sacred relic, such as a scrap of parchment from a chaotic text. The reliquary costs at least 500 gp.

Clone

Necromancy
Level: Sor/Wiz 8
Components: V, S, M, F
Casting Time: 10 minutes
Range: Touch
Effect: One clone
Duration: Instantaneous
Saving Throw: None
Spell Resistance: No

This spell makes an inert duplicate of a creature. If the original individual has been slain, the original's soul transfers to the clone, creating a replacement (provided the soul is free and willing to return; see Bringing Back the Dead, page 153).

The original's physical remains, should they still exist, become inert matter and cannot thereafter be restored to life. If the original has reached the end of its natural life span (died of natural causes), any cloning attempt fails.

To create the duplicate, you must have a piece of flesh (not hair, nails, scales, or the like) taken from the original's living body, with a volume of at least 1 cubic inch. The piece of flesh need not be fresh, but it must be kept from rotting (such as by the *gentle repose* spell). Once the spell is cast, the duplicate must be grown in a laboratory for 2d4 months.

When the clone is completed, if the original is dead, the original's soul enters the clone. The clone has the personality, memories, skills, and levels the original had at the time the piece of flesh was taken. However, the replacement must be at least one level lower than the original was at the time of death. If the original was 1st level, the clone's Constitution score drops by 1; if this would give the clone a Constitution score of 0, the spell fails. If the original creature has lost levels since the flesh sample was taken and died at a lower level than the clone would otherwise be, the clone is at the level at which the original died.

The spell duplicates only the original's body and mind, not its equipment.

A duplicate can be grown while the original still lives, or when the original soul is unavailable, but the resulting creature is merely a soulless bit of inert flesh, which rots if not somehow preserved.

Arcane Material Components: The piece of flesh and various laboratory supplies (cost 1,000 gp).

Focus: Special laboratory equipment (cost 500 gp).

Cloudkill

Conjuration (Creation)
Level: Sor/Wiz 5
Components: V, S
Casting Time: 1 action
Range: Medium (100 ft. + 10 ft./level)
Effect: Cloud spreads 30 ft. wide and 20 ft. high
Duration: 1 minute/level
Saving Throw: See text
Spell Resistance: Yes

This spell generates a bank of fog, similar to a *fog cloud* except that its vapors are ghastly yellowish green and poisonous. They kill any living creature with 3 or fewer HD (no save) and cause creatures with 4 to 6 HD to make Fortitude saving throws or die. Living creatures above 6 HD, and creatures of 4 to 6 HD who make their saving throws, take 1d10 points of poison damage each round while in the cloud. Holding one's breath doesn't help.

Unlike a *fog cloud*, the *cloudkill* moves away from you at 10 feet per round, rolling along the surface of the ground. (Figure out the cloud's new spread each round based on its new point of origin, 10 feet farther away from the point of origin where you cast the spell.) Because the vapors are heavier than air, they sink to the lowest level of the land, even pouring down den or sinkhole openings; thus, the spell is ideal for slaying nests of giant ants, for example. It cannot penetrate liquids, nor can it be cast underwater.

Color Spray

Illusion (Pattern) [Mind-Affecting]
Level: Sor/Wiz 1
Components: V, S, M
Casting Time: 1 action
Range: Close (25 ft. + 5 ft./2 levels)
Area: Cone
Duration: Instantaneous (see text)
Saving Throw: Will negates
Spell Resistance: Yes

A vivid cone of intertwined, clashing colors springs forth from your hand, stunning creatures, blinding them, or even knocking them unconscious. The closest 1d6 creatures in the cone are affected. The spell affects each subject according to its HD:

Up to 2: Unconscious for 2d4 rounds, then blinded for 1d4 rounds, and then stunned for 1 round. (Only living creatures are knocked unconscious.)

3 or 4: Blinded for 1d4 rounds, then stunned for 1 round.

5 or more: Stunned for 1 round.

In addition to the obvious effects, a blinded creature suffers a 50% miss chance in combat (all opponents have full concealment), loses any Dexterity bonus to AC, grants a +2 bonus to attackers' attack rolls (they are effectively invisible), moves at half speed, and suffers a –4 penalty on most Strength- and Dexterity-based skills.

A stunned creature can't act and loses any Dexterity bonus to AC. Attackers gain +2 bonuses to attack it.

Sightless creatures are not affected by *color spray*.

Material Component: A pinch each of powder or sand that is colored red, yellow, and blue.

Command

Enchantment (Compulsion) [Language-
Dependent, Mind-Affecting]
Level: Clr 1
Components: V
Casting Time: 1 action
Range: Close (25 ft. + 5 ft./2 levels)
Target: One living creature

Point of Origin

Affected

Not Affected

Affected

25-foot cone

Color Spray

Duration: 1 round
Saving Throw: Will negates
Spell Resistance: Yes

You give the subject a one-word command, which she obeys to the best of her ability. A very reasonable command causes the subject to suffer a penalty on the saving throw (from –1 to –4, at the DM's discretion). Typical *commands* are "Flee," "Die" (which causes the subject to feign death), "Halt," "Run," "Stop," "Fall," "Go," "Leave," "Surrender," and "Rest." (A *command* of "Suicide" fails because "suicide" is generally used as a noun, not as a command.)

Command Plants

Enchantment (Charm) [Mind-Affecting]
Level: Drd 8, Plant 8
Components: V
Casting Time: 1 action
Range: Close (25 ft. + 5 ft./2 levels)
Targets: Plants and plant creatures (see text)
Duration: 1 day/level or 1 hour/level (see text)
Saving Throw: See text
Spell Resistance: See text

Plants, fungi, plant creatures, and fungus creatures do your bidding.

Charm: Against plant creatures and fungus creatures, *command plants* functions as a *mass charm* spell. You can command a number of plant creatures whose combined level or HD do not exceed three times your level (or at least one creature regardless of HD). No two affected creatures can be more than 30 feet from each other, and each is allowed a Will saving throw to negate the effect. Spell resistance applies. The effect lasts 1 day per caster level. This is a *charm* effect.

Animate: The spell imbues trees or other large, inanimate vegetable life with mobility. The animated plants then attack whomever or whatever you first designate. Animated plants gain human-like senses. The plants' AC, speed, attacks, and special abilities vary with their size and form, as described for animated objects in the *Monster Manual.* You can animate two trees, four shrubs, or eight vines. All plants to be affected must be within 60 feet of each other. You can animate different types of plants if desired (for example, one tree and four vines or a tree and two shrubs). Creatures who have the plants in their possession can prevent the effect with Will saves or spell resistance. The effect lasts 1 hour per caster level.

Entangle: You imbue all plants within range with semimobility, which allows them to entwine around creatures in the area. This duplicates the effect of an *entangle* spell. Spell resistance does not keep creatures from being *entangled.* The effect lasts 1 hour per caster level.

Commune

Divination
Level: Clr 5
Components: V, S, M, DF, XP
Casting Time: 10 minutes
Range: Personal
Target: You
Duration: 1 round/level

You contact your deity—or agents thereof—and ask questions that can be answered by a simple yes or no. (A cleric of no particular deity contacts a philosophically allied deity.) You are allowed one such question per caster level. The answers given are correct within the limits of the entity's knowledge. "Unclear" is a legitimate answer, because powerful beings of the Outer Planes are not necessarily omniscient. In cases where a one-word answer would be misleading or contrary to the deity's interests, the DM should give a short phrase (five words or less) as an answer instead. The spell, at best, provides information to aid character decisions. The entities contacted structure their answers to further their own purposes. If you lag, discuss the answers, or go off to do anything else, the spell ends.

Material Components: Holy (or unholy) water and incense.

XP Cost: 100 XP.

Commune with Nature

Divination
Level: Animal 5, Drd 5
Components: V, S
Casting Time: 10 minutes
Range: Personal
Target: You
Duration: Instantaneous

You become one with nature, attaining knowledge of the surrounding territory. You instantly gain knowledge of up to three facts from among the following subjects: the ground or terrain, plants, minerals, bodies of water, people, general animal population, presence of woodland creatures, presence of powerful unnatural creatures, or even the general state of the natural setting. For example, you could determine the location of any powerful undead creatures, the location of all major sources of safe drinking water, and the location of any buildings (which register as blind spots).

In outdoor settings, the spell operates in a radius of one mile per caster level. In natural underground settings—caves, caverns, etc.—the range is limited to 100 feet per caster level. The spell does not function where nature has been replaced by construction or settlement (such as in dungeons and towns).

Comprehend Languages

Divination
Level: Clr 1, Sor/Wiz 1
Components: V, S, M/DF
Casting Time: 1 action
Range: Personal
Target: You
Duration: 10 minutes/level

You can understand the spoken words of creatures or read otherwise incomprehensible written messages (such as writing in another language). In either case, you must touch the creature or the writing. Note that the ability to read does not necessarily impart insight into the material, merely its literal meaning. Note also that the spell enables you to understand or read an unknown language, not speak or write it.

Written material can be read at the rate of one page (250 words) per minute. Magical writing cannot be read, other than to know it is magical, but the spell is often useful when deciphering treasure maps. This spell can be foiled by certain warding magic (such as the *secret page* and *illusory script* spells). It does not decipher codes or reveal messages concealed in otherwise normal text.

Arcane Material Components: A pinch of soot and a few grains of salt.

Cone of Cold

Evocation [Cold]
Level: Sor/Wiz 5, Water 6
Components: V, S, M/DF
Casting Time: 1 action
Range: Close (25 ft. + 5 ft./2 levels)
Area: Cone
Duration: Instantaneous
Saving Throw: Reflex half
Spell Resistance: Yes

Cone of cold creates an area of extreme cold, originating at your hand and extending outward in a cone. It drains heat, causing 1d6 points of cold damage per caster level (maximum 15d6).

Arcane Material Component: A very small crystal or glass cone.

Confusion

Enchantment (Compulsion) [Mind-Affecting]
Level: Brd 3, Sor/Wiz 4, Trickery 4
Components: V, S, M/DF
Casting Time: 1 action
Range: Medium (100 ft. + 10 ft./level)
Targets: All creatures in a 15-ft. radius
Duration: 1 round/level
Saving Throw: Will negates
Spell Resistance: Yes

Creatures affected by this spell behave randomly, as indicated on the following table:

1d10	Behavior
1	Wander away for 1 minute (unless prevented)
2–6	Do nothing for 1 round
7–9	Attack nearest creature for 1 round
10	Act normally for 1 round

Except on a result of 1, roll again each round to see what the subject does that round. Wandering creatures leave the scene as if disinterested. Attackers are not at any special advantage when attacking them. Behavior is checked at the beginning of each creature's turn. Any *confused* creature who is attacked automatically attacks its attackers on its next turn.

Arcane Material Component: A set of three nut shells.

Consecrate

Evocation
Level: Clr 2
Components: V, S, M, DF
Casting Time: 1 action
Range: Close (25 ft. + 5 ft./2 levels)
Area: 20-ft.-radius emanation
Duration: 2 hours/level
Saving Throw: None
Spell Resistance: No

This spell blesses an area with positive energy. All Charisma checks made to turn undead within this area gain a +3 sacred bonus. Undead entering this area suffer minor disruption, giving them a –1 sacred penalty on attack rolls, damage rolls, and saving throws. Undead cannot be created within or summoned into a *consecrated* area.

If the *consecrated* area contains an altar, shrine, or other permanent fixture dedicated to your deity, pantheon, or aligned higher power, the modifiers listed above are doubled (+6 sacred bonus to turning, –2 penalty to undead rolls). You cannot consecrate an area with a similar fixture of a deity other than your own patron.

Consecrate counters and dispels *desecrate*.

Material Components: A little holy water and 25 gp worth (5 pounds) of silver dust, all of which must be sprinkled around the area.

Contact Other Plane

Divination
Level: Brd 5, Sor/Wiz 5
Components: V
Casting Time: 10 minutes
Range: Personal
Target: You
Duration: Concentration

You send your mind to another plane of existence in order to receive advice and information from powers there. (See the accompanying table for possible consequences and results of the attempt.) The

powers reply in a language you understand, but they resent such contact and give only brief answers to your questions. (The DM answers all questions with "yes," "no," "maybe," "never," "irrelevant," or some other one-word answer.) You must concentrate on maintaining the spell (a standard action) in order to ask questions at the rate of one per round. A question is answered by the power during the same round. For every two caster levels, you may ask one question.

You can contact an Elemental Plane or some plane farther removed. Contact with minds far removed from your home plane increases the probability of suffering an effective decrease to Intelligence and Charisma, but the chance of the power knowing the answer, as well as the probability of the being telling the correct answer, are likewise increased by moving to distant planes. Once the Outer Planes are reached, the power of the deity contacted determines the effects. (Random results obtained from the table are subject to DM changes, the personalities of individual deities, and so on.)

On rare occasions, this divination may be blocked by an act of certain deities or forces.

Contagion

Necromancy
Level: Clr 3, Destruction 3, Drd 3, Sor/Wiz 4
Components: V, S
Casting Time: 1 action
Range: Touch
Target: Living creature touched
Duration: Instantaneous
Saving Throw: Fortitude negates
Spell Resistance: Yes

The subject contracts a disease, which strikes immediately (no incubation period). You infect the subject with blinding sickness, cackle fever, filth fever, mindfire, red ache, the shakes, or slimy doom. See the DUNGEON MASTER'S *Guide* for descriptions of each disease.

Contingency

Evocation
Level: Sor/Wiz 6
Components: V, S, M, F
Casting Time: At least 10 minutes (see text)
Range: Personal
Target: You
Duration: 1 day/level or until discharged

You can place another spell upon your person so that the latter spell comes into effect under some condition you dictate when casting *contingency*. The companion spell and the spell it is to bring into effect are cast at the same time. The 10-minute casting time is the minimum total for both castings; if the companion spell has a casting time longer than 10 minutes, use that casting time instead.

The spell to be brought into effect by the *contingency* must be one that affects your person (*feather fall, levitate, fly, teleport,* and so forth) and be of a spell level no higher than one-third your caster level (rounded down, maximum 6th level).

The conditions needed to bring the spell into effect must be clear, although they can be general. For example, a *contingency* cast with *water breathing* might prescribe that any time you are plunged into or otherwise engulfed in water or similar liquid, the

CONTACT OTHER PLANE

Plane Contacted	Avoid Effective Int/Cha Decrease	True Answer	Don't Know	Lie	Random Answer
Elemental Plane	DC 7/1 week	01–34	35–62	63–83	84–100
(appropriate)	(DC 7/1 week)	(01–68)	(69–75)	(76–98)	(99–100)
Positive/Negative Energy Plane	DC 8/1 week	01–39	40–65	66–86	87–100
Astral Plane	DC 9/1 week	01–44	45–67	68–88	89–100
Outer Plane, demideity	DC 10/2 weeks	01–49	50–70	71–91	92–100
Outer Plane, lesser deity	DC 12/3 weeks	01–60	61–75	76–95	96–100
Outer Plane, intermediate deity	DC 14/4 weeks	01–73	74–81	82–98	99–100
Outer Plane, greater deity	DC 16/5 weeks	01–88	89–90	91–99	100

Avoid Effective Intelligence/Charisma Decrease: You must succeed at an Intelligence check against this DC in order to avoid effective Intelligence and Charisma decrease. If the check fails, your Intelligence and Charisma scores fall to 8 for the stated duration, and you become unable to cast arcane spells. If you lose Intelligence and Charisma, the effect strikes as soon as the first question is asked, and no answer is received. (The entries in parentheses are for questions that pertain to the appropriate Elemental Plane.)

Results of a Successful Contact: The DM rolls d% for the result shown on the table:

True Answer: You get a true, one-word answer. Questions not capable of being answered in this way are answered randomly.

Don't Know: The entity tells you that it doesn't know.

Lie: The entity intentionally lies to you.

Random Answer: The entity tries to lie but doesn't know the answer, so it makes one up.

water breathing spell instantly comes into effect. Or a *contingency* could bring a *feather fall* spell into effect any time you fall more than 4 feet. In all cases, the *contingency* immediately brings into effect the second spell, the latter being "cast" instantaneously when the prescribed circumstances occur. Note that if complicated or convoluted conditions are prescribed, the whole spell combination (*contingency* and the companion magic) may fail when called on. The companion spell occurs based solely on the stated conditions, regardless of whether you want it to.

You can use only one *contingency* spell at a time; if a second is cast, the first one (if still active) is dispelled.

Material Components: Those of the companion spell, plus quicksilver and an eyelash of an ogre mage, ki-rin, or similar spell-using creature.

Focus: A statuette of you carved from elephant ivory and decorated with gems (worth at least 1,500 gp). You must carry the focus for the *contingency* to work.

Continual Flame

Illusion (Figment)
Level: Clr 3, Sor/Wiz 2
Components: V, S, M
Casting Time: 1 action
Range: Touch
Effect: Illusory flame
Duration: Permanent
Saving Throw: None
Spell Resistance: No

A flame, equivalent in brightness to a torch, springs forth from an object that you touch. The flame looks like a regular flame, but it creates no heat and doesn't use oxygen. The flame can be covered and hidden but not smothered or quenched.

Material Component: You sprinkle ruby dust (worth 50 gp) on the item that is to carry the flame.

Control Plants

Transmutation
Level: Drd 4, Plant 4, Rgr 3
Components: V, S, DF
Casting Time: 1 action
Range: Close (25 ft. + 5 ft/2 levels)
Area: Plants within a 25 ft. + 5 ft/2 levels-radius spread, centered on you
Duration: 1 minute/level
Saving Throw: Will negates (see text)
Spell Resistance: No

You can converse, in very rudimentary terms, with all sorts of plants and plantlike creatures (including fungi, molds, and plantlike monsters such as shambling mounds). You automatically exercise limited control over normal plants. Plantlike creatures can negate the control effect with a Will save.

The spell does not enable plants to uproot themselves and move about, but it does allow them to move their branches, stems, and leaves. Thus, you can question plants as to whether or not creatures have passed through them, cause thickets to part to enable easy passage, require vines to entangle pursuers, and command similar services.

The plants can duplicate the effect of an *entangle* spell or free creatures trapped by that spell.

Control Undead

Necromancy
Level: Sor/Wiz 7
Components: V, S, M
Casting Time: 1 action
Range: Close (25 ft. + 5 ft./2 levels)
Targets: Up to 2 HD of undead creatures/level, no two of which can be more than 30 ft. apart
Duration: 1 minute/level
Saving Throw: Will negates
Spell Resistance: Yes

This spell enables you to command undead creatures for a short period of time. You command the creatures by voice. Telepathic communication is not possible, but the creatures understand you no matter what language you speak. Even if vocal communication is impossible (in the area of a *silence* spell, for instance), the controlled undead do not attack you. At the end of the spell, the controlled undead revert to their normal behavior. Intelligent undead remember that you controlled them.

Material Components: A small piece of bone and a small piece of raw meat.

Control Water

Transmutation
Level: Brd 5, Clr 4, Sor/Wiz 6, Water 4
Components: V, S, M/DF
Casting Time: 1 action
Range: Long (400 ft. + 40 ft./level)
Area: Water in a volume of 10 ft./level × 10 ft./level × 2 ft./level (S)
Duration: 10 minutes/level (D)
Saving Throw: None
Spell Resistance: No

Depending on the version you choose, the *control water* spell raises or lowers water.

Lower Water: This causes water (or similar liquid) to sink away to a minimum depth of 1 inch. The depth can be lowered by up to 2 feet per caster level. The water is lowered within a squarish depression whose sides are up to 10 feet long per caster level. In extremely large and deep bodies of water, such as deep ocean, the spell creates a whirlpool that sweeps ships and similar craft downward, putting them at risk and rendering them unable to leave by normal movement for the dura-

tion of the spell. When cast on water elementals and other water-based creatures, this spell acts as a *slow* spell. The spell has no effect on other creatures.

Raise Water: This causes water (or similar liquid) to rise in height, just as the *lower water* version causes it to lower. Boats raised in this way slide down the sides of the hump that the spell creates. If the area affected by the spell includes riverbanks, a beach, or other land near the raised water, the water can spill over onto dry land.

For either version, you may reduce one horizontal dimension by half and double the other horizontal dimension.

Arcane Material Component: A drop of water (to *raise water*) or a pinch of dust (to *lower water*).

Control Weather

Transmutation
Level: Air 7, Brd 6, Clr 7, Drd 7, Sor/Wiz 6
Components: V, S
Casting Time: 10 minutes (see text)
Range: Two miles
Area: Two-mile-radius circle, centered on you (see text)
Duration: 4d12 hours (see text)
Saving Throw: None
Spell Resistance: No

You change the weather in the local area. It takes 10 minutes to cast the spell and an additional 10 minutes for the effects to manifest. The current, natural weather conditions are determined by the DM. You can call forth weather appropriate to the climate and season of the area you are in.

Season	Possible Weather
Spring	Tornado, thunderstorm, sleet storm, or hot weather
Summer	Torrential rain, heat wave, or hailstorm
Autumn	Hot or cold weather, fog, or sleet
Winter	Frigid cold, blizzard, or thaw
Late winter	Hurricane-force winds or early spring (coastal area)

You control the general tendencies of the weather, such as the direction and intensity of the wind. You cannot control specific applications of the weather—where lightning strikes, for example, or the exact path of a tornado. When you select a certain weather condition to occur, the weather assumes that condition 10 minutes later (changing gradually, not abruptly). The weather continues as you left it for the duration, or until you use a standard action to designate a new kind of weather (which fully manifests itself 10 minutes later). Contradictory conditions are not possible simultaneously—fog and strong wind, for example.

Control weather can do away with atmospheric phenomena (naturally occurring or otherwise) as well as create them.

Druids casting this spell double the duration and affect a circle with a three-mile radius.

Control Winds

Transmutation
Level: Air 5, Drd 5
Components: V, S
Casting Time: 1 action
Range: 40 ft./level
Area: 40 ft./level radius centered on you
Duration: 10 minutes/level
Saving Throw: Fortitude negates
Spell Resistance: No

You alter wind force in the area surrounding you. You can make the wind blow in a certain direction or manner, increase its strength, or decrease its strength. The new wind direction and strength persist until the spell ends or you choose to alter your handiwork, which requires concentration. You may create an "eye" of calm air up to 80 feet in diameter at the center of the area if you so desire, and you may choose to limit the effect to any circular area less than your full range (for example, a 20-foot-diameter tornado centered 100 feet away).

Wind Direction: You may choose one of four basic wind patterns to function over the spell's area:

- A downdraft blows from the center outward in equal strength in all directions.
- An updraft blows from the outer edges in toward the center in equal strength from all directions, veering upward before impinging on the eye in the center.
- A rotation causes the winds to circle the center in clockwise or counterclockwise fashion.
- A blast simply causes the winds to blow in one direction across the entire area from one side to the other.

Wind Force: For every three caster levels, you can increase or decrease wind force by one level of strength. (The effects of wind force are described in detail in the DUNGEON MASTER'S *Guide*.) Each round, a creature in the wind must make a Fortitude save or suffer the effect.

Strong winds (21+ mph) make sailing difficult. A severe wind (31+ mph) causes minor ship and building damage. A windstorm (51+ mph) drives most flying creatures from the skies, uproots small trees, knocks down light wooden structures, tears off roofs, and endangers ships. Hurricane force winds (75+ mph) destroy wooden buildings, sometimes uproot even large trees, and cause most ships to founder. A tornado (175+ mph) destroys all nonfortified buildings and often uproots large trees.

Create Food and Water

Conjuration (Creation)
Level: Clr 3
Components: V, S
Casting Time: 10 minutes
Range: Close (25 ft. + 5 ft./2 levels)
Effect: Food and water to sustain three humans or one horse/level for 1 day
Duration: 24 hours (see text)
Saving Throw: None
Spell Resistance: No

The food that this spell creates is simple fare of your choice—highly nourishing, if rather bland. The food decays and becomes inedible within 24 hours, although it can be kept fresh for another 24 hours by casting a *purify food and water* spell on it. The water created by this spell is just like clean rain water. The water doesn't go bad as the food does.

Create Greater Undead

Necromancy [Evil]
Level: Clr 8, Death 8
Components: V, S, M
Casting Time: 1 hour
Range: Close (25 ft. + 5 ft./2 levels)
Target: One corpse
Duration: Instantaneous
Saving Throw: None
Spell Resistance: No

As *create undead*, except that this spell allows you to create more powerful and intelligent sorts of undead. The type of undead created is based on your level. The following types of undead can be created by casters of the specified levels:

Cleric Level	Undead Created
15 or lower	Mummy
16–17	Spectre
18–19	Vampire
20	Ghost*

*Ghosts created by this spell have three ghostly powers in addition to manifestation: malevolence, horrific appearance, and corrupting gaze. See the *Monster Manual* entry on ghosts for details on these powers.

You may attempt to command the undead as it forms with a turning check (see Turn and Rebuke Undead, page 139).

Certain types of undead, such as liches, cannot be created by this spell. Such undead are created in other, very specific ways. See the *Monster Manual* for more information on all types of undead.

Create Undead

Necromancy [Evil]
Level: Clr 6, Death 6, Evil 6
Components: V, S, M
Casting Time: 1 hour
Range: Close (25 ft. + 5 ft./2 levels)
Target: One corpse
Duration: Instantaneous
Saving Throw: None
Spell Resistance: No

A much more potent spell than *animate dead*, this evil spell allows you to create more powerful sorts of undead: ghasts, ghouls, shadow, wights, and wraiths. The following types of undead can be created by casters of the specified levels:

Cleric Level	Undead Created
11 or lower	Ghoul
12–13	Shadow
14–15	Ghast
16–19	Wight
20	Wraith

You may create less powerful undead than your level would indicate if you choose. For example, at 16th level you could decide to create a ghoul or shadow instead of a wight. Doing this may be a good idea, because created undead are not automatically under the control of their animator. You may attempt to command the undead as it forms (see Turn and Rebuke Undead, page 139).

This spell must be cast at night.

Material Components: A clay pot filled with grave dirt and another filled with brackish water. The spell must be cast on a dead body, and the DM may assign specific requirements for various types of undead. You must place a black onyx gem worth at least 50 gp per HD of the undead to be created into the mouth or eye socket of each corpse. The magic of the spell turns these gems into worthless shells.

Create Water

Conjuration (Creation)
Level: Clr 0, Drd 0, Pal 1
Components: V, S
Casting Time: 1 action
Range: Close (25 ft. + 5 ft./2 levels)
Effect: Up to 2 gallons of water/level
Duration: Instantaneous
Saving Throw: None
Spell Resistance: No

This spell generates wholesome, drinkable water, just like clean rain water. Water can be created in an area as small as will actually contain the liquid, or in an area three times as large (possibly creating a downpour or filling many small receptacles).

Note: Conjuration spells can't create substances or objects within a creature. Water weighs about 8 pounds per gallon. One cubic foot of water contains roughly 8 gallons and weighs about 60 pounds.

Creeping Doom

Conjuration (Summoning)
Level: Animal 8, Drd 7
Components: V, S
Casting Time: 1 full round
Range: Close (25 ft. + 5 ft./2 levels)/100 ft. (see text)
Effect: 1,000 insects that fill a 10-ft.-radius spread
Duration: 1 minute/level
Saving Throw: None
Spell Resistance: No

When you utter the spell of *creeping doom*, you call forth a mass of 1,000 venomous, biting and stinging spiders, scorpions, beetles, and centipedes. This carpetlike mass swarms in a square 20 feet on a side. Upon your command, the swarm creeps forth at 10 feet per round toward any prey within 100 feet, moving in the direction you command. Each vermin in the *creeping doom* effect automatically bites a creature for 1 point of damage and then dies. Each creature takes enough damage to kill it, destroying that number of vermin in the process. Thus, a total of 1,000 points of damage can be inflicted on those in the *creeping doom's* effect. These attacks are nonmagical attacks, so creatures with damage reduction, for example, are safe.

If there aren't enough vermin to kill all the creatures in the spell's effect, damage is distributed among the survivors equally.

If *creeping doom* travels more than 100 feet away from you, it loses 50 of its number for each additional 10 feet it travels. For example, at 120 feet, its numbers have shrunk by 100. There are a number of ways to thwart or destroy the creatures forming the swarm. Anything that would deter or destroy normal insects is effective against these insects.

Cure Critical Wounds

Conjuration (Healing)
Level: Brd 4, Clr 4, Drd 5, Healing 4

As *cure light wounds*, except *cure critical wounds* cures 4d8 points of damage +1 point per caster level (up to +20).

Cure Light Wounds

Conjuration (Healing)
Level: Brd 1, Clr 1, Drd 1, Healing 1, Pal 1, Rgr 2
Components: V, S
Casting Time: 1 action
Range: Touch
Target: Creature touched
Duration: Instantaneous
Saving Throw: Will half (harmless) (see text)
Spell Resistance: Yes (harmless)

When laying your hand upon a living creature, you channel positive energy that cures 1d8 points of damage +1 point per caster level (up to +5).

Since undead are powered by negative energy, this spell deals damage to them instead of curing their wounds. An undead creature can attempt a Will save to take half damage.

Cure Minor Wounds

Conjuration (Healing)
Level: Clr 0, Drd 0

As *cure light wounds*, except *cure minor wounds* cures only 1 point of damage.

Cure Moderate Wounds

Conjuration (Healing)
Level: Brd 2, Clr 2, Drd 3, Pal 3, Healing 2

As *cure light wounds*, except *cure moderate wounds* cures 2d8 points of damage +1 point per caster level (up to +10).

Cure Serious Wounds

Conjuration (Healing)
Level: Brd 3, Clr 3, Drd 4, Pal 4, Rgr 4, Healing 3

As *cure light wounds*, except *cure moderate wounds* cures 3d8 points of damage +1 point per caster level (up to +15).

Curse Water

Transmutation [Evil]
Level: Clr 1
Components: V, S, M
Casting Time: 1 minute
Range: Touch
Target: Flask of water touched
Duration: Instantaneous
Saving Throw: Will negates (object)
Spell Resistance: Yes (object)

This transmutation imbues a flask (1 pint) of water with negative energy, turning it into unholy water. Unholy water damages good outsiders the way holy water damages undead.

Material Component: 5 pounds of powdered silver (worth 25 gp).

Dancing Lights

Illusion (Figment)
Level: Brd 0, Sor/Wiz 0
Components: V, S
Casting Time: 1 action
Range: Medium (100 ft. + 10 ft./level)
Effect: Up to four illusionary lights, all within a 10-ft.-radius area
Duration: 1 minute
Saving Throw: Will disbelief (if interacted with)
Spell Resistance: No

Depending on the version selected, you create up to four lights that resemble lanterns or torches (and cast that amount of light), or up to four glowing spheres of light (which look like will-o'-wisps), or one faintly glowing, vaguely humanoid shape. The *dancing lights* must stay within a 10-foot-radius area in relation to each other but otherwise move as you desire (no concentration required): forward or back, up or down, straight or turning corners, etc. The lights can move up to 100 feet a round. A light winks out if the distance between you and it exceeds the spell's range.

Darkness

Evocation [Darkness]
Level: Brd 2, Clr 2, Sor/Wiz 2
Components: V, M/DF
Casting Time: 1 action
Range: Touch
Target: Object touched
Duration: 10 minutes/level (D)
Saving Throw: None
Spell Resistance: No

This spell causes an object to radiate darkness out to a 20-foot radius. Not even creatures who can normally see in the dark (such as with darkvision) can see in an area shrouded in magical *darkness*. Normal lights (torches, candles, lanterns, and so forth) do not work, nor do light spells of lower level (*flare, light, dancing lights*). *Darkness* and the 2nd-level spell *daylight* cancel each other, leaving whatever light conditions normally prevail in the overlapping areas of the spells. Higher-level light spells (such as the 3rd-level cleric spell *daylight*) are not affected by *darkness*.

If the spell is cast on a small object that is then placed inside or under a lightproof covering, the spell's effects are blocked until the covering is removed.

Darkness counters or dispels any light spell of equal or lower level.

Arcane Material Components: A bit of bat fur and either a drop of pitch or a piece of coal.

Darkvision

Transmutation
Level: Sor/Wiz 2
Components: V, S, M
Casting Time: 1 action
Range: Touch
Target: Creature touched
Duration: 1 hour/level
Saving Throw: None
Spell Resistance: Yes (harmless)

The subject gains the ability to see 60 feet even in total darkness. Darkvision is black and white only but otherwise like normal sight. Darkvision does not grant one the ability to see in magical darkness.

Material Component: Either a pinch of dried carrot or an agate.

Daylight

Evocation [Light]
Level: Brd 2, Clr 3, Sor/Wiz 2
Components: V, S
Casting Time: 1 action
Range: Touch
Target: Object touched
Duration: 10 minutes/level
Saving Throw: None
Spell Resistance: No

The object touched sheds light as bright as full daylight in a 60-foot radius. Creatures who suffer penalties in bright light suffer them while exposed to this magical light. If the spell is cast on a small object that is then placed inside or under a lightproof covering, the spell's effects are blocked until the covering is removed.

Daylight brought into an area of magical darkness (or vice versa) is temporarily negated, so that the otherwise prevailing light conditions exist in the overlapping areas of effect.

Daylight counters or dispels any darkness spell of equal or lower level, such as *darkness.*

Daze

Enchantment (Compulsion)
[Mind-Affecting]
Level: Brd 0, Sor/Wiz 0
Components: V, S, M
Casting Time: 1 action
Range: Close (25 ft. + 5 ft./2 levels)
Target: One person
Duration: 1 round
Saving Throw: Will negates
Spell Resistance: Yes

This enchantment clouds the mind of a humanoid of Medium-size or smaller so that he takes no actions. Humanoids of 5 or more HD are not affected. The dazed subject is not stunned (so attackers get no special advantage against him), but he can't move, cast spells, use mental abilities, etc.

Material Component: A pinch of wool or similar substance.

Death Knell

Necromancy [Death, Evil]
Level: Clr 2, Death 2
Components: V, S
Casting Time: 1 action
Range: Touch
Target: Living creature touched
Duration: Instantaneous/10 minutes per target HD (see text)
Saving Throw: Will negates
Spell Resistance: Yes

You draw forth the ebbing life force of a badly wounded creature and use it to fuel your own power. Upon casting this spell, you touch a living creature with –1 hit points or lower. If the subject fails its saving throw, it dies, and you gain 1d8 temporary hit points and +2 Strength. Additionally, your effective caster level goes up by +1, improving spell effects dependent on caster level. (This increase in effective caster level does not grant you access to more spells.) These effects last for 10 minutes per HD of the target creature.

Death Ward

Necromancy
Level: Clr 4, Death 4, Drd 5, Pal 4
Components: V, S, DF
Casting Time: 1 action
Range: Touch
Target: Living creature touched
Duration: 10 minutes/level
Saving Throw: None
Spell Resistance: Yes (harmless)

The subject is immune to all death spells and magical death effects. The spell does not protect against other sorts of attacks, such as hit point loss, poison, petrification, or other effects even if they might be lethal.

Deathwatch

Necromancy
Level: Clr 1
Components: V, S
Casting Time: 1 action
Range: Close (25 ft. + 5 ft./2 levels)
Area: Quarter circle emanating from you to the extreme of the range
Duration: 10 minutes/level
Saving Throw: None
Spell Resistance: No

Using the foul sight granted by the powers of unlife, you can determine the condition of creatures near death within the spell's range. You instantly know whether each creature within the area is dead, fragile (alive and wounded, with 3 or fewer hit points left), fighting off death (alive with 4 or more hit points), undead, or neither alive nor dead (as a construct). This spell foils any spell or ability that allows creatures to feign death.

Deeper Darkness

Evocation [Darkness]
Level: Clr 3
Components: V, S
Casting Time: 1 action
Range: Touch
Target: Object touched
Duration: 1 day/level
Saving Throw: None
Spell Resistance: No

This spell causes the object touched to shed absolute darkness in a 60-foot radius. Even creatures who can normally see in the dark cannot see through this magical darkness. If the spell is cast on a small object that is then placed inside or under a lightproof covering, the spell's effects are blocked until the covering is removed.

Daylight brought into an area of *deeper darkness* (or vice versa) is temporarily negated, so that the otherwise prevailing light conditions exist in the overlapping areas of effect.

Deeper darkness counters or dispels any light spell of equal or lower level, including *daylight* and *light.*

Delay Poison

Conjuration (Healing)
Level: Brd 2, Clr 2, Drd 2, Pal 2, Rgr 1
Components: V, S, DF
Casting Time: 1 action
Range: Touch
Target: Creature touched
Duration: 1 hour/level
Saving Throw: Fortitude negates (harmless)
Spell Resistance: Yes (harmless)

The subject becomes temporarily immune to poison. Any poison in the subject's system, or any poison the subject is exposed to during the spell's duration, does not affect the subject until the spell has expired. *Delay poison* does not cure any damage that poison may have already done.

Delayed Blast Fireball

Evocation [Fire]
Level: Sor/Wiz 7
Duration: Up to 5 rounds (see text)

As *fireball,* except this spell is more powerful and can detonate up to 5 rounds after the spell is cast. The burst of flame detonates with a low roar and delivers 1d8 points of fire damage per caster level.

The glowing bead created by the spell can detonate immediately if you desire, or you can choose to delay the burst for up to 5 rounds. You choose the amount of delay upon completing the spell, and the delay cannot change once it has been set (unless someone touches the bead; see below). If you choose a delay, the glowing bead sits at its destination until it detonates. A creature can pick up and hurl the bead as a thrown weapon (range increment 10 feet). If a creature handles and moves the bead within 1 round of its detonation, there is a 25% chance that the bead detonates while the creature is handling it.

Demand

Enchantment (Compulsion)
[Mind-Affecting]
Level: Sor/Wiz 8
Saving Throw: Will partial
Spell Resistance: Yes

As *sending*, but the message can also contain a suggestion (see the *suggestion* spell), which the subject does her best to carry out. A successful Will save negates the *suggestion* effect but not the contact itself. The demand, if received, is understood even if the creature's Intelligence score is as low as 1. If the message is impossible or meaningless according to the circumstances that exist for the subject at the time the demand comes, the message is understood but the suggestion is ineffective.

The demand's message to the creature must be twenty-five words or less, including the suggestion. The creature can also give a short reply immediately.

Material Component: A short piece of copper wire and some small part of the subject—a hair, a bit of nail, etc.

Desecrate

Evocation
Level: Clr 2, Evil 2
Components: V, S, M, DF
Casting Time: 1 action
Range: Close (25 ft. + 5 ft./2 levels)
Area: 20-ft.-radius emanation
Duration: 2 hours/level
Saving Throw: None
Spell Resistance: Yes

This spell imbues an area with negative energy. All Charisma checks made to turn undead within this area suffer a –3 profane penalty. Undead entering this area gain a +1 profane bonus to attack rolls, damage rolls, and saving throws. Undead created within or summoned into a desecrated area gain +1 hit points per HD.

If the desecrated area contains an altar, shrine, or other permanent fixture dedicated to your deity, pantheon, or aligned higher power, the effects are doubled (turning at –6, +2 profane bonuses to undead rolls, +2 hit points per HD).

If the area contains a similar fixture of a deity, pantheon, or higher power other than your patron, the *desecrate* spell instead curses the area, cutting off its connection with the associated deity or power. This secondary function, if used, does not also grant the bonuses to undead as listed above.

Desecrate counters and dispels *consecrate*.

Material Component: A little unholy water and 25 gp worth (5 pounds) of silver dust, all of which must be sprinkled around the area.

Destruction

Necromancy [Death]
Level: Clr 7, Death 7
Components: V, S, F
Casting Time: 1 action
Range: Close (25 ft. + 5 ft./2 levels)
Target: One creature
Duration: Instantaneous

Saving Throw: Fortitude partial
Spell Resistance: Yes

This awful spell instantly slays the subject and consumes its remains utterly in holy (or unholy) fire. If the target's Fortitude saving throw succeeds, it instead takes 10d6 points of damage. The only way to restore life to a character who has failed to save against this spell is to use *true resurrection*, a carefully worded *wish* spell followed by *resurrection*, or *miracle*.

Focus: A special holy (or unholy) symbol of silver marked with verses of anathema (cost 500 gp).

Detect Animals or Plants

Divination
Level: Drd 1, Rgr 1
Components: V, S
Casting Time: 1 action
Range: Long (400 ft. + 40 ft./level)
Area: Quarter circle emanating from you to the extreme of the range
Duration: Concentration, up to 10 minutes/level (D)
Saving Throw: None
Spell Resistance: No

You can detect a particular type of animal or plant in a quarter circle emanating out from you in whatever direction you face. You must think of a species of animal or plant when using the spell. Each round you can change the animal or plant type. The amount of information revealed depends on how long you search a particular area or focus on a specific type of animal or plant:

1st Round: Presence or absence of the animal or plant type in that quarter.

2nd Round: Number of individuals of the specified type in the area, and the condition of the healthiest specimen.

3rd Round: The condition and location of each individual present. If an animal or plant is outside your line of sight, then you discern its direction but not its exact location.

Conditions: For purposes of this spell, the categories of condition are as follows:

Normal: Has at least 90% of original hit points, free of disease.

Fair: 30% to 90% of original hit points remaining.

Poor: Up to 30% of original hit points remaining, afflicted with a disease, or suffering from a debilitating injury.

Weak: 0 or fewer hit points remaining, afflicted with a disease in the terminal stage, or crippled.

If a creature falls into more than one category, the spell indicates the weaker of the two.

Note: Each round you can turn to detect things in a new area. The spell can penetrate barriers, but 1 foot of stone, 1 inch of common metal, a thin sheet of lead, or 3 feet of wood or dirt blocks it.

The DM decides if a specific type of animal or plant is present.

Detect Chaos

Divination
Level: Clr 1, Rgr 2

As *detect evil*, except that the spell detects chaotic creatures, spells, and magic items, and you are vulnerable to an overwhelming chaotic aura if you are lawful. It does not detect undead.

Detect Evil

Divination
Level: Clr 1, Rgr 2
Components: V, S, DF
Casting Time: 1 action
Range: 60 ft.
Area: Quarter circle emanating from you to the extreme of the range
Duration: Concentration, up to 10 minutes/level (D)
Saving Throw: None
Spell Resistance: No

You can sense the presence of evil. The amount of information revealed depends on how long you study a particular area or subject:

1st Round: Presence or absence of evil.

2nd Round: Number of evil auras (creatures, objects, or spells) in the area and the strength of the strongest evil aura present. If you are of good alignment, the strongest evil aura's strength is "overwhelming" (see below), and the strength is at least twice your character level, you are stunned for 1 round and the spell ends. While you are stunned, you can't act, you lose any Dexterity bonus to AC, and attackers gain +2 bonuses to attack you.

3rd Round: The strength and location of each aura. If an aura is outside your line of sight, then you discern its direction but not its exact location.

Aura Strength: An aura's evil power and strength depend on the type of evil creature or object that you're detecting and its HD, caster level, or (in the case of a cleric) class level.

Creature/Object	Evil Power
Evil creature	HD ÷ 5
Undead creature	HD ÷ 2
Evil elemental	HD ÷ 2
Evil magic item or spell	Caster level ÷ 2
Evil outsider	HD
Cleric of an evil deity	Level

Evil Power	Aura Strength
Lingering	Dim
1 or less	Faint
2–4	Moderate
5–10	Strong
11+	Overwhelming

If an aura falls into more than one strength category, the spell indicates the stronger of the two.

Length Aura Lingers: How long the aura lingers depends on its original strength:

Original Strength	Duration
Faint	1d6 minutes
Moderate	1d6 × 10 minutes
Strong	1d6 hours
Overwhelming	1d6 days

Remember that animals, traps, poisons, and other potential perils are not evil; this spell does not detect them.

Note: Each round, you can turn to detect things in a new area. The spell can penetrate barriers, but 1 foot of stone, 1 inch of common metal, a thin sheet of lead, or 3 feet of wood or dirt blocks it.

Detect Good
Divination
Level: Clr 1, Rgr 2

As *detect evil*, except that the spell detects good creatures, spells, and magic items, and you are vulnerable to an overwhelming good aura if you are evil. It does not detect undead. Also, remember that healing potions, antidotes, and similar beneficial items are not good.

Detect Law
Divination
Level: Clr 1, Rgr 2

As *detect evil*, except that the spell detects lawful creatures, spells, and magic items, and you are vulnerable to an overwhelming lawful aura if you are chaotic. It does not detect undead.

Detect Magic
Universal
Level: Brd 0, Clr 0, Drd 0, Sor/Wiz 0
Components: V, S
Casting Time: 1 action
Range: 60 ft.
Area: Quarter circle emanating from you to the extreme of the range
Duration: Concentration, up to 1 minute/level (D)
Saving Throw: None
Spell Resistance: No

You detect magical auras. The amount of information revealed depends on how long you study a particular area or subject:

1st Round: Presence or absence of magical auras.

2nd Round: Number of different magical auras and the strength of the strongest aura.

3rd Round: The strength and location of each aura. If the items or creatures bearing

the auras are in line of sight, you can make Spellcraft skill checks to determine the school of magic involved in each. (Make one check per aura; DC 15 + spell level, or 15 + half caster level for a nonspell effect.)

Magical areas, multiple types of magic, or strong local magical emanations may confuse or conceal weaker auras.

Aura Strength: An aura's magical power and strength depend on a spell's functioning spell level or an item's caster level.

Strength	Functioning Spell Level	Item Caster Level
Dim	0-level or lingering aura	Lingering aura
Faint	1st–3rd	1st–5th
Moderate	4th–6th	6th–11th
Strong	7th–9th	12th–20th
Overwhelming	Artifact or deity-level magic	Beyond mortal caster

If an aura falls into more than one category, *detect magic* indicates the stronger of the two.

Length Aura Lingers: How long the aura lingers depends on its original strength:

Aura Strength	Duration
Faint	1d6 minutes
Moderate	1d6 × 10 minutes
Strong	1d6 hours
Overwhelming	1d6 days

Note: Each round, you can turn to detect things in a new area. The spell can penetrate barriers, but 1 foot of stone, 1 inch of common metal, a thin sheet of lead, or 3 feet of wood or dirt blocks it. Outsiders and elementals are not magical in themselves, but if they are conjured, the conjuration spell registers.

Detect Poison
Divination
Level: Clr 0, Drd 0, Pal 1, Sor/Wiz 0
Components: V, S
Casting Time: 1 action
Range: Close (25 ft. + 5 ft./2 levels)
Target or Area: One creature, one object, or a 5-ft. cube
Duration: Instantaneous
Saving Throw: None
Spell Resistance: No

You determine whether a creature, object, or area has been poisoned or is poisonous. You can determine the exact type of poison with a successful Wisdom check (DC 20). A character with the Alchemy skill may try an Alchemy check (DC 20) if the Wisdom check fails, or may try the Alchemy check prior to the Wisdom check.

Note: The spell can penetrate barriers, but 1 foot of stone, 1 inch of common metal, a thin sheet of lead, or 3 feet of wood or dirt blocks it.

Detect Scrying
Divination
Level: Brd 4, Sor/Wiz 4
Components: V, S, M
Casting Time: 1 action
Range: 120 ft.
Area: 120-ft.-radius emanation centered on you
Duration: 24 hours
Saving Throw: None
Spell Resistance: No

You immediately become aware of any attempt to observe you by means of *clairaudience/clairvoyance* or *scrying*. The spell's effect radiates from you as you move. The spell also reveals the use of *crystal balls* or other magic scrying devices. You know the location of every magical sensor within the spell's area.

If the scrying attempt originates within the area, you also know its location. If the attempt originates outside this range, you and the scrier immediately make opposed Scry skill checks. (A Scry check is the same as an Intelligence check for a creature without the Scry skill.) If you at least match the scrier's result, you get a visual image of the scrier and a sense of the scrier's direction and distance from you (accurate to within one-tenth the distance).

Material Components: A small piece of mirror and a miniature brass hearing trumpet.

Detect Secret Doors
Divination
Level: Brd 1, Knowledge 1, Sor/Wiz 1
Components: V, S
Casting Time: 1 action
Range: 60 ft.
Area: Quarter circle emanating from you to the extreme of the range
Duration: Concentration, up to 1 minute/level (D)
Saving Throw: None
Spell Resistance: No

You can detect secret doors, compartments, caches, and so forth. Only passages, doors, or openings that have been specifically constructed to escape detection are detected by this spell—an ordinary trapdoor underneath a pile of crates would not be detected. The amount of information revealed depends on how long you study a particular area or subject:

1st Round: Presence or absence of secret doors.

2nd Round: Number of secret doors and the location of each. If an aura is outside your line of sight, then you discern its direction but not its exact location.

Each Additional Round: The mechanism or trigger for one particular secret portal closely examined by you.

Note: Each round, you can turn to detect things in a new area. The spell can penetrate barriers, but 1 foot of stone, 1 inch of common metal, a thin sheet of lead, or 3 feet of wood or dirt blocks it.

Detect Snares and Pits
Divination
Level: Drd 1, Rgr 1
Components: V, S
Casting Time: 1 action
Range: 60 ft.
Area: Quarter circle emanating from you to the extreme of the range
Duration: Concentration, up to 10 minutes/level (D)
Saving Throw: None
Spell Resistance: No

You can detect simple pits, deadfalls, snares of wilderness creatures (trapdoor spiders, giant sundews, ant lions, etc.), and primitive traps constructed of natural materials (mantraps, missile traps, hunting snares, etc.). The spell does not detect complex traps, including trapdoor traps.

The spell does detect certain natural hazards—quicksand (registers as a snare), a sinkhole (pit), or unsafe walls of natural rock (deadfall). However, it does not reveal other potentially dangerous conditions, such as a cavern that floods during rain, an unsafe construction, or a naturally poisonous plant. The spell does not detect magic traps (except those that operate by pit, deadfall, or snaring; see the spell *snare*), nor mechanically complex ones, nor those that have been rendered safe or inactive.

The amount of information revealed depends on how long you study a particular area:

1st Round: Presence or absence of hazards.

2nd Round: Number of hazards and the location of each. If a hazard is outside your line of sight, then you discern its direction but not its exact location.

Each Additional Round: The general type and trigger for one particular hazard closely examined by you.

Note: Each round, you can turn to detect things in a new area. The spell can penetrate barriers, but 1 foot of stone, 1 inch of common metal, a thin sheet of lead, or 3 feet of wood or dirt blocks it.

Detect Thoughts
Divination [Mind-Affecting]
Level: Brd 2, Knowledge 2, Sor/Wiz 2
Components: V, S, F/DF
Casting Time: 1 action
Range: 60 ft.

Area: Quarter circle emanating from you to the extreme of the range
Duration: Concentration, up to 1 minute/level (D)
Saving Throw: Will negates (see text)
Spell Resistance: No

You detect surface thoughts. The amount of information revealed depends on how long you study a particular area or subject:

1st Round: Presence or absence of thoughts (from conscious creatures with Intelligence scores of 1 or higher).

2nd Round: Number of thinking minds and the mental strength of each.

3rd Round: Surface thoughts of any mind in the area. A target's Will save prevents you from reading its thoughts, and you must cast *detect thoughts* again to have another chance. Creatures of animal intelligence (Int 1 or 2) have simple, instinctual thoughts that you can pick up.

Intelligence	Mental Strength
1–2	Animal
3–5	Very low
6–9	Low
10–11	Average
12–15	High
16–17	Very high
18–21	Genius
22–25	Supra-genius
26+	Deific

Note: Each round, you can turn to detect thoughts in a new area. The spell can penetrate barriers, but 1 foot of stone, 1 inch of common metal, a thin sheet of lead, or 3 feet of wood or dirt blocks it.

Arcane Focus: A copper piece.

Detect Undead
Divination
Level: Clr 1, Pal 1, Sor/Wiz 1
Components: V, S, M/DF
Casting Time: 1 action
Range: 60 ft.
Area: Quarter circle emanating from you to the extreme of the range
Duration: Concentration, up to 1 minute/ level (D)
Saving Throw: None
Spell Resistance: No

You can detect the aura that surrounds undead. The amount of information revealed depends on how long you study a particular area or subject:

1st Round: Presence or absence of undead auras.

2nd Round: Number of undead auras in the area and the strength of the strongest undead aura present. If you are of good alignment, and the strongest undead aura's strength is "overwhelming" (see below), and the strength is at least twice your character level, you are stunned for 1 round

and the spell ends. While you are stunned, you can't act, you lose any Dexterity bonus to AC, and attackers gain +2 bonuses to attack you.

3rd Round: The strength and location of each aura. If an aura is outside your line of sight, then you discern its direction but not its exact location.

Aura Strength: The strength of the undead aura is determined by the HD of the undead creature.

Strength	HD
Dim	Lingering aura
Faint	1 or less
Moderate	2–4
Strong	5–10
Overwhelming	11+

Length Aura Lingers: How long the aura lingers depends on its original strength:

Aura Strength	Duration
Faint	1d6 minutes
Moderate	1d6 × 10 minutes
Strong	1d6 hours
Overwhelming	1d6 days

Note: Each round, you can turn to detect things in a new area. The spell can penetrate barriers, but 1 foot of stone, 1 inch of common metal, a thin sheet of lead, or 3 feet of wood or dirt blocks it.

Arcane Material Component: A bit of earth from a grave.

Dictum
Evocation [Lawful, Sonic]
Level: Clr 7, Law 7
Components: V
Casting Time: 1 action
Range: 30 ft.
Area: Creatures in a 30-ft.-radius spread centered on you
Duration: Instantaneous
Saving Throw: None
Spell Resistance: Yes

Uttering *dictum* creates two effects.

If you are on your home plane, nonlawful extraplanar creatures within the area are instantly banished back to their home planes. Creatures so banished cannot return for at least 1 day. This effect takes place regardless of whether the creatures hear the *dictum*.

Creatures native to your plane who hear the *dictum* and are not lawful suffer the following ill effects:

HD	Effect
12 or more	Deafened
Less than 12	*Slowed*, deafened
Less than 8	Paralyzed, *slowed*, deafened
Less than 4	Killed, paralyzed, *slowed*, deafened

The effects are cumulative.

Deafened: The creature is struck deaf (see *blindness/deafness*) for 1d4 rounds.

Slowed: The creature is *slowed*, as by the *slow* spell, for 2d4 rounds.

Paralyzed: The creature is paralyzed and helpless for 1d10 minutes, unable to move or act in any way.

Killed: Living creatures die. Undead creatures are destroyed.

Dimensional Anchor

Abjuration
Level: Clr 4 , Sor/Wiz 4
Components: V, S
Casting Time: 1 action
Range: Medium (100 ft. + 10 ft./level)
Effect: Ray
Duration: 1 minute/level
Saving Throw: None
Spell Resistance: Yes (object)

A green ray springs from your outstretched hand. You must make a ranged touch attack to hit the target. Any creature or object struck is covered with a shimmering emerald field that completely blocks bodily extradimensional travel. Forms of movement barred by the *dimensional anchor* include *astral projection, blink, dimension door, ethereal jaunt, etherealness, gate, maze, plane shift, shadow walk, teleport,* and similar spell-like or psionic abilities. It prevents the use of a *gate* or *teleportation circle* for the duration of the spell.

The *dimensional anchor* does not interfere with the movement of creatures already in ethereal or astral form when the spell is cast, nor does it block extradimensional perception or attack forms such as a basilisk's gaze. Also, it does not prevent summoned creatures from disappearing at the end of a summoning spell.

Dimension Door

Transmutation [Teleportation]
Level: Brd 4, Sor/Wiz 4, Travel 4
Components: V
Casting Time: 1 action
Range: Long (400 ft. + 40 ft./level)
Target: You and touched objects or other touched willing creatures weighing up to 50 lb./level
Duration: Instantaneous
Saving Throw: None and Will negates (object)
Spell Resistance: No and Yes (object)

You instantly transfer yourself from your current location to any other spot within range. You always arrive at exactly the spot desired—whether by simply visualizing the area or by stating direction, such as "900 feet straight downward," or "upward to the northwest, 45-degree angle, 1,200 feet." After using this spell, you can't take any other actions until your next turn.

If you arrive in a place that is already occupied by a solid body, you become trapped in the Astral Plane. Each round that you are trapped in the Astral Plane in this way, you may make a Will save (DC 25) to return to the Material Plane at a random open space on a suitable surface within 100 feet of the intended location. If there is no free space within 100 feet, make a Will save (DC 25) each minute to appear in a free space within 1,000 feet. If there's no free space within 1,000 feet, you are stuck on the Astral Plane until rescued.

Diminish Plants

Transmutation
Level: Drd 3, Rgr 3
Components: V, S, DF
Casting Time: 1 action
Range: See text
Target or Area: See text
Duration: Instantaneous
Saving Throw: None
Spell Resistance: No

This spell has two versions:

Prune Growth: The first version causes normal vegetation (grasses, briars, bushes, creepers, thistles, trees, vines, and so forth) within long range (400 feet + 40 feet per level) to shrink to about a third of their normal size, becoming untangled and less bushy. The affected vegetation appears to have been carefully pruned and trimmed.

At your option, the area can be a circle with a radius of 100 feet, a semicircle with a radius of 150 feet, or a quarter circle with a radius of 200 feet. You may also designate areas within the area that are not affected.

Stunt: The second version targets normal plants within a range of one-half mile, reducing their potential productivity over the course of the following year to one-third below normal.

Diminish plants counters *plant growth*.

Discern Lies

Divination
Level: Clr 4, Pal 3
Components: V, S, DF
Casting Time: 1 action
Range: Close (25 ft. + 5 ft./2 levels)
Targets: One creature/level, no two of which can be more than 30 ft. apart
Duration: Concentration, up to 1 round/level
Saving Throw: Will negates
Spell Resistance: No

Each round, you concentrate on one subject, who must be in range. You know if the subject deliberately and knowingly speaks a lie by discerning disturbances in her aura caused by lying. The spell does not reveal the truth, uncover unintentional inaccuracies, or necessarily reveal

evasions. Each round, you may concentrate on a different subject.

Discern Location

Divination
Level: Clr 8, Knowledge 8, Sor/Wiz 8
Components: V, S, DF
Casting Time: 10 minutes
Range: Unlimited
Target: One creature
Duration: Instantaneous
Saving Throw: None
Spell Resistance: No

A *discern location* spell is among the most powerful means of locating creatures or objects. Nothing short of the direct intervention of a deity keeps you from learning the exact location of a single individual or object. *Discern location* circumvents normal means of protection from scrying or location. The spell reveals the name of the location (place, name, business name, building name, or the like), community, county (or similar political division), country, continent, and plane where the subject lies.

To find a creature with the spell, you must have seen the creature or have some item that once belonged to it. To find an object, you must have touched the object at least once.

Disintegrate

Transmutation
Level: Destruction 7, Sor/Wiz 6
Components: V, S, M/DF
Casting Time: 1 action
Range: Medium (100 ft. + 10 ft./level)
Effect: Ray
Duration: Instantaneous
Saving Throw: Fortitude partial
Spell Resistance: Yes

A thin, green ray springs from your pointing finger, causing the creature or object it strikes to glow and vanish, leaving behind only a trace of fine dust. You must make a successful ranged touch attack to hit. Up to a 10-foot cube of non-living matter is affected, so the spell disintegrates only part of any very large object or structure targeted. The ray affects even magical matter or energy of a magical nature, such as *Bigby's forceful hand* or a *wall of force*, but not a *globe of invulnerability* or an *antimagic field*. A creature or object that makes a successful Fortitude save is only partially affected. It takes 5d6 points of damage instead of disintegrating. Only the first creature or object struck can be affected (that is, the ray affects only one target per casting).

Arcane Material Components: A lodestone and a pinch of dust.

Dismissal

Abjuration
Level: Brd 4, Clr 4, Sor/Wiz 5
Components: V, S, F/DF
Casting Time: 1 action
Range: Close (25 ft. + 5 ft./2 levels)
Target: One extraplanar creature
Duration: Instantaneous
Saving Throw: Will negates
Spell Resistance: Yes

This spell forces an extraplanar creature back to its proper plane. Add the creature's HD to its saving throw and subtract your level as well. If the spell is successful, the creature is instantly whisked away, but there is a 20% chance of actually sending the subject to a plane other than its own.

Arcane Focus: Any item that is distasteful to the subject.

Dispel Chaos

Abjuration [Lawful]
Level: Clr 5, Law 5

As *dispel evil*, except that you are surrounded by constant, blue, lawful energy, and the spell affects chaotic creatures and spells rather than evil ones.

Dispel Evil

Abjuration [Good]
Level: Clr 5, Good 5, Pal 4
Components: V, S, DF
Casting Time: 1 action
Range: Touch
Target or Targets: You and a touched evil creature from another plane; or you and an enchantment or evil spell on a touched creature or object
Duration: 1 round/level or until discharged, whichever comes first
Saving Throw: See text
Spell Resistance: See text

Shimmering, white, holy energy surrounds you. This power has three effects:

1. You gain a +4 deflection bonus to AC against attacks by evil creatures.

2. On making a successful melee touch attack against an evil creature from another plane, you can choose to drive that creature back to its home plane. The creature negates the effects with a Will save (SR applies). This use discharges and ends the spell.

3. With a touch, you can automatically dispel any one enchantment cast by an evil creature or any one evil spell. *Exception:* Spells that can't be dispelled by *dispel magic* also can't be dispelled by *dispel evil*. Saving throws and SR do not apply to this effect. This use discharges and ends the spell.

Dispel Good

Abjuration [Evil]
Level: Clr 5, Evil 5

As *dispel evil*, except that you are surrounded by dark, wavering, unholy energy, and the spell affects good creatures and spells rather than evil ones.

Dispel Law

Abjuration [Chaotic]
Level: Chaos 5, Clr 5

As *dispel evil*, except that you are surrounded by flickering, yellow, chaotic energy, and the spell affects lawful creatures and spells rather than evil ones.

Dispel Magic

Abjuration
Level: Brd 3, Clr 3, Drd 4, Magic 3, Pal 3, Sor/Wiz 3
Components: V, S
Casting Time: 1 action
Range: Medium (100 ft. + 10 ft./level)
Target or Area: One spellcaster, creature, or object; or 30-ft.-radius burst
Duration: Instantaneous
Saving Throw: None
Spell Resistance: No

Because magic is powerful, so, too, is the ability to dispel magic. You can use *dispel magic* to end ongoing spells that have been cast on a creature or object, to temporarily suppress the magical abilities of a magic item, to end ongoing spells (or at least their effects) within an area, or to counter another spellcaster's spell. A dispelled spell ends as if its duration had expired. Some spells, as detailed in their descriptions, can't be defeated by *dispel magic*. *Dispel magic* can dispel (but not counter) the ongoing effects of supernatural abilities as well as spells. *Dispel magic* affects spell-like effects just as it affects spells.

Note: The effects of spells with instantaneous duration can't be dispelled, because the magic effect is already over before the *dispel magic* can take effect. Thus, you can't use *dispel magic* to repair fire damage caused by a *fireball* or to turn a petrified character back to flesh. (The magic has departed, leaving only burned flesh or perfectly normal stone in its wake.)

You choose to use *dispel magic* in one of three ways: a targeted dispel, an area dispel, or a counterspell:

Targeted Dispel: One object, creature, or spell is the target of the spell. You make a dispel check against the spell or against each ongoing spell currently in effect on the object or creature. A dispel check is 1d20 +1 per caster level (maximum +10) against a DC of 11 + the spell's caster level.

For example, Mialee, at 5th level, targets *dispel magic* on a *hasted*, *mage armored*, *strengthened* drow. All three spells were cast on the drow by a 7th-level wizard. Mialee makes a dispel check (1d20+5 against DC 18) three times, once each for the *haste*, *mage armor*, and *strength* effects. If she succeeds at a particular check, that spell is dispelled (the drow's SR doesn't help him); if she fails, that spell remains in effect.

If the spellcaster targets an object or creature who is the effect of an ongoing spell (such as a monster summoned by *monster summoning*), she makes a dispel check to end the spell that conjured the object or creature.

If the object that you target is a magic item, you make a dispel check against the item's caster level. If you succeed, all the item's magical properties are suppressed for 1d4 rounds, after which the item recovers on its own. A suppressed item becomes nonmagical for the duration of the effect. An interdimensional interface (such as a *bag of holding*) is temporarily closed. Remember that a magic item's physical properties are unchanged: A suppressed magic sword is still a sword (a masterwork sword, in fact). Artifacts and creatures of demigod or higher status are unaffected by mortal magic such as this.

You automatically succeed at your dispel check against any spell that you cast yourself.

Area Dispel: The spell affects everything within a 30-foot radius.

For each creature who is the target of one or more spells, you make a dispel check against the spell with the highest caster level. If that fails, you make dispel checks against progressively weaker spells until you dispel one spell (which discharges the *dispel* so far as that target is concerned) or fail all your checks. The creature's magic items are not affected.

For each object that is the target of one or more spells, you make dispel checks as with creatures. Magic items are not affected by area dispels.

For each ongoing area or effect spell centered within the *dispel magic's* area, you make a dispel check to dispel the spell.

For each ongoing spell whose area overlaps that of the dispel, you make a dispel check to end the effect, but only within the area of the *dispel magic*.

If an object or creature who is the effect of an ongoing spell, such as a monster summoned by *monster summoning*, is in the area, you make a dispel check to end the spell that conjured the object or creature (returning it whence it came) in addition to attempting to dispel spells targeting the creature or object.

You may choose to automatically succeed at dispel checks against any spell that you have cast.

Counterspell: The spell targets a spellcaster and is cast as a counterspell (page 152). Unlike a true counterspell, however, *dispel magic* may not work. You must make a dispel check to counter the other spellcaster's spell.

Displacement

Illusion (Glamer)
Level: Brd 3, Sor/Wiz 3
Components: V, M
Casting Time: 1 action
Range: Touch
Target: Creature touched
Duration: 1 round/level
Saving Throw: Will negates (harmless)
Spell Resistance: Yes (harmless)

Emulating the natural ability of the displacer beast, the subject appears to be about 2 feet away from his true location. He benefits from a 50% miss chance as if he had full concealment. However, unlike actual full concealment, *displacement* does not prevent enemies from targeting him normally. *True seeing* reveals his true location.

Material Component: A small strip of leather made from displacer beast hide, twisted into a loop.

Disrupt Undead

Necromancy
Level: Sor/Wiz 0
Components: V, S
Casting Time: 1 action
Range: Close (25 ft. + 5 ft./2 levels)
Effect: Ray
Duration: Instantaneous
Saving Throw: None
Spell Resistance: Yes

You direct a shock wave of positive energy. You must make a ranged touch attack roll to hit, and if the ray hits an undead creature, it deals 1d6 points of damage to it.

Divination

Divination
Level: Clr 4, Knowledge 4
Components: V, S, M
Casting Time: 10 minutes
Range: Personal
Target: You
Duration: Instantaneous

Similar to *augury* but more powerful, a *divination* spell can provide you with a useful piece of advice in reply to a question concerning a specific goal, event, or activity that is to occur within 1 week. The advice can be as simple as a short phrase, or it might take the form of a cryptic rhyme or omen.

For example, suppose the question is "Will we do well if we venture into the ruined temple of Erythnul?" The DM knows that a terrible troll guarding 10,000 gp and a *+1 shield* lurks near the entrance but estimates that your party could beat the troll after a hard fight. Therefore the divination response might be: "Ready oil and open flame light your way to wealth." In all cases, the DM controls what information you receive. Note that if your party doesn't act on the information, the conditions may change so that the information is no longer useful. (For example, the troll could move away and take the treasure with it.)

The base chance for a correct divination is 70% + 1% per caster level. The DM adjusts the chance if unusual circumstances require it (if, for example, unusual precautions against divination spells have been taken). If the dice roll fails, you know the spell failed, unless specific magic yielding false information is at work.

As with *augury*, multiple *divinations* about the same topic by the same caster use the same dice result as the first *divination* and yield the same answer each time.

Material Component: Incense and a sacrificial offering appropriate to your religion, together worth at least 25 gp.

Divine Favor

Evocation
Level: Clr 1, Pal 1
Components: V, S, DF
Casting Time: 1 action
Range: Personal
Target: You
Duration: 1 minute

Calling upon the strength and wisdom of a deity, you gain a +1 luck bonus to attack and weapon damage rolls for every three caster levels you have (at least +1, maximum +6). The bonus doesn't apply to spell damage.

Divine Power

Evocation
Level: Clr 4, War 4
Components: V, S, DF
Casting Time: 1 action
Range: Personal
Target: You
Duration: 1 round/level

Calling upon the divine power of your patron, you imbue yourself with strength and skill in combat. You gain the base attack bonus of a fighter of your total character level, an enhancement bonus to Strength sufficient to raise your Strength score to 18 (if it is not already 18 or higher), and 1 temporary hit point per level.

Dominate Animal

Enchantment (Compulsion)
[Mind-Affecting]
Level: Animal 3, Drd 3
Components: V, S
Casting Time: 1 action
Range: Medium (100 ft. + 10 ft./level)
Target: One animal
Duration: 1 round/level
Saving Throw: Will negates
Spell Resistance: Yes

You can enchant an animal and direct it with simple commands such as "Attack," "Run," and "Fetch." Suicidal or self-destructive commands (including an order to attack a creature two or more size categories larger than the *dominated* animal) are simply ignored.

Dominate animal establishes a mental link between you and the subject animal. The animal can be directed by silent mental command as long as it remains in range. You need not see the animal to control it. You do not receive direct sensory input from the animal, but you know what it is experiencing. Because you are directing the animal with your own intelligence, it may be able to undertake actions normally beyond its own comprehension, such as manipulating objects with its paws and mouth. You need not concentrate exclusively on controlling the animal unless you are trying to direct it to do something it normally couldn't do.

Dominate Monster

Enchantment (Compulsion)
[Mind-Affecting]
Level: Sor/Wiz 9
Target: One creature

As *dominate person*, except that the spell is not restricted by creature type or size.

Dominate Person

Enchantment (Compulsion)
[Mind-Affecting]
Level: Brd 4, Sor/Wiz 5
Components: V, S
Casting Time: 1 action
Range: Medium (100 ft. + 10 ft./level)
Target: One humanoid of Medium-size or smaller
Duration: 1 day/level
Saving Throw: Will negates
Spell Resistance: Yes

You can control the actions of any humanoid that is Medium-size or smaller. You establish a telepathic link with the subject's mind. If a common language is shared, you can generally force the subject to perform as you desire, within the limits of his abilities. If no common language is shared, you can communicate only basic commands, such as "Come here," "Go there," "Fight," and "Stand still." You know what the subject is experiencing, but you do not receive direct sensory input from him.

Subjects resist this control, and those forced to take actions against their nature receive a new saving throw with a bonus of +1 to +4, depending on the type of action required. Obviously self-destructive orders are not carried out. Once control is established, the range at which it can be exercised is unlimited, as long as you and the subject are on the same plane. You need not see the subject to control it.

Protection from evil or a similar spell can prevent you from exercising control or using the telepathic link while the subject is so warded, but it does not prevent the establishment of domination or dispel it.

Doom

Enchantment (Compulsion)
[Fear, Mind-Affecting]
Level: Clr 1
Components: V, S, DF
Casting Time: 1 action
Range: Medium (100 ft. + 10 ft./level)
Target: One living creature
Duration: 1 minute/level
Saving Throw: Will negates
Spell Resistance: Yes

This curse fills a single subject with a feeling of horrible dread and causes her to weaken and lose confidence. The subject suffers a –2 morale penalty to attack rolls, weapon damage rolls, ability checks, skill checks, and saving throws.

Drawmij's Instant Summons

Conjuration (Summoning)
Level: Sor/Wiz 7
Components: V, S, M
Casting Time: 1 action
Range: See text
Target: One object weighing up to 10 lb.
  whose longest dimension is 6 ft. or less
Duration: Permanent until discharged
Saving Throw: None
Spell Resistance: No

You call some nonliving item from virtually any location directly to your hand.

First, you place your *arcane mark* on the item. Then you cast this spell, which magically and invisibly inscribes the name of the item on a sapphire worth at least 1,000 gp. Thereafter, you can summon the item by speaking a special word (set by you when the spell is cast) and crushing the gem. The item appears instantly in your hand. Only you can use the gem in this way.

If the item is in the possession of another creature, the spell does not work, but you know who the possessor is and roughly where he, she, or it is located when the summons is cast.

The inscription on the gem is invisible. It is also unreadable, except by means of a *read magic* spell, to anyone but you.

The item can be summoned from another plane, but only if no other creature has claimed ownership of it.

Material Components: A sapphire worth at least 1,000 gp.

Dream

Illusion (Phantasm) [Mind-Affecting]
Level: Brd 5, Sor/Wiz 5
Components: V, S
Casting Time: 1 minute
Range: Unlimited
Target: One living creature touched
Duration: See text
Saving Throw: None
Spell Resistance: Yes

You, or a messenger touched by you, sends a phantasmal message to others in the form of a dream. At the beginning of the spell, you must name the recipient or identify him by some title that leaves no doubt as to his identity. The messenger then enters a trance, appears in the intended recipient's dream, and delivers the message. The message can be of any length, and the recipient remembers it perfectly upon waking. The communication is one-way. The recipient cannot ask questions or offer information, nor can the messenger gain any information by observing the dreams of the recipient. Once the message is delivered, the messenger's mind returns instantly to her body. The duration of the spell is the time required for the messenger to enter the recipient's dream and deliver the message.

If the recipient is awake when the spell begins, the messenger can choose to wake up (ending the spell) or remain in the trance. She can remain in the trance until the recipient goes to sleep, then enter the recipient's dream and deliver the message as normal. If the messenger is disturbed during the trance, she awakens, and the spell ends.

Creatures who don't sleep or dream (such as elves, but not half-elves) cannot be contacted by this spell.

The messenger is unaware of her own surroundings or the activities around her while in the trance. She is defenseless, both physically and mentally (she always fails any saving throw, for example) while in the trance.

Earthquake

Evocation
Level: Clr 8, Destruction 8, Drd 9, Earth 7
Components: V, S, DF
Casting Time: 1 action
Range: Long (400 ft. + 40 ft./level)
Area: 5 ft./level radius (S)
Duration: 1 round
Saving Throw: See text
Spell Resistance: No

When you cast *earthquake*, an intense but highly localized tremor rips the ground. It knocks creatures down, collapses structures, opens cracks in the ground, and more. The shock lasts 1 round, during which time creatures on the ground can't move or attack. Spellcasters on the ground must make Concentration checks (DC 20 + spell level) or lose any spells they try to cast. The earthquake affects all terrain, vegetation, structures, and creatures in the area. The exact effects depend on the terrain and its features:

Cave, Cavern, or Tunnel: The spell collapses the roof, dealing 8d6 points of damage to any creature caught under the cave-in (Reflex half DC 15). An earthquake cast on the roof of a very large cavern could also endanger those outside the actual area but below the falling debris.

Cliffs: They crumble, causing a landslide that travels horizontally as far as it fell vertically. An earthquake cast at the top of a 100-foot cliff would sweep 100 feet outward from the base of the cliff. Any creature in the path sustains 8d6 points of damage (Reflex half DC 15).

Open Ground: All creatures standing in the area must make Reflex saving throws (DC 15) or fall down. Fissures open in the ground, and every creature on the ground has a 25% chance to fall into one (Reflex save DC 20 to avoid the fissure). At the end of the spell, all fissures grind shut, killing any creatures still trapped within.

Structure: Most structures standing on open ground collapse, dealing 8d6 points of damage to those caught within or beneath the rubble (Reflex half DC 15).

River, Lake, or Marsh: Fissures open underneath the water, draining away the water from that area and forming muddy ground. Soggy marsh or swampland becomes quicksand for the duration of the spell, sucking down creatures and structures. Creatures must make Reflex saving throws (DC 15) or sink down in the mud and quicksand. At the end of the spell, the rest of the body of water rushes in to replace the drained water, possibly drowning those caught in the mud.

Elemental Swarm

Conjuration (Summoning) [see text]
Level: Air 9, Drd 9, Earth 9, Fire 9,
  Water 9
Components: V, S
Casting Time: 10 minutes
Range: Medium (100 ft. + 10 ft./level)
Effect: Two or more summoned creatures, no two of which can be more than 30 ft. apart
Duration: 10 minutes/level (D)
Saving Throw: None
Spell Resistance: No

This spell opens a portal to an Elemental Plane. A druid can choose which plane (air, earth, fire, or water); a cleric opens a portal to the plane matching his domain. You can then summon elementals from that plane.

When the spell is complete, 2d4 Large elementals appear. Ten minutes later, 1d4 Huge elementals appear. Ten minutes after that, one greater elemental appears. Each elemental has at least 5 hit points per HD (that is, at least 60, 80, or 100 hit points, respectively). Once the elementals appear, they serve you for the duration of the spell.

The elementals obey you explicitly and never attack you, even if someone else manages to gain control over them. You do not need to concentrate to maintain control over the elementals. You can dismiss them singly or in groups at any time.

When you use a summoning spell to summon an air, earth, fire, or water creature, it is a spell of that type. For example, *elemental swarm* is a fire spell when you cast it to summon fire elementals and a water spell when you use it to summon water elementals.

motion

Enchantment (Compulsion)
    [Mind-Affecting]
Level: Brd 3, Sor/Wiz 4
Components: V, S
Casting Time: 1 action
Range: Medium (100 ft. + 10 ft./level)
Targets: All living creatures within a
    15-ft. radius
Duration: Concentration
Saving Throw: Will negates
Spell Resistance: Yes

This spell arouses a single emotion of your choice in the subjects. You can choose any one of the following versions:

Despair: The enchanted creatures suffer a –2 morale penalty to saving throws, attack rolls, ability checks, skill checks, and weapon damage rolls. *Emotion (despair)* dispels *emotion (hope)*.

Fear: The enchanted creatures flee from you whenever they are in sight of you. *Emotion (fear)* dispels *emotion (rage)*.

Friendship: The enchanted creatures react more positively toward others. Their attitude on the Influencing NPC Attitude Table (see NPC Attitudes in the DUNGEON MASTER'S *Guide*) shifts to the next more favorable reaction (hostile to unfriendly, unfriendly to indifferent, indifferent to friendly, or friendly to helpful). Creatures involved in combat, however, continue to fight back normally. *Emotion (friendship)* dispels *emotion (hate)*.

Hate: The enchanted creatures react more negatively toward others. Their attitude on the Influencing NPC Attitude Table (see NPC Attitudes in the DUNGEON MASTER'S *Guide*) shifts to the next less favorable reaction (helpful to friendly, friendly to indifferent, indifferent to unfriendly, or unfriendly to hostile). *Emotion (hate)* dispels *emotion (friendship)*.

Hope: The enchanted creatures gain a +2 morale bonus to saving throws, attack rolls, ability checks, skill checks, and weapon damage rolls. *Emotion (hope)* dispels *emotion (despair)*.

Rage: The enchanted creatures gain a +2 morale bonus to Strength and Constitution scores, a +1 morale bonus on Will saves, and a –1 penalty to AC. They are compelled to fight heedless of danger. *Emotion (rage)* does not stack with barbarian rage or with itself. *Emotion (rage)* dispels *emotion (fear)*.

Endurance

Transmutation
Level: Clr 2, Sor/Wiz 2
Components: V, S, DF
Casting Time: 1 action
Range: Touch
Target: Creature touched
Duration: 1 hour/level
Saving Throw: None
Spell Resistance: Yes

The affected creature gains greater vitality and stamina. The spell grants the subject an enhancement bonus (1d4+1 points) to Constitution, adding the usual benefits to hit points, Fortitude saves, Constitution checks, and so forth.

Note: Hit points gained by a temporary increase in Constitution score are not temporary hit points. They go away when the character's Constitution drops back to normal. They are not lost first as temporary hit points are (see page 129).

Endure Elements

Abjuration
Level: Clr 1, Drd 1, Pal 1, Sor/Wiz 1,
    Strength 1, Sun 1
Components: V, S
Casting Time: 1 action
Range: Touch
Target: Creature touched
Duration: 24 hours
Saving Throw: None
Spell Resistance: Yes

This abjuration grants a creature limited protection to damage from whichever one of five energy types you select: acid, cold, fire, electricity, or sonic. Each round, the spell absorbs the first 5 points of damage the creature would otherwise take from the specified energy type, regardless of whether the source of damage is natural or magical. The spell protects the recipient's equipment as well.

Endure elements absorbs only damage. The character could still suffer unfortunate side effects, such as drowning in acid (since drowning damage comes from lack of oxygen) or becoming encased in ice.

Note: *Endure elements* overlaps (and does not stack with) *resist elements* and *protection from elements*. If a character is

warded by *protection from elements* and one or both of the other spells, the *protection* spell absorbs damage until it is exhausted. If a character is warded by *resist elements* and *endure elements* at the same time, the *resist* spell absorbs damage but the *endure* spell does not.

Energy Drain

Necromancy
Level: Clr 9, Sor/Wiz 9
Range: Close (25 ft. + 5 ft./2 levels)
Duration: Instantaneous
Saving Throw: Fortitude negates (see
    text)

As *enervation*, except the creature struck gains 2d4 negative levels, and the negative levels last longer.

Twenty-four hours after gaining any negative levels, the subject must make a Fortitude saving throw (using the spell DC in this case) for each negative level. If the save succeeds, that negative level is negated. If it fails, the negative level goes away, but one of the subject's character levels has been permanently drained.

If the ray strikes an undead creature, that creature gains 2d4×5 temporary hit points.

Enervation

Necromancy
Level: Sor/Wiz 4
Components: V, S
Casting Time: 1 action
Range: Medium (100 ft. + 10 ft./level)
Effect: Ray of negative energy
Duration: Instantaneous
Saving Throw: None
Spell Resistance: Yes

You point your finger and utter the incantation, releasing a black bolt of crackling negative energy that suppresses the life force of any living creature it strikes. You must make a ranged touch attack to hit. If the attack succeeds, the subject gains 1d4 negative levels.

If the subject has at least as many negative levels as HD, he dies. Each negative level gives a creature the following penalties: –1 competence penalty on attack rolls, saving throws, skill checks, ability checks, and effective level (for determining the power, duration, DC, and other details of spells or special abilities). Additionally, a spellcaster loses one spell or spell slot from her highest available level. Negative levels stack.

Assuming the subject survives, he regains lost levels after a number of hours equal to your caster level. Usually, negative levels have a chance of permanently draining the subject's levels, but the negative levels from *enervation* don't last long enough to do so.

If the ray strikes an undead creature, it gives that creature 5 temporary hit points per two caster levels (maximum 25 temporary hit points).

Enlarge

Transmutation
Level: Sor/Wiz 1
Components: V, S, M
Casting Time: 1 action
Range: Close (25 ft. + 5 ft./2 levels)
Target: One creature, or one object of up to 10 cu. ft. per level in volume
Duration: 1 minute/level
Saving Throw: Fortitude negates
Spell Resistance: Yes

This spell causes instant growth of a creature or object, increasing both size and weight. The subject grows by up to 10% per caster level, increasing by this amount in height, width, and depth (to a maximum of 50%). Weight increases by approximately the cube of the size increase, as follows:

Height Increase	Weight Increase
+10% (×1.1)	+30% (×1.3)
+20% (×1.2)	+70% (×1.7)
+30% (×1.3)	+120% (×2.2)
+40% (×1.4)	+170% (×2.7)
+50% (×1.5)	+240% (×3.4)

All equipment worn or carried by a creature is enlarged by the spell. If insufficient room is available for the desired growth, the creature or object attains the maximum possible size, bursting weak enclosures in the process. However, it is constrained without harm by stronger materials—the spell cannot be used to crush a creature by growth.

Magical properties are not increased by this spell—an enlarged +1 *sword* is still only +1, a staff-sized wand is still only capable of its normal functions, a giant-sized potion merely requires a greater fluid intake to make its magical effects operate, and so on. Weight, mass, and strength are affected, though. Thus, a table blocking a door would be heavier and more effective, a hurled stone would have more mass (and cause more damage), chains would be more massive, doors thicker, a thin line turned to a sizable, longer rope, and so on. A creature's hit points, Armor Class, and base attack bonus do not change, but Strength increases along with size. For every 20% of enlargement, the creature gains a +1 enlargement bonus to Strength.

Multiple magical effects that increase size do not stack.

Enlarge counters and dispels *reduce*.

Material Component: A pinch of powdered iron.

Entangle

Transmutation
Level: Drd 1, Plant 1, Rgr 1
Components: V, S, DF
Casting Time: 1 action
Range: Long (400 ft. + 40 ft./level)
Area: Plants in a 40-ft.-radius spread
Duration: 1 minute/level
Saving Throw: Reflex (see text)
Spell Resistance: No

Grasses, weeds, bushes, and even trees wrap, twist, and entwine about creatures in the area or those who enter the area, holding them fast. An *entangled* creature suffers a −2 penalty to attack rolls, suffers a −4 penalty to effective Dexterity, and can't move. An *entangled* character who attempts to cast a spell must make a Concentration check (DC 15) or lose the spell. She can break free and move half her normal speed by using a full-round action to make a Strength check or an Escape Artist check (DC 20). A creature who succeeds at a Reflex saving throw is not *entangled* but can still move at only half speed through the area. Each round, the plants once again attempt to entangle all creatures who have avoided or escaped entanglement.

Note: The DM may alter the effects of the spell somewhat, based on the nature of the entangling plants.

Enthrall

Enchantment (Charm) [Language-Dependent, Mind-Affecting, Sonic]
Level: Brd 2, Clr 2
Components: V, S
Casting Time: 1 full round
Range: Medium (100 ft. + 10 ft./level)
Targets: Any number of creatures
Duration: Up to 1 hour
Saving Throw: Will negates (see text)
Spell Resistance: Yes

If you have the attention of a group of creatures, you can use this spell to hold them spellbound. To cast the spell, you must speak or sing without interruption for 1 full round. Thereafter, those affected give you their undivided attention, ignoring their surroundings. They are considered to have an attitude of friendly while under the effect of the spell (see the DUNGEON MASTER's Guide for information about attitudes). Those of a race or religion unfriendly to yours have a +4 bonus to the saving throw.

Creatures with 4 or more HD or with Wisdom scores of 16 or higher remain aware of their surroundings and have an attitude of indifferent. They gain new saving throws if they witness actions that they oppose.

The enchantment lasts as long as you speak or sing, to a maximum of 1 hour. Those *enthralled* by your words take no

action while you speak or sing, and for 1d3 rounds thereafter while they discuss the topic or performance. Those entering the area during the performance must also successfully save or become *enthralled*. The speech ends (but the 1d3-round delay still applies) if you lose concentration or perform any action other than speaking or singing.

If those not *enthralled* have unfriendly or hostile attitudes toward you, they can collectively make a Charisma check to try to end the spell. This check is based on the character with the highest Charisma and has a +2 bonus for each other jeerer who can make a Charisma check of 10 or higher. The heckling ends the spell if it beats your opposed Charisma check. Only one such challenge is allowed per use of the spell.

If any member of the audience is attacked (or subjected to an overtly hostile act), the spell ends and the audience becomes immediately unfriendly toward you (or hostile, for audience members with 4 or more HD and Wisdom 16 or higher).

Entropic Shield

Abjuration
Level: Clr 1, Luck 1
Components: V, S
Casting Time: 1 action
Range: Personal
Target: You
Duration: 1 minute/level

A magical field appears around you, glowing with a chaotic blast of multicolored hues. This field deflects incoming arrows, rays, and other ranged attacks. Each ranged attack directed at you suffers a 20% miss chance (similar to the effects of concealment). This miss chance affects all ranged attacks for which the attackers make attack rolls, including arrows, magic arrows, *Melf's acid arrow*, *ray of enfeeblement*, and so forth. It does not affect other attacks that simply work at a distance, such as dragon breath.

Erase

Transmutation
Level: Brd 1, Sor/Wiz 1
Components: V, S
Casting Time: 1 action
Range: Close (25 ft. + 5 ft./2 levels)
Target: One scroll or two pages
Duration: Instantaneous
Saving Throw: See text
Spell Resistance: No

Erase removes writings of either magical or mundane nature from a scroll or from up to two pages of paper, parchment, or similar surfaces. It removes *explosive runes*, *glyphs of warding*, *sepia snake sigils*, and *arcane marks*, but it does not remove *illusory script* or *symbols*. Nonmagical writings are automatically erased if you touch them and no one else is holding them. Otherwise, the chance is 90%. Magic writings must be touched, and you must roll 15+ on a caster level check (1d20 + caster level) to succeed. (A natural 1 or 2 is always a miss on this roll.) If you fail to erase *explosive runes*, a *glyph of warding*, or a *sepia snake sigil*, you accidentally activate the runes, glyph, or sigil instead.

thereal Jaunt

Transmutation
Level: Clr 5, Sor/Wiz 7
Components: V, S
Casting Time: 1 action
Range: Personal
Target: You
Duration: 1 round/level (D)

You become ethereal, along with your equipment. You are in a place called the Ethereal Plane, which overlaps the normal, physical, Material Plane.

When the spell expires, you return to material existence.

Note: An ethereal creature is invisible, incorporeal, and capable of moving in any direction, even up or down (albeit at half normal speed). As an incorporeal creature, you can move through solid objects, including living creatures. An ethereal creature can see and hear the Material Plane, but everything looks gray and insubstantial. Sight and hearing onto the Material Plane are limited to 60 feet. Force effects (such as *magic missile* and *wall of force*) and abjurations affect the creature normally. Their effects extend onto the Ethereal Plane from the Material Plane, but not vice versa. An ethereal creature can't attack material creatures, and spells you cast while ethereal affect only other ethereal things. Certain material creatures or objects have attacks or effects that work on the Ethereal Plane (such as the basilisk and its gaze attack). By contrast, treat other ethereal creatures and ethereal objects as if they had become material.

If you end the spell and become material while inside a material object (such as a solid wall), you are shunted off to the nearest open space and take 1d6 points of damage per 5 feet that you so travel.

herealness

Transmutation
Level: Clr 6, Sor/Wiz 8
Range: Touch (see text)
Targets: You and one other touched creature/three levels
Duration: 1 minute/level (D)
Spell Resistance: Yes

As *ethereal jaunt*, except you and other creatures joined by linked hands (along with their equipment) become ethereal.

When a wizard is ethereal, material objects such as this tree appear hazy and insubstantial.

Illus. by D. Martin

Besides yourself, you can bring one creature per three caster levels to the Ethereal Plane. Once ethereal, the creatures need not stay together.

When the spell expires, all affected creatures in the Ethereal Plane return to material existence.

Evard's Black Tentacles

Conjuration (Creation)
Level: Sor/Wiz 4
Components: V, S, M
Casting Time: 1 action
Range: Medium (100 ft. + 10 ft./level)
Effect: 1d4 tentacles + one tentacle/level, all within 15 ft. of a central point
Duration: 1 hour/level
Saving Throw: None
Spell Resistance: No

This spell conjures many rubbery black tentacles. These waving members seem to spring forth from the earth, floor, or whatever surface is underfoot—including water. There are 1d4 such tentacles, plus one per caster level, appearing randomly scattered about the area. Each tentacle is 10 feet long (Large) and saves as you do. It

has AC 16, 1 hit point/per caster level, an attack bonus of +1/per caster level, and a Strength score of 19 (+4 bonus). It is immune to spells that don't cause damage (other than *disintegrate*).

Each round that a tentacle is not already grappling someone or something, starting the round after it appears, it makes a grapple attack at a random creature or object within 10 feet of it. These attacks take place on your turn. The tentacles do not attack each other, nor do they attack objects that are smaller than a Medium-size creature. The attacks are like regular grappling attacks, except that they don't provoke attacks of opportunity from opponents. Also, they cause 1d6 points of normal damage (+4 for Strength), not subdual damage. A tentacle maintains its grapple even after its subject is dying or dead.

The DM can place each tentacle randomly by rolling 1d12 for direction (like the numbers on the face of a clock) and 1d3×5 feet for distance from the central point. Alternatively, the DM can just disperse them more or less evenly across the affected area.

Material Component: A piece of tentacle from a giant octopus or a giant squid.

Expeditious Retreat

Transmutation
Level: Brd 1, Sor/Wiz 1, Travel 1
Components: V, S
Casting Time: 1 action
Range: Personal
Target: You
Duration: 1 minute/level (D)

Expeditious retreat provides you with amazing fleetness of foot, enabling you to run in great leaps and bounds. Your speed and maximum jumping distances both double (see the Jump skill, page 70). These benefits count as enhancement bonuses.

This spell can be used for attack as well as for flight; the name of the spell hints at the typical wizard's attitude toward combat.

Explosive Runes

Abjuration [Force]
Level: Sor/Wiz 3
Components: V, S
Casting Time: 1 action
Range: Touch
Target: One touched object weighing no more than 10 lb.
Duration: Until discharged (D)
Saving Throw: See text
Spell Resistance: Yes

You trace these mystic runes upon a book, map, scroll, or similar object bearing written information. The *runes* detonate when read, dealing 6d6 points of damage. Anyone next to the *runes* (close enough to read them) takes this damage with no saving throw. Others within 10 feet of the *runes* take half damage if they succeed at Reflex saving throws. The object in which the *runes* were written also takes the damage (no saving throw).

As the spellcaster, you and any characters you specifically instruct can read the protected writing without triggering the *runes*. Likewise, you can remove the *runes* whenever desired. Others can remove them with a successful *dispel magic* or *erase* spell. However, attempting to dispel or erase the *runes* and failing to do so triggers the explosion.

Note: Magic traps such as *explosive runes* are hard to detect and disable. A rogue (only) can use the Search skill to find the runes and Disable Device to thwart them. The DC in each case is 25 + spell level, or 28 for *explosive runes*.

Eyebite

Transmutation [see text]
Level: Brd 6, Sor/Wiz 6
Components: V, S
Casting Time: 1 action
Range: Close (25 ft. + 5 ft./2 levels)
Target: You
Duration: 1 round/three levels (see text)

Saving Throw: See text
Spell Resistance: Yes

You can merely meet the gaze of a creature and speak a single word to affect it with one of four magical effects: *charm, fear, sicken,* or *sleep.* You select one of these four possible gaze attacks when casting the spell. You retain the gaze power for 1 round for every three caster levels and can use the gaze attack as a free action each round.

These effects do not affect undead creatures or extend beyond the plane you currently occupy. You are subject to the effects of your reflected gaze and are allowed any applicable saving throw. In the case of a reflected *charm* gaze, you are *held* (as a *hold monster* spell).

The four versions of the spell are as follows:

Charm: Equivalent to the *charm monster* spell, except that the saving throw is based on spell level 6.

Fear: The subject flees in blind terror for 1d4 rounds. Once it stops fleeing, the creature refuses to face you for 10 minutes per your caster level. If subsequently confronted by you, it either cowers or bolts for the nearest cover (50% chance of either). This is an enchantment, compulsion, mind-affecting effect; it can be negated by a Will save (SR applies).

Sicken: Sudden pain and fever sweeps over the subject's body. An affected creature's speed is reduced by half, it loses any Dexterity bonus to Armor Class, and it suffers a –2 penalty to attack rolls. The creature remains stricken for 10 minutes per your caster level. The effects cannot be negated by a *cure disease* or *heal* spell, but a *remove curse* or successful *dispel magic* spell is effective. This is a necromancy effect; it can be negated by a Fortitude save (SR applies).

Sleep: The subject falls asleep. The creature sleeps for your caster level × 10 minutes but can be slapped awake. This is an enchantment, compulsion, mind-affecting effect; it can be negated by a Will save (SR applies).

Note: Each round, a gaze attack automatically works against one creature within range that is looking at (attacking or interacting with) the gazing creature. Creatures can avert their eyes, which grants them a 50% chance to avoid the gaze but in turn grants the gazer one-half concealment (20% miss chance) relative to them. Creatures can close their eyes or turn away entirely; doing so prevents the gaze from affecting them but grants the gazer total concealment (50% miss chance) relative to them.

Fabricate

Transmutation
Level: Sor/Wiz 5
Components: V, S, M

Casting Time: See text
Range: Close (25 ft. + 5 ft./2 levels)
Target: Up to 10 cu. ft./level (see text)
Duration: Instantaneous
Saving Throw: None
Spell Resistance: No

You convert material of one sort into a product that is of the same material. Thus, you can fabricate a wooden bridge from a clump of trees, a rope from a patch of hemp, clothes from flax or wool, and so forth. Creatures or magic items cannot be created or transmuted by the *fabricate* spell. The quality of items made by this spell is commensurate with the quality of material used as the basis for the new fabrication. If you work with a mineral, the target is reduced to 1 cubic foot per level instead of 10 cubic feet.

You must make an appropriate Craft check to fabricate articles requiring a high degree of craftsmanship (jewelry, swords, glass, crystal, etc.).

Casting requires 1 full round per 10 cubic feet (or 1 cubic foot) of material to be affected by the spell.

Material Component: The original material.

Faerie Fire

Evocation
Level: Drd 1
Components: V, S, DF
Casting Time: 1 action
Range: Long (400 ft. + 40 ft./level)
Area: Creature and objects within a 5-ft.-radius burst
Duration: 1 minute/level
Saving Throw: None
Spell Resistance: Yes

A pale glow surrounds and outlines the subjects. Outlined subjects shed light as candles. Outlined creatures do not benefit from the concealment normally caused by darkness, *blur*, displacement, invisibility, or similar effects. The light is too dim to have any special effect on undead or dark-dwelling creatures. The *faerie fire* can be blue, green, or violet, according to your word at the time of casting. The *faerie fire* does not cause any harm to the objects or creatures thus outlined.

False Vision

Illusion (Glamer)
Level: Brd 5, Sor/Wiz 5, Trickery 5
Components: V, S, M
Casting Time: 1 action
Range: Close (25 ft. + 5 ft./2 levels)
Area: 25 ft. + 5 ft/2 levels-radius emanation, centered on the point where you were when you cast the spell
Duration: 1 minute/level
Saving Throw: None
Spell Resistance: No

You and all you desire within the area of the spell become undetectable to scrying (whether by spell or magic device). Furthermore, if you are aware of an attempt to scry, you can create whatever image you desire, including sight and sound, according to the medium of the scrying method. To do this, you must concentrate on the figment you are creating. Once concentration is broken, no further images can be created, although the area remains undetectable for the duration of the spell.

Arcane Material Component: The ground dust of a jade worth at least 250 gp, which is sprinkled into the air when the spell is cast.

Fear

Necromancy [Fear, Mind-Affecting]
Level: Brd 3, Sor/Wiz 4
Components: V, S, M
Casting Time: 1 action
Range: Close (25 ft. + 5 ft./2 levels)
Area: Cone
Duration: 1 round/level
Saving Throw: Will negates
Spell Resistance: Yes

An invisible cone of terror causes living creatures to become panicked. They suffer a –2 morale penalty on saving throws, and they flee from you. A panicked creature has a 50% chance to drop what it's holding, chooses its path randomly (as long as it is getting away from immediate danger), and flees any other dangers that confront it. If cornered, a panicked creature cowers. (See the DUNGEON MASTER'S *Guide* for more information on fear-panicked creatures.)

Material Component: Either the heart of a hen or a white feather.

Feather Fall

Transmutation
Level: Brd 1, Sor/Wiz 1
Components: V
Casting Time: See text
Range: Close (25 ft. + 5 ft./2 levels)
Targets: Any free-falling objects or creatures in a 10-ft. radius whose weight does not total more than 300 lb./level
Duration: Until landing or 1 round/level
Saving Throw: Will negates (object)
Spell Resistance: Yes (object)

The creatures or objects affected fall slowly (though faster than feathers typically do). The rate of falling is instantly changed to a mere 60 feet a round (equivalent to the end of a fall from a few feet), with no damage incurred upon landing while the spell is in effect. However, when the spell duration ceases, a normal rate of fall resumes.

The character can cast this spell with an instant utterance, quickly enough to save herself if she unexpectedly falls. Casting the spell is a free action, like casting a quickened spell, and it counts toward the normal limit of one quickened spell per round.

This spell has no special effect on ranged weapons unless they are falling quite a distance. If the spell is cast on a falling item, such as a boulder dropped from the top of a castle wall, the item does half normal damage based on weight with no bonus for the height of the drop. (See the DUNGEON MASTER'S *Guide* for information on falling objects.)

The spell works only upon free-falling objects. It does not affect a sword blow or a charging or flying creature.

Feeblemind

Enchantment (Compulsion)
[Mind-Affecting]
Level: Sor/Wiz 5
Components: V, S, M
Casting Time: 1 action
Range: Medium (100 ft. + 10 ft./level)
Target: One creature
Duration: Instantaneous
Saving Throw: Will negates (see text)
Spell Resistance: Yes

The subject's Intelligence score drops to 1: roughly the intellect of a lizard. The creature is unable to cast spells, use Intelligence-based skills, or communicate coherently. Still, the creature knows who its friends are and can follow them and even protect them. The creature remains in this state until a *heal, limited wish, miracle,* or *wish* spell is used to cancel the effects. Creatures who can cast arcane spells, such as sorcerers and wizards, or use arcane spell-like effects suffer a –4 penalty on their saving throws.

Material Component: A handful of clay, crystal, glass, or mineral spheres.

Find the Path

Divination
Level: Clr 6, Drd 6, Knowledge 6, Travel 6
Components: V, S, F
Casting Time: 3 rounds
Range: Personal or touch
Target: You or creature touched
Duration: 10 minutes/level
Saving Throw: None or Will negates (harmless)
Spell Resistance: No or Yes (harmless)

The recipient of this spell can find the shortest, most direct physical route to a specified destination, be it the way into or out of a locale. The locale can be outdoors, underground, or even inside a *maze* spell. Note that the spell works with respect to locales, not objects or creatures within a locale. Thus, the spell could not find the way to "a forest where a green dragon lives" or to the location of "a hoard of platinum pieces," but it could find the exit to a labyrinth. The location must be on the same plane as you are at the time of casting.

The spell enables the subject to sense the correct direction that will eventually lead him to his destination, indicating at the appropriate times the exact path to follow or physical actions to take. For example, the spell enables the subject to sense trip wires or the proper word to bypass a *glyph.* The spell ends when the destination is reached or the duration elapses, whichever comes first. The spell frees the subject, and those with him, from a *maze* spell in a single round.

This divination is keyed to the recipient, not his companions, and does not predict or allow for the actions of creatures (including guardians).

Focus: A set of divination counters of the sort favored by you—bones, ivory counters, sticks, carved runes, etc.

Find Traps

Divination
Level: Clr 2
Components: V, S
Casting Time: 1 action
Range: Medium (100 ft. + 10 ft./level)
Target: You
Duration: 1 minute/level

You gain intuitive insight into the workings of traps. You can use your Search skill to detect traps just as a rogue can but gain no special bonus on your Search checks.

Finger of Death

Necromancy [Death]
Level: Drd 8, Sor/Wiz 7
Components: V, S
Casting Time: 1 action
Range: Close (25 ft. + 5 ft./2 levels)
Target: One living creature
Duration: Instantaneous
Saving Throw: Fortitude partial
Spell Resistance: Yes

You can slay any one living creature within range. The subject is entitled to a Fortitude saving throw to survive the attack. If the save is successful, it instead sustains 3d6 points of damage +1 point per caster level. Of course, the subject might die from damage even if it succeeds at its saving throw.

Fireball

Evocation [Fire]
Level: Sor/Wiz 3
Components: V, S, M
Casting Time: 1 action
Range: Long (400 ft. + 40 ft./level)
Area: 20-ft.-radius spread

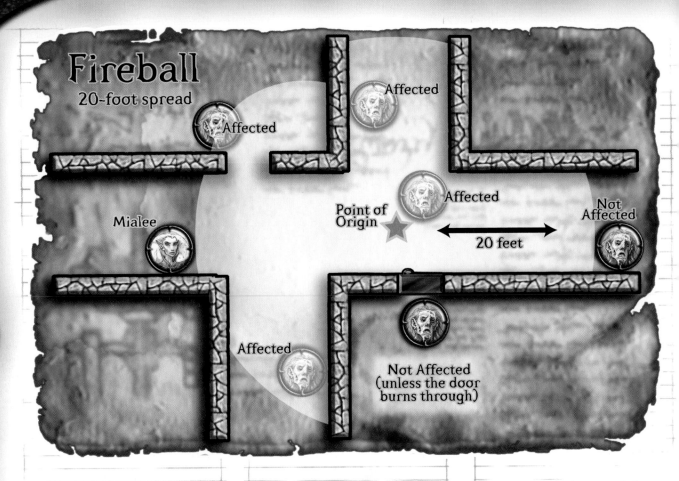

Fireball
20-foot spread

Affected

Affected

Affected

Mialee

Point of Origin

Not Affected

20 feet

Affected

Not Affected (unless the door burns through)

Duration: Instantaneous
Saving Throw: Reflex half
Spell Resistance: Yes

A *fireball* spell is a burst of flame that detonates with a low roar and deals 1d6 points of fire damage per caster level (maximum 10d6) to all creatures within the area. Unattended objects also take this damage. The explosion creates almost no pressure.

You point your finger and determine the range (distance and height) at which the *fireball* is to burst. A glowing, pea-sized bead streaks from the pointing digit and, unless it impacts upon a material body or solid barrier prior to attaining the prescribed range, blossoms into the *fireball* at that point (an early impact results in an early detonation). If you attempt to send the bead through a narrow passage, such as through an arrow slit, you must "hit" the opening with a ranged touch attack, or else the bead strikes the barrier and detonates prematurely.

The *fireball* sets fire to combustibles and damages objects in the area. It can melt metals with a low melting point, such as lead, gold, copper, silver, or bronze. If the damage caused to an interposing barrier shatters or breaks through it, the *fireball* may continue beyond the barrier if the area permits; otherwise it stops at the barrier just as any other spell effect does.

Material Component: A tiny ball of bat guano and sulfur.

Fire Seeds
Conjuration (Creation) [Fire]
Level: Drd 6, Fire 6, Sun 6
Components: V, S, M
Casting Time: 1 action/seed
Range: Touch
Targets: Up to four touched acorns or up to eight touched holly berries
Duration: 10 minutes/level or until used
Saving Throw: Reflex half (see text)
Spell Resistance: Yes

Depending on the version you choose, you turn acorns into grenadelike weapons or holly berries into bombs that you can detonate on command.

Acorn Grenades: Up to four acorns turn into special grenadelike weapons that can be hurled up to 100 feet. A ranged touch attack roll is required to strike the intended target. Each acorn bursts upon striking any hard surface. Together, the acorns are capable of dealing 1d8 points of fire damage per caster level (maximum 20d8), divided up among the acorns as you wish. A 20th-level druid could create one 20d8 missile, two 10d8 missiles, one 11d8 and three 3d8 missiles, or any other combination of d8s totaling up to four acorns and 20d8

points of damage. The acorns deal 1 point of splash damage per die and ignite any combustible materials within 10 feet. If a creature within the burst area makes a successful Reflex saving throw, it takes only half damage; a creature struck directly always sustains full damage (no saving throw).

Holly Berry Bombs: You turn up to eight holly berries into special bombs. The holly berries are usually placed by hand, being too light to make effective thrown weapons (they can be tossed only 5 feet). They burst into flame if you are within 200 feet and speak a word of command. The berries instantly ignite, causing 1d8 points of fire damage +1 point per caster level to creatures and igniting any combustible materials within 5 feet. Creatures who successfully make Reflex saving throws take half damage.

Material Component: The acorns or holly berries.

Fire Shield
Evocation [Fire or Cold]
Level: Fire 5, Sor/Wiz 4, Sun 4
Components: V, S, M/DF
Casting Time: 1 action
Range: Personal
Target: You
Duration: 1 round/level (D)
Saving Throw: None

This spell wreathes you in flame and causes damage to each creature who attacks you in melee. The flames also protect you from either cold-based or fire-based attacks (your choice).

Any creature striking you with its body or handheld weapons deals normal damage, but at the same time the attacker takes 1d6 points of damage +1 point per caster level. This damage is either cold damage (if the *shield* protects against fire-based attacks) or fire damage (if the *shield* protects against cold-based attacks). If a creature has spell resistance, it applies to this damage. Note that weapons with exceptional reach, such as two-handed spears, do not endanger their users in this way.

When casting this spell, you appear to immolate yourself, but the flames are thin and wispy, shedding no heat and giving light equal to only half the illumination of a normal torch (10 feet). The color of the flames is determined randomly (50% chance of either color)—blue or green if the *chill shield* is cast, violet or blue if the *warm shield* is employed. The special powers of each version are as follows.

Warm Shield: The flames are warm to the touch. You take only half damage from cold-based attacks. If that attack allows a Reflex save for half damage, you take no damage on a successful save.

Chill Shield: The flames are cool to the touch. You take only half damage from fire-based attacks. If that attack allows a Reflex save for half damage, you take no damage on a successful save.

Arcane Material Component: A bit of phosphorus for the *warm shield*; a live firefly or glowworm or the tail portions of four dead ones for the *chill shield*.

Fire Storm

Evocation [Fire]
Level: Clr 8, Drd 7, Fire 7
Components: V, S
Casting Time: 1 full round
Range: Medium (100 ft. + 10 ft./level)
Area: Two 10-ft. cubes/level (S)
Duration: Instantaneous
Saving Throw: Reflex half
Spell Resistance: Yes

When a *fire storm* spell is cast, the whole area is shot through with sheets of roaring flame. The raging flames do not harm natural vegetation, ground cover, and plant creatures in the area, if you so desire. Any other creatures (and plant creatures you wish to affect) within the area take 1d6 points of fire damage per caster level (maximum 20d6).

Fire Trap

Abjuration [Fire]
Level: Drd 2, Sor/Wiz 4
Components: V, S, M

Casting Time: 10 minutes
Range: Touch
Target: Object touched
Duration: Permanent until discharged
Saving Throw: Reflex half (see text)
Spell Resistance: Yes

Fire trap creates a fiery explosion when an intruder opens the item that the trap wards. The *fire trap* can ward any closeable item (book, box, bottle, chest, coffer, coffin, door, drawer, and so forth). When casting *fire trap*, you select a point on the item as the spell's center. When someone other than you opens the item, a fiery explosion fills the area within a 5-foot radius around the spell's center. The flames deal 1d4 points of fire damage +1 point per caster level (maximum +20). The item protected by the trap is not harmed by this explosion.

The *fire trapped* item cannot have a second closure or warding spell placed on it.

A *knock* spell does not affect a *fire trap* in any way, because *knock* only opens things and the *fire trap* in no way prevents one from opening the trapped item. An unsuccessful *dispel magic* spell does not detonate the spell.

Underwater, this ward deals half damage and creates a large cloud of steam.

As the caster, you can use the trapped object without discharging it, as can any individual to whom the spell was specifically attuned when cast. "Attuning" usually involves a password that you can share with friends.

Note: Magical traps such as *fire trap* are hard to detect and disable. A rogue (only) can use the Search skill to find the trap and Disable Device to thwart it. The DC in each case is 25 + spell level (DC 27 for a druid's *fire trap* or DC 29 for the arcane version).

Material Components: A half-pound of gold dust (cost 25 gp) sprinkled on the warded object. Attuning the trap to another individual requires a hair or similar object from that individual.

Flame Arrow

Conjuration (Creation) [Fire]
Level: Sor/Wiz 3
Components: V, S, M
Casting Time: 1 action
Range: Medium (100 ft. + 10 ft./level)
Targets or Effect: Up to one projectile/level, all of which must be within 10 ft. of you at the time of casting; or one fiery bolt/four levels
Duration: 1 round/Instantaneous
Saving Throw: See text
Spell Resistance: Yes

You can either create flames that turn normal arrows, bolts, and stones into fiery projectiles, or you can create fiery bolts and shoot them at enemies.

Flaming Normal Projectiles: When choosing this version, you can affect up to one projectile per level. The projectiles must all be within 10 feet of you at the time of casting. If shot before the end of the next round, these projectiles catch fire. If they hit, they deal additional fire damage equal to half your caster level (up to +10). For example, at 9th level, Mialee can affect up to nine arrows (or bolts or stones), which then deal +4 damage each. The flaming projectiles can easily ignite flammable materials or structures. No saving throw is allowed for this version of the spell.

Fiery Bolts: When creating a fiery bolt, you must succeed at a ranged touch attack roll to hit. The bolt deals 4d6 points of fire damage (Reflex save half). If you create extra bolts (at 8th level or higher), all bolts must be aimed at enemies that are all within 30 feet of each other.

Material Components: A drop of oil and a small piece of flint.

Flame Blade

Evocation [Fire]
Level: Drd 2
Components: V, S, DF
Casting Time: 1 action
Range: Touch
Effect: Swordlike beam
Duration: 1 minute/level (D)
Saving Throw: None
Spell Resistance: Yes

A 3-foot-long, blazing beam of red-hot fire springs forth from your hand. You wield this bladelike beam as if it were a scimitar. Attacks with the *flame blade* are melee touch attacks. The blade deals 1d8 points of damage +1 point per two caster levels (maximum +10). Since the blade is immaterial, your Strength modifier does not apply to the damage, which is all fire damage. The *flame blade* can ignite combustible materials such as parchment, straw, dry sticks, and cloth. It can harm any creature who is harmed by magical fire.

The spell does not function underwater.

Flame Strike

Evocation [Fire]
Level: Clr 5, Drd 4, Sun 5, War 5
Components: V, S, DF
Casting Time: 1 action
Range: Medium (100 ft. + 10 ft./level)
Area: Cylinder (10-ft. radius, 40 ft. high)
Duration: Instantaneous
Saving Throw: Reflex half
Spell Resistance: Yes

A *flame strike* produces a vertical column of divine fire roaring downward. The spell deals 1d6 points of damage per caster level (maximum 15d6). Half the damage is fire damage, but the rest results directly from divine power and is therefore not subject to being reduced by *protection from elements (fire)*, *fire shield (chill shield)*, and similar magic.

Flaming Sphere

Evocation [Fire]
Level: Drd 2, Sor/Wiz 2
Components: V, S, M/DF
Casting Time: 1 action
Range: Medium (100 ft. + 10 ft./level)
Effect: 3-ft.-radius sphere
Duration: 1 round/level
Saving Throw: Reflex negates (see text)
Spell Resistance: Yes

A burning globe of fire rolls in whichever direction you point and burns those it strikes. It moves 30 feet per round and can leap up to 30 feet to strike a target. If it enters a space with a creature, it stops moving for the round and deals 2d6 points of fire damage to that creature. (The subject can negate this damage with a successful Reflex save.) The *flaming sphere* rolls over barriers less than 4 feet tall, such as furniture and low walls. The sphere ignites flammable substances it touches and illuminates the same area as a torch.

The *sphere* moves as long as you actively direct it (a move-equivalent action for you); otherwise, it merely stays at rest and burns. It can be extinguished by any means that would put out a normal fire of its size. The surface of the *sphere* has a spongy, yielding consistency and so does not cause damage except by its flame. It cannot push aside unwilling creatures or batter down large obstacles. The *sphere* winks out if it exceeds the spell's range.

Arcane Material Components: A bit of tallow, a pinch of brimstone, and a dusting of powdered iron.

Flare

Evocation [Light]
Level: Brd 0, Drd 0, Sor/Wiz 0
Components: V
Casting Time: 1 action
Range: Close (25 ft. + 5 ft./2 levels)
Effect: Burst of light
Duration: Instantaneous
Saving Throw: Fortitude negates
Spell Resistance: Yes

This cantrip creates a burst of bright light. If you cause the light to burst directly in front of a single creature, that creature is dazzled. A dazzled creature suffers a –1 penalty on attack rolls. The creature recovers in 1 minute. Sightless creatures are not affected by *flare*.

Flesh to Stone

Transmutation
Level: Sor/Wiz 6
Components: V, S, M
Casting Time: 1 action
Range: Medium (100 ft. + 10 ft./level)
Target: One creature
Duration: Instantaneous
Saving Throw: Fortitude negates
Spell Resistance: Yes

The subject and all possessions it carries turn into a mindless, inert statue. If the statue resulting from this spell is broken or damaged, the being (if ever returned to its original state) has similar damage or deformities. The creature is not dead (its soul doesn't pass on), but it does not seem to be alive either (when viewed with spells such as *deathwatch*). Only creatures made of flesh are affected by this spell.

Material Components: Lime, water, and earth.

Fly

Transmutation
Level: Sor/Wiz 3, Travel 3
Components: V, S, F/DF
Casting Time: 1 action
Range: Touch
Target: Creature touched
Duration: 10 minutes/level
Saving Throw: None
Spell Resistance: Yes (harmless)

The spell's subject can fly with a speed of 90 feet (60 feet if the creature wears medium or heavy armor). The subject can fly up at half speed and descend at double speed. The flying subject's maneuverability rating is good. Using the *fly* spell requires as much concentration as walking, so the subject can attack or cast spells normally. The subject of a *fly* spell can charge but not run, and it cannot carry aloft more weight than its maximum load (see page 142), plus any armor it wears.

Should the spell duration expire while the subject is still aloft, the magic fails slowly. The subject drops 60 feet per round for 1d6 rounds. If it reaches the ground in that amount of time, it lands safely. If not, it falls the rest of the distance (falling damage is 1d6 per 10 feet of fall). Since dispelling a spell effectively ends it, the subject also falls in this way if the *fly* spell is dispelled.

Arcane Focus: A wing feather from any bird.

Fog Cloud

Conjuration (Creation)
Level: Sor/Wiz 2, Water 2
Components: V, S
Casting Time: 1 action
Range: Medium (100 ft. + 10 ft. level)
Effect: Fog that spreads in a 30-ft. radius, 20 ft. high
Duration: 10 minutes/level
Saving Throw: None
Spell Resistance: No

A bank of fog billows out from the point you designate. The fog obscures all sight, including darkvision, beyond 5 feet. A creature within 5 feet has one-half concealment (attacks suffer a 20% miss chance). Creatures farther away have total concealment (50% miss chance, and the attacker can't use sight to locate the target).

A moderate wind (11+ mph) disperses the fog in 4 rounds; a strong wind (21+ mph) disperses the fog in 1 round.

The spell does not function underwater.

Forbiddance

Abjuration
Level: Clr 6
Components: V, S, M, DF
Casting Time: 6 rounds
Range: Medium (100 ft. + 10 ft./level)
Area: 60-ft. cube/level (S)
Duration: Permanent
Saving Throw: See text
Spell Resistance: Yes

Forbiddance prevents creatures whose alignments are different from yours from entering the area. Additionally, the spell seals the area against all planar travel into it, including *dimension door, teleport, plane shifting*, astral travel, ethereal travel, and all summoning spells. At your option, the abjuration can be locked by a password, in which case it can be entered only by those speaking the proper words (no saving throw allowed to those who don't speak the password, although SR applies). Otherwise, the effect on those entering the warded area is based on their alignment relative to yours.

Alignments identical: No effect. The creature may enter freely (albeit not by planar travel).

Alignments different with respect to either law/chaos or good/evil: The creature is hedged out and takes 3d6 points of damage. A successful Will save negates both effects, and SR applies.

Alignments different with respect to both law/chaos and good/evil: The creature is hedged out and takes 6d6 points of damage. A successful Will save negates both effects, and SR applies.

Once a saving throw is failed, an intruder cannot enter the forbidden area (future saving throws likewise fail). Intruders who enter by rolling successful saving throws feel uneasy and tense, despite their success.

Dispel magic does not dispel the *forbiddance* effect unless the dispeller's level is at least as high as your caster level.

Material Components: A sprinkling of holy water and rare incenses worth at least 1,500 gp per 60-foot cube. If a password lock is desired, this requires the burning of additional rare incenses worth at least 5,000 gp per 60-foot cube.

Forcecage

Evocation [Force]
Level: Sor/Wiz 7
Components: V, S, M (see text)
Casting Time: 1 action
Range: Close (25 ft. + 5 ft./2 levels)
Area: Barred cage (20-ft. cube) or
windowless cell (10-ft. cube)
Duration: 2 hours/level
Saving Throw: None
Spell Resistance: No

This powerful spell brings into being an immobile cubical prison with bars or solid walls of force (your choice).

Creatures within the area are caught and contained unless they are too big to fit inside or can pass through the slits in the barred cage. All spells and breath weapons can pass through the gaps in the bars. Teleportation and other forms of astral travel provide a means of escape, but the force walls or bars extend into the Ethereal Plane, blocking ethereal travel.

Like a *wall of force* spell, the *forcecage* resists *dispel magic*, but it is vulnerable to a *disintegrate* spell, and it can be destroyed by a *sphere of annihilation* or a *rod of cancellation*.

Barred Cage: The barred cage is a 20-foot cube with bands of force (similar to a *wall of force* spell) for bars. The bands are a half-inch wide, with half-inch gaps between the bars.

Windowless Cell: The cell is a 10-foot cube with no way in and no way out. Solid walls of force form its six sides.

Material Component: The spell needs no material component at the time of casting, but you must have 1,500 gp worth of ruby dust to prepare the spell. Upon completing preparations, you toss the dust into the air and it disappears, leaving only the verbal and somatic components to be provided at the time of casting.

Foresight

Divination
Level: Drd 9, Knowledge 9, Sor/Wiz 9
Components: V, S, M/DF
Casting Time: 1 action
Range: Personal or touch
Target: See text
Duration: 10 minutes/level
Saving Throw: None or Will negates
(harmless)
Spell Resistance: No or Yes (harmless)

This spell grants you a powerful sixth sense in relation to yourself or another. Once the spell is cast, you receive instantaneous warnings of impending danger or harm to the subject of the spell. Thus, if you are the subject of the spell, you would be warned in advance if a rogue were about to attempt a sneak attack on you, or if a creature were about to leap out from an unexpected direction, or if an attacker were specifically targeting you with a spell or ranged weapon. You are never surprised or flat-footed. In addition, the spell gives you a general idea of what action you might take to best protect yourself—duck, jump right, close your eyes, and so on—and gives you a +2 insight bonus to AC and to Reflex saves. This insight bonus is lost whenever you would lose a Dexterity bonus to AC.

When another creature is the object of the spell, you receive warnings about that creature. You must communicate what you learn to the other creature for the warning to be useful, and it can be caught unprepared in the absence of such a warning. Shouting a warning, yanking a person back, and even telepathically communicating (via an appropriate spell) can all be accomplished before some danger befalls the spell subject, provided you act on the warning without delay. The subject, however, does not gain the insight bonus to AC and Reflex saves.

Arcane Material Component: A hummingbird's feather.

Freedom

Abjuration
Level: Sor/Wiz 9
Components: V, S
Casting Time: 1 action
Range: See text
Target: One creature
Duration: Instantaneous
Saving Throw: None
Spell Resistance: Yes

The subject is freed from spells and effects that restrict his movement, including *entangle*, *hold*, *imprisonment*, *paralysis*, *petrification*, *sleep*, *slow*, *stunning*, *temporal stasis*, and *web*. To free someone from *imprisonment*, you must know his name and background, and you must cast this spell at the spot where he was entombed.

Freedom of Movement

Abjuration
Level: Clr 4, Drd 4, Luck 4, Pal 4, Rgr 4
Components: V, S, M, DF
Casting Time: 1 action
Range: Personal or touch
Target: You or creature touched
Duration: 10 minutes/level
Saving Throw: None
Spell Resistance: No or Yes (harmless)

This spell enables you or the creature you touch to move and attack normally for the duration of the spell, even under the influence of magic that usually impedes movement, such as *hold person*, *paralysis*, *solid fog*, *slow*, and *web* spells.

The spell also allows a character to move and attack normally while underwater, even with cutting weapons such as axes and swords and with bludgeoning weapons such as flails, hammers, and maces, provided that the weapon is wielded in the hand rather than hurled. The *freedom of movement* spell does not, however, allow water breathing.

Material Component: A leather thong, bound around the arm or a similar appendage.

Gaseous Form

Transmutation
Level: Air 3, Brd 3, Sor/Wiz 3
Components: S, M/DF
Casting Time: 1 action
Range: Touch
Target: Willing corporeal creature touched
Duration: 2 minutes/level (D)
Saving Throw: None
Spell Resistance: No

The subject and all her gear become insubstantial, misty, and translucent. The subject gains damage reduction 20/+1. Her material armor (including natural armor) becomes worthless, though her size, Dexterity, deflection bonuses, and armor bonuses from force armor (for example, from the *mage armor* spell) still apply. She becomes immune to poison and critical hits. She can't attack or cast spells with verbal, somatic, material, or focus components while in gaseous form. (Note that this does not rule out certain spells that the subject may have prepared using the metamagic feats Silent Spell and Still Spell.) As with *polymorph other*, the subject loses supernatural abilities while in gaseous form. If she has a touch spell ready to use, it is discharged harmlessly when the spell takes effect.

The gaseous creature can't run but she can fly (speed 10, maneuverability perfect). She can pass through small holes or narrow openings, even mere cracks, with all she was wearing or holding in her hands, as long as the spell persists. She is subject to wind. She can't enter water or other liquid.

Arcane Material Components: A bit of gauze and a wisp of smoke.

Gate

Conjuration (Creation, Calling)
Level: Clr 9, Sor/Wiz 9
Components: V, S
Casting Time: 1 action
Range: Medium (100 ft. + 10 ft./level)
Effect: See text
Duration: Instantaneous
Saving Throw: None
Spell Resistance: No

Casting a *gate* spell has two effects. First, it creates an interdimensional connection between your plane of existence and

A sorcerer opens a gate to another plane.

the plane desired, allowing travel between the planes in either direction. Second, you may then call a particular individual or type of being through the *gate*. The *gate* itself is a circular hoop or disk from 5 to 20 feet in diameter (caster's choice), oriented in the direction you desire when it comes into existence (typically vertical and facing you). It is a two-dimensional window into the plane you named, and anyone or anything that moves through is shunted instantly to the other side. The *gate* has a front and a back. Creatures moving through the *gate* from the front are transported to another plane; creatures moving through it from the back are not.

Planar Travel: As a mode of planar travel, *gate* functions much like the *plane shift* spell, except that the *gate* opens precisely at the point you desire (a creation effect). Note that deities and other beings who rule a planar realm can prevent a *gate* from opening in their presence or personal demesnes if they so desire. Travelers need not join hands with you—anyone who chooses to step through the portal is transported. A *gate* cannot be opened to another point on the same plane; the spell works only for interplanar travel.

A clever caster could fill a hallway with the *gate's* opening in order to absorb almost any attack or force coming at her by gating it to the target plane. Whether the denizens of that plane appreciate this tactic is, of course, another matter.

You may hold the *gate* open only for a brief time (no more than 1 round per caster level) and must concentrate on doing so or sever the interplanar connection.

Calling Creatures: The second effect of the *gate* spell is to call an extraplanar creature to your aid (a calling effect). By naming a particular being or type of being as you cast the spell, you may cause the *gate* to open in the immediate vicinity of the desired creature and pull the subject through, willing or unwilling. Deities and unique beings are under no compulsion to come through the *gate*, although they may choose to do so of their own accord. This use of the spell creates a *gate* that remains open just long enough to transport the called creatures.

If you choose to call a type of being instead of a known individual—for instance, a barbezu or a ghaele eladrin—you may call either a single creature (of any HD) or several creatures. If several creatures, you can call and control them as long as their HD total does not exceed your caster level. In the case of a single creature, you can control it if its HD do not exceed twice your caster level. A single creature with more than twice your caster level in HD can't be controlled. Deities and unique beings cannot be controlled in any event. An uncontrolled being acts as it pleases, making the calling of such creatures rather dangerous. An uncontrolled being may return to its home plane at any time.

A controlled creature can be commanded to perform a service for you. These fall into two categories: immediate tasks and contractual service. Fighting for you in a single battle or taking any other actions that can be accomplished within 1 round per caster level counts as an immediate task; you need not make any agreement or pay any reward for the creature's help. The creature departs at the end of the spell.

If you choose to exact a longer or more involved form of service from the called creature, you must offer some fair trade in return for that service. The service exacted must be reasonable with respect to the promised favor or reward. In general, a gift of 100 gp per HD of the called creature per day of service is reasonable. (Unfortunately, some creatures want their payment in "livestock" rather than in coin, which may involve complications.) Immediately upon completion of the service, the being is transported to your vicinity, and you must then and there turn over the

promised reward. After this is done, the creature is instantly freed to return to its own plane.

Failure to fulfill the promise to the letter results in your being subjected to service by the creature or by its liege and master, at the very least. At worst, the creature or its kin may attack you.

Note: When you use a calling spell such as *gate* to call an air, chaotic, earth, evil, fire, good, lawful, or water creature, it becomes a spell of that type. For example, *gate* is a chaotic and evil spell when you cast it to call a demon.

Geas/Quest

Enchantment (Compulsion) [Language-Dependent, Mind-Affecting]
Level: Brd 6, Clr 6, Sor/Wiz 6
Target: One living creature
Saving Throw: None

As *lesser geas*, except that *geas/quest* affects a creature of any HD and allows no saving throw.

Instead of suffering penalties to abilities, the subject takes 3d6 points of damage each day he does not attempt to follow the *geas/quest*. Additionally, each day he must make a Fortitude saving throw or sicken. A sickened creature moves at half his normal speed and suffers –4 penalties on both Strength and Dexterity. He heals damage at one-tenth his normal rate and cannot benefit from any magical healing effects. A sickened creature must make a Fortitude save each day or become crippled. Once crippled, the subject is effectively disabled (as if he had 0 hit points) and can't choose to take strenuous actions. These effects end 1 day after the creature attempts to resume the *geas/quest*.

Remove curse ends the *geas/quest* only if its caster level is at least two higher than your caster level. *Break enchantment* does not end the *geas/quest*, although *limited wish*, *miracle*, and *wish* do.

Wizard and bards usually refer to this spell as *geas*, while clerics call the same spell *quest*.

Gentle Repose

Necromancy
Level: Clr 2, Sor/Wiz 3
Components: V, S, M/DF
Casting Time: 1 action
Range: Touch
Target: Corpse touched
Duration: 1 day/level
Saving Throw: Will negates (object)
Spell Resistance: Yes (object)

You preserve the remains of a dead creature so that they do not decay. Doing so extends the time limit on raising that creature from the dead (see *raise dead*). Days spent under the influence of this spell don't count against the time limit. Additionally, this spell makes transporting a fallen comrade more pleasant.

The spell also works on severed body parts and the like.

Arcane Material Components: A pinch of salt, and a copper piece for each eye the corpse has (or had).

host Sound

Illusion (Figment)
Level: Brd 0, Sor/Wiz 0
Components: V, S, M
Casting Time: 1 action
Range: Close (25 ft. + 5 ft./2 levels)
Effect: Illusory sounds
Duration: 1 round/level (D)
Saving Throw: Will disbelief (if interacted with)
Spell Resistance: No

Ghost sound allows you to create a volume of sound that rises, recedes, approaches, or remains at a fixed place. You choose what type of sound the spell creates when casting the spell and cannot thereafter change its basic character. The volume of sound created, however, depends on your level. You can produce as much noise as four normal humans per caster level (maximum twenty humans). Thus, talking, singing, shouting, walking, marching, or running sounds can be created. The noise a *ghost sound* spell produces can be virtually any type of sound within the volume limit. A horde of rats running and squeaking is about the same volume as eight humans running and shouting. A roaring lion is equal to the noise from sixteen humans, while a roaring dire cat is equal to the noise from twenty humans.

Note that *ghost sound* can enhance the effectiveness of a *silent image* spell.

Material Component: A bit of wool or a small lump of wax.

houl Touch

Necromancy
Level: Sor/Wiz 2
Components: V, S, M
Casting Time: 1 action
Range: Touch
Target: Living humanoid touched
Duration: 1d6+2 rounds
Saving Throw: Fortitude negates
Spell Resistance: Yes

Imbuing you with negative energy, this spell allows you to paralyze a single humanoid for 1d6+2 rounds with a successful melee touch attack. Additionally, the paralyzed subject exudes a carrion stench that causes retching and nausea in a 10-foot radius. Those in the radius (excluding you) must make a Fortitude save or suffer a –2 penalty to all attack rolls, weapon damage rolls, saving throws,

GIANT VERMIN

Caster Level	Target's New HD	New Size	Armor Class	Attack/ Damage	Fortitude	Reflex	Will
7–9	3d8+6	Large	14	+4/1d8+4	+5	+0	+1
10–12	4d8+16	Huge	14	+8/2d6+8	+8	+0	+1
13–15	5d8+20	Huge	14	+8/2d6+8	+8	+0	+1
16–18	6d8+24	Huge	14	+9/2d6+8	+9	+1	+2
19–20	7d8+28	Huge	14	+9/2d6+8	+9	+1	+2

skill checks, and ability checks until the spell ends.

Material Component: A small scrap of cloth taken from clothing worn by a ghoul or a pinch of earth from a ghoul's lair.

Giant Vermin

Transmutation
Level: Clr 4, Drd 4
Components: V, S, DF
Casting Time: 1 action
Range: Close (25 ft. + 5 ft./2 levels)
Targets: Up to three vermin, no two of which can be more than 30 ft. apart
Duration: 1 minute/level
Saving Throw: None
Spell Resistance: Yes

You turn one or more normal-sized insects, arachnids, or other vermin into larger forms resembling the giant vermin described in the *Monster Manual*. Only one type of vermin can be transmuted (so a single casting cannot affect both an ant and a fly), and all must be grown to the same number of HD. The number of vermin and the HD to which they can be grown depends upon your level; see the accompanying table.

The DM should also consult the vermin entry in the *Monster Manual* for more information on what abilities a giant vermin is likely to have. A flying insect can generally carry a rider two size categories smaller than itself.

Any giant vermin created by this spell do not attempt to harm you, but your control of such creatures is limited to simple commands ("Attack," "Defend," "Stop," and so forth). Orders to attack a certain creature when it appears or guard against a particular occurrence are too complex for the vermin to understand. Unless commanded to do otherwise, the giant vermin attack whoever or whatever is near them.

Glitterdust

Conjuration (Creation)
Level: Brd 2, Sor/Wiz 2
Components: V, S, M
Casting Time: 1 action
Range: Medium (100 ft. + 10 ft./level)
Area: Creatures and objects within 10-ft. spread
Duration: 1 round/level
Saving Throw: Will negates (blinding only)
Spell Resistance: Yes

A cloud of glittering golden particles covers everyone and everything in the area, blinding creatures and visibly outlining invisible things. Blindness lasts for the duration of the spell. All within the area are covered by the dust, which cannot be removed and continues to sparkle until it fades.

In addition to the obvious effects, a blinded creature suffers a 50% miss chance in combat (all opponents have full concealment), loses any Dexterity bonus to AC, grants a +2 bonus to opponents' attack rolls (they are effectively invisible), moves at half speed, and suffers a –4 penalty on most Strength- and Dexterity-based skills.

Material Component: Ground mica.

Globe of Invulnerability

Abjuration
Level: Sor/Wiz 6

As *minor globe of invulnerability*, except that it also excludes 4th-level spells and spell-like effects.

Glyph of Warding

Abjuration
Level: Clr 3
Components: V, S, M
Casting Time: 10 minutes
Range: Touch
Target or Area: Object touched or up to 5 sq. ft./level
Duration: Until discharged
Saving Throw: See text
Spell Resistance: Yes (object)

This powerful inscription harms those who enter, pass, or open the warded area or object. A *glyph* can guard a bridge or passage, ward a portal, trap a chest or box, and so on.

You set the conditions of the ward. Typically, any creature violating the warded area without speaking a pass phrase (which you set when casting the spell) is subject to the magic it stores. *Glyphs* can be set according to physical characteristics (such as height or weight) or creature type, subtype, or species (such as "drow" or "aberration"). *Glyphs* can also be set with respect to good, evil, law, or chaos, or to pass those of your religion. They cannot be set according to class, HD, or level. *Glyphs* respond to invisible creatures normally but are not triggered by those who travel past them ethereally. Multiple *glyphs* cannot be cast on the same area. However, if a cabinet had three drawers, each could be separately warded.

When casting the spell, you weave a tracery of faintly glowing lines around the warding sigil. The *glyph* can be placed to conform to any shape up to the limitations of your total square footage. When the spell is completed, the *glyph* and tracery become nearly invisible.

Glyphs cannot be affected or bypassed by such means as physical or magical probing, though they can be dispelled. *Mislead, polymorph,* and *nondetection* can fool a *glyph*.

Read magic allows you to identify a *glyph of warding* with a successful Spellcraft check (DC 13). Identifying the *glyph* does not discharge it and allows you to know the basic nature of the *glyph* (version, type of damage caused, what spell is stored).

The DM may decide that the exact *glyphs* available to a cleric depend on your deity. He or she might also make new *glyphs* available according to the magical research rules.

Note: Magic traps such as *glyph of warding* are hard to detect and disable. A rogue (only) can use the Search skill to find the *glyph* and Disable Device to thwart it. The DC in each case is 25 + spell level, or 28 for *glyph of warding*.

Depending on the version selected, a *glyph* either blasts the intruder or activates a spell.

Blast Glyph: A blast deals 1d8 points of damage per two caster levels to the intruder and to all within 5 feet of the intruder (maximum 5d8). This damage is acid, cold, fire, electricity, or sonic (caster's choice, made at time of casting). Those affected can make Reflex saves to take half damage.

Spell Glyph: You can store any harmful spell of up to 3rd level that you know. All level-dependent features of the spell are based on your level at the time of casting. If the spell has targets, it targets the intruder. If the spell has an area or an amorphous effect (such as a cloud), the area or effect is centered on the intruder. If the spell summons creatures, they appear as close as possible to the intruder and attack. All saving throws operate as normal, except that the DC is based on the level of the *glyph*.

Material Component: You trace the *glyph* with incense, which must first be sprinkled with powdered diamond worth at least 200 gp.

Goodberry

Transmutation
Level: Drd 1
Components: V, S, DF
Casting Time: 1 action
Range: Touch
Targets: 2d4 fresh berries touched
Duration: 1 day/level
Saving Throw: None
Spell Resistance: Yes

Casting *goodberry* upon a handful of freshly picked berries makes 2d4 of them magical. You (as well as any other caster of the same faith and 3rd or higher level) can immediately discern which berries are affected. Each enchanted berry nourishes a creature as if it were a normal meal for a Medium-size creature. The berry also cures 1 point of damage when eaten, subject to a maximum of 8 points of such curing in any 24-hour period.

Grease

Conjuration (Creation)
Level: Brd 1, Sor/Wiz 1
Components: V, S, M
Casting Time: 1 action
Range: Close (25 ft. + 5 ft./2 levels)
Target or Area: One object or a 10-ft. × 10-ft. square
Duration: 1 round/level (D)
Saving Throw: See text
Spell Resistance: No

A *grease* spell covers a solid surface with a layer of slippery grease. Any creature entering the area or caught in it when the spell is cast must make a successful Reflex save or slip, skid, and fall. Those that successfully save can move at half speed across the surface. However, those that remain in the area must each make a new saving throw every round to avoid falling and to be able to move. The DM should adjust saving throws by circumstance. For example, a creature charging down an incline that is suddenly *greased* has little chance to avoid the effect, but its ability to exit the affected area is almost assured (whether it wants to or not).

The spell can also be used to create a greasy coating on an item—a rope, ladder rungs, or a weapon handle, for instance. Material objects not in use are always affected by this spell, while objects wielded or employed by creatures receive a Reflex saving throw to avoid the effect. If the initial saving throw fails, the creature immediately drops the item. A saving throw must be made each round the creature attempts to pick up or use the *greased* item.

Material Component: A bit of pork rind or butter.

Greater Command

Enchantment (Compulsion) [Language-Dependent, Mind-Affecting]
Level: Clr 5
Targets: One creature/level, no two of which can be more than 30 ft. apart
Duration: 1 round/level

As *command,* except that up to one creature per level may be affected. At the start of each *commanded* creature's action after the first, it gets another Will save to attempt to break free from the spell.

Greater Dispelling

Abjuration
Level: Brd 5, Clr 6, Drd 6, Sor/Wiz 6

As *dispel magic,* except that the maximum bonus on the dispel check is +20 instead of +10. Additionally, *greater dispelling* has a chance to dispel any effect that *remove curse* can remove, even if *dispel magic* can't dispel that effect.

Greater Glyph of Warding

Abjuration
Level: Clr 6

As *glyph of warding,* except that the blast deals up to 10d8 damage, and the *greater glyph* can store a harmful spell of up to 6th level.

Material Component: Diamond dust worth at least 400 gp.

Greater Magic Fang

Transmutation
Level: Drd 3, Rgr 3
Range: Close (25 ft. + 5 ft./2 levels)
Target: One living creature
Duration: 1 hour/level

As *magic fang,* except that the enhancement bonus to attack and damage is +1 per three caster levels (maximum +5).

Greater Magic Weapon

Transmutation
Level: Brd 3, Clr 4, Pal 3, Sor/Wiz 3
Components: V, S, M/DF
Casting Time: 1 action
Range: Close (25 ft. + 5 ft./2 levels)
Target: One weapon or fifty projectiles (all of which must be in contact with each other at the time of casting)
Duration: 1 hour/level
Saving Throw: Will negates (harmless, object)
Spell Resistance: Yes (harmless, object)

This spell gives a weapon an enhancement bonus to attack and damage of +1 per three caster levels (maximum +5). An enhancement bonus does not stack with a masterwork weapon's +1 bonus on attacks.

Alternatively, you can affect up to fifty arrows, bolts, or bullets. The projectiles must all be of the same type, and they have to be together in one group (such as in the same quiver). Projectiles (but not thrown weapons) lose their transmutation when used.

If you're a good cleric, the cleric of a good deity, or a paladin, the weapon is considered blessed, which means it has special effects on certain creatures.

Arcane Material Components: Powdered lime and carbon.

Greater Planar Ally
Conjuration (Calling) [see text]
Level: Clr 8
Effect: Up to 24 HD worth of summoned elementals and outsiders, no two of which can be more than 30 ft. apart when they appear

As *lesser planar ally*, except you may call a single creature of up to 24 HD or a number of creatures whose HD total no more than 24. The creatures agree to help you and request your return favor together.

Greater Planar Binding
Conjuration (Calling) [see text]
Level: Sor/Wiz 8
Components: V, S, M
Targets: Up to 24 HD worth of elementals and outsiders, no two of which can be more than 30 ft. apart

As *lesser planar binding*, except you may call a single creature of up to 24 HD or a number of creatures whose HD total no more than 24. Each creature gets a saving throw, makes independent attempts to escape, and must be persuaded to aid you individually.

Greater Restoration
Necromancy
Components: V, S, XP
Level: Clr 7
Casting Time: 10 minutes

As *lesser restoration,* except the spell dispels all negative energy levels afflicting the healed creature, restoring the creature to the highest level it had previously achieved. This reverses level drains by a force or creature. The drained levels are restored only if the time since the creature lost the level is no more than 1 week per caster level.

Greater restoration also dispels all magical effects penalizing the character's abilities, cures all temporary ability damage, and restores all points permanently drained from all ability scores. It also removes all forms of insanity, confusion, and similar mental effects. *Greater restoration* does not restore levels or Constitution points lost due to death.

XP Cost: 500 XP.

Greater Scrying
Divination
Level: Brd 6, Clr 7, Drd 7, Sor/Wiz 7
Components: V, S
Casting Time: 1 action
Duration: 1 hour/level

As *scrying,* except as noted above. All of the following spells can be cast reliably through the sensor: *comprehend languages, darkvision, detect chaos, detect evil, detect good, detect law, detect magic, message, read magic,* and *tongues.*

Greater Shadow Conjuration
Illusion (Shadow)
Level: Sor/Wiz 5

As *shadow conjuration,* except that it can duplicate wizard or sorcerer conjurations of up to 4th level, and the illusory conjurations created are two-fifths (40%) as strong as the real thing instead of one-fifth as strong.

Greater Shadow Evocation
Illusion (Shadow)
Level: Sor/Wiz 6

As *shadow evocation,* but it enables the caster to create partially real, illusory versions of sorcerer or wizard evocations of up to 5th level. If recognized as *greater shadow evocation,* damaging spells deal only two-fifths (40%) of normal damage, with a minimum of 2 points per die of damage. For example, a *greater shadow cloudkill* has a 40% chance to kill creatures of 6 HD or less, and creatures of 4 to 6 HD get a saving throw. Creatures not killed take 1d10 × 0.4 points of damage each round.

Nondamaging effects, such as a *web's* ensnarement, are only 40% likely to work when the *greater shadow evocation* is recognized as mostly illusory (roll separately for each effect and each creature who recognizes the evocation as shadowy).

Guards and Wards
Abjuration
Level: Sor/Wiz 6
Components: V, S, M, F
Casting Time: 30 minutes (D)
Range: Anywhere within the area to be warded
Area: Up to 200 sq. ft./level (S)
Duration: 2 hours/level
Saving Throw: None
Spell Resistance: See text

This powerful spell is primarily used to defend your stronghold. The ward protects 200 square feet per caster level. The warded area can be up to 20 feet high, and shaped as you desire. You can ward several stories of a stronghold by dividing the area among them; you must be somewhere within the area to be warded to cast the spell. The spell creates the following magical effects within the warded area:

Fog: Fog fills all corridors, obscuring all sight, including darkvision, beyond 5 feet. A creature within 5 feet has one-half concealment (attacks suffer a 20% miss chance). Creatures farther away have full concealment (50% miss chance; the attacker cannot use sight to locate the target). Spell resistance: No.

Arcane Locks: All doors in the warded area are *arcane locked.* Spell resistance: No.

Webs: Webs fill all stairs from top to bottom. These strands are identical with those created by the *web* spell, except that they regrow in 10 minutes if they are burned or torn away while the *guards and wards* spell lasts. Spell resistance: Yes.

Confusion: Where there are choices in direction—such as a corridor intersection or side passage—a minor *confusion*-type spell functions so as to make it 50% probable that intruders believe they are going in the exact opposite direction from the one they actually chose. This is an enchantment (mind-affecting) effect. Spell resistance: No.

Lost Doors: One door per caster level is covered by a glamer to appear as if it were a plain wall. Spell resistance: No.

In addition, you can place your choice of one of the following five magical effects:

- *Dancing lights* in four corridors. You can designate a simple program that causes the lights to repeat as long as the *guards and wards* spell lasts. Spell resistance: No.
- A *magic mouth* in two places. Spell resistance: No.
- A *stinking cloud* in two places. The vapors appear in the places you designate; they return within 10 minutes if dispersed by wind while the *guards and wards* spell lasts. Spell resistance: Yes.
- A *gust of wind* in one corridor or room. Spell resistance: Yes.
- A *suggestion* in one place. You select an area up to 5 feet square, and any creature who enters or passes through the area receives the *suggestion* mentally. Spell resistance: Yes.

The whole warded area radiates strong magic of the abjuration school. A *dispel magic* cast on a specific effect, if successful, removes only that effect. A successful *Mordenkainen's disjunction* destroys the entire *guards and wards* effect.

Material Components: Burning incense, a small measure of brimstone and oil, a knotted string, and a small amount of umber hulk blood.

Focus: A small silver rod.

Guidance
Divination
Level: Clr 0, Drd 0
Components: V, S
Casting Time: 1 action

Range: Touch
Target: Creature touched
Duration: 1 minute or until discharged
Saving Throw: None
Spell Resistance: Yes

This spell imbues the subject with a touch of divine guidance. The creature gets a +1 competence bonus on a single attack roll, saving throw, or skill check. It must choose to use the bonus before making the roll to which it applies.

Gust of Wind

Evocation
Level: Brd 3, Sor/Wiz 3
Components: V, S, F
Casting Time: 1 action
Range: Medium (100 ft. + 10 ft./level)
Effect: Gust of wind (10 ft. wide, 10 ft. high) emanating out from you to the extreme of the range
Duration: 1 round
Saving Throw: Fortitude negates
Spell Resistance: Yes

This spell creates a strong blast of air that originates from you and moves in the direction you are facing. The force of this *gust* automatically extinguishes candles, torches, and similar unprotected flames. It causes protected flames, such as those of lanterns, to dance wildly and has a 50% chance to extinguish these lights. Creatures caught in the area may be affected (see the DUNGEON MASTER's *Guide* for details about wind effects on creatures). Any creature is entitled to a saving throw to ignore the *gust's* effects.

A *gust of wind* can do anything a sudden blast of wind would be expected to do. It can create a stinging spray of sand or dust, fan a large fire, overturn delicate awnings or hangings, heel over a small boat, and blow gases or vapors to the edge of the range.
Focus: A tiny leather bellows.

Hallow

Evocation [Good]
Level: Clr 5, Drd 5
Components: V, S, M, DF
Casting Time: One day
Range: Touch
Area: 10-ft./level radius emanating from the touched point
Duration: Instantaneous
Saving Throw: None
Spell Resistance: See text

Hallow makes a particular site, building, or structure a holy site. This has four major effects.

First, the site or structure is guarded by a *magic circle against evil* effect.

Second, all Charisma checks to turn undead gain a +4 sacred bonus and Charisma checks to command undead suffer a –4 sacred penalty. Spell resistance does not apply to this effect. (Note: This provision does not apply to the druid version of the spell.)

Third, any dead body interred in a *hallowed* site cannot be turned into an undead creature.

Finally, you may choose to fix a single spell effect to the *hallow* site. The spell effect lasts for one year and functions throughout the entire consecrated site, regardless of the normal duration and area or effect. You may designate whether the effect applies to all creatures, creatures who share your faith or alignment, or creatures who adhere to another faith or alignment. For example, you may create a *bless* effect that aids all creatures of your alignment or faith in the area, or a *curse* effect that hinders creatures of the opposed alignment or an enemy faith. At the end of the year, the chosen effect lapses, but it can be renewed or replaced simply by casting *hallow* again.

Spell effects that may be tied to a *hallow* site include *aid, bane, bless, cause fear, darkness, daylight, deeper darkness, detect evil, detect magic, dimensional anchor, discern lies, dispel magic, endure elements, freedom of movement, invisibility purge, negative energy protection, protection from elements, remove fear, resist elements, silence, tongues,* and *zone of truth.* Spell resistance might apply to these spells' effects. (See the individual spell descriptions for details.)

An area can receive only one *hallow* (and its associated spell effect) at a time.

Hallow counters or dispels *unhallow.*
Material Components: Herbs, oils, and incense worth at least 1,000 gp, plus 1,000 gp per level of the spell to be included in the hallowed area.

Hallucinatory Terrain

Illusion (Glamer)
Level: Brd 4, Sor/Wiz 4
Components: V, S, M
Casting Time: 10 minutes
Range: Long (400 ft. + 40 ft./level)
Area: One 30-ft. cube/level (S)
Duration: 2 hours/level
Saving Throw: Will disbelief (if interacted with)
Spell Resistance: No

You make natural terrain look, sound, and smell like some other sort of natural terrain. Thus, open fields or a road can be made to resemble a swamp, hill, crevasse, or some other difficult or impassable terrain. A pond can be made to seem like a grassy meadow, a precipice like a gentle slope, or a rock-strewn gully like a wide and smooth road. Structures, equipment, and creatures within the area are not hidden or changed in appearance.
Material Components: A stone, a twig, and a bit of green plant.

Halt Undead

Necromancy
Level: Sor/Wiz 3
Components: V, S, M
Casting Time: 1 action
Range: Medium (100 ft. + 10 ft./level)
Targets: Up to three undead, no two of which can be more than 30 ft. apart
Duration: 1 round/level
Saving Throw: See text
Spell Resistance: Yes

This spell renders up to three undead creatures immobile. Nonintelligent undead (such as skeletons and zombies) get no saving throw; intelligent undead do. If the spell is successful, it renders the undead immobile for the duration of the spell (similar to the effect of *hold person* on a living creature). The effect is broken if the *halted* creatures are attacked or take damage.
Material Components: A pinch of sulfur and powdered garlic.

Harm

Necromancy
Level: Clr 6, Destruction 6, Drd 7
Components: V, S
Casting Time: 1 action
Range: Touch
Target: Creature touched
Duration: Instantaneous
Saving Throw: None
Spell Resistance: Yes

Harm charges a subject with negative energy that causes the loss of all but 1d4 hit points.

If used on an undead creature, *harm* acts like *heal.*

Haste

Transmutation
Level: Brd 3, Sor/Wiz 3
Components: V, S, M
Casting Time: 1 action
Range: Close (25 ft. + 5 ft./2 levels)
Target: One creature
Duration: 1 round/level
Saving Throw: Fortitude negates (harmless)
Spell Resistance: Yes (harmless)

The transmuted creature moves and acts more quickly than normal. This extra speed has several effects.

On his turn, the subject may take an extra partial action, either before or after his regular action.

He gains a +4 haste bonus to AC. He loses this bonus whenever he would lose a dodge bonus.

He can jump one and a half times as far as normal. This increase counts as an enhancement bonus.

Haste dispels and counters *slow*.

Material Component: A shaving of licorice root.

Heal

Conjuration (Healing)
Level: Clr 6, Drd 7, Healing 6
Components: V, S
Casting Time: 1 action
Range: Touch
Target: Creature touched
Duration: Instantaneous
Saving Throw: None
Spell Resistance: Yes (harmless)

Heal enables you to channel positive energy into a creature to wipe away disease and injury. It completely cures all diseases, blindness, deafness, hit point damage, and all temporary ability damage. It neutralizes poisons in the subject's system, so that no additional damage or effects are suffered. It offsets a *feeblemind* spell. It cures those mental disorders caused by spells or injury to the brain. Only a single application of the spell is needed to simultaneously achieve all these effects.

Heal does not remove negative levels, restore permanently drained levels, or restore permanently drained ability scores.

If used against an undead creature, *heal* acts like *harm*.

Healing Circle

Conjuration (Healing)
Level: Brd 5, Clr 5, Drd 6, Healing 5
Components: V, S
Casting Time: 1 action
Range: 20 ft.
Area: All living allies and undead creatures within a 20-ft.-radius burst centered on you
Duration: Instantaneous
Saving Throw: Fortitude half (harmless)
Spell Resistance: Yes (harmless)

Positive energy spreads out in all directions from the point of origin, curing 1d8 points of damage +1 point per caster level (maximum +20) to nearby living allies.

Like *cure* spells, *healing circle* damages undead in its area rather than curing them.

Heal Mount

Conjuration (Healing)
Level: Pal 3
Components: V, S
Casting Time: 1 action
Range: Touch
Target: Your mount touched
Duration: Instantaneous
Saving Throw: None
Spell Resistance: Yes (harmless)

Heal mount enables you to wipe away disease and injury in your special mount (typically a warhorse). It completely cures all diseases, blindness, or deafness of the mount, cures all points of damage taken due to wounds or injury, and repairs temporary ability damage. It cures those mental disorders caused by spells or injury to the brain.

Heal mount does not remove negative levels, restore drained levels, or restore drained ability scores.

Heat Metal

Transmutation
Level: Drd 2, Sun 2
Components: V, S, DF
Casting Time: 1 action
Range: Close (25 ft. + 5 ft./2 levels)
Target: Metal equipment of one creature/two levels, no two of which can be more than 30 ft. apart; or 25 lb. of metal/level, all of which must be within a 30-ft. circle
Duration: 7 rounds
Saving Throw: Will negates (object)
Spell Resistance: Yes (object)

This spell is identical with *chill metal* (page 183) except that it makes metal warm, hot (1d4 points of fire damage), and searing (2d4 points of fire damage) instead of cold, icy, and freezing. Enchanted metal gets a saving throw to resist. Just as damage from *chill metal* negates fire damage, so damage from *heat metal* negates cold damage on a one-for-one basis. If cast underwater, *heat metal* deals half damage and boils the surrounding water.

Heat metal counters and dispels *chill metal*.

Helping Hand

Evocation
Level: Clr 3
Components: V, S, DF
Casting Time: 1 action
Range: Five miles
Effect: Ghostly hand
Duration: 1 hour/level
Saving Throw: None
Spell Resistance: No

You create the ghostly image of a hand, which you can send to find someone within five miles. The hand then beckons to that person and leads her to you if she follows it.

When the spell is cast, the hand appears in front of you. You then specify a person (or any creature) by physical description, which can include race, gender, and appearance but not ambiguous factors such as level, alignment, or class. When the description is complete, the hand streaks off in search of a subject that fits the description. The amount of time it takes to find the subject depends on how far away she is.

Distance	Time to Locate
Up to 100 ft.	1 round
1,000 ft.	1 minute
One mile	10 minutes
Two miles	1 hour
Three miles	2 hours
Four miles	3 hours
Five miles	4 hours

Once the hand locates the subject, it beckons her to follow it. If she follows, the hand points in your direction, leading her in the most direct, feasible route. The hand hovers 10 feet in front of the subject, moving before her at a rate of anywhere up to 240 feet per round. Once the hand leads the subject to you, it disappears.

The subject is not compelled to follow the hand or act in any particular way toward you. If she chooses not to follow, the hand continues to beckon for the duration of the spell, then disappears. If the spell expires while the subject is en route to you, the hand disappears; she will have to rely on her own devices to locate you.

If more than one subject within a five-mile radius meets the description, the hand locates the closest creature. If that creature refuses to follow the hand, the hand does not seek out a second subject.

If, at the end of 4 hours of searching, the hand has found no subject that matches the description within five miles, it returns to you, displays an outstretched palm (indicating that no such creature was found), and disappears.

The ghostly hand has no physical form. It is invisible to anyone except you and potential subjects. It cannot engage in combat or execute any other task aside from locating the subject and leading her back to you. The hand does not pass through solid objects but can ooze through small cracks and slits. The hand cannot travel more than five miles from the spot it appeared when you cast the spell.

Heroes' Feast

Evocation
Level: Clr 6
Components: V, S, DF
Casting Time: 10 minutes
Range: Close (25 ft. + 5 ft./2 levels)
Effect: Feast for one creature/level
Duration: 1 hour + 12 hours (see text)
Saving Throw: None
Spell Resistance: Yes (harmless)

You bring forth a great feast, including a magnificent table, chairs, service, and food and drink. The feast takes 1 hour to consume, and the beneficial effects do not set in until this hour is over. Those partaking of the feast are cured of all diseases, are immune to poison for 12 hours, and are healed of 1d4+4 points of damage after imbibing the nectarlike beverage that is part of the feast. The ambrosial food that is consumed creates an effect equal to *bless* that lasts for 12 hours. During this same period, the people who consumed the feast are immune to magical *fear* and *hopelessness*.

If the feast is interrupted for any reason, the spell is ruined and all effects of the spell are negated.

Hold Animal

Enchantment (Compulsion)
　[Mind-Affecting]
Level: Animal 2, Drd 2, Rgr 2
Components: V, S
Target: One animal

As *hold person*, except the spell affects an animal instead. *Hold animal* does not work on beasts, magical beasts, or vermin. When in doubt about whether something is an "animal" as defined by the spell, check the *Monster Manual*.

Hold Monster

Enchantment (Compulsion)
　[Mind-Affecting]
Level: Brd 4, Law 6, Sor/Wiz 5
Components: V, S, M/DF
Target: One living creature

As *hold person*, except this spell holds any living creature who fails its Will save.

Arcane Material Component: One hard metal bar or rod, which can be as small as a three-penny nail.

Hold Person

Enchantment (Compulsion)
　[Mind-Affecting]
Level: Brd 2, Clr 2, Sor/Wiz 3
Components: V, S, F/DF
Casting Time: 1 action
Range: Medium (100 ft.
　+ 10 ft./level)

Target: One humanoid of Medium-size
　or smaller
Duration: 1 round/level (D)
Saving Throw: Will negates
Spell Resistance: Yes

The subject freezes in place, standing helpless. He is aware and breathes normally but cannot take any physical actions, even speech. He can, however, execute purely mental actions (such as casting a spell with no components).

A winged creature who is *held* cannot flap its wings and falls. A swimmer can't swim and may drown.

Arcane Focus: A small, straight piece of iron.

Hold Portal

Abjuration
Level: Sor/Wiz 1
Component: V
Casting Time: 1 action
Range: Medium (100 ft. + 10 ft./level)
Target: One portal, up to 20 sq. ft./level
Duration: 1 minute/level
Saving Throw: None
Spell Resistance: No

This spell magically bars a door, gate, window, or shutter of wood, metal, or stone. The magic holds the portal fast, just as if it were securely closed and normally locked. A *knock* spell or a successful *dispel magic* spell can negate the *hold portal*. For a portal affected by this spell, add 5 to the normal DC for forcing the portal.

Holy Aura

Abjuration [Good]
Level: Clr 8, Good 8, Luck 8
Components: V, S, F
Casting Time: 1 action
Range: 20 ft.
Targets: One creature/level in a 20-ft.-radius burst centered on you
Duration: 1 round/level (D)
Saving Throw: See text
Spell Resistance: Yes (harmless)

A brilliant divine radiance surrounds the subjects, protecting them from attacks, granting them resistance to spells cast by evil creatures, and blinding evil creatures when they strike the subjects. This abjuration has four effects:

First, the warded creatures gain a +4 deflection bonus to AC and a +4 resistance bonus to saves. Unlike *protection from evil*, this benefit applies against all attacks, not just against attacks by evil creatures.

Second, the warded creatures gain SR 25 against evil spells and spells cast by evil creatures.

Third, the abjuration blocks possession and mental influence, just as *protection from evil* does.

Finally, if an evil creature succeeds at a melee attack against a warded creature, the offending attacker is blinded (Fortitude save negates, as *blindness/deafness*, but against *holy aura's* save DC).

Focus: A tiny reliquary containing some sacred relic, such as a scrap of cloth from a saint's robe or a piece of parchment from a holy text. The reliquary costs at least 500 gp.

Holy Smite

Evocation [Good]
Level: Good 4
Components: V, S
Casting Time: 1 action
Range: Medium (100 ft. + 10 ft./level)
Area: 20-ft.-radius burst
Duration: Instantaneous

Jozan casts holy smite against a succubus.

Saving Throw: Reflex half
Spell Resistance: Yes

You draw down holy power to smite your enemies. Only evil and neutral creatures are harmed by the spell; good creatures are unaffected.

The spell deals 1d8 points of damage per two caster levels (maximum 5d8) to evil creatures and blinds them for 1 round. A successful Reflex saving throw reduces damage to half and negates the blinding effect.

The spell deals only half damage against creatures who are neither good nor evil, and they are not blinded. They can reduce that damage by half (down to one-quarter of the roll) with a successful Reflex save.

In addition to the obvious effects, a blinded creature suffers a 50% miss chance in combat (all opponents have full concealment), loses any Dexterity bonus to AC, grants a +2 bonus to opponents' attack rolls (they are effectively invisible), moves at half speed, and suffers a –4 penalty on most Strength- and Dexterity-based skills.

Holy Sword
Evocation
Level: Pal 4
Components: V, S
Casting Time: 1 action
Range: Touch
Target: Weapon touched
Duration: 1 round/level
Saving Throw: None
Spell Resistance: No

This spell allows you to channel holy power into your sword, or any weapon you choose. The weapon acts as a +5 magic weapon and deals double damage against evil opponents. It emits a *magic circle against evil* (as the spell). If the *magic circle* ends, the sword creates a new one on your turn as a free action. The spell is automatically canceled 1 round after the weapon leaves your hand for any reason. You cannot have more than one *holy sword* at a time.

If this spell is cast on a magic weapon, the powers of the spell supersede any that the weapon normally has, rendering the normal enhancement bonus and powers of the weapon inoperative for the duration of the spell. This spell is not cumulative with *bless weapon* or any other spell that might modify the weapon in any way.

This spell does not work on artifacts.

Note: A masterwork weapon's bonus to attack does not stack with an enhancement bonus to attack.

Holy Word
Evocation [Good, Sonic]
Level: Clr 7, Good 7
Components: V

Casting Time: 1 action
Range: 30 ft.
Area: Creatures in a 30-ft.-radius spread centered on you
Duration: Instantaneous
Saving Throw: None
Spell Resistance: Yes

Uttering *holy word* has two effects.

If you are on your home plane, the spell instantly banishes nongood extraplanar creatures within the area back to their home planes. Creatures so banished cannot return for at least 1 day. This effect takes place regardless of whether the creatures hear the *holy word*.

Creatures native to your plane who hear the *holy word* and are not good suffer the following ill effects:

HD	Effect
12 or more	Deafened
Less than 12	Blinded, deafened
Less than 8	Paralyzed, blinded, deafened
Less than 4	Killed, paralyzed, blinded, deafened

The effects are cumulative.

Deafened: The creature is deafened (see *blindness/deafness*) for 1d4 rounds.

Blinded: The creature is blinded (see *blindness/deafness*) for 2d4 rounds.

Paralyzed: The creature is paralyzed and helpless for 1d10 minutes, unable to move or act in any way.

Killed: Living creatures die. Undead creatures are destroyed.

Horrid Wilting
Necromancy
Level: Sor/Wiz 8, Water 8
Components: V, S, M/DF
Casting Time: 1 action
Range: Long (400 ft. + 40 ft./level)
Targets: Living creatures, no two of whom can be more than 60 ft. apart
Duration: Instantaneous
Saving Throw: Fortitude half
Spell Resistance: Yes

This spell evaporates moisture from the bodies of all the subject living creatures, dealing 1d8 points of damage per caster level (maximum 25d8). This spell is especially devastating to water elementals and plant creatures, who receive a penalty of –2 to their saving throws.

Arcane Material Component: A bit of sponge.

Hypnotic Pattern
Illusion (Pattern) [Mind-Affecting]
Level: Brd 2, Sor/Wiz 2
Components: (V), S, M
Casting Time: 1 action
Range: Medium (100 ft. + 10 ft./level)

Effect: Colorful lights in a 15-ft.-radius spread
Duration: Concentration + 2 rounds
Saving Throw: Will negates
Spell Resistance: Yes

A twisting pattern of subtle, shifting colors weaves through the air, fascinating creatures within it. Roll 2d4 +1 per caster level to determine the total number of HD affected (maximum +10). Creatures with the fewest HD are affected first; and, among creatures with equal HD, those who are closest to the spell's point of origin are affected first. HD that are not sufficient to affect a creature are wasted. Affected creatures gaze at the lights, heedless of all else, acting as if they are affected by *hypnotism*. However, you cannot make suggestions as with *hypnotism*. Sightless creatures are not affected.

A wizard or sorcerer need not utter a sound to cast this spell, but a bard must sing, play music, or recite a rhyme as a verbal component.

Material Component: A glowing stick of incense or a crystal rod filled with phosphorescent material.

Hypnotism
Enchantment (Compulsion) [Mind-Affecting]
Level: Brd 1, Sor/Wiz 1
Components: V, S
Casting Time: 1 action
Range: Close (25 ft. + 5 ft./2 levels)
Area: Several living creatures, no two of which may be more than 30 ft. apart
Duration: 2d4 rounds (D)
Saving Throw: Will negates
Spell Resistance: Yes

Your gestures and droning incantation cause creatures nearby to stop and stare blankly at you, *hypnotized*. You can use their rapt attention to make your suggestions and requests seem more plausible. Roll 2d4 to see how many total HD you affect. Creatures with fewer HD are affected before creatures with more HD. Only creatures who can see or hear you are affected, but they do not need to understand you to be *hypnotized*.

If you use this spell in combat, the targets gain a +2 bonus to their saving throws. If the spell affects only a single creature not in combat at the time, the saving throw has a penalty of –2. While *hypnotized*, a creature's Spot and Listen checks suffer a –4 penalty. Any potential threat (such as an armed party member moving behind the *hypnotized* creature) allows the creature a second saving throw. Any obvious threat, such as casting a spell, drawing a sword, or aiming an arrow, automatically breaks the *hypnotism*, as does shaking or slapping the creature.

A *hypnotized* creature's ally may shake it free of the spell as a standard action.

While the subject is *hypnotized*, you can make a suggestion or request (provided you can communicate with it). The suggestion must be brief and reasonable. An affected creature reacts as though it were two steps more friendly in attitude. (The DUNGEON MASTER's *Guide* has rules for creatures' attitudes.) Even once the spell ends, it retains its new attitude toward you, but only with respect to that particular suggestion.

A creature who fails its saving throw does not remember that you enspelled it.

Ice Storm
Evocation [Cold]
Level: Drd 5, Sor/Wiz 4, Water 5
Components: V, S, M/DF
Casting Time: 1 action
Range: Long (400 ft. + 40 ft./level)
Area: Cylinder (20-ft. radius, 40 ft. high)
Duration: Instantaneous
Saving Throw: None
Spell Resistance: Yes

Great hailstones pound down, dealing 5d6 points of damage to creatures in their path; the damage is 3d6 impact plus 2d6 cold.

Arcane Material Components: A pinch of dust and a few drops of water.

Identify
Divination
Level: Brd 1, Magic 2, Sor/Wiz 1
Components: V, S, M/DF
Casting Time: 8 hours
Range: Touch
Targets: Up to 1 touched object per level
Duration: Instantaneous
Saving Throw: None
Spell Resistance: No

The spell determines the single most basic function of each magic item, including how to activate that function (if appropriate), and how many charges are left (if any). For example, a +2 *vorpal sword*, a +2 *dancing sword*, and a +2 *sword* would all register as "+2 to attack and damage rolls."

If a magic item has multiple different functions that are equally basic, *identify* determines the lowest-level function. If these functions are also of equal level, the DM decides randomly which is identified.

Arcane Material Components: A pearl of at least 100 gp value, crushed and stirred into wine with an owl feather; the infusion must be drunk prior to spellcasting.

Illusory Script
Illusion (Phantasm) [Mind-Affecting]
Level: Brd 3, Sor/Wiz 3
Components: V, S, M
Casting Time: 1 minute or longer (see text)

Range: Touch
Target: One touched object weighing no more than 10 lb.
Duration: 1 day/level
Saving Throw: Will negates (see text)
Spell Resistance: Yes

You write instructions or other information on parchment, paper, or any suitable writing material. The *illusory script* appears to be some form of foreign or magic writing. Only the person (or people) designated by you at the time of the casting are able to read the writing; it's completely unintelligible to any other character, although an illusionist recognizes it as *illusory script*.

Any unauthorized creature attempting to read the script triggers a potent illusory effect and must make a saving throw. A successful saving throw means the creature can look away with only a mild sense of disorientation. Failure means the creature is subject to a *suggestion* implanted in the script by you at the time the *illusory script* spell was cast. The *suggestion* lasts only 30 minutes. Typical *suggestions* include "Close the book and leave," "Forget the existence of the book," and so forth. If successfully dispelled by *dispel magic*, the *illusory script* and its secret message disappear. The hidden message can be read by a combination of the *true seeing* spell with the *read magic* or *comprehend languages* spell.

The casting time depends on how long a message you wish to write, but it is always at least 1 minute.

Material Component: A lead-based ink (cost of not less than 50 gp).

Illusory Wall
Illusion (Figment)
Level: Sor/Wiz 4
Components: V, S
Casting Time: 1 action
Range: Close (25 ft. + 5 ft./2 levels)
Effect: Image 1 ft. × 10 ft. × 10 ft.
Duration: Permanent
Saving Throw: Will disbelief (if interacted with)
Spell Resistance: No

This spell creates the illusion of a wall, floor, ceiling, or similar surface. It appears absolutely real when viewed, but physical objects can pass through it without difficulty. When the spell is used to hide pits, traps, or normal doors, any detection abilities that do not require sight work normally. Touch or probing searches reveal the true nature of the surface, though they do not cause the illusion to disappear.

Imbue with Spell Ability
Evocation
Level: Clr 4, Magic 4

Components: V, S, DF
Casting Time: 10 minutes
Range: Touch
Target: Creature touched
Duration: Until discharged
Saving Throw: Will negates (harmless)
Spell Resistance: Yes (harmless)

You transfer some of your currently prepared spells, and the ability to cast them, to another creature. Only a creature with an Intelligence score of at least 5 and a Wisdom score of at least 9 can receive this bestowal. Only cleric abjurations, divinations, or conjuration (healing) spells can be transferred. The number and level of spells that the subject can be granted depends on her HD; even multiple castings of *imbue with spell ability* can't exceed this limit. If your limit of 4th-level spells decreases, and it drops below the current number of active *imbue with spell ability* spells, the more recently cast imbued spells are dispelled.

HD of Recipient	Spells Imbued
1–2	One 1st-level spell
3–4	Up to two 1st-level spells
5+	Up to two 1st- and one 2nd-level spell

The transferred spell's variable characteristics (range, duration, area, etc.) function according to your level, not the level of the recipient.

Once you cast *imbue with spell ability* on another character, you cannot prepare a new 4th-level spell to replace it until the recipient uses the transferred spells or is slain. In the meantime, you remain responsible to your deity or your principles for the use to which the spell is put.

To cast a spell with a verbal component, the recipient must be able to speak. To cast a spell with a somatic component, she must have humanlike hands. To cast a spell with a material component or focus, she must have the materials or focus.

Implosion
Evocation
Level: Clr 9, Destruction 9
Components: V, S
Casting Time: 1 action
Range: Close (25 ft. + 5 ft./2 levels)
Targets: One corporeal creature/round
Duration: Concentration (up to 4 rounds)
Saving Throw: Fortitude negates
Spell Resistance: Yes

You create a destructive resonance in a corporeal creature's body. For each round you concentrate, you cause one creature to collapse in on itself, killing it. (This effect, being instantaneous, cannot be dispelled.)

You can target a particular creature only once with each casting of the spell.

Implosion has no effect on creatures in gaseous form or on incorporeal creatures.

Imprisonment

Abjuration

Level: Sor/Wiz 9
Components: V, S
Casting Time: 1 action
Range: Touch
Target: Creature touched
Duration: Instantaneous
Saving Throw: None
Spell Resistance: Yes

When you cast *imprisonment* and touch an opponent, he is entombed in a state of suspended animation (see the *temporal stasis* spell) in a small sphere far beneath the surface of the earth. The subject remains there unless a *freedom* spell is cast at the locale where the imprisonment took place. Magical search by a *crystal ball*, a *locate object* spell, or some other similar divination does not reveal the fact that a creature is imprisoned, but *discern location* does. A *wish* or *miracle* spell will not free the recipient but will reveal where it is entombed. The *imprisonment* spell functions only if the target's name and some facts about its life are known.

Improved Invisibility

Illusion (Glamer)

Level: Brd 4, Sor/Wiz 4
Components: V, S
Target: You or creature touched
Duration: 1 minute/level (D)
Saving Throw: Will negates (harmless)

As *invisibility*, except the spell doesn't end if the subject attacks.

Incendiary Cloud

Conjuration (Creation) [Fire]

Level: Fire 8, Sor/Wiz 8
Components: V, S
Casting Time: 1 action
Range: Medium (100 ft. + 10 ft./level)
Effect: Cloud spreads 30 ft. wide and 20 ft. high
Duration: 1 round/level
Saving Throw: Reflex half (see text)
Spell Resistance: Yes (see text)

An *incendiary cloud* spell creates a cloud of roiling smoke shot through with white-hot embers. The smoke obscures all sight as a *fog cloud* does. In addition, the white-hot embers within the cloud deal 4d6 points of fire damage to everything within it each round (half damage on a successful Reflex save).

As with a *cloudkill* spell, the smoke moves away from you at 10 feet per round. Figure

out the smoke's new spread each round based on its new point of origin, 10 feet farther away from where you were when you cast the spell. By concentrating, you can make the cloud (actually its point of origin) move up to 60 feet each round. Any portion of the cloud that would extend beyond your maximum range dissipates harmlessly, reducing the remainder's spread thereafter.

As with *fog cloud*, wind disperses the smoke, and the spell can't be cast underwater.

Inflict Critical Wounds

Necromancy

Level: Clr 4, Destruction 4

As *inflict light wounds*, except you deal 4d8 points of damage +1 point per caster level (maximum +20).

Inflict Light Wounds

Necromancy

Level: Clr 1, Destruction 1
Components: V, S
Casting Time: 1 action
Range: Touch
Target: Creature touched
Duration: Instantaneous
Saving Throw: Will half (see text)
Spell Resistance: Yes

When laying your hand upon a creature, you channel negative energy that deals 1d8 points of damage +1 point per caster level (up to +5).

Since undead are powered by negative energy, this spell cures them of a like amount of damage, rather than harming them.

Inflict Minor Wounds

Necromancy

Level: Clr 0

As *inflict light wounds*, except you deal 1 point of damage.

Inflict Moderate Wounds

Necromancy

Level: Clr 2

As *inflict light wounds*, except you deal 2d8 points of damage +1 point per caster level (maximum +10).

Inflict Serious Wounds

Necromancy

Level: Clr 3

As *inflict light wounds*, except you deal 3d8 points of damage +1 point per caster level (maximum +15).

Insanity

Enchantment (Compulsion)
[Mind-Affecting]

Level: Sor/Wiz 7
Components: V, S
Casting Time: 1 action
Range: Medium (100 ft. + 10 ft./level)
Target: One living creature
Duration: Instantaneous
Saving Throw: Will negates
Spell Resistance: Yes

The enchanted creature suffers from a continuous *confusion* effect.

Remove curse does not remove *insanity*. *Greater restoration*, *limited wish*, *miracle*, and *wish* can restore the creature.

Insect Plague

Conjuration (Summoning) [see text]

Level: Clr 5, Drd 5
Components: V, S, DF
Casting Time: 1 full round
Range: Long (400 ft. + 40 ft./level)
Effect: Cloud of insects 180 ft. wide and up to 60 ft. high
Duration: 1 minute/level
Saving Throw: See text
Spell Resistance: No

A horde of creeping, hopping, and flying insects swarm in a thick cloud when you cast this spell. The insects limit vision to 10 feet, and spellcasting within the cloud is impossible. Creatures inside the *insect plague*, regardless of Armor Class, sustain 1 point of damage at the end of each round they remain within, due to the bites and stings of the insects. Invisibility is no protection. All creatures with 2 or fewer HD are driven from the cloud at their fastest possible speed in a random direction and flee until they are at least 100 feet away from the insects. Creatures with 3 to 5 HD flee as well, though a Will save negates this effect. (This urge to flee is an extraordinary fear effect.)

Heavy smoke drives off insects within its bounds. Fire also drives insects away. For example, a *wall of fire* in a ring shape keeps a subsequently cast *insect plague* outside its confines, but a *fireball* spell simply clears insects from its blast area for 1 round. A single torch is ineffective against this vast horde of insects. Lightning, cold, and ice are likewise ineffective, while a strong wind (21+ mph) that covers the entire *plague* area disperses the insects and ends the spell.

Invisibility

Illusion (Glamer)

Level: Brd 2, Sor/Wiz 2, Trickery 2
Components: V, S, M/DF
Casting Time: 1 action
Range: Personal or touch
Target: You or a creature or object weighing no more than 100 lb./level
Duration: 10 minutes/level (D)

Saving Throw: None or Will negates (harmless, object)

Spell Resistance: No or Yes (harmless, object)

The creature or object touched vanishes from sight, even from darkvision. If the recipient is a creature carrying gear, the gear vanishes, too. If you cast the spell on someone else, neither you nor your allies can see the subject, unless you can normally see invisible things or employ magic to do so.

Items dropped or put down by an invisible creature become visible; items picked up disappear if tucked into the clothing or pouches worn by the creature. Light, however, never becomes invisible, although a source of light can become so (thus, the effect is that of a light with no visible source). Any part of an item that the subject carries but that extends more than 10 feet from it becomes visible, such as a trailing rope.

Of course, the subject is not magically *silenced*, and certain other conditions can render the recipient detectable (such as stepping in a puddle). The spell ends if the subject attacks any creature. For purposes of this spell, an "attack" includes any spell targeting a foe or whose area or effect includes a foe. (Exactly who is a foe depends on the invisible character's perceptions.) Actions directed at unattended objects do not break the spell. Causing harm indirectly is not an attack. Thus, an invisible being can open doors, talk, eat, climb stairs, summon monsters and have them attack, cut the ropes holding a rope bridge while enemies are on the bridge, remotely trigger traps, open a portcullis to release attack dogs, and so forth. If the subject attacks directly, however, it immediately becomes visible along with all its gear. Note that spells such as *bless* that specifically affect allies but not foes are not attacks for this purpose, even when they include foes in their area.

See Table 8–8: Attack Roll Modifiers, page 132, for the effects of invisibility on combat.

Arcane Material Components: An eyelash encased in a bit of gum arabic.

Invisibility Purge
Evocation

Level: Clr 3

Components: V, S

Casting Time: 1 action

Range: Personal

Target: You

Duration: 1 minute/level (D)

You surround yourself with a sphere of power with a radius of 5 feet per caster level that negates all forms of invisibility.

Anything invisible becomes visible while in the area. Only creatures with no visible form, such as an invisible stalker, remain invisible.

Invisibility Sphere
Illusion (Glamer)

Level: Brd 3, Sor/Wiz 3

Components: V, S, M

Area: 10-ft. radius sphere around the creature or object touched

As *invisibility*, except this spell confers invisibility upon all creatures within 10 feet of the recipient. The center of the effect is mobile with the recipient.

Those affected by this spell cannot see each other but can see themselves. Any affected creature moving out of the area becomes visible, but creatures moving into the area after the spell is cast do not become invisible. Affected creatures (other than the recipient) who attack negate the invisibility only for themselves. If the spell recipient attacks, the *invisibility sphere* ends.

Invisibility to Animals
Abjuration

Level: Drd 1

Components: S, DF

Casting Time: 1 action

Range: Touch

Targets: One creature touched/level

Duration: 10 minutes/level

Saving Throw: None

Spell Resistance: Yes

Animals cannot perceive the warded creatures. They act as though the warded creatures are not there. Warded creatures could stand before the hungriest of lions and not be molested or even noticed. If a warded character touches an animal or attacks any creature, even with a spell, the spell ends for all recipients.

Note: Beasts (such as owlbears), magical beasts (such as blink dogs), and vermin (such as giant scorpions) are not "animals" as defined by the spell; see the *Monster Manual*.

Invisibility to Undead
Abjuration

Level: Clr 1

Components: V, S, DF

Casting Time: 1 action

Range: Touch

Targets: One touched creature/level

Duration: 10 minutes/level (D)

Saving Throw: Will negates

Spell Resistance: Yes

Undead cannot perceive the warded creatures. Nonintelligent undead are automatically affected and act as though the warded creatures are not there. Intelligent undead

get saving throws. If they fail, they can't see the warded creatures. However, if they have reason to believe unseen opponents are present, they can attempt to find or strike them. If a warded character attempts to turn or command undead, touches an undead, or attacks any creature (even with a spell), the spell ends for all recipients.

Note: An intelligent undead creature gets one saving throw against the spell. It either sees all the warded creatures or none of them.

Iron Body
Transmutation

Level: Earth 8, Sor/Wiz 8

Components: V, S, M/DF

Casting Time: 1 action

Range: Personal

Target: You

Duration: 1 minute/level (D)

This spell transforms your body into living iron, which grants you several powerful resistances and abilities.

You gain damage reduction 50/+3. You are immune to blindness, critical hits, ability score damage, deafness, disease, drowning, electricity, poison, stunning, and all spells or attacks that affect your physiology or respiration, because you have no physiology or respiration while this spell is in effect. You take only half damage from acid and fire of all kinds. However, you also become vulnerable to all special attacks that affect iron golems.

You gain a +6 enhancement bonus to your Strength score, but you suffer a –6 Dexterity penalty as well (to a minimum Dexterity score of 1), and your speed is reduced to half normal. You have an arcane spell failure chance of 50% and a –8 armor check penalty, just as if you were clad in full plate armor. You cannot drink (and thus can't use potions) or play wind instruments.

Your unarmed attacks deal 1d6 points of lethal damage, and you are considered "armed" when making unarmed attacks (a Small caster deals 1d4 points of damage, not 1d6).

Your weight increases by a factor of ten, causing you to sink in water like a stone. However, you could survive the crushing pressure and lack of air at the bottom of the ocean—at least until the spell expires.

Arcane Material Component: A small piece of iron that was once part of an iron golem, a hero's armor, or a war machine.

Ironwood
Transmutation

Level: Drd 6

Components: V, S

Casting Time: 1 minute/lb. transformed

Range: Touch

Target: 5 lb. of touched wood/level
Duration: 1 day/level (D)
Saving Throw: None
Spell Resistance: No

Ironwood is a magical substance created by druids from normal wood. While remaining natural wood in almost every way, *ironwood* is as strong, heavy, and resistant to fire as steel. Spells that affect metal or iron (such as *heat metal*) do not function on *ironwood*. Spells that affect wood (such as *wood shape*) do affect *ironwood*, although *ironwood* does not burn. Using this spell with *wood shape* or a wood-related Craft check, you can fashion wooden items that function as steel items. Thus, wooden plate armor and wooden swords can be created that are as durable as their normal, steel counterparts. These items are freely usable by druids.

Further, if you make only half as much *ironwood* as the spell would normally allow, any weapon, shield, or suit of armor so transmuted is treated as a +1 magic item.

Jump

Transmutation
Level: Sor/Wiz 1
Components: V, S, M
Casting Time: 1 action
Range: Touch
Target: Creature touched
Duration: 1 minute/level (D)
Saving Throw: None
Spell Resistance: Yes

The subject gets a +30 bonus on Jump checks and does not have the usual maximums for jumping distance. For leaps of maximum horizontal distance, the jump reaches its peak (one-fourth the horizontal distance) at the halfway point.

Material Component: a grasshopper's hind leg, which you break when the spell is cast.

Keen Edge

Transmutation
Level: Brd 3, Sor/Wiz 3
Components: V, S
Casting Time: 1 action
Range: Close (25 ft. + 5 ft./2 levels)
Targets: One weapon or fifty projectiles, all of which must be in contact with each other at the time of casting
Duration: 10 minutes/level
Saving Throw: Will negates (harmless, object)
Spell Resistance: Yes (harmless, object)

This spell makes a weapon magically keen, improving its ability to deal telling blows. This transmutation doubles the threat range of the weapon. A normal threat range becomes 19–20. A threat range of 19–20 becomes 17–20. A threat range of 18–20 becomes 15–20. The spell can be cast only on piercing or slashing weapons (and it does not stack with itself). If cast on arrows or crossbow bolts, the *keen edge* on a particular projectile ends after one use, whether or not the missile strikes its intended target.

Knock

Transmutation
Level: Sor/Wiz 2
Components: V
Casting Time: 1 action
Range: Medium (100 ft. + 10 ft./level)
Target: One door, box, or chest with an area of up to 10 sq. ft./level
Duration: Instantaneous (see text)
Saving Throw: None
Spell Resistance: No

The *knock* spell opens stuck, barred, locked, held, or *arcane locked* doors. It opens secret doors, as well as locked or trick-opening boxes or chests. It also loosens welds, shackles, or chains (provided they serve to hold closures shut). If used to open a *arcane locked* door, the spell does not remove the *arcane lock* but simply suspends its functioning for 10 minutes. In all other cases, the door does not relock itself or becomes stuck again on its own. *Knock* does not raise barred gates or similar impediments (such as a portcullis), nor does it affect ropes, vines, and the like. Note that the effect is limited by the area. A 3rd-level caster can cast a *knock* spell on a door of 30 square feet or less (for example, a standard 4-foot-by-7-foot door). Each spell can undo up to two means of preventing egress through a portal. Thus if a door is locked, barred, and *held*, or quadruple locked, opening it requires two *knock* spells.

Know Direction

Divination
Level: Drd 0
Components: V, S
Casting Time: 1 action
Range: Personal
Target: You
Duration: Instantaneous

You instantly know the direction of north from your current position. The spell is effective in any environment in which "north" exists, but it may not work in extraplanar settings. Your knowledge of north is correct at the moment of casting, but note that you can get lost again within moments if you don't find some external reference point to help you keep track of direction.

Legend Lore

Divination
Level: Brd 4, Knowledge 7, Sor/Wiz 6
Components: V, S, M, F
Casting Time: See text
Range: Personal
Target: You
Duration: See text

Legend lore brings to your mind legends about an important person, place, or thing. If the person or thing is at hand, or if you are in the place in question, the casting time is only 1d4 × 10 minutes. If you have only detailed information on the person, place, or thing, casting time is 1d10 days, and the resulting lore is less complete and specific (though it often provides enough information to help you find the person, place, or thing, thus allowing a better *legend lore* next time). If you know only rumors, casting time is 2d6 weeks, and the resulting lore is vague and incomplete (though it often directs you to more detailed information, thus allowing a better *legend lore*).

During the casting, you cannot engage in other than routine activities: eating, sleeping, etc. When completed, the divination brings legends (if any) about the person, place, or things to your mind. These may be legends that are still current, legends that have been forgotten, or even information that has never been generally known. If the person, place, or thing is not of legendary importance, you gain no information. As a rule of thumb, characters 11th level and higher are "legendary," as are the sorts of creatures they contend with, the major magic items they wield, and the places where they perform their key deeds.

Examples of *legend lore* results:

A divination about a mysterious magic axe you have at hand: "Woe to the evildoer whose hand touches the axe, for even the haft chops the hand of the evil ones. Only a true Son or Daughter of Stone, one who loves Moradin and whom Moradin loves, may awaken the true powers of the axe, and only with the sacred word 'Rudnogg' on the lips."

A divination about a legendary paladin about whom you know many details: "Vanashon has been denied the glory of death and the duty of life. He waits patiently beneath the Forbidden Mountain." (The paladin has been turned to stone in the caverns beneath the mountain.)

A divination about ancient ruins about which you have only a passing reference in a partially damaged tome: "The sorcerer who called herself Ryth built a library without words and a temple without gods. Those who read and those who pray tore it down in a night and a day." (These clues may be enough for you to find out more and get the details you need to cast a better *legend lore.*)

Material Component: Incense worth at least 250 gp.

Focus: Four strips of ivory (worth 50 gp each) formed into a rectangle.

Leomund's Secret Chest

Conjuration (Summoning)
Level: Sor/Wiz 5
Components: V, S, F
Casting Time: 10 minutes
Range: See text
Target: One chest and up to 1 cu. ft. of goods/caster level
Duration: 60 days or until discharged
Saving Throw: None
Spell Resistance: No

You hide a chest on the Ethereal Plane for up to 60 days and can retrieve it at will. The chest can contain up to 1 cubic foot of material per caster level (regardless of the chest's actual size, which is about 3 feet by 2 feet by 2 feet). If any living creatures are in the chest, there is a 75% chance that the spell simply fails. Once the chest is hidden, you can retrieve it by concentrating (a standard action), and it appears next to you.

The chest must be exceptionally well crafted and expensive, constructed for you by master crafters. If made principally of wood, it must be ebony, rosewood, sandalwood, teak, or the like, and all of its corner fittings, nails, and hardware must be platinum. If constructed of ivory, the metal fittings of the chest must be gold. If the chest is fashioned from bronze, copper, or silver, its fittings must be silver or electrum (a valuable metal). The cost of such a chest is never less than 5,000 gp. Once it is constructed, you must make a tiny replica (of the same materials and perfect in every detail), so that the miniature of the chest appears to be a perfect copy. (The replica costs 50 gp.) You can have but one pair of these chests at any given time—even *wishes* do not allow exceptions. The chests themselves are nonmagical and can be fitted with locks, wards, and so on, just as any normal chest can be.

To hide the chest, you cast the spell while touching both the chest and the replica. The chest vanishes into the Ethereal Plane. You need the replica to recall the chest. After 60 days, there is a cumulative chance of 5% per day that it is irretrievably lost. If the miniature of the chest is lost or destroyed, there is no way, not even with a *wish* spell, that the large chest can be summoned back, although an extraplanar expedition might be mounted to find it.

Living things in the chest eat, sleep, and age normally; and they die if they run out of food, air, water, or whatever they need to survive.

Focus: The chest and its replica.

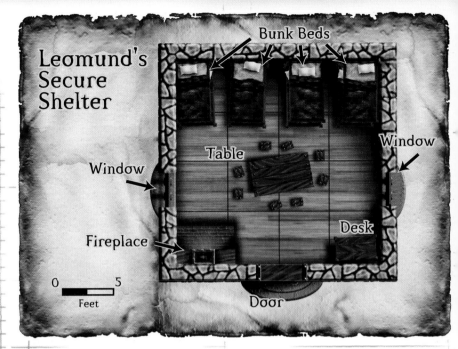

Leomund's Secure Shelter

Leomund's Secure Shelter

Conjuration (Creation)
Level: Brd 4, Sor/Wiz 4
Components: V, S, M/DF (see text)
Casting Time: 10 minutes
Range: Close (25 ft. + 5 ft./2 levels)
Effect: 20-ft.-square structure
Duration: 2 hours/level (D)
Saving Throw: None
Spell Resistance: No

You conjure a sturdy cottage or lodge made of material that is common in the area where the spell is cast—stone, timber, or (at worst) sod. The floor is level, clean, and dry. In all respects the lodging resembles a normal cottage, with a sturdy door, two shuttered windows, and a small fireplace.

The shelter has no heating or cooling source (other than natural insulation qualities). Therefore, it must be heated as a normal dwelling, and extreme heat adversely affects it and its occupants. The dwelling does, however, provide considerable security otherwise—it is as strong as a normal stone building, regardless of its material composition. The dwelling resists flames and fire as if it were stone. It is impervious to normal missiles (but not the sort cast by siege machinery or giants).

The door, shutters, and even chimney are secure against intrusion, the former two being *arcane locked* and the latter secured by an iron grate at the top and a narrow flue. In addition, these three areas are protected by an *alarm* spell. Finally, an *unseen servant* is conjured to provide service to you for the duration of the shelter.

The *secure shelter* contains rude furnishings—eight bunks, a trestle table, eight stools, and a writing desk.

Material Components: A square chip of stone, crushed lime, a few grains of sand, a sprinkling of water, and several splinters of wood. These must be augmented by the components of the *alarm* spell (string and a bit of wood) and the focus of the *alarm* spell (silver wire and a tiny bell) if these benefits are to be included.

Leomund's Tiny Hut

Evocation [Force]
Level: Brd 3, Sor/Wiz 3
Components: V, S, M
Casting Time: 1 action
Range: 20 ft.
Effect: 20-ft.-radius sphere centered on your location
Duration: 2 hours/level (D)
Saving Throw: None
Spell Resistance: No

You create an unmoving, opaque sphere of force of any color you desire around yourself. Half of the sphere projects above the ground, and the lower hemisphere passes through the ground. Up to nine other Medium-size creatures can fit into the field with you; they can freely pass into and out of the *hut* without harming it. However, if you remove yourself from the *hut*, the spell ends.

The temperature inside the *hut* is 70° F if the exterior temperature is between 0° and 100° F. An exterior temperature below 0° or above 100° lowers or raises, respectively, the interior temperature on a 1-degree-for-1 basis (thus, if it's −20° outside, inside it'll be 50°). The *hut* also provides protection against the elements, such as rain, dust, and sandstorms. The *hut* withstands any wind of less than hurricane force, but a hurricane (75+ mph wind speed) or greater force destroys it.

The interior of the *hut* is a hemisphere. You can illuminate it dimly upon command or extinguish the light as desired. Note that although the force field is opaque from the outside, it is transparent from within. Missiles, weapons, and most spell effects can pass through the *hut* without affecting it, although the occupants cannot be seen from outside the hut (they have total concealment).

Material Component: A small crystal bead that shatters when the spell duration expires or the *hut* is dispelled.

Leomund's Trap
Illusion (Glamer)
Level: Sor/Wiz 2
Components: V, S, M
Casting Time: 1 action
Range: Touch
Target: Object touched
Duration: Permanent
Saving Throw: None
Spell Resistance: No

This spell makes a lock or other small mechanism seem to be trapped to anyone who can detect traps. You place the spell upon any small mechanism or device, such as a lock, hinge, hasp, cork, screw-on cap, or ratchet. Any character able to detect traps, or who uses any spell or device enabling trap detection, is 100% certain a real trap exists. Of course, the effect is illusory and nothing happens if the trap is "sprung"; its primary purpose is to frighten away thieves or make them waste precious time.

If another *Leomund's trap* is active within 50 feet when the spell is cast, the casting fails.

Material Component: A piece of iron pyrite touched to the object to be trapped while the object is sprinkled with a special dust requiring 50 gp to prepare.

Lesser Geas
Enchantment (Compulsion) [Language-Dependent, Mind-Affecting]
Level: Brd 3, Sor/Wiz 4
Components: V
Casting Time: 1 action
Range: Close (25 ft. + 5 ft./2 levels)
Target: One living creature of up to 7 HD
Duration: 1 day/level or until discharged (D)
Saving Throw: Will negates
Spell Resistance: Yes

A *lesser geas* places a magical command on a creature to carry out some service or to refrain from some action or course of activity, as desired by you. The creature must have 7 or fewer HD and be able to understand you. While a geas cannot compel a creature to kill itself or perform acts that would result in certain death, it can cause almost any other course of activity. The *geased* creature must follow the given instructions until the geas is completed, no matter how long it takes. If the instructions involve some open-ended task that the recipient cannot complete through his own actions (such as "Wait here" or "Defend this area against attack"), the spell remains in effect for a maximum of 1 day per caster level. Note that a clever recipient can subvert some instructions. For example, if you order the recipient to protect you from all harm, it might place you in a nice, safe dungeon for the duration of the spell.

If the subject is prevented from obeying the *lesser geas* for a whole day, he suffers a –2 penalty on each ability score. Each day, another –2 penalty accumulates, up to a total of –8. Abilities are not reduced below 1. The ability penalties end 1 day after the character resumes obeying the *lesser geas*.

A *lesser geas* (and all ability penalties) can be ended by *break enchantment, limited wish, remove curse, miracle,* or *wish. Dispel magic* does not affect a *lesser geas.*

Lesser Planar Ally
Conjuration (Calling) [see text]
Level: Clr 4
Components: V, S, DF
Casting Time: 10 minutes
Range: Close (25 ft. + 5 ft./2 levels) (see text)
Effect: One summoned elemental or outsider of up to 8 HD
Duration: Instantaneous
Saving Throw: None
Spell Resistance: No

By casting this spell, you request your deity to send you an elemental or outsider (of up to 8 HD) of the deity's choice. If you serve no particular deity, the spell is a general plea answered by a creature sharing your philosophical alignment. If you know an individual creature's name, you may request that individual by speaking the name during the spell (though you might get a different creature anyway).

You may ask the creature to perform one task for you, and the creature may request some service in return. The more demanding your request, the greater return favor the creature asks for. This bargaining takes at least 1 round, so any actions by the creature begin in the round after it arrives. If you agree to the service, the creature performs the task you requested, reports back to you afterward (if possible), and returns to its home plane. You are honor bound to perform the return favor.

A creature may accept some form of payment, such as a magic item, in return for its service. The creature may keep it or may deliver the item to another member of your religion somewhere else, where it can help the religion's cause.

Note: When you use a calling spell that calls an air, chaotic, earth, evil, fire, good, lawful, or water creature, it is a spell of that type. For example, *lesser planar ally* is a fire spell when it calls a fire elemental.

Lesser Planar Binding
Conjuration (Calling) [see text]
Level: Sor/Wiz 5
Components: V, S
Casting Time: 10 minutes
Range: Close (25 ft. + 5 ft./2 levels) (see text)
Target: One elemental or outsider of up to 8 HD
Duration: Instantaneous
Saving Throw: Will negates
Spell Resistance: Yes

Casting this spell attempts a dangerous act: to lure a creature from another plane to a specifically prepared trap, which must lie within the spell's range. The called creature is held in the trap until it agrees to perform one service in return for its freedom.

To create the trap, you must use a *magic circle* spell, focused inward. The type of creature to be bound must be known and stated. If it has a specific, proper, or given name, this must be used in casting the spell.

The target creature must attempt a Will saving throw. If the saving throw succeeds, the creature resists the spell. If the saving throw fails, the creature is immediately drawn to the trap (spell resistance does not keep the creature from being called). The creature can escape from the trap with a successful SR roll, dimensional travel, or a successful Charisma check (DC 15 + 1/2 its level + its Charisma modifier). It can try each method once per day. If it breaks loose, it can flee or attack you. A *dimensional anchor* cast on the creature prevents its escape via dimensional travel. You can also employ a calling diagram (see Calling, page 157) to make the trap more secure.

If the creature does not break free of the trap, you can keep it bound for as long as you dare. You can attempt to compel the creature to perform a service by describing the service and perhaps offering some sort of reward. You make a Charisma check opposed by the creature's Charisma check. The DM then assigns a bonus based on the service and reward, from 0 to +6. This bonus applies to your Charisma check. If the creature wins the opposed check, it refuses service. New offers, bribes, and the like can be made or the old ones reoffered every 24 hours. This can be repeated until the creature promises to serve, until it breaks free, or until you decide to get rid of it by means of some other spell. Impossible demands or unreasonable commands are never agreed to. If you roll a 1 on the Charisma check, the creature breaks free of the binding and can escape or attack you.

Once the requested service is completed, the creature need only so inform you to be instantly sent back whence it came. The creature might later seek revenge. If you assign some open-ended task that the creature cannot complete though its own actions (such as "Wait here" or "Defend this area against attack"), the spell remains in effect for a maximum of 1 day per caster level, and the creature gains an immediate chance to break free. Note that a clever recipient can subvert some instructions.

When you use a calling spell to call an air, chaotic, earth, evil, fire, good, lawful, or water creature, it is a spell of that type. For example, *lesser planar binding* is a water spell when you cast it to call a water elemental.

Lesser Restoration

Conjuration (Healing)
Level: Clr 2, Drd 2
Components: V, S
Casting Time: 3 rounds
Range: Touch
Target: Creature touched
Duration: Instantaneous
Saving Throw: Will negates (harmless)
Spell Resistance: Yes (harmless)

Lesser restoration dispels any magical effects reducing one of the subject's ability scores (such as *ray of enfeeblement*) or cures 1d4 points of temporary ability damage to one of the subject's ability scores (such as from a shadow's touch or poison). It does not restore permanent ability drain (such from a wraith's touch).

Levitate

Transmutation
Level: Brd 2, Sor/Wiz 2
Components: V, S, F
Casting Time: 1 action
Range: Personal or close (25 ft.+ 5 ft./2 levels)
Target: You or one willing creature or one object (total weight up to 100 lb./level)
Duration: 10 minutes/level (D)
Saving Throw: None
Spell Resistance: No

Levitate allows you to move yourself, another creature, or an object up and down as you wish. A creature must be

willing to be *levitated*, and an object must be unattended or possessed by a willing creature. You can mentally direct the recipient to move up or down as much as 20 feet each round; doing so is a move-equivalent action. You cannot move the recipient horizontally, but the recipient could clamber along the face of a cliff, for example, or push against a ceiling to move laterally (generally at half its base speed).

A levitating creature who attacks with a melee or ranged weapon finds itself increasingly unstable; the first attack has an attack roll penalty of –1, the second –2, and so on, up to a maximum penalty of –5. A full round spent stabilizing allows the creature to begin again at –1.

Focus: Either a small leather loop or a piece of golden wire bent into a cup shape with a long shank on one end.

Light

Evocation [Light]
Level: Brd 0, Clr 0, Drd 0, Sor/Wiz 0
Components: V, M/DF
Casting Time: 1 action
Range: Touch
Target: Object touched
Duration: 10 minutes/level (D)
Saving Throw: None
Spell Resistance: No

This spell causes an object to glow like a torch, shedding light in a 20-foot radius from the point you touch. The effect is immobile, but it can be cast on a movable object. Light taken into an area of magical *darkness* does not function.

Arcane Material Component: A firefly or a piece of phosphorescent moss.

Lightning Bolt

Evocation [Electricity]
Level: Sor/Wiz 3
Components: V, S, M
Casting Time: 1 action
Range: Medium (100 ft. + 10 ft./level) or 50 ft. + 5 ft./level
Area: 5 ft. wide to medium range (100 ft. + 10 ft./level); or 10 ft. wide to 50 ft. + 5 ft./level
Duration: Instantaneous
Saving Throw: Reflex half
Spell Resistance: Yes

You release a powerful stroke of electrical energy that deals 1d6 points of damage per caster level (maximum 10d6) to each creature within its area. The bolt begins at your fingertips.

The *lightning bolt* sets fire to combustibles and damages objects in its path. It can melt metals with a low melting point, such as lead, gold, copper, silver, or bronze. If the damage caused to an interposing barrier shatters or breaks through it, the bolt may continue beyond the

barrier if the spell's range permits; otherwise, it stops at the barrier just as any other spell effect does.

Material Components: A bit of fur and an amber, crystal, or glass rod.

Limited Wish

Universal
Level: Sor/Wiz 7
Components: V, S, XP
Casting Time: 1 action
Range: See text
Target, Effect, or Area: See text
Duration: See text
Saving Throw: None
Spell Resistance: Yes

A *limited wish* lets you create nearly any type of effect. A *limited wish* can do any of the following:

- Duplicate any sorcerer/wizard spell of 6th level or lower, provided the spell is not from a school prohibited to you.
- Duplicate any other spell of 5th level or lower, provided the spell is not from a school prohibited to you.
- Duplicate any wizard/sorcerer spell of 5th level or lower even if it's from a prohibited school.
- Duplicate any other spell of 4th level or lower even if it's from a prohibited school.
- Undo the harmful effects of many other spells, such as *geas/quest* or *insanity*.
- Have any other effect whose power level is in line with the above effects, such as a single creature automatically hitting on its next attack or suffering a –7 penalty on its next saving throw.

A duplicated spell allows saving throws and spell resistance as normal (but the save DC is for a 7th-level spell). When a *limited wish* duplicates a spell that has an XP cost, you must pay that cost or 300 XP, whichever is more. When a *limited wish* spell duplicates a spell with a material component that costs more than 1,000 gp, you must provide that component.

XP Cost: 300 XP or more (see above).

Liveoak

Transmutation
Level: Drd 6
Components: V, S
Casting Time: 10 minutes
Range: Touch
Target: Tree touched
Duration: 1 day/level (D)
Saving Throw: None
Spell Resistance: No

This spell turns an oak tree into a protector or guardian. The spell can be cast on only a single tree at a time; while *liveoak* is in effect, you can't cast it again on another tree. The tree on which the spell is cast must be within 10 feet of your dwelling place, within a place sacred to you, or within 300 feet of something that you wish to guard or protect.

Liveoak must be cast on a healthy, Huge oak. A triggering phrase of up to one word per caster level is placed on the targeted oak. For instance, "Attack any persons who come near without first saying 'sacred mistletoe'" is an eleven-word trigger phrase that you could use at 11th level or higher. The *liveoak* spell triggers the tree into animating as a treant. Statistics for a treant can be found in the *Monster Manual*. (At the DM's option, you can extrapolate stats for a smaller tree from the treant statistics if you cast *liveoak* on a smaller oak.)

If *liveoak* is dispelled, the tree takes root immediately, wherever it happens to be. If released by you, it tries to return to its original location before taking root.

ocate Creature

Divination
Level: Brd 4, Sor/Wiz 4
Components: V, S, M
Duration: 10 minutes/level

As *locate object*, except this spell locates a known or familiar creature.

You slowly turn and sense when you are facing in the direction of the creature to be located, provided the creature is within range. You also know in which direction the creature is moving, if any.

The spell can locate a creature of a specific type (such as human or unicorn) or a specific creature known to you. It cannot find a creature of a general type (such as humanoid or beast). To find a type of creature, you must have seen such a creature up close (within 30 feet) at least once.

Running water blocks the spell. It cannot detect objects. It can be fooled by *mislead*, *nondetection*, and *polymorph* spells.

Material Component: A bit of bloodhound's fur.

ocate Object

Divination
Level: Brd 2, Clr 3, Sor/Wiz 2, Travel 2
Components: V, S, F/DF
Casting Time: 1 action
Range: Long (400 ft. + 40 ft./level)
Area: Circle, centered on you, with a radius of 400 ft. + 40 ft./level
Duration: 1 minute/level
Saving Throw: None
Spell Resistance: No

You sense the direction of a well-known or clearly visualized object. The spell locates such objects as apparel, jewelry, furniture, tools, weapons, and even a ladder. You can

search for general items such as a stairway, a sword, or a jewel, in which case you locate the nearest one of its type if more than one is within range. Attempting to find a specific item, such as a particular piece of jewelry, requires a specific and accurate mental image; if the image is not close enough to the actual object, the spell fails. You cannot specify a unique object (such as "Baron Vulden's signet ring") unless you have observed that particular item firsthand (not through divination).

The spell is blocked by lead. Creatures cannot be found by this spell. *Polymorph any object* fools it.

Arcane Focus: A forked twig.

Mage Armor

Conjuration (Creation) [Force]
Level: Brd 1, Sor/Wiz 1
Components: V, S, F
Casting Time: 1 action
Range: Touch
Target: Creature touched
Duration: 1 hour/level (D)
Saving Throw: Will negates (harmless)
Spell Resistance: Yes (harmless)

An invisible but tangible field of force surrounds the subject of *mage armor*, providing a +4 armor bonus to AC. Unlike mundane armor, *mage armor* entails no armor check penalty, arcane spell failure chance, or speed reduction. Since *mage armor* is made of force, incorporeal creatures can't bypass it the way they do normal armor.

Focus: A piece of cured leather.

Mage Hand

Transmutation
Level: Brd 0, Sor/Wiz 0
Components: V, S
Casting Time: 1 action
Range: Close (25 ft. + 5 ft./2 levels)
Target: Nonmagical, unattended object weighing up to 5 lb.
Duration: Concentration
Saving Throw: None
Spell Resistance: No

You point your finger at an object and can lift it and move it at will from a distance. As a move-equivalent action, you can move the object up to 15 feet in any direction, though the spell ends if the distance between you and the object ever exceeds the spell's range.

Magic Circle against Chaos

Abjuration [Lawful]
Level: Brd 3, Clr 3, Law 3, Sor/Wiz 3

As *magic circle against evil*, except that it is similar to *protection from chaos* instead of *protection from evil*.

Magic Circle against Evil

Abjuration [Good]
Level: Brd 3, Clr 3, Good 3, Pal 3, Sor/Wiz 3
Area: Emanates 10 ft. from touched creature
Duration: 10 minutes/level
Spell Resistance: No (see text)

As *protection from evil*, except that it encompasses a much larger area and its duration is longer.

Unlike *protection from evil*, this spell has a special function that you may choose when casting the spell. A *magic circle* can be focused inward rather than outward. In this case, it serves as an immobile, temporary magical prison for a summoned creature. The creature cannot cross the circle's boundaries. (See Summoning, page 157, for more information on using this spell in conjunction with summoning spells.)

You must beat a creature's SR in order to keep it at bay (as in the third function of *protection from evil*), but the deflection and resistance bonuses and the protection from mental control apply regardless of enemies' SR.

If a creature too large to fit into the spell's area is the subject of the spell, the spell acts as a normal *protection from evil* spell for that creature only.

This spell is not cumulative with *protection from evil* and vice versa.

Magic Circle against Good

Abjuration [Evil]
Level: Brd 3, Clr 3, Evil 3, Sor/Wiz 3

As *magic circle against evil*, except that it is similar to *protection from good* instead of *protection from evil*.

Magic Circle against Law

Abjuration [Chaotic]
Level: Brd 3, Chaos 3, Clr 3, Sor/Wiz 3

As *magic circle against evil*, except that it is similar to *protection from law* instead of *protection from evil*.

Magic Fang

Transmutation
Level: Drd 1, Rgr 1
Components: V, S, DF
Casting Time: 1 action
Range: Touch
Target: Living creature touched
Duration: 1 minute/level
Saving Throw: Will negates (harmless)
Spell Resistance: Yes (harmless)

Magic fang gives one natural weapon of the subject a +1 enhancement bonus to attack and damage rolls. The spell can affect a slam attack, fist, bite, or other natural weapon. (The spell does not change an unarmed strike's damage from subdual damage to normal damage.) If you're a good druid, the natural weapon is considered blessed, which means it has special effects on certain creatures.

Magic Jar

Necromancy

Level: Sor/Wiz 5
Components: V, S, F
Casting Time: 1 action
Range: Medium (100 ft.+10 ft./level)
Target: One creature
Duration: 1 hour/level or until you return to your body
Saving Throw: Will negates (see text)
Spell Resistance: Yes

By casting *magic jar*, you place your own soul in a gem or large crystal (known as the *magic jar*), leaving your body lifeless. Then you can attempt to take control of a nearby body, forcing its soul into the *magic jar*. You may move back to the jar (returning the trapped soul to its body) and attempt to possess another body. The spell ends when you send your soul back to your own body (leaving the receptacle empty).

To cast the spell, the *magic jar* must be within spell range and you must know where it is, though you do not need line of sight or effect to it. When you transfer your soul upon casting, your body is, as near as anyone can tell, dead.

While in the *magic jar*, you can sense and attack any life force within 10 feet per caster level (on the same plane). You do need line of effect from the jar to the creatures. You, however, cannot determine the exact creature types or positions of these creatures. In a group of life forces, you can sense a difference of four or more HD and can determine whether a life force is positive or negative energy. (Undead creatures are powered by negative energy. Only sentient undead creatures have, or are, souls.)

For example, if two 10th-level characters are attacking a hill giant (12 HD) and four ogres (4 HD), you could determine that there are three stronger and four weaker life forces within range, all with positive life energy. You could choose to take over either a stronger or a weaker creature, but which stronger or weaker creature you attempt to possess is determined randomly.

Attempting to possess a body is a full-round action. It is blocked by *protection from evil* or a similar ward. You possess the body and force the creature's soul into the *magic jar* unless the subject succeeds at a Will save. Failure to take over the host leaves your life force in the *magic jar*, and the target automatically

A wizard unleashes a magic missile.

succeeds at further saving throws if you attempt to possess its body again.

If successful, your life force occupies the host body, and the host's life force is imprisoned in the *magic jar*. You keep most mental abilities and gain some physical abilities, as with *polymorph other* (except that you get the creature's actual physical abilities, not average ones).

As a standard action, you can shift freely from a host to the *magic jar* if within range, sending the trapped soul back to its body. The spell ends when you shift from the jar to your own body.

If the host body is slain, you return to the *magic jar*, if within range, and the life force of the host departs (that is, it is dead). If the host body is slain beyond the range of the spell, both you and the host die. Any life force with nowhere to go is treated as slain.

If the spell ends while you are in the *magic jar*, you return to your body (or die if your body is out of range or destroyed). If the spell ends while you are in a host, you return to your body (or die, if it is out of range of your current position), and the soul in the *magic jar* returns to its body (or dies if it is out of range). Destroying the receptacle ends the spell, and the spell can be dispelled at either the *magic jar* or the host.

Incorporeal creatures with the magic jar ability can use a handy, nearby object (not just a gem or crystal) as the *magic jar*.

Focus: A gem or crystal worth at least 100 gp.

Magic Missile

Evocation [Force]

Level: Sor/Wiz 1
Components: V, S
Casting Time: 1 action
Range: Medium (100 ft. + 10 ft./level)
Targets: Up to five creatures, no two of which can be more than 15 ft. apart
Duration: Instantaneous
Saving Throw: None
Spell Resistance: Yes

A missile of magical energy darts forth from your fingertip and unerringly strikes its target. The missile deals 1d4+1 points of damage.

The missile strikes unerringly, even if the target is in melee or has anything less than total cover or concealment. Specific parts of a creature cannot be singled out. Inanimate objects (locks, etc.) cannot be damaged by the spell.

For every two levels of experience past 1st, you gain an additional missile. You have two at 3rd level, three at 5th level, four at 7th level, and the maximum of five missiles at 9th level or higher. If you shoot multiple missiles, you can have them strike a single creature or several creatures. A single missile can strike only one creature. You must designate targets before you roll for SR or roll damage.

Magic Mouth

Illusion (Glamer)

Level: Brd 2, Sor/Wiz 2

Components: V, S, M
Casting Time: 1 action
Range: Close (25 ft. + 5 ft./2 levels)
Target: One creature or object
Duration: Permanent until discharged
Saving Throw: Will negates (object)
Spell Resistance: Yes (object)

This spell imbues the chosen object or creature with an enchanted mouth that suddenly appears and speaks its message the next time a specified event occurs. The message, which must be twenty-five or fewer words long, can be in any language known by you and can be delivered over a period of 10 minutes. The mouth cannot speak verbal components, use command words, or activate magical effects. It does, however, move according to the words articulated. For instance, if it were placed upon a statue, the mouth of the statue would actually move and appear to speak. Of course, *magic mouth* can be placed upon a tree, rock, door, or any other object or creature.

The spell functions when specific conditions are fulfilled according to your command as set in the spell. Commands can be as general or as detailed as desired, although only visual and audible triggers can be used, such as the following: "Speak only when a venerable female human carrying a sack sits cross-legged within one foot." Triggers react to what appears to be the case. Disguises and illusions can fool them. Normal darkness does not defeat a visual trigger, but magical *darkness* or *invisibility* does. Silent movement or magical *silence* defeats audible triggers. Audible triggers can be keyed to general types of noises (footsteps, metal clanking) or to a specific noise or spoken word (when a pin drops, when anyone says "Boo"). Note that actions can serve as triggers if they are visible or audible. For example, "Speak when any creature touches the statue" is an acceptable command so long as the creature is visible. A *magic mouth* cannot distinguish invisible creatures, alignments, level, HD, or class except by external garb.

The range limit of a trigger is 15 feet per caster level, so a 6th-level caster can command a *magic mouth* to respond to triggers up to 90 feet away. Regardless of range, the mouth can respond only to visible or audible triggers and actions in line of sight or within hearing distance.

Material Component: A small bit of honeycomb and jade dust worth 10 gp.

Magic Stone
Transmutation
Level: Clr 1, Earth 1
Components: V, S, DF
Casting Time: 1 action
Range: Touch
Targets: Up to three pebbles touched
Duration: 30 minutes or until discharged
Saving Throw: Will negates (harmless, object)
Spell Resistance: Yes (harmless, object)

You transmute up to three pebbles, which can be no larger than sling bullets, so that they strike with great force when thrown or slung. If hurled, they have a range increment of 20 feet. If slung, treat them as sling bullets (range increment 50 feet). The spell gives them a +1 enhancement bonus to attack and damage rolls. The creature using the stones makes a normal ranged attack to use a *magic stone*. Each *magic stone* that hits deals 1d6+1 points of damage (including the enhancement bonus). Against undead creatures, this damage is doubled (2d6+2 points).

Magic Vestment
Transmutation
Level: Clr 3, Strength 3, War 3
Components: V, S, DF
Casting Time: 1 action
Range: Touch
Target: Armor or shield touched
Duration: 1 hour/level
Saving Throw: Will negates (harmless, object)
Spell Resistance: Yes (harmless, object)

You imbue a suit of armor or a shield that you touch with an enhancement bonus of +1 per three caster levels (maximum +5 at 15th level). An outfit of regular clothing counts as a suit of armor that grants no AC bonus for purposes of this spell.

Note: An enhancement bonus increases armor's or a shield's benefit to the wearer's AC. A suit of armor cannot have more than +5 in total bonuses (even if some of its bonus is from other than enhancement).

Magic Weapon
Transmutation
Level: Brd 1, Clr 1, Pal 1, Sor/Wiz 1, War 1
Components: V, S, F, DF
Casting Time: 1 action
Range: Touch
Target: Weapon touched
Duration: 1 minute/level
Saving Throw: Will negates (harmless, object)
Spell Resistance: Yes (harmless, object)

Magic weapon gives a weapon a +1 enhancement bonus to attack and damage rolls. If you're a good cleric, the cleric of a good deity, or a paladin, the weapon is considered blessed, which means it has special effects on certain creatures.

Focus: The weapon.

Major Creation
Conjuration (Creation)
Level: Sor/Wiz 5
Casting Time: 10 minutes
Range: Close (25 ft. + 5 ft./2 levels)
Duration: See text

As *minor creation*, except you can also create an object of mineral nature: stone, crystal, metal, etc. The duration of the created item varies with its relative hardness and rarity:

Hardness and Rarity Examples	Duration
Vegetable matter	2 hours/level
Stone, crystal, base metals	1 hour/level
Precious metals	20 minutes/level
Gems	10 minutes/level
Mithral*	2 rounds/level
Adamantite**	1 round/level

*Includes similar rare metals. Items made of mithral are 50% lighter than similar items made of steel.

**Items made of adamantite weigh 75% as much as similar items made of steel. They are also harder and better capable of retaining an edge, so armor and shields provide 1 higher AC and weapons allow +1 on attack and damage rolls (although the items are not magical).

Major Image
Illusion (Figment)
Level: Brd 3, Sor/Wiz 3
Duration: Concentration + 3 rounds

As *silent image*, except sound, smell, and thermal illusions are included in the spell effect. While concentrating, you can move the image within the range.

The image disappears when struck by an opponent unless you cause the illusion to react appropriately.

Make Whole
Transmutation
Level: Clr 2
Casting Time: 1 action
Range: Close (25 ft. + 5 ft./2 levels)
Target: One object of up to 10 cu. ft./level

As *mending*, except *make whole* completely repairs an object made of any substance, even one with multiple breaks, to be as strong as new. The spell does not restore the magical abilities of a broken magic item made whole, and it cannot mend broken magic rods, staffs, or wands. The spell does not repair items that have been warped, burned, disintegrated, ground to powder, melted, or vaporized.

Mark of Justice
Transmutation
Level: Clr 5
Components: V, S, DF

Casting Time: 10 minutes
Range: Touch
Target: Creature touched
Duration: Permanent (see text)
Saving Throw: None
Spell Resistance: Yes

When moral suasion fails to win a criminal over to right conduct, you can use *mark of justice* to encourage the criminal to walk the straight and narrow path.

You draw an indelible mark on the subject and state some behavior on the part of the subject that will activate the mark. When activated, the mark *curses* the subject. Typically, you designate some sort of criminal behavior that activates the mark, but you can pick any act you please. The effect of the mark is identical with the effect of *bestow curse*.

Since this spell takes 10 minutes to cast and involves writing on the target, you can cast only it on someone who is willing or restrained.

Like *bestow curse*, *mark of justice* cannot be dispelled, but it can be removed with a *break enchantment, limited wish, miracle, remove curse,* or *wish* spell. *Remove curse,* however, works only if the caster is at least as high level as your *mark of justice.* These restrictions apply regardless of whether the mark has activated.

Mass Charm

Enchantment (Charm) [Mind-Affecting]
Level: Sor/Wiz 8
Components: V
Targets: One or more creatures, no two of which can be more than 30 ft. apart
Duration: 1 day/level

As *charm person*, except the spell affects a number of creatures (persons or not) whose combined HD do not exceed twice your level (or at least one creature regardless of HD). If there are more potential targets than you can affect, you choose them one at a time until you choose a creature with too many HD.

Mass Haste

Transmutation
Level: Brd 6, Sor/Wiz 6
Targets: One creature/level, no two of which can be more than 30 ft. apart

As *haste*, except that it affects multiple creatures.

Mass Heal

Conjuration (Healing)
Level: Clr 8, Drd 9, Healing 8
Range: Close (25 ft. + 5 ft./2 levels)
Targets: One or more creatures, no two of which can be more than 30 ft. apart

As *heal*, except as noted above.

Mass Invisibility

Illusion (Glamer)
Level: Sor/Wiz 7
Components: V, S, M
Range: Long (400 ft. + 40 ft./level)
Targets: Any number of creatures, no two of which can be more than 180 ft. apart

As *invisibility*, except the effect is mobile with the group and is broken when anyone in the group attacks. Individuals in the group cannot see each other. The spell is broken for any individual who moves more than 180 feet from the nearest member of the group. (If only two individuals are affected, the one moving away from the other one loses its invisibility. If both are moving away from each other, they both become visible when the distance between them exceeds 180 feet.)

Material Components: An eyelash and a bit of gum arabic, the former encased in the latter.

Mass Suggestion

Enchantment (Compulsion) [Mind-Affecting, Language-Dependent]
Level: Brd 6, Sor/Wiz 6
Range: Medium (100 ft. + 10 ft./level)
Targets: One creature/level, no two of which can be more than 30 ft. apart

As *suggestion*, except that it can affect more creatures. The same *suggestion* applies to all these creatures.

Maze

Conjuration (Creation) [Force]
Level: Sor/Wiz 8
Components: V, S
Casting Time: 1 action
Range: Close (25 ft. + 5 ft./2 levels)
Target: One creature
Duration: See text
Saving Throw: None
Spell Resistance: No

You conjure up an extradimensional labyrinth of force planes, and the subject vanishes into it. If the subject attempts to escape, the time it takes to find the way out depends on its Intelligence score:

Intelligence Score of *Mazed* Creature	Time Trapped in Maze
Under 3	2d4 minutes
3	1d6 minutes
4–5	1d4 minutes
6–8	5d4 rounds
9–12	4d4 rounds
13–15	3d4 rounds
16–17	2d4 rounds
18+	1d4 rounds

If the subject doesn't attempt to escape, the maze disappears after 10 minutes, forcing the subject to leave.

On leaving the maze, the subject reappears in the spot it had been in when the *maze* spell was cast. If this spot is filled with a solid object, the subject appears nearby.

Spells and abilities that move a creature within a plane, such as *teleport* and *dimension door,* do not help a creature escape a *maze* spell, although a *plane shift* spell allows it to exit to whatever plane is designated in that spell. Minotaurs are not affected by this spell.

Meld into Stone

Transmutation
Level: Clr 3, Drd 3
Components: V, S, DF
Casting Time: 1 action
Range: Personal
Target: You
Duration: 10 minutes/level

Meld into stone enables you to meld your body and possessions into a single block of stone. The stone must be large enough to accommodate your body in all three dimensions. When the casting is complete, you and not more than 100 pounds of nonliving gear merge with the stone. If either condition is violated, the spell fails and is wasted.

While in the stone, you remain in contact, however tenuous, with the face of the stone through which you melded. You remain aware of the passage of time and can cast spells on yourself while hiding in the stone. Nothing that goes on outside the stone can be seen, but you can still hear what happens around you. Minor physical damage to the stone does not harm you, but its partial destruction to the extent that you no longer fit within it expels you and deals you 5d6 points of damage. The stone's complete destruction expels you and slays you instantly unless you succeed at a Fortitude save (DC 18).

At any time before the duration expires, you can step out of the stone through the surface that you entered. If the spell's duration runs out or the effect is dispelled before you voluntarily exit the stone, you are violently expelled and take 5d6 points of damage.

The following spells harm you if cast upon the stone that you are occupying: *Stone to flesh* expels you and deals you 5d6 points of damage. *Stone shape* deals you 3d6 points of damage but does not expel you. *Transmute rock to mud* expels you and then slays you instantly unless you succeed at a Fortitude save (DC 18), in which case you are merely expelled. Finally, *passwall* expels you without damage.

Melf's Acid Arrow
Conjuration (Creation) [Acid]
Level: Sor/Wiz 2
Components: V, S, M, F
Casting Time: 1 action
Range: Long (400 ft. + 40 ft./level)
Effect: One arrow of acid
Duration: 1 round +1 round/three levels
Saving Throw: None
Spell Resistance: Yes

A magical arrow of acid springs from your hand and speeds to its target. You must succeed at a ranged touch attack to hit your target. The arrow deals 2d4 points of acid damage. There is no splash damage. For every three caster levels (maximum 18), the acid, unless somehow neutralized, lasts for another round, dealing another 2d4 points of damage for that round. At 3rd–5th level, the acid lasts for 2 rounds; at 6th–8th level, the acid lasts for 3 rounds; and so on, to a maximum of 7 rounds at 18th level.

Material Component: Powdered rhubarb leaf and an adder's stomach.

Focus: A dart.

Mending
Transmutation
Level: Brd 0, Clr 0, Drd 0, Sor/Wiz 0
Components: V, S
Casting Time: 1 action
Range: 10 ft.
Target: One object of up to 1 pound
Duration: Instantaneous
Saving Throw: Will negates (harmless, object)
Spell Resistance: Yes (harmless, object)

Mending repairs small breaks or tears in objects (not warps). In metallic objects, it will weld a broken ring, a chain link, a medallion, or a slender dagger, providing but one break exists. Ceramic or wooden objects with multiple breaks can be invisibly rejoined to be as strong as new. A hole in a leather sack or wineskin is completely healed over by *mending*. The spell can repair a magic item, but the item's magical abilities are not restored. (For restoring a broken magic item's abilities, see the item creation feats in Chapter 5: Feats.) The spell cannot mend broken magic rods, staffs, or wands.

Message
Transmutation [Language-Dependent]
Level: Brd 1, Sor/Wiz 1
Components: V, S, F
Casting Time: 1 action
Range: Medium (100 ft. + 10 ft./level)
Targets: One creature/level
Duration: 10 minutes/level
Saving Throw: None
Spell Resistance: No

You can whisper messages and receive whispered replies with little chance of being overheard. You point your finger at each creature to be included in the spell effect. When you whisper, the whispered message is audible to all of the targeted creatures who are within range. Magical *silence*, 1 foot of stone, 1 inch of common metal (or a thin sheet of lead), or 3 feet of wood or dirt blocks the spell. The message, however, does not have to travel in a straight line. It can circumvent a barrier if there is an open path between you and the subject, and the path's entire length lies within the spell's range. The creatures who receive the message can whisper a reply that you hear. The spell transmits sound, not meaning. It doesn't transcend language barriers.

Note: To speak a message, you must mouth the words and whisper, possibly allowing trained rogues the opportunity to read your lips.

Focus: A short piece of copper wire.

Meteor Swarm
Evocation [Fire]
Level: Sor/Wiz 9
Components: V, S
Casting Time: 1 action
Range: Long (400 ft. + 40 ft./level)
Area: Pattern of *fireball*-like spreads (see text)

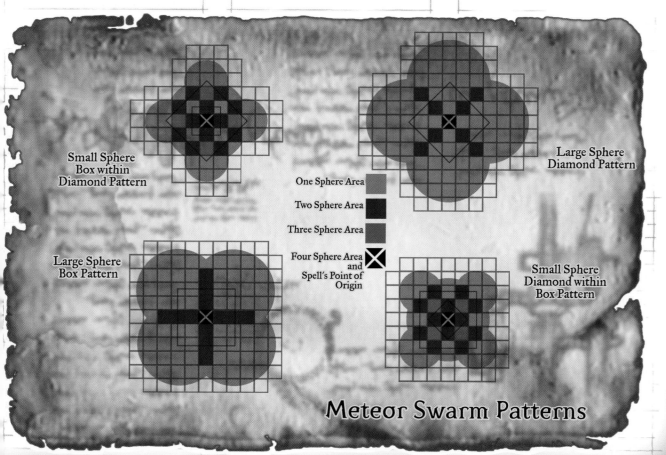

Small Sphere Box within Diamond Pattern

Large Sphere Diamond Pattern

Large Sphere Box Pattern

One Sphere Area
Two Sphere Area
Three Sphere Area
Four Sphere Area and Spell's Point of Origin

Small Sphere Diamond within Box Pattern

Meteor Swarm Patterns

Duration: Instantaneous
Saving Throw: None or Reflex half
 (see text)
Spell Resistance: Yes

Meteor swarm is a very powerful and spectacular spell that is similar to *fireball* in many aspects. When you cast it, either four large spheres (2-foot-diameter) or eight small spheres (1-foot-diameter) spring from your outstretched hand and streak in a straight line to the spot you select. The meteor spheres leave a fiery trail of sparks.

Any creature in the straight-line path of these spheres is struck by each one and takes 24d6 points of fire damage (no save).

If the spheres reach their destination, each bursts like a *fireball* in a spread.

Each large sphere deals 6d6 points of fire damage. The four spheres explode with their points of origin forming a diamond or box pattern around the spell's central point of origin, which you designate upon casting. Each large sphere has a 15-foot-radius spread, and each blast is 20 feet apart along the sides of the pattern, creating overlapping areas of the spell's effect and exposing the center to all four blasts.

The smaller spheres each have a 7 1/2-foot-radius spread, and each deals 3d6 points of fire damage. They explode with their points of origin forming a pattern around the spell's central point of origin (which you designated upon casting) of a box within a diamond or vice versa, with each of the outer sides measuring 20 feet long. The center has four areas of overlapping effect, and numerous peripheral areas have two or three overlapping areas of the spell's effect.

Creatures caught in a blast can attempt Reflex saves for half damage. Creatures struck by multiple blasts save against each blast separately.

Mind Blank

Abjuration
Level: Protection 8, Sor/Wiz 8
Components: V, S
Casting Time: 1 action
Range: Close (25 ft. + 5 ft./2 levels)
Target: One creature
Duration: 1 day
Saving Throw: Will negates (harmless)
Spell Resistance: Yes (harmless)

The subject is protected from all devices and spells that detect, influence, or read emotions or thoughts. This spell protects against all mind-affecting spells and effects as well as information gathering by divination spells or effects. *Mind blank* even foils *limited wish, miracle,* and *wish* when they are used in such a way as to affect the subject's mind or to gain information about him. In the case of scrying that scans an area that the creature is in, such as *arcane eye*, the spell works but the creature simply isn't detected. Scrying attempts that are targeted specifically at the subject do not work at all.

Mind Fog

Enchantment (Compulsion)
 [Mind-Affecting]
Level: Brd 5, Sor/Wiz 5
Components: V, S
Casting Time: 1 action
Range: Medium (100 ft. + 10 ft./level)
Effect: Fog that spreads to fill a 20-ft. cube
Duration: 30 minutes/+2d6 rounds (see text)
Saving Throw: Will negates
Spell Resistance: Yes

Mind fog produces a bank of fog that weakens the mental resistance of those caught in it. Creatures in the *mind fog* suffer a –10 competence penalty to all Wisdom checks and Will saves. (A creature who successfully saves against the fog is not affected and need not make further saves even if it remains in the fog.) Affected creatures suffer the penalty as long as they remain in the fog and for 2d6 rounds thereafter. The fog itself is stationary and lasts for 30 minutes (or until dispersed by wind).

The fog is thin and does not significantly hamper vision.

Minor Creation

Conjuration (Creation)
Level: Sor/Wiz 4
Components: V, S, M
Casting Time: 1 minute
Range: 0 ft.
Effect: Unattended, nonmagical object of nonliving plant matter, up to 1 cu. ft./ level
Duration: 1 hour/level
Saving Throw: None
Spell Resistance: No

You create a nonmagical, unattended object of nonliving, vegetable matter: linen clothes, a hemp rope, a wooden ladder, etc. The volume of the item created cannot exceed 1 cubic foot per caster level. You must succeed at an appropriate skill check to make a complex item, such as a Craft (bowmaking) check to make straight arrow shafts.

Attempting to use any created object as a material component causes the spell to fail.

Material Component: A tiny piece of matter of the same type of item you plan to create with *minor creation*—a bit of twisted hemp to create rope, and so forth.

Minor Globe of Invulnerability

Abjuration
Level: Sor/Wiz 4
Components: V, S, M
Casting Time: 1 action
Range: 10 ft.
Area: 10-ft.-radius spherical emanation, centered on you
Duration: 1 round/level
Saving Throw: None
Spell Resistance: No

An immobile, faintly shimmering magical sphere surrounds you and excludes all spell effects of up to 3rd level. The area or effect of any such spells does not include the area of the *minor globe of invulnerability.* Such spells fail to affect any target located within the globe. This includes spell-like abilities and spells or spell-like effects from devices. However, any type of spell can be cast through or out of the magical globe. Spells of 4th level and higher are not affected by the globe. The globe can be brought down by a targeted *dispel magic* spell, but not by an area *dispel magic.* You can leave and return to the globe without penalty.

Note that spell effects are not disrupted unless their effects enter the globe, and even then they are merely suppressed, not dispelled. For example, creatures inside the globe would still see a *mirror image* created by a caster outside the globe. If that caster then entered the globe, the images would wink out, to reappear when the caster exited the globe. Likewise, a caster standing in the area of a *light* spell would still receive sufficient light for vision, even though that part of the *light* spell volume in the globe would not be luminous.

If a given spell has more than one level depending on which character class is casting it, use the level appropriate to the caster to determine whether *minor globe of invulnerability* stops it.

Material Component: A glass or crystal bead that shatters at the expiration of the spell.

Minor Image

Illusion (Figment)
Level: Brd 2, Sor/Wiz 2
Duration: Concentration+2 rounds

As *silent image,* except this spell includes some minor sounds but not understandable speech.

Miracle

Evocation
Level: Clr 9, Luck 9
Components: V, S, XP (see text)
Casting Time: 1 action
Range: See text
Target, Effect, or Area: See text
Duration: See text
Saving Throw: See text
Spell Resistance: Yes

You don't so much cast a *miracle* as request one. You state what you would like to have happen and request that your deity (or the power you pray to for spells) intercede. The DM then determines the particular effect of the *miracle*.

A *miracle* can do any of the following:

- Duplicate any cleric spell of up to 8th level (including spells to which you have access because of your domains).
- Duplicate any other spell of up to 7th level.
- Undo the harmful effects of certain spells, such as *feeblemind* or *insanity*.
- Have any effect whose power level is in line with the above effects.

If the *miracle* has any of the above effects, casting it carries no experience point cost.

Alternatively, the cleric can make a very powerful request. Casting such a miracle costs the cleric 5,000 XP because of the powerful divine energies involved. Examples of especially powerful *miracles* of this sort could include:

- Swinging the tide of a battle in your favor by raising fallen allies to continue fighting until the end of the battle.
- Moving you and your allies, with all your and their gear, from one plane to another through planar barriers to a specific locale with no chance of error.
- Protecting a city from an earthquake, volcanic eruption, flood, or other major natural disaster.

In any event, a request that is out of line with the deity's (or alignment's) nature is refused.

A duplicated spell allows saving throws and SR as normal (but save DCs are for a 9th-level spell). When a *miracle* duplicates a spell that has an XP cost, you must pay that cost. When a *miracle* spell duplicates a spell with a material component that costs more than 100 gp, you must provide that component.

XP Cost: 5,000 XP (for some uses of the *miracle* spell; see above).

Mirage Arcana
Illusion (Glamer)
Level: Brd 5, Sor/Wiz 5
Components: V, S
Casting Time: 1 action
Area: One 20-ft. cube/level (S)
Duration: Concentration+1 hour/level (D)

As *hallucinatory terrain*, except that it enables you to make any area appear to be something other than it is. The illusion includes audible, visual, tactile, and olfactory elements. Unlike *hallucinatory terrain*, the spell can alter the appearance of structures (or add them where none are present). Still, it can't disguise, conceal, or add creatures (though creatures within the area might hide themselves within the illusion just as they can hide themselves within a real location).

Mirror Image
Illusion (Figment)
Level: Brd 2, Sor/Wiz 2
Components: V, S
Casting Time: 1 action
Range: Personal (see text)
Target: You
Duration: 1 minute/level

Several illusory duplicates of you pop into being, making it difficult for enemies to know which target to attack. The figments stay near you and disappear when struck.

Mirror image creates 1d4 images plus one image per three caster levels (maximum eight images). These figments separate from you and remain in a cluster, each within 5 feet of at least one other figment or you. You can move into and through a *mirror image*. When you and the *mirror image* separate, observers can't use vision or hearing to tell which one is you and which the image. The figments may also move through each other. The figments mimic your actions, pretending to cast spells when you cast a spell,

drink potions when you drink a potion, levitate when you levitate, and so on.

Enemies attempting to attack you or cast spells at you must select from among indistinguishable targets. Generally, roll randomly to see whether the selected target is real or a figment. Any successful attack roll against a figment destroys it. A figment's AC is 10 + size modifier + Dexterity modifier. Figments seem to react normally to area spells (such as looking like they're burned or dead after being struck by a *fireball*).

While moving, you can merge with and split off from figments so that enemies who have learned which image is real are again confounded.

An attacker must be able to see the images to be fooled. If you are invisible or an attacker shuts her eyes, the spell has no effect, though being unable to see carries the same penalties as being blinded: In addition to the obvious effects, a blinded creature suffers a 50% miss chance in combat (all opponents have full concealment), loses any Dexterity bonus to AC, grants a +2 bonus to attackers' attack rolls (they are effectively invisible), moves at half speed, and suffers a –4 penalty on most Strength- and Dexterity-based skills.

Mirror image: Who's the real caster?

Misdirection

Illusion (Glamer)
Level: Brd 2, Sor/Wiz 2
Components: V, S
Casting Time: 1 action
Range: Close (25 ft. + 5 ft./2 levels)
Target: One creature or object, up to a 10-ft. cube in size
Duration: 1 hour/level
Saving Throw: Will negates (object)
Spell Resistance: No

By means of this spell, you misdirect the information from divination spells that reveal auras (including *detect evil*, *detect magic*, *discern lies*, etc.). On casting the spell, you choose another object within range. For the duration of the spell, the subject of *misdirection* is detected as if it were the other object. Detection spells provide information based on the second object rather than on the actual target of the detection unless the caster of the detection succeeds at his save. For instance, you could make yourself detect as a tree if one were within range at casting: not evil, not lying, not magical, neutral in alignment, etc. This spell does not affect other types of divination (*augury*, *detect thoughts*, *clairaudience/clairvoyance*, etc.).

Mislead

Illusion (Figment, Glamer)
Level: Brd 5, Luck 6, Sor/Wiz 6, Trickery 6
Components: S
Casting Time: 1 action
Range: Close (25 ft. + 5 ft./2 levels)
Target/Effect: You/one illusory double
Duration: 1 round/level (D)
Saving Throw: None/Will disbelief (if interacted with)
Spell Resistance: No

An illusory double of you (a figment) appears, and at the same time, you become invisible (as *improved invisibility*, a glamer). You are then free to go elsewhere while your double moves away. The double appears within range but thereafter moves according to your intent at the time of casting. You can make the figment appear superimposed perfectly over your own body so that observers don't notice an image appearing and you turning invisible. You and the figment can then move in different directions. The double moves at your speed, can talk and gesture as if it were real, and even smells and feels real. The double cannot attack or cast spells, but it can pretend to do so.

Modify Memory

Enchantment (Compulsion) [Mind-Affecting]
Level: Brd 4
Components: V, S
Casting Time: 1 action (see text)
Range: Close (25 ft. + 5 ft./2 levels)
Target: One living creature
Duration: Permanent
Saving Throw: Will negates
Spell Resistance: Yes

You reach into the subject's mind and modify up to 5 minutes of her memory in one of the following ways:

- Eliminate all memory of an event the subject actually experienced. This spell cannot negate *charm*, *suggestion*, *geas*, *quest*, or similar spells.
- Allow the subject to recall with perfect clarity an event she actually experienced. For instance, she could recall every word from a 5-minute conversation or every detail from a passage in a book.
- Change the details of an event the subject actually experienced.
- Implant a memory of an event the subject never experienced.

Casting the spell takes 1 action. If the subject fails to save, you proceed with the spell by spending up to 5 minutes (a period of time equal to the amount of memory time you want to modify) visualizing the memory you wish to modify in the subject. If your concentration is disturbed before the visualization is complete, or if the subject is ever beyond the spell's range during this time, the spell is lost.

A modified memory does not necessarily affect the subject's actions, particularly if it contradicts her natural inclinations. An illogical modified memory, such as the subject recalling how much she enjoyed drinking poison, is dismissed by the subject as a bad dream or a memory muddied by too much wine. More useful applications of *modify memory* include implanting memories of friendly encounters with you (inclining the subject to act favorably toward you), changing the details of orders given to the subject by a superior, or causing the subject to forget that she ever saw you or your party. The DM reserves the right to decide whether a modified memory is too nonsensical to significantly affect the subject.

Mordenkainen's Disjunction

Abjuration
Level: Magic 9, Sor/Wiz 9
Components: V
Casting Time: 1 action
Range: Close (25 ft. + 5 ft./2 levels)
Area: All magical effects and magic items within a 30-ft.-radius burst
Duration: Instantaneous
Saving Throw: Will negates (object)
Spell Resistance: No

All magical effects and magic items within the radius of the spell, except for those that you carry or touch, are disjoined. That is, spells and spell-like effects are separated into their individual components (ending the effect as a *dispel magic* spell does), and permanent magic items must make successful Will saves or be turned into normal items. An item in a creature's possession uses its own Will save bonus or its possessor's Will save bonus, whichever is higher.

You also have a 1% chance per caster level of destroying an *antimagic field*. If the *antimagic field* survives the disjunction, no items within it are disjoined.

Even artifacts are subject to disjunction, though there is only a 1% chance per caster level of actually affecting such powerful items. Additionally, if an artifact is destroyed, you must succeed at a Will save (DC 25) or permanently lose all spellcasting abilities. (These abilities cannot be recovered by mortal magic, not even *miracle* or *wish*.)

Note: Destroying artifacts is a dangerous business, and it is 95% likely to attract the attention of some powerful being who has an interest in or connection with the device.

Mordenkainen's Faithful Hound

Conjuration (Creation)
Level: Sor/Wiz 5
Components: V, S, M
Casting Time: 1 action
Range: Close (25 ft. + 5 ft./2 levels)
Effect: Phantom watchdog
Duration: 1 hour/caster level or until discharged, then 1 round/caster level
Saving Throw: None
Spell Resistance: No

You conjure up a phantom watchdog that is invisible to everyone but yourself. It then guards the area where it was conjured. The phantom watchdog immediately starts barking loudly if any Small or larger creature approaches within 30 feet of it. (Those already within 30 feet of the hound when it is conjured may move about in the area, but if they leave and return, they activate the barking.) The hound sees invisible and ethereal creatures. It does not react to figments, but it does react to shadow illusions. It is stationary.

If an intruder approaches to within 5 feet of the watchdog, the dog stops barking and delivers a vicious bite (+10 attack bonus, 2d6+3 points of damage) once per round. The dog also gets the bonuses appropriate to an invisible creature. (For most defenders, the invisible creature gets a +2 attack bonus and the defender loses any Dexterity bonus to AC.) The dog is considered ready to bite intruders, so it delivers its first bite on the intruder's turn. Its bite is the equivalent of a +3 weapon for purposes of damage reduction. The hound cannot be attacked, but it can be dispelled.

The spell lasts for 1 hour per caster level, but once the hound begins barking, it lasts only 1 round per caster level. If you are ever more than 100 feet distant from the watchdog, the spell ends.

Material Component: A tiny silver whistle, a piece of bone, and a thread.

Mordenkainen's Lucubration

Transmutation
Level: Wiz 6
Components: V, S
Casting Time: 1 action
Range: Personal
Target: You
Duration: Instantaneous

You instantly recall any one spell of up to 5th level that you have used during the past 24 hours. The spell must have been actually cast during that time period. The recalled spell is stored in your mind as through prepared in the normal fashion. If the recalled spell requires material components, you must provide these. The recovered spell is not usable until the material components are available.

Mordenkainen's Magnificent Mansion

Conjuration (Creation)
Level: Sor/Wiz 7
Components: V, S, F
Casting Time: 1 action
Range: Close (25 ft. + 5 ft./2 levels)
Effect: Extradimensional mansion, up to three 10-ft. cubes/level (S)
Duration: 2 hours/level
Saving Throw: None
Spell Resistance: No

You conjure up an extradimensional dwelling that has a single entrance on the plane from which the spell was cast. The entry point looks like a faint shimmering in the air that is 4 feet wide and 8 feet high. Only those you designate may enter the mansion, and the portal is shut and made invisible behind you when you enter. You may open it again from your own side at will. Once observers have passed beyond the entrance, they are in a magnificent foyer with numerous chambers beyond. The atmosphere is clean, fresh, and warm.

You can create any floor plan you desire to the limit of the spell's effect. The place is furnished and contains sufficient food-stuffs to serve a nine-course banquet to a dozen people per caster level. There is a staff of near-transparent servants, liveried and obedient, to wait upon all who enter. The servants function as *unseen servant* spells except that they are visible and can go anywhere in the mansion. There are two such servants for each caster level.

Since the place can be entered only through its special portal, outside conditions do not affect the mansion, nor do conditions inside it pass to the plane beyond. Rest and relaxation within the place occurs as normal.

Focus: A miniature portal carved from ivory, a small piece of polished marble, and a tiny silver spoon.

Mordenkainen's Sword

Evocation [Force]
Level: Sor/Wiz 7
Components: V, S, F
Casting Time: 1 action
Range: Close (25 ft. + 5 ft./2 levels)
Effect: One sword
Duration: 1 round/level (D)
Saving Throw: None
Spell Resistance: Yes

You bring into being a shimmering, swordlike plane of force. The sword strikes at any opponent within its range, as you desire, starting the round that you cast the spell. The sword attacks its designated target once each round. Its attack bonus is your level + your Intelligence bonus or your Charisma bonus (for wizards and sorcerers, respectively) with a +3 enhancement bonus. As a force effect, it can strike ethereal and incorporeal creatures. It deals 4d6+3 points of damage, with a threat range of 19–20 and a crit of ×2.

The sword always strikes from your direction. It does not get a flanking bonus or help a combatant get one. If the sword goes beyond the spell range from you, if it goes out of your sight, or if you are not directing it, the sword returns to you and hovers.

Each round after the first, you can use a standard action to switch the sword to a new target. If you do not, the sword continues to attack the previous round's target. The sword cannot be attacked or harmed by physical attacks, but *dispel magic*, *disintegrate*, a *sphere of annihilation*, or a *rod of cancellation* affects it. The sword's AC against touch attacks is 13.

If an attacked creature has SR, the resistance is checked the first time *Mordenkainen's sword* strikes it. If the sword is successfully resisted, the spell is dispelled. If not, the sword has its normal full effect on that creature for the duration of the spell.

Focus: A miniature platinum sword with a grip and pommel of copper and zinc. It costs 250 gp to construct.

Mount

Conjuration (Summoning)
Level: Sor/Wiz 1
Components: V, S, M
Casting Time: 1 full round
Range: Close (25 ft. + 5 ft./2 levels)
Effect: One mount
Duration: 2 hours/level
Saving Throw: None
Spell Resistance: No

You summon a light horse or a pony (your choice) to serve you as a mount. The steed serves willingly and well. The mount comes with a bit and bridle and a riding saddle.

Material Component: A bit of horse hair.

Move Earth

Transmutation
Level: Sor/Wiz 6
Components: V, S, M
Casting Time: See text
Range: Long (400 ft. + 40 ft./level)
Area: Dirt in an area up to 750 ft. square and up to 10 ft. deep (S)
Duration: Instantaneous
Saving Throw: None
Spell Resistance: No

Move earth moves dirt (clay, loam, sand), possibly collapsing embankments, moving hillocks, shifting dunes, etc. However, in no event can rock formations be collapsed or moved. The area to be affected determines the casting time. For every 150-foot square (up to 10 feet deep), casting takes 10 minutes. The maximum area, 750 feet by 750 feet, takes 4 hours and 10 minutes to move.

This spell does not violently break the surface of the ground. Instead, it creates wavelike crests and troughs, with the earth reacting with glacierlike fluidity until the desired result is achieved. Trees, structures, rock formations, and such are mostly unaffected except for changes in elevation and relative topography.

The spell cannot be used for tunneling and is generally too slow to trap or bury creatures. Its primary use is for digging or filling moats or for adjusting terrain contours before a battle.

Material Components: A mixture of soils (clay, loam, and sand) in a small bag, and an iron blade.

Negative Energy Protection

Abjuration
Level: Clr 3
Components: V, S
Casting Time: 1 action
Range: Touch
Target: Living creature touched
Duration: 1 round/level
Saving Throw: Will negates (harmless)
Spell Resistance: Yes (harmless)

The warded creature gains partial protection from undead creatures who use negative energy (such as shadows, wights, wraiths, spectres, or vampires) and certain weapons and spells that drain energy levels. The *negative energy protection* spell uses positive energy, which can offset the effects of a negative energy attack. Each time the warded creature is struck by a negative energy attack that drains levels or ability scores, it rolls 1d20 + caster level against a DC of 11 + the attacker's HD.

If the warded creature succeeds, the energies cancel with a bright flash of light and a thunderclap. The warded creature takes only hit point damage from the attack and does not suffer any drain of experience levels or ability scores, regardless of the number of levels or ability score points the attack would have drained. An attacking undead creature takes 2d6 points of damage from the positive energy. An attacking caster or weapon receives no damage.

If the warded creature does not succeed, the negative energy attack deals its normal damage. An attacking undead creature in such a situation does not take any positive energy damage.

Neutralize Poison

Conjuration (Healing)
Level: Brd 4, Clr 4, Drd 3, Pal 4, Rgr 3
Components: V, S, M/DF
Casting Time: 1 action
Range: Touch
Target: Creature or object of up to 1 cu. ft./level touched
Duration: Instantaneous
Saving Throw: Will negates (harmless, object)
Spell Resistance: Yes (harmless, object)

You detoxify any sort of venom in the creature or object touched. A poisoned creature suffers no additional damage or effects from the poison, and any temporary effects are ended, but the spell does not reverse instantaneous effects, such as hit point damage, temporary ability damage, or effects that don't go away on their own. For example, if a poison has dealt 3 points of temporary Constitution damage to a character and threatens to deal more damage later, this spell prevents the future damage but does not repair the damage already done.

This spell also neutralizes the poison in a poisonous creature or object. A poisonous creature, such as a wyvern, replenishes its poison at its normal rate.

Arcane Material Component: A bit of charcoal.

Nightmare

Illusion (Phantasm) [Mind-Affecting, Evil]
Level: Brd 5, Sor/Wiz 5
Components: V, S
Casting Time: 10 minutes
Range: Unlimited
Target: One living creature
Duration: Instantaneous
Saving Throw: Will negates
Spell Resistance: Yes

You send a hideous and unsettling phantasmal vision to a specific creature whom you name or otherwise specifically designate. The nightmare prevents restful sleep and causes 1d10 points of damage. The nightmare leaves the subject tired out and unable to regain arcane spells for the next 24 hours.

Dispel evil cast on the subject while you are casting the spell dispels the *nightmare* and stuns you for 10 minutes per caster level of the *dispel evil*. While you are stunned, you can't act, you lose any Dexterity bonus to AC, and attackers get a +2 bonus against you.

If the recipient is awake when the spell begins, you can choose to cease casting (ending the spell) or enter a trance until the recipient goes to sleep, whereupon you become alert again and complete the casting. If you are disturbed during the trance, the spell ends.

If you choose to enter a trance, you are not aware of your surroundings or the activities around you while in the trance. You are defenseless, both physically and mentally, while in the trance. (You always fail any saving throw, for example.)

Creatures who don't sleep or dream (such as elves, but not half-elves) are immune to this spell.

Nondetection

Abjuration
Level: Rgr 4, Sor/Wiz 3, Trickery 3
Components: V, S, M
Casting Time: 1 action
Range: Touch
Target: Creature or object touched
Duration: 1 hour/level
Saving Throw: Will negates (harmless, object)
Spell Resistance: Yes (harmless, object)

The warded creature or object becomes difficult to detect by divination spells such as *clairaudience/clairvoyance*, *locate object*, and detection spells. *Nondetection* also prevents location by such magic items as *crystal balls*. If a divination is attempted against the warded creature or item, the caster of the divination must succeed at a caster level check (1d20 + caster level) against a DC of 11 + the caster level of the spellcaster who cast *nondetection*. If you cast *nondetection* on yourself or on an item currently in your possession, the DC is 15 + your caster level.

If cast on a creature, *nondetection* wards the creature's gear as well as the creature itself.

Material Component: A pinch of diamond dust worth 50 gp.

Nystul's Magic Aura

Illusion (Glamer)
Level: Sor/Wiz 1
Components: V, S, F
Casting Time: 1 action
Range: Touch
Target: One touched object weighing up to 5 lb./level
Duration: 1 day/level
Saving Throw: None (see text)
Spell Resistance: No

You make an item's aura register to detection spells (and similar spells) as though it were either a magic item of the type that you specify or the subject of a spell that you specify. You could make an ordinary sword register as a *+2 vorpal sword* as far as magical detection is concerned or make a *+2 vorpal sword* register as if it were a *+1 sword*.

If the object bearing *Nystul's magic aura* has *identify* cast on it or is similarly examined, the examiner recognizes that the aura is false and detects the object's actual qualities if he succeeds at a Will save. Otherwise, he believes the aura and no amount of testing reveals what the true magic is.

If the targeted item's own aura is exceptionally powerful (if it is an artifact, for instance), *Nystul's magic aura* doesn't work.

Note: A magic weapon, shield, or suit of armor must be a masterwork item, so a sword of average make, for example, looks suspicious if it has a magical aura.

Focus: A small square of silk that must be passed over the object that receives the aura.

Nystul's Undetectable Aura

Illusion (Glamer)
Level: Magic 1, Sor/Wiz 1
Components: V, S, F
Casting Time: 1 action
Range: Touch
Target: Object touched weighing up to 5 lb./level
Duration: 1 day/level
Saving Throw: None (see text)
Spell Resistance: No

This spell allows you to mask a magic item's aura from detection. If the object bearing *Nystul's undetectable aura* has *identify* cast on it or is similarly examined, the examiner recognizes that the aura is false and detects the object's actual qualities if he succeeds at a Will save.

Focus: A small square of silk that must be passed over the object.

Obscure Object

Abjuration
Level: Brd 2, Clr 3, Sor/Wiz 2
Components: V, S, M/DF
Casting Time: 1 action
Range: Touch

Target: One object touched of up to 100 lb./level
Duration: 8 hours
Saving Throw: Will negates (object)
Spell Resistance: Yes (object)

This spell hides an object from location by a spell, a *crystal ball*, and other forms of scrying.

Arcane Material Component: A piece of chameleon skin.

Obscuring Mist

Conjuration (Creation)
Level: Air 1, Clr 1, Drd 1, Sor/Wiz 1, Water 1
Components: V, S
Casting Time: 1 action
Range: 30 ft.
Effect: Cloud centered on you spreads 30 ft. and is 20 ft. high
Duration: 1 minute/level
Saving Throw: None
Spell Resistance: No

A misty vapor arises around you. It is stationary once created. The vapor obscures all sight, including darkvision, beyond 5 feet. A creature 5 feet away has one-half concealment (attacks have a 20% miss chance). Creatures farther away have total concealment (50% miss chance, and the attacker cannot use sight to locate the target).

A moderate wind (11+ mph), such as from the *gust of wind* spell, disperses the fog in 4 rounds. A strong wind (21+ mph) disperses the fog in 1 round. A *fireball*, *flame strike*, or similar spell burns away the fog in the explosive or fiery spell's area. A *wall of fire* burns away the fog in the area into which it deals damage.

This spell does not function underwater.

Open/Close

Transmutation
Level: Brd 0, Sor/Wiz 0
Components: V, S, F
Casting Time: 1 action
Range: Close (25 ft. + 5 ft./2 levels)
Target: Portal or object that can be opened or closed
Duration: Instantaneous
Saving Throw: Will negates (object)
Spell Resistance: Yes (object)

You can open or close (caster's choice) a door, chest, box, window, bag, pouch, bottle, or other container. If anything resists this activity (such as a bar on a door or a lock on a chest), the spell fails. In addition, the spell can only open and close things that are of standard weight (see Table 7–7: Goods and Services, page 108, and Table 7–8: Containers and Carriers, page 110). The lid of a big chest or an oversized door is beyond the spell's capability.

Focus: A brass key.

Order's Wrath

Evocation [Lawful]
Level: Law 4
Components: V, S
Casting Time: 1 action
Range: Medium (100 ft. + 10 ft./level)
Area: Nonlawful creatures within a burst that fills a 30-ft. cube
Duration: Instantaneous (1 round)
Saving Throw: Reflex partial (see text)
Spell Resistance: Yes

You channel lawful power to smite enemies. The power takes the form of a three-dimensional grid of energy. Only chaotic and neutral (not lawful) creatures are harmed by the spell.

The spell deals 1d8 points of damage per caster level (maximum 5d8) to chaotic creatures and dazes them for 1 round. A dazed creature can take no actions but suffers no penalties when attacked. A successful Reflex save reduces the damage to half and negates the daze effect.

The spell deals only half damage to creatures who are neither chaotic nor lawful, and they are not dazed. They can reduce the damage in half again (down to one-quarter of the roll) with a successful Reflex save.

Otiluke's Freezing Sphere

Evocation [Cold]
Level: Sor/Wiz 6
Components: V, S, F
Casting Time: 1 action
Range: See text
Target, Effect, or Area: See text
Duration: See text
Saving Throw: See text
Spell Resistance: Yes

Otiluke's freezing sphere is a multipurpose spell. You can cast any one of the following three versions:

Frigid Sphere: A tiny sphere of freezing matter steaks from your fingertips to up to long range (400 feet + 40 feet/level) to strike a body of water or a liquid that is principally water. When it strikes such a target, it freezes the liquid to a depth of 6 inches over an area equal to 100 square feet (a 10-foot square) per caster level. This ice lasts for 1 round per caster level. The sphere has no effect if it strikes a creature, even a water-based creature, but creatures swimming on the surface of frozen water become trapped in the ice. Attempting to break free is a full-round action. A trapped creature must succeed at a Strength check (DC 25) to do so.

Arcane Focus: A thin sheet of crystal about 1 inch square.

Cold Ray: A ray of cold springs from your hand to close range (25 feet + 5 feet/2 levels). You must succeed at a ranged touch attack to hit your target. The ray instantaneously deals 1d6 points of cold damage per caster level (maximum 20d6).

Arcane Focus: A small, white ceramic cone or prism.

Globe of Cold: You create a small globe about the size of a sling stone, cool to the touch but not harmful. This globe is a grenadelike weapon and can be hurled either as a thrown weapon (range increment 20 feet) or in a sling. The globe bursts on impact, dealing 6d6 points of cold damage instantaneously to all targets within a 10-foot radius. Affected creatures can attempt Reflex saves for half damage. If you do not hurl the globe, it bursts on its own after 1 round per caster level. You can command the globe to burst sooner if you wish, but the time cannot be changed once set (though it still bursts on impact after being hurled).

Focus: A small crystal sphere.

Otiluke's Resilient Sphere

Evocation [Force]
Level: Sor/Wiz 4
Components: V, S, M
Casting Time: 1 action
Range: Close (25 ft. + 5 ft./2 levels)
Effect: 1-ft.-diameter/level sphere, centered around a creature
Duration: 1 minute /level
Saving Throw: Reflex negates
Spell Resistance: Yes

A globe of shimmering force encloses a creature, provided it is small enough to fit within the diameter of the sphere. The sphere contains its subject for the spell's duration. The sphere is not subject to damage of any sort except from a *rod of cancellation*, a *wand of negation*, *disintegrate*, or a targeted *dispel magic* spell. These destroy the sphere without harm to the subject. Nothing can pass through the sphere, inside or out, though the subject can breathe normally. The subject may struggle, but the only effect that act produces is to move the sphere slightly. The globe can be physically moved either by people outside it or by the struggles of those within. (See Lifting and Dragging, page 142, for rules on pushing heavy objects.)

Material Components: A hemispherical piece of clear crystal and a matching hemispherical piece of gum arabic.

Otiluke's Telekinetic Sphere

Evocation [Force]
Level: Sor/Wiz 8
Components: V, S, M
Casting Time: 1 action
Range: Close (25 ft. + 5 ft./2 levels)
Effect: 1-ft.-diameter/level sphere, centered around creatures or objects
Duration: 1 minute/level (D)
Saving Throw: Reflex negates (object)
Spell Resistance: Yes (object)

As *Otiluke's resilient sphere*, with the addition that the creatures or objects inside the globe are nearly weightless. Anything contained within an *Otiluke's telekinetic sphere* weighs only one-sixteenth of its normal weight. You can telekinetically lift anything in the sphere that normally weighs up to 5,000 pounds. The range of the telekinetic control extends to a maximum distance of medium range from you (100 feet + 10 feet per caster level) after the sphere has succeeded in encapsulating its contents.

You move objects or creatures in the sphere that weigh up to a total of 5,000 pounds by concentrating on the sphere. You can begin moving a sphere the round after casting the spell. A round's concentration (a standard action) moves the sphere up to 30 feet. If you cease concentrating, the sphere does not move that round (if on a level surface) or descends at its falling rate (if aloft) until it reaches a level surface, the spell's duration ends, or you begin concentrating again. If you cease concentrating (voluntarily or due to failing a Concentration check), you can resume concentrating on your next turn or any later turn during the spell's duration.

Note that even if more than 5,000 pounds of weight is englobed, the perceived weight is only one-sixteenth of the actual weight, so the orb can be rolled without exceptional effort. The sphere falls at a rate of only 60 feet per round, which is not fast enough to cause damage to the contents of the sphere.

You can move the sphere telekinetically even if you are in it.

Material Components: A hemispherical piece of clear crystal, a matching hemispherical piece of gum arabic, and a pair of small bar magnets.

Otto's Irresistible Dance

Enchantment (Compulsion)
[Mind-Affecting]
Level: Sor/Wiz 8
Components: V
Casting Time: 1 action
Range: Touch
Target: Living creature touched
Duration: 1d4+1 rounds
Saving Throw: None
Spell Resistance: Yes

The subject feels an undeniable urge to dance and begins doing so, complete with foot shuffling and tapping. The dance makes it impossible for the subject to do anything other than caper and prance, worsens the Armor Class of the creature by –4, makes Reflex saves impossible except on a roll of 20, and makes it impossible to use a shield.

Passwall

Transmutation
Level: Sor/Wiz 5
Components: V, S, M
Casting Time: 1 action
Range: Close (25 ft. + 5 ft./2 levels)
Effect: 5 ft. × 8 ft. opening, 1 ft./level deep
Duration: 1 hour/level (D)
Saving Throw: None
Spell Resistance: No

You create a passage through wooden, plaster, or stone walls, but not through metal or other harder materials. If the wall's thickness is more than 1 foot per caster level, then a single *passwall* simply makes a niche or short tunnel. Several *passwall* spells can then form a continuing passage to breach very thick walls. When *passwall* ends, creatures within the passage are ejected out the nearest exit. If someone dispels the *passwall* or you dismiss it, creatures in the passage are ejected out the far exit if there is one or out the sole exit if there is only one.

Material Component: A pinch of sesame seeds.

Pass without Trace

Transmutation
Level: Drd 1, Rgr 1
Components: V, S, DF
Casting Time: 1 action
Range: Touch
Targets: One creature/level touched
Duration: 10 minutes/level
Saving Throw: Will negates (harmless)
Spell Resistance: Yes (harmless)

The subjects can move through any type of terrain—mud, snow, dust, etc.—and leave neither footprints nor scent. Tracking the subject is impossible by nonmagical means.

Permanency

Universal
Level: Sor/Wiz 5
Components: V, S, XP
Casting Time: 2 rounds
Range: See text
Target, Effect, or Area: See text
Duration: Permanent (see text)
Saving Throw: None
Spell Resistance: No

This spell makes certain other spells permanent. Depending on the spell, you must be at least a minimum level and must expend a number of XP.

You can make these spells permanent in regard to yourself:

Spell	Minimum Level	XP Cost
Comprehend languages	9th	500 XP
Darkvision	10th	1,000 XP
Detect magic	9th	500 XP
Protection from arrows	11th	1,500 XP
Read magic	9th	500 XP
See invisibility	10th	1,000 XP
Tongues	11th	1,500 XP

You cast the desired spell and then follow it with the *permanency* spell. You cannot cast these spells on other creatures. This application of *permanency* can be dispelled only by a caster of greater level than you were when you cast the spell.

In addition to personal use, *permanency* can be used to make the following spells permanent on yourself, another creature, or an object (as appropriate):

Spell	Minimum Level	XP Cost
Enlarge	9th	500 XP
Magic Fang	9th	500 XP
Resistance	9th	250 XP

Additionally, the following spells can be cast upon objects or areas only and rendered permanent:

Spell	Minimum Level	XP Cost
Alarm	9th	500 XP
Dancing lights	9th	500 XP
Ghost sound	9th	500 XP
Gust of wind	11th	1,500 XP
Invisibility	10th	1,000 XP
Magic mouth	10th	1,000 XP
Phase door	15th	3,500 XP
Prismatic sphere	17th	4,500 XP
Shrink item	11th	1,500 XP
Solid fog	12th	2,000 XP
Stinking cloud	11th	1,500 XP
Symbol	16th	4,000 XP
Teleportation circle	17th	4,500 XP
Wall of fire	12th	2,000 XP
Wall of force	13th	2,500 XP
Web	10th	1,000 XP

Spells cast on other creatures, objects, or locations (not on you) are vulnerable to *dispel magic* as normal.

The DM may allow other selected spells to be made permanent. Researching this possible application of a spell costs as much time and money as independently researching the selected spell (see the DUNGEON MASTER's *Guide*). If the DM has already determined that the application is not possible, the research automatically fails. Note that you never learn what is possible except by the success or failure of your research.

XP Cost: See tables above.

Permanent Image

Illusion (Figment)

Level: Brd 6, Sor/Wiz 6
Effect: Figment that cannot extend beyond a 20-ft. cube + one 10-ft. cube/level (S)
Duration: Permanent (D)

As *silent image*, except the figment includes visual, auditory, olfactory, and thermal elements, and the spell is permanent. By concentrating, you can move the image within the limits of the range, but it is static while you are not concentrating.

Material Component: A bit of fleece plus powdered jade worth 100 gp.

Persistent Image

Illusion (Figment)

Level: Brd 5, Sor/Wiz 5
Duration: 1 minute/level (D)

As *silent image*, except the figment includes visual, auditory, olfactory, and thermal components, and the figment follows a script determined by you. The figment follows that script without your having to concentrate on it. The illusion can include intelligible speech if you wish. For instance, you could create the illusion of several orcs playing cards and arguing, culminating in a fistfight.

Material Components: A bit of fleece and several grains of sand.

Phantasmal Killer

Illusion (Phantasm) [Fear, Mind-Affecting]

Level: Sor/Wiz 4
Components: V, S
Casting Time: 1 action
Range: Medium (100 ft. + 10 ft./level)
Target: One living creature
Duration: Instantaneous
Saving Throw: Will disbelief (if interacted with), then Fortitude partial
Spell Resistance: Yes

You create the phantasmal image of the most fearsome creature imaginable to the subject simply by forming the fears of the subject's subconscious mind into something that its conscious mind can visualize: this most horrible beast. Only the spell's subject can see the phantasmal killer. You see only a shadowy shape. The subject first gets a Will save to recognize the image as unreal. If the subject fails, the phantasm touches him, and he must succeed at a Fortitude save or die from fear. Even if the Fortitude save is successful, the subject takes 3d6 points of damage.

If the subject of a *phantasmal killer* attack succeeds in disbelieving and he is wearing a *helm of telepathy*, the beast can be turned upon you. You must then disbelieve it or suffer its deadly fear attack.

Phantom Steed

Conjuration (Creation)

Level: Brd 3, Sor/Wiz 3
Components: V, S
Casting Time: 10 minutes
Range: 0 ft.
Effect: One quasi-real, horselike creature
Duration: 1 hour/level
Saving Throw: None
Spell Resistance: No

You conjure a quasi-real, horselike creature. The steed can be ridden only by you or by the one person for whom you specifically created the mount. A phantom steed has a black head and body, gray mane and tail, and smoke-colored, insubstantial hooves that make no sound. It has what seems to be a saddle, bit, and bridle. It does not fight, but all normal animals shun it and refuse to attack it. (Dire animals and nonintelligent creatures, such as vermin, can attack it.)

The mount has an Armor Class of 18 (−1 size, +4 natural armor, +5 Dex) and 7 hit points +1 hit point per caster level. If it loses all its hit points, the phantom steed disappears. A phantom steed has a speed of 20 feet per caster level, to a maximum of 240 feet. It can bear its rider's weight plus up to 10 pounds per caster level.

These mounts gain certain powers according to caster level. A mount's abilities include those of mounts of lower caster levels. Thus, the mount created by a 12th-level caster has the 8th, 10th, and 12th caster level abilities.

8th Level: The mount can ride over sandy, muddy, or even swampy ground without difficulty or decrease in speed.

10th Level: The mount can ride over water as if it were firm, dry ground.

12th Level: The mount can ride in the air as if it were firm land, so chasms and the like can be crossed without benefit of a bridge. The mount cannot simply take off and fly. It can only ride horizontally across the air. After 1 round in the air, the mount falls.

14th Level: The mount can fly at its speed. It has a maneuverability rating of average.

Phase Door

Conjuration (Creation)

Level: Sor/Wiz 7, Travel 8
Components: V
Casting Time: 1 action
Range: Touch
Effect: Ethereal 5 ft. × 8 ft. opening, 1 ft./level deep
Duration: One usage/two levels
Saving Throw: None
Spell Resistance: No

This spell creates an ethereal passage through wooden, plaster, or stone walls, but not other materials. The *phase door* is invisible and inaccessible to all creatures except you, and only you can use the passage. You disappear when you enter the *phase door* and appear when you exit. If you desire, you can take one other creature (Medium-size or smaller) through the door. This counts as two uses of the door. The door does not allow light, sound, or spell effects through it, nor can you see through it without using it. Thus, the spell can provide an escape route, though certain creatures, such as phase spiders, can follow with ease. *Gems of true seeing* and similar magic reveal the presence of a *phase door* but do not allow its use.

A *phase door* is subject to *dispel magic*. If anyone is within the passage when it is dispelled, he is harmlessly ejected just as if he were inside a *passwall* effect.

A *phase door* can be made permanent with a *permanency* spell. You can allow other creatures to use the *phase door* by setting some triggering condition for the door. Such conditions can be as simple or elaborate as you desire. They can be based on a creature's name, identity, or alignment, but otherwise must be based on observable actions or qualities. Intangibles such as level, class, HD, and hit points don't qualify.

Planar Ally

Conjuration (Calling) [see text]

Level: Clr 6
Effect: Up to 16 HD worth of summoned elementals and outsiders, no two of which can be more than 30 ft. apart when they appear

As *lesser planar ally*, except you may call a single creature of up to 16 HD or a number of creatures whose HD total no more than 16. The creatures, as a group, agree to perform one task for you and request one favor in return.

Planar Binding

Conjuration (Summoning) [see text]

Level: Sor/Wiz 6
Components: V, S, M
Targets: Up to 16 HD worth of elementals and outsiders, no two of which can be more than 30 ft. apart when they appear

As *lesser planar binding*, except you may call a single creature of up to 16 HD or a number of creatures whose HD total no more than 16. Each creature gets a save, makes an independent attempt to escape, and must be individually persuaded to aid you.

Plane Shift

Transmutation

Level: Brd 6, Clr 5, Sor/Wiz 7
Components: V, S, F
Casting Time: 1 action
Range: Touch

Target: Creature touched, or up to eight willing creatures joining hands
Duration: Instantaneous
Saving Throw: Will negates
Spell Resistance: Yes

You move yourself or some other creature to another plane of existence or alternate dimension. If several willing persons link hands in a circle, up to eight can be affected by the *plane shift* at the same time. Pinpoint accuracy as to a particular arrival location on the intended plane is nigh impossible. From the Material Plane, you can reach any other plane, though you appear 5 to 500 miles (5d%) from your intended destination.

Note: *Plane shift* transports the creatures instantaneously and then ends. The creatures need to find other means if they are to travel back.

Focus: A small, forked metal rod. The size and metal type dictates to which plane of existence or alternate dimension the spell sends the affected creatures. Forked rods keyed to certain planes may be difficult to come by, as decided by the DM.

Plant Growth

Transmutation
Level: Drd 3, Plant 3, Rgr 3
Components: V, S, DF
Casting Time: 1 action
Range: See text
Target or Area: See text
Duration: Instantaneous
Saving Throw: None
Spell Resistance: No

Plant growth has different effects depending on the version chosen.

Overgrowth: The first effect causes normal vegetation (grasses, briars, bushes, creepers, thistles, trees, vines, etc.) within long range (400 feet + 40 feet per level) to become thick and overgrown. The plants entwine to form a thicket or jungle that creatures must hack or force a way through. Speed drops to 5 feet, or 10 feet for Large or larger creatures. (The DM may allow faster movement for very small or very large creatures.) The area must have brush and trees in it for this spell to take effect.

At your option, the area can be a circle with a radius of 100 feet, a semicircle with a radius of 150 feet, or a quarter circle with a radius of 200 feet. You may also designate areas within the area that are not affected.

Enrichment: The second effect targets plants within a range of one-half mile, raising their potential productivity over the course of the next year to one-third above normal.

In many farming communities, clerics or druids cast this spell at planting time as part of the spring festivals.

Plant growth counters *diminish plants*.

Poison

Necromancy
Level: Clr 4, Drd 3
Components: V, S, DF
Casting Time: 1 action
Range: Touch
Target: Living creature touched
Duration: Instantaneous (see text)
Saving Throw: Fortitude negates (see text)
Spell Resistance: Yes

Calling upon the venomous powers of natural predators, you inflict the subject with a horrible poison by making a successful melee touch attack. The poison deals 1d10 points of temporary Constitution damage immediately and another 1d10 points of temporary Constitution damage 1 minute later. Each instance of damage can be negated by a Fortitude save (DC 10 + one-half caster level + caster's Wisdom modifier).

Polymorph Any Object

Transmutation
Level: Sor/Wiz 8, Trickery 8
Components: V, S, M/DF
Casting Time: 1 action
Range: Close (25 ft. + 5 ft./2 levels)
Target: One creature or object
Duration: See text
Saving Throw: Will negates (object) (see text)
Spell Resistance: Yes (object)

As *polymorph other*, except this spell changes one object or creature into another. The duration of the spell depends on how radical a change is made from the original state to its enchanted state. The DM determines the duration by using the following guidelines:

Changed Subject Is:	Increase to Duration Factor*
Same kingdom (animal, vegetable, mineral)	+5
Same class (mammals, fungi, metals, etc.)	+2
Same size	+2
Related (twig is to tree, wolf fur is to wolf, etc.)	+2
Same or lower Intelligence	+2

*Add all that apply. Look up the total on the next table.

Duration

Factor	Example	Duration
0	Pebble to human	20 minutes
2	Marionette to human	1 hour
4	Human to marionette	3 hours
5	Lizard to manticore	12 hours
6	Sheep to wool coat	2 days
7	Shrew to manticore	1 week
9+	Manticore to shrew	Permanent

Unlike *polymorph other*, *polymorph any object* does grant the creature the Intelligence score of its new form. If the original form didn't have a Wisdom or Charisma score, it gains those scores of the new form.

As with other polymorph spells, damage sustained in the new form can result in the injury or death of the polymorphed creature. For example, it is possible to polymorph a creature into rock and grind it to dust, causing damage, perhaps even death. If the creature was changed to dust to start with, more creative methods to damage it would be needed. Perhaps you could use a *gust of wind* spell to scatter the dust far and wide. In general, damage occurs when the new form is changed through physical force, although the DM will have to adjudicate many of these situations.

Also note that a polymorph effect often detracts from an item's or creature's powers but does not add new powers except perhaps movement capabilities not present in the old form. A nonmagical object cannot be made magical by this spell. A magic item or weapon or other object can be polymorphed into another type of magic object, but it never gains abilities superior to those of the original object.

This spell cannot create material of great intrinsic value, such as copper, silver, gems, silk, gold, and platinum.

This spell can also be used to duplicate the effects of *polymorph other*, *flesh to stone*, *stone to flesh*, *transmute mud to rock*, *transmute water to dust*, or *transmute rock to mud*.

Arcane Material Components: Mercury, gum arabic, and smoke.

Polymorph Other

Transmutation
Level: Sor/Wiz 4
Components: V, S, M
Casting Time: 1 action
Range: Medium (100 ft. + 10 ft./level)
Target: One creature
Duration: Permanent
Saving Throw: Fortitude negates
Spell Resistance: Yes

Polymorph other changes the subject into another form of creature. The new form can range in size from Diminutive to one size larger than the subject's normal form. Upon changing, the subject regains lost hit points as if having rested for a day (though this healing does not restore temporary ability damage and provide other benefits of resting for a day; and changing back does not heal the creature further). If slain, the polymorphed creature reverts to its original form, though it remains dead.

The polymorphed creature acquires the physical and natural abilities of the creature it has been polymorphed into while retaining its own mind. Physical abilities include natural size and Strength,

Dexterity, and Constitution scores. Natural abilities include armor, attack routines (claw, claw, and bite; swoop and rake; and constriction; but not petrification, breath weapons, energy drain, energy effects, etc.), and similar gross physical qualities (presence or absence of wings, number of extremities, etc.). Natural abilities also include mundane movement capabilities, such as walking, swimming, and flight with wings, but not magical flight and other magical forms of travel, such as *blink*, *dimension door*, *phase door*, *plane shift*, *teleport*, and *teleport without error*. Extremely high speeds for certain creatures are the result of magical ability, so they are not granted by this spell. Other nonmagical abilities (such as an owl's low-light vision) are considered natural abilities and are retained.

Any part of the body or piece of equipment that is separated from the whole reverts to its original form.

The creature's new scores and faculties are average ones for the race or species into which it has been transformed. You cannot, for example, turn someone into a mighty weight lifter to give the subject great Strength.

The subject retains its Intelligence, Wisdom, and Charisma scores, level and class, hit points (despite any change in its Constitution score), alignment, base attack bonus, and base saves. (New Strength, Dexterity, and Constitution scores may affect final attack and save bonuses.) The subject retains its own type (for example, "humanoid"), extraordinary abilities, spells, and spell-like abilities, but not its supernatural abilities. The subject can cast spells for which it has components. It needs a humanlike voice for verbal components and humanlike hands for somatic components. The subject does not gain the spell-like abilities of its new form. The subject does not gain the supernatural abilities (such as breath weapons and gaze attacks) or the extraordinary abilities of the new creature.

The new form can be disorienting. Any time the polymorphed creature is in a stressful or demanding situation (such as combat), the creature must succeed at a Will save (DC 19) or suffer a –2 penalty on all attack rolls, saves, skill checks, and ability checks until the situation passes. Creatures who are polymorphed for a long time (years and years) grow accustomed to their new form and can overcome some of these drawbacks (DM's discretion).

When the polymorph occurs, the creature's equipment, if any, transforms to match the new form. If the new form is a creature who does not use equipment (aberration, animal, beast, magical beast, construct, dragon, elemental, ooze, some outsiders, plant, some undead creatures, some shapechangers, or vermin), the equipment melds into the new form and

becomes nonfunctional. Material components and focuses melded in this way cannot be used to cast spells. If the new form uses equipment (fey, giant, humanoid, some outsiders, many shapechangers, many undead creatures), the subject's equipment changes to match the new form and retains its properties. If in doubt about the new form's ability to use equipment, refer to its entry in the *Monster Manual*.

You can freely designate the new form's minor physical qualities (such as hair color, hair texture, and skin color) within the normal ranges for a creature of that type. The new form's significant physical qualities (such as height, weight, and gender) are also under your control, but must fall within the norms for the new form's species. The subject can be changed into a member of its own species or even into itself. (If changed into itself, it does not suffer the abovementioned penalties from the disorientation of a new form.)

The subject is effectively disguised as an average member of the new form's race. If you use this spell to create a disguise, you get a +10 bonus on your Disguise check.

Incorporeal or gaseous forms cannot be assumed, and incorporeal or gaseous creatures are immune to being polymorphed. A natural shapeshifter (a lycanthrope, doppelganger, experienced druid, etc.) can take its natural form as a standard action.

Material Component: An empty cocoon.

Polymorph Self

Transmutation
Level: Rgr 4, Sor/Wiz 4
Components: V
Casting Time: 1 action
Range: Personal
Target: You
Duration: 1 hour/level (D)

As *polymorph other*, except that you assume the form of a different creature.

You can change your form as often as desired for the duration of the spell simply by willing it so. Each change is a full-round action. You regain hit points as if having rested for a day only from the initial transformation, however.

Power Word, Blind

Conjuration (Creation)
Level: Sor/Wiz 8, War 8
Components: V
Casting Time: 1 action
Range: Close (25 ft. + 5 ft./2 levels)
Area: Creatures with up to 200 total hit points within a 15-ft.-radius sphere
Duration: See text
Saving Throw: None
Spell Resistance: Yes

This spell creates a wave of magical energy that blinds one or more creatures. It

affects the creatures with the lowest hit point totals first, selecting subjects one at a time until the next target would put it over the limit of 200. (Creatures with negative hit points count as having 0 hit points.)

The duration of the spell depends on the total hit points of the affected creatures:

Hit Points	Duration
Up to 50	Permanent
51 to 100	1d4+1 minutes
101 to 200	1d4+1 rounds

Power Word, Kill

Conjuration (Creation) [Death]
Level: Sor/Wiz 9, War 9
Components: V
Casting Time: 1 action
Range: Close (25 ft. + 5 ft./2 levels)
Target or Area: One living creature or one or more creatures within a 15-ft.-radius sphere
Duration: Instantaneous
Saving Throw: None
Spell Resistance: Yes

When *power word, kill* is uttered, you can either target a single creature or let the spell affect a group.

If *power word, kill* is targeted at a single creature, that creature dies if it has 100 or fewer hit points.

If *power word, kill* is cast as an area spell, it kills creatures in a 15-foot-radius sphere. It kills only creatures who have 20 or fewer hit points, and only up to a total of 200 hit points of such creatures. The spell affects creatures with the lowest hit point totals first until the next creature would put the total over the limit of 200. (Creatures with negative hit points count as having 0 hit points.)

Power Word, Stun

Conjuration (Creation)
Level: Sor/Wiz 7, War 7
Components: V
Casting Time: 1 action
Range: Close (25 ft. + 5 ft./2 levels)
Target: One creature with up to 150 hit points
Duration: See text
Saving Throw: None
Spell Resistance: Yes

When a *power word, stun* spell is uttered, one creature of your choice is stunned, whether the creature can hear the word or not. A creature with 50 or fewer hit points remains stunned for 4d4 rounds, one with 51 to 100 hit points is stunned for 2d4 rounds, one with 101 to 150 hit points is stunned for 1d4 rounds, and a creature with 151 hit points or more is not affected.

A stunned creature can't act and loses any Dexterity bonus to AC. Attackers gain +2 bonuses to attack it.

Prayer

Conjuration (Creation)
Level: Clr 3, Pal 3
Components: V, S, DF
Casting Time: 1 action
Range: 30 ft.
Area: All allies and foes within a 30-ft.-radius burst centered on you
Duration: 1 round/level
Saving Throw: None
Spell Resistance: Yes

You bring special favor upon your allies (and possibly yourself) and bring disfavor to your enemies. You and your allies gain a +1 luck bonus on attack rolls, weapon damage rolls, saves, and skill checks, while foes suffer a –1 penalty on such rolls.

Prestidigitation

Universal
Level: Brd 0, Sor/Wiz 0
Components: V, S
Casting Time: 1 action
Range: 10 ft.
Target, Effect, or Area: See text
Duration: 1 hour
Saving Throw: See text
Spell Resistance: No

Prestidigitations are minor tricks that novice spellcasters use for practice. Once cast, the *prestidigitation* spell enables you to perform simple magical effects for 1 hour. The effects are minor and have severe limitations. Prestidigitations can slowly lift 1 pound of material. They can color, clean, or soil items in a 1-foot cube each round. They can chill, warm, or flavor 1 pound of nonliving material. They cannot inflict damage or affect the concentration of spellcasters. *Prestidigitation* can create small objects, but they look crude and artificial. The materials created by a *prestidigitation* spell are extremely fragile, and they cannot be used as tools, weapons, or spell components. Finally, a prestidigitation lacks the power to duplicate any other spell effects. Any actual change to an object (beyond just moving, cleaning, or soiling it) persists only 1 hour.

Characters typically use prestidigitations to impress common folk, amuse children, and brighten dreary lives. Common tricks with prestidigitations include producing tinklings of ethereal music, brightening faded flowers, creating glowing balls that float over your hand, generating puffs of wind to flicker candles, spicing up aromas and flavors of bland food, and making little whirlwinds to sweep dust under rugs.

Prismatic Sphere

Abjuration
Level: Protection 9, Sor/Wiz 9, Sun 9
Components: V
Range: 10 ft.
Effect: 10-ft.-radius sphere centered on you

As *prismatic wall*, except you conjure up an immobile, opaque globe of shimmering, multicolored light that surrounds you and protects you from all forms of attack. The sphere flashes in all colors of the visible spectrum.

The sphere's blindness effect on creatures with less than 8 HD lasts 2d4 × 10 minutes.

You can pass into and out of the *prismatic sphere* and remain near it without harm. However, when you're inside it, the sphere blocks any attempt to project something through the sphere (including spells). Other creatures who attempt to attack you or pass through suffer the effects of each color, one at a time.

Typically, only the upper hemisphere of the globe will exist, since you are at the center of the sphere, so the lower half is usually excluded by the floor surface you are standing on.

The colors of the sphere have the same effects as the colors of a *prismatic wall*.

Prismatic Spray

Evocation
Level: Sor/Wiz 7
Components: V, S
Casting Time: 1 action
Range: Close (25 ft. + 5 ft./2 levels)
Area: Cone
Duration: Instantaneous
Saving Throw: See text
Spell Resistance: Yes

This spell causes seven shimmering, intertwined, multicolored beams of light to spray from your hand. Each beam has a different power. Creatures in the area of the spell with 8 HD or less are automatically blinded (see *blindness/deafness*) for 2d4 rounds. All creatures in the area are randomly struck by one or more beams, which have additional effects.

1d8	Color of Beam	Effect
1	Red	20 points fire damage (Reflex half)
2	Orange	40 points acid damage (Reflex half)
3	Yellow	80 points electricity damage (Reflex half)
4	Green	Poison (Kills; Fortitude partial, take 20 points of damage instead)
5	Blue	Turned to stone (Fortitude negates)
6	Indigo	Insane, as *insanity* spell (Will negates)
7	Violet	Sent to another plane (Will negates)
8		Struck by two rays; roll again twice, ignoring any "8" results.

Prismatic Wall

Abjuration
Level: Sor/Wiz 8
Components: V, S
Casting Time: 1 action
Range: Close (25 ft. + 5 ft./2 levels)
Effect: Wall 4 ft./level wide × 2 ft./level high
Duration: 10 minutes/level
Saving Throw: See text
Spell Resistance: See text

Prismatic wall creates a vertical, opaque wall—a shimmering, multicolored plane of light that protects you from all forms of attack. The wall flashes with seven colors, each of which has a distinct power and purpose. The wall is immobile, and you can pass through and remain near the wall without harm. However, any other creature with fewer than 8 HD that is within 20 feet of the wall is blinded (see *blindness/deafness*) for 2d4 rounds by the colors if it looks at the wall.

The wall's maximum proportions are 4 feet wide per caster level and 2 feet high per caster level. A *prismatic wall* spell cast to materialize in a space occupied by a creature is disrupted, and the spell is wasted.

Each color in the wall has a special effect. The accompanying table shows the seven colors of the wall, the order in which they appear, their effects on creatures trying to attack you or pass through the wall, and the magic needed to negate each color.

The wall can be destroyed, color by color, in consecutive order, by various magical effects; however, the first must be brought down before the second can be affected, and so on. A *rod of cancellation* or a *Mordenkainen's disjunction* spell destroys a *prismatic wall*, but an *antimagic field* fails to penetrate it. *Dispel magic* and *greater dispelling* cannot dispel the wall or anything beyond it. Spell resistance is effective against a *prismatic wall*, but the caster level check must be repeated for each color present.

Produce Flame

Evocation [Fire]
Level: Drd 2, Fire 2
Components: V, S
Casting Time: 1 action
Range: Touch
Effect: Flame in your palm
Duration: 1 round/level (D)
Saving Throw: None
Spell Resistance: Yes

Flames appear in your hand. You can hurl them or use them to touch enemies. The bright flames, which illuminate out to 20 feet as torches do, appear in your open hand and harm neither you nor your equipment.

Prismatic wall makes an effective barrier.

RISMATIC WALL

Color	Order	Effect of Color	Negated By
Red	1st	Stops nonmagical ranged weapons.	*Cone of cold*
		Deals 20 points of fire damage (Reflex half).	
Orange	2nd	Stops magical ranged weapons.	*Gust of wind*
		Deals 40 points of acid damage (Reflex half).	
Yellow	3rd	Stops poisons, gases, and petrification.	*Disintegrate*
		Deals 80 points of electricity damage (Reflex half).	
Green	4th	Stops breath weapons.	*Passwall*
		Poison (Kills; Fortitude partial to take 20 points of damage instead).	
Blue	5th	Stops divination and mental attacks.	*Magic missile*
		Turned to stone (Fortitude negates).	
Indigo	6th	Stops all spells.	*Daylight*
		Will save or become insane (as *insanity* spell).	
Violet	7th	Energy field destroys all objects and effects.*	*Dispel magic*
		Creatures sent to another plane (Will negates).	

*The violet effect makes the special effects of the other six colors redundant, but they are included here because certain magic items can create prismatic effects one color at a time, and SR might render some colors ineffective (see above).

You can strike opponents with a melee touch attack, dealing fire damage equal to 1d4 +1 point per two caster levels (maximum +10). Alternatively, you can hurl the flames up to 120 feet as a thrown weapon. When doing so, you attack with a ranged touch attack (with no range penalty) and deal the same damage as with the melee attack. No sooner do you hurl the flames than a new set appears in your hand.

The spell does not function underwater.

Programmed Image
Illusion (Figment)
Level: Brd 6, Sor/Wiz 6
Effect: Visual figment that cannot extend beyond a 20-ft. cube + one 10-ft. cube/level (S)
Duration: Permanent until triggered, then 1 round/level

As *silent image*, except this spell's figment activates when a specific condition occurs. The figment includes visual, auditory, olfactory, and thermal elements, including intelligible speech.

You set the triggering condition (which may be a special word) when casting the spell. The event that triggers the illusion can be as general or as specific and detailed as desired but must be based on an audible, tactile, olfactory, or visual trigger. The trigger cannot be based on some quality not normally obvious to the senses, such as alignment. (See *magic mouth* for more details about such triggers.)

Material Component: A bit of fleece and jade dust worth 25 gp.

Project Image
Illusion (Shadow)
Level: Brd 6, Sor/Wiz 6
Components: V, S, M
Casting Time: 1 action
Range: Medium (100 ft. + 10 ft./level)
Effect: One shadow duplicate
Duration: 1 round/level (D)
Saving Throw: Will disbelief (if interacted with)
Spell Resistance: No

You create a shadow duplicate of yourself; it looks, sounds, and smells like you but is intangible. The shadow mimics your actions (including speech) unless you concentrate on making it act differently. You can see through its eyes and hear through its ears as if you were standing where it is, and during your turn in a round you can switch from seeing through its eyes to seeing normally, or back again. If you desire, any spell you cast whose range is touch or greater can originate from the shadow instead of from you. (The shadow is quasi-real, just real enough to cast spells that you originate.) The shadow can cast spells on itself only if those spells affect shadows.

You must maintain line of effect to the shadow at all times. If your line of effect is obstructed, the spell ends. If you use *dimension door, teleport, plane shift,* or a similar spell that breaks your line of effect, even momentarily, the spell ends.

Material Component: A small replica of you (a doll).

Protection from Arrows
Abjuration
Level: Sor/Wiz 2
Components: V, S, F
Casting Time: 1 action
Range: Touch

Target: Creature touched
Duration: 10 minutes/level or until discharged
Saving Throw: Will negates (harmless)
Spell Resistance: Yes (harmless)

The warded creature gains resistance to ranged weapons. The subject gains damage reduction 10/+1 against ranged weapons. It ignores the first 10 points of damage each time it takes damage from a ranged weapon, though a weapon with a +1 enhancement bonus or any magical attack bypasses the reduction. The damage reduction increases with the caster level to 10/+2 at 5th, 10/+3 at 10th, 10/+4 at 15th, and 10/+5 at 20th. Once the spell has prevented a total of 10 points of damage per caster level (maximum 100 points), it is discharged.

Focus: A piece of shell from a tortoise or a turtle.

Protection from Chaos
Abjuration [Lawful]
Level: Brd 1, Clr 1, Law 1, Sor/Wiz 1

As *protection from evil*, except that the deflection and resistance bonuses apply to attacks from chaotic creatures, and chaotic summoned or conjured creatures cannot touch the subject.

Protection from Elements
Abjuration
Level: Clr 3, Drd 3, Luck 3, Protection 3, Rgr 2, Sor/Wiz 3
Components: V, S, DF
Casting Time: 1 action
Duration: 10 minutes/level or until discharged

As *endure elements*, but *protection from elements* grants temporary invulnerability to the selected energy type. When the spell absorbs 12 points per caster level of elemental damage, it is discharged.

Note: Protection from elements overlaps (and does not stack with) *resist elements* and *endure elements*. If a character is warded by *protection from elements* and one or both of the other spells, the *protection* spell absorbs damage until it is exhausted. If a character is warded by *resist elements* and *endure elements* at the same time, the *resist* spell absorbs damage but the *endure* spell does not.

Protection from Evil
Abjuration [Good]
Level: Brd 1, Clr 1, Good 1, Pal 1, Sor/Wiz 1
Components: V, S, M/DF
Casting Time: 1 action
Range: Touch
Target: Creature touched
Duration: 1 minute/level (D)
Saving Throw: Will negates (harmless)
Spell Resistance: No (see text)

This spell wards a creature from attacks by evil creatures, from mental control, and from summoned or conjured creatures. It creates a magical barrier around the subject at a distance of 1 foot. The barrier moves with the subject and has three major effects:

First, the subject gets a +2 deflection bonus to AC and a +2 resistance bonus on saves. Both these bonuses apply against attacks made by evil creatures.

Second, the barrier blocks any attempt to possess the warded creature (as by a *magic jar* attack) or to exercise mental control over the creature (as by a vampire's supernatural domination ability, which works similar to *dominate person*). The protection does not prevent a vampire's domination itself, but it prevents the vampire from mentally commanding the protected creature. If the *protection from evil* effect ends before the domination effect does, the vampire would then be able to mentally command the controlled creature. Likewise, the barrier keeps out a possessing life force but does not expel one if it is in place before the spell is cast. This second effect works regardless of alignment.

Third, the spell prevents bodily contact by summoned or conjured creatures (see the *Monster Manual*). This causes the natural weapon attacks of such creatures to fail and the creatures to recoil if such attacks require touching the warded creature. Good elementals and outsiders are immune to this effect. The protection against contact by summoned or conjured creatures ends if the warded creature makes an attack against or tries to force the barrier against the blocked creature. Spell resistance can allow a creature to overcome this protection and touch the warded creature.

Arcane Material Component: A little powdered silver with which you trace a 3-foot-diameter circle on the floor (or ground) around the creature to be warded.

Protection from Good
Abjuration [Evil]
Level: Brd 1, Clr 1, Evil 1, Sor/Wiz 1

As *protection from evil*, except that the deflection and resistance bonuses apply to attacks from good creatures, and good summoned or conjured creatures cannot touch the subject.

Protection from Law
Abjuration [Chaotic]
Level: Brd 1, Chaos 1, Clr 1, Sor/Wiz 1

As *protection from evil*, except that the deflection and resistance bonuses apply to attacks from lawful creatures, and lawful summoned or conjured creatures cannot touch the subject.

Protection from Spells
Abjuration
Level: Magic 8, Sor/Wiz 8
Components: V, S, M, F
Casting Time: 1 action
Range: Touch
Targets: Up to one creature/four levels touched
Duration: 10 minutes/level
Saving Throw: Will negates (harmless)
Spell Resistance: Yes (harmless)

Subjects gain a +8 resistance bonus on saving throws against spells and spell-like abilities (but not against supernatural and extraordinary abilities).

Material Component: A diamond of at least 500 gp value, which must be crushed and sprinkled over the spell recipients.

Focus: One 1,000 gp diamond per creature granted the protection. Each recipient must carry one such gem for the duration of the spell. If a recipient loses the gem, the spell ceases to affect him.

Prying Eyes
Divination
Level: Sor/Wiz 5
Components: V, S, M
Casting Time: 1 minute
Range: One mile
Effect: Creates 1d4 levitating eyes +1 eye/level
Duration: 1 hour/level (see text)
Saving Throw: None
Spell Resistance: No

You create ten or more semitangible, visible magical orbs (called "eyes") that move out, scout around, and return as you direct them when casting the spell. When an eye returns, it relays what it has seen to you and then disappears. Each eye is about the size of a small apple and can see 120 feet (normal vision only) in all directions.

The spell conjures 1d4 eyes plus one eye per caster level. While the individual eyes are quite fragile, they're small and difficult to spot. Each eye is a Fine construct that has 1 hit point, has AC 18 (+8 bonus for its size), flies at a speed of 30 feet with perfect maneuverability, and a +16 skill modifier on Hide checks. The eyes are subject to illusions, darkness, fog, and any other factors that would affect your ability to receive visual information about your surroundings. An eye traveling through darkness must find its way by touch.

When you create the eyes, you specify instructions you want the eyes to follow in a command of up to twenty-five words. Any knowledge you possess is known by the eyes as well, so if you know, for example, what a typical merchant looks like, the eyes do as well. Sample commands might include:

"Surround me at a range of four hundred feet and return if you spot any dangerous creatures." The phrase "Surround me" directs the eyes to form an equally spaced, horizontal ring at whatever range you indicate, and then move with you. As eyes return or are destroyed, the rest automatically space themselves to compensate. In the case of this sample command, an eye returns only if it spots a creature whom you would regard as dangerous. A "peasant" that is actually a *shapechanged* dragon wouldn't trigger an eye's return. Ten eyes can form a ring with a radius of 400 feet and among themselves see everything that crosses the ring.

"Spread out and search the town for Arweth. Follow him for three minutes, staying out of sight, and then return." The phrase "Spread out" directs the eyes to move away from you in all directions. In this case, each eye would separately follow Arweth for three minutes once it spots him.

Other commands that might be useful include having the eyes form a line in a certain manner, making them move at random within a certain range, or have them follow a certain type of creature. The DM is the final judge of the suitability of your directions.

In order to report their findings, the eyes must return to your hand. Each replays in your mind everything it has seen during its existence. It takes an eye only 1 round to replay 1 hour of recorded images.

If an eye ever gets more than one mile distant from you, it instantly ceases to exist. However, your link with the eye is such that you won't know if the eye was destroyed because it wandered out of range or because of some other event.

The eyes exist for up to 1 hour per caster level or until they return to you. After relaying its findings, an eye disappears. *Dispel magic* can destroy eyes. Roll separately for each eye caught in an area dispel. Of course, if the eye is sent into darkness, then it's very possible that it could hit a wall or similar obstacle and destroy itself.

Material Component: A handful of crystal marbles.

Purify Food and Drink

Universal
Level: Clr 0, Drd 0
Components: V, S
Casting Time: 1 action
Range: 10 ft.
Target: 1 cu. ft./level of contaminated food and water
Duration: Instantaneous
Saving Throw: Will negates (object)
Spell Resistance: Yes (object)

This spell makes spoiled, rotten, poisonous, or otherwise contaminated food and water pure and suitable for eating and drinking. This spell does not prevent subsequent natural decay or spoilage. Unholy water and similar food and drink of significance is spoiled by *purify food and drink*, but the spell has no effect on creatures of any type nor upon magic potions.

Note: Water weighs about 8 pounds per gallon. One cubic foot of water contains roughly 8 gallons and weighs about 60 pounds.

Pyrotechnics

Transmutation
Level: Brd 2, Sor/Wiz 2
Components: V, S, M
Casting Time: 1 action
Range: Long (400 ft. + 40 ft./level)
Target: One fire source, up to a 20-ft. cube
Duration: 1d4+1 rounds or 1d4+1 rounds after creatures leave the smoke cloud (see text)
Saving Throw: Will negates or Fortitude negates (see text)
Spell Resistance: Yes or No (see text)

Pyrotechnics turns a fire into either a burst of blinding fireworks or a thick cloud of choking smoke, depending on the version you choose.

Fireworks: The fireworks are a flashing, fiery, momentary burst of glowing, colored aerial lights. This effect blinds creatures within 120 feet of the fire source for 1d4+1 rounds (Will negates). These creatures must have line of sight to the fire to be affected. Spell resistance can prevent blindness. In addition to the obvious effects, a blinded creature suffers a 50% miss chance in combat (all opponents have full concealment), loses any Dexterity bonus to AC, grants a +2 bonus to attackers' attack rolls (they are effectively invisible), moves at half speed, and suffers a –4 penalty on most Strength- and Dexterity-based skills.

Smoke Cloud: The smoke is a writhing stream of smoke billowing out from the source and forming a choking cloud. The cloud spreads 20 feet in all directions and lasts for 1 round per caster level. All sight, even darkvision, is ineffective in or through the cloud. All within the cloud suffer –4 penalties to Strength and Dexterity scores (Fortitude negates). These effects last for 1d4+1 rounds after the cloud dissipates or after the character leaves the area of the cloud. Spell resistance does not apply.

Material Component: The spell uses one fire source, which is immediately extinguished. A fire so large that it exceeds a 20-foot cube is only partly extinguished. Magical fires are not extinguished, although a fire-based creature (such as a fire elemental) used as a source takes 1 point of damage per caster level.

Quench

Transmutation
Level: Drd 4
Components: V, S, DF
Casting Time: 1 action
Range: Medium (100 ft. + 10 ft./level)
Area or Target: One 20-ft. cube/level (S) or one fire-based magic item
Duration: Instantaneous
Saving Throw: None or Will negates (object)
Spell Resistance: No or Yes (object)

Quench is often used to put out forest fires and other conflagrations. It extinguishes all nonmagical fires in its area. The spell also dispels fire spells in the area, though you must succeed at a dispel check of 1d20 +1 per caster level (maximum +15) against each spell to dispel it. The DC to dispel such spells is 11 + the caster level of the fire spell. Fire-based creatures within the area take 1d6 points of damage per caster level from the spell (maximum 15d6, no save allowed).

Alternatively, you can target the spell on a single magic item that creates or controls flame, such as a *wand of fireball* or a *flame tongue sword*. The item loses all its fire-based magical abilities permanently unless it succeeds at a Will save. (Artifacts are immune to this effect.)

Rainbow Pattern

Illusion (Pattern) [Mind-Affecting]
Level: Brd 4, Sor/Wiz 4
Components: (V), S, M, F (see text)
Casting Time: 1 action
Range: Medium (100 ft. + 10 ft./level)
Effect: Colorful lights with a 15-ft.-radius spread
Duration: Concentration+1 round/level (D)
Saving Throw: Will negates
Spell Resistance: Yes

A glowing, rainbow-hued pattern of interweaving colors captivates those within it. *Rainbow pattern* captivates a maximum of 24 HD of creatures. Creatures with the fewest HD are affected first. Among creatures with equal HD, those who are closest to the spell's point of origin are affected first. Affected creatures who fail their saves are captivated by the pattern. Captivated creatures cannot move away from the pattern, nor can they take actions other than to defend themselves. Thus, a captivated fighter cannot run away or attack but suffers no penalties when attacked. An attack on a captivated creature frees it from the spell immediately.

With a simple gesture (a free action), you can make the *rainbow pattern* move up to 30 feet per round (moving its effective point of origin). All captivated creatures follow the moving rainbow of light, trying to get or remain within the effect. Captivated creatures who are restrained and removed from the pattern still try to follow it. If the pattern leads its subjects into a dangerous area (through flame, off a cliff, etc.), each captivated creature gets a second save. If the view of the lights is completely blocked (by an *obscuring mist* spell, for instance), creatures who can't see them are no longer affected.

The spell does not affect sightless creatures.

Verbal Component: A wizard or sorcerer need not utter a sound to cast this spell, but a bard must sing, play music, or recite a rhyme as a verbal component.

Material Component: A piece of phosphor.

Focus: A crystal prism.

Raise Dead

Conjuration (Healing)
Level: Clr 5
Components: V, S, M, DF
Casting Time: 1 minute
Range: Touch
Target: Dead creature touched
Duration: Instantaneous
Saving Throw: None (see text)
Spell Resistance: Yes (harmless)

The cleric restores life to a deceased creature. The cleric can raise creatures who have been dead only up to 1 day per caster level. In addition, the subject's soul must be free and willing to return (see Bringing Back the Dead, page 153). If the subject's soul is not willing to return, the spell does not work; therefore, subjects who want to return receive no saving throw. The subject loses a level (or 1 Constitution point, if she's 1st level) when raised.

Raise dead cures hit point damage up to a total of 1 hit point per Hit Die. Any ability scores damaged to 0 are raised to 1. Normal poison and normal disease are cured in the process of raising the subject, but magical diseases and curses are not undone. While the spell closes mortal wounds and repairs lethal damage of most kinds, the body of the creature to be raised must be whole. Otherwise, missing parts are still missing when the creature is brought back to life. None of the dead creature's equipment or possessions are affected in any way by this spell.

A creature who has been turned into an undead creature or killed by a death effect can't be raised by this spell. Constructs, elementals, outsiders, and undead creatures can't be raised. The spell cannot bring back a creature who has died of old age.

Coming back from the dead is an ordeal. The subject of the spell loses one level when it is raised, just as if it had lost a level to an energy-draining creature. This level loss cannot be repaired by any spell. If the subject is 1st level, it loses 1 point of Constitution instead. A character who died with spells prepared has a 50% chance of losing any given spell upon being raised, in addition to losing spells for losing a level. A character with spellcasting capacity (such as a sorcerer) has a 50% chance of losing any given spell slot, in addition to losing spell slots for losing a level.

Material Component: A diamond worth at least 500 gp.

Random Action

Enchantment (Compulsion)
[Mind-Affecting]
Level: Clr 1
Components: V, S, DF
Casting Time: 1 action
Range: Close (25 ft. + 5 ft./2 levels)
Target: One living creature
Duration: 1 round
Saving Throw: Will negates
Spell Resistance: Yes

The enchanted creature is compelled to act randomly for 1 round. Rather than deciding its action for itself, the subject of the spell takes an action determined randomly on the following table:

1d8	Action
1	Attack self (succeed on any roll other than a natural 1).
2	Attack nearest being (for this purpose, a familiar counts as part of the subject's "self").
3	Flee away from caster at top possible speed.
4	Drop anything held.
5	Stand motionless (as if stunned).
6	Do nothing but defend (total defense).
7	Speak (in the subject's native tongue, usually regarding surface thoughts) or make noises (if not capable of speech).
8	Attack caster with melee or ranged weapons (or close with caster if attacking is not possible).

Nothing can affect this die roll in any way. It is always entirely random.

Note: Nonintelligent creatures are immune to mind-affecting spells.

Rary's Mnemonic Enhancer

Transmutation
Level: Wiz 4
Components: V, S, M, F
Casting Time: 10 minutes
Range: Personal

Target: You
Duration: Instantaneous

You prepare or retain additional spells. In either event, the spell or spells prepared or retained fade after 24 hours (if not cast). Pick one of these two versions:

- *Prepare:* You prepare up to three additional levels of spells (such as three 1st-level spells, a 2nd-level and a 1st-level spell, or a 3rd-level spell). A cantrip counts as one-half level for these purposes. You prepare and cast these spells normally.
- *Retain:* You retain any spell up to 3rd level that you had cast up to 1 round before you started casting the *mnemonic enhancer*. This restores the previously cast spell to your mind.

Material Components: A piece of string, and ink consisting of squid secretion with black dragon's blood.

Focus: An ivory plaque of at least 50 gp value.

Rary's Telepathic Bond

Divination
Level: Sor/Wiz 5
Components: V, S, M
Casting Time: 1 action
Range: Close (25 ft. + 5 ft./2 levels)
Targets: One creature/three levels, no two of which can be more than 30 ft. apart
Duration: 10 minutes/level
Saving Throw: None
Spell Resistance: No

You forge a telepathic bond among creatures, each of which must have an Intelligence score of 6 or higher. Each creature included in the link is linked to all the others. The bond can be established only among willing subjects, which therefore receive no saving throw or SR. The creatures can communicate telepathically through the bond regardless of language. No special power or influence is established as a result of the bond. Once the bond is formed, it works over any distance (although not from one plane to another).

A *wish* spell can make a *Rary's telepathic bond* permanent, but it can bond only two people per *wish*.

Material Components: A piece of eggshell from two different species of creature.

Ray of Enfeeblement

Necromancy
Level: Sor/Wiz 1
Components: V, S
Casting Time: 1 action
Range: Close (25 ft. + 5 ft./2 levels)
Effect: Ray
Duration: 1 minute/level

Saving Throw: Fortitude negates
Spell Resistance: Yes

A coruscating ray springs from your hand. You must succeed at a ranged touch attack to strike a target. The subject suffers a −1d6 enhancement penalty to Strength, with an additional −1 per two caster levels (maximum additional penalty of −5). The subject's Strength score cannot drop below 1.

Ray of Frost
Conjuration (Creation) [Cold]
Level: Sor/Wiz 0
Components: V, S
Casting Time: 1 action
Range: Close (25 ft. + 5 ft./2 levels)
Effect: Ray
Duration: Instantaneous
Saving Throw: None
Spell Resistance: Yes

A ray of freezing air and ice projects from your pointing finger. You must succeed at a ranged touch attack with the ray to deal damage to a target. The ray deals 1d3 points of cold damage.

Read Magic
Universal
Level: Brd 0, Clr 0, Drd 0, Pal 1, Rgr 1, Sor/Wiz 0
Components: V, S, F
Casting Time: 1 action
Range: Personal
Target: You
Duration: 10 minutes/level

By means of *read magic*, you can read magical inscriptions on objects—books, scrolls, weapons, and the like—that would otherwise be unintelligible. This deciphering does not normally invoke the magic contained in the writing, although it may do so in the case of a cursed scroll. Furthermore, once the spell is cast and you have read the magical inscription, you are thereafter able to read that particular writing without recourse to the use of *read magic*. You can read at the rate of one page (250 words) per minute. The spell allows you to identify a *glyph of warding* with a successful Spellcraft check against DC 13 or a *symbol* with a successful Spellcraft check against DC 19.

Focus: A clear crystal or mineral prism.

Reduce
Transmutation
Level: Sor/Wiz 1
Components: V, S, M
Casting Time: 1 action
Range: Close (25 ft. + 5 ft./2 levels)
Target: One creature or object of up to 10 cu. ft./caster level
Duration: 1 minute/level

Saving Throw: Fortitude negates (object)
Spell Resistance: Yes (object)

This spell causes instant diminution of a creature or object, decreasing its size and weight. Its height shrinks by up to 10% per caster level, to a maximum reduction of 50%. The reduced weight is proportional to the cube of the new height, as follows:

Height Decrease	Weight Decrease
−10% (× 0.9)	−30% (× 0.7)
−20% (× 0.8)	−50% (× 0.5)
−30% (× 0.7)	−60% (× 0.4)
−40% (× 0.6)	−80% (× 0.2)
−50% (× 0.5)	−90% (× 0.1)

All equipment worn or carried by a creature is reduced by the spell. Magical properties are not decreased by this spell—a smaller +3 *sword* is still +3, a smaller wand is still capable of its normal functions, and a smaller dose of a potion still has its normal effects. Weight, mass, and strength are affected, though. Thus, a hurled stone would have less mass (and cause less damage),

chains would be easier to burst, a rope made thinner and easier to sever, and so on. A creature's hit points, Armor Class, and attack rolls do not change, but Strength decreases with size. For every 10% of reduction, a creature's Strength score suffers an enlargement penalty of −1, to a minimum score of 1.

A shrinking object may damage weaker materials affixed to it, but a reduced object shrinks only as long as the object itself is not damaged.

Multiple magical effects that reduce size do not stack.

Reduce counters and dispels *enlarge*.

Material Component: A pinch of powdered iron.

Refuge
Transmutation [Teleportation]
Level: Clr 7, Sor/Wiz 9
Components: V, S, M
Casting Time: 1 action
Range: Touch
Target: Object touched
Duration: Permanent until discharged
Saving Throw: None
Spell Resistance: No

You create powerful magic in some specially prepared object—a statuette, a jeweled rod, a gem, etc. This object contains the power to instantaneously transport its possessor across any distance within the same plane to your abode. Once the item is transmuted, you must give it

A wizard uses a ray of frost.

willingly to an individual and at the same time inform him of a command word to be spoken when the item is to be used. To make use of the item, the subject speaks the command word at the same time that he rends or breaks the item (a standard action). When this is done, the individual and all that he is wearing and carrying (up to a maximum of 50 lb./level) are instantaneously transported to your abode. No other creatures are affected (aside from a familiar that is touching the subject).

You can alter the spell when casting it so that it transports you to within 10 feet of the possessor of the item when it is broken and the command word spoken. You will have a general idea of the location and situation of the item possessor at the time the *refuge* spell is discharged, but once deciding to alter the spell in this fashion you have no choice whether or not to be transported.

Material Component: The specially prepared object, whose construction includes gems worth 1,500 gp.

Regenerate

Conjuration (Healing)
Level: Clr 7, Healing 7
Components: V, S, DF
Casting Time: 3 full rounds
Range: Touch
Target: Living creature touched
Duration: Instantaneous
Saving Throw: Fortitude negates (harmless)
Spell Resistance: Yes (harmless)

The subject's severed body members (fingers, toes, hands, feet, arms, legs, tails, or even heads of multiheaded creatures), broken bones, and ruined organs grow back. After the spell is cast, the physical regeneration is complete in 1 round if the severed members are present and touching the creature. It takes 2d10 rounds otherwise. *Regenerate* also cures 1d8 points of damage +1 point per caster level (up to +20).

Reincarnate

Transmutation
Level: Drd 4
Components: V, S, DF
Casting Time: 10 minutes
Range: Touch
Target: Dead creature touched
Duration: Instantaneous
Saving Throw: None (see text)
Spell Resistance: Yes (harmless)

With this spell, you bring back a dead creature in another body, provided death occurred no more than 1 week before the casting of the spell and the subject's soul is free and willing to

return (see Bringing Back the Dead, page 153). If the subject's soul is not willing to return, the spell does not work; therefore, subjects who want to return receive no saving throw. Since the dead creature is returning in a new body, all physical ills and afflictions are repaired. The magic of the spell creates an entirely new young adult body for the soul to inhabit from the natural elements at hand. This process requires 1 hour to complete. When the body is ready, the subject is reincarnated.

A character reincarnated recalls the majority of his former life and form. He retains his Intelligence, Wisdom, and Charisma scores, as well as any class abilities or skills he formerly possessed. His class, base attack bonus, base save bonuses, and hit points are unchanged. Strength, Dexterity, and Constitution scores depend partly on his new body. First eliminate the character's racial adjustments (since he is no longer of his previous race) and then apply the adjustments found below. The character's level is reduced by 1. (If the character was 1st level, his new Constitution score is reduced by 1.)

It's quite possible for the change in the character's ability scores to make it difficult for him to pursue his previous character class. If this happens, the character is well advised to become a multiclass character.

The new incarnation is determined on the following table or by DM choice.

d%	Incarnation	Str	Dex	Con
01–03	Badger	+4	+8	+4
04–09	Bear, black	+8	+2	+4
10–13	Bear, brown	+15	+2	+8
14–17	Boar	+4	0	+6
18–25	Centaur	+8	+4	+4
26–28	Dryad	0	+4	0
29–32	Eagle	0	+4	+2
33–42	Elf	0	+2	–2
43–46	Gnome	–2	0	+2
47–48	Hawk	–4	+6	0
49–58	Halfling	–2	+2	0
59–78	Human	0	0	0
79–80	Leopard	+6	+8	+4
81–82	Owl	–4	+6	0
83–85	Pixie	–4	+8	0
86–88	Satyr	0	+2	+2
89–90	Sprite	–4	+6	0
91–96	Wolf	+2	+4	+4
97–99	Wolverine	+10	+8	+8
100	Other	?	?	?
	(DM's choice)			

Some bodies may make it impossible for the reincarnated character to use some of his class abilities. For example, a caster reincarnated as a hawk can't cast spells with somatic components because he doesn't have hands. The reincarnated

character does gain any powers or abilities associated with his new form, including forms of movement and speeds, natural armor, natural attacks, etc. Refer to the *Monster Manual* for exact figures. A humanoid reincarnated into an animal body can speak the languages it formerly knew and is a magical beast.

A *wish* spell can restore a reincarnated character to his original form.

Remove Blindness/Deafness

Conjuration (Healing)
Level: Clr 3, Pal 3
Components: V, S
Casting Time: 1 action
Range: Touch
Target: Creature touched
Duration: Instantaneous
Saving Throw: Fortitude negates (harmless)
Spell Resistance: Yes (harmless)

Remove blindness/deafness cures blindness or deafness (caster's choice), whether the effect is normal or magical. The spell does not restore ears or eyes that have been lost, but it repairs them if they are damaged.

Remove blindness/deafness counters and dispels *blindness/deafness*.

Remove Curse

Abjuration
Level: Brd 3, Clr 3, Sor/Wiz 4
Components: V, S
Casting Time: 1 action
Range: Touch
Target: Creature or item touched
Duration: Instantaneous
Saving Throw: Will negates (harmless)
Spell Resistance: Yes (harmless)

Remove curse instantaneously removes all curses on an object or a person. *Remove curse* does not remove the curse from a cursed shield, weapon, or suit of armor, although the spell typically enables the person afflicted with any such cursed item to remove and get rid of it. Certain special curses may not be countered by this spell or may be countered only by a caster of a certain level or higher.

Remove curse counters and dispels *bestow curse*.

Remove Disease

Conjuration (Healing)
Level: Brd 3, Clr 3, Drd 3, Rgr 3
Components: V, S
Casting Time: 1 action
Range: Touch
Target: Creature touched
Duration: Instantaneous
Saving Throw: Fortitude negates (harmless)
Spell Resistance: Yes (harmless)

Remove disease cures all diseases that the subject is suffering from. The spell also kills parasites, including green slime, rot grubs, and others.

Note: Since the spell's duration is instantaneous, it does not prevent reinfection after a new exposure to the same disease at a later date.

Remove Fear
Abjuration
Level: Clr 1
Components: V, S
Casting Time: 1 action
Range: Close (25 ft. + 5 ft./2 levels)
Targets: One creature plus one additional creature/four levels, no two of which can be more than 30 ft. apart
Duration: 10 minutes and see text
Saving Throw: Will negates (harmless)
Spell Resistance: Yes (harmless)

You instill courage in the subject, granting the creature a +4 morale bonus against *fear* effects for 10 minutes. If the subject is suffering from a *fear* effect when receiving the spell, it gets a new save with a +4 morale bonus.

Remove fear counters and dispels *cause fear*.

Remove Paralysis
Conjuration (Healing)
Level: Clr 2, Pal 2
Components: V, S
Casting Time: 1 action
Range: Close (25 ft. + 5 ft./2 levels)
Targets: Up to four creatures, no two of which can be more than 30 ft. apart
Duration: Instantaneous
Saving Throw: Will negates (harmless)
Spell Resistance: Yes (harmless)

You can free one or more creatures from the effects of any temporary paralysis or from related magic, including a ghoul's touch, a *hold* spell, or a *slow* spell. If the spell is cast on one creature, the paralysis is negated. If cast on two creatures, each receives another save against the effect that afflicts it with a +4 resistance bonus. If cast on three or four creatures, each receives another save with a +2 resistance bonus.

The spell does not restore ability scores reduced by penalties, damage, or loss.

Repel Metal or Stone
Abjuration
Level: Drd 8
Components: V, S
Casting Time: 1 action
Range: Medium (100 ft. + 10 ft./level)
Area: Path 120 ft. wide and 10 ft. high, emanating from you
Duration: 1 round/level
Saving Throw: None
Spell Resistance: No

Like *repel wood*, this spell creates waves of invisible and intangible energy that roll forth from you. All metal or stone objects in the path of the spell are pushed away from you to the limit of the range. Fixed metal or stone objects larger than 3 inches in diameter and loose objects weighing more than 500 pounds are not affected. Anything else, including animated objects, small boulders, and creatures in metal armor, moves back. Fixed objects 3 inches in diameter or smaller bend or break, and the pieces move with the wave of energy. Objects affected by the spell are repelled at the rate of 40 feet per round.

Objects such as metal armor, swords, etc. are pushed back, dragging their bearers with them. Even magic items with metal components are repelled, although an *antimagic field* blocks the effects.

The waves of energy continue to sweep down the set path for the spell's duration. After casting the spell, the path is set, and you can then do other things or go elsewhere without affecting the spell's power.

Repel Vermin
Abjuration
Level: Animal 4, Clr 4, Drd 4
Components: V, S, DF
Casting Time: 1 action
Range: 10 ft.
Area: 10-ft.-radius emanation centered on you
Duration: 10 minutes/level
Saving Throw: None or Will negates (see text)
Spell Resistance: Yes

An invisible barrier holds back vermin. A vermin with less than one-third your level in HD cannot penetrate the barrier. A vermin with at least one-third your level in HD can penetrate the barrier if it succeeds at a Will save. Even so, crossing the barrier deals the vermin 2d6 points of damage, and pressing against the barrier causes pain, which deters less aggressive vermin.

Repel Wood
Transmutation
Level: Drd 6, Plant 6
Components: V, S
Casting Time: 1 action
Range: Medium (100 ft. + 10 ft./level)
Area: Path 120 ft. wide and 10 ft. high, emanating from you
Duration: 1 minute/level
Saving Throw: None
Spell Resistance: No

Waves of energy roll forth from you, moving in the direction that you determine, causing all wooden objects in the path of the spell to be pushed away from you to the limit of the range. Wooden objects larger than 3 inches in diameter that are fixed firmly are not affected, but loose objects (barrels, siege towers, etc.) are. Objects 3 inches in diameter or smaller that are fixed in place splinter and break, and the pieces move with the wave of energy. Objects affected by the spell are repelled at the rate of 40 feet per round.

Objects such as wooden shields, spears, wooden weapon shafts and hafts, and arrows and bolts are pushed back, dragging those carrying them with them. (A creature being dragged by an item it is carrying can let go. A creature being dragged by a shield can unlimber it as a move-equivalent action.) If a spear is planted (set) to prevent this forced movement, it splinters. Even magic items with wooden sections are repelled, although an *antimagic field* blocks the effects.

The waves of energy continue to sweep down the set path for the spell's duration. After casting the spell, the path is set, and you can then do other things or go elsewhere without affecting the spell's power.

Repulsion
Abjuration
Level: Brd 6, Clr 7, Protection 7, Sor/Wiz 6
Components: V, S, F/DF
Casting Time: 1 action
Range: Up to 10 ft./level
Area: Up to 10-ft.-radius/level emanation centered on you
Duration: 1 round/level (D)
Saving Throw: Will negates
Spell Resistance: Yes

An invisible, mobile field surrounds you and prevents creatures from approaching you. You decide how big the field is at the time of casting (up to the limit your level allows). Creatures within or entering the field must attempt saves. If they fail, they become unable to move toward you for the duration of the spell. Repelled creatures' actions are not otherwise restricted. They can fight other creatures and can cast spells and attack you with ranged weapons. If you move closer to an affected creature, nothing happens. (The creature is not forced back.) The creature is free to make melee attacks against you if you come within reach. If a repelled creature moves away from you and then tries to turn back toward you, it cannot move any closer if it is still within the spell's area.

Arcane Focus: A pair of small iron bars attached to two small canine statuettes, one black and one white.

Resistance
Abjuration
Level: Brd 0, Clr 0, Drd 0, Pal 1, Sor/Wiz 0
Components: V, S, M/DF

Casting Time: 1 action
Range: Touch
Target: Creature touched
Duration: 1 minute
Saving Throw: Will negates (harmless)
Spell Resistance: Yes (harmless)

You imbue the subject with magical energy that protects her from harm, granting her a +1 resistance bonus on saves.

Arcane Material Component: A miniature cloak.

Resist Elements

Abjuration
Level: Clr 2, Drd 2, Fire 3, Pal 2, Rgr 1, Sor/Wiz 2
Components: V, S, DF
Casting Time: 1 action
Duration: 1 minute/level

As *endure elements*, except *resist elements* absorbs the first 12 points of damage each round.

Note: *Resist elements* overlaps (and does not stack with) *endure elements* and *protection from elements*. If a character is warded by *protection from elements* and one or both of the other spells, the *protection* spell absorbs damage until it is exhausted. If a character is warded by *resist elements* and *endure elements* at the same time, the *resist* spell absorbs damage but the *endure* spell does not.

Restoration

Conjuration (Healing)
Level: Clr 4
Components: V, S, M

As *lesser restoration*, except the spell also dispels negative energy levels and restores one experience level to a creature who has had a level drained. The drained level is restored only if the time since the creature lost the level is equal to or less than 1 day per caster level. Thus, if a 10th-level character has been struck by a wight and drained to 9th level, *restoration* brings the character up to exactly the minimum number of experience points necessary to restore her to 10th level (45,000 XP), gaining her an additional HD and level functions accordingly.

Restoration cures all temporary ability damage, and it restores all points permanently drained from a single ability score (caster's choice if more than one is drained).

Restoration does not restore levels or Constitution points lost due to death.

Material Component: Diamond dust worth 100 gp that is sprinkled over the target.

Resurrection

Conjuration (Healing)
Level: Clr 7
Casting Time: 10 minutes

As *raise dead*, except you are able to restore life and complete strength to any deceased creature. The condition of the remains is not a factor. So long as some small portion of the creature's body still exists, it can be resurrected, but the portion receiving the spell must have been part of the creature's body at the time of death. (The remains of a creature hit by a *disintegrate* spell count as a small portion of its body.) The creature can have been dead no longer than 10 years per caster level.

Upon completion of the spell, the creature is immediately restored to full hit points, vigor, and health, with no loss of prepared spells. However, the subject loses one level (or 1 point of Constitution if the subject was 1st level).

You can revive someone killed by a death effect or someone who has been turned into an undead creature and then destroyed. You cannot revive someone who has died of old age.

Material Components: A sprinkle of holy water and a diamond worth at least 500 gp.

Reverse Gravity

Transmutation
Level: Drd 8, Sor/Wiz 7
Components: V, S, M/DF
Casting Time: 1 action
Range: Medium (100 ft. + 10 ft./level)
Area: Up to one 10-ft. cube/2 levels (S)
Duration: 1 round/level (D)
Saving Throw: None (see text)
Spell Resistance: No

This spell reverses gravity in the spell's area, causing all unattached objects and creatures within it to fall upward and reach the top of the area in 1 round. If some solid object (such as a ceiling) is encountered in this fall, falling objects and creatures strike it in the same manner as they would during a normal downward fall. If an object or creature reaches the top of the area without striking anything, it remains there, oscillating slightly, until the spell ends. At the end of the spell duration, affected objects and creatures fall downward.

Provided there's something for them to hold onto, creatures caught in the area can attempt Reflex saves to secure themselves when the spell strikes. Creatures who can fly or levitate can keep themselves from falling.

Arcane Material Components: A lodestone and iron filings.

Righteous Might

Transmutation
Level: Clr 5, Strength 5
Components: V, S, DF
Casting Time: 1 action
Range: Personal
Target: You
Duration: 1 round/level

You grow to double your height, and your gear grows proportionally. This increase has the following effects:

- You gain a +4 enlargement bonus to Strength.
- Your size becomes one step larger. That alters your size modifier for AC and attacks (reducing each by 1 if you were originally Tiny, Small, Medium-size, or Large).
- Mass increases by a factor of eight.
- Weapons increase in size one step, increasing their damage as shown below.

Old Damage	New Damage
1d2	1d3
1d3	1d4
1d4	1d6
1d6	1d8
1d8	2d6
1d10	2d6
1d12	2d8

For example, Jozan, a human, casts *righteous might*. He becomes Large, loses 1 from his AC and base attack bonus, and gains +4 to his Strength score (from 12 to 16), for an additional +2 ability bonus on melee attacks and damage. Additionally, his morningstar is now Large, and it deals 2d6 points of damage instead of 1d8 (plus whatever magical bonuses may apply).

Magical properties of magic items that get bigger do not change.

Rope Trick

Transmutation
Level: Sor/Wiz 2
Components: V, S, M
Casting Time: 1 action
Range: Touch
Target: One touched piece of rope from 5 to 30 ft. long
Duration: 1 hour/level (D)
Saving Throw: None
Spell Resistance: No

When this spell is cast upon a piece of rope from 5 to 30 feet long, one end of the rope rises into the air until the whole rope hangs perpendicular, as if affixed at the upper end. The upper end is, in fact, fastened to an extradimensional space that is outside the multiverse of extradimensional spaces ("planes"). You and up to seven others can climb up the rope and disappear into this place of safety where no creature can find you. Climbing the rope counts as climbing a knotted rope, which requires a Climb check against DC 5 (see the skill description, page 64). The rope can be taken into the extradimensional space if fewer than eight persons have climbed it; otherwise, it simply stays hanging in the air. Pulling the rope free requires succeeding at a Strength check (DC 30).

Spells cannot be cast across the inter-dimensional interface, nor can area effects cross it. Those in the extradimensional space can see out of it as if a 3-foot-by-5-foot window were centered on the rope. Anything inside the extradimensional space drops out when the spell ends. The rope can be climbed by only one person at a time. The *rope trick* spell enables climbers to reach a normal place if they do not climb all the way to the extradimensional space.

Note: Creating an extradimensional space within or taking an extradimensional space into an existing extradimensional space is hazardous.

Material Components: Powdered corn extract and a twisted loop of parchment.

usting Grasp

Transmutation
Level: Drd 4
Components: V, S, DF
Casting Time: 1 action
Range: Touch
Target: One nonmagical ferrous object (or the volume of the object within 3 ft. of the touched point) or one ferrous creature
Duration: See text
Saving Throw: None
Spell Resistance: No

You corrode iron and iron alloys at a touch. Any iron or iron alloy item you touch becomes instantaneously rusted, pitted, and worthless, effectively destroyed. If the item is so large that it cannot fit within a 3-foot radius (a large iron door or a *wall of iron*), a 3-foot-radius volume of the metal is rusted and destroyed. Magical metal items are immune to this spell.

You may employ *rusting grasp* in combat with a successful melee touch attack. *Rusting grasp* used in this way instantaneously destroys 1d6 points of Armor Class gained from metal armor (up to the maximum amount of protection the armor offered) through corrosion. For example, full plate armor (AC +8) could be reduced to +7 or as low as +2 in protection, depending on the die roll.

Weapons in use by an opponent targeted by the spell are more difficult to grasp. You must succeed at a melee touch attack against the weapon. (See Strike a Weapon, page 136.) A metal weapon that is hit is instantaneously destroyed. Note: Striking at an opponent's weapon provokes an attack of opportunity. Also, you must touch the weapon and not the other way around.

Against ferrous creatures, *rusting grasp* instantaneously deals 3d6 points of damage +1 per caster level (maximum +15) per successful attack. The spell lasts for 1 round per level, and you can make one melee touch attack per round.

Sanctuary

Abjuration
Level: Clr 1, Protection 1
Components: V, S, DF
Casting Time: 1 action
Range: Touch
Target: Creature touched
Duration: 1 round/level
Saving Throw: Will negates
Spell Resistance: No

Any opponent attempting to strike or otherwise directly attack the warded creature, even with a targeted spell, must attempt a Will save. If the save succeeds, the opponent can attack normally and is unaffected by that casting of the spell. If the save fails, the opponent can't follow through with the attack, that part of the attacker's action is lost, and the attacker can't directly attack the warded creature for the duration of the spell. Those not attempting to attack the subject remain unaffected. This spell does not prevent the warded creature from being attacked or affected by area or effect spells (*fireball, summon monster IV*, etc.). While protected by this spell, the subject cannot attack without breaking the spell but may use nonattack spells or otherwise act. This allows a warded cleric to heal wounds, for example, or to *bless*, perform an *augury*, summon creatures, cast a *light* spell in the area, and so on.

Scare

Necromancy [Fear, Mind-Affecting]
Level: Brd 2, Sor/Wiz 2
Components: V, S, M
Casting Time: 1 action
Range: Medium (100 ft. + 10 ft./level)
Targets: All creatures within a 15-ft. radius
Duration: 1 round/level
Saving Throw: Will negates
Spell Resistance: Yes

As *cause fear*, except this spell causes all targeted creatures of less than 6 HD to become frightened.

Material Component: A bit of bone from an undead skeleton, zombie, ghoul, ghast, or mummy.

Screen

Illusion (Glamer)
Level: Sor/Wiz 8, Trickery 7
Components: V, S
Casting Time: 10 minutes
Range: Close (25 ft. + 5 ft./2 levels)
Area: 30-ft. cube/level (S)
Duration: 1 day
Saving Throw: None or Will disbelief (if interacted with) (see text)
Spell Resistance: No

This spell combines several elements to create a powerful protection from scrying and direct observation. When the spell is cast, you dictate what will and will not be observed in the spell's area. The illusion created must be stated in general terms. Thus, you could specify the illusion of yourself and another character playing chess for the duration of the spell, but you could not have the illusory chess players take a break, make dinner, and then resume their game. You could have a cross-roads appear quiet and empty even while an army is actually passing through the area. You could specify that no one be seen (including passing strangers), that your troops be undetected, or even that every fifth person or unit should be visible. Once the conditions are set, they cannot be changed.

Attempts to scry the area automatically detect the image stated by you with no save allowed. Sight and sound are appropriate to the illusion created. A band of people standing in a meadow could be concealed as an empty meadow with birds chirping, for instance.

Direct observation may allow a save (as per a normal illusion), if there is cause to disbelieve what is seen. Certainly onlookers in the area would become suspicious if the column of a marching army disappeared at one point to reappear at another. Even entering the area does not cancel the illusion or necessarily allow a save, assuming that hidden beings take care to stay out of the way of those affected by the illusion.

Scrying

Divination
Level: Brd 3, Clr 5, Drd 4, Sor/Wiz 4
Components: V, S, M/DF, F
Casting Time: 1 hour
Range: See text
Effect: Magical sensor
Duration: 1 minute/level
Saving Throw: None
Spell Resistance: No

You can see and hear some creature, who may be at any distance. You must succeed at a Scry check to do so. The difficulty of the task depends on how well you know the subject and what sort of physical connection (if any) you have to that creature. Furthermore, if the subject is on another plane, you get a –5 penalty on the Scry check.

Knowledge	DC
None*	20
Secondhand (you have heard of the subject)	15
Firsthand (you have met the subject)	10
Familiar (you know the subject well)	5

*You must have some sort of connection to a creature you have no knowledge of.

Connection	Scry Check Bonus
Likeness or picture	+5
Possession or garment	+8
Body part, lock of hair, nail clippings, etc.	+10

This spell creates a magical sensor located near the subject. Any creature with Intelligence 12 or higher can notice the sensor by making a Scry check (or an Intelligence check) against DC 20.

The following spells can be cast through a *scrying* spell: *comprehend languages, read magic, tongues,* and *darkvision*. The following spells have a 5% chance per caster level of operating correctly: *detect magic, detect chaos, detect evil, detect good, detect law,* and *message*.

Arcane Material Components: The eye of a hawk, an eagle, or even a roc, and nitric acid, copper, and zinc.

Wizard, Sorcerer, or Bard Focus: A mirror of finely wrought and highly polished silver costing not less than 1,000 gp. The mirror must be at least 2 feet by 4 feet.

Cleric Focus: A holy water font costing not less than 100 gp.

Druid Focus: A natural pool of water.

Sculpt Sound
Transmutation
Level: Brd 3
Components: V, S
Casting Time: 1 action
Range: Close (25 ft. + 5 ft./2 levels)
Targets: One creature or object/level, no two of which can be more than 30 ft. apart
Duration: 1 hour/level (D)
Saving Throw: Will negates (object)
Spell Resistance: Yes (object)

You change the sounds that creatures or objects make. You can create sounds where none exist (such as making trees sing), deaden sounds (such as making a party of adventurers silent), or transform sounds into other sounds (such as making a caster's voice sound like a pig snorting). All affected creatures or objects must be transmuted in the same way. Once the transmutation is made, you cannot change it.

You can change the qualities of sounds but cannot create words with which you are unfamiliar yourself. For instance, you can't change your voice so that it sounds as though you are giving the command word to activate a magic item unless you know that command word.

A spellcaster whose voice is changed dramatically (such as into that of the aforementioned snorting pig) is unable to cast spells with verbal components.

Searing Light
Evocation
Level: Clr 3, Sun 3
Components: V, S

Casting Time: 1 action
Range: Medium (100 ft. + 10 ft./level)
Effect: Ray
Duration: Instantaneous
Saving Throw: None
Spell Resistance: Yes

Focusing holy power like a ray of the sun, you project a blast of light from your open palm. You must succeed at a ranged touch attack to strike your target. A creature struck by this ray of light takes 1d8 points of damage per two caster levels (maximum 5d8). Undead creatures take 1d6 points of damage per caster level (maximum 10d6), and undead creatures particularly vulnerable to sunlight, such as vampires, take 1d8 points of damage per caster level (maximum 10d8). Constructs and inanimate objects take only 1d6 points of damage per two caster levels (maximum 5d6).

Secret Page
Transmutation
Level: Sor/Wiz 3
Components: V, S, M
Casting Time: 10 minutes
Range: Touch
Target: Page touched, up to 3 sq. ft. in size
Duration: Permanent
Saving Throw: None
Spell Resistance: No

Secret page alters the actual contents of a page so that they appear to be something entirely different. Thus, a map can be changed to become a treatise on burnishing ebony walking sticks. The text of a spell can be changed to show a ledger page or even another spell. *Explosive runes* or *sepia snake sigil* can be cast upon the *secret page*.

A *comprehend languages* spell alone cannot reveal the *secret page's* contents. You are able to reveal the original contents by speaking a special word, perusing the actual page, and then returning it to its *secret page* form at will. You can also remove the spell by double repetition of the special word. A *detect magic* spell reveals dim magic on the page in question but does not reveal its true contents. *True seeing* reveals the presence of the hidden material but does not reveal the contents unless cast in combination with *comprehend languages*. *Secret page* can be dispelled, and the hidden writings can be destroyed by means of an *erase* spell.

Material Components: Powdered herring scales and will-o'-wisp essence.

See Invisibility
Divination
Level: Brd 2, Sor/Wiz 2
Components: V, S, M
Casting Time: 1 action

Range: Medium (100 ft. + 10 ft./level)
Area: Cone
Duration: 10 minutes/level (D)
Saving Throw: None
Spell Resistance: No

You see any objects or beings that are invisible, as well as any that are astral or ethereal, as if they were normally visible.

The spell does not reveal the method used to obtain invisibility, though an astral traveler is easy to identify if he has a silver cord. It does not reveal illusions or enable you to see through opaque objects. It does not reveal creatures who are simply hiding, concealed, or otherwise hard to see.

Material Components: A pinch of talc and a small sprinkling of powdered silver.

Seeming
Illusion (Glamer)
Level: Sor/Wiz 5
Components: V, S
Casting Time: 1 action
Range: Close (25 ft. + 5 ft./2 levels)
Targets: One person/two levels, no two of which can be more than 30 ft. apart
Duration: 12 hours
Saving Throw: Will negates or Will disbelief (if interacted with)
Spell Resistance: Yes or No

As *change self*, except you can change the appearance of other people as well. Affected creatures resume their normal appearances if slain.

Unwilling targets can negate the spell's effect on them by making Will saves or with SR.

Sending
Evocation
Level: Clr 4, Sor/Wiz 5
Components: V, S, M/DF
Casting Time: 10 minutes
Range: See text
Target: One creature
Duration: 1 round (see text)
Saving Throw: None
Spell Resistance: No

You contact a particular creature with whom you are familiar and send a short message of twenty-five words or less to the subject. The subject recognizes you if it knows you. It can answer in like manner immediately. Creatures with Intelligence scores as low as 1 can understand the sending, though the subject's ability to react is limited normally by its Intelligence. Even if the sending is received, the subject is not obligated to act upon it in any manner.

If the creature in question is not on the same plane of existence as you are, there is a 5% chance that the sending does not arrive. (Local conditions on other planes may worsen this chance considerably, at the option of the DM.)

Arcane Material Component: A short piece of fine copper wire.

epia Snake Sigil

Conjuration (Creation) [Force]
Level: Brd 3, Sor/Wiz 3
Components: V, S, M
Casting Time: 10 minutes
Range: Touch
Target: One touched book or written work
Duration: Permanent or until discharged; until released or 1d4 days +1 day/level (see text)
Saving Throw: Reflex negates
Spell Resistance: No

When you cast *sepia snake sigil*, a small symbol appears in the text of one written work such as a book, scroll, or map. When this symbol is read, the sepia snake springs into being and strikes at the nearest living creature (but does not attack you). The target is entitled to a save to evade the snake's strike. If it succeeds, the sepia snake dissipates in a flash of brown light accompanied by a puff of dun-colored smoke and a loud noise. If the target fails its save, it is engulfed in a shimmering amber field of force and immobilized until released, either at your command or when 1d4 days +1 day per caster level have elapsed.

While trapped in the amber field of force, the subject does not age, breathe, grow hungry, sleep, or regain spells. He is preserved in a state of suspended animation, unaware of his surroundings. He can be damaged by outside forces (and perhaps even killed), since the field provides him with no protection against physical injury. However, if he is reduced to –1 to –9 hit points, he does not lose hit points or stabilize until the spell ends.

The hidden sigil cannot be detected by normal observation, and *detect magic* reveals only that the entire text is magical. A *dispel magic* can remove the sigil. An *erase* spell destroys the entire page of text. *Sepia snake sigil* can be cast in combination with

other spells that hide or garble text, such as *secret page*.

Material Components: 500 gp worth of powdered amber, a scale from any snake, and a pinch of mushroom spores.

Sequester

Abjuration
Level: Sor/Wiz 7
Components: V, S, M
Casting Time: 1 action
Range: Touch
Target: One creature or object (up to a 2-ft. cube/level) touched
Duration: 1 day/level (D)

A shadow conjured pegasus.

Saving Throw: Will negates (object)
Spell Resistance: Yes (object)

When cast, this spell not only prevents divination spells from working to detect or locate the creature or object affected by *sequester*, it also renders the affected creature or object invisible to any form of sight or seeing. Thus, *sequester* can mask a secret door, a treasure vault, etc. The spell does not prevent the subject from being discovered through tactile

means or through the use of devices (such as a *robe of eyes* or a *gem of seeing*). Living creatures (and even undead creatures) affected by *sequester* become comatose and are effectively in a state of suspended animation until the spell wears off or is dispelled.

Note: The Will save prevents a character from being sequestered. There is no save to see the sequestered creature or object or to detect it with a divination spell.

Material Components: A basilisk eyelash, gum arabic, and a dram of whitewash.

Shades

Illusion (Shadow)
Level: Sor/Wiz 6

As *shadow conjuration*, except that it mimics sorcerer and wizard conjuration spells of up through 5th level, and these conjurations are three-fifths (60%) as strong as the real things.

Shadow Conjuration

Illusion (Shadow)
Level: Sor/Wiz 4
Components: V, S
Casting Time: 1 action
Range: See text
Effect: See text
Duration: See text
Saving Throw: Will disbelief (if interacted with); varies (see text)
Spell Resistance: No (see text)

You use material from the Plane of Shadow to shape quasi-real illusions of one or more creatures, objects, or forces. *Shadow conjuration* can mimic any sorcerer or wizard conjuration spell of 3rd level or lower. Shadow conjurations are actually one-fifth (20%) as strong as the real things, though creatures who believe the shadow conjurations to be real are affected by them at full strength.

All those that interact with the conjured object, force, or creature can make Will saves to recognize its shadowy nature. Those who succeed do so.

Attack spells, such as *flame arrow*, have normal effects unless those affected succeed at Will saves. Each disbelieving creature takes only one-fifth damage from the attack. If the disbelieved attack has a special effect other than damage, that effect is one-fifth as strong (if applicable) or only 20% likely to occur. Mimicked spells allow the normal saves and SR.

Shadow objects or substances, such as *obscuring mists*, have normal effects except against those who disbelieve them. Against disbelievers, they are one-fifth strength or 20% likely to work. For instance, a shadow *obscuring mist* only provides one-half concealment at 25 feet, not 5 feet.

Shadow creatures have one-fifth the normal hit points (regardless of whether they're recognized as shadowy). They deal normal damage and have all normal abilities and weaknesses. Against a creature who recognizes them as shadowy, however, such a creature's damage is one-fifth normal, and all special abilities that do not produce normal damage (in hit points) are only 20% likely to work. (Roll for each use and each affected character separately.) Furthermore, the shadow creature's AC bonuses are one-fifth as large (so a +7 total bonus resulting in AC 17 would change to a +1 total bonus for a new AC of 11).

Those who succeed at their saves see the *shadow conjurations* as transparent images superimposed on vague, shadowy forms.

Shadow Evocation

Illusion (Shadow)
Level: Sor/Wiz 5
Components: V, S
Casting Time: 1 action
Range: See text
Effect: See text
Duration: See text
Saving Throw: Will disbelief (if interacted with)
Spell Resistance: Yes

You tap energy from the Plane of Shadow to cast a quasi-real, illusory version of a wizard or sorcerer evocation of 4th level or lower. (For a spell with more than one level, use the best one applicable to you.) For example, this spell can be *magic missile, fireball, lightning bolt,* or so on. If recognized as a *shadow evocation*, a damaging spell deals only one-fifth normal damage. Regardless of the result of the save to disbelieve, affected creatures are also allowed any save the spell being simulated allows, but set the save DC according to *shadow magic*'s level (5th) rather than the spell's normal level. Nondamaging effects (such as *web*'s ensnarement) have no effect when the shadow magic is recognized as mostly illusory.

Shadow Walk

Illusion (Shadow)
Level: Sor/Wiz 7
Components: V, S
Casting Time: 1 action
Range: Touch
Targets: Up to one touched creature/level
Duration: 1 hour/level (D)
Saving Throw: Will negates
Spell Resistance: Yes

To use the *shadow walk* spell, you must be in an area of heavy shadows. You and any creature you touch are then transported along a coiling path of shadow-stuff to the edge of the Material Plane where it borders the Plane of Shadow. The effect is largely illusory, but the path is quasi-real. You can take more than one creature along with you (subject to your level limit), but all must be touching each other.

In the region of shadow, you can move at a rate of up to seven miles every 10 minutes, moving normally on the borders of the Plane of Shadow but much more rapidly relative to the Material Plane. Thus, a character can use this spell to travel rapidly by stepping onto the Plane of Shadow, moving the desired distance, and then stepping back onto the Material Plane. You know where you will come out on the Material Plane.

Shadow walk can also be used to travel to other planes that border on the Plane of Shadow, but this requires the potentially perilous transit of the Plane of Shadow to arrive at a border with another plane of reality. The transit of the Plane of Shadow requires 1d4 hours.

Any creatures touched by you when *shadow walk* is cast also make the transition to the borders of the Plane of Shadow. They may opt to follow you, wander off through the plane, or stumble back into the Material Plane (50% chance for either of the latter results if they are lost or abandoned by you). Creatures unwilling to accompany you into the Plane of Shadow receive a Will saving throw, negating the effect if successful.

Shambler

Conjuration (Creation)
Level: Drd 9, Plant 9
Components: V, S
Casting Time: 1 action
Range: Medium (100 ft. + 10 ft./level)
Effect: Three or more shambling mounds, no two of which can be more than 30 ft. apart (see text)
Duration: Seven days or seven months (D) (see text)
Saving Throw: None
Spell Resistance: No

Shambler creates 1d4+2 shambling mounds of 11 HD. (See the *Monster Manual* for details about shambling mounds.) The creatures willingly aid you in combat or battle, perform a specific mission, or serve as bodyguards. The creatures remain with you for seven days unless you dismiss them. If the shamblers are created only for guard duty, however, the duration of the spell is seven months. In this case, the shamblers can only be ordered to guard a specific site or location. Shamblers

summoned to guard duty cannot move outside the spell's range, which is measured from the point where each first appeared.

The shamblers have resistance to fire as normal shambling mounds do only if the terrain is rainy, marshy, or damp.

Shapechange

Transmutation
Level: Animal 9, Drd 9, Sor/Wiz 9
Components: V, S, F
Casting Time: 1 action
Range: Personal
Target: You
Duration: 10 minutes/level

As *polymorph other*, except this spell enables you to assume the form of any single creature of less than deity status (including unique dragon types, or the like) or any single object. The assumed form can be no smaller than a flea and no larger than 200 feet in its largest dimension. Unlike *polymorph other*, this spell allows incorporeal forms to be assumed.

Your new form works like a *polymorph other* form. You still do not gain the supernatural or spell-like abilities of your new form, though you do gain its extraordinary abilities while keeping your own. You also gain the type of the new form (for example, "dragon" or "magical beast") in place of your own. The new form does not disorient you. Parts of your body or pieces of equipment that are separated from you do not revert to their original forms. Thus, a new form's poison bite is effective.

You can become just about anything you are familiar with. You can change form once each round as a free action. The change takes place either immediately before your regular action or immediately after it, but not during the action. For example, you are in combat and assume the form of a will-o'-wisp. When this form is no longer useful, you change into a stone golem and walk away. When pursued, you change into a flea, which hides on a horse until it can hop off. From there, you can become a dragon, an ant, or just about anything you are familiar with.

If you use this spell to create a disguise, you get +10 on your Disguise check.

Focus: A jade circlet worth no less than 1,500 gp, which you must place on your head when casting the spell. (The focus melds into your new form when you change shape.)

Shatter

Evocation [Sonic]
Level: Brd 2, Chaos 2, Clr 2, Destruction 2, Sor/Wiz 2
Components: V, S, M/DF
Casting Time: 1 action

Range: Close (25 ft. + 5 ft./2 levels)
Area or Target: 3-ft.-radius spread; or one solid object or one crystalline creature
Duration: Instantaneous
Saving Throw: Will negates (object); Will negates (object) or Fortitude half (see text)
Spell Resistance: Yes (object)

Shatter creates a loud, ringing noise that shatters brittle, nonmagical objects; sunders a single solid, nonmagical object; or damages a crystalline creature.

Used as an area attack, *shatter* destroys nonmagical objects of crystal, glass, ceramic, or porcelain, such as vials, bottles, flasks, jugs, windows, mirrors, and so forth. All such objects within a 3-foot radius of the point of origin are smashed into dozens of pieces by the spell. Objects weighing more than 1 pound per your level are not affected, but all other objects of the appropriate composition are shattered.

Alternatively, you can target *shatter* against a single solid object, regardless of composition, weighing up to 10 pounds per caster level.

Targeted against a crystalline creature (of any weight), *shatter* deals 1d6 points of damage per caster level (maximum 10d6), with a Fortitude save for half damage.

Arcane Material Component: A chip of mica.

Shield

Abjuration [Force]
Level: Sor/Wiz 1
Components: V, S
Casting Time: 1 action
Range: Personal
Target: You
Duration: 1 minute/level (D)

Shield creates an invisible, mobile disk of force that hovers in front of you. It negates *magic missile* attacks directed at you. The disk also intercepts attacks, providing three-quarters cover (+7 AC and +3 on Reflex saves against attacks that affect an area). The disk moves out of the way when you attack, so it does not provide cover to opponents. The disk protects you only against *magic missiles* and attacks from one direction. You designate half the battlefield (with yourself on the dividing line) as being blocked by the shield. The other half is not. You can change the defensive direction of the *shield* (that is, rotate the dividing line) once as a free action on each of your turns.

Shield of Faith

Abjuration
Level: Clr 1
Components: V, S, M
Casting Time: 1 action

Range: Touch
Target: Creature touched
Duration: 1 minute/level
Saving Throw: Will negates (harmless)
Spell Resistance: Yes (harmless)

This spell creates a shimmering, magical field around the touched creature that averts attacks. The spell grants the subject a +2 deflection bonus, with an additional +1 to the bonus for every six levels you have (maximum +5 deflection bonus).

Material Component: A small parchment with a bit of holy text written upon it.

Shield of Law

Abjuration [Lawful]
Level: Clr 8, Law 8
Components: V, S, F
Casting Time: 1 action
Range: 20 ft.
Targets: One creature/level in a 20-ft.-radius burst centered on you
Duration: 1 round/level (D)
Saving Throw: See text
Spell Resistance: Yes (harmless)

A dim, blue glow surrounds the subjects, protecting them from attacks, granting them resistance to spells cast by chaotic creatures, and *slowing* chaotic creatures when they strike the subjects. This abjuration has four effects:

First, the warded creatures gain a +4 deflection bonus to AC and a +4 resistance bonus to saves. Unlike *protection from chaos*, this benefit applies against all attacks, not just against attacks by chaotic creatures.

Second, the warded creatures gain SR 25 against chaotic spells and spells cast by chaotic creatures.

Third, the abjuration blocks possession and mental influence, just as *protection from chaos* does.

Finally, if a chaotic creature succeeds at a melee attack against a warded creature, the attacker is *slowed* (Will save negates, as the *slow* spell, but against *shield of law's* save DC).

Focus: A tiny reliquary containing some sacred relic, such as a scrap of parchment from a lawful text. The reliquary costs at least 500 gp.

Shield Other

Abjuration
Level: Clr 2, Pal 2, Protection 2
Components: V, S, F
Casting Time: 1 action
Range: Close (25 ft. + 5 ft./2 levels)
Target: One creature
Duration: 1 hour/level (D)
Saving Throw: Will negates (harmless)
Spell Resistance: Yes (harmless)

This spell wards the subject and creates a mystic connection between you and the subject so that some of the subject's wounds are transferred to you. The subject gains a +1 deflection bonus to AC and a +1 resistance bonus to saves. Additionally, the subject takes only half damage from all wounds and attacks (including those inflicted by special abilities) that deal it hit point damage. The amount of damage not taken by the warded creature is taken by you. Forms of harm that do not involve hit points, such as *charm* effects, temporary ability damage, level draining, and *disintegration*, are not affected. If the subject suffers a reduction of hit points from a lowered Constitution score, the reduction is not split with you because it is not hit point damage. When the spell ends, subsequent damage is no longer divided between the subject and you, but damage already split is not reassigned to the subject.

If you and the subject of the spell move out of range of each other, the spell ends.

Focus: A pair of platinum rings (worth at least 50 gp each) worn by both you and the warded creature.

Shillelagh

Transmutation
Level: Drd 1
Components: V, S, DF
Casting Time: 1 action
Range: Touch
Target: One touched nonmagical oak club or quarterstaff
Duration: 1 minute/level
Saving Throw: Will negates (object)
Spell Resistance: Yes (object)

Your own oak cudgel or unshod quarterstaff becomes a weapon with a +1 enhancement bonus to attack and damage rolls that deals 1d10 points of damage (+1 point for the enhancement bonus) when you wield it. If you do not wield it, it behaves as if unaffected by this spell.

Shocking Grasp

Transmutation [Electricity]
Level: Sor/Wiz 1
Components: V, S
Casting Time: 1 action
Range: Touch
Target: Creature or object touched
Duration: Until discharged
Saving Throw: None
Spell Resistance: Yes (object)

This spell imbues your hand with a powerful electrical charge that you can use to damage an opponent. Your successful melee touch attack deals 1d8 points of electrical damage +1 point per caster level (maximum +20). When delivering the jolt, you gain a +3 attack bonus if the opponent is wearing metal armor (or made out of metal, carrying a lot of metal, etc.).

Shout

Evocation [Sonic]
Level: Brd 4, Sor/Wiz 4
Components: V
Casting Time: 1 action
Range: Close (25 ft. + 5 ft./2 levels)
Area: Cone
Duration: Instantaneous
Saving Throw: Fortitude partial (see text) (object)
Spell Resistance: Yes (object)

You emit an ear-splitting yell that deafens and damages creatures in its path. Any creature within the area is deafened for 2d6 rounds and takes 2d6 points of damage. A successful save negates the deafness and reduces the damage by half. Any exposed brittle or crystalline object or crystalline creature takes 1d6 points of damage per caster level (maximum 15d6). Crystalline creatures are allowed Fortitude saves to reduce the damage by half, and creatures holding fragile objects can negate damage to them with successful Reflex saves.

A deaf character, in addition to the obvious effects, suffers a –4 penalty on initiative and a 20% chance to miscast and lose any spell with a verbal (V) component that he tries to cast.

The *shout* spell cannot penetrate the spell *silence*.

Shrink Item

Transmutation
Level: Sor/Wiz 3
Components: V, S
Casting Time: 1 action
Range: Touch
Target: One touched object of up to 2 cu. ft./level
Duration: 1 day/level (see text)
Saving Throw: Will negates (object)
Spell Resistance: Yes (object)

You are able to shrink one nonmagical item (if it is within the size limit) to one-twelfth of its normal size in each dimension (to about 1/2,000th the original volume and mass). Optionally, you can also change its now-shrunken composition to a clothlike one. Objects changed by a *shrink item* spell can be returned to normal composition and size merely by tossing them onto any solid surface or by a word of command from the original caster. Even a burning fire and its fuel can be shrunk by this spell. Restoring the shrunken object to its normal size and composition ends the spell.

If *shrink item* is made permanent (see the *permanency* spell), the affected object can be shrunk and expanded an indefinite number of times, but only by the original caster.

Silence

Illusion (Glamer)
Level: Brd 2, Clr 2
Components: V, S
Casting Time: 1 action
Range: Long (400 ft. + 40 ft./level)
Area: 15-ft.-radius emanation centered on a creature, object, or point in space
Duration: 1 minute/level
Saving Throw: Will negates or none (object)
Spell Resistance: Yes or no (object)

Upon the casting of this spell, complete silence prevails in the affected area. All sound is stopped: Conversation is impossible, spells with verbal components cannot be cast, and no noise whatsoever issues from, enters, or passes through the area. The spell can be cast on a point in space, but the effect is stationary unless cast on a mobile object. The spell can be centered on a creature, and the effect then radiates from the creature and moves as it moves. An unwilling creature can attempt a Will save to negate the spell and can use SR, if any. Items in a creature's possession or magic items that emit sound receive saves and SR, and unattended objects and points in space do not. This spell provides a defense against sonic or language-based attacks, such as *command*, harpy song, a *horn of blasting*, etc.

Silent Image

Illusion (Figment)
Level: Brd 1, Sor/Wiz 1
Components: V, S, F
Casting Time: 1 action
Range: Long (400 ft. + 40 ft./level)
Effect: Visual figment that cannot extend beyond four 10-ft. cubes + one 10-ft. cube/level (S)
Duration: Concentration
Saving Throw: Will disbelief (if interacted with)
Spell Resistance: No

This spell creates the visual illusion of an object, creature, or force, as visualized by you. The illusion does not create sound, smell, texture, or temperature. You can move the image within the limits of the size of the effect.

Focus: A bit of fleece.

Simulacrum

Illusion (Shadow)
Level: Sor/Wiz 7
Components: V, S, M, XP
Casting Time: 12 hours
Range: Touch
Effect: One duplicate creature
Duration: Instantaneous
Saving Throw: None
Spell Resistance: No

Simulacrum creates an illusory duplicate of any creature. The duplicate creature is partially real and formed from ice or snow. The duplicate appears to be exactly the same as the original, but there are differences: The simulacrum has only 51% to 60% (50%+1d10%) of the hit points, knowledge (including level, skills, and speech), and personality of the real creature. Creatures familiar with the original might detect the ruse with a successful Spot check. You must make a Disguise check when you cast the spell to determine how good the likeness is.

At all times the simulacrum remains under your absolute command. No special telepathic link exists, so command must be exercised in some other manner. The simulacrum has no ability to become more powerful. It cannot increase its level or abilities. If destroyed, it reverts to snow and melts instantly into nothingness. A complex process requiring at least 1 day, 100 gp per hit point, and a fully equipped magical laboratory can repair damage to the simulacrum.

Material Component: The spell is cast over the rough snow or ice form, and some piece of the creature to be duplicated (hair, nail, etc.) must be placed inside the snow or ice. Additionally, the spell requires powdered ruby worth 100 gp.

XP Cost: 1,000 XP.

Slay Living

Necromancy [Death]
Level: Clr 5, Death 5
Components: V, S
Casting Time: 1 action
Range: Touch
Target: Living creature touched
Duration: Instantaneous
Saving Throw: Fortitude partial
Spell Resistance: Yes

You can slay any one living creature. You must succeed at a melee touch attack to touch the subject, and the subject can avoid death with a successful Fortitude save. If she succeeds, she instead takes 3d6 points of damage +1 point per caster level. (Of course, the subject might die from damage even if she succeeds at her save.)

Sleep

Enchantment (Compulsion) [Mind-Affecting]
Level: Brd 1, Rgr 2, Sor/Wiz 1
Components: V, S, M/DF
Casting Time: 1 action
Range: Medium (100 ft. + 10 ft./level)
Area: Several living creatures within a 15-ft.-radius burst
Duration: 1 minute/level
Saving Throw: Will negates
Spell Resistance: Yes

A *sleep* spell causes a comatose slumber to come upon one or more creatures. Roll 2d4 to determine how many total HD of creatures can be affected. Creatures with the fewest HD are affected first. Among creatures with equal HD, those who are closest to the spell's point of origin are affected first. No creature with 5 or more HD is affected, and HD that are not sufficient to affect a creature are wasted.

Creatures with fewer HD are affected first. For example, Mialee casts *sleep* at three kobolds (1/2 HD), two gnolls (2 HD), and an ogre (4 HD). The roll (2d4) result is 4. All three kobolds and one gnoll are affected (1/2 + 1/2 + 1/2 + 2 = 3 1/2 HD). The remaining 1/2 HD is not enough to affect the last gnoll or the ogre. Mialee can't choose to have *sleep* affect the ogre or the two gnolls.

Sleeping creatures are helpless. Slapping or wounding awakens affected creatures, but normal noise does not. Awakening a creature is a standard action (an application of the aid another action).

Sleep does not target unconscious creatures, constructs, or undead creatures.

Note: Extra hit points are irrelevant for determining how many HD a creature has. An ogre with 4d8+8 hit points still has only 4 HD and can be affected by the spell.

Arcane Material Component: A pinch of fine sand, rose petals, or a live cricket.

eet Storm

Conjuration (Creation) [Cold]
Level: Drd 4, Sor/Wiz 3
Components: V, S, M/DF
Casting Time: 1 action
Range: Long (400 ft. + 40 ft./level)
Effect: Sleet spreads 40 ft., 20 ft. high
Duration: 1 round/level
Saving Throw: Reflex partial
Spell Resistance: No

Driving sleet blocks all sight (even darkvision) within it and causes the ground in the area to be icy, slowing movement to one-half normal. Additionally, any creature in sleet that attempts to move must succeed at a Reflex save or fall down instead. The sleet extinguishes torches and small fires.

Arcane Material Components: A pinch of dust and a few drops of water.

ow

Transmutation
Level: Brd 3, Sor/Wiz 3
Components: V, S, M
Casting Time: 1 action
Range: Close (25 ft. + 5 ft./2 levels)
Targets: One creature/level, no two of which can be more than 30 ft. apart
Duration: 1 round/level
Saving Throw: Will negates
Spell Resistance: Yes

Affected creatures move and attack at a drastically slowed rate. *Slowed* creatures can take only a partial action each turn. Additionally, they suffer –2 penalties to AC, melee attack rolls, melee damage rolls, and Reflex saves. *Slowed* creatures jump half as far as normal.

Slow counters and dispels *haste* but does not otherwise affect magically speeded or slowed creatures.

Material Component: A drop of molasses.

Snare

Transmutation
Level: Rgr 2, Drd 3
Components: V, S, DF
Casting Time: 3 rounds
Range: Touch
Target: Touched nonmagical circle of vine, rope, or thong with a 2 ft. diameter + 2 ft./level
Duration: Until triggered or broken
Saving Throw: None
Spell Resistance: No

This spell enables you to make a snare that functions as a magic trap. The snare can be made from any supple vine, a thong, or a rope. When you cast *snare* upon it, the cordlike object blends with its surroundings (DC 23 Search check for a rogue [only] to locate). One end of the snare is tied in a loop that contracts around one or more of the limbs of any creature stepping inside the circle. (Note that the head of a worm or a snake could be thus ensnared.)

If a strong and supple tree is nearby, the *snare* can be fastened to it. The spell causes the tree to bend and then straighten when the loop is triggered, dealing 1d6 points of damage to the creature trapped and lifting it off the ground by the trapped limb or limbs. If no such tree is available, the cordlike object tightens around the creature, causing no damage but tightly binding it.

An entangled creature suffers a –2 penalty to attack rolls and suffers a –4 penalty to effective Dexterity. If the snare is anchored to an immobile object, the entangled character cannot move. Otherwise, he can move at half speed, but can't run or charge. A character capable of spellcasting who is bound by this spell must succeed at a Concentration check (DC 15) to cast a spell.

The *snare* is magical. To escape, the trapped creature must succeed at an Escape Artist check (DC 23) or a Strength check (DC 23) that is a full-round action. The snare has 5 hit points and AC 7. A successful escape from the *snare* breaks the loop and ends the spell.

Soften Earth and Stone

Transmutation
Level: Drd 2, Earth 2
Components: V, S, DF
Casting Time: 1 action
Range: Close (25 ft. + 5 ft./2 levels)
Area: 10-ft. square/level (see text)
Duration: Instantaneous
Saving Throw: None
Spell Resistance: No

When this spell is cast, all natural, undressed earth or stone in the spell's area is softened. Wet earth becomes thick mud; dry earth becomes loose sand or dirt; and stone becomes soft clay that is easily molded or chopped. You affect a 10-foot-square area to a depth of 1 to 4 feet, depending on the toughness or resilience of the ground at that spot (DM's option). Magical, enchanted, dressed, or worked stone cannot be affected. Earth or stone creatures are not affected.

Creatures in mud must succeed at Reflex saves or be caught for 1d2 rounds and unable to move, attack, or cast spells. Creatures who succeed at their saves can move through the mud at half speed, and they can't run or charge.

Loose dirt is not as troublesome as mud, but all creatures in the area are reduced to half their normal speed and can't run or charge over the surface.

Stone softened into clay does not hinder movement, but it does allow characters to cut, shape, or excavate areas they may not have been able to affect before. For example, a party of adventurers trying to break out of a cavern might use this spell to soften a wall. While *soften earth and stone* does not affect dressed or worked stone, vertical surfaces such as cliff faces or cavern ceilings can be affected. Usually, this causes a moderate collapse or landslide as the loosened material peels away from the face or the wall or roof and falls.

A moderate amount of structural damage can be dealt to a manufactured structure (such as a wall or a tower) by softening the ground beneath it, causing it to settle. However, most well-built structures will only be damaged by this spell, not destroyed.

Solid Fog

Conjuration (Creation)
Level: Sor/Wiz 4
Components: V, S, M
Duration: 1 minute/level

As *fog cloud*, but in addition to obscuring sight, the *solid fog* is so thick that any creature attempting to move through it progresses at one-tenth normal speed, and all melee attack and melee damage rolls suffer a –2 penalty. The vapors prevent effective ranged weapon attacks (except for magic rays and the like). A creature or object that falls into *solid fog* is slowed, so that each 10 feet of vapor that the creature or objects passes through reduces falling damage by 1d6.

However, unlike normal fog, only a severe wind (31+ mph) disperses these vapors, and it does so in 1 round.

Material Components: A pinch of dried, powdered peas combined with powdered animal hoof.

Soul Bind

Necromancy
Level: Clr 9, Sor/Wiz 9
Components: V, S, F
Casting Time: 1 action
Range: Close (25 ft. + 5 ft./2 levels)
Target: Corpse
Duration: Permanent
Saving Throw: Will negates
Spell Resistance: No

You draw the soul from a newly dead body and imprison it in a black sapphire gem. The subject must have been dead no more than 1 round per caster level. The soul, once trapped in the gem, cannot be returned through *clone, raise dead, reincarnation, resurrection, true resurrection,* or even a *miracle* or a *wish.* Only by destroying the gem or dispelling the spell on the gem can one free the soul (which is then still dead).

Focus: A black sapphire of at least 1,000 gp value for every Hit Die possessed by the creature whose soul is to be bound. If the gem is not valuable enough, it shatters when the binding is attempted. (While characters have no concept of level or Hit Dice as such, the value of the gem needed to trap an individual can be researched. Remember that this value can change over time as characters advance.)

Sound Burst

Evocation [Sonic]
Level: Brd 2, Clr 2
Components: V, S, F/DF
Casting Time: 1 action
Range: Close (25 ft. + 5 ft./2 levels)
Area: 10-ft.-radius spread
Duration: Instantaneous
Saving Throw: Will partial
Spell Resistance: Yes

You blast an area with a tremendous cacophony. Creatures in the area take 1d8 points of sonic damage and must succeed at Will saves to avoid being stunned for 1 round. A stunned creature can't act and loses any Dexterity bonus to AC. Attackers gain +2 bonuses to attack it.

Deafened creatures are not stunned but are still damaged.

Arcane Focus: A small musical instrument.

Speak with Animals

Divination
Level: Clr 2, Drd 2, Rgr 1
Components: V, S
Casting Time: 1 action
Range: Personal
Target: You
Duration: 1 minute/level

You can comprehend and communicate with animals. You are able to ask questions of and receive answers from animals, although the spell doesn't make animals any more friendly or cooperative than normal. Furthermore, wary and cunning animals are likely to be terse and evasive, while the more stupid ones make inane comments. If the animal is friendly, it may do some favor or service for you (as determined by the DM).

Note: This spell does not work on beasts, magical beasts, or vermin.

Speak with Dead

Necromancy [Language-Dependent]
Level: Clr 3
Components: V, S, DF
Casting Time: 10 minutes
Range: 10 ft.
Target: One dead creature
Duration: 1 minute/level
Saving Throw: Will negates (see text)
Spell Resistance: No

You grant the semblance of life and intellect to a corpse, allowing it to answer several questions that you put to it. You may ask up to one question per two caster levels. Unasked questions are wasted if the duration expires. The corpse's knowledge is limited to what the creature knew during life, including the languages it spoke (if any). Answers are usually brief, cryptic, or repetitive. If the creature's alignment was different from yours, the corpse gets a Will save to resist the spell as if it were alive.

If the corpse has been subject to *speak with dead* within the past week, the new spell fails. You can cast this spell on a corpse that has been deceased for any amount of time, but the body must be mostly intact to be able to respond. A damaged corpse may be able to give partial answers or partially correct answers, but it must at least have a mouth in order to speak at all.

This spell does not let you actually speak to the person (whose soul has departed). It instead draws on the imprinted knowledge stored in the corpse. The partially animated body retains the imprint of the soul that once inhabited it, and thus it can speak with all the knowledge that the creature had while alive. The corpse, however, cannot learn new information. Indeed, it can't even remember being questioned.

Any corpse that has been turned into an undead creature can't be spoken to with *speak with dead.*

Speak with Plants

Divination
Level: Clr 3, Drd 3, Rgr 2
Components: V, S
Casting Time: 1 action
Range: Personal
Target: You
Duration: 1 minute/level

You can comprehend and communicate with plants, including normal plants and plant creatures. You are able to ask questions of and receive answers from plants. A regular plant's sense of its surroundings is limited, so it won't be able to give (or recognize) detailed descriptions of creatures or answer questions about events outside its immediate vicinity.

The spell doesn't make plant creatures any more friendly or cooperative than normal. Furthermore, wary and cunning plant creatures are likely to be terse and evasive, while the more stupid ones may make inane comments. If the plant creature is friendly, it may do some favor or service for you (as determined by the DM).

Spectral Hand

Necromancy
Level: Sor/Wiz 2
Components: V, S
Casting Time: 1 action
Range: Medium (100 ft. + 10 ft./level)
Effect: One spectral hand
Duration: 1 minute/level (D)
Saving Throw: None
Spell Resistance: No

A ghostly, glowing hand shaped from your life force materializes and moves as you desire, allowing you to deliver low-level, touch range spells at a distance. On casting the spell, you lose 1d4 hit points that return when the spell ends (even if it is dispelled), but not if the hand is destroyed. (The hit points can be healed as normal.) For as long as the spell lasts, any touch range spell that you cast of 4th level or lower can be delivered by the *spectral hand.* The spell gives you a +2 bonus to your melee touch attack roll, and attacking with the hand counts normally as an attack. The hand always strikes from your direction. The hand can flank targets like a creature can. If the hand goes beyond the spell range, goes out of your sight, or if you are not directing it, the hand returns to you and hovers.

The hand is incorporeal and thus cannot be harmed by normal weapons. It has improved evasion (one-half damage on a failed save against an area spell and no damage on a successful save), your save bonuses, and an AC of at least 22. Your Intelligence modifier applies to the hand's AC as if it were the hand's

Dexterity modifier. The hand has 1 to 4 hit points, the same number that you lost in creating it.

Spell Immunity
Abjuration
Level: Clr 4, Protection 4, Strength 4
Components: V, S, DF
Casting Time: 1 action
Range: Touch
Target: Creature touched
Duration: 10 minutes/level
Saving Throw: Will negates (harmless)
Spell Resistance: Yes (harmless)

The warded creature is immune to the effects of one specified spell for every four levels you have. The spells must be of 4th level or lower. The warded creature effectively has unbeatable SR regarding the specified spell or spells. Naturally, that spell immunity doesn't protect a creature from spells for which SR doesn't apply. *Spell immunity* protects against spells, spell-like effects of magic items, and innate spell-like abilities of creatures. It does not protect against supernatural or extraordinary abilities, such as breath weapons or gaze attacks. Only a particular spell can be protected against, not a certain domain or school of spells or a group of spells that are similar in effect. Thus, a creature given immunity to *lightning bolt* is still vulnerable to *shocking grasp* or *chain lightning*.

A creature can have only one *spell immunity* spell in effect on it at a time.

Spell Resistance
Abjuration
Level: Clr 5, Magic 5, Protection 5
Components: V, S, DF
Casting Time: 1 action
Range: Touch
Target: Creature touched
Duration: 1 minute/level
Saving Throw: Will negates (harmless)
Spell Resistance: Yes (harmless)

The creature gains SR equal to 12 + caster level.

In order to affect a creature who has SR with a spell, a spellcaster must roll the creature's SR or higher on 1d20 + caster level. A creature with SR may voluntarily lower it in order to accept a spell.

Spellstaff
Transmutation
Level: Drd 6
Components: V, S, F
Casting Time: 10 minutes
Range: Touch
Target: Wooden quarterstaff touched
Duration: Permanent until discharged (D)
Saving Throw: Will negates (object)
Spell Resistance: Yes (object)

You store one spell that you can normally cast in a wooden quarterstaff. Only one such spell can be stored in a staff at a given time, and you cannot have more than one *spellstaff* at any given time. You can cast a spell stored within a staff just as though it were among those you had prepared, but it does not count against your normal total for a given day. You use up any applicable material components required to cast the spell when you store it in the *spellstaff*.

Focus: The staff that stores the spell.

Spell Turning
Abjuration
Level: Luck 7, Magic 7, Sor/Wiz 7
Components: V, S, M/DF
Casting Time: 1 action
Range: Personal
Target: You
Duration: Until expended or 10 minutes/ level

Spells (and spell-like effects) targeted against you rebound on the original caster. The abjuration turns only spells that have you as a target. Effect and area spells are not affected. *Spell turning* also fails to affect touch range spells. Thus, a *charm person* spell cast at you could be turned back upon and possibly enable you to charm the caster, but a *fireball* could not be turned back, and neither could *inflict critical wounds*.

From seven to ten (1d4+6) spell levels are affected by the turning. The DM secretly rolls the exact number. Each spell turned subtracts its level from the amount of spell turning left.

A spell might be only partially turned. Subtract the 1d4+6 result from the spell level of the incoming spell. Divide the remaining levels of the incoming spell by the spell level of the incoming spell to see what fraction of the effect gets through. For damaging spells, you and the caster each take a fraction of the damage. For nondamaging spells, each of you has a proportional chance to be affected.

If you and a spellcasting attacker are both warded by *spell turning* effects in operation, a resonating field is created. Roll randomly to determine the result:

d%	Effect
01–70	Spell drains away without effect.
71–80	Spell affects both of you equally at full effect.
81–97	Both turning effects are rendered nonfunctional for 1d4 minutes.
98–100	Both of you go through a rift into another plane.

Arcane Material Component: A small silver mirror.

Spider Climb
Transmutation
Level: Sor/Wiz 1
Components: V, S, M
Casting Time: 1 action
Range: Touch
Target: Creature touched
Duration: 10 minutes/level
Saving Throw: Will negates (harmless)
Spell Resistance: Yes (harmless)

The subject can climb and travel on vertical surfaces or even traverse ceilings as well as a spider does. The affected creature must have bare hands and feet to climb in this manner. The subject climbs at half its speed. A creature with a Strength score of at least 20 +1 per caster level can pull the subject off a wall.

Material Components: A drop of bitumen and a live spider, both of which must be eaten by the subject.

Spike Growth
Transmutation
Level: Drd 3
Components: V, S, DF
Casting Time: 1 action
Range: Medium (100 ft. + 10 ft./level)
Area: One 20-ft. square/level
Duration: 1 hour/level (D)
Saving Throw: Reflex partial
Spell Resistance: Yes

Any ground-covering vegetation in the spell's area becomes very hard and sharply pointed without changing its appearance. In areas of bare earth, roots and rootlets act in the same way. Typically, *spike growth* can be cast in any outdoor setting except open water, ice, heavy snow, sandy desert, or bare stone. Any creature moving on foot into or through the spell's area takes 1d4 points of damage for each 5 feet of movement through the spiked area.

Any creature who sustains damage from this spell must also succeed at a Reflex save or suffer injuries to its feet and legs that slow its speed by one-third. This speed penalty lasts for 24 hours or until the injured creature receives a *cure* spell (which also restores lost hit points). Another character can remove the penalty by taking 10 minutes to dress the injuries and succeeding at a Heal check against the spell's save DC.

Spike growth is a magic trap that can't be disabled with the Disable Device skill.

Note: Magic traps such as *spike growth* are hard to detect. A rogue (only) can use the Search skill to find the *spike growth*. The DC is 25 + spell level, or DC 28 for *spike growth*.

Spike Stones
Transmutation
Level: Drd 4, Earth 4
Components: V, S, DF

Casting Time: 1 action
Range: Medium (100 ft. + 10 ft./level)
Area: One 20-ft. square/level
Duration: 1 hour/level (D)
Saving Throw: Reflex partial
Spell Resistance: Yes

Rocky ground, stone floors, and similar surfaces shapes themselves into long, sharp points that blend into the background. The spike stones impede progress through an area and deal damage. Any creature moving on foot into or through the spell's area takes 1d8 points of damage for each 5 feet of movement through the spiked area. In addition, ground speed through the spell's area is reduced by half.

Any creature who sustains damage from this spell must also succeed at a Reflex save or suffer injuries to its feet and legs that slow its speed by one-third. This movement penalty lasts for 24 hours or until the injured creature receives a *cure* spell (which also restores lost hit points). Another character can remove the penalty by taking 10 minutes to dress the injuries and succeeding at a Heal check against the spell's save DC.

Spike stones is a magic trap that can't be disabled with the Disable Device skill.

Note: Magic traps such as *spike stones* are hard to detect. A rogue (only) can use the Search skill to find the *spike stones*. The DC is 25 + spell level, or DC 29 for *spike stones*.

Spiritual Weapon

Evocation [Force]
Level: Clr 2, War 2
Components: V, S, DF
Casting Time: 1 action
Range: Medium (100 ft. + 10 ft./level)
Effect: Magic weapon of force
Duration: 1 round/level (D)
Saving Throw: None
Spell Resistance: Yes

A melee weapon made of pure force springs into existence and attacks opponents at a distance, as you direct it, dealing 1d8 damage per hit. The weapon takes the shape of a weapon favored by your deity or a weapon with some spiritual significance or symbolism to you (see below) and has the same threat range and critical multipliers as a real weapon of its form. It strikes the opponent you designate, starting with one attack the round the spell is cast and continuing each round thereafter. It uses your base attack bonus as its attack bonus (possibly allowing it multiple attacks per round in subsequent rounds). It strikes as a spell, not as a weapon, so, for example, it can strike incorporeal creatures. The weapon always strikes from your direction. It does not get a flanking bonus or help a combatant get one. Your feats (such as Weapon Focus) or combat

actions (such as charge) do not affect the weapon. If the weapon goes beyond the spell range, if it goes out of your sight, or if you are not directing it, the weapon returns to you and hovers.

Each round after the first, you can use a standard action to switch the weapon to a new target. If you do not, the weapon continues to attack the previous round's target. On any round that the weapon switches targets, it gets one attack. Subsequent rounds of attacking that target allow the weapon to make multiple attacks if your base attack bonus would allow it to. The *spiritual weapon* cannot be attacked or damaged.

If an attacked creature has SR, the resistance is checked the first time the *spiritual weapon* strikes it. If the weapon is successfully resisted, the spell is dispelled. If not, the weapon has its normal full effect on that creature for the duration of the spell.

The weapon that you get is often a force replica of your deity's own personal weapon, many of which have individual names. A cleric without a deity gets a weapon based on his alignment. A neutral cleric without a deity can create a spiritual weapon of any alignment provided he is acting at least generally in accord with that alignment at the time. The weapons of each deity or alignment are:

Deity or Alignment	Spiritual Weapon
Boccob	Quarterstaff
Corellon Larethian	Longsword, "Sahandrian"
Ehlonna	Longsword
Erythnul	Morningstar (with a blunt, stone head)
Fharlanghn	Quarterstaff
Garl Glittergold	Battleaxe, "Arumdina"
Gruumsh	Spear
Heironeous	Longsword, "The Blade of Valor"
Hextor	Flail
Kord	Greatsword
Moradin	Warhammer, "Soulhammer"
Nerull	Scythe
Obad-Hai	Quarterstaff
Olidammara	Rapier
Pelor	Mace
St. Cuthbert	Mace
Vecna	Dagger
Wee Jas	Dagger
Yondalla	Short sword, "Hornblade"
Good	Hammer, "The Hammer of Justice"
Evil	Flail, "The Scourge of Souls"
Law	Sword, "The Sword of Truth"
Chaos	Battleaxe, "The Blade of Change"

Statue

Transmutation
Level: Sor/Wiz 7
Components: V, S, M
Casting Time: 1 action
Range: Touch
Target: Creature touched
Duration: 1 hour/level (D)
Saving Throw: Will negates (harmless)
Spell Resistance: Yes (harmless)

A *statue* spell turns the subject to solid stone, along with any garments and equipment worn or carried. The initial transformation from flesh to stone requires 1 full round after the spell is cast. In statue form, the subject gains hardness 8. The subject retains its own hit points.

The subject can see, hear, and smell normally, but does not need to eat or breathe. Feeling is limited to those sensations that can affect the granite-hard substance of the individual's body. Chipping is equal to a mere scratch, but breaking off one of the statue's arms is serious damage.

The individual under the magic of a *statue* spell can return to his normal state, act, and then return instantly to the statue state (a free action) if he so desires, as long as the spell duration is in effect.

Material Components: Lime, sand, and a drop of water stirred by an iron bar, such as a nail or spike.

Status

Divination
Level: Clr 4
Components: V, S
Casting Time: 1 action
Range: Touch
Targets: One creature touched/three levels
Duration: 1 hour/level
Saving Throw: Will negates (harmless)
Spell Resistance: Yes (harmless)

When a cleric needs to keep track of comrades that may get separated, *status* allows him to mentally monitor their relative position and general condition. The cleric is aware of direction and distance to the creatures and their status: unharmed, wounded, disabled, staggered, unconscious, dying, dead, etc. Once the spell has been cast upon the subjects, the distance between them and the caster does not affect the spell as long as they are on the same plane of existence. If they leave it, the spell ceases to function for them.

Stinking Cloud

Conjuration (Creation)
Level: Sor/Wiz 3
Components: V, S, M
Casting Time: 1 action
Range: Medium (100 ft. + 10 ft./level)

Effect: Cloud that spreads in 30-ft. radius, 20 ft. high
Duration: 1 round/level
Saving Throw: Fortitude negates (see text)
Spell Resistance: Yes

Stinking cloud creates a bank of fog like that created by *fog cloud*, except that the vapors are nauseating. Living creatures in the cloud are nauseated (Fortitude negates), making them unable to attack, cast spells, concentrate on spells, and so on. The only action a nauseated character can take is a single move (or move-equivalent action) per turn. These effects last as long as the character is in the cloud and for 1d4+1 rounds after he or she leaves the cloud. (Roll separately for each nauseated character.) Those who succeed at their saves but remain in the cloud must continue to save each round.

Material Component: A rotten egg or several skunk cabbage leaves.

Stone Shape

Transmutation
Level: Clr 3, Drd 3, Earth 3, Sor/Wiz 5
Components: V, S, M/DF
Casting Time: 1 action
Range: Touch
Target: Stone or stone object touched, up to 10 cu. ft. +1 cu. ft./level
Duration: Instantaneous
Saving Throw: None
Spell Resistance: No

You can form an existing piece of stone into any shape that suits your purpose. For example, you can make a stone weapon, a special trapdoor, or a crude idol. *Stone shape* also permits you to reshape a stone door to make an exit where one didn't exist or to seal a door shut. While it's possible to make crude coffers, doors, and so forth with *stone shape*, fine detail isn't possible. There is a 30% chance that any shape including moving parts simply doesn't work.

Arcane Material Component: Soft clay, which must be worked into roughly the desired shape of the stone object and then touched to the stone while the verbal component is uttered.

Stoneskin

Abjuration
Level: Earth 6, Sor/Wiz 4, Strength 6
Components: V, S, M
Casting Time: 1 action
Range: Touch
Target: Creature touched
Duration: 10 minutes/level or until discharged
Saving Throw: Will negates (harmless)
Spell Resistance: Yes (harmless)

The warded creature gains resistance to blows, cuts, stabs, and slashes. The subject gains damage reduction 10/+5. (It ignores the first 10 points of damage each time it takes damage, though a weapon with a +5 enhancement bonus or any magical attack bypasses the reduction.) Once the spell has prevented a total of 10 points of damage per caster level (maximum 150 points), it is discharged.

Material Components: Granite and 250 gp worth of diamond dust sprinkled on the target's skin.

Stone Tell

Divination
Level: Drd 6
Components: V, S, DF
Casting Time: 10 minutes
Range: Personal
Target: You
Duration: 1 minute/level

You gain the ability to speak with stones, which relate to you who or what has touched them as well as revealing what is covered or concealed behind or under them. The stones relate complete descriptions if asked. Note that a stone's perspective, perception, and knowledge may prevent the stone from providing the details you are looking for (as determined by the DM). You can speak with natural or worked stone.

Stone to Flesh

Transmutation
Level: Sor/Wiz 6
Components: V, S, M
Casting Time: 1 action
Range: Medium (100 ft. + 10 ft./level)
Target: One petrified creature or a cylinder of stone from 1 ft. to 3 ft. in diameter and up to 10 ft. long
Duration: Instantaneous
Saving Throw: Fortitude negates (object) (see text)
Spell Resistance: Yes

This spell restores a petrified creature to its normal state, restoring life and goods. The creature must succeed at a Fortitude save (DC 15) to survive the process. Any petrified creature, regardless of size, can be restored.

The spell also can convert a mass of stone into a fleshy substance. Such flesh is inert and lacking a vital life force unless a life force or magical energy is available. (For example, this spell would turn a stone golem into a flesh golem, but an ordinary statue would become a corpse.) You can affect an object that fits within a cylinder from 1 foot to 3 feet in diameter and up to 10 feet long or a cylinder of up to those dimensions in a larger mass of stone.

Material Components: A pinch of earth and a drop of blood.

Storm of Vengeance

Conjuration (Summoning)
Level: Clr 9
Components: V, S
Casting Time: 1 full round
Range: Long (400 ft. + 40 ft./level)
Effect: 360-ft.-radius storm cloud
Duration: Concentration (maximum 10 rounds) (D)
Saving Throw: See text
Spell Resistance: Yes

This spell creates an enormous black storm cloud. Lightning and crashing claps of thunder appear within the storm. Creatures beneath the cloud must succeed at Fortitude saves or be deafened (see *blindness/deafness*) for 1d4×10 minutes.

If you do not maintain concentration on the spell after casting it, the spell ends. If you continue to concentrate, the spell generates additional effects in each following round, as noted below. Each effect occurs during your turn.

Second Round: Acid rains down in the area, dealing 1d6 points of acid damage. No save is allowed.

Third Round: You call six bolts of lightning down from the cloud. You decide where the bolts strike. All may be directed at a single target, or they may be directed at up to six separate targets. Each bolt deals 10d6 points of electricity damage. Creatures struck can attempt Reflex saves for half damage.

Fourth Round: Hailstones rain down in the area, dealing 5d6 points of damage (no save).

Fifth through Tenth Rounds: Violent rain and wind gusts reduce visibility. The rain obscures all sight, including darkvision, beyond 5 feet. A creature 5 feet away has one-half concealment (attacks suffer a 20% miss chance). Creatures farther away have total concealment (50% miss chance, and the attacker cannot use sight to locate the target). Speed is reduced by three-quarters. Ranged attacks within the area of the storm are impossible. Spells cast within the area are disrupted unless the caster succeeds at a Concentration check against a DC equal to the *storm of vengeance*'s save + the level of the spell the caster is trying to cast.

Suggestion

Enchantment (Compulsion) [Mind-Affecting, Language-Dependent]
Level: Brd 2, Sor/Wiz 3
Components: V, M
Casting Time: 1 action
Range: Close (25 ft. + 5 ft./2 levels)
Target: One living creature
Duration: 1 hour/level or until completed

Saving Throw: Will negates
Spell Resistance: Yes

You influence the actions of the enchanted creature by suggesting a course of activity (limited to a sentence or two). The suggestion must be worded in such a manner as to make the activity sound reasonable. Asking the creature to stab itself, throw itself onto a spear, immolate itself, or do some other obviously harmful act automatically negates the effect of the spell. However, a suggestion that a pool of acid is actually pure water and that a quick dip would be refreshing is another matter. Urging a red dragon to stop attacking your party so that the dragon and party could jointly loot a rich treasure elsewhere is likewise a reasonable use of the spell's power.

The suggested course of activity can continue for the entire duration, such as in the case of the red dragon mentioned above. If the suggested activity can be completed in a shorter time, the spell ends when the subject finishes what he was asked to do. You can instead specify conditions that will trigger a special activity during the duration. For example, you might suggest that a noble knight give her warhorse to the first beggar she meets. If the condition is not met before the spell expires, the activity is not performed.

A very reasonable suggestion causes the save to be made with a penalty (such as –1, –2, etc.) at the discretion of the DM.

Material Components: A snake's tongue and either a bit of honeycomb or a drop of sweet oil.

Summon Monster I

Conjuration (Summoning) [see text]
Level: Brd 1, Clr 1, Sor/Wiz 1
Components: V, S, F/DF
Casting Time: 1 full round
Range: Close (25 ft. + 5 ft./2 levels)
Effect: One summoned creature
Duration: 1 round/level (D)
Saving Throw: None
Spell Resistance: No

This spell summons an outsider (extraplanar creature) that attacks your enemies. It appears where you designate and acts immediately, on your turn. It attacks your opponents to the best of its ability. If you can communicate with the outsider, you can direct it not to attack, to attack particular enemies, or to perform other actions. Summoned creatures act normally on the last round of the spell and disappear at the end of their turn.

Choose a 1st-level monster from the Summon Monster table.

When you use a summoning spell to summon an air, chaotic, earth, evil, fire, good, lawful, or water creature, it is a spell of that type. For example, *summon monster I* is a lawful and evil spell when cast to summon a dire rat.

Arcane Focus: A tiny bag and a small (not necessarily lit) candle.

Summon Monster II

Conjuration (Summoning) [see text]
Level: Brd 2, Clr 2, Sor/Wiz 2

SUMMON MONSTER

Creature	Alignment
1st Level	
Celestial dog (animal)	LG
Celestial badger (animal)	CG
Fiendish dire rat	LE
Fiendish hawk (animal)	CE
2nd Level	
Celestial eagle (animal)	CG
Formian worker	LN
Lemure (devil)	LE
Fiendish squid (animal)	LE
Fiendish wolf (animal)	LE
Fiendish shark, Medium-size (animal)	NE
Fiendish viper, Tiny (animal)	CE
Fiendish hyena [treat as wolf (animal)]	CE
Fiendish octopus (animal)	CE
3rd Level	
Celestial bear, black (animal)	LG
Celestial bison (animal)	NG
Triton	NG
Celestial dire badger	CG
Azer	LN
Elemental, Small	N
Thoqqua	N
Fiendish dire weasel	LE
Fiendish gorilla (animal)	LE
Fiendish snake, constrictor (animal)	LE
Fiendish boar	NE
Fiendish dire bat	NE
Fiendish lizard, giant (animal)	NE
Salamander, Small	NE
Fiendish shark, Large (animal)	NE
Fiendish viper, Small snake (animal)	CE
Fiendish crocodile (animal)	CE
Dretch	CE
Fiendish leopard (animal)	CE
Fiendish wolverine (animal)	CE
4th Level	
Lantern archon (celestial)	LG
Giant owl	NG
Giant eagle	CG
Celestial lion (animal)	CG
Tojanida, Small	N
Xorn, Small	N
Arrowhawk, Small	N
Magmin	CN
Imp (devil)	LE
Fiendish dire ape	LE
Fiendish dire wolf	LE
Hell hound	LE
Varguouille	NE
Fiendish viper, Medium-size snake (animal)	CE
Howler	CE
5th Level	
Celestial bear, brown (animal)	LG
Hound archon (celestial)	LG
Celestial orca, whale (animal)	NG
Celestial pegasus	CG
Celestial dire lion	CG
Formian warrior	LN
Elemental, Medium-size	N
Mephit, any	N
Arrowhawk, Medium-size	N
Tojanida, Medium-size	N
Achaierai	LE
Fiendish griffon	LE
Fiendish snake, giant constrictor (animal)	LE
Yeth hound	NE
Fiendish dire boar	NE
Fiendish rhinoceros (animal)	NE
Fiendish shark, Large (animal)	NE
Salamander, Medium-size	NE
Shadow mastiff	NE
Fiendish viper, Large (animal)	CE
Quasit	CE
Fiendish dire wolverine	CE
Fiendish giant crocodile (animal)	CE
Fiendish tiger (animal)	CE
Fiendish girallon	CE
6th Level	
Celestial dire bear	LG
Celestial unicorn	CG
Elemental, Large	N
Rast	N
Xorn, Medium-size	N
Slaad, red	CN
Chaos beast	CN
Kyton	LE
Barbazu (devil)	LE
Bezekira	LE
Erinyes (devil)	LE
Belker	NE
Fiendish viper, Huge snake (animal)	CE
7th Level	
Celestial elephant (animal)	NG
Avoral guardinal (celestial)	NG
Djinni	CG
Ravid [alone]	N
Elemental, Huge	N
Invisible stalker	N
Xorn, Large	N
Arrowhawk, Large	N
Tojanida, Large	N
Slaad, blue	CN
Hamatula (devil)	LE
Osyluth (devil)	LE
Fiendish dire tiger	CE
Bebilith	CE
Fiendish octopus, giant (animal)	CE
8th Level	
Lillend	CG
Formian taskmaster [alone]	LN
Janni (genie)	N
Elemental, greater	N
Barghest, Medium-size	LE
Cornugon (devil)	E
Fiendish squid, giant (animal)	LE
Salamander, Large	NE
Succubus (demon)	CE
9th Level	
Lammasu	LG
Couatl	LG
Astral deva (celestial)	NG
Ghaele eladrin (celestial)	CG
Elemental, elder	N
Barghest, Large	LE
Xill	LE
Rakshasa	LE
Gelugon (devil)	LE
Night hag	NE
Nightmare	NE
Vrock (demon)	CE

Mialee summons a couatl.

Effect: One or more summoned creatures, no two of which can be more than 30 ft. apart

As *summon monster I*, except you can summon one outsider from the 2nd-level list or 1d3 outsiders of the same type from the 1st-level list.

Summon Monster III

Conjuration (Summoning) [see text]
Level: Brd 3, Clr 3, Sor/Wiz 3
Effect: One or more summoned creatures, no two of which can be more than 30 ft. apart

As *summon monster I*, except you can summon one creature from the 3rd-level list, 1d3 creatures of the same type from the 2nd-level list, or 1d4+1 creatures of the same type from the 1st-level list.

Summon Monster IV

Conjuration (Summoning) [see text]
Level: Brd 4, Clr 4, Sor/Wiz 4
Effect: One or more summoned creatures, no two of which can be more than 30 ft. apart

As *summon monster I*, except you can summon one creature from the 4th-level list, 1d3 creatures of the same type from the 3rd-level list, or 1d4+1 creatures of the same type from a lower-level list.

Summon Monster V

Conjuration (Summoning) [see text]
Level: Brd 5, Clr 5, Sor/Wiz 5
Effect: One or more summoned creatures, no two of which can be more than 30 ft. apart

As *summon monster I*, except you can summon one creature from the 5th-level list, 1d3 creatures of the same type from the 4th-level list, or 1d4+1 creatures of the same type from a lower-level list.

Summon Monster VI

Conjuration (Summoning) [see text]
Level: Brd 6, Clr 6, Sor/Wiz 6
Effect: One or more summoned creatures, no two of which can be more than 30 ft. apart

As *summon monster I*, except you can summon one creature from the 6th-level list, 1d3 creatures of the same type from the 5th-level list, or 1d4+1 creatures of the same type from a lower-level list.

Summon Monster VII

Conjuration (Summoning) [see text]
Level: Clr 7, Sor/Wiz 7

As *summon monster I*, except you can summon one creature from the 7th-level list, 1d3 creatures of the same type from the 6th-level list, or 1d4+1 creatures of the same type from a lower-level list.

Summon Monster VIII

Conjuration (Summoning) [see text]
Level: Clr 8, Sor/Wiz 8

As *summon monster I*, except you can summon one creature from the 8th-level list, 1d3 creatures of the same type from the 7th-level list, or 1d4+1 creatures of the same type from a lower-level list.

Summon Monster IX

Conjuration (Summoning) [see text]
Level: Chaos 9, Clr 9, Evil 9, Good 9, Law 9, Sor/Wiz 9

As *summon monster I*, except you can summon one creature from the 9th-level list, 1d3 creatures of the same type from the 8th-level list, or 1d4+1 creatures of the same type from a lower-level list.

Summon Nature's Ally I
Conjuration (Summoning) [see text]
Level: Drd 1, Rgr 1
Components: V, S, DF
Casting Time: 1 full round
Range: Close (25 ft. + 5 ft./2 levels)
Effect: One summoned creature
Duration: 1 round/level (D)
Saving Throw: None
Spell Resistance: No

This spell summons a natural creature who attacks your enemies. It appears where you designate and acts immediately, on your turn. It attacks your opponents to the best of its ability. If you can communicate with the creature, you can direct it not to attack, to attack particular enemies, or to perform other actions. Summoned creatures act normally on the last round of the spell and disappear at the end of their turn.

Choose a 1st-level creature from the Summon Nature's Ally table. All the creatures on the table are neutral unless otherwise noted.

Summon Nature's Ally II
Conjuration (Summoning) [see text]
Level: Drd 2, Rgr 2
Effect: One or more creatures, no two of which can be more than 30 ft. apart

As *summon nature's ally I*, except that you can summon one 2nd-level creature or 1d3 1st-level creatures of the same type.

Summon Nature's Ally III
Conjuration (Summoning) [see text]
Level: Drd 3, Rgr 3
Effect: One or more creatures, no two of which can be more than 30 ft. apart

As *summon nature's ally I*, except that you can summon one 3rd-level creature, 1d3 2nd-level creatures of the same type, or 1d4+1 1st-level creatures of the same type.

When you use a summoning spell to summon an air, chaotic, earth, evil, fire, good, lawful, or water creature, it is a spell of that type. For example, *summon nature's ally III* is an evil and fire spell when you cast it to summon a salamander.

Summon Nature's Ally IV
Conjuration (Summoning) [see text]
Level: Drd 4, Rgr 4
Effect: One or more creatures, no two of which can be more than 30 ft. apart

As *summon nature's ally I*, except that you can summon one 4th-level creature, 1d3 3rd-level creatures of the same type, or 1d4+1 lower level creatures of the same type.

When you use a summoning spell to summon an air, chaotic, earth, evil, fire, good, lawful, or water creature, it is a spell of that type.

Summon Nature's Ally V
Conjuration (Summoning) [see text]
Level: Drd 5
Effect: One or more creatures, no two of which can be more than 30 ft. apart

As *summon nature's ally I*, except that you can summon one 5th-level creature, 1d3 4th-level creatures of the same type, or 1d4+1 lower level creatures of the same type.

When you use a summoning spell to summon an air, chaotic, earth, evil, fire, good, lawful, or water creature, it is a spell of that type.

Summon Nature's Ally VI
Conjuration (Summoning) [see text]
Level: Drd 6
Effect: One or more creatures, no two of which can be more than 30 ft. apart

As *summon nature's ally I*, except that you can summon one 6th-level creature, 1d3 5th-level creatures of the same type, or 1d4+1 lower level creatures of the same type.

When you use a summoning spell to summon an air, chaotic, earth, evil, fire, good, lawful, or water creature, it is a spell of that type.

Summon Nature's Ally VII
Conjuration (Summoning) [see text]
Level: Drd 7
Effect: One or more creatures, no two of which can be more than 30 ft. apart

As *summon nature's ally I*, except that you can summon one 7th-level creature, 1d3

SUMMON NATURE'S ALLY

1st Level
Badger (animal)
Dire rat
Dog (animal)
Hawk (animal)
Viper, Tiny (animal)

2nd Level
Eagle (animal)
Hyena [treat as wolf (animal)]
Octopus (animal)
Shark, Medium-size (animal)
Squid (animal)
Wolf (animal)
Viper, Small (animal)

3rd Level
Ape (animal)
Bear, black (animal)
Bison
Boar
Crocodile (animal)
Dire badger
Dire bat
Dire weasel
Elemental, Small

Leopard (animal)
Lizard, giant (animal)
Salamander, Small [neutral evil]
Satyr [without pipes]
Shark, Large (animal)
Snake, constrictor (animal)
Thoqqua
Viper, Medium-size (animal)
Wolverine (animal)

4th Level
Arrowhawk, Small
Assassin vine
Dire ape
Dire wolf
Giant eagle [chaotic good]
Giant owl [neutral good]
Grig (sprite) [without pipes, neutral good]
Lion (animal)
Phantom fungus
Tojanida, Small
Viper, Large (animal)
Xorn, Small

5th Level
Arrowhawk, Medium-size
Bear, brown (animal)
Dire boar
Dire lion
Dire wolverine
Elemental, Medium-size
Giant crocodile (animal)
Rhinoceros (animal)
Salamander, Medium-size [neutral evil]
Satyr [with pipes]
Shark, Large (animal)
Snake, giant constrictor (animal)
Tiger (animal)
Tojanida, Medium-size
Viper, Huge (animal)
Whale, orca (animal)

6th Level
Dire bear
Elemental, Large
Shambling mound
Tendriculos
Unicorn [chaotic good]
Xorn, Medium-size

7th Level
Arrowhawk, Large
Dire tiger
Elemental, Huge
Elephant
Octopus, giant (animal)
Pixie [can't cast *Otto's irresistible dance*, neutral good]
Tojanida, Large
Treant [neutral good]
Xorn, Large

8th Level
Elemental, greater
Salamander, Large [neutral evil]
Squid, giant (animal)

9th Level
Elemental, elder
Pixie [can cast *Otto's irresistible dance*, neutral good]

6th-level creatures of the same type, or 1d4+1 lower level creatures of the same type.

When you use a summoning spell to summon an air, chaotic, earth, evil, fire, good, lawful, or water creature, it is a spell of that type.

Summon Nature's Ally VIII
Conjuration (Summoning) [see text]
Level: Drd 8
Effect: One or more creatures, no two of which can be more than 30 ft. apart

As *summon nature's ally I*, except that you can summon one 8th-level creature, 1d3 7th-level creatures of the same type, or 1d4+1 lower level creatures of the same type.

When you use a summoning spell to summon an air, chaotic, earth, evil, fire, good, lawful, or water creature, it is a spell of that type.

Summon Nature's Ally IX
Conjuration (Summoning) [see text]
Level: Drd 9
Effect: One or more creatures, no two of which can be more than 30 ft. apart

As *summon nature's ally I*, except that you can summon one 9th-level creature, 1d3 8th-level creatures of the same type, or 1d4+1 lower level creatures of the same type.

When you use a summoning spell to summon an air, chaotic, earth, evil, fire, good, lawful, or water creature, it is a spell of that type.

Summon Swarm
Conjuration (Summoning)
Level: Brd 2, Drd 2, Sor/Wiz 2
Components: V, S, M/DF
Casting Time: 1 full round
Range: Close (25 ft. + 5 ft./2 levels)
Effect: Swarm of small creatures in a 5-ft. spread
Duration: Concentration + 2 rounds
Saving Throw: None
Spell Resistance: No

A swarm of little creatures carpets the effect's area, viciously attacking all other creatures there. (Roll on the table below to see what sort of creature is summoned.) A creature in the swarm who takes no actions other than fighting off the creatures takes 1 point of damage on its turn. A creature in the swarm who takes any other action, including leaving the swarm, takes 1d4 points of damage +1 point per three caster levels. Spellcasting or concentrating on spells within the swarm is impossible.

1d20	Swarm Type*
1–8	Rats (animals)
9–14	Bats (animals)
15–16	Spiders (vermin, poisonous)
17–18	Centipedes (vermin, poisonous)
19–20	Flying beetles (vermin)

*The creature types (in parentheses) indicate what sorts of spells and effects might aid a subject against the swarm.

A swarm of poisonous creatures deals no damage to creatures who are immune to poison, though it still prevents spellcasting and concentration. The creatures' attacks are nonmagical. Damage reduction, being incorporeal, and other special abilities also make a creature immune to damage from the swarm.

The swarm cannot be fought effectively with weapons, but fire and damaging area effects can force it to disperse. The swarm disperses when it has taken a total of 2 hit points of damage per caster level from these attacks. Certain area or effect spells, such as *gust of wind* and *stinking cloud*, disperse a swarm immediately if appropriate to the swarm summoned. (For example, only fliers are affected by a *gust of wind*.)

The swarm is stationary once summoned. A druid caster, however, can (as a move-equivalent action) direct the swarm to move up to 30 feet per round (or 90 feet per round if she has summoned bats or beetles).

Arcane Material Component: A square of red cloth.

Sunbeam
Evocation
Level: Drd 7, Sun 7
Components: V, S, DF
Casting Time: 1 action
Range: Medium (100 ft. + 10 ft./level)
Area: Beam 5 feet wide and 100 ft. + 10 ft./level long, starting at a point right in front of you
Duration: 1 round/level or until all beams are exhausted
Saving Throw: Reflex negates and half (see text)
Spell Resistance: Yes

For the duration of this spell, you can use a standard action to evoke a dazzling beam of intensely hot light each round. You can call forth one beam per three caster levels (maximum six beams at 18th level). The spell ends when its duration runs out or your allotment of beams is exhausted.

All creatures in the beam are blinded and take 3d6 points of damage. (A successful Reflex save negates the blindness and reduces the damage by half.) In addition to the obvious effects, a blinded creature suffers a 50% miss chance in combat (all opponents have full concealment), loses any Dexterity bonus to AC, grants a +2 bonus to attackers' attack rolls (they are effectively invisible), moves at half speed, and suffers a –4 penalty on most Strength- and Dexterity-based skills. Creatures to whom sunlight is harmful or unnatural take double damage.

Undead creatures caught within the ray are dealt 1d6 points of damage per caster level (maximum 20d6), or half damage if a Reflex save is successful. In addition, the ray results in the destruction of undead creatures specifically affected by sunlight if they fail their saves.

The ultraviolet light generated by the spell deals damage to fungi, mold, oozes, slimes, jellies, puddings, and fungoid creatures just as if they were undead creatures.

Sunburst
Evocation
Level: Drd 8, Sor/Wiz 8, Sun 8
Components: V, S, M/DF
Casting Time: 1 action
Range: Long (400 ft. + 40 ft./level)
Area: 10 ft./level-radius burst
Duration: Instantaneous
Saving Throw: Reflex partial (see text)
Spell Resistance: Yes

Sunburst causes a globe of searing heat and radiance to explode silently from a point you select. All creatures in the globe are blinded and are dealt 3d6 points of damage. (A successful Reflex save negates the blindness and reduces the damage by half.) In addition to the obvious effects, a blinded creature suffers a 50% miss chance in combat (all opponents have full concealment), loses any Dexterity bonus to AC, grants a +2 bonus to attackers' attack rolls (they are effectively invisible), moves at half speed, and suffers a –4 penalty on most Strength- and Dexterity-based skills. Creatures to whom sunlight is harmful or unnatural take double damage.

Undead creatures caught within the globe are dealt 1d6 points of damage per caster level (maximum 25d6), or half damage if a Reflex save is successful. In addition, the burst results in the destruction of undead creatures specifically affected by sunlight if they fail their saves.

The ultraviolet light generated by the spell deals damage to fungi, mold, oozes, slimes, jellies, puddings, and fungoid creatures just as if they were undead creatures.

Arcane Material Components: A piece of sunstone and a naked flame.

Symbol
Universal [see text]
Level: Clr 8, Sor/Wiz 8
Components: V, S, M/DF (or V, S, M for carefully engraved)
Casting Time: 1 action or 10 minutes
Range: Touch
Effect: One symbol

Duration: See text
Saving Throw: See text
Spell Resistance: Yes

This spell allows you to scribe any of the potent runes described below. A *symbol* can be quickly scribed in the air or on some surface. Alternatively, you can carefully inscribe it on a surface. The *symbol* harms those who trigger it (usually those who pass over it, touch it, read it, etc.)

A quickly scribed *symbol* has a casting time of 1 action. The resulting rune becomes active immediately. It lasts 10 minutes per caster level and glows faintly while it lasts. *Symbols of fear, hopelessness, pain,* or *persuasion* can be used in this manner. *Symbols of death, discord, insanity, pain, sleep,* and *stunning* cannot.

A carefully engraved *symbol* has a casting time of 10 minutes. The *symbol* is inactive when finished and remains so until triggered. Once triggered, it becomes active and glows, usually lasting 10 minutes per caster level. Some *symbols* can last indefinitely once triggered. For example, a *symbol of death* ends when it has slain 150 hit points worth of creatures.

To be effective, a *symbol* must always be placed in plain sight and in a prominent location. Covering or hiding the rune renders the *symbol* ineffective.

As a default, a *symbol* is triggered whenever a creature does one or more of the following, as you select: reads, touches, or passes over the rune, looks at the rune, or passes through a portal bearing the rune.

In this case, "reading" the rune means any attempt to study it, identify it, or fathom its meaning. Throwing a cover over a *symbol* to render it inoperative triggers it if it reacts to touch. To trigger a *symbol*, a creature must be within 60 feet of the rune.

You can set special triggering conditions of your own. These can be as simple or elaborate as you desire. Special conditions for triggering a *symbol* can be based on a creature's name, identity, or alignment, but otherwise must be based on observable actions or qualities. Intangibles such as level, class, HD, and hit points don't qualify. For example, a *symbol* can be set to activate when a lawful good creature approaches, but not when a paladin approaches.

A *symbol's* triggering conditions must always be defensive in nature. A touch-triggered *symbol* remains untriggered if an item bearing the *symbol* is used to touch a creature. Likewise, a *symbol* cannot be placed on a weapon and set to activate when the weapon strikes a foe.

Once the spell is cast, a *symbol's* triggering conditions cannot be changed.

You ignore the effects of your own *symbols* and cannot inadvertently trigger them. When scribing a *symbol* quickly, you can instantly attune any number of creatures to the *symbol*, rending them immune to its effects, provided the creatures are within 60 feet of the rune when it is created and that you are aware of their presence.

When creating a carefully inscribed *symbol*, you can specify a password or phrase that prevents a creature using it from triggering the *symbol*. You also can attune any number of creatures to the *symbol*, but doing this can extend the casting time. Attuning one or two creatures takes negligible time, and attuning a small group (up to ten creatures) takes 1 hour. Attuning a large group (up to twenty-five creatures) takes 1 day. Attuning larger groups takes proportionately longer, as the DM sees fit.

When triggered, a *symbol* affects all creatures within a 60-foot radius except for you and any individuals attuned to it. If a *symbol* has a password, anyone using the password remains immune to that particular rune's effects so long as the character remains within 60 feet of the rune. If the character leaves the radius and returns later, he must use the password again. Once triggered, a *symbol* remains active until its duration expires. Creatures who subsequently meet an active *symbol's* triggering conditions suffer its effects.

A successful *dispel magic* removes the effects of a *symbol* from a creature unless the *symbol's* effect is instantaneous (*death, stunning*) or the description specifies another remedy (*insanity*). The rune itself can be removed by a successful *dispel magic* targeted solely on the rune. An *erase* spell has no effect on a *symbol*. Destruction of the surface where a *symbol* rests destroys the *symbol* but also triggers its effects.

Jozan casts symbol of pain.

Read magic allows you to identify a *symbol* with a successful Spellcraft check (DC 19). Identifying the *symbol* does not discharge it and allows you to know the version of the *symbol*.

Note: Magic traps such as *symbol* are hard to detect and disable. A rogue (only) can use the Search skill to find a *symbol* and Disable Device to thwart it. The DC in each case is 25 + spell level, or 33 for *symbol*.

A *symbol* can be rendered permanent with the *permanency* spell, provided it is carefully engraved upon a permanent, nonportable surface such as a wall or door. A *permanency* spell extends a *symbol's* basic duration of 10 minutes per caster level indefinitely. When triggered, a permanent *symbol* usually glows and is active for about 10 minutes, but there is no limit to how many times it can be triggered. If the *symbol* can affect only a limited number of hit points worth of creatures, the limit applies each 10 minutes. For example, a permanent symbol of *death* could slay 150 hit points worth of creatures every 10 minutes.

Known symbols include:

Death: One or more creatures within the radius, whose combined total hit points do not exceed 150, must succeed at Fortitude saves or die. The *symbol* affects the closest creatures first, skipping creatures with too many hit points to affect. This *symbol* must be carefully engraved on a surface. Once triggered, the symbol lasts until it has affected 150 hit points worth of creatures.

Discord: All creatures with an Intelligence score of 3 or higher within 60 feet immediately fall into loud bickering and arguing. Meaningful communication is impossible. If the affected creatures have different alignments, there is a 50% chance that they attack each other. Bickering lasts 5d4 rounds. Fighting begins 1d4 rounds into the bickering and lasts 2d4 rounds. This *symbol* must be carefully engraved on a surface. Once triggered, the *symbol* lasts 10 minutes per caster level. This version is a mind-affecting spell.

Fear: This *symbol* can be scribed quickly or carefully engraved on a surface. Creatures within the radius are afflicted by a powerful version of the *fear* spell. If scribed in the air, this symbol requires a Will save to resist. If the rune is carefully inscribed, the save DC increases by 4. Once triggered, the symbol lasts 10 minutes per caster level. This version is a mind-affecting spell.

Hopelessness: All creatures within the radius must attempt Will saves. If the rune is carefully engraved on a surface, the save DC increases by 4. If the save fails, the creature suffers from hopelessness for 3d4×10 minutes and submits to

simple demands from foes, such as to surrender or get out. The effect is similar to that of the *suggestion* spell. If no foes are present to make demands, there is a 25% chance that a hopeless creature proves unable to take any action except hold its ground. If the creature remains free to act, there is a 25% chance it retreats from the rune at normal speed. In either case, the creature can defend normally if attacked. Once triggered, the *symbol* lasts 10 minutes per caster level. This version is a mind-affecting spell.

Insanity: One or more creatures within the radius, whose combined total hit points do not exceed 150, become insane (as the *insanity* spell; Will negates). The *symbol* affects the closest creatures first, skipping creatures with too many hit points to affect. This *symbol* must be carefully engraved on a surface. Once triggered, the *symbol* lasts until it has affected 150 hit points worth of creatures. This version is a mind-affecting spell.

Pain: Creatures within the radius suffer wracking pains that reduce Dexterity scores by 2 and impose a –4 penalty on attack rolls, skill checks, and ability checks (Fortitude negates). Both effects last 2d10×10 minutes. This *symbol* can be scribed quickly or carefully engraved on a surface. If carefully inscribed, the save DC increases by 4. Once triggered, the *symbol* lasts 10 minutes per caster level.

Persuasion: This *symbol* can be scribed quickly or carefully engraved on a surface. All creatures within the radius must succeed at Will saves to resist. If the symbol is carefully inscribed, the save DC increases by 4. If the save fails, the creature becomes the same alignment as you for 1d20 × 10 minutes. During this time, affected creatures become friendly to you as though subjected to *charm person*. This version is a mind-affecting spell.

Sleep: Creatures within the radius fall into a catatonic slumber if they have 8 or fewer HD (Will negates). Sleeping creatures cannot be awakened for 3d6×10 minutes. This *symbol* must be carefully engraved on a surface. Once triggered, the *symbol* lasts 10 minutes per caster level. This version is a mind-affecting spell.

Stunning: One or more creatures within the radius whose total hit points do not exceed 250 become stunned (Fortitude negates). The *symbol* affects the closest creatures first, skipping creatures with too many hit points to affect. A stunned creature can't act and loses any Dexterity bonus to AC. Attackers gain +2 bonuses to attack it. In addition, the stunned creatures drop what they are holding. This *symbol* must be carefully engraved on a surface.

Arcane Material Components (Quickly Scribed Symbol): A small amount of mercury and phosphorus.

Material Components (Carefully Engraved Symbol): Mercury and phosphorus, plus powdered diamond and opal with a total value of at least 5,000 gp each.

Sympathy

Enchantment (Compulsion) [Mind-Affecting]
Level: Drd 9, Sor/Wiz 8
Components: V, S, M
Casting Time: 1 hour
Range: Close (25 ft. + 5 ft./2 levels)
Target: One location (up to a 10-ft. cube/level) or one object
Duration: 2 hours/level
Saving Throw: Will negates (see text)
Spell Resistance: Yes

You cause an object or location to emanate magical vibrations that attract either a specific type of intelligent creature or creatures of a particular alignment, as defined by you. The particular type of creature to be affected must be named specifically—for example, red dragons, hill giants, wererats, lammasu, catoblepas, vampires, etc. Larger groups, such as "goblinoids," are not specific enough. Likewise, the specific alignment must be named—for example, chaotic evil, chaotic good, lawful neutral, or true neutral.

Creatures of the type or alignment feel elated and pleased to be in the area or desire to touch or to possess the object. The compulsion to stay in the area or touch the object is overpowering. If the save is successful, the creature is released from the enchantment, but a subsequent save must be made 1d6 × 10 minutes later. If this save fails, the affected creature attempts to return to the area or object.

Sympathy counters and dispels *antipathy*.

Material Components: 1,500 gp worth of crushed pearls and a drop of honey.

Tasha's Hideous Laughter

Enchantment (Compulsion)
Level: Brd 2, Sor/Wiz 2
Components: V, S, M
Casting Time: 1 action
Range: Close (25 ft. + 5 ft./2 levels)
Target: One creature (see text)
Duration: 1d3 rounds
Saving Throw: Will negates
Spell Resistance: Yes

This spell afflicts the subject with uncontrollable laughter. It collapses into gales of manic laughter, falling prone. The subject can take no actions while laughing. After the spell ends, it can act normally.

Creatures with Intelligence scores of 2 or lower are not affected. A creature whose type (such as humanoid or dragon) is different from the caster's receives a +4 bonus on its saving throw, because humor doesn't "translate" well.

Material Component: Tiny tarts that are thrown at the target and a feather that is waved in the air.

Telekinesis
Transmutation
Level: Sor/Wiz 5
Components: V, S
Casting Time: 1 action
Range: Long (400 ft. + 40 ft./level)
Target or Targets: See text
Duration: Concentration (up to 1 round/level) or instantaneous (see text)
Saving Throw: Will negates (object) (see text)
Spell Resistance: Yes (object) (see text)

You move objects or creatures by concentrating on them. Depending on the version selected, the spell can provide either a gentle, sustained force or a single short, violent thrust.

Sustained Force: A sustained force moves a creature or object weighing up to 25 pounds per caster level up to 20 feet per round. A creature can negate the effect against itself or against an object it possesses with a successful Will save or with SR.

This version of the spell lasts up to 1 round per caster level, but it ends if you cease concentration. The weight can be moved vertically, horizontally, or both. An object cannot be moved beyond your range. The spell ends if the object is forced beyond the range. If you cease concentration for any reason, the object falls or stops.

An object can be telekinetically manipulated as if with one hand. For example, a lever or rope can be pulled, a key can be turned, an object rotated, and so on, if the force required is within the weight limitation. You might even be able to untie simple knots, though delicate activities such as these require Intelligence checks against a DC set by the DM.

Violent Thrust: Alternatively, the spell energy can be expended in a single round. You can hurl one or more objects or creatures who are within range and all within 10 feet of each other toward any target within 10 feet/level of all the objects. You can hurl up to a total weight of 25 pounds per caster level.

You must succeed at attack rolls (one per creature or object thrown) to hit the target with the items, using your base attack bonus + your Intelligence modifier. Weapons cause standard damage (with no Strength bonus). Other objects cause damage ranging from 1 point per 25 pounds (for less dangerous objects such as a barrel) to 1d6 points of damage per 25 pounds (for hard, dense objects such as a boulder).

Creatures who fall within the weight capacity of the spell can be hurled, but they are allowed Will saves to negate the effect, as are those whose held possessions are targeted by the spell. If a telekinesed creature is hurled against a solid surface, it takes damage as if it had fallen 10 feet (1d6 points).

Teleport
Transmutation [Teleportation]
Level: Sor/Wiz 5, Travel 5
Components: V
Casting Time: 1 action
Range: Personal and touch
Target: You and touched objects or other touched willing creatures weighing up to 50 lb./level
Duration: Instantaneous
Saving Throw: None and Will negates (object)
Spell Resistance: No and Yes (object)

This spell instantly transports you to a designated destination. Distance is not a factor, but interplanar travel is not possible. You can bring along objects and willing creatures totaling up to 50 pounds per caster level. As with all spells where the range is personal and the target is you, you need not make a saving throw, nor is SR applicable to you. Only objects held or in use (attended) by another person receive saving throws and SR.

You must have some clear idea of the location and layout of the destination. You can't simply teleport to the warlord's tent if you don't know where that tent is, what it looks like, or what's in it. The clearer your mental image, the more likely the teleportation works. Areas of strong physical or magical energies may make teleportation more hazardous or even impossible.

Note: Teleportation is instantaneous travel through the Astral Plane. Anything that blocks astral travel also blocks teleportation.

To see how well the teleportation works, roll d% and consult the Teleport table. Refer to the following information for definitions of the terms on the table.

Familiarity: "Very familiar" is a place where you have been very often and where you feel at home. "Studied carefully" is a place you know well, either because you've been there often or you have used other means (such as *scrying*) to study the place. "Seen casually" is a place that you have seen more than once but with which you are not very familiar. "Viewed once" is a place that you have seen once, possibly using magic. "Description" is a place whose location and appearance you know through someone else's description, perhaps even from a precise map.

"False destination" is a place that doesn't exist, such as if you have mistranslated an ancient tome and tried to teleport into a nonexistent treasure vault that you believe you read about, or if a traitorous guide has carefully described an enemy's sanctum to you when that sanctum is completely different from what the traitor described. When traveling to a false destination, roll 1d20+80 to obtain results on the table, rather than rolling d%, since there is no real destination for you to hope to arrive at or even be off target from.

On Target: You appear where you want to be.

Off Target: You appear safely a random distance away from the destination in a random direction. Distance off target is 1d10 × 1d10% of the distance that was to be traveled. For example, if you tried to travel 120 miles, landed off target, and rolled 5 and 3 on the two d10s, then you would be 15% off target. That's 18 miles, in this case. The DM determines the direction off target randomly, such as by rolling 1d8 and designating 1 as north, 2 as northeast, etc. If you were teleporting to a coastal city and wound up 18 miles out at sea, you could be in trouble.

Similar Area: You wind up in an area that's visually or thematically similar to the target area. A wizard heading for her home laboratory might wind up in another wizard's laboratory or in an alchemy supply shop that has many of the same tools and implements as in her laboratory. Generally, you appear in the closest similar place, but since the spell has no range limit, you could conceivably wind up somewhere else across the globe.

Mishap: You and anyone else teleporting with you have gotten "scrambled." You each take 1d10 points of damage, and you reroll on the chart to see where you wind

TELEPORT

Familiarity	On Target	Off Target	Similar Area	Mishap
Very familiar	01–97	98–99	100	—
Studied carefully	01–94	95–97	98–99	100
Seen casually	01–88	89–94	95–98	99–100
Viewed once	01–76	77–88	89–96	97–100
Description	01–52	53–76	77–92	93–100
False destination (1d20+80)	—	—	81–92	93–100

264

up. For these rerolls, roll 1d20+80. Each time "Mishap" comes up, the characters take more damage and must reroll.

Teleportation Circle

Transmutation [Teleportation]
Level: Sor/Wiz 9
Components: V, M
Casting Time: 10 minutes
Range: Touch
Effect: Circle up to 5 ft. in radius that teleports those who activate it
Duration: 10 minutes/level (D)
Saving Throw: None
Spell Resistance: Yes

You create a circle on the floor or other horizontal surface that teleports, as *teleport without error*, any creature who stands on it to a designated spot. Once you designate the destination for the circle, you can't change it. The spell fails if you attempt to set the circle to teleport creatures into a solid object, to a place with which you are not familiar and have no clear description, or to another plane.

The circle itself is subtle and nearly impossible to notice. If you intend to keep creatures from activating it accidentally, you need to mark the circle in some way, such as by placing it on a raised platform.

Note: Magic traps such as *teleportation circle* are hard to detect and disable. A rogue (only) can use the Search skill to find the circle and Disable Device to thwart it. The DC in each case is 25 + spell level, or 34 in the case of *teleportation circle*.

Material Component: Amber dust to cover the area of the circle (cost 1,000 gp).

Teleport without Error

Transmutation [Teleportation]
Level: Sor/Wiz 7, Travel 7

As *teleport*, except there is no chance you arrive off target. You must have at least a reliable description of the place to which you are teleporting. If you attempt to teleport with insufficient information (or with misleading information), you disappear and simply reappear in your original location.

Temporal Stasis

Transmutation
Level: Sor/Wiz 9
Components: V, S, M
Casting Time: 1 action
Range: Touch
Target: Creature touched
Duration: Permanent
Saving Throw: None
Spell Resistance: Yes

You must succeed at a melee touch attack. You place the subject into a state of suspended animation. For the creature, time ceases to flow and its condition becomes fixed. The creature does not grow older. Its body functions virtually cease, and no force or effect can harm it. This state persists until the magic is removed by a successful *dispel magic* spell.

Material Component: A powder composed of diamond, emerald, ruby, and sapphire dust with a total value of at least 5,000 gp.

Tenser's Floating Disk

Evocation [Force]
Level: Sor/Wiz 1
Components: V, S, M
Casting Time: 1 action
Range: Close (25 ft. + 5 ft./2 levels)
Effect: 3-ft.-diameter disk of force
Duration: 1 hour/level
Saving Throw: None
Spell Resistance: No

You create a slightly concave, circular plane of force that follows you about and carries loads for you. The disk is 3 feet in diameter and 1 inch deep at its center. It can hold 100 pounds of weight per caster level. (If used to transport a liquid, its capacity is 2 gallons.) The disk floats approximately 3 feet above the ground at all times and remains level. It floats along horizontally within spell range and will accompany you at a rate of no more than your normal speed each round. If not otherwise directed, it maintains a constant interval of 5 feet between itself and you. The disk winks out of existence when the spell duration expires. The disk also winks out if you move beyond range (by moving too fast or by such means as a *teleport* spell) or try to take the disk more than 3 feet away from the surface beneath it. When the disk winks out, whatever it was supporting falls to the surface beneath it.

Material Component: A drop of mercury.

Tenser's Transformation

Transmutation
Level: Sor/Wiz 6
Components: V, S, M
Casting Time: 1 action
Range: Personal
Target: You
Duration: 1 round/level

You become a virtual fighting machine—stronger, tougher, faster, and more skilled in combat. Your mind-set changes so that you relish combat and you can't cast spells, even from magic items.

You gain 1d6 temporary hit points per caster level, a +4 natural armor bonus to AC, a +2d4 Strength enhancement bonus, a +2d4 Dexterity enhancement bonus, a +1 base attack bonus per two caster levels (which may give you an extra attack), a +5

competence bonus on Fortitude saves, and proficiency with all simple and martial weapons. You attack opponents with melee or ranged weapons if you can, even resorting to unarmed attacks if that's all you can do.

Material Component: A *potion of Strength*, which you drink (and whose effects are subsumed by the spell effects).

Time Stop

Transmutation
Level: Sor/Wiz 9, Trickery 9
Components: V
Casting Time: 1 action
Range: Personal
Target: You
Duration: 1d4+1 rounds (apparent time)

This spell seems to make time cease to flow for everyone but you. In fact, you speed up so greatly that all other creatures seem frozen, though they are actually still moving at their normal speeds. You are free to act for 1d4+1 rounds of apparent time. Normal and magical fire, cold, gas, and the like can still harm you. While the *time stop* is in effect, other creatures are invulnerable to your attacks and spells; however, you can create spell effects and leave them to take effect when the *time stop* spell ends. (The spells' durations do not begin until the *time stop* is over.)

You cannot move or harm items held, carried, or worn by a creature stuck in normal time, but you can affect any item that is not in another creature's possession.

You are undetectable while *time stop* lasts. You cannot enter an area protected by an *antimagic field*, or by *protection from chaos/evil/good/law*, or by a *magic circle* spell, while under the effects of *time stop*.

Tongues

Divination
Level: Brd 2, Clr 4, Sor/Wiz 3
Components: V, M/DF
Casting Time: 1 action
Range: Touch
Target: Creature touched
Duration: 10 minutes/level
Saving Throw: None
Spell Resistance: No

This spell grants the creature touched the ability to speak and understand the language of any intelligent creature, whether it is a racial tongue or a regional dialect. Naturally, the subject can speak only one language at a time, although she may be able to understand several languages. *Tongues* does not enable the subject to speak with creatures who don't speak. The subject can make herself understood as far as her voice carries. This spell does not predispose any creature addressed toward the subject in any way.

Arcane Material Component: A small clay model of a ziggurat, which shatters when the verbal component is pronounced.

Transmute Metal to Wood

Transmutation
Level: Drd 7
Components: V, S, DF
Casting Time: 1 action
Range: Long (400 ft. + 40 ft./level)
Area: All metal objects within a 40-ft.-radius burst
Duration: Instantaneous
Saving Throw: None
Spell Resistance: Yes (object; see text)

This spell enables you to change all metal objects within its area to wood. Weapons, armor, and other metal objects carried by creatures are affected as well. Magic objects made of metal effectively have SR 20 + caster level against this spell. Artifacts cannot be transmuted. Weapons converted from metal to wood suffer a –2 penalty to attack and damage rolls. Armor converted from metal to wood loses 2 points of AC bonus. Weapons changed by this spell splinter and break on any natural attack roll of 1 or 2, and armor changed by this spell loses an additional point of AC bonus every time it is struck by a natural attack roll of 19 or 20.

Only a *limited wish, miracle,* or *wish* or similar magic can restore a transmuted object to its metallic state. Otherwise, for example, a metal door changed to wood is forevermore a wooden door.

Transmute Mud to Rock

Transmutation
Level: Drd 5, Sor/Wiz 5
Components: V, S, M/DF
Casting Time: 1 action
Range: Medium (100 ft. + 10 ft./level)
Area: Up to two 10-ft. cubes/level (S)
Duration: Permanent
Saving Throw: See text
Spell Resistance: No

This spell transforms normal mud or quicksand of any depth into soft stone (sandstone or a similar mineral) permanently. Creatures in the mud are allowed a Reflex save to escape before the area is hardened to stone.

Transmute mud to rock counters and dispels *transmute rock to mud.*

Arcane Material Component: Sand, lime, and water.

Transmute Rock to Mud

Transmutation
Level: Drd 5, Sor/Wiz 5
Components: V, S, M/DF
Casting Time: 1 action
Range: Medium (100 ft. + 10 ft./level)
Area: Up to two 10-ft. cubes/level (S)
Duration: Permanent (see text)
Saving Throw: See text
Spell Resistance: No

This spell turns natural, uncut or unworked rock of any sort into an equal volume of mud. If the spell is cast upon a boulder, for example, the boulder collapses into mud. Magical or enchanted stone is not affected by the spell. The depth of the mud created cannot exceed 10 feet. Creatures unable to levitate, fly, or otherwise free themselves from the mud sink until hip- or chest-deep, reducing their speed to 5 feet and giving them –2 penalties on attack rolls and AC. Brush thrown atop the mud can support creatures able to climb on top of it. Creatures large enough to walk on the bottom can wade through the area at a speed of 5 feet.

If *transmute rock to mud* is cast upon the ceiling of a cavern or tunnel, the mud falls to the floor and spreads out in a pool at a depth of 5 feet. For example, a 10th-level caster could convert twenty 10-foot cubes into mud. Pooling on the floor, this mud would cover an area of forty 10-foot squares to a depth of 5 feet. The falling mud and the ensuing cave-in deal 8d6 points of damage to anyone caught directly beneath the area, or half damage to those who succeed at Reflex saves.

Castles and large stone buildings are generally immune to the effects of the spell, since *transmute rock to mud* can't affect worked stone and doesn't reach deep enough to undermine such buildings' foundations. However, small buildings or structures often rest upon foundations shallow enough to be damaged or even partially toppled by this spell.

The mud remains until a successful *dispel magic* or *transmute mud to rock* spell restores its substance—but not necessarily its form. Evaporation turns the mud to normal dirt over a period of days. The exact time depends on exposure to the sun, wind, and normal drainage.

Arcane Material Component: Clay and water.

Transport via Plants

Transmutation
Level: Drd 6
Components: V, S
Casting Time: 1 action
Range: Unlimited
Target: You
Duration: 1 round

You can enter any normal plant (Medium-size or larger) and pass any distance to a plant of the same species in a single round, regardless of the distance separating the two. The entry plant must be alive. The destination plant need not be familiar to you, but it also must be alive. If you are uncertain of the location of a particular kind of destination plant, you need merely designate direction and distance ("an oak tree one hundred miles due north of here"), and the *transport via plants* spell moves you as close as possible to the desired location. If a particular destination plant is desired (the oak tree outside your druid grove, for instance), but the plant is not living, the spell fails and you are ejected from the entry plant.

This spell does not function with plant creatures such as shambling mounds and treants.

The destruction of an occupied plant slays you.

Trap the Soul

Conjuration (Summoning)
Level: Sor/Wiz 8
Components: V, S, M, (F)
Casting Time: 1 action or see text
Range: Close (25 ft. + 5 ft./2 levels)
Target: One creature
Duration: Permanent (see text)
Saving Throw: See text
Spell Resistance: Yes (see text)

Trap the soul forces a creature's life force (and its material body) into a gem.

The gem holds the trapped entity indefinitely or until the gem is broken and the life force is released, which allows the material body to reform. If the trapped creature is a powerful creature from another plane (which could mean a character trapped by an inhabitant of another plane when the character is not on the Material Plane), it can be required to perform a service immediately upon being freed. Otherwise, the creature can go free once the gem imprisoning it is broken.

Depending on the version selected, the spell can be triggered in one of two ways.

Spell Completion: First, the spell can be completed by speaking its final word as a standard action as if you were casting a regular spell at the subject. This allows SR (if any) and a Will save to avoid the effect. If the creature's name is spoken as well, any SR is ignored and the save DC increases by 2. If the save or SR is successful, the gem shatters.

Trigger Object: The second method is far more insidious, for it tricks the subject into accepting a trigger object inscribed with the final spell word, automatically placing the creature's soul in the trap. To use this method, both the creature's name and the trigger word must be inscribed on the trigger object when the gem is enchanted. A *sympathy* spell can also be placed on the trigger object. As soon as the subject picks up or accepts the trigger object, its life force is automatically transferred to the gem without the benefit of SR or a save.

Material Component: Before the actual casting of *trap the soul*, you must procure a gem of at least 1,000 gp value for every Hit Die possessed by the creature to be trapped (for example, it requires a gem of 10,000 gp value to trap a 10 HD creature). If the gem is not valuable enough, it shatters when the entrapment is attempted. (While characters have no concept of level as such, the value of the gem needed to trap an individual can be researched. Remember that this value can change over time as characters advance.)

Focus (Trigger Object Only): If the trigger object method is used, a special trigger object, prepared as described above, is needed.

Tree Shape

Transmutation
Level: Drd 2, Rgr 3
Components: V, S, DF
Casting Time: 1 action
Range: Personal
Target: You
Duration: 1 hour/level (D)

By means of this spell, you are able to assume the form of a small, living tree or shrub or a large, dead tree trunk with a small number of limbs. The closest inspection cannot reveal that the tree in question is actually a magically concealed creature. To all normal tests you are, in fact, a tree or shrub, although a *detect magic* spell reveals a faint transmutation on the tree. While in tree form, you can observe all that transpires around you just as if you were in your normal form, and your hit points and saves remain unaffected. You gain a +10 natural armor bonus to AC but have an effective Dexterity score of 1. You are immune to critical hits while in tree form. All clothing and gear carried or worn changes with you.

You can dismiss *tree shape* as a free action (instead of as a standard action).

Tree Stride

Transmutation [Teleportation]
Level: Drd 5, Rgr 4
Components: V, S, DF
Casting Time: 1 action
Range: Personal
Target: You
Duration: 1 hour/level or until expended (see text)

You gain the ability to enter trees and move from inside one tree to inside another tree. The first tree you enter and all others you enter must be of the same type, must all be living, and must have girth at least equal to yours. By moving into an oak tree (for example), you instantly know the location of all other oak trees within transport range (see

below) and may choose whether you want to pass into one or simply step back out of the tree you moved into. You may choose to pass to any tree of the appropriate kind within the transport range shown in the following table:

Type of Tree	Range of Transport
Oak, ash, yew	3,000 feet
Elm, linden	2,000 feet
Other deciduous	1,500 feet
Any coniferous	1,000 feet
All other trees	500 feet

You may move into a tree up to one time per level (passing from one tree to another counts only as moving into one tree). The spell lasts until the duration is expended or you exit a tree. In a thick oak forest, this means that a 10th-level druid could make ten transports over the course of 10 rounds, traveling up to 30,000 feet (about six miles) by doing so. Each transport is a full-round action.

You can, at your option, remain within a tree without transporting yourself, though you are forced out when the spell ends. If the tree in which you are concealed is chopped down or burned, you are slain if you do not exit before the process is complete.

True Resurrection

Conjuration (Healing)
Level: Clr 9, Healing 9
Casting Time: 10 minutes

As *raise dead,* except the cleric can resurrect a creature who has been dead up to 10 years per caster level. This spell can even bring back creatures whose bodies have been wholly destroyed, provided you unambiguously identify the deceased in some fashion (reciting the deceased's time and place of birth or death is the most common method).

Upon completion of the spell, the creature is immediately restored to full hit points, vigor, and health, with no loss of level (or Constitution point) or prepared spells.

You can revive someone killed by a death effect or someone who has been turned into an undead creature and then destroyed.

Even *true resurrection* can't restore to life a creature who has died of old age.

Material Components: A sprinkle of holy water and a diamond worth at least 5,000 gp.

True Seeing

Divination
Level: Clr 5, Drd 7, Knowledge 5, Sor/Wiz 6
Components: V, S, M
Casting Time: 1 action

Range: Touch
Target: Creature touched
Duration: 1 minute/level
Saving Throw: Will negates (harmless)
Spell Resistance: Yes (harmless)

You confer on the subject the ability to see all things as they actually are. The subject sees through normal and magical darkness, notices secret doors hidden by magic, sees the exact locations of creatures or objects under *blur* or *displacement* effects, sees invisible creatures or objects normally, sees through illusions, and sees the true form of polymorphed, changed, or transmuted things. Further, the subject can focus her vision to see into the Ethereal Plane. The range of *true seeing* conferred is 120 feet.

True seeing, however, does not penetrate solid objects. It in no way confers X-ray vision or its equivalent. It does not cancel concealment, including that caused by fog and the like. *True seeing* does not help the viewer see through mundane disguises, spot creatures who are simply hiding, or notice secret doors hidden by mundane means. In addition, the spell effects cannot be further enhanced with known magic, so one cannot use *true seeing* through a *crystal ball* or in conjunction with *clairaudience/clairvoyance.*

Additionally, the divine version of this spell allows the subject to see auras, noting alignments of creatures at a glance.

Material Component: An ointment for the eyes that costs 250 gp and is made from very rare mushroom powder, saffron, and fat.

True Strike

Divination
Level: Sor/Wiz 1
Components: V, F
Casting Time: 1 action
Range: Personal
Target: You
Duration: 1 round

You gain temporary, intuitive insight into the immediate future during your next attack. Your next single attack roll (within the duration of the spell) gains a +20 insight bonus. Additionally, you are not affected by the miss chance that applies to attacks against a concealed target.

Focus: A small wooden replica of an archery target.

Undetectable Alignment

Abjuration
Level: Brd 2, Clr 2, Pal 2
Components: V, S
Casting Time: 1 action
Range: Close (25 ft. + 5 ft./2 levels)
Target: One creature or object

Duration: 24 hours
Saving Throw: Will negates (object)
Spell Resistance: Yes (object)

An *undetectable alignment* spell conceals the alignment of an object or a creature from all forms of divination.

Unhallow

Evocation [Evil]
Level: Clr 5, Drd 5
Components: V, S, M
Casting Time: One day
Range: Touch
Area: 10-ft./level radius emanating from the touched point
Duration: Instantaneous
Saving Throw: None
Spell Resistance: See text

Unhallow makes a particular site, building, or structure an unholy site. This has three major effects.

First, the site or structure is guarded by a *magic circle against good* effect.

Second, all turning checks to turn undead suffer a –4 profane penalty and turning checks to rebuke undead gain a +4 profane bonus. Spell resistance does not apply to this effect. (Note: This provision does not apply to the druid version of the spell.)

Finally, you may choose to fix a single spell effect to the *unhallow* site. The spell effect lasts for one year and functions throughout the entire consecrated site, regardless of its normal duration and area or effect. You may designate whether the effect applies to all creatures, creatures who share your faith or alignment, or creatures who adhere to another faith or alignment. For example, you may create a *bless* effect that aids all creatures of like alignment or faith in the area, or a *curse* effect that hinders creatures of the opposite alignment or an enemy faith. At the end of the year, the chosen effect lapses, but it can be renewed or replaced simply by casting *unhallow* again.

Spell effects that may be tied to an *unhallow* site include *aid, bane, bless, cause fear, darkness, daylight, deeper darkness, detect magic, detect good, dimensional anchor, discern lies, dispel magic, endure elements, freedom of movement, invisibility purge, negative energy protection, protection from elements, remove fear, resist elements, silence, tongues,* and *zone of truth.* Spell resistance might apply to these spells' effects. (See the individual spell descriptions for details.)

An area can receive only one *unhallow* (and its associated spell effect) at a time.

Unhallow counters and dispels *hallow*.

Material Components: Herbs, oils, and incense worth at least 1,000 gp, plus 1,000 gp per level of the spell to be tied to the unhallowed area.

Unholy Aura

Abjuration [Evil]
Level: Clr 8, Evil 8
Components: V, S, F
Casting Time: 1 action
Range: 20 ft.
Targets: One creature/level in a 20-ft.-radius burst centered on you
Duration: 1 round/level (D)
Saving Throw: See text
Spell Resistance: Yes (harmless)

A malevolent darkness surrounds the subjects, protecting them from attacks, granting them resistance to spells cast by good creatures, and weakening good creatures when they strike the subjects. This abjuration has four effects:

First, the warded creatures gain a +4 deflection bonus to AC and a +4 resistance bonus to saves. Unlike the effect of *protection from good,* this benefit applies against all attacks, not just against attacks by evil creatures.

Second, the warded creatures gain SR 25 against good spells and spells cast by good creatures.

Third, the abjuration blocks possession and mental influence, just as *protection from good* does.

Finally, if a good creature succeeds at a melee attack against a warded creature, the offending attacker takes 1d6 points of temporary Strength damage (Fortitude save negates).

Focus: A tiny reliquary containing some sacred relic, such as a piece of parchment from an unholy text. The reliquary costs at least 500 gp.

Unholy Blight

Evocation [Evil]
Level: Evil 4
Components: V, S
Casting Time: 1 action
Range: Medium (100 ft. + 10 ft./level)
Area: 20-ft.-radius spread
Duration: Instantaneous
Saving Throw: Fortitude partial
Spell Resistance: Yes

You call up unholy power to smite your enemies. The power takes the form of a cold, cloying cloud of greasy darkness. Only good and neutral (not evil) creatures are harmed by the spell.

The spell deals 1d8 points of damage per two caster levels (maximum 5d8) to good creatures and sickens them for 1d4 rounds. A sickened creature suffers a –2 penalty on attack rolls, weapon damage rolls, saves, skill checks, and ability checks. A successful Fortitude save reduces damage to half and negates the sickening effect.

The spell deals only half damage to creatures who are neither evil nor good, and they are not sickened. They can

reduce the damage in half again (down to one-quarter of the roll) with a successful Reflex save.

Unseen Servant

Conjuration (Creation)
Level: Brd 1, Sor/Wiz 1
Components: V, S, M
Casting Time: 1 action
Range: Close (25 ft. + 5 ft./2 levels)
Effect: One invisible, mindless, shapeless servant
Duration: 1 hour/level
Saving Throw: None
Spell Resistance: No

The unseen servant is an invisible, mindless, shapeless force that performs simple tasks at your command. It can run and fetch things, open unstuck doors, and hold chairs, as well as clean and mend. The servant can perform only one activity at a time, but it repeats the same activity over and over again if told to do so, thus allowing you to command the servant to clean the floor and then turn your attention elsewhere as long as you remain within range. It can open only normal doors, drawers, lids, etc. It has an effective Strength score of 2 (so it can lift 20 pounds or drag 100 pounds). It can trigger traps and such, but it can exert only 20 pounds of force, and that is not enough to activate certain pressure plates and other devices. Its speed is 15 feet.

The servant cannot attack in any way; it is never allowed an attack roll. It cannot be killed, but it dissipates if it takes 6 points of damage from area attacks. (It gets no saves against attacks.) If you attempt to send it beyond the spell's range (measured from your current position), the servant ceases to exist.

Material Components: A piece of string and a bit of wood.

Vampiric Touch

Necromancy
Level: Sor/Wiz 3
Components: V, S
Casting Time: 1 action
Range: Touch
Target: Living creature touched
Duration: Instantaneous/1 hour (see text)
Saving Throw: None
Spell Resistance: Yes

You must succeed at a melee touch attack. Your touch deals 1d6 points of damage per two caster levels (maximum 10d6). You gain temporary hit points equal to the damage you inflict. However, you can't gain more than the subject's current hit points +10, which is enough to kill the subject. The temporary hit points disappear 1 hour later.

Vanish

Transmutation [Teleportation]
Level: Sor/Wiz 7
Range: Touch
Target: One touched object of up to 50 lb./level and 3 cu. ft./level
Saving Throw: Will negates (object)
Spell Resistance: Yes (object)

As *teleport*, except it teleports an object, not you. Creatures and magical forces (such as a *delayed blast fireball* bead) cannot be made to *vanish*. There is a 1% chance that a vanished item is disintegrated instead.

If desired, a vanished object can be sent to a distant location on the Ethereal Plane. In this case, the point from which the object vanished remains faintly magical until the item is retrieved. A successful targeted *dispel magic* spell cast on that point brings the vanished item back from the Ethereal Plane.

Veil

Illusion (Glamer)
Level: Brd 6, Sor/Wiz 6
Components: V, S
Casting Time: 1 action
Range: Long (400 ft. + 40 ft./level)
Targets: One or more creatures, no two of which can be more than 30 ft. apart
Duration: Concentration + 1 hour/level (D)
Saving Throw: Will negates (see text)
Spell Resistance: Yes (see text)

You instantly change the appearance of the subjects and then maintain that appearance for the spell's duration. You can make the subjects appear to be anything you wish. A party might be made to resemble a mixed band of brownies, pixies, and faeries led by a treant. The subjects look, feel, and smell just like the creatures the spell makes them resemble. Affected creatures resume their normal appearances if slain. You must succeed at a Disguise check to duplicate the appearance of a specific individual. This spell gives you a +10 bonus on the check.

Unwilling targets can negate the spell's effect on them by making Will saves or with SR. Those who interact with the subjects can attempt Will disbelief saves to see through the glamer, but SR doesn't help.

Ventriloquism

Illusion (Figment)
Level: Brd 1, Sor/Wiz 1
Components: V, F
Casting Time: 1 action
Range: Close (25 ft. + 5 ft./2 levels)
Effect: Intelligible sound, usually speech
Duration: 1 minute/level (D)
Saving Throw: Will disbelief (if interacted with)
Spell Resistance: No

You can make your voice (or any sound that you can normally make vocally) seem to issue from someplace else, such as from another creature, a statue, from behind a door, down a passage, etc. You can speak in any language you know. With respect to such voices and sounds, anyone who hears it and rolls a successful save recognizes the sound as illusory (but still hears it).

Focus: A parchment rolled up into a small cone.

Virtue

Transmutation
Level: Clr 0, Drd 0, Pal 1
Components: V, S, DF
Casting Time: 1 action
Range: Touch
Target: Creature touched
Duration: 1 minute
Saving Throw: Yes (harmless)
Spell Resistance: Yes (harmless)

The subject gains 1 temporary hit point.

Vision

Divination
Level: Sor/Wiz 7
Components: V, S, M, XP
Casting Time: 1 action

As *legend lore*, except *vision* works more quickly but produces some strain on you. You pose a question about some person, place, or object, then cast the spell. If the person or object is at hand or if you are in the place in question, you receive a vision about it with a successful Scry check (DC 10). If only detailed information on the person, place, or object is known, the DC is 15, and the information gained is incomplete. If only rumors are known, the DC is 20, and the information gained is vague.

XP Cost: 100 XP.

Wail of the Banshee

Necromancy [Death, Sonic]
Level: Death 9, Sor/Wiz 9
Components: V
Casting Time: 1 action
Range: Close (25 ft. + 5 ft./2 levels)
Area: One living creature/level within a 30-ft.-radius spread
Duration: Instantaneous
Saving Throw: Fortitude negates
Spell Resistance: Yes

You emit a terrible scream that kills creatures who hear it (except for yourself). The spell affects up to one creature per caster level. Creatures closest to the point of origin are affected first.

Wall of Fire

Evocation [Fire]
Level: Drd 5, Fire 4, Sor/Wiz 4
Components: V, S, M/DF
Casting Time: 1 action
Range: Medium (100 ft. + 10 ft./level)
Effect: Opaque sheet of flame up to 20 ft. long/caster level or a ring of fire with a radius of up to 5 ft./two caster levels; either form 20 ft. high
Duration: Concentration + 1 round/level
Saving Throw: See text
Spell Resistance: Yes

An immobile, blazing curtain of shimmering violet fire springs into existence. One side of the wall, selected by you, sends forth waves of heat, dealing 2d4 points of fire damage to creatures within 10 feet and 1d4 points of fire damage to those past 10 feet but within 20 feet. The wall deals this damage when it appears and each round that a creature enters or remains in the area. In addition, the wall deals 2d6 points of fire damage +1 point of fire damage per caster level (maximum +20) to any creature passing through it. The wall deals double damage to undead creatures.

If you evoke the wall so that it appears where creatures are, each creature takes damage as if passing through the wall. Each such creature can avoid the wall by making a successful Reflex save. (If the creature ends up on the hot side of the wall, it takes 2d4 points of damage, as normal.)

If any 5-foot length of wall takes 20 points of cold damage or more in 1 round, that length goes out. (Do not divide cold damage by 4, as normal for objects.)

Arcane Material Component: A small piece of phosphorus.

Wall of Force

Evocation [Force]
Level: Sor/Wiz 5
Components: V, S, M
Casting Time: 1 action
Range: Close (25 ft. + 5 ft./2 levels)
Effect: Wall whose area is up to one 10-ft. square/level or a sphere or hemisphere with a radius of up to 1 ft./level
Duration: 1 minute/level (D)
Saving Throw: None
Spell Resistance: No

A *wall of force* spell creates an invisible wall of force. The *wall of force* cannot move, it is immune to damage of all kinds, and it is totally unaffected by most spells, including *dispel magic*. However, *disintegrate* immediately destroys it, as does a *rod of cancellation*, a *sphere of annihilation*, and *Mordenkainen's disjunction*. Spells and breath weapons cannot pass through the wall in either direction, although *dimension door*, *teleport*, and similar effects can bypass the barrier. It blocks ethereal creatures as well as material creatures (though ethereal creatures can usually get around the wall by floating under or over it through material floors and ceilings). Gaze attacks can operate through the *wall of force*.

The caster can form the wall into a flat, vertical plane whose area is up to one 10-foot square per level, or into a sphere or hemisphere with a radius of up to 1 foot per level.

The *wall of force* must be continuous and unbroken when formed. If its surface is broken by any object or creature, the spell fails.

Material Component: A pinch of powder made from a clear gem.

Wall of Ice

Evocation [Cold]
Level: Sor/Wiz 4
Components: V, S, M
Casting Time: 1 action
Range: Medium (100 ft. + 10 ft./level)
Effect: Anchored plane of ice, up to one 10-ft. square/level, or hemisphere of ice with a radius of up to 3 ft. +1 ft./level
Duration: 1 minute/level
Saving Throw: See text
Spell Resistance: Yes

This spell creates an anchored plane of ice or a hemisphere of ice, depending on the version selected. A wall of ice cannot form in an area occupied by physical objects or creatures. Its surface is smooth and unbroken when created. Fire, including *fireball* and red dragon breath, can melt a wall of ice. It deals full damage to the wall (instead of the normal half damage suffered by objects). Suddenly melting the *wall of ice* creates a great cloud of steamy fog that lasts for 10 minutes.

Ice Plane: A sheet of strong, hard ice appears. The wall is 1 inch thick per caster level. It covers up to a 10-foot-square area per caster level (so a 10th-level wizard can create a wall of ice 100 feet long and 10 feet high, a wall 50 feet long and 20 feet high, etc.). The plane can be oriented in any fashion as long as it is anchored. A vertical wall need only be anchored on the floor, while a horizontal or slanting wall must be anchored on two opposite sides.

The wall is primarily defensive in nature and is used to stop pursuers from following you and the like. Each 10-foot square of wall has 3 hit points per inch of thickness. Creatures can hit the wall automatically. A section of wall whose hit points drop to 0 is breached. If a creature tries to break through the wall with a single attack, the DC for the Strength check is 15 + caster level.

Even when the ice has been broken through, a sheet of frigid air remains. Any creature stepping through it (including the one who broke through the wall) takes 1d6 points of cold damage +1 point per caster level.

Hemisphere: The wall takes the form of a hemisphere whose maximum radius is 3 feet +1 foot per caster level. Thus, a 7th-level caster can create a hemisphere 10 feet in radius. It is as hard to break through as the ice plane form, but it does not deal damage to those who go through a breach.

You can create the hemisphere so that it traps one or more creatures, though these creatures can avoid being trapped by the hemisphere by making successful Reflex saves.

Material Component: A small piece of quartz or similar rock crystal.

Wall of Iron

Conjuration (Creation)
Level: Sor/Wiz 5
Components: V, S, M
Casting Time: 1 action
Range: Medium (100 ft. + 10 ft./level)
Effect: Iron wall whose area is up to one 5-ft. square/level (see text)
Duration: Instantaneous
Saving Throw: See text
Spell Resistance: No

You cause a flat, vertical iron wall to spring into being. This wall can be used to seal off a passage or close a breach, for the wall inserts itself into any surrounding nonliving material if its area is sufficient to do so. The wall cannot be conjured so that it occupies the same space as a creature or another object. It must always be a flat plane, though you can shape its edges to fit the available space.

The *wall of iron* is 1 inch thick per four caster levels. You can double the wall's area by halving its thickness. Each 5-foot square of the wall has 30 hit points per inch of thickness. Creatures can hit the wall automatically, but it is so hard that the first 10 points of damage from each blow are ignored. (For example, a blow of 17 points of damage deals only 7 to the wall.) A section of wall whose hit points drop to 0 is breached. If a creature tries to break through the wall with a single attack, the DC for the Strength check is 25 + 2 per inch of thickness.

If you desire, the wall can be created vertically resting on a flat surface but not attached to the surface so that it can be tipped over to fall on and crush creatures beneath it. The wall is 50% likely to tip in either direction if left unpushed. Creatures can push the wall in one direction rather than letting it fall randomly. A creature must succeed at a Strength check (DC 40) to push the wall over. Creatures with room to flee the falling wall may do so by making

successful Reflex saves. Large and smaller creatures who fail take 10d6 points of damage. The wall cannot crush Huge and larger creatures.

Like any iron wall, this wall is subject to rust, perforation, and other natural phenomena.

Material Component: A small piece of sheet iron plus gold dust worth 50 gp (1 pound of gold dust).

Wall of Stone

Conjuration (Creation)
Level: Clr 5, Drd 6, Earth 5, Sor/Wiz 5
Components: V, S, M/DF
Casting Time: 1 action
Range: Medium (100 ft. + 10 ft./level)
Effect: Stone wall whose area is up to one 5-ft. square/level (S)
Duration: Instantaneous
Saving Throw: See text
Spell Resistance: No

This spell creates a wall of rock that merges into adjoining rock surfaces. It is typically employed to close passages, portals, and breaches against opponents. The *wall of stone* is 1 inch thick per four caster levels and composed of up to one 5-foot square per level. You can double the wall's area by halving its thickness. The wall cannot be conjured so that it occupies the same space as a creature or another object.

Unlike a *wall of iron*, you can create a *wall of stone* in almost any shape you desire. The wall created need not be vertical, nor rest upon any firm foundation; however, it must merge with and be solidly supported by existing stone. It can be used to bridge a chasm, for instance, or as a ramp. For this use, if the span is more than 20 feet, the wall must be arched and buttressed. This requirement reduces the spell's area by half. Thus, a 20th-level caster can create a span with a surface area of ten 5-foot squares. The wall can be crudely shaped to allow crenellations, battlements, and so forth by likewise reducing the area.

Like any other stone wall, this one can be destroyed by *disintegrate* or by normal means such as breaking and chipping. Each 5-foot square has 15 hit points per inch of thickness. Creatures can hit the wall automatically, but the wall is so hard that the first 8 points of damage from each blow are ignored. A section of wall whose hit points drop to 0 is breached. If a creature tries to break through the wall with a single attack, the DC for the Strength check is 20 + 2 per inch of thickness.

It is possible, but difficult, to trap mobile opponents within or under a *wall of stone*, provided the wall is shaped so it can hold the creatures. Creatures avoid entrapment with successful Reflex saves.

Arcane Material Component: A small block of granite.

Wall of Thorns

Conjuration (Creation)
Level: Drd 5, Plant 5
Components: V, S
Casting Time: 1 action
Range: Medium (100 ft. + 10 ft./level)
Effect: Wall of thorny brush, up to one 10-ft. cube/level (S)
Duration: 10 minutes/level (D)
Saving Throw: None
Spell Resistance: No

The *wall of thorns* spell creates a barrier of very tough, pliable, tangled brush bearing needle-sharp thorns as long as a person's finger. Any creature forced into or attempting to move through the *wall of thorns* takes 25 points of damage per round of movement, minus 1 point for each point of the creature's AC. Dexterity bonuses to AC and dodge bonuses do not count for this calculation. (Creatures with an Armor Class of 25 or higher take no damage from contact with the wall.)

You can make the wall as thin as 5 feet thick, which allows you to shape the wall as a number of 10-by-10-by-5-foot blocks equal to caster level ×2. This has no effect on the damage inflicted by the thorns, but any creature attempting to break through takes that much less time to force its way through the barrier.

Creatures can force their way slowly through the wall. To make any progress, a creature must succeed at a Strength check (DC 20). A successful creature moves a number of feet equal to its Strength check result minus 19, so a creature who rolled 24 on its Strength check could move 5 feet in a round. Of course, moving or attempting to move through the thorns incurs damage as described above. A creature trapped in the thorns can choose to remain motionless in order to avoid taking any more damage.

Any creature within the area of the spell when it is cast takes damage as if it had moved into the wall and is caught inside. In order to escape, it must attempt to push its way free, or it can wait until the spell ends. Creatures with the ability to pass through overgrown areas unhindered can pass through a *wall of thorns* at their normal speed without taking damage.

A *wall of thorns* can be carefully breached by slow work with edged weapons.

Chopping away at the wall creates a safe passage 1 foot deep for every 10 minutes of work. Normal fire cannot harm the barrier, but magical fire burns away the barrier in 10 minutes.

Warp Wood

Transmutation
Level: Drd 2
Components: V, S
Casting Time: 1 action
Range: Close (25 ft. + 5 ft./2 levels)
Target: 1 lb. of wood/level, all within a 20-ft. radius

Web can effectively entangle several foes at once.

Duration: Instantaneous
Saving Throw: Will negates (object)
Spell Resistance: Yes (object)

You cause wood to bend and warp, permanently destroying its straightness, form, and strength. At 1st level, you can warp a handaxe handle or ten crossbow bolts. At 3rd level, you can warp the shaft of a typical shortspear. Boards or planks can also be affected, causing a door to be sprung or a boat or ship to leak. Warped ranged weapons are useless. Warped melee weapons suffer a –4 penalty to their attack rolls.

Alternatively, you can unwarp wood (effectively warping it back to normal) with this spell, straightening wood that has been warped by this spell or by other

means. *Make whole,* on the other hand, does no good in repairing a warped item.

Water Breathing

Transmutation
Level: Clr 3, Drd 3, Sor/Wiz 3, Water 3
Components: V, S, M/DF
Casting Time: 1 action
Range: Touch
Target: Living creatures touched
Duration: 2 hours/level (see text)
Saving Throw: Will negates (harmless)
Spell Resistance: Yes (harmless)

The transmuted creatures can breathe water freely. Divide the duration evenly among all the creatures you touch.

The spell does not make creatures unable to breathe air.
Arcane Material Component: A short reed or piece of straw.

Water Walk

Transmutation
Level: Clr 3, Rgr 3
Components: V, S, DF
Casting Time: 1 action
Range: Touch
Targets: One touched creature/level
Duration: 10 minutes/level
Saving Throw: Will negates (harmless)
Spell Resistance: Yes (harmless)

The transmuted creatures can tread on any liquid as if it were firm ground. Mud, oil, snow, quicksand, running water, ice, and even lava can be traversed easily, since the subjects' feet hover an inch or two above the surface. (Creatures crossing molten lava still take damage from the heat.) The creatures can walk, run, charge, or otherwise move across the surface as if it were normal ground.

If the spell is cast underwater (or while the subjects are partially or wholly submerged in whatever liquid they are in), the subjects are borne toward the surface at 60 feet per round until they can stand on it.

Web

Conjuration (Creation)
Level: Sor/Wiz 2
Components: V, S, M
Casting Time: 1 action
Range: Medium (100 ft. + 10 ft./level)
Effect: Webs in a 20-ft.-radius spread
Duration: 10 minutes/level
Saving Throw: Reflex negates (see text)
Spell Resistance: Yes

Web creates a many-layered mass of strong, sticky strands. These strands trap those caught in them. The strands are similar to spider webs but far larger and tougher. These masses must be anchored to two or more solid and diametrically opposed points—floor and ceiling, opposite walls, etc.—or else the web collapses upon itself and disappears. Creatures caught within a *web* or simply touching its strands become *entangled* among the gluey fibers.

An *entangled* creature suffers a −2 penalty to attack rolls, suffers a −4 penalty to effective Dexterity, and can't move. An *entangled* character who attempts to cast a spell must make a Concentration check (DC 15) or lose the spell.

Anyone in the effect's area when the spell is cast must make a Reflex save. If this save succeeds, the creature is not stuck in the webs and is free to act, though moving may be a problem (see below). If the save fails, the creature is stuck. A stuck creature can break loose by spending 1 round and succeeding at a Strength check (DC 20) or an Escape Artist check (DC 25). Once loose (either by making the initial Reflex save or a later Strength check or Escape Artist check), a creature may progress through the web very slowly. Each round devoted to moving allows the creature to make a new Strength check or Escape Artist check. The creature moves 5 feet for each full 5 points by which the check result exceeds 10.

The web provides one-quarter cover for every 5 feet of the substance between you and an opponent—one-half cover for 10 feet of web, three-quarters for 15 feet, and total cover for 20 feet or more. (See Table 8–9: Cover, page 133.)

The strands of a *web* spell are flammable. A magic *flaming sword* can slash them away as easily as a hand brushes away cobwebs. Any fire—a torch, burning oil, a flaming sword, etc.—can set them alight and burn away 5 square feet in 1 round. All creatures within flaming webs take 2d4 points of damage from the flames.

Material Component: A bit of spider web.

Weird

Illusion (Phantasm) [Fear, Mind-
  Affecting]
Level: Sor/Wiz 9
Targets: Any number of creatures, no
  two of which can be more than 30 ft.
  apart

As *phantasmal killer*, except it can affect more than one creature. Only the affected creatures see the phantasmal creatures attacking them, though you see the attackers as shadowy shapes.

If a subject's Fortitude save succeeds, the subject still takes 3d6 points of damage and is stunned for 1 round. The subject's Strength score also drops 1d4 points for 10 minutes. A stunned creature can't act and loses any Dexterity bonus to AC. Attackers gain +2 bonuses to attack it.

Whirlwind

Evocation [Air]
Level: Air 8, Drd 8
Components: V, S, DF
Casting Time: 1 action
Range: Long (400 ft. + 40 ft./level)
Effect: Cyclone 10 ft. wide at base,
  30 ft. wide at top, and 30 ft. tall
Duration: 1 round/level
Saving Throw: Reflex negates (see text)
Spell Resistance: Yes

This spell creates a powerful cyclone of raging wind that moves through the air, along the ground, or over water at a speed of 60 feet per round. You can concentrate on controlling the cyclone's every movement or specify a simple program, such as move straight ahead, zigzag, circle, or the like. Directing the cyclone's movement or changing its programmed movement is a standard action for you. The whirlwind always moves during your turn in the initiative order. If the cyclone exceeds the spell's range, it moves in a random, uncontrolled fashion for 1d3 rounds—possibly endangering you or your allies—and then dissipates. (You can't regain control of the cyclone, even if comes back within range.)

Any Large or smaller creature who comes in contact with the whirlwind must succeed at a Reflex save or take 3d6 points of damage. Medium-size or smaller creatures who fail their first save must succeed at a second one or be picked up bodily by the whirlwind and held suspended in its powerful winds, taking 1d8 points of damage each round with no save allowed. You may direct the cyclone to eject any carried creatures whenever you wish, depositing the hapless souls wherever the whirlwind happens to be when they are released.

Whispering Wind

Transmutation
Level: Brd 2, Sor/Wiz 2
Components: V, S
Casting Time: 1 action
Range: One mile/level
Area: 10-ft.-radius spread
Duration: Until discharged (destina-
  tion is reached) or no more than
  1 hour/level
Saving Throw: None
Spell Resistance: No

You send a message or sound on the wind to a designated spot. The *whispering wind* travels to a specific location within range that is familiar to you, provided that it can find a way to the location. (It can't pass through walls, for instance.) The *whispering wind* is as gentle and unnoticed as a zephyr until it reaches the location. It then delivers its whisper-quiet message or other sound. Note that the message is delivered regardless of whether anyone is present to hear it. The wind then dissipates. You can prepare the spell to bear a message of up to twenty-five words, cause the spell to deliver other sounds for 1 round, or merely have the *whispering wind* seem to be a faint stirring of the air. You can likewise cause the *whispering wind* to move as slowly as one mile per hour or as quickly as one mile per 10 minutes. When the spell reaches its objective, it swirls and remains until the message is delivered. As with *magic mouth*, *whispering wind* cannot speak verbal components, use command words, or activate magical effects.

Wind Walk

Transmutation
Level: Clr 6, Drd 7
Components: V, S, DF
Casting Time: 1 action
Range: Touch
Targets: You and one touched creature/
  three levels
Duration: 1 hour/level (D)
Saving Throw: No and Will negates
  (harmless)
Spell Resistance: No and Yes (harmless)

You alter the substance of your body to a cloudlike vapor and move through the air, possibly at great speed. You can take other creatures with you, each of which acts independently.

A magical wind wafts a wind walker along at up to 600 feet per round (60 mph) or as slow as 5 feet per round (1/2 mph), as the walker wills. Wind walkers are not invisible but rather appear misty and translucent. If fully clothed in white, they are 80% likely to be mistaken for clouds, fog, vapors, etc.

A wind walker can regain her physical form as desired and later resume the cloud form. Each change to and from vaporous form requires 5 rounds. You, however, may dismiss the spell, ending it immediately. You may even dismiss it for individual wind walkers and not others. While in vaporous form, subjects gain damage reduction 20/+1, though they may sustain damage from high winds (as determined by the DM). No spellcasting is possible in vaporous form.

For the last minute of the spell, a wind walker automatically descends 60 feet per round (for a total of 600 feet), though she may descend faster if she wishes. This descent serves as a warning that the spell is about to end.

Wind Wall
Evocation
Level: Air 2, Brd 3, Clr 3, Rgr 4, Sor/Wiz 3
Components: V, S, M/DF
Casting Time: 1 action
Range: Medium (100 ft. + 10 ft./level)
Effect: Wall up to 10 ft./level long and 5 ft./level high (S)
Duration: 1 round/level
Saving Throw: None (see text)
Spell Resistance: Yes

An invisible vertical curtain of wind appears. It is 2 feet thick and of considerable strength. It is a roaring blast sufficient to blow away any bird smaller than an eagle or tear papers and similar materials from unsuspecting hands. (A Reflex save allows a creature to maintain its grasp on an object.) Tiny and Small flying creatures cannot pass through the barrier. Loose materials and cloth garments fly upward when caught in a *wind wall*. Arrows and bolts are deflected upward and miss, while any other normal ranged weapon passing through the wall suffers a 30% miss chance. (A giant-thrown boulder, a siege projectile, and other massive ranged weapons are not affected.) Gases, most gaseous breath weapons, and creatures in gaseous form cannot pass through the wall (although it is no barrier to incorporeal creatures).

While the wall must be vertical, you can shape it in any continuous path along the ground that you like. It is possible to create cylindrical or square wind walls to enclose specific points. A 5th-level caster can create a wall up to 50 feet long and up to 25 feet high, which is sufficient to form a cylinder of wind 15 feet in diameter.

Arcane Material Components: A tiny fan and a feather of exotic origin.

Wish
Universal
Level: Sor/Wiz 9
Components: V, XP
Casting Time: 1 action
Range: See text
Target, Effect, or Area: See text
Duration: See text
Saving Throw: See text
Spell Resistance: Yes

Wish is the mightiest spell a wizard or sorcerer can cast. By simply speaking aloud, you can alter reality to better suit you. Even *wish*, however, has its limits.

A *wish* can do any one of the following:

- Duplicate any wizard or sorcerer spell of 8th level or lower, provided the spell is not from a school prohibited to you.
- Duplicate any other spell of 6th level or lower, provided the spell is not from a school prohibited to you.
- Duplicate any wizard or sorcerer spell of 7th level or lower even if it's from a prohibited school.
- Duplicate any other spell of 5th level or lower even if it's from a prohibited school.
- Undo the harmful effects of many other spells, such as *geas/quest* or *insanity*.
- Create a valuable item, even a magic item, of up to 15,000 gp in value.
- Grant a creature a +1 inherent bonus to an ability score. Two to five *wish* spells cast in immediate succession can grant a creature a +2 to +5 inherent bonus to an ability score (two wishes for a +2 inherent bonus, three for a +3 inherent bonus, and so on). Inherent bonuses are instantaneous, so they cannot be dispelled. Note: An inherent bonus may not exceed +5 for a single ability score, and inherent bonuses to a particular ability score do not stack, so only the best one applies.
- Remove injuries and afflictions. A single *wish* can aid one creature per caster level, and all subjects must be cured of the same type of affliction. For example, you could heal all the damage your party has suffered, or remove all the poison effects from the party, but not do both with the same *wish*. A *wish* can never restore the experience point loss from casting a spell or the level or Constitution loss from being raised from the dead.
- Revive the dead. A *wish* can bring a dead creature back to life by duplicating a *resurrection* spell. A *wish* can revive a dead creature whose body has been destroyed, but the feat takes two *wishes*, one to recreate the body and another to infuse the body with life again. A *wish* cannot prevent a character who was brought back to life from losing an experience level.
- Transport travelers. A *wish* can lift one creature per caster level from anywhere on any plane and place these creatures anywhere else on any plane regardless of local conditions. An unwilling target gets a Will save to negate and SR.
- Undo misfortune. A *wish* can undo a single recent event. The *wish* forces a reroll of any roll made within the last round (including your last turn). Reality reshapes itself to accommodate the new result. For example, the *wish* could undo an opponent's successful save, a foe's successful critical hit

(either the attack roll or the critical roll), a friend's failed save, and so on. The reroll, however, may be as bad as or worse than the original roll. An unwilling target gets a Will save to negate and SR.

You may wish for greater effects than these, but doing so is dangerous. Such a *wish* gives you the opportunity to fulfill your request without fulfilling it completely. (The *wish* may pervert your intent into a literal but undesirable fulfillment or only a partial fulfillment.) For example, wishing for a *staff of the magi* might get you instantly transported to the presence of the staff's current owner. Wishing to be immortal could get you imprisoned in a hidden extradimensional space (as in *imprisonment*), where you could "live" indefinitely.

Duplicated spells allow saves and SR as normal (but save DCs are for 9th-level spells). When a *wish* duplicates a spell that has an XP cost, you must pay 5,000 XP or that cost, whichever is more. When a *wish* duplicates a spell with a material component that costs more than 10,000 gp, you must provide that component.

XP Cost: 5,000 XP or more (see above).

Wood Shape
Transmutation
Level: Drd 2
Components: V, S, DF
Casting Time: 1 action
Range: Touch
Target: One touched piece of wood no larger than 10 cu. ft. + 1 cu. ft./level
Duration: Instantaneous
Saving Throw: Will negates (object)
Spell Resistance: Yes (object)

Wood shape enables you to form one existing piece of wood into any shape that suits your purpose. For example, you can make a wooden weapon, fashion a special trapdoor, or sculpt a crude idol. This spell also permits you to reshape a wood door to make an exit where one didn't exist or to seal a door shut. While it is possible to make crude coffers, doors, and so forth, fine detail isn't possible. There is a 30% chance that any shape that includes moving parts simply doesn't work.

Word of Chaos
Evocation [Chaotic, Sonic]
Level: Chaos 7, Clr 7
Components: V
Casting Time: 1 action
Range: 30 ft.
Area: Creatures in a 30-ft.-radius spread centered on you
Duration: Instantaneous

Saving Throw: None
Spell Resistance: Yes

Uttering *word of chaos* creates two effects:

If you are on your home plane, non-chaotic extraplanar creatures within the area are instantly banished back to their home planes. Creatures so banished cannot return for at least 1 day. This effect takes place regardless of whether the creatures hear the *word of chaos*.

Creatures native to your plane who hear the *word of chaos* and are not chaotic suffer the following ill effects:

HD	Effect
12 or more	Deafened
Less than 12	Stunned, deafened
Less than 8	Confused, stunned, deafened
Less than 4	Killed, confused, stunned, deafened

The effects are cumulative.

Deafened: The creature is struck deaf (see *blindness/deafness*) for 1d4 rounds.

Stunned: The creature is stunned for 1 round. A stunned creature can't act and loses any Dexterity bonus to AC. Attackers gain +2 bonuses to attack it.

Confused: The creature is confused, as by the *confusion* spell, for 1d10 minutes. This is a mind-affecting enchantment.

Killed: Living creatures die. Undead creatures are destroyed.

Word of Recall

Transmutation [Teleportation]
Level: Clr 6, Drd 8
Components: V
Casting Time: 1 action
Range: Unlimited
Target: You and objects and willing creatures totaling up to 50 lb./level
Duration: Instantaneous
Saving Throw: None or Will negates (harmless, object)
Spell Resistance: No or Yes (harmless, object)

Word of recall teleports you instantly back to your sanctuary when the word is uttered. You must designate the sanctuary when you prepare the spell, and it must be a very familiar place. The actual point of arrival is a designated area no larger than 10 feet by 10 feet. You can be transported any distance within a plane but cannot travel between planes. You can transport, in addition to yourself, objects and creatures weighing up to 50 pounds per caster level. Thus, a 15th-level cleric could transport his person and objects or creatures weighing an additional 750 pounds. Exceeding this limit causes the spell to fail.

An unwilling creature can't be teleported by *word of recall*. Likewise, a creature's Will save (or SR) prevents items in its possession from being teleported. Unattended, nonmagical objects receive no saving throw.

Zone of Truth

Enchantment (Compulsion) [Mind-Affecting]
Level: Clr 2
Components: V, S, DF
Casting Time: 1 action
Range: Close (25 ft. + 5 ft./2 levels)
Area: 5-ft.-radius/level emanation
Duration: 1 minute/level
Saving Throw: Will negates
Spell Resistance: Yes

Creatures within the emanation area (or those who enter it) can't speak any deliberate and intentional lies. Creatures are allowed a save to avoid the effects when the spell is cast or when they first enter the emanation area. Affected creatures are aware of this enchantment. Therefore, they may avoid answering questions to which they would normally respond with a lie, or they may be evasive as long as they remain within the boundaries of the truth. Creatures who leave the area are free to speak as they choose.

Appendix: General Guidelines and Glossary

The general rules for what to do when rounding fractions and when several multipliers apply to a die roll (often encountered as what to do when doubling something that is already doubled) are recorded below, followed by a glossary of game terms.

ROUNDING FRACTIONS

In general, if you wind up with a fraction, round down, even if the fraction is one-half or larger. For example, if a *fireball* deals you 17 points of damage, but you succeed at your saving throw and only take half damage, you take 8 points of damage.

Exception: Certain rolls, such as damage and hit points, have a minimum of 1.

MULTIPLYING

Sometimes a special rule makes you multiply a number or a die roll. As long as you're applying a single multiplier, multiply the number normally. When two or more multipliers apply, however, combine them into a single multiple, with each extra multiple adding 1 less than its value to the first multiple. Thus, a double (×2) and a double (×2) applied to the same number results in a triple (×3, because 2 + 1 = 3).

For example, Tordek, a high-level dwarven fighter, deals 1d8+6 damage with a warhammer. With a critical hit, a warhammer deals triple damage, so that's 3d8+18 damage for Tordek. A magic *dwarven thrower* warhammer deals double damage (2d8+12 for Tordek) when thrown. If Tordek scores a critical hit while throwing the *dwarven thrower*, his player rolls quadruple damage (4d8+24) because 3 + 1 = 4.

Another way to think of it is to convert the multiples into additions. Tordek's critical hit increase his damage by 2d8+12, and the *dwarven thrower's* double increases his damage by 1d8+6, so both of them together increase his damage by 3d8+18 for a grand total of 4d8+24.

GLOSSARY

0-level spell: A spell of the lowest possible level. Arcane spellcasters often call their 0-level spells "cantrips," and divine spellcasters often call them "orisons."

5-foot step: A small position adjustment that does not count as a move in combat. Usually (but not always), a 5-foot step is permitted in conjunction with a full-round action and may be taken at any point in the round. Most partial actions also permit a 5-foot step. This movement does not provoke an attack of opportunity.

ability: One of the six basic character qualities: Strength (Str), Dexterity (Dex), Constitution (Con), Intelligence (Int), Wisdom (Wis), and Charisma (Cha). See ability score.

ability check: A check of 1d20 + the appropriate ability modifier.

ability damage: A temporary loss of 1 or more ability score points. Lost points return at a rate of 1 point per day. This differs from an effective ability decrease, which ends when the condition causing it does.

ability drain: A permanent decrease in an ability score. Such a loss is permanent; that is, the character can only regain the lost points through magical means.

ability modifier: The bonus or penalty associated with a particular ability score. Ability modifiers apply to die rolls for character actions involving the corresponding abilities.

ability score: The numeric rating of one of the six character abilities (see ability). Some creatures lack certain ability scores; others cannot be rated in particular abilities.

AC: Armor Class.

action: A character activity. Actions are subdivided into the following categories according to the time required to perform them (from most time required to least): full-round actions, standard actions, partial actions, move-equivalent actions, and free actions.

adventuring party: A group of characters who adventure together. An adventuring party is composed of player characters plus any followers, familiars, associates, cohorts, or hirelings they might have.

alignment: One of the nine descriptors of morality for intelligent creatures: lawful good (LG), neutral good (NG), chaotic good (CG), lawful neutral (LN), neutral (N), chaotic neutral (CN), lawful evil (LE), neutral evil (NE), and chaotic evil (CE).

animal: A classification of creature that includes all natural animals and their giant forms (see the *Monster Manual*).

arcane spell failure: The chance that a spell fails and is cast to no effect because the caster's ability to use a somatic component was hampered by armor.

arcane spells: Arcane spells involve the direct manipulation of mystic energies rather than the intervention of higher powers or forces (see divine spells). Bards, sorcerers, and wizards cast arcane spells.

armor bonus: Armor (either mundane or magical) grants the wearer an armor bonus to Armor Class, as do various spells, magic effects, and magic items. Armor bonuses stack with natural armor bonuses and shield bonuses. An armor bonus granted by a spell or magic item typically takes the form of an invisible, tangible field of force around the recipient.

Armor Class: A number representing a creature's ability to avoid being hit in combat. An opponent's attack roll must equal or exceed the target creature's Armor Class to hit it. Armor Class = 10 + all modifiers that apply (typically armor bonus, shield bonus, Dexterity modifier, and size modifier).

Astral Plane: An open, weightless plane that connects with all other planes of existence and is used for transportation among them. Certain spells (such as *astral projection*) allow access to this plane.

attack: Any of numerous actions intended to harm, disable, or neutralize an opponent. The result of an attack is determined by an attack roll.

attack of opportunity: A single extra melee attack per round that a combatant can make when an opponent within reach takes an action that provokes attacks of opportunity. One-half or better cover prevents attacks of opportunity.

attack roll: A roll to determine whether an attack hits. To make an attack roll, roll 1d20 and add the appropriate modifiers for the attack type, as follows: melee attack roll = 1d20 + base attack bonus + Strength modifier + size modifier; ranged attack roll = 1d20 + base attack bonus + Dexterity modifier + size modifier + range penalty. In either case, the attack hits if the result is at least as high as the target's Armor Class.

automatic hit: An attack that hits regardless of target AC. Automatic hits occur on an attack roll of natural 20 or as a result of certain spells. A natural 20 attack roll is also a threat—a possible critical hit.

automatic miss: An attack that misses regardless of target AC. Automatic misses occur on an attack roll of natural 1.

Bbn: Barbarian.

Brd: Bard.

base attack bonus: An attack roll bonus derived from character class and level. Base attack bonuses increase at different rates for different character classes. A character gains a second attack when his or her base attack bonus reaches +6, a third with a base attack bonus of +11 or better, and a fourth with a base attack bonus of +16 or better. Base attack bonuses gained from multiple classes, as when a character is multiclassed, stack.

base save bonus: A saving throw modifier derived from character class and level. Base save bonuses increase at different rates for different character classes.

base speed: The speed a character can move while unarmored. Base speed is derived from character race.

blinded: Unable to see. A blinded character suffers a 50% miss chance in combat (all opponents are considered to have full concealment), loses any Dexterity bonus to AC, moves at half speed, and suffers a –4 penalty on Search checks and on most Strength- and Dexterity-based skill checks. Any skill check that relies on vision (such as Spot) automatically fails. Opponents of a blinded character gain a +2 bonus to their attack rolls, since they are effectively invisible.

bolster undead: A supernatural ability of evil clerics (and some neutral ones). Bolstering undead increases the resistance of undead creatures to turning attempts.

bonus: A positive modifier to a die roll.

cantrip: An arcane 0-level spell.

cast a spell: Trigger the magical or divine energy of a spell by means of words, gestures, focuses, and/or special materials. Spellcasting requires uninterrupted concentration during the requisite casting time. Disruption forces the caster to make a successful Concentration check or lose the spell. Successful casting brings about the spell's listed effect or effects.

caster level: A measure of the power with which a spellcaster casts a spell. Generally, a spell's caster level is the spellcaster's class level.

caster level check: A roll of 1d20 + the caster level (in the relevant class). If the result equals or exceeds the DC (or the spell resistance, in the case of caster level checks made for spell resistance), the check succeeds.

casting time: The time required to cast a spell. Spells with a casting time of 1 action are cast as standard actions. Those requiring 1 full round to cast are cast as full-round actions. Spells with casting times longer than 1 round count as full-round actions for all the rounds encompassed in the casting time.

(cc): Cross-class (a skill that's not a class skill).

Cha: Charisma.

channel energy: Tap and direct energy from another source (often extraplanar) to create a desired effect.

character: A fictional individual within the confines of a fantasy game setting. The words "character" and "creature" are often used synonymously within these rules, since almost any creature could be a character within the game, and every character is a creature (as opposed to an object).

character class: One of the following eleven player character types: barbarian, bard, cleric, druid, fighter, monk, paladin, ranger, rogue, sorcerer, and wizard. Class defines a character's predominant talents and general function within an adventuring party. Character class may also refer to a nonplayer character class or a prestige class (see the DUNGEON MASTER's Guide).

character level: A character's total level. For a single-classed character, class level and character level are the same thing.

check: A method of deciding the result when a character attempts an action (other than an attack or a saving throw) that has a chance of failure. Checks are based on a relevant character ability, skill, or other characteristic. Most checks are either ability checks or skill checks, though special types such as turning checks, caster level checks, dispel checks, and initiative checks also exist. The specific name of the check usually corresponds to the skill or ability used. To make a check, roll 1d20 and add any relevant modifiers. (Higher results are always better.) If this check result equals or exceeds the Difficulty Class number assigned by the DM (or the opponent's check, if the action is opposed), the check succeeds.

checked: Prevented from achieving forward motion by an applied force, such as wind. Checked creatures on the ground merely stop. Checked flying creatures move back a distance specified in the description of the specific effect.

circumstance modifier: A bonus or penalty based on situational factors rather than on innate character abilities. Such bonuses or penalties may apply either to a character's check or to the DC for that check. Circumstance modifiers stack with each other unless otherwise specified.

class: See character class.

class feature: Any special characteristic derived from a character class.

class level: A character's level in a single class. Class features generally depend on class level rather than character level.

class skill: A skill to which characters of a particular class have easier access than characters of other classes. Characters may buy class skills at a rate of 1 rank per skill point, as opposed to a half rank per skill point for cross-class skills. The maximum rank for a class skill is 3 plus the character's level.

Clr: Cleric.

Colossal: A Colossal creature is typically 64 feet or more in height or length and weighs 250,000 pounds or more.

command word item: A magic item that activates when the user speaks a particular word or phrase. Activating a command word item does not require concentration and does not provoke attacks of opportunity.

command undead: The supernatural ability of evil clerics and some neutral clerics to control undead creatures by channeling negative energy. See also turning check, turning damage, rebuking undead, and turn undead.

competence bonus: A bonus that improves a character's performance at a particular task. Such a bonus may apply to attack rolls, saving throws, skill checks, or any other checks to which a bonus relating to level or skill ranks would normally apply. It does not apply to ability checks, initiative checks, and so on.

Con: Constitution.

concealment: Something that prevents an attacker from clearly seeing his or her target. Concealment creates a chance that an otherwise successful attack misses (a miss chance).

confused: Befuddled and unable to determine a course of action due to a spell or magical effect. A *confused* character's actions are determined by rolling 1d10 for each round the condition is in effect. On a result of 1, the character wanders away (unless prevented) for 1 minute. On a result of 2–6, the character does nothing for 1 round. On a result of 7–9, the character attacks the nearest creature for 1 round. On a result of 10, the character acts normally for 1 round. Any *confused* creature who is attacked, however, automatically responds in kind at the next opportunity, regardless of the die roll results.

continuous damage: Damage from a single attack that continues to inflict injury every round without the need for additional attack rolls.

coup de grace: (Pronounced "koo-day-*grah*.") An action that allows an attacker to attempt a killing blow against a helpless opponent. A coup de grace can be administered with a melee weapon, or with a bow or crossbow if the attacker is adjacent to the opponent. An attacker delivering a coup de grace automatically scores a critical hit, after which the defender must make a successful Fortitude save (DC 10 + damage inflicted) or die. Rogues also gain their extra sneak attack damage for this attack. Delivering a coup de grace provokes attacks of opportunity from threatening foes. A coup de grace is not possible against a creature immune to critical hits.

cover: Any barrier between an attacker and defender. Such a barrier can be an object, a creature, or a magical force. Cover grants the defender a bonus to AC.

cowering: Frozen in fear and unable to take combat or movement actions. Cowering creatures lose all Dexterity bonuses, and attacks against them gain a +2 bonus.

cp: Copper piece.

creature: A living or otherwise active being, not an object. The terms "creature" and "character" are sometimes used interchangeably.

creature type: One of several broad categories of creatures. The creature types are aberration, animal, beast, construct, dragon, elemental, fey, giant, humanoid, magical beast, monstrous humanoid, ooze, outsider, plant, shapechanger, undead, and vermin. (See the *Monster Manual* for full descriptions.)

crit: Critical hit.

critical hit (crit): A hit that strikes a vital area and therefore deals double damage or more. To score a critical hit, an attacker must first score a threat (usually a natural 20 on an attack roll) and then succeed on a critical roll (just like another attack roll). Critical hit damage is usually double normal damage, which means rolling damage twice, just as if the attacker had actually hit the defender two times. (Any bonus damage dice, such as from a rogue's sneak attack, are not rolled multiple times, but added to the total at the end of the calculation.)

critical roll: A special second attack roll made in the event of a threat to determine whether a critical hit has been scored. If the critical roll is a hit against the target creature's AC, then the original attack is a critical hit. Otherwise, the original attack is a regular hit.

cross-class (cc) skill: A skill that is neither a class skill for a character nor an exclusive skill. Characters may buy cross-class skills at the rate of a half rank per skill point, as opposed to 1 rank per skill point for class skills. The maximum rank a character can achieve in a cross-class skill is one-half of the class skill maximum (3 plus the character's level), rounded neither up nor down.

cure spell: Any spell with the word "cure" in its name, such as *cure minor wounds*, *cure light wounds*, or *cure critical wounds*.

current hit points: A character's hit points at a given moment in the game. Current hit points go down when the character suffers damage and go back up upon recovery.

damage: A decrease in hit points, an ability score, or other aspects of a character caused by an injury, illness, or magical effect. The three main categories of damage are normal damage, subdual damage, and ability damage. In addition, wherever it is relevant, the type of damage an attack inflicts is specified, since natural abilities, magic items, or spell effects may grant immunity to certain types of damage. Damage types include weapon damage (subdivided into bludgeoning, slashing, or piercing) and energy damage (positive, negative, acid, cold, electricity, fire, or sonic). Modifiers to melee damage rolls apply to both subcategories of weapon damage (melee and unarmed). Some modifiers apply to both weapon and spell damage, but only if so stated. Damage points are deducted from whatever character attribute has been harmed—normal and subdual damage from current hit points, and ability damage from the relevant ability score. Damage heals naturally over time, but can also be negated wholly or partially by curative magic.

damage reduction: A special defense that allows a creature to ignore a set amount of damage from most weapons, but not from energy attacks, spells, spell-like abilities, and supernatural abilities. Barbarians have damage reduction as a class feature, but theirs is a special type that negates a set amount of damage from any source.

dazed: Unable to act normally. A dazed character can take no actions, but can defend against attacks normally.

dazzled: Unable to see well because of overstimulation of the eyes. A dazzled creature suffers a –1 penalty on attack rolls until the effect ends.

DC: Difficulty Class.

dead: A character dies when his or her hit points drop to –10 or lower. A character also dies when his or her Constitution drops to 0, and certain spells or effects (such as failing a Fortitude save against massive damage) can also kill a character outright. Death causes the victim's soul to leave the body and journey to an Outer Plane. Dead characters cannot benefit from normal or magical healing, but they can be restored to life via magic. A dead body decays normally unless magically preserved, but magic that restores a dead character to life also restores the body either to full health or to its condition at the time of death (depending on the spell or device).

deafened: Unable to hear. A deafened character suffers a –4 penalty to initiative, automatically fails Listen checks, and has a 20% chance of spell failure when casting spells with verbal components.

deal damage: Cause damage to a target with a successful attack. How much damage is dealt is usually expressed in terms of dice (for example, 2d6+4) and may have a situational modifier as well.

However, damage dealt by a weapon or spell does not necessarily equal damage taken by the target, because the target may have special defenses that negate some or all of the damage.

deflection bonus: A deflection bonus increases the recipient's AC by making attacks veer off harmlessly.

Dex: Dexterity.

Difficulty Class (DC): The target number that a player must meet or beat for a check or saving throw to succeed. Difficulty Classes other than those given in specific spell or item descriptions are set by the DM using the skill rules as a guideline.

Diminutive: A Diminutive creature is typically between 6 inches and 1 foot in height or length and weighs between 1/8 of a pound and 1 pound.

disabled: At exactly 0 current hit points. A disabled character is horribly wounded, but not unconscious. Such a character can move at half normal speed and take a partial action each round without risking further damage, but cannot perform any strenuous action. Taking a strenuous action while disabled causes the loss of 1 hit point at the end of that action, changing the character's status from disabled to dying, unless the act served to increase current hit points.

dispel: Negate, suppress, or remove one or more existing spells or other effects on a creature, item, or area. Dispel usually refers to a *dispel magic* spell, though other forms of dispelling are possible. Certain spells cannot be dispelled, as noted in the individual spell descriptions.

dispel check: A roll of 1d20 + caster level of the character making the attempt to dispel (usually used with *dispel magic*). The DC is 11 plus the level of the spellcaster who initiated the effect being dispelled.

dispel turning: Channel negative energy to negate a successful turning undead attempt by a good cleric or a paladin.

divine spells: Spells of religious origin powered by faith or by a deity. Clerics, druids, paladins, and rangers cast divine spells.

DM: Dungeon Master.

dodge bonus: A bonus to Armor Class (and sometimes Reflex saves) resulting from physical skill at avoiding blows and other ill effects. Dodge bonuses are never granted by spells or magic items. Any situation or effect (except wearing armor) that negates a character's Dexterity bonus also negates any dodge bonuses the character may have. Dodge bonuses stack with other dodge bonuses.

domain: A granted power and a set of nine divine spells (one each of 1st through 9th level) themed around a particular concept and associated with one or more deities. The available domains are: Air, Animal, Chaos, Death, Destruction, Earth, Evil, Fire, Good, Healing, Knowledge, Law, Luck, Magic, Plant, Protection, Strength, Sun, Travel, Trickery, War, and Water.

domain spell: A divine spell belonging to a domain. Each domain offers one spell of each spell level. In addition to their normal daily complement of spells, clerics can cast one domain spell per day for each spell level that their caster levels allow. This spell may be from either of their domains. Domain spells cannot be exchanged for *cure* or *inflict* spells.

double weapon: A weapon with two ends, blades, or heads that are both intended for use in combat. Any weapon for which two damage ranges are listed is a double weapon. Double weapons can be used to make an extra attack as if the wielder were fighting with two weapons (light weapon in the off hand).

Drd: Druid.

Dungeon Master (DM): The player who portrays nonplayer characters, makes up the story setting for the other players, and serves as a referee.

dying: Near death and unconscious. A dying character has –1 to –9 current hit points and can take no actions. Each round, a dying character loses 1 hit point unless the player succeeds at a 10% roll, in which case the character stops losing hit points every round.

effective ability decrease: A decrease in an ability score that ends when the condition causing it does.

effective hit point increase: Hit points gained through temporary increases in Constitution score. Unlike temporary hit points, points gained in this manner are not lost first, and must be subtracted from the character's current hit points at the time the Constitution increase ends.

electrum: A naturally occurring alloy of gold and silver.

Elemental Plane: One of the Inner Planes consisting entirely of one type of matter: Air, Earth, Fire, or Water.

end of round: The point in a combat round when all the participants have completed all their allowed actions. End of round occurs when no one else involved in the combat has an action pending for that round.

energy damage: Damage caused by one of five types of energy (not counting positive and negative energy): acid, cold, electricity, fire, and sonic.

energy drain: An attack that saps a living opponent's vital energy giving the creature negative levels, which might permanently drain the creature's levels.

Energy Plane: An Inner Plane, either the Positive Energy Plane or the Negative Energy Plane.

engaged: Threatening or being threatened by an enemy. (Held, unconscious, or otherwise immobilized characters are not considered engaged unless they are actually being attacked.)

enhancement bonus: A bonus that represents an increase in the hardness and/or effectiveness of armor or a weapon, or a general bonus to an ability score.

enlargement modifier: A modifier to Strength (and sometimes Constitution) based on magical alteration of a creature's size. Size increases result in enlargement bonuses; size decreases result in enlargement penalties.

entangled: Ensnared. Entanglement impedes movement, but does not entirely prevent it unless the bonds are anchored to an immobile object or tethered by an opposing force. An entangled creature moves at half speed, cannot run or charge, and suffers a −2 penalty to attack rolls and a −4 penalty to its effective Dexterity score.

ethereal: On the Ethereal Plane. An ethereal creature is invisible and intangible to creatures on the Material Plane, but visible and corporeal to creatures on the Ethereal Plane. As such, such a creature is capable of moving through solid objects on the Material Plane and in any direction (even up or down, albeit at half normal speed). Ethereal beings can see and hear what is happening in the same area of the Material Plane to a distance of 60 feet, but everything looks gray and insubstantial. Force effects originating on the Material Plane can affect items and creatures that are ethereal, but the reverse is not true.

Ethereal Plane: A gray, foggy plane parallel to the Material Plane at all points. Creatures within the Ethereal Plane can see and hear into the Material Plane, though the reverse is not usually true. Force effects originating on the Material Plane can affect items and creatures on the Ethereal Plane, but the reverse is not true.

exclusive skill: A skill in which ranks can be purchased only by characters for whom they are class skills.

exhausted: Tired to the point of significant impairment. A fatigued character becomes exhausted by doing something else that would normally cause fatigue. An exhausted character moves at half normal speed and suffers an effective ability decrease of −6 to both Strength and Dexterity. After 1 hour of complete rest, an exhausted character becomes fatigued.

experience points (XP): A numerical measure of a character's personal achievement and advancement. Characters earn experience points by defeating monsters and other opponents. At the end of each adventure, the DM assigns experience to the characters based on what they have accomplished. Characters continue to accumulate experience points throughout their adventuring careers, gaining new levels in their character classes at certain experience point totals.

extraordinary ability (Ex): A nonmagical special ability (as opposed to a spell-like or supernatural ability).

face: The amount of floor space a creature requires to fight effectively. Face determines how many creatures can fight side by side in a corridor, as well as how many creatures can attack a single opponent at once. A creature's face depends upon both its size and its body shape. A character's face is generally 5 feet on a side.

fail: Achieve an unsuccessful result for a check, saving throw, or other determination involving a die roll.

fatigued: Tired to the point of impairment. A fatigued character can neither run nor charge and suffers an effective ability decrease of −2 to both Strength and Dexterity. After 8 hours of complete rest, fatigued characters are back to normal.

fear effect: Any spell or magical effect that causes the victim to become cowering, frightened, or panicked, or to suffer from some other fear-based effect defined in the description of the specific spell or item in question.

Fine: A Fine creature is typically 6 inches or less in height or length and weighs 1/8 pound or less.

flank: To be directly on the other side of an enemy that is threatening the enemy a character is attacking. A flanking attacker gains a +2 flanking bonus to attack rolls against the defender. A rogue can sneak attack a defender that she is flanking.

flat-footed: Especially vulnerable to attacks at the beginning of a battle. Characters are flat-footed until their first turns in the initiative cycle. Flat-footed creatures cannot use their Dexterity bonuses to AC or make attacks of opportunity.

Fortitude save: A type of saving throw, related to a character's ability to withstand damage thanks to his physical stamina.

free action: Free actions consume a negligible amount of time, and one or more such actions can be performed in conjunction with actions of other types.

frightened: Fearful of a creature, situation, or object. Frightened creatures flee from the source of their fear as best they can. If unable to flee, they may fight, but suffer a −2 morale penalty to all their attack rolls, weapon damage rolls, and saving throws.

Ftr: Fighter.

full-round action: Full-round actions consume all of a character's effort during a round. The only movement possible in conjunction with a full-round action is a 5-foot step, which can occur before, after, or during the action. Some full-round actions (as specified in their descriptions) do not allow even this much movement. When using a full-round action to cast a spell whose casting time is 1 full round, the spell is not completed until the beginning of the caster's next turn.

Gargantuan: A Gargantuan creature is typically between 32 and 64 feet in height or length and weighs between 32,000 and 250,000 pounds.

gp: Gold piece.

grab: The initial attack required to start a grapple. To grab a target, the character must make a successful melee touch attack.

granted power: The special ability a cleric gains from each of his selected domains.

grapple check: An opposed check that determines a character's ability to struggle in a grapple. Grapple check = 1d20 + base attack modifier + Strength modifier + special size modifier (+4 for every size above Medium-size or −4 for every size below Medium-size).

grappled: Engaged in wrestling or some other form of hand-to-hand struggle with one or more attackers. A grappled character cannot move, cast a spell, fire a ranged weapon, or undertake any action more complicated than making a barehanded attack, attacking with a Small weapon, or attempting to break free from the opponent. In addition, grappled characters do not threaten any area and lose any Dexterity bonuses to AC against opponents they aren't grappling. For creatures, grappling can also mean trapping opponents in any number of ways (in a toothy maw, under a huge paw, and so on).

grenadelike weapon: A ranged weapon that splashes on impact, dealing damage to creatures who are within 5 feet of the spot where it lands as well as to targets it actually hits. Attacks with grenadelike weapons are ranged touch attacks.

hardness: A measure of an object's ability to resist damage. Only damage in excess of the object's hardness is actually deducted from the object's hit points upon a successful attack.

haste bonus: A bonus resulting from a magical effect that causes the subject to move faster than normal.

HD: Hit Die (or Hit Dice).

held: Immobile as the result of a spell or magical enchantment effect (such as *hold person*). *Held* characters are helpless and can't perform any physical actions. Such characters continue to breathe normally, however, and can take purely mental actions.

helpless: Paralyzed, bound, *held*, sleeping, unconscious, or otherwise completely at an opponent's mercy. An attacker can use a coup de grace against a helpless target.

hit: Make a successful attack roll.

Hit Die (HD): A die rolled to generate a creature's hit point total. The term Hit Dice is synonymous with character level for spells, magic items, and magical effects that affect a certain number of Hit Dice of creatures.

hit point total: An individual character's maximum hit points when undamaged.

hit points (hp): A measure of character health or object integrity. Damage decreases current hit points, and lost hit points return with healing or natural recovery. A character's hit point total increases permanently with additional experience and/or permanent increases in Constitution, or temporarily through the use of various special abilities, spells, magic items, or magical effects (see temporary hit points and effective hit point increase).

hp: Hit points.

Huge: A Huge creature is typically between 16 and 32 feet in height or length and weighs between 4,000 and 32,000 pounds.

incorporeal: Having no physical body. Incorporeal creatures are immune to all nonmagical attack forms. They can be harmed only by other incorporeal creatures, +1 or better magical weapons, spells, spell-like effects, or supernatural effects. Even when struck by spells, magical effects, or magic weapons, however, they have a 50% chance to ignore any damage from a corporeal source. In addition, rogues cannot employ sneak attacks against incorporeal beings, since such opponents have no vital areas to target. An incorporeal creature has no natural armor bonus, but does have a deflection bonus equal to its Charisma modifier or +1, whichever is greater. Such creatures can pass through solid objects at will, but not through force effects. Therefore, their attacks negate the bonuses provided by natural armor, armor, and shields, but deflection bonuses and force effects (such as *mage armor*) work normally against them. Incorporeal creatures move silently, so they cannot be heard with Listen checks unless they wish it.

inflict spell: A spell with the word "inflict" in its name, such as *inflict light wounds*, *inflict moderate wounds*, or *inflict critical wounds*.

inherent bonus: A bonus to an ability score resulting from powerful magic, such as a *wish*. Inherent bonuses cannot be dispelled. A character is limited to a total inherent bonus of +5 to any ability score. Inherent bonuses to a particular ability score do not stack, so only the best one applies.

initiative: A system of determining the order of actions in battle. Before the first round of combat, each combatant makes a single initiative check. Each round, the participants act in order from the highest initiative result to the lowest.

initiative check: A Dexterity check used to determine a creature's place in the initiative order for a combat.

initiative modifier: A bonus or penalty to initiative.

Inner Plane: One of several portions of the planar landscape that contain the primal forces—those energies and elements that make up the building blocks of reality. The Elemental Planes and the Energy Planes are Inner Planes.

insight bonus: An insight bonus improves performance at a given activity by granting the character an almost precognitive knowledge of what might occur.

Int: Intelligence.

invisible: Visually undetectable. Invisible creatures gain a +2 bonus to attack rolls and negate Dexterity bonuses to their opponents' AC.

known spell: A spell that an arcane spellcaster has learned and can prepare. For wizards, knowing a spell means having it in their spellbooks. For sorcerers and bards, knowing a spell means having selected it when acquiring new spells as a benefit of level advancement.

Large: A Large creature is typically between 8 and 16 feet in height or length and weighs between 500 and 4,000 pounds.

level: A measure of advancement or power applied to several areas of the game. See caster level, character level, class level, and spell level.

light weapon: A weapon with a size category smaller than that of the wielder.

line of effect: A straight, unblocked line between two points relevant to a spell's effect.

line of sight: An unobstructed line between two points such that a creature at one point can see the other.

luck bonus: A modifier that represents good fortune.

massive damage: At least 50 points of damage resulting from a single attack.

masterwork: Exceptionally well-made, generally adding +1 to attack rolls (if the item is a weapon), reducing the armor check penalty by 1 (if the item is armor), or adding +2 to relevant skill checks (if the item is a tool). A masterwork weapon's bonus to attack rolls does not stack with enhancement bonuses.

Material Plane: The "normal" plane of existence.

Medium-size: A Medium-size creature is typically between 4 and 8 feet in height or length and weighs between 60 and 500 pounds.

melee: Melee combat consists of physical blows exchanged by opponents close enough to threaten one another's space, as opposed to ranged combat.

melee attack: A physical attack suitable for close combat.

melee attack bonus: A modifier applied to a melee attack roll.

melee attack roll: An attack roll within melee combat, as opposed to a ranged attack roll. See attack roll.

melee touch attack: A touch attack made in melee, as opposed to a ranged touch attack. See touch attack.

melee weapon: A handheld weapon designed for close combat.

miss chance: The possibility that a successful attack roll misses anyway because of the attacker's uncertainty about the target's location. See concealment.

miss chance roll: A d% roll to determine the success of an attack roll to which a miss chance applies.

modifier: Any bonus or penalty applying to a die roll. A positive modifier is a bonus, and a negative modifier is a penalty. Modifiers with specific descriptors generally do not stack with others of the same type. If more than one modifier of a type is present, only the best bonus or worst penalty in that grouping applies. Bonuses or penalties that do not have descriptors stack with those that do.

Mnk: Monk.

morale bonus: A bonus representing the effects of greater hope, courage, and determination.

move-equivalent action: An action that takes the place of moving at normal speed. A character can take a move-equivalent action instead of moving at normal speed in a standard action or as a partial action, or two move-equivalent actions instead of a double move.

mundane: Normal, commonplace, or everyday.

natural: A natural result on a roll or check is the actual number appearing on the die, not the modified result obtained by adding bonuses or subtracting penalties.

natural ability: A nonmagical capability, such as walking, swimming (for aquatic creatures), and flight (for winged creatures).

natural armor bonus: A bonus to AC resulting either from a creature's naturally tough hide or from a spell, magic item, or magical effect that toughens the subject's skin.

natural weapon: A creature's body part that deals normal damage in combat. Natural weapons include teeth, claws, horns, tails, and other appendages.

nauseated: Experiencing stomach distress. Nauseated creatures are unable to attack, cast spells, concentrate on spells, or do anything else requiring attention. The only action such a character can take is a single move (or move-equivalent action) per turn.

negate: Invalidate, prevent, or end an effect with respect to a designated area or target.

negative energy: A black, crackling energy that originates on the Negative Material Plane. In general, negative energy heals undead creatures and hurts the living.

Negative Energy Plane: The Inner Plane from which negative energy originates.

negative level: A loss of vital energy resulting from energy drain, spells, magic items, or magical effects. For each negative level gained, a creature suffers a –1 penalty to all skill checks, ability checks, attack rolls, and saving throws, plus a –1 effective level penalty. (That is, whenever the creature's level is used in a die roll or calculation, reduce its value by 1 for each negative level.) In addition, a spellcaster so affected loses access to one spell per negative level from the highest spell level castable. If two or more spells fit this criterion, the caster decides which one becomes inaccessible. The lost spell becomes available again as soon as the negative level is removed, providing the caster would be capable of using it at that time. Negative levels remain in place for 24 hours after acquisition or until removed. After that period, the negative level goes away, but the afflicted creature must attempt a Fortitude save (DC = 10 + 1/2 the attacker's Hit Dice + the attacker's Charisma modifier) to determine whether there is a lasting effect. If the saving throw succeeds, there is no harm to the character. Otherwise, the creature's character level drops by one and any benefits acquired with that level are lost. The afflicted creature must make a separate saving throw for each negative level possessed.

nonintelligent: Lacking an Intelligence score. Mind-affecting spells do not affect nonintelligent creatures.

nonplayer character (NPC): A character controlled by the Dungeon Master rather than by one of the other players in a game session, as opposed to a player character.

normal: Unharmed and unafflicted, or standard (as in "normal damage").

NPC: Nonplayer character.

off hand: A character's weaker or less dexterous hand (usually the left). An attack made with the off hand incurs a –4 penalty to the attack roll. In addition, only one-half of a character's Strength bonus may be added to damage dealt with a weapon held in the off hand.

one-handed weapon: A weapon with a size category the same as that of the wielder.

orison: A divine 0-level spell.

Outer Plane: One of several planes of existence where spirits of mortal beings go after death. These planes are the homes of powerful beings, such as demons, devils, and deities. Individual Outer Planes typically exhibit the traits of one or two specific alignments associated with the beings who control them.

overlap: Coexist with another effect or modifier in the same area or on the same target. Bonuses that do not stack with each other overlap instead, such that only the largest bonus provides its benefit.

Pal.: Paladin.

panicked: A panicked creature must drop anything it holds and flee at top speed from the source of its fear, as well as any other dangers it encounters, along a random path. In addition, the creature suffers a –2 morale penalty on saving throws. If cornered, a panicked creature cowers and does not attack, typically using the total defense action in combat.

paralyzed: Unable to move or act physically. Paralyzed characters have effective Dexterity and Strength scores of 0 and are helpless.

partial action: An abbreviated action. Characters do not choose to take partial actions, but they are sometimes mandated by situations, such as a character's condition or a previous decision. Generally, a character can accomplish either portion of a standard action (that is, moving full speed or attacking) during a partial action, but not both. (The partial charge is the sole exception to this.) A 5-foot step is usually permitted in conjunction with a partial action.

party: An adventuring party.

PC: Player character.

penalty: A negative modifier to a die roll.

petrified: Turned to stone. Petrified characters cannot move or take actions of any kind, and they have effective Strength and Dexterity scores of 0. They are completely unaware of what occurs around them, since all of their senses have ceased to operate. If a petrified character cracks or breaks, but the broken pieces are joined with the body as it returns to flesh, the character is unharmed. Otherwise, the DM must assign some amount of permanent hit point loss and/or debilitation.

pinned: Held immobile (but not helpless) in a grapple.

plane of existence: One of many dimensions that may be accessed by spells, spell-like abilities, magic items, or specific creatures. These planes include (but are not limited to) the Astral Plane, the Ethereal Plane, the Inner Planes, the Outer Planes, the Plane of Shadow, and various other realities. The "normal" world is part of the Material Plane.

Plane of Shadow: A plane of existence that pervades the Material Plane. The Plane of Shadow may be accessed and manipulated from the Material Plane through shadows. Shadow spells make use of the substance of this plane in their casting.

player character (PC): A character controlled by a player other than the Dungeon Master, as opposed to a nonplayer character.

point of origin: The location in space where a spell or magical effect begins. The caster designates the point of origin for any spells in which it is variable.

points of damage: A number by which an attack reduces a character's current hit points.

positive energy: A white, luminous energy that originates on the Positive Material Plane. In general, positive energy heals the living and hurts undead creatures.

Positive Energy Plane: The Inner Plane from which positive energy originates.

pp: Platinum piece.

prerequisite: A requirement that must be fulfilled before a given benefit can be gained.

profane bonus: A bonus that stems from the power of evil.

projectile weapon: A device, such as a bow, that uses mechanical force to propel a projectile toward a target.

prone: Lying on the ground. An attacker who is prone has a –4 penalty to melee attack rolls and cannot use a ranged weapon (except for a crossbow). Melee attacks against a prone defender have a +4 bonus, and ranged attacks against a prone character have a –4 penalty.

racial bonus: A bonus granted because of the culture a particular creature was brought up in or because of innate characteristics of that type of creature.

range increment: Each full range increment of distance between an attacker using a ranged weapon and a target gives the attacker a cumulative –2 penalty to the ranged attack roll. Thrown weapons have a maximum range of five range increments. Projectile weapons have a maximum range of ten range increments.

range penalty: A penalty applied to a ranged attack roll based on distance. See range increment.

ranged attack: Any attack made at a distance with a ranged weapon, as opposed to a melee attack.

ranged attack roll: An attack roll made with a ranged weapon. See attack roll.

ranged touch attack: A touch attack made at range, as opposed to a melee touch attack. See touch attack.

ranged weapon: A thrown or projectile weapon designed for ranged attacks.

ray: A beam created by a spell. The caster must succeed at a ranged touch attack to hit with a ray.

reach weapon: A long melee weapon, or one that has a long haft. Reach weapons allow the user to threaten or strike at opponents 10 feet away with a melee attack roll. Most such weapons cannot be used to attack adjacent foes, however.

rebuke undead: A supernatural ability to make undead cower by channeling negative energy.

Reflex save: A type of saving throw, related to a character's ability to withstand damage thanks to his agility or quick reactions.

regenerate: Regrow severed body parts and ruined organs, repair broken bones, and heal other damage. Severed body parts that are not reattached simply die, and the regenerating creature grows replacements at a rate specified in the individual spell or monster description. Most damage dealt to a naturally regenerating creature is treated as subdual damage, which heals at a fixed rate. However, certain attack forms (typically fire and acid) deal damage that does not convert to subdual damage. Such damage is not regenerated. Regeneration does not alter conditions that do not deal damage in hit points, such as poisoning and disintegration.

resistance bonus: A bonus to saving throws that provides extra protection against harm.

result: The numerical outcome of a check, attack roll, saving throw, or other 1d20 roll. The result is the sum of the natural die roll and all applicable modifiers.

Rgr: Ranger.

Rog: Rogue.

round: A 6-second unit of game time used to manage combat. Every combatant may take at least one action every round.

sacred bonus: A bonus that stems from the power of good.

save: Saving throw.

saving throw (save): A roll made to avoid (at least partially) damage or harm. The three types of saving throws are Fortitude, Reflex, and Will.

school of magic: A group of related spells that work in similar ways. The eight schools of magic available to spellcasters are Abjuration, Conjuration, Divination, Enchantment, Evocation, Illusion, Necromancy, and Transmutation.

score: The numerical rating associated with an ability.

scribe: Write a spell onto a scroll.

scry: See and hear events from afar through the use of a spell or a magic item.

shield bonus: A bonus to Armor Class gained by using a shield (either mundane or magical).

size: The physical dimensions and/or weight of a creature or object. The sizes, from smallest to largest, are Fine, Diminutive, Tiny, Small, Medium-size, Large, Huge, Gargantuan, and Colossal.

size modifier: The bonus or penalty derived from a creature's size category. Size modifiers of different types apply to Armor Class, attack rolls, Hide checks, grapple checks, and various other checks.

skill: A talent that a character acquires and improves through training.

skill check: A check relating to use of a skill. The basic skill check = 1d20 + skill rank + the relevant ability modifier (or simply 1d20 + skill modifier).

skill modifier: The bonus or penalty associated with a particular skill. Skill modifier = skill rank + ability modifier + miscellaneous modifiers. (Miscellaneous modifiers include racial bonuses, armor check penalty, situational modifiers, etc.). Skill modifiers apply to skill checks for character actions that make use of the corresponding skills.

skill points: A measure of a character's ability to gain and improve skills. At each level, a character gains skill points and spends them to buy skill ranks. Each skill point buys 1 rank in a class skill or a half rank in a cross-class skill.

skill rank: A number indicating how much training or experience a character has with a given skill. Skill rank is incorporated into the skill modifier, which in turn improves the chance of success for skill checks with that skill.

Small: A Small creature is typically between 2 feet and 4 feet in height or length and weighs between 8 pounds and 60 pounds.

Sor: Sorcerer.

sp: Silver piece.

speed: The number of feet a creature can move when taking a standard action.

spell: A one-time magical effect. The two primary categories of spells are arcane and divine. Clerics, druids, paladins, and rangers cast divine spells, while wizards, sorcerers, and bards cast arcane spells. Spells are further grouped into eight schools of magic.

spell completion item: A magic item (typically a scroll) that contains a partially cast spell. Since the spell preparation step has already been completed, all the user need do to cast the spell is complete the final gestures, words, etc., normally required to trigger it. To use a spell completion item safely, the caster must be high enough level in the appropriate class to cast the spell already, though it need not be a known spell. A caster who does not fit this criterion has a chance of spell failure. Activating a spell completion item is a standard action and provokes attacks of opportunity just as casting a spell does.

spell failure: The chance that a spell fails and is ruined when cast under less than ideal conditions; when a spell is cast to no effect.

spell level: A number from 0 to 9 that indicates the general power of a spell.

spell-like ability (Sp): A special ability with effects that resemble those of a spell. In most cases, a spell-like ability works just like the spell of the same name.

spell preparation: Part of the spellcasting process for wizards, clerics, paladins, rangers, and druids. Preparing a spell requires careful reading from a spellbook (for wizards) or devout prayers or meditation (for divine spellcasters). The character actually casts the first and lengthiest part of the spell during the preparation phase, leaving only the very end for completion at another time. To use a prepared spell, the character finishes the casting with the appropriate spell components—a few special words, some complex gestures, a specific item, or a combination of the three. A prepared spell is used up once cast and cannot be cast again until the spellcaster prepares it again. Sorcerers and bards need not prepare their spells.

spell resistance (SR): A special defensive ability that allows a creature or item to resist the effects of spells and spell-like abilities. Supernatural abilities are not subject to spell resistance.

spell slot: The "space" in a spellcaster's mind dedicated to holding a spell of a particular spell level. A spellcaster has enough spell slots to accommodate an entire day's allotment of spells. Spellcasters who must prepare their spells in advance generally fill their spell slots during the preparation period, though a few slots can be left open for spells prepared later in the day. A spellcaster can always opt to fill a higher-level spell slot with a lower-level spell, if desired.

spell trigger item: A magic item (such as a wand) that produces a particular spell effect. Any spellcaster whose class spell list includes a particular spell knows how to use a spell trigger item that duplicates it, regardless of whether the character knows (or could know) that spell at the time. The user must determine what the spell stored in the item is before trying to use it. To activate the item, the user must speak a word, but no gesture or spell finishing is required. Activating a spell trigger item is a standard action and does not provoke attacks of opportunity.

spell version: One of several variations of the same spell. The caster must select the desired version of the spell at the time of casting. *Symbol*, *dispel magic*, and *ice storm* each have multiple versions.

spontaneous casting: The special ability of a cleric to drop a prepared nondomain spell to gain a *cure* or *inflict* spell of the same level or lower. Since the substitution of spells occurs on the spur of the moment, clerics need not prepare their *cure* or *inflict* spells in advance.

SR: Spell resistance.

stable: Unconscious but not dying, with a current hit point total between –1 and –9. A dying character who is stabilized regains no hit points, but stops losing them at a rate of 1 per round.

stack: Combine for a cumulative effect. In most cases, modifiers to a given check or roll stack if they have different descriptors, but do not stack if they have the same descriptors, regardless of their sources. If the modifiers to a particular roll do not stack, only the best bonus or worst penalty applies. Dodge bonuses, circumstance bonuses, and synergy bonuses, however, do stack with one another unless otherwise specified. Also, an armor bonus from a shield stacks with an armor bonus from armor. Spell effects that do not stack may overlap, coexist independently, or render one another irrelevant, depending on their exact effects.

staggered: Having subdual damage equal to current hit points. Staggered characters can only take partial actions. Characters are no longer staggered once their current hit points exceed their subdual damage.

standard action: The most basic type of action. Standard actions allow a character to perform an activity (attack, cast a 1-action spell, use a skill, etc.) and move a distance less than or equal to his or her speed. The character can move either before or after the activity.

Str: Strength.

stunned: A stunned creature can't take actions and loses any positive Dexterity modifier to AC. Each attacker gains a +2 bonus to attack rolls against that creature. In addition, stunned characters immediately drop anything they are holding.

subdual damage: Nonlethal damage typically resulting from an unarmed attack, an armed attack delivered with intent to subdue, a forced march, or a debilitating condition such as heat or starvation.

subject: A creature affected by a spell.

supernatural ability (Su): A magical power that produces a particular effect, as opposed to a natural, extraordinary, or spell-like ability. Using a supernatural ability generally does not provoke an attack of opportunity. Supernatural abilities are not subject to dispelling, disruption, or spell resistance. However, they do not function in areas where magic is suppressed or negated, such as inside an *antimagic field*.

suppress: Cause a magical effect to cease functioning without actually ending it. When the suppression ends, the spell effect returns, provided it has not expired in the meantime.

surprise: A special situation that occurs at the beginning of a battle if some (but not all) combatants are unaware of their opponents' presence. In this case, a surprise round happens before regular rounds begin. In initiative order (highest to lowest), those combatants who started the battle aware of their opponents each take a partial action during the surprise round. Creatures unaware of opponents are flat-footed through the entire surprise round and do not enter the initiative cycle until the first regular combat round.

synergy bonus: A modifier resulting from an unusually beneficial interaction between two related skills.

take damage: Sustain damage (either real or subdual) from a successful attack. Note that damage dealt by an opponent does not necessarily equal damage taken, as various special defenses may reduce or negate damage from certain kinds of attacks.

take 10: To reduce the chances of failure on certain skill checks by assuming an average die roll result (10 on a 1d20 roll).

take 20: To greatly reduce the chances of failure for certain skill checks by assuming that a character makes sufficient retries to obtain the maximum possible check result (as if a 20 were rolled on 1d20).

target: The intended recipient of an attack, spell, supernatural ability, extraordinary ability, or magical effect. If a targeted spell is successful, its recipient is known as the subject of the spell.

temporary hit points: Hit points gained for a limited time through certain spells (such as *aid*) and magical effects.

threat: A possible critical hit.

threaten: To be able to make an attack of opportunity against an opponent within reach. Creatures threaten all areas into which they can make melee attacks, even when it is not their turn to take an action.

threatened area: An area within an opponent's reach. Generally, characters threaten all areas within 5 feet of them, though reach weapons can alter this range. Certain actions provoke attacks of opportunity when taken within a threatened area.

threat range: All natural die roll results that constitute a threat when rolled for an attack roll. For most weapons, the threat range is 20, but some weapons have threat ranges of 19–20 or even 18–20. However, any attack roll that does not result in a hit is not a threat, whether or not it lies within the weapon's threat range.

thrown weapon: A ranged weapon that a character hurls at an enemy, such as a spear, as opposed to a projectile weapon.

Tiny: A Tiny creature is typically between 1 and 2 feet in height or length and weighs between 1 and 8 pounds.

touch attack: An attack in which the attacker must connect with an opponent but does not need to penetrate armor. Touch attacks may be either melee or ranged. The target's armor bonus, shield bonus, and natural armor bonus do not apply to AC against a touch attack.

touch spell: A spell that delivers its effect when the caster touches a target creature or object. Touch spells are delivered to unwilling targets by touch attacks.

trained: Having at least 1 rank in a skill. Many skills can be used untrained by making a successful skill check using 0 skill ranks. Others, such as Spellcraft, can be used only by characters who are trained in that skill.

turn: The portion of each combat round in which a particular character acts.

turn undead: The supernatural ability to drive off or destroy undead by channeling positive energy.

turned: Affected by a turn undead attempt. Turned undead flee for 10 rounds (1 minute) by the best and fastest means available to them. If they cannot flee, they cower.

turning check: A roll of 1d20 + Charisma modifier to determine how much positive or negative energy is able to be channeled when attempting to turn or rebuke undead.

turning damage: The number of Hit Dice of undead that are turned or rebuked with a particular turning check. Turning damage = 2d6 + cleric level + Charisma modifier.

two-handed weapon: A weapon with a size category one step larger than that of the wielder.

unarmed attack: A melee attack made with no weapon in hand.

unarmed strike: A successful blow, typically for subdual damage, from a character attacking without weapons. Monks can deal normal damage with an unarmed strike, but others deal subdual damage.

unconscious: Knocked out and helpless. Unconsciousness can result from having current hit points between –1 and –9, or from subdual damage in excess of current hit points.

untrained: Having no ranks in a skill. Many skills can be used untrained by making a successful skill check using 0 ranks and including all other modifiers as normal. Other skills can be used only by characters who are trained in that skill.

use-activated item: A magic item that activates upon typical usage for a normal item of its type. For example, a character can activate a potion by drinking it, a magic sword by swinging it, a lens by looking through it, or a cloak by wearing it. Characters do not learn what a use-activated item does just by wearing or using it unless the benefit occurs automatically with use.

Will save: A type of saving throw, related to a character's ability to withstand damage thanks to his mental toughness.

Wis: Wisdom.

Wiz: Wizard.

XP: Experience points.

Index

PLAYTESTER CREDITS

Special thanks to: Jim Lin, Richard Garfield, Skaff Elias, Andrew Finch

John Amos, Ruari Armstrong, Alastair Damon, Jo Damon, Rupert Johnson, Jon Kenny, Robert Kenny, Alan Mead, Andy Mussell, Joy Mussell, Alison Whetton; Todd Antill, Chris Altnau, Brandy Antill, Alan Apperson, Joe Parish, Adam Revia; David Arneson; Rich Baker, Michele Carter, Andy Collins, Bruce Cordell, Dale Donovan, Miranda Horner, Shaun Horner, Scott Magner, Steve Miller, Chris Perkins, John Rateliff, Keri Reynolds, Sean Reynolds; Mark Barnabo, Morgan Albert, Douglas Dean, Maurice Doucette, Paul Gosselin, Timothy Harrigan, Earl Horner, Brett Kearney, John Page, George Miller, Rachel Nicholson, Lee Patten, Cheryl Rasmussen, Eric Rasmussen, Ron Shigeta, Mark Solvang, Mark Terilli, Craig Young, Glen Young; Matthew Barrett, Alan Crawford, Eric Garling, Robbie Hart, Rick Preston, Llywellyn Stengel, Melissa Thom; Kevin Baumann, Sharon Baumann, Paul Coveney, Robert Gallant, Michael Hallet; Wolfgang Baur, Michael Alex, Vince Alvarez, Charles Cowan, Karl Hubbs, Scott Kupec, Gerald Linn; Linda Baxter, Craig Baxter, Matthew Baxter, Gina Gibson, Bill Nelson, Trisha Nelson; Jim Bishop, René Flores, Michael Kent, Siobhan Rix, Jay Stull; William David Clarke III, Jeff Bolger, Kevin Ray Ford, Jr., Scott Hogan, Michael Irwin, Jr., William Patrick Jacobs, Eric Montgomery, Jeff Simmons, Shawn Smith, Jason Smith, Robert Turner, Rick L. Wyatt; James Bologna, Andy Cancellieri, Jim Clardy, Paul Dawson, Patrick Hart. Patti O'Connell, Chris Riedmueller, Nathaniel White; Brannon Boren, Gene Guthrie, Mark Richards, Shannon Richards, Charles Wittenberg; Lloyd Brown, Anthony Branco, Carol Brown, James Kahre, Philip Pettit, Aaron Riley, Warren Riley, Jose Villanueva; Mark Bruce, John Baker, John Donahie, Christine Johnson, Lisa Lappert, Kevin Min; Tom Burnett, Lisa Burnett, Jonathan Collins, Caroline Kealy, Caroline Martens, Charles Wallace, Anton Zieren; Jim Butler, Steve Enemark, Eric Haddock, James Jacobs, Jerry Jensen, Julia Martin, Patrick Ryan, Paul Takahashi, Terry Wilcox; Adam Canning, Mark Bristow, Graeme Bradbury, Michael Penberthy, Richard Rowlands, Charles Taylor; Andy Collins, Greg Collins, Chris Galvin, Joe Hauck, Viet Nguyen, Scott Smith, Dennis Worrell; Joseph Cottin, Layne Bradford, Bob Hafer, Duane Nelson, Eric Nelson, Harold Nelson, Don Schotte, Stephen Snipes, James Walden; Jeremiah Cronk, Bridget Cronk, Kristen Dawes, Kevin Pogue, John Waters, Nathan Wilder; David Darnell, Michelle Beazley, Ben Bizzell, Peter Blanton, Sean Bradley, Larry Carl, Tom Hamilton, Tim Joslin, David Quick, Anita Resnick, Andy Resnick, Cindy Steely, Eric Steely, John Steely; John Deiley, Jeremy Barnes, Gregory Baumeister, John Deiley, Brian Freyermuth, Michael Greene, Floyd Grubb, David Hendee, Jeff Jirsa, Scott McKelvey, Kyle Schubel; Mike Eckrich, David Antonelli, Shawn Bemis, Russell Bird, Chuck Clarke, David Eckhard, Bill Forisha, Bryan Gilles, Scott Gowins, Phon Huynh, Steven Neel, Doug Ort, Marshall Ronningen, Jesse Salazar, Greg Sanchez, Michael Schellhorn, Richard Whipple, Mike Ziesmer; Robert Emerson, Jacob Blackmon, Rick Blakeley, Lyle Hale, M. Brock Harris, William Hezeltine, Matthew Johnson, John Malohney, Tammy Overstreet, Daniel Thibadeau, Sandi Thibadeau; Joshua C. J. Fischer, Chris Adams, Karol Fuentes, Jason Iha, Bob Landowski, James "Kimo" Saper, Casey Teschner, Liz Tuttle; David Flemming, Rob Albrecht, Patrick James Collins, Dan Cunningham, Thomas Flemming, Robert Penwell, Eric Woollums; Jeff Fox, Laurie Fox, Andrew Alton, Kevin Blake, James Bowers, Eric Cook, Abigail Dailey, Phoebe Fox, Lance Nichols; John Grose, Eric Apjoke, Christian Canada, Dana Harrod-Paul, Ray Holding, Brady Hustad, Kelli Hustad, Pete Indge, Brett Paul, Eric Scott; Dave Gross, Steve Earth; Gary Gygax; Keith Hoffman, Michael Coyle, Sue Coyle, Claire Hoffman, David Hirst, Jeff Richards, Cheryl Richards; Nicolai Imset, Thomas Brevik, Jarle Hauglum, Andre Mathisen, Terje Sandal, Dag Traaholt; Scott Jacobowitz, Sean Borjes, Michael Goldman, Steve Gorman, David Katz, Phil Martinez, Robert Posada, Ilya Rakhlin, Lawrence Ramirez, Steve Turney, Dave Wolin, Alison Wolin; Mike Jensen; Daniel Kaufman, Bob Blazak, Mary Kay Gillngham, Michael Lee, Colin McClod, Troy Tortorich, Mark Waldron; Stephen Kenson, Andrew Frades, Lyle Hinckley, Sean Johnson, William Michie, Richard Tomasso; Michael König, Markus Ames, Marc Dengel, Daniel Klein, Alexander Pfeifer; Eric Kukielka, Michael Gellett, Heather Jardine, Tracey Rodell, Richard Rooney, Jennifer Roth, Matthew Shenck,

Don Warden, Hayo Vanderberg; Kevin Kulp, Michael Beaver, Jeremy Bernstein, Dorian Hart, Tonia Lopez-Fresquet, Peggy O'Connell; Robin D. Laws; Hee-Sang Lee, Seuk-Won Kang, Jong-Bum Park, Dong-Sup Rhee, Dong-Kwan Shin, Jong-Ho Song; Robert Lee, David Alexander, David Anderson, Randy Anderson, Karl Haynes, Angela Lee, Brian Patterson, Clinton Roberts; Phil Lewis, Richard Bligh, Vickie Bligh, James Hamilton, Richard C. Lewis; Ian Malcomson, Kevin Collings, Claire Gentle, Paula-Jane Gentle, Caroline Malcomson, Jason Sidwell; Thomas McCambley, Jean-Gabriel Bergeron, Bart Breedyk, Scott Delahunt, Darryl Farr, Mark Templeton; Leonard McGillis, Jon Creech, Deb Creech, Robby Duncan, Deneen Olsen, Mary Ruger, Tulene Ruger, John Taylor; Todd Meyer, Steve Bachus, Tom Dowd, John Granack, Steve Jessen, Mike Kearns, David Locke, Noel Llopis, Kevin Pierce, Michael Rae, Jim Washburn, Edwin Way, Brian Whooley; Mark Middleton, Pat Connolly, Paul Dorthy, Troy Daniels, Bruce Finch, Jeff Greenwood, Mark Jindra, Aaron Martin, Chip Slicer, Mike White; Kimberly Ann Moser, Chris Goodman, Tammy Lynn Hart, Walter Glenn Hart, Gregory Alan Moser; Wes Nicholson, Rob Aked, Natalie Aked, David Lundquest, Jon Naughton, Wes Nicholson, Adam Reeve; Christian Nielsen, Rune Aamund, Kim Bak, Jens Peter Engelund, Niels Krogsgaard Handest, Rune Lysell, Karsten Bjerregaard Nielsen, Søren Smith, John Christian Outhwaite Spence, Michael Svejgaard; Anibal Onnis, Diego Jose Condomi Alcorta, Braulio Firpo Banegas, German Bollmann, Adrian Antonio Troccoli; Rasmus Pechuel, Matthias Depka, Daniel Oster, Dominik Roesch, Danyel Rohmann; Jonathan Philpot, Sam Alanddin, Casey Lusk, Jon Sharp; Richard Poffley, Albert Davies, Keith Hughes, John Lindley, Alex Nicole; Vic Polites, Cindy Alberg, Erik Alberg, Jeremy Boersma, Esther Chonowski, Matt Hellens, Shoji Koreeda, David Laswell; Benjamin Messer; Thomas Reid, Eric Cagle, Adam Conus, Ed Stark; Stuart Renton, Gavin Birch, David Crookes, Dorian Hawkins, F.M. Rickard; Jason Reynolds, Robert Drinkwater, Richard Ellerton, Richard Thorne; David Roberts, Fiona Brewster, Tim Collinson, John Fowler, Justin Price, David Roberts, Jo Roberts, Mookie Roberts, Stuart Sands; Rich Robinson, Andrew Steel, Vaughan Thomas; David Roomes, Dana Bachens, Elizabeth Dupke, Mark Price, Jared Rydrych, Nathan Sherman, Eric Weakland; Todd Schoonover, Michael Bentley, Tony Gray, Allen MacDonnell, Jamie MacDonnell, Krista Moody, Ryan Wiatrowski, Thomas Wilson; Jefferson M. Shelley, Randy Brühl, Hans Reifenrath, Ben Tracy, Sam Wood; Steve Shropshire, John Beck, Jeffrey Byron, Chad Harball, Elizabeth Kelley, Nathan Kostel, Jeff Kragkovic, Robert Parker, Jeff Patten, Kathleen Patten; Paul Smith, Jason Arsenault, Jason Burchstead, Griffin Felt, Mark Gionet, Mike Kennedy, Julio Rodriguez, Paul Smith; Leon Sniegowski, Ronald James Ellis, John Payne, David Peterson, LeAnn Peterson, Jeff Pfaff, Lori Schenning; Ryk Spoor, Steven Franceschetti, George Green, Greg King, Eric Palmer; Hauke Stammer, Michael Borchert, Fly Christensen, Rouven Ebsen, Jan Evers; Owen Stephens, Stephanie Michelle Ellison, Carl Gilchrist, LJ Stephens, Greg Surber; Nathan Stiles, Mike Davis, David Figueroa, George Meyers, Richard Sewell, Arthur Thomas; Sean Taterczynski, Kate Appelman, Peter Appelman, Colin Couchman, CJ Gregory, Mark Hunt, Cliff Jones; Jeffrey E. Thetford, Andy Easton, Gerald Emert, Dorian Gaines, David Moore, Curry Russell, Miles R. Russell; Marco Torres, Andrew Brooks, John Carey, Melissa Fizer, David Lindgren, Michael Sterken, Hugo Torres, Tania Torres; Jay Tummelson; Stuart Turner, Andrew Ellis, Chris Johnson, Nick Kabilafkas, Kon Kabilafkas, David Devjack, Martin Rowe; Jonathan Tweet, Brannon Boren, Shawn Carnes, Jennifer Clarke-Wilkes, Andrew Finch, Robert Gutschera, Rob Heinsoo, Mark Jessup, Eric Tumbleson; Steven Van Dalem, Senechal Alain, Sue Ketels, Raes Peter, Cordewiner Wouter; George Vellella, George Henion, Nick Ruosch, Mark Schmitt, Pete Shackelford, Jennifer Tyacke, GJ Vellella III, Susan Vellella; David E. Wall, Theodore Coop, Ryan Hicks, Raymond Miller, Jaxon Ravens, Paul Schaaf, William Stier; Dean Waltenberger, Jim Anderegg, Jim Brown, Mike Capps, Mark Capps, Steve Dillard, Dan Doty, Daron Dierkes, Perry Jaynes, Chris McLean, Rusty Schodroski, Craig Slate, Tammy Slate; Peter Whitley, David Guckian, Frank Hussey, Kevin McKee, Scott Sauer, Dan Thayer, Lonny Washburn; David Wilson, Larry Herrin, Julie Weatherspoon, Tricia Wilson; Bryon Wischstadt, Kathy Bowen, Jay Doscher, Patrick Dwyer, Mike Jones, Shannon McGrath, Shawn McGrath, Kevin Mohondro; James Wyatt, Geoffrey Gowan, Steven Johnson, Thor Sparks, John Wunder

CHARACTER NAME

PLAYER

DUNGEONS & DRAGONS®
CHARACTER RECORD SHEETS

CLASS RACE ALIGNMENT DEITY

LEVEL SIZE AGE GENDER HEIGHT WEIGHT EYES HAIR

ABILITY NAME	ABILITY SCORE	ABILITY MODIFIER	TEMPORARY SCORE	TEMPORARY MODIFIER
STR STRENGTH				
DEX DEXTERITY				
CON CONSTITUTION				
INT INTELLIGENCE				
WIS WISDOM				
CHA CHARISMA				

HP HIT POINTS — TOTAL — WOUNDS/CURRENT HP — SUBDUAL DAMAGE

SPEED

AC ARMOR CLASS — TOTAL — = 10+ — ARMOR BONUS + SHIELD BONUS + DEX MOD + SIZE MOD + MISC MOD — ARCANE SPELL FAILURE — ARMOR CHECK PENALTY

ARMOR TYPE

INITIATIVE MODIFIER — TOTAL — = DEX MOD + MISC MOD

BASE ATTACK BONUS

SKILLS
MAX RANKS /

CROSS CLASS	SKILL NAME	KEY ABILITY	SKILL MOD	ABILITY MOD	RANKS	MISC MOD

SAVING THROWS

	TOTAL	BASE SAVE	ABILITY MODIFIER	MAGIC MODIFIER	MISC. MODIFIER	TEMP. MODIFIER
FORTITUDE (CONSTITUTION)	=	+	+	+		
REFLEX (DEXTERITY)	=	+	+	+		
WILL (WISDOM)	=	+	+	+		

CONDITIONAL MODIFIERS

	TOTAL	BASE ATTACK BONUS	STR MOD	SIZE MOD	MISC MOD	TEMP. MODIFIER
MELEE ATTACK BONUS	=	+	+	+		
RANGED ATTACK BONUS	=	+	+	+		
	TOTAL	BASE ATTACK BONUS	DEX MOD	SIZE MOD	MISC MOD	

CONDITIONAL MODIFIERS

WEAPON		TOTAL ATTACK BONUS	DAMAGE	CRITICAL

RANGE	WEIGHT	SIZE	TYPE	SPECIAL PROPERTIES

WEAPON		TOTAL ATTACK BONUS	DAMAGE	CRITICAL

RANGE	WEIGHT	SIZE	TYPE	SPECIAL PROPERTIES

WEAPON		TOTAL ATTACK BONUS	DAMAGE	CRITICAL

RANGE	WEIGHT	SIZE	TYPE	SPECIAL PROPERTIES

ARMOR/PROTECTIVE ITEM		TYPE	ARMOR BONUS	CHECK PENALTY

MAX DEX	SPELL FAILURE	SPEED	WEIGHT	SPECIAL PROPERTIES

SHIELD/PROTECTIVE ITEM	ARMOR BONUS	WEIGHT	SPELL FAILURE	CHECK PENALTY

SPECIAL PROPERTIES

AMMUNITION

CHARACTER ILLUSTRATION

LIFT OVER HEAD
EQUALS MAX LOAD

LIFT OFF GROUND
2 × MAX LOAD

PUSH OR DRAG
5 × MAX LOAD

CAMPAIGN

EXPERIENCE POINTS

GEAR

ITEM	ITEM

MONEY

SPELLS

SPELL SAVE

DC MOD

NUMBER OF SPELLS KNOWN (BARDS & SORCERERS ONLY)

0 _____ 1ST _____ 2ND _____ 3RD _____ 4TH _____
5TH _____ 6TH _____ 7TH _____ 8TH _____ 9TH _____

SPELLS

SPELL SAVE DC	LEVEL	SPELLS PER DAY	BONUS SPELLS
	0		0
	1ST		
	2ND		
	3RD		
	4TH		
	5TH		
	6TH		
	7TH		
	8TH		
	9TH		

LANGUAGES

SPECIAL ABILITIES/FEATS

NOTES

2000 SURVIVAL KIT

You've pored over the spells, played out the combats in your head, and dreamed up a thousand new characters. But the *Player's Handbook* is only the first of three core books for the DUNGEONS & DRAGONS game. The DUNGEON MASTER's *Guide*, available in September 2000, gives the DM all the tools to create and run fantastic D&D adventures. And the *Monster Manual*, available in October 2000, offers more than 500 fair and foul creatures.

But until you've got your hands on those books, you can put your new D&D characters through their paces with the monsters, magic items, and rules we've provided here. Consider this final chapter a temporary substitute until the DUNGEON MASTER's *Guide* and *Monster Manual* are available. We've condensed many of the rules, and we've had to leave a lot out. But what remains should give you enough to start D&D adventures of your own—and give you a taste of what's to come.

DUNGEON MASTER's Guide

Here are just some of the things you'll find in the *Dungeon Master's Guide* (DMG):

- Prestige classes that require characters to perfect aspects of adventuring before they can multiclass into them. Examples include the dwarven defender, the assassin, and the arcane archer.
- Advice for creating your own races and classes.
- Expanded rules for helpful companions like hirelings, cohorts, and allies.
- Traps, poisons, diseases, and other noncombat hazards.
- More than 800 magic items, not including the thousands possible from the custom design system.
- Advice for creating your own adventures, campaigns, and worlds.
- Random encounter tables, lair generators, and on-the-fly town demographics.

Monster Manual

The *Monster Manual* has 560 monsters in it, so it's obviously important. But in addition to 560 challenges to overcome, the *Monster Manual* offers all of the following:

- Template creatures. That werewolf might have been the village cobbler before being infected with lycanthropy. But what if that werewolf was once a 10th-level sorcerer? In minutes you'll be able to create custom monsters designed to provide your characters with challenges appropriate to their level.
- Challenge Ratings. We've taken some of the guesswork out of adventure design by assigning each monster a Challenge Rating. You'll know whether a given monster is too tough, too weak, or just right for your party.
- Brand new monsters like the stealthy, tentacled grick, the high-flying arrowhawk, and the just plain weird tojanida.
- The return of old favorite creatures. Your characters will be able to battle demons and devils from the Lower Planes or consult with celestials and devas from the Upper Planes.

- Scalable monsters. The bigger they are, the harder you'll fall. You can summon Small elementals or face a Colossal zombie. Scalable monsters stay tough no matter what level your adventurers are. Even a single skeleton can pose a challenge for 7th-level characters—if it's big enough.

Fair Warning

Not everything you'll find in this chapter is exactly the way it'll appear in the DUNGEON MASTER's *Guide* and *Monster Manual*. Some rules were condensed, simplified, or omitted so the rest would fit. And as this chapter is being written, substantial changes are still being made to those two books.

> Information in the DUNGEON MASTER's *Guide* or *Monster Manual* supersedes information in this chapter.

What's to Come This Fall

Beyond the DUNGEON MASTER's *Guide* and *Monster Manual*, you can look forward to *The Sunless Citadel*, an adventure that takes beginning characters into an underground forest full of menace.

EXPERIENCE

The DUNGEON MASTER's *Guide* devotes most of a chapter to awarding experience, but here you'll find a summary that'll guide you through your first few sessions. Play by the rules below, and your campaign will stay balanced, though you might miss a nuance or two.

How to Award Experience Points

In the D&D game, characters earn experience for overcoming monsters and NPCs that oppose them. "Did the characters overcome the challenge?" is the key question the DM should ask herself before awarding experience.

The adventurers don't need to defeat every last monster to earn experience for all of them. If the characters are facing eight goblins, defeat five, and force three to flee, they've earned experience for all eight goblins.

SINGLE MONSTER CHALLENGE RATING

Party Level	—Experience Points—									
	1	2	3	4	5	6	7	8	9	10
1–3	300	600	900	1,350	1,800	2,700	3,600	5,400	7,200	10,8
4	300	600	800	1,200	1,600	2,400	3,200	4,800	6,400	9,6
5	300	500	750	1,000	1,500	2,250	3,000	4,500	6,000	9,0
6	300	450	600	900	1,200	1,800	2,700	3,600	5,400	7,2
7	263	394	525	700	1,050	1,400	2,100	3,150	4,200	6,3
8	200	300	450	600	800	1,200	1,600	2,400	3,600	4,8
9	*	225	338	506	675	900	1,350	1,800	2,700	4,05
10	*	*	250	375	563	750	1,000	1,500	2,000	3,0

They've overcome the challenge that the goblins posed. Conversely, if the adventurers defeat five goblins, then decide to retreat, they receive no experience award.

It's possible for clever players to earn experience points without ever drawing a sword. If the characters' goal is to retrieve an idol from a hidden temple, they'll earn experience points for the ogre guard even if they wait until it falls asleep before sneaking in. But if they were just wandering around and encountered a sleeping ogre, they wouldn't earn experience points for sneaking past it.

Experience in Four Easy Steps

Each monster has a Challenge Rating (CR) that determines how much experience it's worth. The numbers range from fractions (such as goblins, who are CR 1/4) to 20 (such as really big dragons and creatures from other planes).

First, figure out the average level of the adventurers. Simply sum the character level of each character, then divide by the number of characters and round down.

Second, find the CR for each defeated monster or NPC. Monster CRs are listed in the monster descriptions, and an NPC has a CR equal to its level.

Third, cross-index the party level with each opponent on the table above. Challenge Ratings run along the top of the table, and average party levels are along the left edge. The table is designed to provide less experience for tough characters who fight weak monsters, and more experience for the reverse. For monsters with fractional Challenge Ratings, simply group them together so you have a group worth CR 1. For example, a goblin is worth CR 1/4, so eight goblins are worth two CR 1 monsters.

Fourth, sum the experience point awards for each monster in the encounter. Then divide by the number of characters that started the encounter. Characters earn experience even if they were paralyzed, turned to stone, or killed during the battle. They won't earn a[ny] more experience beyond this point, but they get f[ull] experience for the battle they just fought.

Example: A party of five 4th-level PCs defeats tw[o] ogres. An ogre is Challenge Rating 3, so the party ear[ns] 800 XP per monster, for a total of 1,600 XP. There a[re] five characters in the party, so they each get 320 X[P].

Example: Four characters attack an ogre strongho[ld]. A 5th-level sorcerer, 5th-level paladin, 4th-level cler[ic], and 2nd-level rogue/1st-level wizard manage to defea[t 8] goblins, 2 hobgoblins, an ogre, and its hell hound p[et]. The party's average level is $(5 + 5 + 4 + 3) \div 4$, or just ov[er] 4. The 8 goblins (CR 1/4) are grouped into two sets [of] four, and each set is worth 300 XP. The two hobgobli[ns] (CR 1/2) form a single set worth another 300 XP. T[he] ogre is CR 2 and is worth 600 XP, and the hell houn[d is] CR 3 and worth 800. The experience point total is 2,3[00], so each character earns 575 XP.

Why the Chart Looks Like It Does

The experience point system is designed to give char[ac]ters an extra level after roughly fourteen encounters, [if] the characters are facing appropriate opponents. [A] single monster with a CR equal to the average par[ty] level is an appropriate challenge, as is a group of weak[er] monsters worth equivalent XP. An appropriate cha[l]lenge should use up between a sixth and a quarter of t[he] characters' resources (spells, hit points, and so on).

The DMG Has More

Chapter 7: Rewards in the DUNGEON MASTER's Guide h[as] the full Single Monster Challenge Rating Table, not ju[st] the first quarter of it. You'll also find tips for balanci[ng] an encounter to match your specific party, Challen[ge] Ratings for traps, ad hoc experience point awards, exp[e]rience for solving puzzles, and story and roleplayi[ng] awards.

MONSTERS

...ed Dragon, Mature Adult

Huge Dragon (Fire)

...t Dice:	25d12+150 (312 hp)
...itiative:	+4 (Improved Initiative)
...eed:	40 ft., fly 150 ft. (poor)
...::	32 (–2 size, +24 natural)
...tacks:	Bite +34 melee, 2 claws +29 melee, 2 wings +29 melee, tail slap +29 melee; or crush +34 melee
...amage:	Bite 2d8+11; claw 2d6+5; wing 1d8+5; tail slap 2d6+16; crush 2d8+16
...ce/Reach:	10 ft. by 40 ft./10 ft.
...ecial Attacks:	Breath weapon, frightful presence, spells, spell-like abilities
...ecial Qualities:	Immunities, damage reduction 10/+1, SR 23, blindsight, keen senses
...ves:	Fort +20, Ref +14, Will +18
...ilities:	Str 33, Dex 10, Con 23, Int 18, Wis 19, Cha 18
...ills:	Bluff +29, Concentration +31, Diplomacy +29, Escape Artist +25, Intimidate +29, Jump +36, Knowledge (arcana) +29, Knowledge (history) +29, Listen +31, Scry +29, Search +29, Spellcraft +29, Spot +31
...ats:	Alertness, Cleave, Flyby Attack, Improved Initiative, Power Attack, Quicken Spell-like Ability, Weapon Focus (claw)
...imate/Terrain:	Temperate and warm hills, mountains, and underground
...rganization:	Solitary, pair, or family (1–2 and 1d4+1 offspring)
...allenge Rating:	13
...easure:	Triple standard
...ignment:	Always chaotic evil
...vancement Range:	26–27 HD (Huge)

Red dragons range from Tiny wyrmlings to Colossal great wyrms. Here's an example of a fairly powerful mature adult red dragon to show you what a truly powerful monster looks like.

Red dragons lair in large caves that extend deep into the earth, that shimmer with the heat of their bodies, and are marked by a sulfurous, smoky odor. However, they always have a high perch nearby from which to haughtily survey their territory, which they consider to be everything in sight.

Combat

Dragons prefer to fight on the wing, staying out of reach until they have worn down the enemy with ranged attacks. Dragons do not favor grapple attacks, though their crush attack uses normal grapple rules.

Because red dragons are so confident, they seldom pause to appraise an adversary. On spotting a target they make a snap decision whether to attack, using one of many strategies worked out ahead of time. A red dragon will land to attack small, weak creatures with its claws and bite rather than obliterating them with its breath weapon, so as not to destroy any treasure they might be carrying.

Breath Weapon (Su): A red dragon can breathe a cone of fire 50 feet long once every 1d4 rounds as a standard action. Creatures caught in the cone take 14d10 points of damage. A successful Reflex save (DC 28) halves the damage.

Locate Object (Sp): The dragon can use this ability seven times per day.

Frightful Presence (Ex): The dragon can unsettle foes with its mere presence whenever it attacks, charges, or flies overhead. Creatures with 24 or fewer Hit Dice (except for other dragons) within 210 feet of the dragon must succeed at a Will save (DC 26) to avoid this *fear* effect. On a failure, creatures with 4 or fewer HD become panicked for 4d6 rounds and those with 5 or more HD become shaken for 4d6 rounds.

Spells: The dragon knows and casts arcane spells as a 9th-level sorcerer, and can also cast cleric spells and those from the Chaos, Evil, and Fire domains as arcane spells. The save DC, where applicable, is 14 + spell level.

Spell-Like Abilities: Seven times a day—*locate object*; three times a day—*suggestion*; once a day—*eyebite* and *discern location*. These abilities are as the spells cast by a 9th-level sorcerer. The save DC, where applicable, is 14 + spell level.

Immunities (Ex): Red dragons have fire immunity and are immune to *sleep* and *paralysis* effects.

Blindsight (Ex): The dragon can ascertain creatures by nonvisual means (mostly hearing and scent, but also by noticing vibration and other environmental clues) with a range of 210 feet.

Keen Senses (Ex): The dragon sees four times as well a human in low-light conditions and twice as well in normal light. It also has darkvision with a range of 700 feet.

Feats: The dragon has the following bonus feats.
Flyby Attack: The dragon can attack at any point during, before, or after its move if it is flying.
Quicken Spell-Like Ability: The dragon can use one of its spell-like abilities each round as a free action.

3

Gelatinous Cube

Huge Ooze

Hit Dice:	4d10+36 (58 hp)
Initiative:	−5 (Dex)
Speed:	15 ft.
AC:	3 (−2 size, −5 Dex)
Attacks:	Slam +1 melee
Damage:	Slam 1d6+4 and acid 1d6
Face/Reach:	10 ft. by 10 ft./10 ft.
Special Attacks:	Engulf, paralysis, acid
Special Qualities:	Blindsight, transparent, electricity immunity, ooze
Saves:	Fort +5, Ref −4, Will +1
Abilities:	Str 10, Dex 1, Con 19, Int —, Wis 11, Cha 1
Climate/Terrain:	Underground
Organization:	Solitary
Challenge Rating:	3
Treasure:	1/10th coins; 25% goods (metal and stone goods only); 25% items (metal and stone items only)
Alignment:	Always neutral
Advancement Range:	5–12 HD (Huge); 13–24 HD (Gargantuan)

The nearly transparent gelatinous cube travels slowly along dungeon corridors and cave floors, absorbing carrion, creatures, and trash. Inorganic material remains trapped and visible inside the cube's body.

A typical gelatinous cube is 10 feet on a side and weighs about 10,000 pounds, though much larger specimens are not unknown.

Combat

A gelatinous cube attacks by slamming its body into its prey. It is capable of lashing out with a pseudopod, but usually engulfs foes.

Engulf (Ex): Although it moves slowly, a gelatinous cube can simply mow down Large or smaller creatures as a standard action. It cannot make a slam attack during a round in which it engulfs. The gelatinous cube merely has to move over the opponents, affecting as many as it can cover with its movement. Opponents can make opportunity attacks against the cube, but if they do so they are not entitled to a saving throw. Those who do not attempt opportunity attacks must succeed at Reflex saves (DC 13) or be engulfed. On a success, they are pushed back or aside (opponent's choice) as the cube moves forwa[rd]. Engulfed creatures are subject to the cube's paralysis a[nd] acid, and are considered to be grappled and trapp[ed] within its body.

Paralysis (Ex): Gelatinous cubes secrete an an[es]thetizing slime. A target hit by a cube's melee or eng[ulf] attack must succeed at a Fortitude save (DC 16) or [be] paralyzed for 3d6 rounds. The cube can automatica[lly] engulf a paralyzed opponent.

Acid (Ex): Any melee hit by the cube deals ac[id] damage. The cube's acid does not harm metal or sto[ne].

Transparent (Ex): Gelatinous cubes are hard to s[ee] even under ideal conditions, and it takes a success[ful] Spot check (DC 15) to notice one. Creatures who fail [to] notice a cube and walk into it are automatically engulf[ed].

Ooze: Immune to mind-influencing effects, pois[on,] sleep, paralysis, stunning, and polymorphing. Not su[b]ject to critical hits.

Blindsight (Ex): A gelatinous cube is blind, but [its] entire body is a primitive sensory organ that c[an] detect and locate prey by scent and vibration with[in] 60 feet.

Ghoul

	Ghoul	Ghast
	Medium-Size Undead	Medium-Size Undead
Hit Dice:	2d12 (13 hp)	4d12 (26 hp)
Initiative:	+2 (Dex)	+2 (Dex)
Speed:	30 ft.	30 ft.
AC:	14 (+2 Dex, +2 natural)	16 (+2 Dex, +4 natural)
Attacks:	Bite +3 melee;	Bite +4 melee;
	2 claws +0 melee	2 claws +1 melee
Damage:	Bite 1d6+1 and paralysis;	Bite 1d8+1 and paralysis;
	claw 1d3 and paralysis	claw 1d4 and paralysis
Face/Reach:	5 ft. by 5 ft./5 ft.	5 ft. by 5 ft./5 ft.
Special Attacks:	Paralysis	Stench, paralysis
Special Qualities:	Undead	Undead
Saves:	Fort +0, Ref +2, Will +5	Fort +1, Ref +3, Will +6
Abilities:	Str 13, Dex 15, Con —,	Str 13, Dex 15, Con —,
	Int 13, Wis 14, Cha 16	Int 13, Wis 14, Cha 16
Skills:	Climb +6, Escape Artist +7, Hide +7,	Climb +6, Escape Artist +8, Hide +8,
	Intuit Direction +3, Jump +6, Listen +7,	Intuit Direction +3, Jump +6, Listen +8,
	Move Silently +7, Search +6, Spot +7	Move Silently +7, Search +6, Spot +8
Feats:	Multiattack, Weapon Finesse (bite)	Multiattack, Weapon Finesse (bite)
Climate/Terrain:	Any land and aquatic	Any land and underground
Organization:	Solitary, gang (2–4), or pack (7–12)	Solitary, gang (2–4), or pack (2–4, plus 7–12 ghouls)
Challenge Rating:	3	4
Treasure:	None	Standard
Alignment:	Always chaotic evil	Always chaotic evil
Advancement Range:	2–3 HD (Medium-size)	3–6 HD (Medium-size)

Ghouls haunt graveyards, battlefields, and other places rich with the carrion they hunger for. These terrible creatures lurk wherever the stench of death hangs heavy, ready to devour the unwary.

Ghouls are said to be created on the death of a living man or woman who savored the taste of human flesh. This may or may not be true, but it does explain the disgusting behavior of these cannibalistic undead. Some believe that anyone of exceptional debauchery and wickedness runs the risk of becoming a ghoul.

That ghouls were once human is obvious to those with the courage to look upon them. Although they still appear more or less human, their mottled, decaying flesh is drawn tight across clearly visible bones. The transformation from living beings into fell things of the night has warped their minds, making them cunning and feral. Their eyes burn like hot coals in their sunken sockets.

Ghouls speak Common.

Combat

Ghouls try to attack with surprise whenever possible. They strike from behind tombstones, leap from mausoleums, and burst from shallow graves.

Paralysis (Ex): Those hit by a ghoul's attack must succeed at a Fortitude save (DC 14) or be paralyzed for 1d6+2 minutes. Elves are immune to this paralysis.

Undead: Immune to mind-influencing effects, poison, sleep, paralysis, stunning, and disease. Not subject to critical hits, subdual damage, ability damage, energy drain, or death from massive damage.

Spawn

In most cases, ghouls devour those they kill. From time to time, however, the bodies of their victims lie where they fell, to rise as ghouls themselves in 1d4 days. Casting *bless* on a body before the end of that time averts the transformation.

Lacedon

These aquatic cousins of the ghoul lurk near hidden reefs or other places where ships are likely to meet their end. They have a swim speed of 30 feet.

Ghast

Although these creatures look just like their lesser kin, they are far more deadly and cunning.

Combat

Stench (Ex): The stink of death and corruption surrounding these creatures is sickening. Those within 10 feet must succeed at a Fortitude save (DC 15) or be racked with nausea, suffering a –2 morale penalty to all attacks, saves, and skill checks for 1d6+4 minutes.

Paralysis (Ex): Those hit by a ghast's attack must succeed at a Fortitude save (DC 15) or be paralyzed for 1d6+4 minutes. Even elves are vulnerable to this paralysis.

Goblin

Small Humanoid (Goblinoid)

Hit Dice:	1d8 (4 hp)
Initiative:	+1 (Dex)
Speed:	30 ft.
AC:	15 (+1 size, +1 Dex, +3 studded leather)
Attacks:	Morningstar +0 melee; or javelin +2 ranged
Damage:	Morningstar 1d8–1; javelin 1d6–1
Face/Reach:	5 ft. by 5 ft./5 ft.
Special Qualities:	Darkvision 60 ft.
Saves:	Fort +0, Ref +3, Will +0
Abilities:	Str 8, Dex 13, Con 11, Int 10, Wis 11, Cha 8
Skills:	Hide +6, Listen +3, Move Silently +5, Spot +3
Feats:	Alertness
Climate/Terrain:	Temperate and warm land and underground
Organization:	Gang (4–9), band (10–100 goblins, plus 1 leader of 4th to 6th level and 1 3rd-level sergeant per 20 adults), war band (10–24 goblins with worg mounts), or tribe (40–400 goblins, plus 1 leader of 6th to 8th level, 1–2 lieutenants of 4th to 5th level, and 1 3rd-level sergeant per 20 adults, plus 10–24 worgs and 2–4 dire wolves)
Challenge Rating:	1/4
Treasure:	Standard
Alignment:	Usually neutral evil
Advancement Range:	By character class

Goblins are small humanoids that many consider little more than a nuisance. However, if unchecked, their great numbers, rapid reproduction, and evil dispositions let them overrun and despoil civilized areas.

Goblins have flat faces, broad noses, pointed ears, wide mouths, and small, sharp fangs. Their foreheads slope back, and their eyes are usually dull and glazed, varying in color from red to yellow. They walk upright, but their arms hang down almost to their knees. Goblins' skin color ranges from yellow through any shade of orange to a deep red; usually all members of a single tribe are about the same color. They wear clothing of dark leather, tending toward drab, soiled-looking colors.

Goblins speak Goblin; those with Intelligence scores of 12 or above also speak Common.

Combat

Being bullied by bigger, stronger creatures has taught goblins to exploit what few advantages they have: sheer numbers and malicious ingenuity. The concept of a "fair fight" is meaningless in their society. They favor ambushes, overwhelming odds, dirty tricks, and any other edge they can devise.

Goblins have a poor grasp of strategy and are cowardly by nature, tending to flee the field if a battle turns against them. With proper supervision, though, they can implement reasonably complex plans. In such circumstances, their numbers can be a deadly advantage.

Skills: Goblins receive a +4 racial bonus to Move Silently checks. Goblin cavalry (mounted on worgs) receive a +6 bonus to Ride checks and the Mounted Combat feat. (Neither are included above.)

Goblin Characters

A goblin's favored multiclass is rogue; goblin leaders tend to be rogues or fighter/rogues. Goblin clerics can choose two of the following domains: Chaos, Evil, and Trickery. Most goblin spellcasters, however, are adepts (see "NPC Classes" in Chapter 2: Characters in the DUNGEON MASTER's *Guide*). Goblin adepts favor spells that fool or confuse enemies.

Goblin Society

Goblins are tribal. Their leaders are generally the biggest, strongest, and sometimes even the smartest around. They have almost no concept of privacy, living and sleeping in large common areas; only the leaders live separately. Goblins survive by raiding and stealing (preferably from those who cannot defend themselves easily), sneaking into lairs, villages, and even towns by night to take what they can. They are not above waylaying travelers on the road or in forests and stripping them of all possessions, up to and including the clothes on their backs. Goblins sometimes capture slaves to perform hard labor in the tribe's lair or camp.

These creatures live wherever they can, from dank caves to dismal ruins, and their lairs are always smelly and filthy due to an utter lack of sanitation. Goblins often settle near civilized areas to raid for food, livestock, tools, weapons, and supplies. Once a tribe has despoiled a locale, they simply pack up and move on to the next convenient area. Hobgoblins and bugbears are sometimes found in the company of goblin tribes, usually in leadership roles. Some goblin tribes form alliances with worgs, which allow themselves to be ridden into combat.

The chief goblin deity is Maglubiyet, who urges his worshipers to expand their numbers and overwhelm their competitors.

ell Hound

Medium-Size Outsider (Evil, Fire, Lawful)

Dice:	4d8+4 (22 hp)
iative:	+5 (+1 Dex, +4 Improved Initiative)
ed:	40 ft.
:	16 (+1 Dex, +5 natural)
acks:	Bite +5 melee
mage:	Bite 1d8 +1
e/Reach:	5 ft. by 5 ft./5 ft.
ecial Attacks:	Breath weapon
ecial Qualities:	Scent, fire defenses
ves:	Fort +5, Ref +5, Will +4
ilities:	Str 13, Dex 13, Con 13, Int 6, Wis 10, Cha 6
lls:	Hide +11, Listen +5, Move Silently +13, Spot +15,
ts:	Improved Initiative
mate/Terrain:	Any land and underground
ganization:	Solitary, pair, or pack (5–12)
allenge Rating:	3
asure:	None
gnment:	Always lawful evil
vancement Range:	3–4 HD (Medium-size); 5–8 HD (Large)

Hell hounds are aggressive, fire-breathing canines of extraplanar origin. Specimens are frequently brought to the Material Plane to serve evil beings, and many have established indigenous breeding populations.

A hell hound resembles a large, powerfully built dog with short, rust-red or reddish-brown fur; its markings, teeth, and tongue are sooty black. It is easily distinguished from normal hounds by its red glowing eyes. A typical hell hound stands about 4 1/2 feet high at the shoulder and weighs approximately 120 pounds.

Hell hounds do not speak but understand Infernal.

ombat

Hell hounds are efficient hunters. A favorite tactic is to surround prey quietly, then attack with one or two hounds, driving the prey with their fiery breath toward the rest of the pack. If it doesn't run, the pack closes in. Hell hounds track fleeing prey relentlessly.

Breath Weapon (Su): Hell hounds can breathe cones of fire 30 feet long once every 1d4 rounds. Those within the cone must succeed at a Reflex save (DC 13) or take 1d6+1 points of damage. The fiery attack also ignites any flammable materials within the cone. Hell hounds can use their breath weapon while biting.

Fire Defenses: Fire immunity, double damage from cold on a failed save.

Skills: Hell hounds receive a +5 racial bonus to Hide and Move Silently checks, and a +8 racial bonus to Spot checks and Wilderness Lore checks when tracking by scent, due to their keen sense of smell.

Ogre

Large Giant

Hit Dice:	4d8+8 (26 hp)
Initiative:	–1 (Dex)
Speed:	30 ft.
AC:	16 (–1 size, –1 Dex, +5 natural, +3 hide)
Attacks:	Huge greatclub +8 melee; Huge longspear +1 ranged
Damage:	Huge greatclub 2d6+7; Huge longspear 2d6+7
Face/Reach:	5 ft. by 5 ft./10 ft. (15–20 ft. with longspear)
Saves:	Fort +6, Ref +0, Will +1
Abilities:	Str 21, Dex 8, Con 15, Int 6, Wis 10, Cha 7
Skills:	Climb +5, Listen +3, Spot +3
Feats:	Weapon Focus (greatclub)
Climate/Terrain:	Any land, aquatic, and underground
Organization:	Solitary, pair, gang (2–4), or band (5–8)
Challenge Rating:	2
Treasure:	Standard
Alignment:	Usually chaotic evil
Advancement Range:	By character class

Ogres are big, ugly, greedy creatures who live by raiding and scavenging. They join other monsters to prey on the weak and associate freely with giants and trolls.

Lazy and bad-tempered, ogres solve problems by smashing them; what they can't smash they either ignore or flee. Dwelling in small tribal groups, ogres occupy any convenient location and eat nearly anything they can catch, steal, or slay. Ogres sometimes accept mercenary service with other evil humanoids (including humans).

Adult ogres stand 9 to 10 feet tall and weigh 300 to 350 pounds. Their skin color ranges from dull yellow to dull brown. Their thick hides are often covered in dark warty bumps, and their hair is long, unkempt, and greasy. Their clothing consists of poorly cured furs and hides, which add to their naturally repellent odor.

Ogres speak Giant, and those specimens who boast Intelligence scores of at least 10 also speak Common.

Combat

Ogres favor overwhelming odds, sneak attacks, a ambushes to a fair fight. They are intelligent enough—barely—to fire ranged weapons first to soften up th foes before closing, but ogre gangs and bands fight unorganized individuals.

Merrow (Aquatic Ogre)

The merrow are a variety of ogre that dwell in freshw ter lakes and rivers. Apart from their habitat, spe (swim 40 ft.), and their penchant for longspears (atta +7 melee, damage 1d8+7), they are identical to the landbound cousins.

Skeleton

	Small Skeleton Small Undead	Medium-Size Skeleton Medium-Size Undead	Large Skeleton Large Undead
Hit Dice:	1/2 d12 (3 hp)	1d12 (6 hp)	2d12 (13 hp)
Initiative:	+5 (+1 Dex, +4 Improved Initiative)	+5 (+1 Dex, +4 Improved Initiative)	+5 (+1 Dex, +4 Improved Initiativ
Speed:	30 ft.	30 ft.	40 ft.
AC:	13 (+1 size, +1 Dex, +1 natural)	13 (+ 1 Dex, +2 natural)	13 (–1 size, +1 Dex, +3 natur
Attacks:	2 claws +0 melee	2 claws +0 melee	2 claws +2 melee
Damage:	Claw 1d3–1	Claw 1d4	Claw 1d6+2
Face/Reach:	5 ft. by 5 ft./5 ft.	5 ft. by 5 ft./5 ft.	5 ft. by 5 ft./10 ft.
Special Qualities:	Undead, immunities	Undead, immunities	Undead, immunities
Saves:	Fort +0, Ref +1, Will +2	Fort +0, Ref +1, Will +2	Fort +0, Ref +1, Will +3
Abilities:	Str 8, Dex 12, Con —,	Str 10, Dex 12, Con —,	Str 14, Dex 12, Con —,
	Int —, Wis 10, Cha 11	Int —, Wis 10, Cha 11	Int —, Wis 10, Cha 11
Feats:	Improved Initiative	Improved Initiative	Improved Initiative
Climate/Terrain:	Any land and underground		
Organization:	Tiny and Small—Squad (6–10) or mob (11–20); Medium-size—Gang (2–5), squad (6–10), or mob (11–20)		
Challenge Rating:	Small 1/4, Medium-size 1/3, Large 1		
Treasure:	None		
Alignment:	Always neutral		
Advancement Range:	Small and Medium-size —; Large 3 HD (Large)		

Skeletons are the animated bones of the dead, mindless automatons that obey the orders of their evil masters.

These undead creatures are seldom garbed with any-

thing more than the rotting remnants of any armor th were wearing when slain. Pinpoints of red light sm der in their empty eye sockets.

Skeletons do only what they are ordered to do. Th can draw no conclusions of their own and take no init tive. Because of this, their instructions must always simple, such as "Kill anyone who enters this chambe

Combat

Skeletons attack until destroyed, for that is what th were created to do. The threat posed by a group of ske tons depends primarily on their size.

Undead: Immune to mind-influencing effect poison, sleep, paralysis, stunning, and disease. Not su ject to critical hits, subdual damage, ability damag energy drain, or death from massive damage.

Immunities (Ex): Skeletons have cold immunit Because they lack flesh or internal organs, they are n damaged by piercing weapons and take only ha damage from slashing weapons.

More Monsters

Here are some more monsters in an abbreviated format. Here's what these statistic block entries mean:

Creature's name (# appearing): SZ (size) and creature type; HD (Hit Dice); hp (hit points); Init (initiative modifier); Spd (speed); AC (Armor Class); Atk: attack modifiers (damage/attack); Face; Reach; SA (special attacks); SQ (special qualities); SR (spell resistance); SV (saving throws); Ability Scores; AL (alignment). Skills and Feats (if any).

Badger: SZ T (animal); HD 1d8+2; hp 6; Init +4; Spd 20, burrow 10; AC 16 (+2 size, +4 Dex); Atk: 2 claws +4 (1d2+2), bite −1 (1d3+1); Face 2.5 ft. × 2.5 ft.; Reach 0 ft.; SQ scent; SV Fort +4, Ref +6, Will +1; Str 14, Dex 19, Con 15, Int 2, Wis 12, Cha 6; AL N. Skills: Escape Artist +7, Listen +4, Spot +4.

When a badger takes damage in combat, it goes berserk on the next round for the rest of the fight, gaining +2 Strength, +2 Constitution, and −2 AC. Badgers can also scent creatures within 30 feet and can discern their direction as a partial action. They are CR 1/2.

Dire Rat: SZ S (animal); HD 1d8+1; hp 5; Init +3; Spd 40, climb 20; AC 15 (+1 size, +3 Dex, +1 natural); Atk: bite +2 (1d4); Face 5 ft. × 5 ft.; Reach 5 ft.; SA disease; SQ scent; SV Fort +3, Ref +5, Will +3; Str 10, De 17, Con 12, Int 1, Wis 12, Cha 4; AL N. Skills Climb +11, Hide +11, Move Silently +6. Feats: Weapon Finesse (bite).

Those hit by a dire rat's bite must make a DC 11 Fortitude save or catch a disease with an incubation period of 1d3 days. The initial damage is 1 point of Constitution damage, and the secondary damage is 1 point of Dexterity damage and 1 point of Constitution damage. Dire rats can also scent their prey. They detect creatures within 30 feet and can discern their direction as a partial action. They are CR 1/2.

Dwarf Warrior: SZ M (humanoid); HD 1d8+1; hp 5; Init +0; Spd 15; AC 16 (+4 scale mail, +2 large shield); Atk: dwarven waraxe +1 (1d10) or shortbow +1 (1d6); Face 5 ft. × 5 ft.; Reach 5 ft.; SA dwarven traits; SQ dwarven traits; SV Fort +3, Ref +0, Will +0; Str 11, Dex 10, Con 13, Int 10, Wis 10, Cha 8; AL LG. Skills: Listen +1, Spot +1. Feats: Exotic Weapon Proficiency (dwarven waraxe).

Dwarven warriors gain all the benefits for dwarves listed in Chapter 2: Races. They are CR 1/2.

Dog: SZ S (animal); HD 1d8+1; hp 5; Init +3; Spd 40; AC 14 (+1 size, +3 Dex); Atk: bite +2 (1d4+2); Face 5 ft. × 5 ft.; Reach 5 ft.; SQ scent; SV Fort +3, Ref +5, Will +1; Str 11, Dex 17, Con 13, Int 2, Wis 12, Cha 6; AL N. Skills Listen +6, Spot +6.

Dogs can scent creatures within 30 feet and can discern their direction as a partial action. They are CR 1/3.

Hawk: SZ T (animal); HD 1d8; hp 4; Init +3; Spd 10, fly 60; AC 17 (+2 size, +3 Dex, +2 natural); Atk: claw +5 (1d4−2); Face 2.5 ft. × 2.5 ft.; Reach 0 ft.; SV Fort +2, Ref +5, Will +2; Str 6, Dex 17, Con 10, Int 2, Wis 14, Cha 6; AL N. Skills: Spot +6.

Hawks gain a +8 bonus to Spot checks in daylight. They are CR 1/3.

Hobgoblin: SZ M (humanoid); HD 1d8+1; hp 5; Init: +1; Spd 30; AC 15 (+1 Dex, +3 studded leather, +1 small shield); Atk: longsword +0 (1d8) or javelin +1 (1d6); Face 5 ft. × 5 ft.; Reach 5 ft.; SV Fort +3, Ref +1, Will +0; Str 11, Dex 13, Con 13, Int 10, Wis 10, Cha 10; AL LE. Skills: Hide +1, Listen +4, Move Silently +3, Spot +4. Feats: Alertness.

Hobgoblins, larger versions of goblins, have CR 1/2.

Human Warrior: SZ M (humanoid); HD 1d8; hp 4; Init +0; Spd 20; AC 16 (+4 scale mail, +2 large shield); Atk: longsword +1 (1d8) or crossbow +1 (1d8); Face 5 ft. × 5 ft.; Reach 5 ft.; SV Fort +3, Ref +0, Will +0; Str 11, Dex 10, Con 11, Int 10, Wis 10, Cha 10; AL NE. Skills: Listen +1, Spot +1, Search +1. Feats: Weapon Focus (longsword), Point-Blank Shot.

These humans are typical bandits or soldiers. They are CR 1/2.

Orc: SZ M (humanoid); HD 1d8; hp 4; Init +0; Spd 20; AC 14 (+4 scale mail); Atk: greataxe +2 (1d12+3) or javelin +0 (1d6+2); Face 5 ft. × 5 ft.; Reach 5 ft.; SV Fort +2, Ref +0, Will −1; Str 15, Dex 10, Con 11, Int 9, Wis 8, Cha 8; AL CE. Skills: Listen +4, Spot +3. Feats: Alertness.

Orcs suffer a −1 penalty to attack rolls in bright sunlight or within the radius of a *daylight* spell. They are CR 1/2.

Unicorn: SZ L (magical beast); HD 4d10+20; hp 42; Init +3; Spd 60; AC: 18 (−1 size, +3 Dex, +6 natural); Atk: horn +11 (1d8+8), 2 hooves +3 (1d4+2); Face 5 ft. × 10 ft.; Reach 5 ft. (10 ft. with horn); SQ spell-like abilities, immunities; SV Fort +5, Ref +3, Will +5; Str 20, Dex 17, Con 21, Int 10, Wis 21, Cha 24; AL CG. Skills: Animal Empathy +10, Listen +10, Move Silently +7, Spot +10, Wilderness Lore +9. Feats: Alertness.

Unicorns have *magic circle against evil* at all times. They can *detect evil* at will and use *teleport without error* once per day. Each day, they can *cure light wounds* three times, *cure moderate wounds* once, and *neutralize poison* once. They are immune to poisons, *charm*, and *hold*. They are CR 3.

Zombie: SZ M (undead); HD 2d12; hp 16; Init −1; Spd 30; AC 11 (−1 Dex, +2 natural); Atk: +2 melee (1d6+1 bash); Face 5 ft. × 5 ft.; Reach 5 ft.; SQ undead immunities, partial actions only; SV Fort +0, Ref +1, Will +2; Str 13, Dex 8, Con —, Int —, Wis 10, Cha 11; AL N. Feat: Toughness.

Zombies follow simple instructions set by their creator. They have the same undead immunities that skeletons do. Zombies are CR 1/2.

Familiars

Bat: HD 1/4d8; Init +2, Spd fly 40; AC 16; Atk: none; SV Fort +2, Ref +4, Will +2. Skills: Listen +9, Move Silently +4, Spot +9.

Cat: HD 1/2d8; Init +2, Spd 30; AC 14; Atk: 2 claws +3 (1), bite −2 (1); SV Fort +2, Ref +4, Will +1. Skills: Climb +5, Hide +13, Listen +6, Move Silently +5, Spot +6.

Owl: HD 1d8, Init +3, Spd fly 40; AC 17, claw +5 (1d4−2); SV Fort +2, Ref +5, Will +2. Skills: Listen +14, Move Silently +14, Spot +6.

Rat: HD 1/4d8; Init +2, Spd 15 (can climb); AC 14; Atk: bite +4 (1); SV Fort +2, Ref +4, Will +1. Skills: Climb +12, Hide +18, Move Silently +10.

Raven: HD 1/4d8; Init +2, Spd fly 40; AC 14; Atk: claw +3 (1); SV Fort +2, Ref +4, Will +2. Skills: Spot +7, Listen +7.

Snake: HD 1/4d8; Init +3, Spd 15 (can climb or swim); AC 17; Atk: bite +5 (Fort DC 11 or 1d6 Con); SV Fort +2, Ref +5, Will +1. Skills: Climb +14, Hide +19, Listen +9, Spot +9.

Toad: HD 1/4d8; Init +1, Spd 5; AC 15; Atk: none; SV Fort +2, Ref +3, Will +2. Skills: Hide +21, Listen +5, Spot +5.

Weasel: HD 1/2d8; Init +2, Spd 20 (climb 30); AC 14; Atk: bite +4 (1); SV Fort +2, Ref +4, Will +1. Skills: Climb +10, Hide +14, Move Silently +14, Spot +5.

TREASURE

Until you have access to the full treasure system in the *Dungeon Master's Guide*, here's a simple system that provides reasonably balanced results. Feel free to deviate from the tables below for variety or to suit the needs of your specific campaign.

Treasure in Three Easy Steps

First, figure out how much treasure you want to have in a particular location. In general, a 4th-level treasure is guarded by a single CR 4 monster or a number of weaker monsters worth equivalent XP. But it's a good idea to vary this somewhat, because not all monsters care about treasure. You'll still have a balanced adventure, for example, if half the monsters have no treasure at all and the other half have double treasure. But keeping treasure equal to CR is a good rule of thumb, so that's how we'll treat it here.

Second, use the table below to determine the overall contents of the treasure. Roll d% three times: once for coins, once for goods, and once for items. On any roll, you roll 96–100, keep what you roll, then roll again for that category on the next-higher level. For example, if you roll 98 on a 3rd-level coin roll, you'll get both 1d10×10 pp and whatever you roll on the 4th-level section of the Treasure Table for coins.

TREASURE TABLE

Level		—Coins—		—Goods—		—Items—
1	01–14	—	01–90	—	01–71	—
	15–29	1d6×1000 cp	91–95	1 gem	72–95	1 mundane
	30–52	1d8×100 sp	96–100	1 art	96–100	1 minor
	53–95	2d8×10 gp				
	96–100	1d4×10 pp				
2	01–13	—	01–81	—	01–49	—
	14–23	1d10×1,000 cp	82–95	1d3 gems	50–85	1 mundane
	24–43	2d10×100 sp	96–100	1d3 art	86–100	1 minor
	44–95	4d10×10 gp				
	96–100	2d8×10 pp				
3	01–11	—	01–77	—	01–49	—
	12–21	2d10×1,000 cp	78–95	1d3 gems	50–79	1d3 mundane
	22–41	4d8×100 sp	96–100	1d3 art	86–100	1 minor
	42–95	1d4×100 gp				
	96–100	1d10×10 pp				
4	01–11	—	01–70	—	01–42	—
	12–21	3d10×1,000 cp	71–95	1d4 gems	43–62	1d4 mundane
	22–41	4d12×1,000 sp	96–100	1d3 art	63–100	1 minor
	42–95	1d6×100 gp				
	96–100	1d8×10 pp				
5	01–10	—	01–60	—	01–57	—
	11–19	1d4×10,000 cp	61–95	1d4 gems	58–67	1d4 mundane
	20–38	1d6×1,000 sp	91–100	1d4 art	68–100	1d3 minor
	39–95	1d8×100 gp				
	96–100	1d10×10 pp				

Third, determine the exact nature of the gems, art, mundane items, and magic items.

Gems

d%	Value	Example
01–25	4d4 gp (avg. 10 gp)	Hematite
26–50	2d4 ×10 gp (50)	Onyx
51–70	4d4 ×10 gp (100)	Pearl
71–90	2d4 ×100 gp (500)	Topaz
91–99	4d4 ×100 gp (1,000)	Sapphire
100	2d4 ×1,000gp (5,000)	Diamond or ruby

Art Objects

d%	Value
01–10	1d10 ×10 gp (avg. 55 gp)
11–25	3d6 ×10 gp (105)
26–40	1d6 ×100 gp (350)
41–50	1d10 ×100 gp (550)
51–60	2d6 ×100 gp (700)
61–70	3d6 ×100 gp (1,050)
71–80	4d6 ×100 gp (1,400)
81–85	5d6 ×100 gp (1,750)
86–90	1d4 ×1,000 gp (2,500)
91–95	1d6 ×1,000 gp (3,500)
96–99	2d4 × 1,000 gp (5,000)
100	2d6 ×1,000 gp (7,000)

Mundane Items: Mundane items run the gamut from alchemist's fire to masterwork bows. Pick an unusual item from Chapter 7: Equipment. On average, each mundane item should be worth about 275 gp, but they vary widely.

Minor Magic Items: A sampling of minor magic items follows on the next page.

MAGIC ITEMS

It takes the largest chapter of the DUNGEON MASTER's Guide to explain the ins and outs of magic items, and we aren't going to try to duplicate that here. Instead, you'll find some examples of minor magic items—the sort beginning characters are most likely to discover, buy, or find in the hands of antagonists. The DUNGEON MASTER's Guide has hundreds more minor magic items, plus rules and descriptions for medium and major magic items. You'll also find rules for artifacts of unsurpassed power in the DUNGEON MASTER's Guide.

Scrolls

A scroll is a spell (or collection of spells) that has been stored in written form. A spell on a scroll can be used only once. The writing vanishes from the scroll when the spell is activated. Minor scrolls typically have 1d3 1st- through 3rd-level spells. Example minor scrolls include *burning hands* (25 gp), *sleep* (25 gp), *bless* (25 gp), *summon swarm* (150 gp), and *hold person* (150 gp).

Using a scroll requires these steps:

1. Decipher the Writing: This requires a *read magic* spell or a successful Spellcraft skill check at a DC of 15 + the spell's level.

Deciphering a scroll to determine its contents does not activate its magic. A character can decipher the writing on a scroll in advance so that she can proceed directly to the next step when the time comes to use the scroll.

2. Activate the Spell: Activating a scroll requires reading the spell aloud from the scroll. The character must be able to see and read the writing on the scroll and must be able to speak unless the spell has no verbal component.

Activating a scroll spell requires no material components or focuses. (The creator of the scroll provided these when scribing the scroll.) Activating a scroll spell is subject to disruption just as casting a spell is. Scrolls are spell completion activation items, and using a spell on a scroll takes the same time as casting the spell would take.

To have any chance of activating a scroll spell, the user must be able to cast spells of the correct type (arcane or divine), the user must have the spell on her class list, and the user must have the requisite ability score (15 Intelligence for a wizard casting a 5th-level spell, for example).

If the user meets all the requirements noted above and is high enough level to cast the spell, she can automatically activate the spell. But if her own level is below the scroll's caster level, then she has to make a caster level check to cast the spell successfully. Roll 1d20 and add her level. The DC for this check is the scroll's caster level + 1.

3. Determine the Effect: A spell successfully activated from a scroll works exactly like a spell prepared and cast the normal way. Assume the scroll spell's caster level is always the minimum level required to cast the spell for the character who scribed the scroll (usually twice the spell's level, minus 1).

Whether the activation is successful or not, the writing for an activated spell disappears from the scroll.

If the user failed to activate the spell successfully, she must roll 1d20 and add her class level. If the result is not at least equal to the level that she would have to be to cast the spell, then there is a mishap. A mishap is some harmful misfire, as determined by the DM, but a mishap defaults to a surge of uncontrolled magical energy that deals 1d6 damage per spell level.

Potions

Potions are also stored spells, but they don't require a knowledgeable caster. Simply drink the potion, and it's as if the spell were cast on you. All potions duplicate spell effects exactly, and any choices were made when the creator brewed the potion. A *potion of protection from elements*, for example, already has which element it protects from specified.

Regular potions duplicate the effects of 3rd or lower level spells. Each is good for one use. A typical potion or oil consists of an ounce of liquid held in a ceramic, glass, or metal vial fitted with a tight stopper. The stoppered container is usually no more than 1 inch wide and 2 inches high. Typical glass and ceramic potion vials have a base AC of 9, a hardness of 0, 5 hit points, and a break DC of 12.

Example minor potions: *cure light wounds* (50 gp), *spider climb* (50 gp), *aid* (300 gp), *invisibility* (300 gp), *neutralize poison* (750 gp).

Rods, Staffs, and Wands

Wands and staffs have up to 50 charges (when new) and store spells. Like scrolls, they require the user to be a spellcaster with the appropriate spell on his class list. But activating the spell within the wand or staff is automatic when a word is spoken. Wands have one spell stored within them, and staffs have more than one kind of spell. Rods never have charges and don't directly duplicate spells.

Rods: Rods are scepterlike, unique items and do not have charges. Anyone can use a rod. Details relating to rod use vary from rod to rod. Rods all weigh approximately 5 pounds. They range from 2 feet to 3 feet long and are usually made of iron or some other metal. (Many can function as light maces or at least clubs due to their sturdy construction.) These sturdy items have an AC of 9, a hardness of 10, 10 hit points, and a break DC of 27.

There are no minor rods. An example rod is a *rod of metal and mineral detection* (10,500 gp). This rod pulses in the wielder's hand and points to the largest mass of metal within 30 feet. However, the wielder can concentrate on a specific metal or mineral (gold, platinum, quartz, beryl, diamond, corundum, etc.). If the specific mineral is within 30 feet, the rod points to any and all places it is located, and the rod possessor knows the approximate quantity as well. If more than one deposit of the specified metal or mineral is within range, the rod points to the largest cache first. Each operation requires a full-round action.

Caster Level: 9th; *Prerequisites:* Craft Rod, *locate object*; *Market Price:* 10,500 gp

Staffs: Staffs are long shafts of wood that serve as multiple spell storage items. A typical staff is 4 feet to 7 feet long and 2 inches to 3 inches thick. It weighs about 5 pounds. Most staffs are wood, but a rare few are bone, metal, or even glass. Staffs are often decorated with carvings or runes. Each staff is unique and has a maximum of 50 charges. The only limit to the number of spells a staff can hold is the number the creator is willing to place within it. Only casters who have the staff's spells on their spell list can use those spells. Using a staff requires the same casting time as for the spell

stored within it. A staff's user must hold it forth in [at] least one hand (or whatever passes for a hand for no[n]humanoid creatures) to invoke its abilities. Typic[al] staffs are thick wooden shafts—like walking stick[s,] quarterstaffs, or cudgels. They have an AC of 7, a har[d]ness of 5, 10 hit points, and a break DC of 24.

There are no minor staffs. An example staff is a *staff [of]* *size alteration* (6,500 gp). Stout and sturdy, this staff [of] dark wood allows use of either *enlarge* spells or *redu[ce]* spells at a cost of 1 charge each.

Wands: A wand is a thin baton that contains a spe[ll.] A typical wand is 6 inches to 12 inches long and abo[ut] 1/4 inch thick. They often weigh no more than [an] ounce. Most wands are wood, but some are bone. Ea[ch] wand can have up to 50 charges, allowing the wan[d's] stored spell to be used once for each charge. A wan[d] that runs out of charges is just a stick. Wands are sp[ell] knowledge activation items. Using a wand requires t[he] same casting time as for the spell stored within it. Usi[ng] a wand requires that the wand be held in the user's han[d] (or whatever passes for a hand for a nonhumanoid cre[a]ture) and pointed in the general direction of the targe[t] or area. A successful attack on the wand can destroy [it.] Typical wands are thin and fragile, being made of woo[d] or bone. They have an AC of 7, a hardness of 5, 5 h[it] points, and a break DC of 16.

Minor wands have a 1st- through 3rd-level spe[ll] within them. Example minor wands include *wands [of] detect magic* (375 gp), *magic missile* (750 gp), *charm perso[n]* (750 gp), *cure light wounds* (750 gp), and *ghoul tou[ch]* (4,500 gp).

Rings

Rings are finger jewelry that bestow magical powe[r] upon their wearers. Only a rare few have charge[s.] Anyone can use a ring. Ring use details vary from rin[g] to ring.

Unless otherwise noted, rings are command wo[rd] activation items, which means that they can be act[i]vated as a standard action by the use magic item actio[n] and not provoke attacks of opportunity.

Rings have an AC of 13, a hardness of 10, 2 hit poin[ts,] and a break DC of 25.

The following are some typical minor rings:

Climbing: This ring is actually a magic leather co[rd] that ties around a finger. It grants the wearer a +[1] bonus to Climb checks.

Market Price: 2,900 gp

Counterspells: This ring might seem to be a *ring [of] spell storing* upon first examination. However, while [it] allows a single spell of 1st through 6th level to be ca[st] into it, that spell cannot be cast out of it again. Instea[d,] should that spell ever be cast upon the wearer, the spe[ll] is immediately countered, as a counterspell actio[n] requiring no action (or even knowledge) on the weare[r's]

part. Once so used, the spell cast within the ring is gone. A new spell (or the same one again) may be placed in it again.

Market Price: 4,000 gp

Elemental Resistance (Minor): This reddish iron ring protects the wearer from damage from one type of energy—fire, cold, electricity, acid, or sonic. When the wearer would normally take such damage, subtract 15 points of damage per round from the total to account for the ring's effect.

Market Price: 16,000 gp

Force Shield: An iron band, this simple ring generates a large shield-sized (and shield-shaped) *wall of force* that stays with the ring and can be wielded by the wearer as if it were a normal shield (+2 AC). This special creation, since it can be activated and deactivated at will (a free action), offers no armor check penalty nor arcane spell failure chance.

Market Price: 8,500 gp

Protection: This ring offers magical protection in the form of a +1 or +2 deflection bonus.

Market Price: 2,000 gp (+1 ring) or 8,000 gp (+2 ring)

Ram: The *ring of the ram* is an ornate ring forged of hard metal, usually iron or an iron alloy. It has the head of a ram or of a buck goat as its device.

The wearer can cause the ring to give forth a ramlike force, manifested by a vaguely discernible shape that resembles the head of a ram or goat. This force strikes a single target, dealing 1d6 points of damage if one charge is expended, 2d6 points if two charges are used, or 3d6 points if three charges (the maximum) are used. Treat this as a ranged attack with a 50-foot maximum range and no penalties for distance. The ring is quite useful for knocking opponents off parapets or ledges, among other things.

The force of the blow is considerable, and those struck by the ring are subject to a bull rush if within 30 feet of the ring-wearer. (The ram has a Strength score of 25 and is considered Large.) The ram gains a +1 bonus to the bull rush attempt if two charges are expended, or a +2 if three charges are expended.

In addition to its attack mode, the *ring of the ram* also has the power to open doors as if it were a person of 25 Strength. If two charges are expended, the effect is equivalent to a character of 27 Strength. If three charges are expended, the effect is that of a character of 29 Strength.

The ring can have 50 charges at a time.

Market Price: 8,500 gp

Magic Armor

All magic armor and shields begin as masterwork items and then are enchanted to provide even more protection. As masterwork items, their check penalties are 1 lower than normal armor or shield of that type.

To figure out the market price for magic armor or shields, start with a masterwork version, then add 1,000 gp for +1 armor or a +1 shield, or 4,000 gp for +2 armor or a +2 shield. Remember that +1 armor with a special ability counts as +2 armor for pricing purposes.

Minor magic armor or shields are enchanted to +1 or +2 enhancement bonus. In place of the second plus of bonus, a magic weapon can have any one of the following special abilities:

Bashing (Shield Only): This shield is made to make a shield bash. No matter what the size of the attacker, a large bashing shield deals 1d8 base damage and a small bashing shield deals 1d6 base damage. The shield acts as a *+1 weapon* when used as such.

Blending (Armor Only): A suit of armor with this capability appears normal. However, upon command, the armor changes shape and form, assuming the appearance of a normal set of clothing. The armor retains all its properties (including weight) when disguised. Only a *true seeing* spell or similar magic reveals the true nature of the armor when disguised.

Blinding (Shield Only): A shield with this enchantment flashes with a brilliant light up to twice per day upon the command of the wielder. All within 20 feet except the wielder must make a Reflex saving throw (DC 13) or be blinded for 1d4 rounds.

Minor Reinforcement: This suit of armor or shield protects vital areas of the wearer more effectively. When a critical hit is scored on the wearer, there is a 25% chance that the critical is negated and damage is rolled normally.

Spell Resistance (Armor Only): This enchantment grants the wearer of the armor spell resistance 11 while she wears it.

Magic Weapons

Magic weapons also begin as masterwork items, but their attack bonuses are supplanted by the enhancement bonuses that enchantment provides.

To figure out the market price for a magic weapon, start with a masterwork version of the weapon, then add 2,000 gp for a +1 weapon or 8,000 gp for a +2 weapon. A +1 weapon with a special ability counts as a +2 weapon for pricing purposes.

Minor magic weapons are enchanted to +1 or +2 enhancement bonus. In place of the second plus of bonus, a magic weapon can have any one of the following special abilities:

Distance: This enchantment can only be placed on a ranged weapon. A weapon of distance doubles its range increment.

Flaming: A flaming weapon, upon command, is sheathed in fire. The fire does not harm the hands that hold the weapon. Flaming weapons deal an additional 1d6 points of fire damage upon a successful hit. This

additional damage is not multiplied by a critical hit. Bows, crossbows, and slings so enchanted bestow the energy upon their ammunition.

Frost: A frost weapon, upon command, is sheathed in icy cold. The cold does not harm the hands that hold it. Frost weapons deal an additional 1d6 points of cold damage upon a successful hit. This additional damage is not multiplied by a critical hit. Bows, crossbows, and slings so enchanted bestow the energy upon their ammunition.

Keen Weapon: This enchantment doubles the threat range of a weapon. If placed on a longsword with a threat range of 19–20, the keen longsword scores a threat on a 17–20. Only slashing and piercing weapons can be enchanted to be keen.

Mighty Cleaving: A mighty cleaving weapon allows a wielder with the Cleave feat to make one additional cleave attempt in a round. Only one extra cleave attempt is allowed per round.

Returning: This enchantment can only be placed on a weapon that can be thrown. A returning weapon returns through the air back to the creature that threw it. It returns on the round following the round that it was thrown just before its throwing creature's turn. It is therefore ready to use again that turn.

Shock: Upon command, a shock weapon is sheathed in crackling electricity. The electricity does not harm the hands that hold the weapon. Shock weapons deal an additional 1d6 points of electrical damage upon a successful hit. This additional damage is not multiplied by a critical hit. Bows, crossbows, and slings so enchanted bestow the energy upon their ammunition.

Throwing: This enchantment can only be placed on a melee weapon. A melee weapon enchanted with this ability can be thrown up to 30 feet (maximum) without incurring a range penalty by a wielder proficient in its normal use.

Wondrous Items

This is a catch-all category for everything that doesn't fit elsewhere. The following are some typical minor items:

Bag of Holding: This appears to be a common cloth sack about 2 feet by 4 feet in size. The *bag of holding* opens into a nondimensional space: Its inside is larger than its outside dimensions. Regardless of what is put into the bag, it always weighs a fixed amount. This weight and the limits in weight and volume of the bag's contents depend on the bag's type, as shown on the table below:

Bag Type	Bag Weight	Contents Weight Limit	Contents Volume Limit	Market Price
Bag 1	15 lb.	250 lb.	30 cu. ft.	2,500 gp
Bag 2	25 lb.	500 lb.	70 cu. ft.	5,000 gp

If overloaded, or if sharp objects pierce it (from inside or outside), the bag ruptures and is ruined. All contents are lost forever. If a *bag of holding* is turned inside out, its contents spill out, unharmed, but the bag must be put right before it can be used again. If living creatures are placed within the bag, they can survive for up to 10 minutes, after which time they suffocate.

Boots of Elvenkind: These soft boots enable the wearer to move quietly in virtually any surroundings, granting a +10 enhancement bonus to Move Silently checks.

Market Price: 2,000 gp; *Weight:* 1 lb.

Cloak of Resistance: These garments offer magic protection in the form of a +1 or +2 resistance bonus for all saving throws (Fortitude, Reflex, Will).

Market Price: 1,000 gp (+1) or 4,000 gp (+2); *Weight:* 1 lb.

Gauntlets of Ogre Power: These gauntlets, made of tough leather with iron studs running across the back of the hand and fingers, grant the wearer great strength. Add a +2 enhancement bonus to the wearer's Strength score.

Market Price: 4,000 gp; *Weight:* —

Horn of Goodness/Evil: This trumpet adapts itself to the alignment of its possessor, so it produces either a good or an evil effect depending on the alignment of its owner. If the possessor is neither good nor evil, the horn has no power whatsoever. If the owner is good or evil, then blowing the horn has the effect of a *magic circle against evil* or a *magic circle against good* (as appropriate), and this protection lasts 10 rounds. The horn can be blown once per day.

Market Price: 4,500 gp; *Weight:* 1 lb.

Rope of Climbing: A 60-foot-long *rope of climbing* is no thicker than a slender wand, but it is strong enough to support 3,000 pounds. Upon command, the rope snakes forward, upward, downward, or any other direction at 10 feet per round and attaches itself securely wherever desired. It returns or unfastens itself in a similar manner. A *rope of climbing* can also be commanded to knot or unknot itself. This causes large knots to appear at 1-foot intervals along the rope. Knotting shortens the rope to a 50-foot length until the knots are untied. A creature must hold one end of the rope when its magic is invoked.

Market Price: 3,000 gp; *Weight:* 3 lb.

DO-IT-YOURSELF DUNGEON

Want to try out these new rules? Here's a rudimentary dungeon suitable for four 1st- and 2nd-level characters.

Step 1: Find four friends (besides yourself). Choose one person to be the Dungeon Master. That person should complete Steps 2, 3, and 4 below while everybody else creates 1st-level characters using this book. It's a good idea to have characters who are good in combat, and at least one cleric. If the DM reads this book ahead of time, it's okay to create the dungeon before everyone gathers to play. That way the DM can help everyone else create characters.

Step 2: Roll 18 times on the table below. Write down what you get each time. Note that this will leave eight empty rooms.

d20	Encounter
1	1d6 Medium-size skeletons guarding a 1st-level treasure.
2	1d4 zombies guarding a 1st-level treasure.
3	1d3 ghouls guarding a 2nd-level treasure.
4	1d8 goblins guarding a 1st-level treasure.
5	1d4 hobgoblins guarding a 1st-level treasure.
6	1 gelatinous cube guarding a 3rd-level treasure.
7	1 hell hound guarding a 3rd-level treasure.
8	1 ogre guarding a 2nd-level treasure.
9	1d8 orcs guarding a 2nd-level treasure.
10	1d3 dire rats guarding a 1st-level treasure.
11	1d4 human warriors, CE alignment, guarding a 1st-level treasure.
12	Human rogue, 3rd-level, NE alignment. Has 1,500 in equipment.
13	1 unicorn. Might help adventurers.
14	1d4 dwarf warriors, LG alignment. Might help adventurers.
15	Gnome wizard (illusion specialty), 1st-level, N alignment. Has starting package equipment. Might help adventurers.
16	Elf ranger, 2nd-level. CG alignment. Has 900 gp in equipment. Might help adventurers.
17	Trap.
18	Trap.
19	DM's choice, or make something up.
20	Another adventuring party. DM chooses alignment and treasure.

If you rolled a trap above, determine what kind of trap it is below.

d6	Trap Type
1	Arrow trap. Arrow has a +10 attack bonus and deals 1d6 points of damage (×3 crit).
2	Gas trap. Gas affects characters as a *sleep* spell centered on the trap.
3	Pit trap. A 10-ft. pit deals 1d6 points of damage from falling.
4	Flame trap. Reflex save (DC 13) avoids 1d6 points of fire damage.
5	Magical trap. A globe of cold deals 1d6 cold damage to everyone within 10 feet. Fortitude save (DC 13) for half damage.
6	Poison needle trap. Reflex save (DC 15) or take 1 point of temporary Con damage now. In 1 minute, make another Reflex save (DC 15) or take 1d2 points of temporary Con damage.

Note: The exact location of the trap and the nature of its trigger mechanism are up to the DM. Treasure chests often set off traps when opened, sections of floor might conceal a pressure-plate, and door-traps sometimes catch unwary rogues trying to pick a lock.

If you rolled the rogue, the wizard, the ranger, or the adventuring party, you'll need to create them, just as if you were making up a character yourself.

Step 3: Look at the map on the next page, and place one encounter in each room. It's a good idea to group similar monsters together. For example, if you rolled goblins, hobgoblins, and ogre, perhaps they're all working together. The ogre is in charge, the hobgoblins are his warriors, and the goblins wait on him hand and foot. Maybe he keeps dire rats as pets. Remember that eight rooms will be empty. Either leave them that way, or invent their contents yourself.

Next, sketch in some doors, making sure there's at least one way to get into every room. You can make some of them secret doors, if you like. Include one door that leads to the outside.

Step 4: Think about the plot. Why would the characters come into this dungeon? Maybe they're looking for captives, or they've been hired by a local lord.

Also, think about how the monsters will react. Maybe the gnolls in room 22 can hear a fight involving the hell hounds in room 23. If they make a Listen check, they might decide to head out into the hall and surprise the party by attacking from their rear.

Step 5: The characters should introduce themselves to each other and make up a story that explains why they're adventuring together. Then the adventure begins with the characters standing outside the door to room 1.

While the Adventure Is Running

Here are some tips for the DM:

- **Doors**: Roll percentile dice whenever the characters first come to a door. On a 01–50, the door is locked (and requires an Open Lock check at DC 20). Doors in this dungeon have hardness of 5, 10 hit points (18 points to break), and can be bashed open with a Strength check (DC 18).
- **Dungeon Dressing**: Feel free to put normal items like furniture, chests, tapestries, and cobwebs in your dungeon. Few monsters live in otherwise empty rooms.
- **Retreating**: Wounded characters can retreat to town if they wish. Monsters will generally pursue them within the dungeon but won't follow them to the surface. Monsters will heal and might be better prepared for the players when they return.

Scale: One Square Equals 5 Feet